Praise for

OF IRISH BLOOD

"Fascinating story. Engrossing, with an endearing central character and a wonderful, rich historical background."

—Mary Higgins Clark, international and
New York Times bestselling author of *I've Got My Eyes on You*

"Kelly is a wonderful, creative, intelligent writer who's endowed with a sense of humor. I highly recommend *Of Irish Blood*."

—Malachy McCourt, *New York Times* bestselling author of
A Monk Swimming

"Kelly captures the drama, the turmoil, the excitement of the complex history of Irish and Irish Americans in the early twentieth century [through] the perspective of a daring, uncompromising woman who is at the center of the great movements of her time, and illuminates the arduous task of finding a true self in the heart of a whirlwind."

—Mary Gordon, award-winning author of *The Company of Women*

"A sweeping historical novel played on one of the world's richest stages—Paris in the teens and twenties, where Irish expats mingle with Americans and fascinating fictional characters rub elbows with Hemingway, Gertrude Stein, and even Coco Chanel. The book trembles with the intrigues of international politics, thunders with the distant sounds of strife, and pulses with life. Like other great Irish yarns, spun by great Irish storytellers, it's complex, lively, wildly romantic, and hugely entertaining."

—William Martin, *New York Times* bestselling author
of *Bound for Gold*

"A gripping story about passionate people, [and] an exploration of the depth and heights of that explosive word, Irish. There is heartbreak in the word—and exaltation. A rare reading experience."

—Thomas Fleming, *New York Times* bestselling author of
The Secret Trial of Robert E. Lee

"A feisty Irish-American girl from Chicago discovers love, independence, and what it means to be Irish. . . . Vivid and full of passion, *Of Irish Blood* will sweep you away." —Lynn Garafola, author of *Diaghilev's Ballets Russes*

"A passionately told tale of romance and revolution that brushes away the dust and cobwebs of history to bring alive a time when the fates of individuals and nations hung in the balance. The writing is vivid, the characters fiery real, and the story irresistible. *Of Irish Blood* is a book to savor and remember."
—Peter Quinn, winner of the American Book Award for *Banished Children of Eve*

"Mary Pat is an incredible writer; there is really no one better to capture the sophisticated, original, and slightly offbeat Parisian fashion of the Roaring Twenties as seen through the eyes of a younger generation."
—Tommy Hilfiger, iconic fashion designer

"A riveting novel that brings the heroines of the Irish Revolution to vivid life. Told from the viewpoint of Nora Kelly, 'a new woman,' it's a great read and a wonderful addition to every Irish American's library."
—Patricia Harty, cofounder and editor of *Irish America*

"Inspired by the life of the author's (*Galway Bay*) great-aunt, Nora's story is a broad, sweeping historical saga; what sets it apart from other novels about the Irish War of Independence is its feisty character development, feminist viewpoint, and excellent writing. It will have wide appeal to readers of both Irish history and historical novels, as well as those wishing to sink their teeth into a really good story."
—*Library Journal* (starred review)

OTHER BOOKS BY MARY PAT KELLY

FICTION

Special Intentions
Galway Bay
Irish Above All

NONFICTION

Martin Scorsese: The First Decade
Martin Scorsese: A Journey
Home Away from Home: The Yanks in Ireland
Proudly We Served: The Men of the USS Mason
Good to Go: The Rescue of Scott O'Grady from Bosnia

OF IRISH BLOOD

MARY PAT KELLY

A TOM DOHERTY ASSOCIATES BOOK
NEW YORK

This is a work of fiction. All of the characters, organizations, and events portrayed in this novel are either products of the author's imagination or are used fictitiously.

OF IRISH BLOOD

Copyright © 2015 by Mary Pat Kelly

Designed by Greg Collins

A Forge Book
Published by Tom Doherty Associates
175 Fifth Avenue
New York, NY 10010

www.tor-forge.com

Forge® is a registered trademark of Macmillan Publishing Group, LLC.

The Library of Congress has cataloged the hardcover edition as follows:

Kelly, Mary Pat, author
   Of Irish blood / Mary Pat Kelly.—First edition.
     p. cm.
   "A Tom Doherty Associates book."
   ISBN 978-0-7653-2913-4 (hardcover)
   ISBN 978-1-4299-8737-0 (ebook)
1. Young women—Ireland—Fiction. 2. Home rule—Ireland—Fiction. 2. Ireland—History—Easter Rising, 1916—Fiction. 3. Ireland—History—War of Independence, 1919–1921—Fiction. 4. Ireland—History—20th century—Fiction. I. Title.
   PS3561.E39463 O35 2015
   813'.54—dc23
                                         2015295056

ISBN 978-1-250-20349-6 (trade paperback)

Our books may be purchased in bulk for promotional, educational, or business use. Please contact your local bookseller or the Macmillan Corporate and Premium Sales Department at 1-800-221-7945, extension 5442, or by email at MacmillanSpecialMarkets@macmillan.com.

First Edition: February 2015
First Trade Paperback Edition: January 2019

Printed in the United States of America

0 9 8 7 6 5 4 3 2 1

In New York, Loretta Brennan Glucksman is an encouraging friend and Carole Hart is an inspiration. Thanks to Jean Doumanian, Dee Ito, Laura Jackson, Sheila Cox, Laura Aversano, and to Colleen Ambrose and Pamela Craig Delaney for their hospitality and counsel. I am very grateful to Lynn Garafola, Daria Rose Foner, and Eric Foner. Thank you to Mary Gordon, Mary Higgins Clark, Peter Quinn, Malachy McCourt, Alfie McCourt, Tim O'Brien, Brian Brown, Michael Carty, Jr., Ellen McCourt, Julia Judge, Charlotte Moore, Ciaran O'Reilly, the Irish American Writers and Artists, as well as The Kelly Gang.

In Paris, I appreciate the help Sheila Pratschke, director of The Irish Cultural Centre (formerly The Irish College) gave me. Thanks also to Marcel and Elizabeth Gruenspan, as well as Dominique Faugeras.

Thanks to Roberta Aria Sorvino, MaryAnne Kelly De Fuccio, Monique Dubois Inzinna, Danielle Inzinna, and Diana Berndt. In Ireland, I'm grateful to Patsy O'Kane and all at Beech Hill House Hotel, Aine and Colm O'Keefe, as well as Roisin Nevin, Pauline Ross, Antoinette O'Ceallaigh, Geraldine Folam, Maire O'Connor at Lough Inagh Lodge, and Sister Maive MacNaillais. Thanks to all in Kansas City, especially Marilyn Stearns, Jacob and Audrey Kenemore, Rosemary Stipe, Nancy Wormington, and the O'Neills. Thank you, Barbara Leahy Sutton, for a lifetime of friendship and support.

A special roll of honor for those who helped prepare the *Of Irish Blood* manuscript—Kathy Danzer, Azure Bourne, Mary Kanak, Deb Spohnheimer, Nicolette Richardson, Alexi Schwartzkopff, Adrienne Royals, Katie McGale, the great Madeline Hart, and Jim and Toni Hart.

All Irish Americans owe much to Patricia Harty, founding editor of *Irish America* magazine. So do I.

Though a work of fiction, much research went into *Of Irish Blood* as I tried to get the history right. Specific references and a discussion of what is fact and what is fiction is on my website: marypatkelly.com. Thank you, librarians in Chicago, New York, Dublin, Galway, Paris, and Three Lakes, Wisconsin, for your help.

I am very happy to be published by Tom Doherty/Forge and thank Tom Doherty; my one-of-a-kind editor, Robert Gleason; Kelly Quinn; Elayne Becker; and Terry McGarry. My agent, Susan Gleason, is a gift to me in every way. Thanks!

To my husband, Martin Sheerin—your love, patience, intelligence, and knowledge of all things Irish fill me with gratitude always.

For my mother,

Mariann Williams Kelly,

and my aunt,

Marguerite Kelly McGuire,

the matriarchs,

with love and gratitude

ACKNOWLEDGMENTS

I am grateful to so many people, not only for their help with *Of Irish B*
but also for their embrace of *Galway Bay*, which made this sequel possi
Thank you to my sisters, Randy, Mickey, Susie, and Nancy, to my brot
Michael, to my brothers-in-law, Ernie Strapazon, Ed Panian, and B
Jarchow, and to my sister-in-law, Martha Hall Kelly, with whom I shar
memorable research trip to Paris as she was writing her novel *The Ra*
of Ravensbruck. Thank you to all my nephews and nieces, who inspire
to write these stories, and to my cousins, those I've always known
those I met through *Galway Bay*, especially Tom Rauch and Nicole Te
our genealogists, and Tom McGuire, whose kindness makes so
happen. We are all grateful to the welcoming Keeleys in Carna, C
Galway—Padraig Keeley, Erin Gibbons, her husband, Ned Kelly, and
children, Olwen, MacDarra, Rosa, and Fiona.

I feel great gratitude toward all my readers and am touched by those
who tell me my books make you want to learn more about your own far

Thanks to the amazing Irish-American organizations who have i
me to their events and festivals. I think I wrote *Of Irish Blood* so you
me back! And book clubs. What fun it's been to visit you in person
the phone. I also loved speaking at universities, schools, librarie
parish churches, and thank the extraordinary singers Catherine O'C
and Mary Deady, for making many of these appearances so speci
enjoyed going to bookstores, and especially thank Elizabeth Me
Titcomb's Bookshop, Beverly Schreck of Barnes & Noble in Fort C
Colorado, and John Barry and all at Paddy's On the Square.

In Chicago, I thank Mary Evers, Marilyn Antonik, Father Roger
John Fitzgerald, Darrell Windle, the always wonderful Dave Sar
Polo Café, Rick Kogan, Katie O'Brien, Skinny and Houli, the paris
of St. James, Roseann Finnegan LeFevour, Joan O'Leary, Cliff C
all at IBAM, and, of course, The Group.

Twenty million Americans of Irish Blood—
surely enough to free Ireland.

—MAUD GONNE MACBRIDE, 1895

1

BRIDGEPORT, CHICAGO

JUNE 23, 1903

"We'll have to run for it, Ag." I can see Johnny Murphy forcing his old nags into the traffic on Archer Avenue. Miss the horse tram and I'll be late for work—again—and my niece Agnella for class at St. Xavier's High School.

"Come on," I say to her.

"Oh, Aunt Nonie. He's pulled away from our stop. We'll never catch up," she says, panting.

"Ah, now," I shout, "what God has for ye won't go past ye," imitating my Granny Honora's brogue. I start running.

"You shouldn't make fun, Aunt Nonie!" Agnella says, but begins trotting along beside me. One block left to Archer and Arch, where the brown brick bulk of St. Bridget's chides us. Should have left earlier.

Full summer now and the sun, finally serious about Chicago, turning our few trees green. A warm breeze too but from the west. So all clogged with the smell of the Stockyards.

Now Agnella and I pound along faster. I'm too old and too corseted to be running hell for leather through the neighborhood, as I'll be told by somebody I'm sure. Maybe my hobble skirt's a bit too tight around the ankles. Fashionable though. We're almost to Archer Avenue. I'm twenty-four, Agnella's fourteen, but she's already up to my shoulder. Her pleated black serge school uniform makes for easy running. Another tall Kelly woman. Though she's a blue-eyed blonde, and I have ginger hair and greenish eyes.

Johnny Murphy, the driver, sees us. I wave, but what does the *amadán* do but slap the reins on his swaybacked horses, making good his threat of yesterday morning. "I've my schedule, Miss Nora Kelly, and I can't be waiting for you every day." Leaving us, when it's not my fault we're late.

A big row at the breakfast table started by my sister Henrietta, Agnella's mother. Some nonsense about my not wringing out my shift properly and who but her had to wipe up the drips on the bathroom floor. You'd think she'd be grateful we have an indoor privy—all thanks to our big brother Mike, the master plumber. Henrietta railed on about me to poor Mike, who was trying to enjoy a second cup of coffee before heading to his job site. Supervisor now. Doesn't have to go out at the crack of dawn like my other brother Mart, who meets the fellows delivering newspapers to the little candy store Mike bought for him. Or James the youngest boy, who works for the railroad. My sister Annie's out early too. A policewoman, if you could feature it, but then we're four years into the twentieth century and we women are coming into our own, though Henrietta's too busy feeling sorry for herself to see any opportunity. Not easy for her, widowed at twenty-one from a husband called Kelly, would you believe? She and her three children having to move back in with the family. Still that was years ago. Mam spoke up for me at breakfast but Henrietta got all offended and asked Mam didn't she appreciate her and the way she runs the house and maybe she should leave and take the children with her though how they'd survive, she didn't know. And that stopped Mam because it's looking as if Henrietta's kids might be the only grandchildren she'll ever know, what with Mike coming up to forty already and not married, and the rest of us four stair-steps the same.

Only my brother Edward has a wife, and they live away in Indiana with her people. Mam always says her greatest sorrow is that her own mother back in Ireland never knew any of us. And Granny Honora had agreed. Bad enough to have to say farewell to your children but to never set eyes on grandchildren . . .

I remember Mam talking to Granny Honora right before Granny died, the two of them wondering why we didn't find mates when even in the worst times in Ireland and the early days in Chicago people couldn't wait to pair up. Better chance with two working together, Mam said, and now with plenty of good jobs going and her children blessed with work, they stayed clustered at home.

Granny said, "Ah well, maybe they're only taking their time. I'd say young Honora won't be lollygagging."

But that was then. Granny's gone four years now and me still not married. Granny was the only one called me Honora. Named after her. But I was always Nora in school, and Nonie in the family, which seemed right because she, Granny, was the true Honora Kelly. Henrietta held my name against me. Said she should've been called after Granny. "You carry the name of two women who helped this family," Granny had told her which shut Henrietta up. Still, there'd be no bickering at the breakfast table if Granny Honora were still alive.

Nor would we be rushing out at the last minute and have to run for our lives to catch Johnny Murphy.

"Johnny!" I shout. He's trying to maneuver the tram past—of all things—a Model T Ford bumping along leading the parade. Rare enough in Bridgeport. I'm trying to talk Mike into getting an auto. Now that would be the bee's knees.

"Wait! Wait!" I yell.

So close now—if I can get a grip on that pole—I stretch out my right hand, pulling Agnella along with my left. Suddenly I'm flying, swinging up onto the platform with Agnella beside me, just like that. And each of us held by one big hand of this fellow. Now I stumble into to him and doesn't he hug me to himself, laughing.

And that starts it, God forgive me. A kind of enchantment. In Granny Honora's stories, women in Ireland are whisked off to fairyland where they dance and feast through the night, only to come home the next morning to find a century has passed. Is that what's happening to me?

"Thank you," I say when I get my breath. Agnella and I stare at this giant of a fellow. She nods and hurries toward the back of the car, but I smile right into his face. "One in the eye for Johnny Murphy," I say, "but I'd best pay my fare now."

"No, no," he says. "All taken care of. When I saw you and your sister . . ."

"Niece."

"Niece, then—but the both of you running flat out, you reminded me of this game filly I own who can't bear to lose so I had to lend a hand."

"Game filly? A horse?" I say, ready to get mad but he laughs again and raises his straw boater hat. Wearing one of those new cream-colored suits that show the dirt.

"I'm Tim McShane, miss. Or is it missus?"

"Miss," I say, "Miss Nora Kelly," and stick out my hand. And doesn't he take it in both of his and wink at me. Much too bold for the Archer Avenue tram at eight in the morning with every eye on us.

I pull my hand away and walk back to where Agnella waits with our friends Rose and Mame McCabe in the seats they save for us every morning since they board the tram earlier at the Brighton Park stop near where they live in a boardinghouse run by my Aunt Kate. The sisters work with me at Montgomery Ward, telephone operators too, taking orders for the catalog, the three of us, which my sister Henrietta finds suspect.

"Nattering away to strangers all day? Not what I'd call proper." But my brother Mike loves to get us telling stories about the orders we get. He calls us "the Trio"—me the oldest at twenty-four. Rose with her big hazel eyes and round, sweet face is twenty-two. Mame's just twenty-one but regal somehow—dark eyes, high cheekbones, straight nose . . . mine turns up a bit. All of us old to be unmarried, as Henrietta reminds me often. "Old maids, the lot of you," she'll say to me.

"Better than being a crabbed widow like you," I say back to her. Cruel, I know, but that tongue of hers sets me off before I even realize it.

Henrietta loves to tear down the McCabes. Jealous because we three are always so well turned out thanks to Rose's skill as a seamstress. Any outfit I can draw Rose can make. Mame's wearing one of mine now—deep brown skirt with a burnt-orange fitted jacket. Though Rose copied her own navy blue cotton from *Woman's Home Companion*. I had offered to design a dress for Henrietta that Rose would sew. She'd only laughed.

But now both McCabes shake their heads at me. Rose clicks her tongue.

"Oh, Nonie," Rose says. "That's Tim McShane."

"I know," I say. "He introduced himself."

"No decent woman in Brighton Park would even speak to him." Agnella nods along with Rose and then Mame speaks up.

"He is a bit of a bad hat, Nonie. Trains racehorses at the track in the Park."

"So? What's wrong with that? Mike and my cousin Ed go to the track all the time."

"But they don't spend their time with gangsters. They say Tim McShane does all kinds of things to the horses to make them win," Mame says.

"Or lose," Rose puts in. "And he's Dolly McKee's fancy man."

"The singer, Dolly McKee? But she must be years older than he is," I say.

I was twelve years old the first time Mam took me to the McVicker's Theatre to see Dolly McKee perform and Dolly wasn't young then. Still gorgeous though up there under the spotlight in that sparkly dress, singing "Love's Old Sweet Song" with Mam crying next to me thinking of my father, who died so young. Still able to fill a theater all these years later is Dolly McKee, and living like a queen in the Palmer House. So she picked out Tim McShane. Interesting.

"Dolly is always at the track, and they say she owns the horses Tim trains. Took up with him years ago," Rose goes on.

"You two have his seed, breed, and generation," I say. "Why haven't you talked about him before?"

"There's a new boarder come to Aunt Kate's who works at the track. A little runt of a Cavan fellow. He's been telling us all about Tim McShane," Mame says.

"And now he's very kindly rescued Ag and me. I wonder, did I thank him properly?" I stand up but Ag and Rose pull me down.

"Nonie! Please!"

"Maybe I'll ask him for tickets to Dolly's show," I say.

"Oh, Nonie! You wouldn't!" Rose says.

"Not like you two to be so skittery," I say.

"A man to stay away from," Mame says. "According to the little Cavan fellow."

"Look there, he's getting off anyway," Rose says.

The tram stops at LaSalle right near the new City Hall. Tim McShane steps off then looks up to see the four of us pressed against the window. He tips his hat and gives a half bow. The McCabes and Ag lean back, but I wave at Tim McShane and incline my head. He smiles. Oh!

And, of course, our supervisor Miss Allen is annoyed as the three of us come sliding into our chairs and clap the headphones over our ears just as the nine o'clock start bell rings. Mad at us for cutting the time so close and madder still that we'd made it and she couldn't scold us. Not a bad sort really, Miss Allen, but not from Chicago, unmarried, no family here, a neat, well-dressed woman. Devoted to the company.

"You are Montgomery Ward to the world," she says to us now as she does every morning. "Your voice, your diction, your cool professional manner creates confidence in our customers. They need to trust you."

I take out the dog-eared script she's written for us and begin. Twenty of us in a long row push the plugs into the switchboard, then say in the clear, unaccented voice that Miss Allen demands, "Good morning. I am a Montgomery Ward operator, ready to take your order." No deviation, as Miss Allen walks along behind us, listening.

We start together. The Good-Morning Chorus, Rose calls us, but with each call and order the pace changes. "What sizes? What colors? How many?" we ask.

"How much?" they come back. "How long before my order gets there?" Men mostly.

My first caller's new to the telephone. I imagine him standing next to the cracker barrel at a country store, shouting into the round black receiver. Had to be heard in Chicago, after all. He repeats his name and address twice, sure I wouldn't get it right the first time.

"I'll send your seeds out COD on the next train," I say to him three times.

"Nora," Miss Allen says to me, "keep it short."

My voice tangles with the others as words twist up and down the rows.

Miss Allen moves to the other end of the row and I hear Mame, beside me, say, "Thank God your wheat is growing well!" She pauses and then says, "Yes, rain is a blessing. Though when I was a little girl in Ireland I thought God blessed us too well!" Another pause. "Oh, Sweden? How lovely. We have a large community of Swedish people living right here in Chicago. My sister and I buy the best rye bread there." A pause, then, "Your wife makes rye? Wonderful," and, "Yes, please send me the recipe. Address it to . . ."

Rose hisses at Mame but it's too late. Miss Allen is standing behind them.

"Not again, Miss McCabe! How many times do I have to tell you, we do not engage the customers in private conversation?" Miss Allen leans over Mame and speaks right into the telephone: "Thank you, sir, for your order . . . Yes, I'll tell the sweet little Irish girl." She chomps out the words. Mame still has a hint of the lilt that came with her across the ocean.

Miss Allen ends the call, turns to Mame. "That's it, Miss McCabe! You have been warned innumerable times. Now come with me to Mr. Bartlett's office. You are fired."

Rose stands up. "She was only being nice, Miss Allen."

"You are here to take orders, not to be nice."

I get up then.

"Now, Miss Allen, be honest. Doesn't Mame get bigger orders than any of us? The customer starts talking and remembers something else he wants to buy."

"That's true, Miss Allen," Mame says. "Why, yesterday this fellow had completely forgotten his wedding anniversary until I asked him how he met his wife and then . . ."

"You what?" Miss Allen says. "This is beyond anything I can even imagine!"

"Oh, for God's sake, Miss Allen," I say. "I chat a bit, too, if the customer is willing. So what?"

"Time, Miss Kelly. Time and money. Come with me, Miss McCabe."

"If you're firing her, better fire me too," I say.

Rose has already taken off her headset.

"And me," she says.

The switchboard buzzes away, but no one is answering the calls. Every one of the girls is watching and listening to us.

I remember my great-uncle Patrick's story of the strike he led of the fellows digging the Illinois and Michigan Canal and wonder if I say, "Girls, rise up!," will they follow me?

Mame smiles at Miss Allen.

"I know why you're upset with me," she says. "You think I'm being disrespectful, that I ignore all your teachings and don't deserve the money Mr. Ward pays me. But say that fellow does send his wife's recipe to me, and I maybe write a note saying thanks. Wouldn't he be more likely to think of Ward's instead of Sears when he wants a new tractor?"

"That's beside the point," Miss Allen says.

She realizes the rest of the girls are ignoring the ringing phones. "Girls! Man your stations!" she shouts, and the "Good morning"s start up.

"Mame won't do it again," Rose says.

"Why not?" I say. "Miss Allen, take all three of us to Mr. Bartlett. You make your case, and we'll make ours."

Just then Josie Schmidt calls out from the end of the row. "I've a man here wants to give his order to the Irish girl who spoke to him in Polish. He and three other farmers have pitched in to buy a harvester, and he wants . . ."

"Tell him she doesn't work here anymore," I shout back.

Miss Allen doesn't like that one bit. "Go and take the order, Miss McCabe," she says, and to us, "You two get back to work."

⊱❖⊰

"Let's go to Henricci's for lunch," I say when noon finally comes.

"Oh, Nonie," Rose says, "that place's wildly expensive."

"So? We're celebrating!"

"Celebrating?" Mame asks.

"A victory over Miss Allen. Hurrah for the working woman."

Usually we duck into one of the tearooms or cafés around Ward's that have discreet signs in the windows—LADIES WELCOME—because ladies aren't welcome in most of the bars and restaurants downtown. Still a novelty for women to be out and about working. Lady shoppers could eat lunch at Field's Walnut Room, but not in the establishments along LaSalle or State Street where the businessmen and politicians of Chicago gather to do their deals and slap each other's backs. Henricci's is the back-slappingest of them all and right near City Hall.

The headwaiter stands near the door, one of those starched white aprons covering him from his chest to the floor.

"His wife must spend half her days washing it," Rose whispers to me as the man frowns at us and starts a lot of blather about a nice tearoom around the corner—not a Bridgeport fellow, not Irish even, but luckily Rick Garvey, a big-shot lawyer, is coming in right behind us and he says, "Hello, Nora," and to the waiter, "You must know Nora Kelly, Mike Kelly's sister, Ed's cousin. Her uncles are Dominic and Luke and Steve and . . ."

I smile at Rick and say to the waiter, "I've loads of relations. Do I have to name them all for us to get a table?"

"No," he says, and with a kind of snotty nod to Rick, he leads us past the tables with Reserved signs to the very back of the restaurant.

I can just about see the entrance from my seat. We order and eat chicken pot pies and drink two glasses each of root beer. "Let's have sundaes," I say. Not ready to leave. Keeping an eye on the door as I scoop up the last of the hot fudge taking my time. "For heaven's sake, Nonie. Come on," Rose says. "We have to get back. Can't be late after all the bother this morning."

"Bother?" I say. "What we should do is organize the girls into a union and march right out of Montgomery Ward's. Why can't Mame chat to the customers and make them laugh? I'm tired of all the rules and regulations they put on us! Jesus, that last memo Miss Allen pinned to the bulletin board— 'Operators should not adjust their underwear while at the switchboard'— all because Janie O'Brien loosened her stays. When women get the vote we won't allow such nonsense!"

"There she goes," Mame says to Rose. "She'll have us standing on our chairs denouncing Mr. Henricci for putting us back here in the ladies' section."

"Not a bad idea," I say, and pretend to climb onto my chair. And then I see him . . .

Tim McShane coming right through the door as if I'd conjured him out of the air, much taller than the headwaiter. Taking his hat off. Blond curly hair, big shoulders, those massive hands. And that cream-colored suit.

The headwaiter is laughing. Not so uppity now, bowing and scraping to a fare-thee-well.

Tim McShane doesn't see us. The waiter leads him to a table by the window, and takes away the Reserved sign.

"Look," I say to Rose and Mame, "it's Tim McShane. What's to stop me from going over there and saying, 'What a coincidence!' and 'Thank you again for your rescue!'"

"We'll stop you," Rose says, pulling me back into my seat. "He's a scoundrel, Nonie. Please."

"Oh, Rose, you're too good for this world. So he's not a saint. So he's . . ."

But the rest of the sentence sputters because who's sailing into Henricci's, flags and feathers flying, but only Chicago's most famous soprano Dolly McKee herself. A woman who looks as if she doesn't give a snap of her fingers about goodness. Lunchtime at Henricci's, and she's dressed for dinner at the Palmer House. All in black, with jet beads sewn over the front of her dress and the neckline cut so low her white bosom shines across the room.

I remember how, as a lone figure in the spotlight, she reached Mam and me high in the balcony of the McVicker's Theatre. Now she overwhelms Henricci's, moving toward her table and Tim McShane, who stands up. She offers him her hand, and doesn't he kiss it.

I sit down. So does Dolly.

"Jesus, Mary, and Joseph," I say.

"He's devoted to her. That's what they say," Mame says.

Awfully bright at that window table, the light ducks under the brim of Dolly's hat, hits her across her face. Wrinkles under all that powder and rouge. Fifty at least, I think. But every fellow in the place is looking over at her. Now the county clerk, the assesor, and two aldermen walk over to her table. She says a word or two to each man and then, with a lovely half wave, sends him on his way.

"Well, that's that," I say to Mame and Rose. "Let's go."

How I wish for a back door. None in Henricci's. So the three of us have to walk right past Queen Dolly and her courtier to get out of the place.

He won't see me, I think. Too dazzled. I have my hand on the first panel of the revolving door when his voice catches me.

"Well, if it isn't the nearly late Miss Kelly." Calling out to me while he lounges in his chair. Laughing. Making a show of me in front of everyone.

I turn—with Rose and Mame on each side of me—stand very straight, and nod. "Good afternoon, Mr. McShane, Mrs. McKee," I say.

"Come over," Tim says, waving his cigar.

Drinking, I think. The table full of beer steins and not two o'clock. I know I should leave. But don't I walk right over with Rose and Mame following. Is this what happens to the women in Granny's stories of enchantment? Do their minds melt away and their bodies pull them forward?

"Dolly, here's the girl I told you about," Tim McShane says.

"The damsel in distress," Dolly says, nodding her head to me. "And Tim saved you."

The feathers on her hat point straight at my heart. "Well," I say, "I could have caught the next car."

"What you should have done," she says. "Long ago I stopped running. I stand still and draw good things to myself."

"Fine for you," I say, "but I'll keep sprinting while I'm able."

A snort from Mame—suppressing a laugh.

"These are my friends, Rose and Mame McCabe."

"Ah, sisters," Dolly says. "I was never blessed with sisters. Born in a trunk and raised on the Orpheum Circuit, me and Georgie Cohan growing up together." Now she spreads her arms wide. "Warmhearted show people my only family! And you are unmarried women, earning your own way in the world, I understand." She bows her head and sighs, and suddenly we three are characters drawn into a melodrama.

"I see someone's been inquiring about us," I say, looking at Tim McShane.

"City Hall is a great place for information," he says. "And, of course, I've had the pleasure of seeing the McCabe sisters at Mass at St. Agnes in Brighton Park." He inclines his head toward them.

Jesus, are we in some kind of play? The big phony. I'd say it's far from Mass at St. Agnes Tim McShane is on a Sunday morning.

Rose, of course, takes him at his word and says, "Strange. I've never seen you."

"Well, I stand at the back," he says.

But Mame isn't letting him get away with such palaver. "Very far in the back, I'd say. The street, even," she says.

He laughs at that.

"Or, do you just tip your hat as you go by?" I ask.

"I do, indeed."

Rose speaks up. "When I pass a church, I always make a visit so when they roll my body up the aisle the Lord won't say, 'Who is it?'"

I laugh, but Dolly McKee lifts up her eyes, aiming for heaven I suppose, but hitting Henricci's ceiling. She touches some imagined moisture under her eyes. "Ah yes, that day will come for all of us. My late husband was a strapping, healthy young man one day and gone the next."

Very quickly gone, I think. Most people assume Dolly's "Mrs." is a title she's given herself as some women performers do. Lends a bit of respectability. Silly, I think. Sarah Bernhardt doesn't hide behind an imagined husband, nor did Jenny Lind or Lillie Langtry, but Dolly's dabbing away at the memory of great sorrow, her eyes closed.

How in the hell does Tim McShane put up with her? I wonder. But then Dolly opens her eyes and looks right at me.

Whoa. The mind behind her histrionics shows itself. Applaud and move on if you know what's good for you, those dark eyes say.

Now she stares at Tim, who stands up immediately and says, "So nice to see you again, ladies," and then to Dolly, "We must give these girls some tickets for your appearance at the Lyric Opera."

She smiles. "Best if they wait until I'm in a vaudeville show at the

McVicker's again. I've agreed to appear with the Cohans next month. More pleasurable for you than my opera repertoire," she says, still looking at me. "What's your name again?"

"Kelly," I say. And right there in front of God and man and the head-waiter I sing:

> *"Has anybody here seen Kelly?*
> *K-E-double-L-Y?*
> *Has anybody here seen Kelly?*
> *Have you seen him smile?*
> *Oh, his hair is red and his eyes are blue*
> *And he's Irish through and through*
> *Has anybody here seen Kelly?*
> *Kelly from the Emerald Isle?"*

And don't the fellows at the next table start clapping, Mame and Rose along with them.

Dolly doesn't applaud. "I'll remember the name," she says.

Tim McShane says nothing as we leave.

We wait until we get around the corner to State Street, and then slip into the doorway of Marshall Field's and kill ourselves laughing.

"Oh, Nonie!" Rose says. "Singing like that right in the restaurant!"

"I just couldn't take another minute of her looking down her nose at us," I say.

"She is beautiful," Mame says. "Maybe theater people are just different from regular people."

"You mean members of the great family of show business?"

"Nice to see the Cohans," Rose says. "Do you think she'll really give us tickets?"

"Now Rose, you're the one warning me off Tim McShane, and you'd take tickets from him?"

"No, I guess we can't," she says.

"Well, that was a waste of a dollar," I say.

"Why?" Rose says. "It was a lovely lunch, and we met Dolly McKee!"

"And you did see Tim McShane, Nonie," Mame says.

"Oh." Rose catching on. "So that's why we went."

"Pathetic to see a grown man at that woman's beck and call," I say.

"Maybe he loves her," Mame says.

"I'm sure he loves training her horses," I say. "Do they live together?"

"Nonie," Mame says, "they're not married. Even Dolly McKee wouldn't dare."

"No decent person would ever attend another one of her shows," Rose says.

"Whatever their relationship is, it's no concern of ours, is it, Nonie?" Mame says to me.

"None at all," I say.

We have to run the last three blocks to Ward's, keeping our eyes on that golden angel on the top of the building. He's blowing his horn right at us. "Late again," he trumpets.

Miss Allen leads the three of us right up to Mr. Bartlett's office.

"Miss Allen tells me you three girls have had quite a day," he says—new to Ward's, a short, plumpish man with black hair, the color of his very serious suit. "You've disobeyed every one of Miss Allen's rules, and are one hour late coming from lunch." He opens a file folder.

"I have quite a number of complaints from Miss Allen." But then he smiles. Strange.

Now, any other two girls working there would've put blame right on me, wouldn't have been able to help themselves, but the McCabes are two of the best, and say nothing. Not a word from any of the three of us.

Fire us, fire us, get it over with, I think.

"Miss Allen says you three are insubordinate and undisciplined," Mr. Bartlett says, paging through the folder.

"Irish," Miss Allen says.

"That's it," I say. "I quit!"

"Now, just a minute," Mr. Bartlett says. "I believe in listening to my employees."

All right . . . What did I have to lose? So I start. "First of all, don't blame Rose and Mame for being late. It was my fault."

Mame interrupts. "We went to lunch because Miss Allen was cross with *me*. And Dolly McKee was in the restaurant and she spoke to us. So how could we rush out? That would be very rude."

"Dolly McKee?" Mr. Bartlett says. "Yes, she would be hard to break away from."

Miss Allen holds up her hand. "You see what I mean, Mr. Bartlett? These girls are always full of some story or another. Distracting, that's what they are, and this one," she points at Mame, "goes on and on to the customers and promises to send them recipes and all kinds of folderol."

"What about the Polish farmers and the harvester, Miss Allen?" I say.

"What harvester?" he asks.

So I tell Mr. Bartlett about Mame making friends with the farmer, and how he joined together with his friends to buy a harvester from us instead of at Sears or John Deere, and Mr. Bartlett nods so I go on. "You don't understand. Mame is not just a good talker, she's a great writer and understands people."

"I hardly think . . ." Miss Allen starts but now she is the one gestured into silence by Mr. Bartlett's hand.

"Go on," he says to me.

"Well, you know how the *Tribune* has an essay contest every year for students, 'Why I'm a Patriot'?"

"I do. A good promotion," he says.

"Well, Mame won it when she was thirteen. First prize! And she didn't write it about the Founding Fathers or wars or the Constitution. She wrote about coming to America. Her mother and sister—Rose here—had gone ahead, so Mame was a ten-year-old girl traveling alone with only a neighbor to watch her on that ship during the long, long voyage. What was the name of the ship, Mame?" I ask her.

"The *Compania*," she says.

"Oh, Nonie, Mr. Bartlett isn't interested," Rose says.

"No, go on," he says.

"Well, when the ship sailed into New York Harbor and Mame saw the Statue of Liberty, she thought it was a giant statue of Our Lady, the mother of Jesus, holding up a light and showing Mame the way to America and her own mother. Isn't that right, Mame?"

"I did," she says. "You see, Mr. Bartlett, I was very young and I'd been so lonely, knowing my mother and sister only through letters, and here was the biggest Blessed Mother I've ever seen saying 'All will be well.'"

"Tell him about the train trip, Mame," I say.

"Well, our neighbor from Cavan, Mary Clarke, took care of me on the ship then traveled with me to Chicago. Loads of people on that train, sharing all kinds of different food with each other—German sausage, Polish pierogies, mozzarella on Italian bread—things I'd never tasted. As I ate, I stared out the window. So many trees! In Ireland only the rich have trees but in America trees cover the place and anybody can stretch out under their shade. We came to Union Station and then my mother and Rose were rushing up to me, hugging me close. So I wrote that America was a generous mother sharing her love with the whole world, taking you into the family, setting out a picnic under shady trees, serving food from all over the world and saying, 'Eat. You're home,' and that's why I'm a patriot."

"And won first prize," I finish for her.

"Interesting," he says. And then to me, "And you, Miss Kelly, are you a writer too?"

I shake my head, no, but Rose speaks up. "Nora's an artist. She can draw anything and anybody. See the dress she's wearing? She designed it."

"And Rose made the pattern and sewed it for me," I say. "Not easy to get a hobble skirt right and . . ."

"Really, girls," Miss Allen says. "I apologize, Mr. Bartlett. I didn't intend to waste your time this way. I just can't have such flibbertigibbets among my operators. They are a bad influence. And this one," she points at me, "is always talking to the girls about how women should vote, and all kinds of socialist nonsense."

"Yes, these three are a challenge," Mr. Bartlett says. "I see your problem and agree with you, these girls are not suited to be order takers. Would you three wait in the outer office please."

I hear Miss Allen let out a breath and say, "Thank you, sir, thank you. Two weeks' pay in lieu of notice would be fine," as we leave the office.

"Why is he making us wait," I say. "Fire us and be done with it."

But a few minutes later Mr. Bartlett calls us back in. Miss Allen's slumped down in her chair, silent.

"Miss Allen and I agree that her department is not the right place for you three," Mr. Bartlett says, "but Montgomery Ward doesn't want to lose such talented young women. Miss McCabe, I could use a good writer to answer the questions and suggestions customers send me. Do you think you could handle such correspondence?"

At first I don't take in what he's saying. But then I blurt out, "Mame has lovely handwriting."

"Montgomery Ward just has purchased typewriters, Miss Kelly," he says. "We feel women with their smaller fingers and ability to endure repetitive motion might be well suited to the typewriter. Miss McCabe, do you mind being part of such an experiment?"

"Not at all, Mr. Bartlett," Mame says.

"And you two," he says, "might collaborate on women's fashions. Montgomery Ward has wanted to add such a section to our catalog. But our customers would not be interested in European styles or even New York imports. We want nice dresses with easy-to-follow patterns. Turn around, Miss Kelly . . . Yes, plain but fashionable garments like your dress will do very nicely. Don't you agree, Miss Allen?"

She barely lifts her head. "I suppose so," she says.

"I'm thinking of setting up Miss Kelly and Miss Rose McCabe as our new Ladies' Fashion Department. We'll try, say, seven different pieces illustrated by Miss Kelly's design sketches in the catalog, then duplicate and sell Miss McCabe's patterns. We'll raise your salaries by one dollar a week."

This shocks Miss Allen. "But," she says, "they'll be making five dollars a week, and that's what I'm paid!"

"And you're worth every penny."

Then Mr. Bartlett says to me, "Montgomery Ward will own the designs and patterns outright, you understand that Miss Kelly?"

Wow. Is he really offering to pay me to make sketches of clothes when every teacher I've ever had has reprimanded me for doodling? And isn't my sister Henrietta death on me for "littering the house with useless scraps of paper"? Mr. Bartlett will put my sketches in the catalog with Rose's patterns for women to buy? I can do seven sketches in a day, so many ideas rattling around inside my head. Let Montgomery Ward own them. What am I going to do with them? Not likely Rose and I would ever set up as dressmakers. I can't see myself passing a tape measure around some lady's hips with my mouth full of pins. If I'd imagined a perfect job, drawing would be it, and for five dollars a week! Wait until Henrietta hears about this.

"Why not take the rest of the day off," Mr. Bartlett says. "Miss Allen will find some space for the Fashion Department, and put a desk and a typewriter in my outer office for you, Miss McCabe. Thank you, girls. Good afternoon."

We three can't move. Stunned is the least of it.

Finally Rose says, "Thank you, Mr. Bartlett. Thank you very much."

Mame adds, "We're very grateful."

And I say, "We will do a good job for you."

"I believe you will," he says, "and Miss Kelly, please give my regards to your brother Mike."

"You know him?"

"I do. And your cousin Ed, too, a fine boxer."

"You, you don't go to the Brighton Park Athletic Club, do you?" I ask.

"Sometimes," he said. "On Saturday when I visit my grandmother, Kate O'Connor."

"Of the shop?" says Rose. "Are you her daughter Mary's son?"

"Yes," he says.

"But Aunt Kate Larney says Mary O'Connor married a rich Protestant and left the neighborhood."

"Not entirely," he says, and then, "Miss Allen, close your mouth." He smiles at us. "I married a McCarthy from the Patch. My wife and I are at Faith, Hope and Charity in Winnetka. I've had my eye on you three for a while."

"Oh Jesus," I say. "You had us shaking in our boots, not knowing you were one of us."

"I am first and foremost an employee of Montgomery Ward. I am offering you these jobs because I believe you have talents that will benefit the company. But there will be no favoritism, and certainly no disruptions of our labor force by troublemakers of any denomination. Is that understood, Miss Kelly?"

"I'm a Democrat, not an agitator," I say. "But I do want women to vote and workers to be treated fairly. What's wrong with that?"

"Nothing," he says, "as long as you do a good day's work."

"Oh, we will, we will," Rose says.

"Come on, Nonie," Mame says, "before our afternoon off is over. We'll be back promptly at nine, Miss Allen."

Our former supervisor stands up, straightens her back.

"Eight-forty-five," she says.

"But . . ." I start.

The McCabes take my arm and push me out the door.

"For Lord's sake, Nonie," Mame says to me when we are safely down the stairs and in the hallway. "Were you trying to talk the man into changing his mind?"

"What do we tell the others?" I say as we stand before the door to the telephone room.

"They're probably sure we've been fired," Mame says. "They'll be happy for us."

"Will they?" I say. I'm thinking of Henrietta's begrudgery and wondering how I'd react to such a tale of good fortune. Jealousy and Envy—two of the deadly sins according to the catechism.

I want to hold on to the good news, to protect it, but Mame's through the door saying, "Girls! Girls! We didn't get fired! We have lovely new jobs! Isn't that wonderful?"

All of them look at us, surprised, and I see some of that deadly sinfulness on a few faces.

But then Alice Jennings, who sits next to Mame, gets up, comes over, and hugs her. "I'm so glad!"

And then from the others, "Good on you! Good girls, yourselves!"

Well, I think, Tim McShane should know that Dolly McKee's not the only professional woman going. What God has for you won't go past you.

2

When I tell them at dinner that night that I'm a dress designer now, making money from my sketches, Agnella, good girl that she is, is over the moon, which annoys Henrietta no end, especially when Mam says, "I loved to draw when I was a girl in Mayo. I used a charred stick and a bit of slate to get the look of our cottage and the fields around it. Such a lovely little place."

Mam mourns for Auld Ireland just as Granny Honora did. As a little kid and the youngest grandchild I loved hearing Granny's stories about her home on the shores of Galway Bay. At fourteen, I stopped listening to her stories.

"Too busy, Granny," I said, rushing out to St. Xavier's High School myself or to the dances at St. Bridget's parish hall, one thing always leading to another. By good luck Ag was living with us then and glad enough to settle herself into Granny Honora's lap and listen. Especially after Granny took us all to the World's Fair and the Irish Village. Four years old, Ag was, and thought she somehow saw Galway Bay from above. "No Ag," I told her, the two of us sitting at the kitchen table, her watching me do my homework, a year or so after the Fair. "We went up in the air in the Ferris wheel and looked down on the thatched cottages of the Irish Village on Lake Michigan. That is what you remember."

"But I can close my eyes right now and see Ireland," she said. "The green grass, the hills, the white cottages, the blue water rushing in to break on the stones."

"Well, Ag," I told her, "I see that too, in my imagination. I suppose all of us whose parents or grandparents came from Ireland have pictures in our heads that come from their songs and stories." And then I sang to her, "'When the fields are fresh and green, I will take you to your home, Kathleen.'"

My great-aunt Máire, walking through the kitchen, heard us. "I'm one who doesn't want to go home," she said. "The songs don't talk about people starving to death and bodies laying in the street and the landlord stepping over them. Be glad you are in Amerikay, girls. I am."

I knew Máire's children had a landlord for their father. It was her son, my cousin Thomas, told me that day at the Fair when we were all having our dinner at Mrs. Hart's Donegal Castle. The menu said, "Ye Olde Medieval Fare," but it was corned beef and cabbage.

Thomas had settled in San Francisco and must have been about fifty then, never married, and a dour kind of fellow, not laughing and chatting away like the rest of us. A drinker, nipping from the silver pocket flask he offered to no one. He leaned over to me and said, "I own a real castle in Ireland, my father's, and I'm his oldest son."

I saw Aunt Máire watching us and later as we walked along the midway she took me aside.

"Thomas blathering away to you about his lost inheritance?" she asked me.

"A bit," I said.

"Poor Thomas," she said, "made up a story in his head and I haven't the heart to tell him his grandfather Pyke was a monster and the son, his father, not much better."

She pointed ahead to where my great-uncle Patrick—my grandda Michael's brother—and Granny Honora walked together. Married to each other now. Something to get your head around. "Your uncle Patrick told my sons Thomas and Daniel that their father, Robert Pyke, had died a soldier's death in India. Knew it would please them. Though why anyone would be glad to see the English taking some other poor country by the throat I don't know."

When I was small I thought Uncle Patrick was my grandda. But Uncle

Patrick said I'd had the best grandfather in the world, his brother Michael Kelly. "A better man than I am."

"But he's dead," I said. I was about ten. I liked to help him dig potatoes from the patch he cultivated in a clear space not far from the riverbank where he told me the last Potawatomi family in Bridgeport had camped. Lots of good stories from Uncle Patrick.

"And what does how long a fellow lives have to do with his greatness?" he asked me.

"But isn't living better than dying?" I said.

"Not always," he said.

And I wonder if that wasn't the day I started turning away from the stories Granny and the black-shawled chorus of women who gathered at our fire told. Such sad tales—lovers separated, soldiers dead, ships going down. In Chicago, Irish people lived happily ever after. Danced to Mc-Namara's band, the finest in the land, got better jobs, bigger houses, sent their sons to Notre Dame, and cheered the "Fighting Irish" to victory after victory. We lost in Auld Ireland but we are winning in Chicago. Look at me: head of design for Ladies' Fashion at Montgomery Ward. "Hurrah for me!"

Except Henrietta's saying, "Montgomery Ward must be soft in the head. No one's going to buy some silly dress that you've concocted, Nonie. Something else is going on here. What's this Bartlett expect from you?"

Mam and Agnella only look to her, not understanding, but Mike speaks up sharply.

"Now Henrietta, that's enough. Al Bartlett is a fine fellow and a member of the Knights of Columbus. Nonie has plenty of talent."

"Thanks, Mike," I say. "Besides, I've Rose McCabe helping me."

"And Mame?" Mike asks. "Is she part of this new enterprise?"

"She's got her own job writing letters to customers as Mr. Bartlett's special assistant."

"Now that's wonderful," Mam says. "Such a nice young woman, Mame."

And Henrietta grunts—the noise coming through her clenched teeth. "When I think of how I worked," she says, "scrubbing floors for those ungrateful bitches on Michigan Avenue . . ."

"Language, Henrietta!" Mam says.

"That's right! Criticize me when I'm only telling the truth. But then no one cares about what I think, not when Miss Nora Kelly, who's too good to lift a hand to help keep this house clean and tidy, is bragging away about herself."

"Oh, Mother," Agnella says, reaching her hand out to touch Henrietta's shoulder.

"Don't 'oh Mother' me, Agnella Kelly. Letting yourself become infected by Nonie. I named you for my own teacher, Sister Agnella, who appreciated me and to have you, my own daughter . . ." And then Henrietta stands, her face all red and squinched up, forces out whatever stray tears she can muster, and leaves the table.

Ag gets up to go after her, but Mam says, "Finish your dinner, Agnella," and follows Henrietta to her room.

So, there we sit, picking at the food on our plates. Deflated.

"She holds us all hostage," I say. "With her begrudgery and . . ."

"Please, Nonie," Mike says, and points at Agnella and her brothers— Bill, a silent little fellow at twelve, and Ed, ten, a charmer who entertains us all with his stories. Both are subdued now. And Annie—the police- woman who arrested a bank robber, for God's sake—looking out into space and shaking her head. Jim and Mart silent.

"Well, not me," I say. "Tell Mam I'm going to spend the evening with the McCabes." I get up and walk out.

I stomp down the stairs and onto Hillock. Henrietta ruins everything, and we let her. The worst kind of begrudger, Granny Honora's word for somebody who resents someone else's success. I know she's had a hard time of it, widowed and all, but Jesus, Mary, and Joseph, she's never missed a meal. Mike bears the biggest share of the burden but all of us contribute to the rent and the food, supporting her and her children. I clench my fist so tightly my fingernails cut into my palms. She makes me so angry. "Ignore her," I tell myself over and over. But I can't.

A lovely evening and the wind blowing from the Lake, pushing away smells from the stockyards. Seven o'clock, still light. The clouds cluster around the sun just starting to set over the prairie. The West. Uncle Stephen, Ed's father, tells stories about how covered wagons gathered right here at the edge of Bridgeport, ready to follow Archer Avenue until it disappeared into the high grass and open spaces. If I saw a wagon taking off right this minute, I'd climb on it no question. California, here I come.

Instead I walk west for two miles until I reach Brighton Park ard Aunt

Kate Larney's boardinghouse, where Rose and Mame McCabe live. The sisters are sitting on the porch with Aunt Kate's son John Larney, a pleasant-looking man of about thirty. You'd not guess he was a police detective unless you noticed how his body seemed packed into the navy blue suit he's wearing.

Rose gets up and comes to the top step. "Nonie, what's wrong? Somebody sick?"

"Not physically," I say.

"What . . ." Rose starts.

I run up the steps to her and say, "Not to worry, Rose, I'm out for an evening stroll."

"And just in time to celebrate with us," John says. "Your new jobs and the return of the wanderer."

The door into the house opens and out comes Ed with two pitchers, one of beer and the other of lemonade, followed by Aunt Kate with a plate of cookies.

"Ed," I say, "when did you come home?"

"Just today, a little while ago," he says, setting the pitchers down on the big white wicker table on the porch.

"Looking fit," I say. He's taken his suit jacket off, wearing a very white starched shirt and bow tie.

He's added some muscle out there surveying with the army. Always tall, the Kelly men, both Ed and Mike well over six feet but Ed the only red-head among the boys and men, and me the only girl with red hair.

"The Twins," Granny Honora called us, though Ed was three years older than I. Always a special bond between us. Funny how I could tell him things I couldn't talk about to my own brothers. Maybe because Mike and Mart and Jim only saw me as the little sister.

I was so happy when Henrietta brought me Agnella. Finally a little sister for me. I loved Henrietta's boys, too. Only babies when they first came to us. Hard for them growing up around that gang of big men, their uncles, tromping in and out of the place, filling our small apartment, beds in every room. Mam, Granny Honora, Annie, and I in one bedroom, with the four boys sharing the second and the third for Henrietta and her children.

"This is how we lived when we came from Ireland," Granny Honora would say. "Máire and I with nine children between us."

"I moved out as soon as I could," Máire had whispered to me.

And then the visitors; some fellow connected to us somehow coming from 'Auld Ireland,' sleeping up in the parlor for a month or two until he found work and a place of his own.

Wouldn't I love a room to myself in Aunt Kate's boardinghouse, I think as I settle myself in one of the wicker chairs. John Larney and Rose share the swing, moving with a breeze that brings the freshness of Lake Michigan to us. And now Ed sits next to Mame on the loveseat.

Aunt Kate pours out lemonade for Rose and Mame and me and beer for the boys and herself. Kate's father was German and her mother was Irish, and although she and her sister—my aunt Nelly, Ed's mother—have both married Irishmen, they still take a glass or two of Pilsen at night. A no-nonsense woman Aunt Kate, with her flowered apron and thick-soled shoes, gray hair pulled back in a knob. But kind. A second mother to Rose and Mame McCabe, who'd lost their own so young.

Ed begins to tell us about his adventures with the army surveying team that was plotting a route for a new canal through the wilds of Michigan to connect with the Great Lakes.

"At first," he says, "I was rod man, only holding the rods while the others measured. All of the rest had gone to university. And here I was with only my night school learning. But I had on-the-job training at the Sanitary District, I told them, starting as an axe-man cutting trees along the canal. So then I worked my way from rod-man to full-fledged surveyor. At camp, after dinner, I'd get Captain Lewis to discuss the work. Asked him a lot of questions about the best way to blast through the rocks, how to test the soil, things like that. He gave me more and more responsibility. Said every important engineering project depends on an accurate survey. Have to know the lay of the land first. I told him that was true of most things."

John tells Ed he's sure the army boys were impressed and hoped they would send a good report back to the Sanitary District. "You're going to need help getting your old job back, Ed, with the Republicans in charge," he says.

John and Ed are off and running about who had been elected and whose brother-in-law had gotten the top job until Mame says, "Politics. You two always end up going on about politics. Can't we talk about something else?"

Ed smiles at her. "Sorry, Mame. Don't mean to bore you."

Bore her? Politics are Ed's lifeblood and he's apologizing? What's going on between him and Mame? And now he's asking her all about our pro-motions and the letters she plans to write. Taking in every word.

So. No wonder he stopped by here before he came to tell us he was home. Yet Mame hasn't said one word to me about Ed, nor Ed about Mame. Had she forgotten "the Pact" we three girls made last summer on this very porch? We promised each other we wouldn't be panicked into getting married. I think the McCabes wanted to support me after I said no to Joe Murphy. A nice enough fellow but not a bit of chat in him. I couldn't un-derstand why he was even courting me except he was a friend of Mart's and lived next door and thought it was time to go for a bride. He started appearing in our parlor on Sundays and after about a month he followed me into the kitchen and said, "So what about it?"

"What about what?" I asked, thinking he wanted a cup of tea or a glass of beer, but no, marriage was the "it" though I had to drag the words from him.

"Me, marry you, Joe?"

"Well," he said, "I've a good job in the quarry and likely to be the fore-man soon. My mother's dead, so she wouldn't have to live with us. All my sisters are married. We'd have the place to ourselves, which I thought you'd like."

God, did our house look so crowded he thought I'd marry him just to get some space?

"And do you have feelings for me, Joe?" I asked.

"Well, you're a good-looking woman, Nonie. And all your chattering doesn't bother me since, as you might have noticed, I'm not a great talker and so you could fill up the silence in any way you wanted."

"Well, Joe, that's nice of you, I'm sure, but I don't think we're really suited."

"Oh, sorry, I forgot. I love you, Nonie. Mart told me to say that first, but I get so nervous."

"Mart told you?" I said.

"He did. We were thinking you and me are both getting on in years . . ."

"You're forty, I'm twenty-three," I told him.

"You're as old as that?" he said. "I wasn't sure. Well, most of my friends and your friends are married and there's not all that many left to choose from. Mart said as well me as any other, since I'm steady and not a drinker and that you'd grab at your last chance to get married." And then he rubbed his eyes. "Whew, that's a lot of words came out of me at one time," he said, as if he'd surprised himself.

I smiled at him and thanked him for the effort, but I wasn't going to marry a fellow because he used up a week's worth of talk on me. I blathered on a bit about the great honor and what a fine husband he'd make some lucky girl.

"I might even be able to go for a younger one," he said.

I agreed that age wasn't as much of an issue for a fellow. He seemed happy, and I thought I'd done very well, keeping my temper when I wanted to blast him, telling myself he was only a shy *guilpín*. But then he asked would I help him propose to Rose or Mame McCabe.

"Which one?" I said, sarcastic now.

And he said, "Which do you think would have me?"

The eejit. And then I lost the run of myself a bit and said that all women weren't as desperate to get married as maybe his sisters had been. Mart had come over to tell me to keep my voice down. I could be heard in the parlor. And I'd told him if he'd mind his own business I wouldn't have to raise up and defend myself since it seemed my own brother was so anxious to get rid of me.

Joe spoke up and said, "Don't blame Mart. He only said you were always moaning about not being heard, and all I've done my whole life is listen."

Well, I couldn't keep raging at him, remembering how the Murphy girls would go on and on and on. Not worth yelling at Mart either, and I did make a good story of Joe's proposal for Rose and Mame. That's when we resolved not to marry at all unless we felt well and truly in love with a man who loved and appreciated us. If any such fellow showed up, we'd present him to the other two, who'd vote on him. Maybe women couldn't select the president of the United States but we could help each other pick the best man for an even more important job.

"And if we don't find such a fellow," I said, "we have our work and each other."

I stretched my hand out, and Mame put hers on top of mine with Rose covering Mame's, as the Three Musketeers did in the novel we'd all read, and we swore our oath.

Now here's Rose with John Larney and Mame with Ed and not a word to me from any of them. I look over at Aunt Kate, wondering. Is she the matchmaker? Snagging Mame for her sister's son and Rose for her own? A neat enough situation and she knew the McCabe girls were fine women, not silly young girls. Mike liked to quote the saying, "It's not the years in your life, it's the life in your years." Abraham Lincoln. The only good Republican ever.

Now, I am not in any way, shape, or form a begrudger. Living with Henrietta made me swear never to fall into that trap. I'm only thinking that somebody could have said something to me, and I wonder will they have a double wedding, with me a double bridesmaid? And maybe Ed would ask his father, my uncle Steve, to walk the girls down the aisle, though that might be odd, him being the father of the groom. My brother Mike might be more suited.

But here I am, planning their wedding, and them not even telling me! I assume they'd want me to stand up for them, but for all I know they might ask somebody else. Secrets! I hate secrets. And I thought we were so close.

Just then I hear the most god-awful racket out on the street, the blurt of an engine and then a rattling sound.

"An automobile," says Ed, and we all stand up and go to the porch rail.

Dusk now, but easy enough to see two big lights mounted on the hood of the horseless carriage as it gets closer. For all the talk of automobiles as the coming thing, there are very few around the place. Some in the Loop, which is what we call the heart of downtown where the horse tram tracks turn around on themselves. And, of course, the likes of Mrs. Potter Palmers and Marshall Field have chauffeur-driven vehicles, but not many automobiles come bouncing down Hillock or Archer either.

"An Oldsmobile," Ed says, "the latest model."

Like a carriage, all right, tall with four big wheels, the backseat higher than the front.

"All that noise," Aunt Kate says, "and the smell."

"Gasoline exhaust," Ed says.

"I like it," I say. "Better than horse manure."

Always talk about limiting Chicago's growth because the city's being overrun by piles and piles of the stuff left by the hundreds of horses filling our streets. No room for more wagons when we already have all that muck splattering our clothes. Well, compared to the stink of horse droppings, automobile exhaust smells like lemon verbena.

Now the automobile stops right in front of Aunt Kate's. A man gets out wearing a long black duster coat with goggles over his face. He starts up the sidewalk leading to the porch.

"Engine trouble," John says.

"Maybe the transmission," Ed says.

"Probably a valve overheated," John says.

"Or he needs water for the radiator," Ed says.

How knowledgeable the fellows are.

Already tossing off words like "radiator" and "transmission." Huge arguments around our dinner table about horseless carriages, with Mike all for them and Mart completely against.

"Toys for the rich," Mart said. "How many children will be run down and killed?"

Henrietta agreed, saying, "The likes of us will never be able to afford an automobile, that's for sure. One more way to mock the poor."

But Mam was more concerned about our uncle Michael's blacksmith business. "Blackshirt Mike" they called him and he was great for giving jobs to men just arrived from Ireland. My own grandfather Michael Kelly had wielded a hammer onto an anvil, Mam told us, and his grandfather before him, Granny Honora had said.

"Always will need blacksmiths, if only for racehorses," my brother James put in.

"You should know," Henrietta said. "The money you waste betting at Brighton Park track."

So a split vote on automobiles in our house, but now I can go home and say I've seen one.

The fellow climbs the steps and even before he pushes the goggles up on his head I know. Tim McShane, standing right in front of us. Jesus, Mary, and Joseph.

Ed speaks up first. "Quite a beautiful motorcar. An Oldsmobile, right?"

"Did it break down?" John asks.

"Not at all," Tim says. "I'm on my way to check my horses, and I saw you all in the shadows. Such a pleasant group, I couldn't help but stop. Hello, Mrs. Larney. Are those the famous cookies your son keeps talking about?"

"Well, John does like my *engelsaugen*," Aunt Kate says. "My German father taught my Irish mother the recipe."

John walks over to him. "I don't remember discussing my mother's cookies with you, Mr. McShane," he says.

"I suppose a police detective's life is so full he's bound to forget a few things," Tim says.

Aunt Kate looks from John to Tim and back, aware of the tension. And surprised at her son's bad manners. But she's too hospitable and too curious about the automobile not to invite Tim to join us. John's shaking his head as I say, "*Engelsaugen* mean's angel eyes."

And doesn't Tim McShane wink at me.

"I look forward to sampling them," Tim says.

"I'll just get another glass," Aunt Kate says.

"Let me, Aunt Kate," I say, and head into the house, passing Tim as he takes the empty chair next to mine.

"Hurry," he says to me softly.

My hand actually trembles as I take a glass from the kitchen cabinet. In Granny's stories, fairies or a pooka arrive riding a magic horse. Dear God, are they using automobiles now?

On the porch Tim touches my hand as he takes the glass, and I feel the spell taking hold. Pull away, Nonie, pull away, I tell myself.

"Thank you, Miss Kelly," he says.

"You're welcome, Mr. McShane."

"Tim—please. This is our third meeting."

"Third?" Ed says.

"All by accident," I say. "On the tram, at Henricci's, and now here."

"Oh yes, all accidental," Tim says.

John looks a question at Rose but she nods and smiles. Thinking of tickets for Dolly McKee's concert, I bet, while I'm drowning.

"Happy accidents," Tim says, biting into a cookie. "Wonderful." He smiles at Aunt Kate, who nods at him. "Angel eyes," he says to me.

"So nice to have young people together," Aunt Kate says. And doesn't she tell him about our new jobs—my designs for dresses, Rose's patterns, and Mame's letter writing.

And Tim McShane says, "Such talented women, and beautiful too."

John just grunts.

But Rose speaks up. "And how is Mrs. McKee, Mr. McShane?"

"Tim, please," he says. "Fine, excellent. Onstage right now and taking her bows."

"I'd have thought you'd be there," I say.

"No, Nora. We lead quite separate lives. Very good friends though, and have been for a long time."

"So I hear," I say.

"She owns the team of champion horses I train. I met her when I was a young lad cleaning stables and exercising the horses for Jim Boyle. This grand lady came sweeping in telling Jim she was moving all of her horses to his stable. Took an interest in me."

"And were your parents in the racing business, too, Tim?" Aunt Kate asks.

"Yes, but my dad died young, Mrs. Larney. We lived in Saratoga, and my father was a trainer."

"Saratoga—a place I've always wanted to visit," Mame says.

"Nothing better than a long soak in those mineral springs," he says, looking at me again.

I can't help but see him stretched out naked, water bubbling around him, and damn if he doesn't know what I'm thinking.

"And did your parents drown?" John says, which makes Rose poke him with her elbow.

"Sadly my father was kicked to death by a stallion who was mounting a mare," Tim says. "Animal passion hard to control." He catches my eye. The nerve of him. "My mother died soon after. I was fourteen."

"Very sad," Aunt Kate says.

"At least automobiles don't kick people to death," Ed says.

"They will," John Larney says. "Crashes already."

"That'll be sorted out when drivers are better," Ed says. Always up for whatever's new, Ed is.

As I sit in the warm darkness of that summer evening, I accept the tale. The poor but honest young orphan being scooped up by a grande dame, too naive to understand her intention. How well I listen, embroidering his story for him in my mind.

"I'd like to take you out for a drive sometime, Ed," Tim says.

Ed nods. "Machines will change everything. The roads we'll build . . . Captain Lewis and I used to talk about a great highway going along Lake Michigan. Parks and fine buildings on the shoreline and automobiles sailing by."

"But much of the shore is swamp," Tim says, which allows Ed to talk about landfill and reinforced concrete.

Ed's been dreaming of creating a new lakefront for Chicago since we watched the World's Fair buildings that made up the White City burn to the ground. Right before he left for the surveying we walked along Lake

Michigan past the piles of rusting tin cans and pieces of all kinds of junk that cover the shore. Even a decaying railroad car on the rocks just east of Michigan Avenue.

"What kind of city turns its most beautiful feature into a garbage dump?" Ed said.

"A city that works hard," I answered.

"More to Chicago than our sweat," Ed said. "Don't you remember Granny Honora taking us on picnics at the Lake, to that stretch of sand she found, south of Burnham Harbor, and how she made us half close our eyes and pretend the Lake was Galway Bay?"

"I do," I said, "and not one beautiful vista left."

And here's Ed going on about his dream for the lakefront to Tim Mc-Shane, who keeps nodding, agreeing with him.

"A real disgrace," Tim says. "Those of us who appreciate the finer things must band together and speak up. The grand mansions north of the city monopolize our lakefront. That's not fair."

"Exactly," Ed says. "Families from Bridgeport and Brighton Park and Bronzeville want to enjoy the green spaces too. We're the ones need to get out of the slums and into the fresh air."

"I couldn't agree more," Tim says. "My morning ride is the highlight of my day. To be up on a horse and see the sun climb out of the lake, hear the birds singing . . ." He sighs.

"I wouldn't have taken you for an early riser," I say to him.

"Not saying I'd been asleep, Nora," he says.

And now John Larney stands up. "Very nice of you to stop by, Mr. McShane, but we *are* early risers around here, and it's past ten o'clock. Come on, Nonie. I'll see you home."

"I'll come along," Ed says, "to say hello to Mike. Good night, Tim."

"But, lads, I thought you'd want to take a better look at the Oldsmobile. Run your hands along its withers as it were," Tim says.

"I'm sure we'd all like to pet your machine," I say. "Right, Mame? Rose? Aunt Kate?"

So we troop down and circle the Oldsmobile, standing under the new electric streetlight. Tim climbs into the front seat then rubs his hand along the upholstery.

"Genuine leather," Tim says. "Look at the curved dashboard. You steer with that stick."

Ed reaches out to touch it.

"Come on. Climb up," Tim says. "I'll teach you to drive her right now!"

"No," John says.

"I was asking Ed," Tim says.

And Ed steps away. John Larney is against Tim McShane, and Ed's ready to back John.

"Let's go, Nonie," John says. "Ed and I will walk you home now."

"Walking?" Tim says. "When this fine machine can carry Miss Kelly to her door in under ten minutes?"

Ed and John say, "No," at the same time.

Aunt Kate looks at them. "I suppose riding in such a thing could be dangerous," she says.

"Extremely," John says.

Rose and Mame stay silent. They step away from the automobile and say, "Good night, Nonie."

"Come on, Ed, Nonie," John says, very sharpish as he takes my arm.

Then Tim says to me, "I didn't realize you took orders from the Chicago Police Department."

I pull away from John. "I don't," I say. "Only John's very protective and Ed should know better. I'd go with you but I don't have the gear."

"I've some ladies' wear." He gets out, opens a compartment in the back of the car, and takes out a duster, goggles, and scarf. "This is to keep your hat on, but I see you don't wear one. Not very proper, Miss Kelly," he says. "To be out bareheaded."

"Nora was coming a short distance to visit family," Rose says to him.

"Didn't think you'd be so concerned about etiquette, Mr. McShane," I say.

"I'm not," he says, and starts to drape the scarf over my hair.

I grab the two ends and tie the silk square together.

"Nonie, don't," Rose says.

I know I shouldn't go, but maybe because I resent the McCabes' imagined double wedding or relish the shock on Henrietta's face when I pull up to our house in an Oldsmobile or maybe it's a fairy spell, but I button myself into the duster while Tim McShane climbs into the automobile. He leans over and offers me his hand and up I go.

"Is that the horn?" I ask, pointing to the rubber bulb.

"It is," he says.

I squeeze out a loud squeaking sound and turn to wave at Aunt Kate, John and Ed, and the McCabes. Short of manhandling me out of the horseless carriage, which would have upset his mother, John can do nothing.

Tim moves the stick and the motor rumbles. "See, no crank needed," he says to Ed, who is leaning close to watch. "Put her in gear and off we go," Tim says. "Sound the horn again, Nora."

I do. The automobile lurches forward. I look back to see a dark cloud coming from the machine. A bad smell, no question, trailing behind us as we turn onto Archer Avenue, stirring up the dust. Cattle herded along here. I'm glad for the goggles.

"Move closer to me," Tim shouts to me over the hiccoughing engine. "Center of gravity," he says, and points to a space nearer him. "Better to ride flank-to-flank. Don't want to tip over."

I slide next to him but don't let my leg touch his.

"Afraid?" he says.

"Not at all. We are not exactly speeding," I say.

"We're moving at twelve miles an hour," he says. "I can go faster."

"Bouncy," I say to him as we hit a deep rut in the road.

"I like the vibration," he says. "Lively."

Just room enough on the bridge over the canal for the automobile. We turn and drive along Bubbly Creek.

"Lucky there's no traffic," I shout.

"Yes. All these bridges will have to be rebuilt. Makes a man want to go into the construction business. Exciting times," he says, and pats my knee. And leaves his hand there. "I'll teach you to drive," he says.

I push his hand away. "Concentrate on *your* driving," I say.

"I'm a man able to do a number of things at the same time," he says, but doesn't touch me again.

He knows my address without asking, steers the automobile to the curb in front of 2703, and stops under the gas lamp. No electricity on Hillock yet.

"One of the old houses, I see," he says, pointing at our front door below street level.

"Lifted the road for the sewers," I say. "Years ago."

"Shouldn't be talking plumbing on such a night," he says. "Nice moon." Quick, get out, I tell myself. Don't talk about the moon or the stars. Don't let him walk you to the door. Don't stand with him in the cramped hidden space under the street. I start to unfasten the buttons of the duster.

"Let me help," he says, leaning over to me and running his fingers over the top button.

"Stop," I say, slapping his hand away. "You might not be used to respectable women, but we don't let strange men . . ."

Tim takes me by the shoulders, pulls me to him, and kisses me right on the lips.

"There," he says. "I've wanted to do that since I pulled you onto the tram."

"How dare you," I say, and stand up. "My brothers are right upstairs and I will—"

"Sit down, Nora. You're not a young girl. You're not a girl at all, but a twenty-five-year-old woman."

"Twenty-four," I say.

"A woman nonetheless, in spite of the fact that I'd wager you've never been with a man. Oh, I'm not saying you haven't given a fellow or two a wee court, but you have no idea—"

"I'm getting out of here," I say, and swing my legs over the side of the automobile. Very high up it is.

"You'll break your ankle," he says.

I wrap the duster around my legs and start to ease myself down from the high seat.

He grabs my arm. "For God's sake. I thought we wouldn't have to pretend. I thought I'd finally met a woman who could be honest about how she felt. Who'd be brave enough to take her pleasure like a man does."

"Let me go or I'll shout for my brothers," I say.

"No, you won't," he says. "You're not married and I'd say you could be, so what's stopping you? An instinct? Not willing to waste yourself on some clumsy fellow who'll come home from a night's drinking to roll over on you and . . ."

"Shut up!" I say.

"Ah, Nora, be sensible. The attraction between us is the most natural thing in the world and . . ."

"Are you proposing to me?" I ask.

"Yes, I am."

"You want to marry me?"

He laughs. "Come now, Nora Kelly, catch yourself on. Why would the likes of us want to be married? Aren't you launched on a great career, and don't I have certain obligations?"

"Dolly McKee," I say.

"Yes, Dolly and I are business associates."

"And lovers."

"Not sure if I'd say that but yes, there are physical duties."

I laugh. "You have some nerve, Tim McShane," I say.

He laughs too. "We'd have a bit of fun. What's the harm? And I know about protection so no worries about getting you in the family way. I'd just like to see you let out a bit of the spirit you're holding down. No one the wiser. And if the time comes when you feel you need a bunch of kids, and want to find some nice fellow, well, I'd not stand in your way. Friends at the end and no hard feelings. Nora, darling." He traces the shape of my lips with his fingers. "Be brave."

Honora Bridget Kelly, St. Xavier's graduate, Montgomery Ward designer, descendant of the Kelly kings of Ireland, slides out of that machine, climbs up the steps, and never sees Tim McShane again. Ah, but the fairy woman who's taken me over lifts her face up and kisses Tim McShane.

After that first long kiss, I do put my hand on his chest, push away, get out of the automobile, run up the three flights of stairs, and go through our front door and down the long hall into our kitchen.

Safe.

Except . . .

"Mam." She stands at the stove waiting for the kettle to boil. "You're up late. Making me a nice cup of tea?" I ask, and kiss her on the cheek. Get out of my mind, Tim McShane. Now.

Not often I'm alone with Mam, and the kitchen so quiet and cozy.

"A cup of tea, is it? I should box your ears. Fighting with Henrietta and then out until all hours."

"Now, Mam. You've never struck any one of us. Why start now?"

She laughs. "How are the McCabes and Kate?"

"Fine. Rose and John Larney are definitely courting. Ed Kelly was there. Home from the wilds. I think he has a notion of Mame McCabe."

Mam nods. "She'd be doing well with him working for the city and opening that wake house with What's-his-name Doran."

"It's called a funeral parlor, Mam. The coming thing. Better than having the corpse in the house. Creepy, that."

"Not when it's the body of someone you love, Nonie. I would never have let your father rest in some strange place! What would he think of me? We gave him a grand funeral, didn't we?"

"Grand, Mam."

"You were probably too young to remember, only five years old."

"I remember, Mam."

"Such a comfort for your granny Honora to know that when her time came she had a neat grave next to him in Calvary under that big tree."

I get two mugs for the tea down from the cabinet.

But Mam says, "I'm boiling water for Jim. He started coughing after dinner. All stuffed up. This steam should help."

"Thirty years old and still being looked after by his mother. And you wonder why none of us leave home?" I say.

"Oh, you'll be going, Nonie. You're not meant to be a home bird. You'll meet the right fellow one day. No rush."

And I almost tell her. Say, "Mam, something's taken me by the throat, and I don't know what to do." But instead I find a big kitchen towel, lift the kettle, and follow Mam, who carries a bowl into the parlor, where Jim lies half-asleep on the horsehair sofa.

I help sit him up and drape the towel over his head while Mam pours the boiling water into the white bowl and holds it under his chin.

"Breathe in the steam," Mam says to him.

Jim tries, but hard as he sniffs he can't pull the steam into his blocked nose.

"Try through your mouth," I say.

He gulps but then starts coughing, a deep rasping sound. I can smell the mentholated grease Mam has rubbed into his chest.

"I only wish we had Uncle Patrick's salve," she says. Some Indian concoction from my great-uncle Patrick's Ojibwa pals, the remedy of my growing up, gone since Uncle Patrick died ten years ago, with Great-Aunt Máire and Granny Honora following close behind him. Not one of them making it into the twentieth century.

"I'm burning up, Mam," Jim says.

"Dear God, Mam," I say. "Should I go for the doctor?"

"Dr. Haley was here earlier. 'A bad cold,' he says, but this weather. I'm afraid it could turn into pneumonia."

Some lore brought over from Ireland that the start of summer holds special dangers. Warm days turning into cold nights, confusing the body, leaving it open to invasion.

We sit with Jim until he finally falls asleep.

"He'll be grand in the morning, Mam," I say.

Mike and Mart and Henrietta's boys are snoring away in their room, and Henrietta and Agnella asleep, too, in theirs.

Mam follows me into our room. Annie wakes up.

"How is he?" she asks.

"Sleeping," I say, and settle myself next to Mam on the bed we share.

A quiet sleeper is Mam and never moves much, but all the same I'm ashamed at how my mind goes back into the Oldsmobile with Tim Mc-Shane while my mother breathes so close to me. "Take your pleasure like a man does," he'd said, but here I am sleeping with my mother and my sister in the next bed. Not a place to think about taking pleasure like a man. I could never . . . Could I?

The next morning Jim isn't better. Coughing and spitting out wads of green and yellow phlegm, and Mam is worried.

"I'll stay home, Mam," I tell her. Though I'll hate to miss the first day of my new job.

"Go, Nonie. Henrietta's here."

"I am, Mam," Henrietta says—too loud, I think. "I'm here."

Mr. Bartlett is as good as his word. He's set up Rose and me in a "studio"—yes, he uses that word—with a long countertop, a wooden table, and four chairs.

He points to the big window. "North light."

"Oh, Rose," I say when he's left. "Remember what Sister Immaculée called those Paris painter's studios? Ateliers? We have our very own atelier."

"Except we need paper and pins and scissors and . . . Oh, Nonie, do you think they'll get me a sewing machine?"

"Let's make a list. 'In for a penny, in for a pound,'" I say, using Granny Honora's brogue.

And how fast the day goes. We don't even think of lunch. I forget about

Jim's cold and we wave Mame away when she comes by for a chat. Rose and me in a fever—our place, our studio.

Atelier, I whisper to myself. The Fairy Woman can't get me here. More pleasure in working than from kissing Tim McShane. Taking my pleasure like an artist, I think.

Late when we leave, and later still when I get home. Long past dinner, startled to see every light on in the parlor. Jim . . .

Dr. Haley is leaving when I come in, standing in the doorway talking to Mike. I hear him say, "Keep them drinking water and hot tea, steam to help them breathe, and hope their lungs can throw it off."

Them?

"Is Jim worse, Mike?" I ask.

"He is, Nonie. And Mam's . . . Henrietta said she started coughing this morning. Couldn't stop."

"Did Henrietta try tea with lemon and honey? Did she call the doctor right away?" I say.

Henrietta comes out of the bedroom. I start to go to Mam but Henrietta puts her hand on my arm.

"Mam's finally sleeping," she says. "Leave her alone."

But I shake off Henrietta and go in. Annie is sitting in the chair next to the bed watching Mam. Terrible jagged gulps of air Mam is taking in, not breathing easy in sleep.

Annie takes my hand. "She's strong. She's not old like Granny Honora."

Yes, I think. Mam's only fifty-three and she's never been sick. Had seven children and not a bother on her. Only a young girl when she traveled from Ireland with her brothers, her parents dead, the worst of the Great Starvation over, but bad times nevertheless. Always proud she lived in New York.

"Well, Jersey City, really, but I've walked the streets of Manhattan, I have," she'd say.

"Are they paved with gold, Mam?" I asked, teasing her.

"They were, Nonie, because my brothers were well paid for paving them."

Her brothers. Luke and Dominic. Do they know?

I go out to the kitchen to ask Henrietta has she told them Mam is sick.

"No need to make a show of ourselves," Henrietta says. "Mam'll be fine, and we don't want to look like fools alarmed over nothing."

Saturday the next day, thank God, and my day off, though I'd not have gone in to work anyway. Late afternoon when Jim becomes delirious, trying to get out of bed. Mike has to hold him down. Jim is saying that he has to help Da at the blacksmith shop, the place he'd worked as a boy.

Mam says nothing. Coughing and coughing, her shoulders shaking. We try steam, me holding the towel over her head and Annie offering the bowl while Agnella sits on the floor next to her holding Mam's hand.

Henrietta comes marching in. "Too many people," she says, and makes us leave.

We wait in the kitchen, taking our turns sitting with her. No change Sunday. Jim in the parlor, Mam in the bedroom as Dr. Haley goes from one to the next not saying much. We eat cold spuds and chunks of ham for dinner, but that night Joe Murphy's wife brings a pot of stew and loaves of fresh-baked brown bread. I don't go to work on Monday. Rose comes by. She'll tell Mr. Bartlett why I'm missing.

Mam's brothers come, and Aunt Kate and Aunt Nelly with Uncle Stephen, and Uncle Michael and his wife, Mary Chambers. Dr. Haley only allows each one a few minutes.

"How're you keeping, Bridey?" they say to her, and Mam tries to smile.

Two days of this and Dr. Haley says, "That's it. She must rest."

What with sleeping and coughing, Mam is only able to take a little soup, some tea.

"Mam, Mam," I murmur over and over when it is my time to sit with her. She tries to talk but then the coughing takes over. "Don't, Mam, stay still."

We don't tell her when Jim dies, early in the morning on June 30th. Jim—my silent brother—keeping himself to himself but a good fellow. Oh, Jim, I hardly knew you! Lost in our big chattering family. Me, too busy bickering with Henrietta to take much notice of you. Dear Jim, forgive me. Rest in peace. And then another prayer. Dear God, you took my brother. Leave my mother, please God. Please!

Ed lays Jim out at his new funeral home. Only one night for the wake, and the funeral Mass is the next morning. I stay with Mam while the rest go to church.

She wakes up. "Jim, Nonie. How's Jim?"

"He's fine," I start.

But she tries to sit up. "Jim?" she calls out. "Jim?"

"He's . . . he's gone, Mam. The Mass is going on now."

She turns, reaching under her pillow, grabbing for something.

"Your beads, Mam?"

"Please."

I take the rosary from the dresser and put them in Mam's hands. She lies back against the pillows and starts fingering the wooden beads Da carved for her.

She crosses herself. "In the name of the Father," she manages to say before the coughing shakes her. "And of the Son and of the Holy Ghost," I finish. Then I say the Our Father, the first Hail Mary.

The spasms weaken Mam but she tries to pray with me. I hate saying "now and at the hour of our death."

"Hold on, Mam," I whisper to her. "Outlast it."

"I'm tired, Nonie. So tired."

"Rest, Mam," I say.

"Nonie," she says. "You must be good, Nonie. Promise me. A woman has only her good name and without it . . ." Another spasm.

"Quiet, Mam."

I stroke her forehead. Now why would she say such a thing? I haven't seen Tim McShane—or thought of him even—since last week. Far too worried about Mam.

"Mam," I whisper.

She closes her eyes. Breathing easier. Asleep. She'll wake up better. But she doesn't.

Thank God all of us are with her as the end comes. Even my brother Ed and his wife come from Indiana.

Henrietta kneels at the side of her bed, sobbing. Annie stands between Mart and Mike, not moving, Ed next to Agnella behind them, Henrietta's boys in the doorway, and me sitting on the bed beside my mother, stroking her hair, holding her hand . . . not sure she is still alive.

But then she opens her eyes. "Paddy," she says, looking off toward the window, and then clear as anything to us: "Your father's come to take me home."

Gone in that moment. Her spirit free before that awful sound—the death rattle—goes through her body.

Gone. And the rest of us more alone than ever before.

Tim McShane comes to my mother's wake, he and Dolly McKee marching right into the Kelly and Doran Funeral Parlor. Dolly stands by the coffin and sings an "Ave Maria" that no one will ever forget. I feel nothing when Tim shakes my hand. Thank God. Only thinking of Mam. How can I go on without her?

"You'll feel her presence," Aunt Nelly promises me.

And I do have a sense that she's glad to take her place next to Da, not in Calvary. No room. We bury them both in the new cemetery Mount Carmel. Ed arranges everything, buys the plot, sends a crew from the Sanitary District to dig Da's coffin up in Calvary, drive it to Mount Carmel. All done in one day, and Da ready to be buried with Mam.

"Excessive," Henrietta says. "Expensive."

But Jesus Christ, don't we want them to be together?

"What about Granny Honora?" I say to Ed. "You left her there in Calvary."

"She's with Aunt Máire, Uncle Patrick, and Maire's son Johnny Og," Ed says. "Colonel Mulligan's there too, all the soldiers from the Civil War. Let her be, Nonie."

Jim and Mam, gone within a week. I can't even form the thought. Still expect Mam to walk into the kitchen . . .

⸎

Another week before I can go back to work. Awful staying home with Henrietta. I resolved for Mam's sake to be kind and loving to her. After all, we share the same sorrow but, dear God, Henrietta would try the patience of a saint.

"If only you had told me that first night," she said to me. "Jim should have been moved to the hospital. Wouldn't have infected Mam. Could have saved them both." Ridiculous but still . . .

Glad to be in the studio with Rose again.

"You'll never get over losing her," Rose says. "But your mother'll be with you. And you will be happy again, Nonie. I know it seems impossible, but she'll make sure of that. She wants you to be happy. I know she does."

And some solace in the work. We get the new Singer and Rose makes a dress from one of my sketches that Mr. Bartlett approves. The pattern will be sold in the catalog.

But I'm so lonely for Mam! A month somehow passes. And then one night I come out of Ward's to find Tim McShane standing on the corner. He takes my arm and leads me across the street to where the Oldsmobile is parked.

He helps me up, and I sit close to him as we drive north and then east to a small hotel on State Street and a shabby room where the Fairy Woman takes me over.

And so it begins.

3

STATE STREET HOTEL

1903–1911

Now, in Granny Honora's stories the women do not go back and forth to
fairyland, but that's me during the next eight years. For all Tim's talk about
how he and Dolly McKee live separate lives, they reside together. He has a
suite down the hall from hers at the Palmer House. But he also rents a
room in that small hotel on State Street near Holy Name Cathedral and
the big white stone church reproaches me every time I pass it on my way
back from Tim's to my real life. We meet every Tuesday and Thursday
from four to seven when Dolly has her special beauty treatments, though
not during Christmas when I'm with my family or in August when Tim
and Dolly go to Saratoga.

Sometimes he'll telephone me at Montgomery Ward. Bold as you
please, telling my assistant that Mrs. Dolly McKee would like to see Miss
Kelly's latest sketches or wants to try on a dress. Yes, believe it or not, Tim
makes Dolly our go-between. She doesn't know it, or so I think, and of
course everyone at Montgomery Ward's only too delighted to have the
great Dolly McKee actually ordering our designs. No one more than Rose,
who not only makes the patterns for Dolly, but sews them into beautiful
dresses for her. Not the fabulous gowns Dolly wears onstage, or even the

daytime costumes she appears in for her lunches at Henricci's or the Berg-hoff. No, our dresses are the simple clothes she wears "in my private time" as she told the *Tribune* in the article Tim arranged to have written with my sketches of Dolly in our dresses as illustrations.

Now, I thought I'd be so consumed with guilt that I wouldn't be able to look Dolly McKee in the face, but instead I laugh with her over lunch, and take my entire family to McVicker's Theatre when the Cohans come to town. Dolly sings "Believe Me, if All Those Endearing Young Charms"—going on about love's constancy to George M. while offstage Tim and I betray her every week.

Oh, I am bothered at the beginning. During that first year I resolved over and over not to climb the stairs to that room ever again. But Tim said I was helping Dolly really, as he was much kinder and more caring with her now that we had our afternoons on North State Street. I have to admit I was nicer to Henrietta, too. She didn't annoy me as much. Still ranting and raging at the drop of a hat but now I'd say to myself, "She's frustrated," because Tim had told me women needed sex just as much as men did only most of them didn't know it.

"Always going on about love when it's really sex they want," he'd say, as if love was the greatest fool's game going.

"And you're speaking from experience, I suppose," I said as we got dressed one afternoon a year and a half into our, well, our "special friend-ship," as Tim called it.

"I am. 'Do you love me?'" he said in a high voice. "How the hell do I know? No such foolishness with Dolly or you either, Nonie. Sorry, *Nora*."

I insisted from the beginning that he call me only Nora. Nonie was the real me, the Bridgeport girl who went to ten o'clock Mass at St. Bridget's on Sundays and gave Henrietta a share of her pay every Friday, who danced at Rose's wedding when she married John Larney in 1905 and walked along the Lake with Ed two years later when he told me with a kind of matter-of-fact sadness why he and Mame would never marry.

"Politics," he'd said. "She doesn't understand why I spend so much time on campaigns and elections. I told her what Uncle Patrick said. Remember?" he asked me.

Of course I did. Drummed into our heads. Politics would save us. The Irish died during the Great Starvation because they didn't have their own aldermen and precinct captains.

"If our people had been in office all that food would not have been sent out of the country. One million people would not have been murdered," Uncle Patrick told us.

"I don't know, Ed," I said to him. "Sometimes it's hard to see fellows like Bathhouse John Kelly or Hinky Dink McKenna as noble figures. What would Uncle Patrick think of them?"

"A few bad apples," Ed said.

"Well, you know, Ed," I said. "Mame's not fond of drink or drinkers, and politics always seems to happen in saloons."

"What do you expect when half the City Council members own one or more bars?" Ed said. "Where else can workingmen gather? All right for the rich with their gentlemen's clubs."

"Seems like a lot of these champions of the common man are getting rich themselves," I said.

"So what, Nonie? A bigger house, a car. That's not being really rich. Our boys don't own companies that gouge workers. They stand up for us. Where would I be right now without Tom Casey?"

As John Larney had predicted, Ed's old job at the Sanitary District was given to the brother-in-law of a Republican alderman while Ed was away with the army surveyors. Tom Casey, our Democratic alderman, had enough clout to get it back for him.

"But that was only right. You were the best man for the job," I said.

And Ed only laughed.

I didn't tell him that I thought there might be another reason for Mame's reluctance. At Rose's wedding she told me she was in love with someone, waiting for him, though she wouldn't tell me who it was.

"Is he, uhm, involved with someone else?" Hoping she'd say yes, God forgive me. Share my guilt a bit.

"You mean married?" she asked. "He's not, but he has family obligations." And she refused to say more.

But then Rose and Mame and I didn't talk to each other as freely as we did. Mame was living with Rose and John now, and I walled off a whole part of my life from them.

I watched every word. Well into the third year I felt so full of shame I told Tim that it was over, we were finished. And he made a show of being a gentleman, and said of course, if that was what I wanted. But then he started going on about how much he cared for me, hadn't he even fallen in love with me, much to his surprise, and he wanted nothing more than to marry me.

"Dolly isn't really well," he said. "Always had a weak heart. She won't see sixty."

And then he dropped hints about what he'd inherit in Dolly's will. He said he knew money didn't mean all that much to me, but we'd be very comfortable. He could provide for our children. On and on and then he put his head in his hands and cried. And I thought, "The big galoot is in love for the first time in his life," and well, we made it up. Now I hadn't been much good at the lovemaking itself in the beginning but Tim liked teaching me. Patient—from training horses I guess. I was surprised at how I got the hang of it. The Fairy Woman all pleased with herself and taking me over completely.

But then two years later on my thirtieth birthday, April 18, 1909, all of a sudden I wanted to have a child. Decided I couldn't wait much longer. Not that women in Bridgeport didn't go on bearing children well into their forties, but I surprised myself with a kind of longing to hold my own baby. I thought raising Agnella had filled that need once and for all, and that she'd marry and bring her kids over to me. Plenty of babies to cuddle then send home.

But at seventeen, Agnella joined the BVMs, Sisters of Charity of the Blessed Virgin Mary in Dubuque, Iowa. Over the moon Henrietta was. The whole family celebrated.

"Your mam would be proud and your granny Honora would have been so pleased," Ed's mother, Aunt Nelly, said to me. "She always said the Kellys owed a daughter to the convent, what with her changing her mind about becoming a nun when your grandfather came to her naked out of the waves of Galway Bay."

"What?" I said. "Now that's a story she never told me!"

I wondered if I could have talked to Granny Honora about Tim Mc-Shane were she alive. Surely, Aunt Máire would've understood. I remember the night Henrietta accused me of having Aunt Máire's bad blood in me. I must have been seventeen or eighteen. Henrietta had caught me kissing Kevin Connelly in the gangway. I only did it because Kevin was such a gormless fellow, and I knew he'd be over the moon if I gave him the slightest peck and really what harm? Late and Mam and Granny Honora asleep—Henrietta too I thought but she saw us from the window and began screaming: "You harlot! You're disgracing your family!" and then, "It's Máire's bad blood!!" A warm night and every house on Hillock with their windows open listening to her screech and looking down on us. Kevin had run away, left me turning around like a rabbit on a spit, cooked in the stares of the neighbors. I came upstairs, ready for Mam's scolding, but she got angry at Henrietta. "You would not be living right now except for your great-aunt Máire and the help she gave Granny Honora. Two women running for their lives with eight children and Granny Honora expecting."

Aunt Máire must have been in her seventies then. She lived away from Bridgeport in her own wonderful place on Michigan Avenue but she heard about my disgrace soon enough and came to the house the next night with a package wrapped in brown paper. She brought me up to the attic storage space way at the top of the house and we sat there, the two of us, smoking one of her cigarettes. "Never let what other people do or say push through to your real self," she told me. In Ireland she'd been forced to work in the Big House. Have sex—she said it right out—with the landlord's son. I knew he was my cousin Thomas's father, and Daniel and Grace were his children too. She said that the landlords of Ireland made a practice of taking a bride's first night. "They had a fancy French name for it, 'droit du seigneur,' but it was rape," she said.

"And no one stopped them, Aunt Máire?"

"Who would?" she said. "Anyone who raised a hand against the landlord would be evicted or worse. One more weapon they used to keep us in our place."

"Oh God, Aunt Máire, how did you survive it?"

"Survive?" she said. "I didn't just survive. I beat him. We won, Nora. Your granny and me, we're the victors and you are the proof. We got out. We spit in their eye, Nora. We truly did."

"You are so brave, Aunt Máire," I said.

Still are, I thought, because I knew there were some women in Bridgeport who'd objected to Máire living on her own and even now whispered about her "past" and her "gentlemen friends." Máire took no notice. Then she unwrapped the package and shook out a red silk shawl, the fringe floating through the air. She told me that the colored nun who'd taken the family in when they arrived in New Orleans from Ireland gave it to her.

After Aunt Máire left I went into the bedroom, wrapped myself in the shawl, and walked into the parlor. When she saw me Henrietta screamed herself hoarse. Me flaunting myself. Shaming her. I started crying until Mam took her into the bedroom. Granny Honora made me a cup of tea, and told me if I was going to wear Aunt Máire's shawl I'd best show a little of her spirit, and then told me the rest of the story. How the Scoundrel Pyke, their landlord, really wanted to take Granny Honora on her wedding day and . . . Granny couldn't say the word.

"Rape you?" I said.

She nodded.

"Your aunt Máire stepped in. Her, a young widow already expecting her dead husband's child. She took my place, and if she hadn't, Honora, you might not be standing here for your grandfather was a young man and too brave for his own good and might very well have gone for the landlord's son who was a soldier and allowed to shoot dead anyone who attacked him."

When Sister Henrietta, the colored nun who helped them in New Orleans, heard that story she gave Aunt Máire the red shawl as a badge of honor and protection, Granny told me. "Your namesake," I said to Henrietta after I repeated Granny's story to her. "Shut up," she replied. Dead now—Granny Honora, Aunt Máire. Would I be carrying on with Tim if they were living?

Sometimes after I come home from my few hours with Tim, I slip into the bedroom and settle the smooth silk over my shoulders and pray to Aunt Máire. What am I doing? Can I believe all his talk about his change of heart and us getting married? And did I even want to marry him? Tim was a crook, pure and simple, doping his horses and gambling and I didn't want to know what else. Being a fallen woman when no one knew was one thing, but Mrs. Tim McShane? Was a baby worth that?

As much as I miss Agnella I'm glad she's gone to the convent. Hard to lie to her. Sometimes I want to confess to Rose but she is deep in sorrow, three miscarriages already, and one born two months early, a boy who lived for an hour. I went with Rose to arrange a funeral Mass for the poor little guy but Father Sullivan said no funeral because the child hadn't been baptized. I told him that the baby's own father poured water over his head and said the words while Rose held him, and that any child of Rose McCabe Larney would be welcomed into heaven by every angel in the place. Still he'd refused us. Priests! What if he knew. I was at the communion rail every Sunday while "having carnal knowledge with a man not my husband"?

That's what the priest at St. Michael's German church on North Avenue called it when I stopped by there that Saturday afternoon a few weeks after I turned thirty-one. Here's the place to get right with God, I thought. And then . . . marry Tim? Find another fellow? Maybe if my soul were clean I'd know what to do.

Any luck and the German priest won't understand a word I say, I thought. But wouldn't you know the fellow had a brogue. And very impatient. A warm day in May and I could smell the sweat off him. He told me to speak up and get to the point. So I said this man and I were acting like we were husband and wife and we weren't. He said, "Carnal knowledge with a man not your husband is a mortal sin," and asked me if he the man was married.

"No," I said.

"Haven't you a father or brother who'd make the man marry you?" he said.

"I'm not sure I want . . ." I started.

"So you like sinning? You enjoy being a fallen woman?"

I almost said, "At times I do, and that's the problem."

He went on and on, and after he wrestled a firm promise of amendment from me he mumbled *"Absolvo te"* in Latin and gave me ten rosaries as a penance.

I stepped out of the box into the gilt and glory of St. Michael's Church, so different from the Irish plainness of St. Bridget's. The archangel himself, dressed in shiny armor, held pride of place over the altar. This had been Aunt Nelly and Aunt Kate's church as girls, and it reminded me of the Christmas cakes their German father taught their Irish mother to make. Ten layers stacked up and held together by different kinds of jams and jellies—apricot, strawberry—and drenched with whipped cream. *"Schlag"* they called it, and marzipan fruit sunk into the top and pushed into the sides, covering every inch. Good, but so rich. St. Bridget's looked more like the devil's food cake with white boiled frosting that Mam made for our birthdays. Delicious and you could eat more than one piece.

So, Blessed Mother, I said, kneeling in front of the altar that displayed her picture as Our Lady of Perpetual Help. What do I do? The priest accused me of enjoying my sin and, well, I do. If I didn't, there'd be no problem. Not proper, I suppose, to speak to you about carnal knowledge. But I've checked every statue in the place trying to find a "Holy Woman, neither Virgin nor Martyr" like the missal says. Such saints did exist, but most of them were queens, Elizabeth of Hungary and Bridget of Sweden and Elizabeth of Portugal.

"Powerful women, girls," Sister Ruth Eileen had told us during religion class at St. Xavier's, "who served God and helped their husbands."

Most of them had hotfooted it into the convent as soon as their husbands died, but at least they'd been with men. They were saints and yet they might understand why what happened with Tim in that small room seemed so natural. So, well, pleasant. In fact, when Tim wanted to hurry through our encounters to get back to his horses or collect Dolly, it was me who tried to prolong our sessions. I wonder, was it the same for those noble ladies? The kings, their husbands, off to the cabinet meeting and them in the bed ready for more?

I glanced up at Our Lady of Perpetual Help. A queen herself, outlined in gold and stern-faced with an oddly shaped infant Jesus sitting bolt upright in her arms. Greek, and the original painted by St. Luke, Sister Ruth Eileen had told me.

And then the prayer jumped out of me. Oh please, Mary, give me the strength to leave Tim. That's what I want! Get away from him. Sure now. I'm so tired of being a sinner.

But then that Fairy Woman spoke up. What harm are you doing?

Well, there's Dolly, I said.

That got a laugh.

And I'm lying all the time. Living two lives.

So. You earn good money, are your own boss, and have never done better work.

True enough.

After her marriage to John Larney, Rose left the studio and I acquired a staff of three girls to make patterns of my sketches and sew up sample dresses. I sat in my studio and sketched away, humming and singing, the pencil moving by itself as I drew skirts and blouses, added flounces and feathers.

And I must say, I was easier to be with at home after my time with Tim. I stayed on at Hillock. Getting my own place as Aunt Máire had would have led to talk. Important not to arouse suspicion. We Kellys weren't the only family of aging brothers and sisters in Bridgeport living together.

Ten rosaries!, I thought. I'll say them on the tram, I told Our Lady. Too quiet in here, too many voices.

I stood up and noticed a box built into the altar rail with a sign that said, PETITIONS. Next to it, a stack of papers with a pencil tied on a string.

Petitions. But what should I ask for? I remembered that the sisters at St. Xavier's had an all-purpose category. "Pray for a special intention," they'd say. So I wrote "Special Intention" on the paper and put it through the slit in the box. Not even sure what I wanted.

As I had left the church I thought of another saint—Augustine. "Make me chaste, Lord, but not now." Amen to that.

But that winter I begin to take chances. Staying late with Tim after work, missing dinner, getting home at midnight.

And then early one morning in January 1911, I found Henrietta waiting up for me.

"Where have you been?" she asked.

"I got inspired," I said, "stayed in the studio, lost track of time."

"Inspired? Is that what it's called nowadays? I saw you get out of an automobile. Whose?" Henrietta said.

"The night porter gave me a lift home."

Actually I was driving Tim's car, while he nodded off in the passenger seat. Proud of the driving skills he had taught me.

"What's his name?"

"Martin Smith. He lives way out south near Fifty-fifth Street. You wouldn't know him." I would have come up with a better name but Henrietta wasn't really listening, only shaking her head.

"You're spoiled. Always have been. And now you're disgracing the family!"

"What?" Oh dear God, did she know?

"Coming in all hours. Riding with the porter, no less!"

Thank God she's such a snob.

"Henrietta, would you give it a rest. I'm going to bed."

"And I'm going to wake Mike and tell him what his highfalutin sister's really like."

I grabbed Henrietta's arm. "Don't you go near Mike, Henrietta, or I'll . . ."

"You'll what?" She laughed. Here come the hysterics. But no, she stopped laughing and smiled.

"You think Mike won't believe me. But I'll get proof. I've known for a long time you've been up to something. I'll find you out, Nonie. I will." And just like that, she went up to bed.

Oh, great. Now I have her stirred up. Jesus Christ. Blessed Mother. Help.

But the next morning Henrietta said no more so here I am, running for the tram and off to work every morning as always. Though now automobiles clog Archer Avenue. Model Ts mostly. Prices have come down so much working fellows can afford to buy an automobile. Mike says that the man who makes them, Henry Ford, is Irish though Ford doesn't make much of his heritage. Still Mike felt a kind of connection to Ford or Forde as the name should be spelled, Mike said, when he bought the automobile. Doing very well, Mike is.

Mike and Ed and their friends have started what they call the Irish Fellowship Club and love to trade stories about successful Irishmen. All the boys in the club are making money and not just from taverns or politics. Look at John M. Smyth with his furniture store, though Mike says it's a shame he's not called Murphy so everyone knows he's Irish. And there are lawyers and doctors falling out of the trees now and building big houses far from the old neighborhoods. A march of new parishes as the Irish on the way up go farther south or west or north, depending on whether they'd started in South, West, or North Side neighborhoods. No more from Henrietta and I'm grateful. Glad almost when August comes and Tim's gone to Saratoga.

On Sundays, Mike takes us for spins in his automobile. Henrietta climbs up next to Mike in the front seat of the Model T, while Mart, Annie, Henrietta's kids, and I fit ourselves into the back, and we cruise the boulevards that link one park to the next. Garfield Boulevard is Henrietta's favorite. She knows who owns every house.

SEPTEMBER 1911

We're out for our Sunday drive on Garfield Boulevard to see the fancy new houses south of Bridgeport.

"See, there's the place Mrs. O'Leary's son built," Henrietta says. A lovely fall day—the trees along the avenue bright yellow. Warm.

"Look there, a bust of her carved into the post for all to see. That's a devoted son," Henrietta goes on.

"Didn't Mrs. O'Leary burn down the city?" Henrietta's son Eddie says. We call him Toots—so many Eds in our family.

"She did not," Henrietta says. "They blame her just because she's Irish."

Mike says that Mrs. O'Leary's devoted son makes his money from casinos.

"Why can't we buy a big place on the boulevard? Crazy to be still renting in Bridgeport when all the best people are moving out," Henrietta says to Mike.

Mike says nothing. "We could be evicted," Henrietta says. "Just like the people in Ireland."

"Never," I say. "Mike's put in all those bathrooms for the landlord. He'd beg us to stay."

"Why take on a mortgage?" Mike says, and asks Henrietta if she really she wants to leave St. Bridget's and all her friends.

"My friends are moving too," Henrietta says as we get out of our Model T and climb the stairs of 2703. "Nobody's in the old neighborhoods anymore."

"That's not true, Henrietta," I say. "Our cousin Ed and Mary Roche are still in Brighton Park."

Ed married the daughter of an alderman. The Democratic Party could turn her parlor into a small-scale convention hall as far as she's concerned. Born to it, she is.

"I don't mind the men," she said to me once, "but the smoke! Can't see my hand in front of my face. Sometimes I worry about little Eddie breathing in all those cigars, but Ed says he might as well get used to it."

A fine sturdy little boy, their son. Two years old. And redheaded like Ed and me. Three of us now.

Henrietta is always asking Ed's wife why they stayed in Brighton Park. "Ed's getting rich. You could move to the avenue."

"But this is his base," Mary Roche tells her.

Not that Ed intends to run for office himself. He tried that six or seven years ago, going for a place as trustee of the Sanitary District. But that was a Republican year and he lost big. "Better to be the man choosing the candidate than out there yourself," he told me, and I think he was quoting his friend Pat Nash. I met him at Ed and Mary's a time or two.

Older than Ed, tall and quiet, Pat is one of the boys in the know, no question, and shares Ed's dream of building Chicago into one of the great cities of the world. And Pat can do it. Owns a big construction company.

OCTOBER 1911

Then, about a month after that Sunday drive, October it is, Mame comes up to my studio at Ward's. Unusual for her. She has her own office way on the other side of the building. When I stop by for a chat her head will be down, fingers pushing the keys of the big black typewriter that looks to me like a giant insect striking out with its spindly legs leaving a trail of words on the paper. I'll call her name at least three times before she looks up. That machine of hers is bewitched. Not natural. Something about having a pencil in your hand, forming the letters yourself, that feels human, but to turn your power over to a machine . . . Still Mame was connected to her typewriter and never left it to wander the halls.

So what is she doing here, I wonder, as she stands in the doorway of my busy workshop.

Five women now cut out the patterns, and three are making samples on sewing machines. They are as tied to their contraptions as Mame is to her typewriter. Startled when I tap them on the shoulder to ask them a question. Still a pleasant place, my studio. No one bothers me as long as we meet our deadlines. Mr. Bartlett promoted high up in Montgomery Ward—a vice-president now, on the strength of the success of our ladies' dresses.

"Nonie," Mame says, "come out in the hall."

"Oh God, is something wrong? Has Rose miscarried again?" I whisper. "No, no."

I follow her out onto the fire escape. "What?"

"Good news, Nonie, great news. I'm getting married."

"Married? Mame, my God! Is it the fellow with the obligations? Jerry Kehoe, I bet. His mother just died and . . ."

"Not Jerry, Nonie."

"Well, who? You're not a very good friend to keep such a secret!"

"Ah well, Nonie, I promised I'd say nothing until the time was right. Save a lot of upset."

"But still . . ."

Mame lifts her finger. "Nonie, sometimes saying nothing's best. I haven't been quizzing you about your life, have I? We're not girls together anymore. I always liked the bit in the Bible where Jesus says, 'Judge not and you shall not be judged.'"

She knows, I think. Oh my God, she knows!

But she smiles and says, "I hope you understand, Nonie. It's Mike. I'm marrying Mike."

"Mike? Mike who?"

"Michael J. Kelly. Your brother."

"My brother!? Oh Mame, but he's . . . forty-five years old!"

"And I'm twenty-nine," she says.

"But you're young . . ."

"Young enough, I hope. We want a family. A big family. We plan to marry in November. Oh Nonie, we've found the most beautiful house out of the city, in Argo."

"House? Argo?"

"Well, I could hardly move in with all of you. Mike waited until Henrietta's boys were working and all of you settled and, well, I've loved him for the longest time. We write to each other. He's been worried about your sister Henrietta's reaction but really, if we want a family we can't wait any longer."

"You can't," I say. At least one of the Trio with children. How I'll love Mike and Mame's babies!

Mike and Mame. Perfect. Mam would have been over the moon. I wonder, did Our Lady of Perpetual Help get mixed up and think *this* was my special intention? Fair play to her. But Mike and Mame McCabe moving into a house . . . Our Lady better start dumping grace on my sister Henrietta. All hell is about to break loose.

❧

"Dolly wants to come to the wedding," Tim tells me as we get dressed one evening a week before Mame and Mike are to be married, on November 11th at St. Agnes Church in Brighton Park. If only Mam were here to see them wed, I think, still aching for her nearly nine years after her death.

I designed a dress for Mame, and Rose came back to the studio to run it up on the sewing machine.

Henrietta shouted and roared about the place for weeks after Mike told her he and Mame were to marry. She said she would not come to the wedding. "Never!"

Mike looked up from reading his newspaper to say, "All right, Henrietta. We'll miss you, but do what you must."

After days and days of silence she announced at breakfast, "I'm coming for Mam's sake. Though what she'd say about your breaking the promise you gave her on her deathbed, I can't say."

Henrietta remembered whole conversations with Mam that none of us had ever heard. Still hard to think about those last, sad days. Mam had said "Be good, Nonie," to me. Ah, well, Mam, I tried. We'd all heard her call for my da at the end, but no messages to Henrietta that anyone else remembered.

"Mike, how can you leave us to eviction or worse?" Henrietta asked him—a sob in her voice.

"I paid the rent for the next year, Henrietta. There are four people working in this house and more now that your boys have jobs."

Generous when Mike will have his own family to support, please God. But through all Henrietta's raving, Mike stands firm. Surprising really, but he waited so long for Mame, writing letters to her for years, as I found out. And saying nothing to me, either one of them.

"You would have told Henrietta," Mame said to me.

"I would not," I started, but stopped. She was right. I probably would have thrown it at Henrietta during one of the arguments that flared up out of nothing, leaving me guilty and saying, "Sorry." If Henrietta ever found out about Tim McShane . . . And if Dolly and Tim were at the wedding . . . Henrietta's not stupid. Always ready to believe the worst about people, and too often right.

"Jesus, Tim, I don't think that's a good idea," I say to him.

"Dolly gets these notions, Nora. She says you're like a sister to her and she's always admired Mike Kelly, and your cousin Ed is a good man to know."

I do like Dolly even though I'm betraying her every Tuesday and Thursday and sometimes on the weekends.

"She just bought herself a diamond necklace for ten thousand dollars and wants to wear it. She's taking out mortgages on property all over the place. But when I told her we needed a new car, she wouldn't discuss it!"

For all Tim's bluster, Dolly rules the roost. When she'd decided to sell all of her horses after Brighton Park closed, nothing he could do but say, "All right, Dolly."

She finally agreed to set him at Arlington Racetrack, but its more expensive there, and not as easy to "help" one horse win or slow down another. Racetrack officials watching. So Dolly bought Tim a share in Jake Logan's casino to keep him occupied. Now he spent his nights there, swanning around, and gambling with her money—which Dolly doesn't know.

"Be careful, Tim," I said and told him what James McKenna said to me when he'd taken over the tavern his father and grandfather had run.

"I never touch alcohol," James had said. "Too many fellows drink their own bars away."

"Easy to lose your shirt gambling," I told Tim.

"Not when you own the place."

"You only have a share," I said. "And those partners of yours *will* collect from you one of these days."

He ignored me. Be glad he's not your husband, I tell myself. Not my worry. But to have him enter my real life, be around my family?

"No, Tim, you can't come to the wedding," I say. "Please, no."

But at her next fitting Dolly catches my eyes in the mirror and holds them. "Looking forward to the wedding, Nora," she says.

Does she know? Is she planning a showdown in front of everyone? Oh, please, dear God. Please! I know I've done nothing to deserve your help but think of Mame. Don't let Dolly make a scene—I'm the sinner. Punish me. Leave my family alone and don't give Henrietta the satisfaction. Bad for her character. Please!

Mame chose November 11th for her wedding day because she is sure 11/11/11 would be lucky. And she seems to be right. I mean we're having summer weather! Seventy-five degrees, unheard of in Chicago, when Rose and I arrive in the vestibule of St. Agnes Church.

Dolly's all smiles as she comes in on Tim McShane's arm. He doesn't look at me. She wears a dress the like of which I've never seen except in a magazine, swishing a big feathered fan in front of her.

"My gown is from Paris," she says to Rose and me.

"Charles Worth?" I ask.

"Better. Madame Simone," she says.

"Whoever that is," I say to Rose as we wait for Mame and Ed. Ed is giving the bride away, standing in for the father, who died before Mame was born. Rose and I watch Dolly, calculating yardage and counting pleats and tucks, as she and Tim move up the aisle and sit right behind our family.

John Larney turns his head so sharply I think I hear his neck crack, but he says nothing to his mother or the cousins next to her. His family's very well dressed. His two uncles' grocery store at Larney's Corner in Brighton Park's becoming very prosperous.

And all our Kelly relations look polished and presentable too. The men wear new suits, the women lovely dresses and expensive hats. Doing all right for ourselves in America.

But the bride could have walked up the aisle in her shift and would have still outshone everyone. The happiness pouring from Mame lights up the gloomy church. Mike waits at the altar, grinning. My serious big brother—forty-five years old now, president of the Knights of Columbus, the master plumber, the head of our family since the age of eighteen—is suddenly young.

Thank you, Mame, I think. Mike is happy. I'm sure he'd never even hoped for such a thing.

"'Oh, how we danced on the night we were wed,'" Dolly sings as Mike and Mame move across the polished wooden floor of the gym at the Brighton Park Athletic Club, the boxing ring put away for the occasion.

I see Tim talking to a few fellows around the punch bowl, my brother Mart and Joe Murphy among them, all of them laughing out loud, not listening to Dolly's performance. He still hasn't spoken to me, thank God.

I see Dolly look over at Tim. Does he ever think of her happiness? Or mine, for that matter? I can't do this anymore. Not to Dolly, not to myself. There. My special intention answered. I know my time with Tim is over. The Fairy Woman gone. Free of him, I think, as Dolly finishes to applause.

I am happy when I'm working in my studio, the "atelier," I think, sketching dresses in that sunlit space, the sewing machines whirring. I find joy in my family, in the babies—a whole raft of new cousins: not only Ed's red-headed two-year-old boy but his brother Evan's little girl. My cousin Ella's married to Joe O'Donnell. They have two children. Uncle Mike's youngest, George, who looks so like Ed, has three little ones now. All of these new Kellys, the second generation born in America. I belong with them.

I look at Tim—getting fat now. His face red—drinking too much. Not much pleasure in our afternoons anymore. Habit more like it and to be honest, a bit of fear. Especially on that last afternoon before the wedding. He, well, had trouble and said it was me. Squeezed a roll of flesh above my waist. "Get rid of this," he said. "It's putting me off."

"I wouldn't talk, Tim," I said, and he took me by the shoulders and shook me hard.

"Jesus, Tim," I started—mad—but I don't know, a look about him that made me go very quiet. "You're right, Tim," I said. "Best stop eating Aunt Kate's cookies." I forced myself to laugh. He let go.

"Look what you made me do with that smart mouth of yours," he said.

I dressed fast that afternoon.

Now Tim looks up from the punch bowl, sees me staring at him and winks at me. What's that about? Then says something to my brother Mart and Joe. They all laugh. What is he saying? He's drunk. Can I slip away?

I see Ed introduce Dolly to Edward Dunne and his wife Elizabeth, who's a Kelly. Probably some kin to us. Dunne was mayor and running for governor now. Not here at the wedding because of politics though or at least not Chicago politics. Dunne's father P.J. was a Fenian friend of my uncle Patrick. The two of them plotting in our parlor. Pat Nash and his wife, also a Kelley but with an "e," join the group. Dolly going on about something. Now's my chance. Go.

But then Uncle Stephen leads Aunt Nelly onto the dance floor with Uncle Mike and his wife, Mary Chambers, following. Granny Honora's sons, my father's brothers, my da and Uncle James gone, but these aunts and uncles still connecting me to my father, to Mam and Granny Honora.

Tommy McGuire, the bandleader, says, "And now a reel!"

The whole crowd applauds and quickly lines up in pairs, shouting, "Good man, Tommy!"

"The Siege of Limerick!" he calls out.

The sets form: Mame and Mike; Rose and John; Ed and Mary take the lead. Annie out there too with some policeman friend of hers, and even Henrietta in the dance partnered by Toots. The Dunnes and Nashes part of the reel.

"Come on, Nonie," my cousin Bill, Ed's little brother, says to me.

But just then, Tim McShane comes up behind us with Dolly on his arm, both of them smiling.

"Good-bye, Nora," Dolly is saying. "I have to leave. I've a show tonight."

"Thank you for coming, for singing," I say.

"My pleasure," she says. She touches my shoulder with her finger and then points at the dancers. "And thank your cousin Ed," she says. "Tell him I enjoyed meeting Pat Nash and the governor-to-be."

"Dolly's thinking of buying a chunk of land out south, going to build herself a castle," Tim says.

"A quiet retreat," Dolly says to me.

"But she wants to make sure the city will put in sewers and roads for her. Why she came today," Tim adds.

"That's not true," she says.

"Be honest, Dolly, for once!" he says.

"Well, of course I'm interested in Chicago's growth and whether my little plot of land will . . ."

"Shove it," Tim says.

He is very drunk, I think, or he wouldn't dare speak to Dolly like that.

"Oh, Mrs. McKee." Henrietta's left the dance to slip between Tim Mc-Shane and Dolly. "I just wanted to tell you how honored we Kellys are that you came!"

Babbling away as if she hadn't tried her best to ruin the wedding, weeping even this morning, sitting at the kitchen table while the rest of us dressed, with Mike telling her he'd understand if she wanted to stay home, that Mame wouldn't hold it against her. I said we'd be glad not to have her there, more peaceful. And now she's making over Dolly McKee as if Henrietta herself were the bride's mother.

"Such a lovely dress, Mrs. McKee, and that necklace—are those really diamonds?"

"Better be," Tim says.

Henrietta looks up at him. "Good evening. I'm Mrs. Henrietta Kelly. Henrietta Kelly Kelly, really. Born a Kelly and married a Kelly!"

"Good for you," Tim says.

"My poor husband Bill's been dead these many years, but he gave me his name and three beautiful children. One is a holy sister now. A BVM."

"A blessing, certainly," Dolly says.

Dear God, I've complained about my sister Henrietta to Tim many times, told him things. He's in such a strange mood . . . what if he repeats something now—insults her?

But he only says, "So long, Mrs. Kelly Kelly," to Henrietta.

Good. Go!

But Henrietta's still talking to Dolly, turning Dolly away from Tim and me.

Tim leans close and whispers, "I could ruin you now. A few words to this crowd and they'd turn on you fast."

"Shut up," I say. Thank God Dolly and Henrietta are paying no attention to us and the music is so loud no one else can hear Tim.

But he won't stop.

"All of them, the aunts, uncles, that big brother of yours, the stuck-up Larneys, the politicians . . . Everyone in Bridgeport and Brighton Park will despise you. Father Sullivan will preach against your whoredom from the pulpit of St. Bridget's Church." He laughs. "This will be fun!" He waves his arms. "Ladies and gentlemen," his voice loud now and a few people turn around to look at him.

"Please, Tim. Please," I say.

Tommy McGuire, at the bandstand, sees him. He smiles at Tim and holds up his hand, slowing the band, stopping the reel.

Tommy thinks Tim's signaling that Dolly wants to sing again. Soon there'll be silence and Tim will destroy me.

The dancers wait.

"An announcement!" Tim calls out.

Dolly looks at me, those eyes stare into mine.

She knows what he intends, I think. Here it is, her chance for revenge. Even Rose and Mame wouldn't, couldn't understand. Mike's wedding destroyed. A bitter memory. No joy. Only their disappointment in me.

Henrietta's still smiling like a fool.

Then Dolly speaks to Tim. "No." Only that, "No," thrusting the word at him. She takes Tim's arm, gestures with her other hand to Tommy, tracing an explanation in the air: Time to go. Too tired. Good-bye. She throws Tommy a kiss.

Tommy nods, and directs the band to pick up the tempo and the reel begins again.

Dolly moves Tim to the door behind us and they leave.

My legs are trembling but somehow I walk to a chair and sit down. "Jesus H. Christ," I say.

Aloud.

Henrietta hears me as she plops down next to me. "Nonie, really," she says. "Taking our Lord's name in vain. What would people think if they heard you!"

I start to laugh. If you only knew.

Thank you, Blessed Mother. Thank you, Mam. Thank you Holy Women, neither virgins nor martyrs. Thank you.

No more. I promise all of you. No more. Good-bye Tim McShane.

Freezing when we leave the hall. The temperature has dropped from 75 degrees to 13 degrees. Astounding even for Chicago. The "Blue Norther," the Sunday papers call it. An omen, I think. Nature itself telling me to get away from Tim McShane.

4

Hard to leave the house that Monday morning, so sure am I that Tim McShane will bushwhack me before I get to work.

"I could ruin you." His words in my head. But then Dolly would know. Still, she *must* know. She stopped him. "No." The way he looked at her. He hates us both. Drink taken. The booze making him mean. Tim probably doctored the punch. Even Mart was full when we got home. Henrietta tipsy too, yakking away about Dolly and Tim until I wanted to scream the truth at her. "I could ruin you!" he said. I might blurt out my own destruction.

No Oldsmobile idles near Ward's. A relief to get to the studio. My sanctuary. I take out a large sheet of paper and start sketching Dolly's gown. What I remember. Never get all the pleats and tucks, but maybe I can suggest them . . . Done in satin perhaps, as a wedding dress. Our customers might buy a "Paris creation" for a very special occasion. Complicated though.

Since Rose left, Susie Hanrahan works out the patterns. A young one from Bridgeport, ambitious but courting, she probably won't be working with me much longer. Though she told me she intends to keep on here even after she married, and said her mother could look after her babies. "My Frank will understand. He'd better!" Good luck to her.

Now Susie grabs the sketch and begins pulling out bolts of fabric. "Marshall Field sends buyers over to the Paris fashion shows," she says. "They buy the real thing for their rich society lady customers. Why couldn't we give our women a good copy?"

Mr. Bartlett is intrigued when we show him the sketches. "All right, Miss Kelly. A one-off for the spring catalog and we'll see what response we get."

Susie and I stay late wrapping each other in fabrics.

"I suppose Dolly would never lend us the dress itself," Susie says as I pinch and pleat the swathes of satin I drape over her. "You being so friendly with her and her husband."

"He's not her husband," I say. "Her manager."

Susie says nothing. Does she know? Does everyone? Over. It's over.

⎯⎯❦⎯⎯

Tim is stretched out on the bed naked when I let myself in the next day, Tuesday. Late. Six o'clock and the Angelus ringing at Holy Name. No sheets. Only the dirty mattress.

I have my speech all ready. We had a good run of it, I'll say. We'll part as friends, and on and on. But under all the calm words I'm frightened. I think of how he took me by the shoulders, shook me. So ugly when he said, "I could ruin you." Careful. I'll be careful.

I've always welcomed the isolation of this dim room. The courtyard-facing window lets only the barest bit of light in through its grimy cover. A space apart, the Fairy Woman's cave.

But now I feel trapped. No big speeches, Nonie, I say to myself. A few words and skedaddle.

Tim's half asleep, the heft of him like some reclining giant. Balor of the One-Eye, the villain in so many of Granny's stories. And I can't let the sleeping giant lie. No, I start talking, trying to make him understand, to justify the last eight years to him and to me. I sit on a chair next to the bed and go on about our great passionate love that just couldn't be. "Apologize for your behavior at the wedding, and then I'll go."

"Shut your gob," he says.

"What?"

"Dolly's going to Paris. Leaving on the train for New York tomorrow morning," he says. "I'm staying. She'll be gone a month. You'll move in here. Time I started getting more out of you. Sick of your high-hatting family. You'll come with me to the casino at night."

"No. No, I won't. Didn't you hear me? It's over between us." How could he think I would want to be seen with him?

"Take your clothes off. Hurry up. I'm meeting a fellow at the casino at seven."

I stand up. A dignified good-bye and I'll be gone.

"I'm leaving, and won't be back," I say.

He grabs my skirt, jerks me back down onto the chair, clamps one big hand on my arm and holds me still as he sits up and leans toward me.

"Didn't you hear me? I said strip."

"If you think I'm going to . . ."

"You want me to smack you right in the puss?"

"Are you drunk?"

He gets out of the bed, picks me up, and flings me down onto the mattress. When I try to sit up he shoves me back down.

"God, Nora, the way you cover everything with palaver. A woman's a place to park my pod. I've taken more trouble with you than any man should have to. At first I liked making you holler. The little virgin begging for more. But now . . ." He holds my chin and turns my face toward him. "Lines around your eyes, Nora. Getting old. Be glad I still want you. Start unbuttoning."

"Tim, I'm not, I . . ."

And he slaps my face. Hits me with his open hand, a hard blow.

I scream and turn away from him. "Stop!" I say.

"Shut up," he says, and hits me again, using the back of his hand this time.

I kick up at him and he laughs. Oh dear God he's enjoying this. He's going to beat me and be glad. Help me! Help me, God. Please!

"Not so stuck up now, are you? Where's that fine family of yours now? No Kellys. Only you and me. Whore. Dolly said a girl like you'd be perfect. No trouble. Dying for it. But Jesus, I'm fed up to the teeth with you and your yammering. Take off your clothes or I'll tear them off."

In terror now, my heart racing. He's on the bed, kneeling over me. He slides his hand up my breasts to my throat, mocking the touches I'd responded to so many times.

"How easy to squeeze the life out of you," he says. "Leave your body out in the gangway. Another prossie done in, the police would think. Might never identify you. Or maybe Detective John Larney, that pompous ass, would be strolling through the morgue and see you naked on a slab—'No-nee, No-nee.'"

Mad. Mad altogether. His fingers tighten around my throat. A voice in my head tells me, Don't whimper, don't scream . . . smile. I do. Somehow I do. Then wink at him, which startles him. He lets go.

"Jesus, Tim, you would do well writing penny dreadful novels," I say. "I didn't know you had such an imagination." Got to make him laugh.

But he slaps me again, harder.

"Will you never learn to shut up?"

He starts to pull at the neck of my blouse but the tip of a whalebone stay cuts his finger.

"Blood," he says, lifts his finger to his lips and rolls onto his back.

"My best blouse, Tim," I say. "Let me take it off." Somehow I'm able to unfasten the top button. I sit up.

"Let me go to the bathroom to get myself ready for you. All that"—how I hate saying the words—"masculine force is very exciting altogether, Tim."

He looks from me to his bleeding finger, and I ease myself off the bed. The toilet is in the hall. If I . . .

"Take off your shoes," he says. "Leave them here."

"Yes, Tim," and I unfasten them.

"You can't run from me," he says. "I'd find you anywhere you go."

"Then come with me to the toilet," I say. I'm standing now, looking down at his naked body—the body I thought I'd loved. "Take your pleasure like a man," he said. What a fool I was.

"Go. Go," he says. "But make it fast. That fellow'll be waiting for me."

I get by him and I'm into the hall. Then I'm running down the stairs and into the street. Piles of dirty snow on the State Street sidewalk and I've no shoes, but I don't feel the cold. Tim'll have to get dressed. I have a few minutes. Where to go? Holy Name Cathedral. I could hide in a confessional. No, he'll look in the church. The rectory? And explain my plight to the priest's housekeeper? Hardly. The convent? I wouldn't put it past Tim to come battering at the nuns' door. Can't go home. He'll go there surely. Besides, I can't run shoeless and coatless all the way to Bridgeport. Not a penny on me. I suppose a tram driver might let me on, but there's none coming. Besides, the passengers would stare at me. What if I see someone I knew? No way to get to Mike's or Rose and John's. And Tim might go to their houses. The police? "Good evening, I'm Nora Kelly," I imagine myself saying to the desk sergeant. "I've just been beaten up by a man I thought I loved." Oh God, the newspaper boys have tipsters at all the police stations. A juicy story—"City Official's Relative Attacked by Gangster Lover . . ."

A good three blocks away now and I stop. I haven't noticed other people on the street, but now I look behind me, see two men I must've passed, standing, looking at me.

"You need help?" one asks.

"Thank you," I start. "Maybe you could . . ."

But then the other says, "Lose your customer? I'll oblige you." He laughs.

"Go to hell," I say.

"Only joking," he says, and walks toward me.

Then I hear the sound of an automobile. Of course, he'd come after me in the Oldsmobile. I run behind a building and look down State Street. I see the car pull up in front of Holy Name. He goes into the church. Thank God I didn't go there, but where now?

The church bell rings eight o'clock. The streets are empty. He'll have no trouble finding me. Hide in a tavern or a restaurant? Only a few around here. Wouldn't take long for him to find me. The thought of Tim crashing in and dragging me out of the place. Where?

I come to the bridge across the river. My feet are wet and my toes burn with cold. I'm shivering and, wouldn't you know, it starts snowing. Big flakes slapping at me, dropping into the river. The bridge is slippery and I have to hold on to the rails as I go across. All I need now is to fall in the river. Suicide, on top of everything else.

The thought makes me laugh. And then, oh Jesus, the sound of the Oldsmobile again!

I start running, turn onto Wacker. Please God, he'll go straight south expecting me to make for Bridgeport. I turn right, and there in front of me is a huge block of gray stone holding its own against the snow. The Opera House. People inside and warmth. Maybe I could sneak in a side door . . .

What's wrong with me? Dolly's performing there tonight, playing the Merry Widow in Lehár's operetta. Tim always bragged to me that he never picked up Dolly after the theater. Not at her beck and call. She had her own car and driver and she could join him at the casino or go back to the Palmer House. He'd be there or not, as it suited him.

Dolly. Dolly. Would she help me? The way she'd said, "No" . . . But then hadn't Tim said something about Dolly thinking I'd be the kind of girl who'd give no trouble?

The old fellow at the stage door stands for a long time looking at me—a wet mess by now. He stares at my shoeless feet. I say I'm here to see Mrs. McKee.

"I don't know. Mrs. McKee didn't say nothing to me about nobody coming. She's particular."

"Please, just put me in some corner down in the basement until the performance is over and then give her my name. I'll write it down. I'm sure she'll see me. Please."

"All right, all right. Cold enough outside to freeze a witch's tit. I'll let you into her dressing room, but don't steal nothing."

And I'm in Dolly's lavish space. A big sofa against the far wall. To sit down! Thank you, God, thank you! I pull off my stockings and start rubbing feeling back into my feet. My blouse and skirt are soaked.

The door opens. Not Dolly, but Carrie O'Toole, her dresser, a woman I know from Dolly's fittings. Must be well into her seventies, from Brooklyn, New York, as she's told me often enough. The only one I've ever seen razz Dolly and get away with it.

"Look what the cat's dragged in," she says.

"Oh, Carrie, I'm . . ."

"I can see," she says. "Take off those wet clothes and I'll give you one of Her Highness's robes."

"I don't think . . ."

"Hurry up. Dolly's got a quick change coming up, and I've got to go out and help her."

I start to fumble with the buttons on my blouse, but my fingers are so cold, stiff and trembling . . .

Then Carrie is helping me. She looks at the torn collar and up at me. She undoes my blouse and starts to loosen my corset. I yelp. "Sore?" she says.

"I . . . I . . ."

"Bumped into a door?" she says. She lifts the corset off. "Bruise already turning purple."

The skin on my chest's an awful color.

"Anything broken?" Carrie asks.

"I don't know. I don't think so."

"Take a deep breath," she says.

I do.

"You can breathe. You're probably all right. Go in and take a hot bath. This place's got amazing plumbing."

"I know. My brother Mike put in the system."

"Isn't that nice?" she says, shakes her head, and starts laughing.

"Sorry," I begin. "Ridiculous thing to say. It's just . . . Carrie, I can't believe what just happened. I mean, out of nowhere this, this friend turned on me."

"Hey, Nora, don't pretend with me. I know who smacked you around. I'd be lying if I said I was surprised. Just go in and soak yourself. Use the bath salts in there. Being clean and smelling good helps."

"You know? You've been, uhm, hit?"

"Not me, but . . ." She rolls her eyes, cocks her head at the dressing table covered with framed photographs of Dolly and her admirers.

"Dolly? He'd never dare lay a hand on Dolly!"

"Oh, wouldn't he?"

A knock at the door. "Two minutes," a voice says.

"I'd better get going," Carrie says. "Take a nap on the chaise longue after your bath. You're safe enough. You got away. Smart girl." She looks me over. "Didn't let him break your front tooth. You've an hour before the final curtain."

In the lavender-scented hot water the muscles in my shoulders let go. My whole chest aches. The purple bruise has spread across both breasts. Breathe. Breathe, I tell myself, and start to doze in the bath. Then I think, what if Tim breaks the door down right now? Decides to come here and . . .

I get out of the bath, dry off. Look for my clothes in the dressing room. Gone. Carrie has taken them, tricking me. She and Dolly are afraid of Tim. They'll tell him where I am.

The dressing room door is opening. I duck behind the chaise longue. Carrie walks in, alone. Thank God.

"Here," she says. "All Dolly's things are too big, but one of the girls in the chorus gave me these." She hands me a skirt and blouse—black serge wool.

"Got the outfit for a funeral. Says you can keep them. She doesn't want sad clothes anymore. Your blouse's all ripped and the skirt not much better. Toss them. You won't want to wear them again."

She's right. She gives me a pair of Dolly's shoes which do fit.

"Oh Carrie, what if Tim comes here?"

"He doesn't usually. But just in case I had a word with Charlie on the door. We got stagehands here who could clean Tim's clock, he starts anything. Well-behaved when there's fellows as strong as him around."

I hear applause, shouting. The final curtain. Dolly taking her bows.

"I should leave, Carrie."

But she is rummaging through the drawer of an ornate white dresser. She tosses me some bloomers and a shift and a card of pins. I start to dress, making the underwear fit, already imagining Tim brawling with the stagehands.

"I've got to go," I say to Carrie. "Get away before Dolly . . ."

Then there she is. Dolly, standing still in the doorway, the skirt of her costume blocking the entranceway. And Tim behind her? No, thank God. She says nothing. Carrie points at my chest, the bruise darker above the top of the shift. I pull on the black blouse as Carrie moves to help Dolly out of her costume, unbuttoning the bodice of the frilly white gown.

"I'm sorry for you, Nora," Dolly says. "I really am. I thought he'd gotten that temper of his under control. What did you say to him?"

"Me? Say to him? What do you mean? This wasn't temper, Dolly. He wanted to beat me. Cold about it. Deliberate."

Dolly steps out of the gown and into the robe Carrie holds. She sits down in front of her dressing table mirror, begins to take off the stage makeup, rubbing cream all over her face until her features disappear behind the white film. I watch as she uses a wad of cotton to wipe away the Merry Widow. Never have seen Dolly's face bare. The harsh lights around the mirror show the fine wrinkles scoring her cheeks and forehead. A blankness around her eyes. She turns around to me. I'm dressed now.

"So where can we stash you?" she says. "I'd say stay here, but there's the off chance that Tim . . . You can go home with Carrie."

"Jesus Christ, Dolly, remember last time? He broke my Belleek bowl out of pure badness when he didn't find you at my place," Carrie says.

"Someone he doesn't know," Dolly says to me. "Not your relatives."

"How about a hotel?" Carrie says.

"I . . . I don't have any money," I say.

Dolly waves her fingers at me. She applies a tinted cream over her face, then outlines her eyes with a black kohl pencil. Creating herself.

"By tomorrow Tim'll be recovered. Come to your door with an armload of roses. Very sorry, he always is," Dolly says.

"Always? Dear God, Dolly, how can you let him?"

"He doesn't mean any harm. Not easy for him to be in my shadow. I make allowances."

A clicking sound from Carrie.

"And am I an allowance too?" I ask Dolly.

"You see, Tim is a man of great appetite," she says. "And I . . ." She stops.

"Can't be bothered," Carrie says.

"Not true," Dolly says. "I am a woman of passion, of course, but my energy has to go into my work."

"So I spelled you. Is that it?" I say.

"Better you than some goofy chorus girl who fancies herself in love with him," Dolly says.

Carrie speaks up. "And threatens to go to the coppers. Remember that little Italian girl whose father came here, said he'd make a lot of trouble, tell the newspapers? Cost you a lot more than a night in a hotel will," she says.

"Go to the newspapers?" I say. "I never want anyone to know. I am so ashamed!"

"*He* hit *you*," Carrie says, "not the other way around. He's the one should be ashamed."

"Still, you must have provoked him," Dolly says.

"No, no, I didn't."

"Did you get mad at him for threatening you at the wedding?" she asks.

"Mad? Not really. I only said we couldn't go on. Dolly, he would have told my whole family if you hadn't stopped him."

She sighs.

"He does have it in for you Kellys and hates that detective. What's his name? Larney. Says your brother and cousin look down on him. Wants to wipe those smug looks off their faces, he says."

"He told you all this? That's awful."

When I was a little girl I got up one night to find a neighbor woman sitting at our kitchen table. Three little boys with her, crying. Mam making tea, Granny Honora holding her hand. Uncle Patrick and Da went out.

"They'll have a word with him," Granny said to the woman.

"It's the drink," the woman said. "The devil gets into him."

Uncle Patrick and Da came back and the woman left with them.

"Made him see sense," Uncle Patrick said to Granny when he and my da returned. "One of those fellows who hangs his fiddle behind the door."

"Angel in the street, devil in the house," Granny Honora said.

The next morning I asked Mam what Uncle Patrick and Granny meant.

"Oh Nonie," she said. "Some fellows charm the world but torture the people who love them."

"Why, Mam? Why?"

"I suppose because they can," she said.

"Will he hit that lady again?"

"I hope not, Nonie. Your father and uncle threw a good scare into him. Better if she could get away from him. But where would she go? Not even a mother living here. In Ireland she'd have loads of relatives though no guarantee she'd be welcomed. Poor thing."

Poor thing. Dolly, with all her money and fame, ready to let Tim knock her around and then take him back. Tolerate his other women. "I am a woman of passion," she said. Well, if that's passion, please God, save me from it! Love. I really thought I'd loved him. A man who was only a squeeze of his fingers away from killing me.

Nowhere to go? I'll find somewhere. Not for me, roses and apologies. I'm awake now, the fairy kingdom left far behind me, the Fairy Woman flown.

Dolly stands up. Carrie removes her robe. Well-corseted is Dolly, her flesh pushed up and overflowing. Formidable. He hits *her*? What would he do to me?

"You're a fool, Dolly," Carrie says. "Tim is getting worse. He's going to kill somebody one of these days. And it could be you!"

Dolly laughs from under the dress over her head. "I'm the director of this drama," she says when she reemerges. "Tim always comes to heel."

Carrie shakes her head and says, "You never threw him out, told him you were done like Nora did." She looks at me. "He won't like that, Nora. Dangerous. I'd get as far away from Chicago as I could," she says.

Dolly smooths down the skirt of her dress, pleated at the waist and falling in easy folds that disguise her bulk. She sees me looking.

"Curious about my gown?" she asks.

"Well, it is very flattering," I say.

Can't believe I'm letting myself be distracted by a design when I should be running for my life right now.

"Made by the Paris dressmaker, Madame Simone," Dolly says.

"Who did the dress you wore to Mame's wedding?"

"Yes, she . . ."

"Are you two nuts?" Carrie shouts. Then puts on a falsetto. "Mmmm, I wonder what Nora should wear in her coffin?"

She snaps her fingers in front of Dolly's face.

"We've got to find a place for this kid," Carrie says.

But Dolly fingers the fabric of her gown. "Velvet," she says. "Made in France."

"Dolly," I say. "Carrie's right. Tim might be on his way here right now."

"I'm supposed to take the train to New York tomorrow morning. Then sail to Paris. Pick up the wardrobe I ordered from Madame Simone. I have my passage booked."

"Dolly, for God's sake," Carrie starts.

"Be quiet, Carrie," Dolly says. "I'm thinking." She looks at me. "You could go instead," she says. "Easy enough to change the ticket to your name."

"Me go to Paris?"

"I wasn't all that interested in making the trip. Don't like winter crossings. But thought Tim should worry a bit about what I'd be doing when I was away. Get his attention. But now . . ."

Carrie laughs.

"Paris?" I say again. "Impossible. I can't go to Europe. Leave my family, my job? I've relatives in Galena—maybe . . ."

A knock at the door. Then a voice.

"McShane's here." It's Charlie, the doorman. "Drunk. A couple of the stagehands got him in the green room. Gave him a bottle. But he's cutting up rough, Dolly," he says.

"Thanks, Charlie. Tell Tim I'll be there in a minute."

Dolly sits down at her dressing table, writes a note, puts it in an envelope, which she addresses

"Take this to Madame Simone. Her shop's on the rue de Rivoli," Dolly says. "Near the rue Saint-Honoré where the fashion houses are."

Honoré, I think. Granny Honora. Guiding me? Hadn't she saved her children, my own da, from starving to death by running for her life with four little ones and a baby on the way. Surely I can rescue myself from one man. Go, I tell myself.

"I'll go," I say. "Thank you, Dolly, thank you!"

She opens her dressing table, takes out a small purse. Counts out twenty-five dollars.

"Take this. My wardrobe's paid for. You check it and arrange with Madame Simone to ship it to me. In the note I suggested she give you a job."

"A job," I say. "In Paris?"

"Nora!" Carrie says. "In three minutes McShane could be breaking down this door. No more questions."

Dolly rubs some rouge into her cheeks. Stands up.

"Go to the Drake," she says to Carrie. "Have the concierge send a wire to the French Line office. Substitute Nora's name for mine. The *Chicago* sails Thursday, Nora," Dolly says. "You'll have to get the morning train to New York."

"Wait," I say. "The name of the ship is the *Chicago*?"

"Didn't I just say that?" Dolly says.

The *Chicago*. Another good omen.

"Leave through the front of the house," Dolly says to us. "I'll take care of Tim."

She smiles at us and leaves.

"The lion tamer," Carrie says.

❧

I follow Carrie through the lobby of the Drake and up to the front desk. She gives the concierge Dolly's instructions and a five-dollar bill. The telegram to the shipping line will go out immediately, he says. Done.

Our room faces the dark expanse of Lake Michigan. We stand looking out.

"Far too much water for me," Carrie says. "I'm from Tipperary. Never saw the sea until I sailed across it when I was nineteen. Met Dolly when I went for a job as a cleaner in a theater in New York forty years ago."

"Forty? Then Dolly's . . ."

"Old enough to know better, but this McShane's got the kibosh on her. Only a big boob to me, for all his winning ways." She turns to me. "I'm glad you're going far away. He's getting worse. Dolly indulges him. Maybe if she'd taken a firmer hand with him in the beginning." She shrugs. "I don't know. Men who hit their women see nothing wrong with it. Like she's theirs to do with whatever they want."

"I'm so grateful. I can't believe Dolly's so generous," I say.

"Cheaper than paying for a lawyer to defend Tim on a murder rap after he kills you! Once you go, Dolly will bring him back into line. He didn't want her to go to Paris. She'll say she changed her mind for him."

Carrie walks away from the window and turns down the two beds. "There's a nightgown for you in that bag," she says.

I pull out a long silk garment with a plunging neckline edged in lace and hold it up to me.

"One of Dolly's. Always has the right costume for the scene, does Dolly," Carrie says. "Why she needs a leading man. Me, I prefer flannel."

"I think I'll sleep in my clothes, just in case I have to get up and run," I say. Still in the black funeral dress.

"McShane doesn't know where you are. Besides, the house dick here's a tough old bird. Sleep will put one night between you and what happened."

But I can't undress. I lie awake clutching the sheets, listening for footsteps in the hotel hallway. I had wanted to send a note to Henrietta by way of Dolly's chauffeur.

But Carrie said, "Oh great. And what if Tim's casing your joint and sees Raymond pull up in Dolly's Daimler?"

"But I have no clothes," I said. "Only this black dress."

"Buy them in New York," she told me. "Go to Delancey Street."

New York? Paris? The farthest I've been from Chicago is Eagle River, Wisconsin, where Ed has a summer cabin. I'll never close my eyes again, I think. But I do.

The rising sun wakes me. Confused, I look around the strange room but then I sit straight up and remember. Tim. Dolly. Paris. Carrie is snoring away.

Ashamed to put words to what happened, even to myself. Couldn't tell Mike. He'd do more than have a word with Tim McShane. He'd tear his head off, or try to anyway. God knows what Tim would do in return. Doesn't bear thinking about. Tim's got a gun.

What now? I have to let someone know I'm leaving. Ed, I think. Ed, who'll be heading toward me right now. An odd habit he has of running along the Lake at sunrise even in winter. Some old boxer had told him an hour of pounding along was all the training he'd ever need for the ring.

"You'll have two strong legs, powerful lungs, and a fixed mind," the fellow told him.

Ed said it worked. Hadn't he been undefeated in every Brighton Park match? Told me he outlasted his opponents. Something to be said for staying on your feet no matter the blows rained on you, he said.

I teased him: "Jesus, Ed, you're too skinny to be the next Jack Dempsey, so why bother?"

"It's enough to be Champ of Brighton Park," he told me.

His fighting days long past. A serious engineer but still there at ringside for every bout. And he runs each morning, then ducks into early Mass at Holy Name. I take the boat ticket, money, write a note to Carrie, then leave the room.

I find Ed rounding the corner of Michigan Avenue right under the Drake Hotel sign. The sun is pushing itself out of the Lake.

"Ed." I stand in front of him.

"Nonie? What? Did somebody die?" Looking at me dressed in the chorus girl's funeral clothes.

"Nobody died, Ed, but I have to talk to you."

The sun's up now, turning the dark water of the Lake blue.

"Let's go down to the shore," he says.

I nod but, my God, what a hike, through a wasteland of weeds and bits of wood and trash washed up from the Lake. Train tracks built on a trestle right in the water. I hear the whistle of the Illinois Central Railroad.

And, of course, Ed starts up again about how there should be beaches here sweeping from the north to the south, and families strolling along grass instead of picking their way through decayed animal carcasses and rotting piles of garbage. As if the rich will ever let people from the slums into their front yards on Sunday afternoon.

He's waving his hands and saying "Granny Honora" and "Galway Bay" and "Chicago could be as green as Ireland" until I shout: "Ed! I'm in trouble."

I see his face.

"No, I'm not having a child, but . . ."

I walk over to a flat rock and sit down, patting a place for him next to me. He sits.

"I have to leave Chicago."

"Good to travel a bit," he says. "Gives perspective. After being away with the surveying team I saw that Chicago will never take its place among the great cities of the world until our lakefront—"

"Please, Ed! I have to leave today!"

Damn. I'm sniveling. Can't cry. So I start to talk fast. I make myself tell him everything. The words pour out of me. My years with Tim and last night. Ed gets up, pacing as I speak. Not looking at me.

I finish with, "Tim McShane says he'll kill me if I leave him and I've left him."

"Mike and I'll have a word with McShane. Don't you worry."

"No, Ed, he's a black-hearted bastard. I've been pretending not to see it for years. No telling what he'll do."

"Let him take a swing at me. I'll flatten him just like I knocked out that foreman." Ed's finest hour. He hit a fellow who'd been abusing him and the rest of the crew. Sent to Colonel Robert McCormick, head of the Sanitary District, to be fired. Turned out McCormick liked a man who stood up for himself, promoted Ed and they'd been friends ever since, even though McCormick was a die-hard Republican.

"But McShane's got a pistol. I have to get away. Please. Listen to me!"

Finally Ed nods. "Well, we've family in Galena."

"I'm afraid he'll come looking for me. I'm going to Paris."

"I suppose that's far enough south," Ed says. "And I've a friend—"

"Not Paris, Illinois, Ed. Paris, France."

That gets him.

"Nonie, you're nuts!"

"I can't tell you any details, but a friend's giving me a ticket and the chance of a job."

Ed's shaking his head. About to argue.

"Tim's dangerous, Ed," I say. "He'll go to the newspapers. He'll use me to get at you, the family."

"He may do it anyway."

"Once I'm gone, Dolly will handle him. Please, Ed."

He looks at me for a long time. "Okay," he says. "You'll need money. We'll go to the bank and . . ."

"I have to go now! Catch the nine o'clock train to New York. I have twenty-five dollars."

"Not enough," he says.

I follow him onto Delaware Street where his Packard is parked. We get in the big car.

"We'll stop at my house, then I'll drive you to the train."

"Oh Ed. Thank you! You're being so good to me. I can't thank you . . . I'm so ashamed . . . I . . ."

"Whist!" Granny Honora's word. "You're a Kelly, Nonie—my own flesh and blood."

"Flesh and blood," I say. "What will Mike think. He'll hate me! I'll never be able to face him. I . . ."

"Never is a long time, Nonie."

"You're not going to tell him about . . . Tim McShane."

"Not as big a secret as you think, Nonie," he says.

"Oh, God, Mike knows?"

"McShane's a braggart and, well one night at the Palmer House bar he hinted around to Mike that you were . . ."

"And Mike?"

"Called him a liar and walked out. McShane was drunk."

"Oh, no. When?"

"Must be a year ago."

"And neither of you said anything?"

"I asked my wife and she said the fellow was crazy. That you would never . . ."

"Ed, you told Mary . . . and did Mike tell Mame?" I can hardly say the words.

"I told you Nonie, we decided it wasn't true and it's not. Deny everything. His word against yours."

His wife Mary lets us in to his house, says nothing but "Good morning, Nonie," and goes back to feeding baby Eddie his breakfast. Lovely little fellow, the spit of Ed, this third Kelly redhead.

Amazing that she asks me no questions. We chat about the baby while Ed goes into another room. A good politician's wife.

Ed hands me an envelope. Twenty-five dollars inside.

"Let's go," he says.

We're on Archer, almost downtown at the station, when I say, "Ed. I'm so sorry. I can't believe I let myself . . ." I stop. "Do you hate me, Ed? Will the others?"

He turns and smiles. Thank God.

"I love you, Nonie. We're the redheads, the Twins. People make mistakes. It's what they do afterwards that counts."

"What will you tell the family? What about Mr. Bartlett? My job?"

"I'll tell Al Bartlett you had to settle family business in Ireland. And as for the family. Maybe better they don't know where you're going if McShane comes looking for you."

The thought of that. Dolly won't let him. Dolly will . . .

"What about a passport?" Ed asks me.

"Passport? I don't even have underwear," I say.

"Not required to have a passport really," he says. "But it might not be a bad idea for you to carry some document. It's just eight o'clock. Pat'll be in his office."

"Pat?"

"Pat Nash. He'll have an idea."

We pull into Nash Brothers construction yard. A whole block on West Eighteenth Street.

"Stay here, Nonie," Ed says.

I'm glad to sit in the car. Wouldn't want to try to explain myself to Pat Nash.

In ten minutes Ed trots back to the car.

"We have to hurry. Matt's waiting at his house."

So. I leave Chicago with fifty dollars, Madame Simone's address, and a temporary passport issued by Federal Judge Matthew Craig.

"I'll be back in the spring," I tell Ed as I board the train. I'll write to the others. I will, I think as we pull out of the station. But now it's relief I feel.

Glad when the last bit of Chicago slides by. Get away. Get away. Get away.

5

PARIS 1911–1914

NOVEMBER 1911

I stand in front of the Gare Saint-Lazare repeating to myself the name of the Paris hotel I want. "L'Hôtel Jeanne d'Arc," the steward on the S.S. *Chicago* had said. A Frenchman and a good fellow. Somehow knew how lost I felt on that huge ship full of fancy people. Overwhelmed by the luxury of the first-class cabin where I spent most of the voyage. Sick. The steward had brought me the few meals I could eat. And afraid too. What if Tim Mc-Shane had somehow followed me? On the ship. Ready to pounce.

Crazy I know, but if you've ever been really afraid you understand how your own mind can make the impossible seem all too probable. That noise at midnight? Tim McShane waiting outside my cabin door, going to break it down. And my heart beat fast and my throat went dry and . . .

Well, anyway, now I'm in Paris. Safe, I tell myself . . . safe. If only I can find somewhere to sleep tonight.

"Pas cher," the steward said about the hotel, which is good because though the bank on the ship had magically changed the forty dollars I had left after buying a wardrobe from the pushcart on Delancey Street into two hundred francs, which sounds like a fortune, the steward told me that much money will see me through two months at the most. I'll get that

job with Madame Simone, please God, as Granny Honora would say. Don't start thinking about the family or home. Get yourself to the Jeanne d'Arc.

"Not 'Joan of Arc,'" Sister Mary Agnes our French teacher would tell us in class. "Jan Dark." Rapping the syllables at us. "The Maid, La Pucelle, France's great heroine and a true saint, no matter what some say." Very annoyed that nearly five hundred years after her birth, Joan had still not been canonized. "Politics," Sister said. "The English."

For all her love of things French, Sister Mary Agnes remained Chicago Irish to her core and was convinced of the perfidiousness of Albion. "Jeanne's enemies are still powerful," she'd tell us as we wrote a monthly letter to the Pope urging him to hurry up Joan's cause.

"It took the Church nearly four hundred years to even start the canonization process and now they drag their feet!" Sister Agnes had said, and explained how the devil's advocate defamed "Jan," casting doubt on her voices and demeaning her accomplishments. "A warning, girls. The world uses powerful women and casts them aside." Joan finally beatified two years ago though not a saint yet.

But Sister had cemented the name in my brain.

"Jan Dark," I say, speaking louder and louder until the poor woman I'd stopped in front of the train station shakes off my hand from her arm. "Joan of Arc," I try, enunciating the English words, but she hurries away.

I rummage in my pocket for the small piece of paper where I'd written the hotel's name and wait. Here's a younger woman, not in such a hurry— good. I stop her.

"*Pardon,*" I start, wishing I'd paid more attention to Sister Mary Agnes when she shouted declensions at us. I have a slew of French words rattling around in my brain but putting one word next to the other with plenty of space between seems exactly the wrong way to get the French to understand me. So I rush a phrase at this girl, hoping I hit a word or two right. "*L'hôtel, s'il vous plaît,*" I say, and point to the paper.

She looks, smiles, and takes me by the elbow. She knows, I think. Her family stays at the Jeanne d'Arc when they come in from the country! It's only steps away.

"*Ici,*" she says, pointing to a line of automobiles. "*Taxi.*"

"*Taxi,*" I repeat. It becomes my most useful French word.

My bags and I fit ourselves in the back of a taxi and go rushing toward what the taxi man calls "Jan Dark Ma-ray," adding the location of the hotel to her name.

Midafternoon now, not as cold as a November day in Chicago but brisk enough. Splashes of sun hit the grand buildings I crane my neck to see from the taxi windows. Wow. I open the window. A smell of gasoline exhaust in the air. More cars here than in Chicago. Fewer horse-drawn carriages and no stockyard stench. I inhale.

We follow a twist of streets until we reach a square—"Sainte Kat-ereen," the driver says, which I assume means St. Catherine. He stops at a white building with "Jan's" name embellished in golden letters on the front.

"Please, Joan, help me," I pray to the painting in the lobby. She holds up a sword and wears armor—reassuring. Tim McShane might be an ocean away but the memory of his hands squeezing my throat can surprise me at the odd moment. Nice to have an armed woman guarding me.

The desk clerk speaks a kind of English. He's young—twenty-five at the most—thin, long hair, very thick eyebrows.

"I am Etienne, Stefan."

He has a single room *"pas cher."* Five francs. Thirty if I take it for a week. Geeze Louise that's six dollars! A one-bedroom apartment in Chicago's only twenty dollars a month!

"Too much," I say.

He shrugs.

"Try the other hotels. All cost more."

He looks at my bags and so do I.

The taxi from the station cost five francs. Do I spend more money going from hotel to hotel?

"For the month—one hundred francs," Stefan says. With breakfast— *petit déjeuner*—not too petite I hope because to get this *"bon prix"* I have to pay in advance. I only have ninety-five francs—nineteen dollars—left.

The room's small, good. I can see every corner from the bed. No place for Tim to lurk. I touch the beams that hold up the ceiling, running my hands over their pitted surface. Rough-hewn and sagging but they've felt the weight of centuries and held.

The bed's firm, the sheets clean and smooth, with a big fluffy cover on top. A long sleep, I think, as I pull it up around me. But after a few hours

I wake to darkness. Why is the ship so still? Then I remember. I'm here. I've arrived. Tim can't get me.

I get up. Push the windows open. St. Catherine's Square is below me. Quiet. Hours until dawn.

The sky edges from black to gray. I see humps of chimneys stuck here and there on the Paris roofs. So different from the straight up-and-down of Chicago buildings. Centuries jam together here. Maybe the eight years I lost to Tim McShane aren't as long in Paris as in Chicago. God, I'd love a cup of coffee—*café*. At least I can say that. Seven, Stefan said is when they start serving breakfast. Soon I'll be one night closer to getting back to myself, whoever that is. The woman looking out at the rooftops of Paris, is she Honora Bridget Kelly? Nora? Nonie? Mademoiselle?

I'm the first one down when the coffee comes from the kitchen.

"Café au lait?" Stefan is the waiter now.

"Oui, oui," I say. A lovely taste both smooth and bitter, a perfect complement to the warm bread that I slather with sweet butter and raspberry jam. Eat enough bread and I'll get through the day.

An older couple comes carefully into the small breakfast room. He, tall and lean, nods at me. She, shorter and rounder, smiles.

"Bonjour," I say. Might as well try.

And they respond, though their *"Bonjour, mademoiselle"* goes up and down the scale in a way that would be considered showing off in Sister Mary Agnes's class, who I now realize fit French into her own Chicago speech pattern.

A retired teacher and his wife, I decide.

Stefan brings them their coffee and gives me a new pot. *"Un croissant?"* he asks me, and drops a flaky horn-shaped pastry on my plate. So soft I hardly feel my teeth go through it. I eat a second. A clatter of crumbs falls onto the front of my blouse.

Coming from the station I noticed the Paris women were all turned out in muted colors, well-cut jackets and skirts. I wonder if this yellow and red plaid dress with a sailor collar I got on Delancey Street isn't a bit loud. Ah well, I'm here to learn from them.

After breakfast I show Stefan the address of Dolly's seamstress, 374 rue de Rivoli.

He takes out a map.

"We are here," he says. "Le Marais—it means the marsh. This *quartier* was built on swampy ground."

"Like Chicago," I say.

He starts telling me the history of the neighborhood. The Knights Templar were the first to move in when they came back from the Holy Land in twelve something.

"The Crusades," I say. Lots about the Crusades at St. Xav's.

Stefan is going on about some king who built a palace somewhere called the place des Vosges, which is around the corner though I don't find it for days. But that's Paris for you. Hides its treasures down pokey streets nobody in Chicago would even want to live on.

Stefan's drawing lines on the map now. *"Rue de Rivoli, à droite."*

A street to love the rue de Rivoli! If it doesn't go there, neither will I. I see that I can walk the whole Right Bank then over one of the bridges over the Seine and be in la Rive Gauche. Rue de Rivoli doesn't wiggle or squiggle or change its name—a reliable rue. This first morning it leads me through my own *quartier* past men with long beards and round black hats. Stefan says Le Marais is a Jewish neighborhood, and the Hebrew lettering on some of the stores reminds me of Maxwell Street.

I stop to gawk at the Hôtel de Ville—City Hall from what I can figure out. This close to Christmas our City Hall would have been decorated with pine boughs and tinsel. Not an ornament in sight here. But imagine setting up as mayor in that place! Only for my having seen the White City at the World's Fair could I take in the scope and scale of the building. Stone recesses are full of statues. And this is a place for city business? What will the churches look like?

The rue de Rivoli and I hit what first seems a massive wall that goes on for blocks and blocks. I pause under the arches that cover the sidewalk. A man walking behind collides with me. A middle-aged fellow, somberly dressed.

I smile, trying to say, "Sorry, all my fault," in French, then I point. *"Qu'est-ce que c'est ça?"* I ask.

He almost drops the rolled umbrella he carries.

He answers in English, "That, madame, is the Palais du Louvre, the most important museum in the world," he says, using the tip of his umbrella to underline each word.

I apologize for my ignorance and say, "The *Mona Lisa*," but he's on his way.

Of course, Sister Mary Agnes had gone on and on about the Louvre but she hadn't told us the place sprawled in all directions.

I continue on the rue de Rivoli, and there waiting for me all golden and shining against the gray sky—Jeanne d'Arc herself, mounted on a powerful-looking horse. Her face is young but resolute. She looks straight at me holding high a banner. Unfurled, no matter how strong the wind. A saint, title or no title. And I stand up straighter. You and me, Joan. You'll help me, I know.

Rue de Rivoli delivers me to the place de la Concorde. I look up at the obelisk Sister Mary Agnes said Napoleon stole from the Egyptians. My Paris life almost ends as I try to cross four lanes of traffic. Automobiles, horse-drawn hacks, and carriages all come at me. Madness. I stand paralyzed until I see an old woman plunge right into the middle of it all. I follow her across, throw a few *"Mercis"* in her direction. Then scatter more "Thank you"s into the air.

Number 374 rue de Rivoli doesn't have a grand façade or a big window displaying the latest fashions as do some of the other shops I passed along rue Saint-Honoré, which I guess is Paris's State Street. A small card with "Madame Simone, Couturier, 1er Etage" written in flowing handwriting fits into a slot under a brass hand that rests on the black lacquer door. The knocker makes a satisfying bang when I lift it then let it go.

A young girl in a black dress opens the door.

"Vite, vite," she says, and practically pulls me into a dark hallway and up a set of winding stairs because the first floor here is actually the second. Strange. The large room we enter is very like my studio at Montgomery Ward: counters covered with fabrics, dress dummies, a mirrored wall, and standing in the center of it on a round platform the client—plumpish, maybe sixty, being fitted by a woman who kneels at her feet with pins in her mouth. Her blond hair's pulled into a bun. In her fifties I'd say. She wears a black dress with a high gathered waist and gored skirt. No sailor collars here or red plaid either.

"Madame Simone," the girl says to her. *"Ici. La femme de traducteur."*

"Bon," Madame Simone says, and tosses a spate of French through the pins at me.

"Please," I say in English, then try to tell her in French that I can't understand when she speaks so quickly.

"Too *vite*," I say. *"Lentment*, slowly, *s'il vous plaît."*

She looks at me and starts muttering in French.

"Please, madame," I say. "Here."

I give her Dolly's letter, but before she can open it the client says, "An American! Oh, thank God! Can you tell this woman she's got to finish this dress today! We're going to dinner at Maxim's tonight and I must wear it."

"I'll try," I say. "My French is not great."

"But aren't you the translator? The concierge at the Ritz said he'd send over someone who spoke English and French," she says.

"Well, I do speak English very well," I say.

Madame Simone stares at us trying to will herself into comprehension. I sympathize with her. All right, here goes . . .

"Pardon, madame," I say. *"Cette femme."* I point at the client. *"Vouloir le gown."* I touch the skirt which poufs out impressively and is covered with tiny crystals. *"Pour cette nuit. Maintenant."* Then I throw in, *"Très nécessaire."*

Madame Simone looks puzzled.

"What's wrong?" the client says. "I understand every word you say."

"But you don't speak French," I say.

I try again, pretend I am putting on the dress, then mime sitting down at table and eating. *"Maintenant,"* I say.

"N'est ce pas un restaurant, mademoiselle," the maid says to me.

"Non, non. La femme va à Maxim's." And I twirl around as if delighted with my new gown. *"Ce soir.* Tonight."

And now Madame Simone nods. She rubs her thumb and two fingers together in a gesture that needs no translating.

"Combien?" I say.

She holds up ten fingers, five times.

"You have to pay her an extra fifty francs," I say to the American woman. So much. The client will never . . .

"Fine," she says.

"D'accord," I say to Madame.

And Madame Simone smiles.

The woman's name is Mary Zander and she wants to see Paris. Will I be her guide while Madame Simone finishes her gown?

Madame looks at me. *"Comment?"* What's the woman asking for now?

I try to explain, pointing to Mary Zander and then to myself.

"Le Louvre," I say. *"Le place de la Concorde, Eiffel Tower."*

"*Tour Eiffel*," Madame Simone corrects me. She understands. "Georgette," she says to the maid, and makes show-them-out gestures.

"*Va*," Madame says to us. "*Va! Va!*"

Mary Zander changes into a navy blue serge dress with sailor collar and we *va*. The blind leading the blind I think. But so what? Back we go to the rue de Rivoli.

"May I present the Louvre," I say to Mary Zander.

"Marvelous," she says. She doesn't even need to go in. Happy to walk through the Tuileries.

"Nice day," I say. "Indian summer."

Mary smiles. "Yes. Do you think there is any way to say *that* in French?"

We walk up the Champs-Élysées and nod at the Arc de Triomphe. I find a taxi stand and we head for her hotel, the Ritz on the place Vendôme.

"Beautiful, isn't it?" Mary says to me as we get out and look at the façades on the place Vendôme.

"Wow," I say.

We lunch or *déjeuner* at the Ritz. Mary has learned to say *steak et pommes frites*, "the only thing without all those sauces." I get the same. Delicious.

The Zanders are from Buffalo, she tells me. Her husband is if not *the* grain king at least a well-placed grain prince. She finds interacting with the French an ordeal. She needs not just a guide but a go-between, a friend. But most importantly she wants to share the naked wonder of Paris with someone who won't react with cool French amusement to her enthusiasm. I am happy to fill the bill.

After lunch we go to the Eiffel Tower. That's easy to spot. "Isn't it great?" I say to Mary. "All these sights we've seen only in pictures and now here's the real thing."

Mary smiles and nods.

The maid, Georgette, is waiting at the Ritz with Mary's gown when we return. I notice the box has THE HOUSE OF CHARLES WORTH embossed on it. Georgette sees Mary give me ten francs. We wave at Mary as she goes up the marble and gilt staircase, the bellman following her with the box. Georgette looks at me, says "*Madame Simone, demain*," and rubs her fingers together. So I guess I pay Madame a share.

But I've two more dollars now, and a full stomach. Not too bad for my first day. I sleep through the night.

The next morning I go back to Madame Simone's studio. Cold today and raining. Madame greets me with an outstretched hand. No words needed. I put a franc on her palm. She just looks at it until I add four more. She walks over to a table, pushes fabric aside, sits down. Takes a black leather box from a drawer and puts the money away.

Dolly's letter is open in front of her. I look down, see that it's written in French, thank God. Madame Simone points to a rack of gowns.

"*Pour Dolly*," she says.

I walk over and look at the four. Very fancy. Sequins and feathers on each. Beautifully made. I lift the hem. Tiny even stitches.

"*C'est bon*," I say.

"*Bon?*" Madame says. "*Bon? Non. Magnifique.*"

"*Oui, oui,*" I say. "That too."

Georgette brings out a big box, takes a gown down, and begins to carefully wrap it in tissue paper. Getting the shipment ready? "*Aujourd'hui,*" she says. Going out today, I guess.

"*Merci, mademoiselle,*" Madame Simone says to me. "*Au revoir.*"

Good-bye? No. Didn't Dolly tell her I need a job? I point to the letter.

"*Travaillez pour vous s'il vous plaît?*" I say.

"*Comment?*" Madame says. Doesn't understand me. The train station all over again.

I take the folded sketches of my designs from my bag and set them next to Dolly's letter on the table. Madame Simone puts a finger on one and pushes it toward me.

"*Vous,*" I say. "Sew-ez," making imaginary stitches in the air. "*Le* dresses *de moi.*"

"*Comment?*" she says again.

I repeat the charade and now Georgette is watching.

"Ahh," she says, and rattles away in French to Madame Simone.

"*Vous,*" Madame Simone says, pointing at me. "*Une couturière?*" She starts laughing and the maid joins in. Very amused. What's so funny? I want to tell them that Montgomery Ward's sold lots of my dress patterns in the catalog. But of course I don't. How can I find the words?

Madame Simone picks up a sketch. "*Vous?*" She mimes drawing.

"*Oui oui,*" I say. And I sketch a design in the air. Then another and another. Silence from Madame though Georgette laughs. "*Peut-être,*" Madame says.

That means perhaps. A chance. "*Peut-être?*"

"*Moi?*" I say. "*Traivaillez pour vous?*"

Madame Simone nods.

"I've got the job, I'm a designer?" I say, which Madame doesn't under-stand at all. It's the maid, Georgette, who sets me straight. Very good at pantomime is Georgette.

I find out that Madame Simone copies the designs of big names like Charles Worth and Paul Poiret then makes up the gowns in very good fabrics. Nothing chintzy about Madame Simone's creations, Georgette lets me know. She has me touch the velvet skirt of a dress. But Madame Sim-one's versions cost half what the original would. Madame has a few French customers, but she specializes in tourists. The concierges at the best hotels drop hints about a fine dressmaker, "*pas cher,*" and well . . . Madame makes good money.

Except no couturier allows Madame or anyone known to be on her staff to attend their shows or enter the sacred ground of their fashion houses. So she has to wait until the finished dresses appear in the illustrated maga-zines like *Le Bon Temps* or *Art et Décoration.*

Now I am to pretend to be a rich American on the couturier circuit. The concierge at the Ritz will arrange the appointments. I'll ask to make some notes, quickly sketch the gowns, and voilà.

Dishonest, right? Bad enough Madame Simone laughs at my designs but now she wants me to become a crook. Because it is stealing to copy someone else's work, isn't it? But try to get that concept across in high school French and charades. Though I think Madame Simone understands. In fact she says to me in surprising English, "I not steal, I adapt. *Les couturiers* give me inspiration."

So do I say "no" or "*non*" and storm out? Well, I want to but then she says she'll pay me five francs a dress, a dollar. What do I do? I put my hands on my head and move them back and forth trying to show I'm thinking. "*Demain,*" I say. "Can I let you know tomorrow?"

Georgette sees me out. At the downstairs door she points to me and then to herself. "*Aidez Madame,*" she says. "*Et moi et les autres.*" Which I guess means she and the seamstresses need the jobs that come from Madame Simone's business. Maybe Madame's "inspiration" has been running dry because Georgette takes my hand and says, "*S'il vous plaît.*"

I really don't know what to do. I mean, I'm not exactly a virtuous woman. Not after eight years of sneaking off to see Tim McShane. But I guess I've made kind of a bargain with God. If I'm good in other aspects of my life, then He'll forgive me for my sins of the flesh. After all, Tim Mc-Shane almost murdered me. If there's a category of saint "martyr neither virgin," that could have been me. Surely facing death grants some kind of absolution. But will I start this new life as a thief? I wander back to the hotel, walking along the rue de Rivoli but seeing nothing.

That night I ask Stefan for a good place for dinner. That morning's petit déjeuner has disappeared after twelve hours. Stefan suggests a nearby restaurant around the corner called L'Impasse because it's located on an impasse, a dead end. It allows "*les femmes,* women," he says. I guess Paris is the same as Chicago. Lone women can't just go anywhere to eat. I find the restaurant on impasse Guéménée.

Stefan told me the restaurant is owned by the Collard family. Their busiest time is lunch, he said, when they serve the merchants from the local market and sell animal fodder, which somehow makes them more open-minded.

The restaurant is empty when I arrive at seven. Early, but *"Je suis une Americaine,"* I say to Madame Collard, a heavyset woman in a black skirt and blouse who sits behind a desk on a high stool just inside the door. I pat my stomach, which confuses her because she smiles, says "aahh," and pretends to rock a baby. She's fifty maybe but has one of those full faces that don't wrinkle.

"You think I'm pregnant," I say in English. Then *"Non, non"* while rocking the baby myself.

"Faim," I say, "hungry."

"Henri," she calls out. *"Mon fils Henri parle anglais."*

Well, sort of English.

"Hello. Hello," the young fellow says. Henri leads me to a table. Early twenties, handsome in a skinny kind of way. No beard or mustache.

I don't even pretend to read the menu. But say to Henri, *"S'il vous plaît."*

"Bon," Henri says. A few seconds later he's pulling a cork from a bottle of wine. *"Pommard,"* he says. "Burgundy." He pours a little in my glass. I take a sip. Indian summer, it tastes like Indian summer. Those last warm days, sunlight on orange leaves, the sky that bright blue.

"Wow," I say, and he fills my glass to the top. Who knew I loved wine? Not me.

"Merci," I say. *"Merci."*

I'd be happy to just drink the wine and eat the crusty bread but then he brings out the soup. Creamy, first of all, not watery. Delicious. What is it?

"Choufleur," Henri tells me, and searches for the English word. Finally he brings me a head of cauliflower from the kitchen. This from that? I don't even like cauliflower but I'd ask for more, except he takes the bowl away.

"Coq au vin," Henri says, setting down a plate. Chicken I guess, but no Chicago chicken ever got this treatment. Covered in mushrooms with roast potatoes on the side and the sauce . . .

"Trés, trés bon," I tell Henri.

Dessert's cream puffs stuffed with ice cream, covered with hot fudge.

"Profiteroles," Henri says.

I repeat the word three times. I want *"profiteroles"* in my French vocabulary.

Monsieur Collard, the chef, comes out. Roly-poly I'd call him. Red-faced from the kitchen in a white chef's hat and apron. He kisses my hand. Dear God, Paris. Hurrah.

Henri gives me the bill. Five francs—a whole dollar. Yikes! The most expensive dinner at the Berghoff is only fifty cents. But then I've never eaten like this at the Berghoff.

More customers are arriving as I leave. Henri puts the half-full bottle of Pommard on the shelf and says *"Pour vous au revoir,"* mine for the next time, I guess.

Stefan wants to know did I enjoy my dinner.

"Oui," I say. "But *cher.*"

"How much?"

"Five francs," I say.

"Very reasonable for Paris," he tells me, sniffing.

I calculate. Including the five francs from Mary Zander I have enough money for twenty dinners. What do I do? Eat twice a week? And I do want to eat. I want more coq au vin and profiteroles and a glass of wine from my own bottle of Burgundy waiting around the corner. Now I understand the dreamy tone in Aunt Máire's voice when she talked about New Orleans, the port where she and Granny Honora landed, when they came from Ireland. "Beignets at Café du Monde," she'd say. She'd wanted to stay there. "I would have done anything to stay," she told me once, and I knew *anything* involved the red silk fringed shawl. Now I understand. I'm considering becoming a thief to pay for profiteroles.

I don't sleep much that night and I'm up early. Mary Zander leaves to-day. I want to catch her. Get her opinion on abetting Madame Simone and her fiddle.

Breakfast at the Ritz is not petite at all. Funny how the rich get so much for free. Mary tells the waiter to give me anything I want. So I order *"une omelette avec jambon."*

"Ham," he says in English.

I choose the words for my dilemma carefully. After all, Mary Zander went to Maxim's in an imitation Charles Worth gown. I stumble around until she stops me.

"Madame Simone provides a service," she says. "My husband would never allow me to buy a *real* Worth. He says becoming rich hasn't made him stupid. Value for money is his motto, and if people in Buffalo think my gown's authentic, so what? In a way I'm advertising Worth, getting new customers for him."

"So you don't tell your friends about Madame Simone?"

Mary Zander laughs. "Only very, very close friends. Oh, Nora, you have a very delicate conscience for a woman making her way alone in Paris."

She has a point, I think. By five o'clock the omelette's only a memory. I'm hungry. No L'Impasse tonight. I pick up a hunk of *fromage* for one franc, the cheapest of the huge selection at the shop called a fromagerie on the nearby rue Saint-Antoine. Loads of food stores each displaying a specialty—fruit, vegetables, meat, fish. On the corner there's a glass and marble bakery with cases full of pastries shining with cream and choco-late. All very *cher*. I keep my eyes on the floor as I buy a baguette for fifty centimes. Cheap enough. Riots in Paris if the bread costs too much. Wasn't that what got Marie Antoinette in trouble? "No bread? Let them eat cake." Not at these prices.

Stefan notices my baguette and package of cheese as I walk through the lobby.

"No job?" he says.

"No," I say. I explain what Madame Simone wants me to do. "I can work, but as a spy," I say. "I don't want to steal the designs of great couturi-ers," I say. "Join Madame Simone in her fraud."

He laughs.

"You're worrying about stealing from the ruling class who abuse their workers and promote a system of false values that poisons *tout la Paris?*" he asks.

Sometimes his English is really good.

"You sound like a Bolshevik," I say. "We have those in Chicago."

Stefan stops laughing. Pounds the desk and says, "Chicago! The Haymarket. A disgrace!"

Now, you don't mention the Haymarket incident in my family. I was only seven when a big squad of police started to break up a meeting of workingmen only to have a bomb thrown at them. One policeman was hit by a fragment and died. The other cops started shooting. Thirty people dead including a good number of police, shot by their own fellows in the confusion. Ed's father, my uncle Steve, was one of the policemen, while my uncle Mike and his friends from the blacksmiths' union were in the crowd at the meeting.

"A massacre," Uncle Mike always said. "What were we—only workers trying to get decent wages. A peaceful demonstration against the bloodsucking plutocrats."

"Anarchists! Bolsheviks!" Uncle Steve would yell. "Foreign agitators. Violent."

Now Stefan is saying proudly, "I'm not only a Bolshevik, I am a follower of Vladimir Lenin." Then:

"Take the job, you imbecile," Stefan says. "You have a chance to strike at the parasites, support the workers."

I am the only one at breakfast the next morning. Stefan allows me a second croissant but not a third.

"You have decided?" he asked.

"I will take the job," I say to him. See, I really like the idea of being in Madame Simone's studio with other women at work making something. Who knows? If I help with her "inspirations" maybe she'll look at my sketches again. And there's dinners at L'Impasse. Stefan kisses me on both cheeks. *"Citoyenne,"* he says.

You're a long way from Chicago, Nonie, I tell myself.

Madame Simone asks me no questions when I arrive, only says, *"Vite. Vite."* Georgette explains that the fashion houses will soon close for the *"vacances de Noël,"* Christmas vacation I guess. Getting the hang of French. Madame's clients want gowns for holiday parties. Georgette hands me a magazine with a photograph of a woman in an Oriental-looking outfit. Beautiful really, the photo's like a painting almost. I point at it and make sewing motions. Why can't Madame Simone copy the photograph?

"Non," Georgette says. *"Il faut présenter les nouveaux."* Madame shows me the names of five women who want gowns for Noël. Today is December 5th. How can they make five couturier gowns in ten days? By rushing.

In less than an hour, I'm on my way to Paul Poiret's House of Fashion. I wear one of Madame Simone's royal blue costumes with a fur cape wrapped around me. The note I carry from Alain at the Ritz introduces me as Madame Smith. Imaginative right? Well, it's easy to remember.

Now here's a fellow Marshall Field would like I think standing in front of his shop near the place Vendôme. Merchandise jams the window. A mannequin dressed in a gold lamé skirt and a purple velvet tunic stands surrounded by figures costumed like the sultan's favorites, called in to entertain His Majesty. The few masculine mannequins wear long embroidered coats, and one has a peacock feather stuck into his turban.

I walk in.

"Wow!" I say to the woman clerk who comes up to me. She covers her slight wince with an automatic smile and says in an English accent, "You're an American, I assume."

"I am," I say. "So happy you speak English."

God, I'd hate to try out my charades on this one.

"Quite a display on your window," I say.

"A scene from Mr. Poiret's famous party this summer, the One Thousand and Two Arabian Nights," she says.

"Oh, I get it," I say. "Adding to the One Thousand and One."

She nods and leads me to a large photograph. Points. "Here's Monsieur himself dressed as a caliph," she says. "And there's Lord Acton. He makes a very good Oriental potentate, don't you think?"

He looks ridiculous, but I don't say anything.

"I'm visiting Paris," I tell her, "with my husband who's in grain."

She nods again.

No racks to go through like in Field's basement, I'll tell you that. You sit down and models parade by you. Beautiful women. I wonder what they're paid. Not much I'd say.

I tell Miss Rule Britannia I'd like to make a few notes. I get out my pad. Oh dear God, she's staring right at me. How can I start to sketch?

The first outfit has a silk hobble skirt in red satin and a jacket encrusted with jewels.

"Gosh," I say to her. "Are those real?"

"Semiprecious stones," she says.

"How much?" I ask.

"Five hundred francs," she says.

"One hundred dollars!" I try not to let my voice squeak. That's as much as a Model T costs.

She watches me write "$100" on my pad.

"Would you like to sketch this gown?" she says.

What?

"Well, yes I would," I say.

"Your pencil doesn't seem very sharp," she says.

I look at the point.

"It's okay," I say to her.

"I could sharpen it for you for a small charge," she answers.

"Oh," I say.

"Ten francs."

"What?" Now my voice does squeak.

"I'll let you sketch five gowns."

"But . . ."

"All right. Ten gowns. Remember the models will have to stand very still."

"And will they get a, er, consideration too?" I say.

"They will," she says.

Another Bolshevik? What can I do?

"Well Miss Lenin." That freezes her. "I guess we can do business."

"I'm Miss Jones, Mrs. Smith, and we will never meet again."

I thought I'd have a hard time explaining to Madame Simone how Mademoiselle Jones spotted me and demanded a bribe. But all I have to do is mime sketching, then count out ten francs, and she understands.

"C'est la vie," she says.

I think about my brother Mart paying the fellows who deliver the *Tribune* and the *Chicago American* a dollar so he'd get the bundles of newspapers before 7:00 a.m. And what were those Christmas envelopes I gave to the janitor at Ward's? Bribes of a kind. Greases the wheels, Mike would say about extra payments to plumbing suppliers and contributions to the aldermen's campaign funds.

Maybe Paris and Chicago are not so different after all.

I do well. Madame Simone picks five sketches, gives me twenty-five francs. Subtract the ten I gave to Miss Jones and I'd made fifteen francs, three dollars, and still had five sketches to sell. I feel very businesslike altogether. I expect the guilt to catch up with me that night, but I elude it by eating *boeuf bourguignonne* at L'Impasse and finishing my bottle of Pommard.

By Christmas I've made one hundred francs, doubled my money.

So. I have my Christmas dinner with Madame Simone and Stefan at L'Impasse, which is open for special customers. But I do not go to church. Midnight Mass would overwhelm me with longing for home and my family. And well, why give the Fairy Woman a chance to remind me of my shame? In January Madame Simone tells me it's foolish to pay for another month in a hotel. You must get a "residence." She's says all this in French, but the words are starting to make sense if she talks slowly and looks right at me.

Madame Simone finds me a huge room looking out on the place des Vosges next to the building where Victor Hugo lived. "The maids' dormitory," she says. The landlord has shoehorned a tiny sink, toilet, and bidet, which she explains, into the space under the eaves. The kitchen's in a corner.

"Not suitable for a family, really," Madame Simone tells him, and then points out that no artist wants to live so far away from the Left Bank or Montmartre. She tells him that he's lucky I'm interested. A single woman, a careful housekeeper—quiet. After an hour of negotiating with Madame Simone, the poor landlord begs me to take the flat at a very reasonable rent. Seventy francs a month, fourteen dollars. Very *pas cher*, I suppose. But, I hesitate. I'll be alone here. What if Tim McShane. . . .

The afternoon sun comes through the casement windows, makes squares of light on the walls. My atelier. Tim McShane is far away.

I look at Stefan, Madame, and the landlord, all so pleased to offer me such a place. I take a breath and say yes, or rather, *"Oui, oui, monsieur. Merci. Merci."*

Madame Simone, Georgette, and I spend that Sunday cleaning the place. Madame helps me buy a bed, a sofa, a table—all bargains from the flea market at the edge of the city. I group the furniture around the small fireplace. Georgette tells me I'll need lots of coal for a room so big and drafty, and coal costs money. Well, the tourists will be returning to Paris soon. Madame Simone will offer me to her customers as a guide, she says. With those fees and my undercover work in couturier, I can pay my bills and start saving. Madame insists I open a bank account. I chose a small bank on, of course, the rue de Rivoli. The manager assures me, when I ask in a carefully couched way, that no one could trace me through my account. Shocked to think the bank would divulge private information. At that moment the sheer monumentalness of Paris makes Tim McShane seem very small.

A new life.

I miss Rose and Mame McCabe and my family, Mike and Ed especially. Though I'm glad enough to be away from Henrietta's accusing finger pointing out my flaws. And yet, renting an apartment and banking money makes my separation from home seem somehow permanent. Not simply here for work staying at a hotel. My own place. Starting over.

But every time I pass a church, I feel strange. Guilty, I guess. And in Paris you can't look down a row of buildings without noticing a spire or two. Even in my neighborhood, Le Marais, churches rub shoulders with the synagogues: St. Paul's, St. Antoine's, Notre-Dame-des-Blancs-Manteaux— Our Lady of the White Habits, named for the nuns whose convent church it was—and St. Martin and St. Nicholas, also formerly parts of an abbey, then Saint-Denis-du-Saint-Sacrement, to distinguish it from all the other churches in Paris dedicated to St. Denis. All those saints I've known all my life. Reproaching me.

Let me see a Gothic façade, pass a carved wooden door, or hear the Angelus bell and a queasy net of regret drops over me. I'd been bad, no other word for it. Fornicating to beat the band, all the while pretending to be a virtuous woman, sidling up to Communion every Sunday. Hypocrite. "Be good, Nonie," Mam's dying words. And I wasn't. Even Paris can't completely distract me from my own guilt and remorse. Ah, well. I'll stay out of the churches. Stick with Joan of Arc. She'll understand.

6

SPRING 1912

So. Happy to see crews of workmen planting flowers in the Tuileries and the chestnut trees unfurling their leaves. Not many meals at L'Impasse that first winter. Careful with my money. Still avoiding churches and the saints. Tough when every other rue or boulevard's named for one. But busy enough now.

Madame Simone's American clients return, drawn by Paris in the spring. They pay my fee of five francs to Madame Simone. I get four. But often the ladies add a generous tip, usually in dollars, which the bank changes for me. I'm buying crepes on the street and eating at L'Impasse. Not hard to show the ladies the Paris they want to see: the Louvre, the Place de la Concorde, the Arc de Triomphe, and, of course, the Eiffel Tower—the sites people at home will ask about.

Then tea at the Ritz, or a glass of champagne at Foquets—all part of the tour.

And I continue to copy Madame's inspirations. Nervous though the first time I sit in the back row of Charles Worth's fashion show. Then I notice men openly sketching the gowns. Gentlemen of the press, I see. Legitimate. So I pull out my notebook. "Le Tribune Chicago," I say to the usher who stands behind me. No one notices me. Another twelve francs in the bank.

So I'm happy this May morning. Not really thinking of going home. Chicago seems very far away.

A proper Midwestern wife, Cornelia Wilson of South Bend, Indiana, arrives all delighted with herself and the new hat she'd purchased around the corner on rue Cambon from a woman called Gabrielle Chanel.

Madame Simone only grunts.

The hat has none of the fruit and flowers usually piled onto the chapeaus of fashionable Paris, but I like its spare and simple shape and the one white feather.

"And," Cornelia Wilson says, "Miss Chanel says she's going to sell dresses. I saw a sample, such odd colors, gray and black, made of a soft material."

"Jersey," Madame Simone says to me. "I know all about Madame Chanel's experiments. Tell this woman her husband would not approve. Chanel does not dress respectable women."

"What is she saying?" Cornelia asks.

"She thinks Chanel may be too, well, advanced for you."

"No corsets," Cornelia says. "That's probably what Madame Simone means. But why," she says, lifting up her arms, "do we have to bind ourselves? We went to see Isadora Duncan's recital last night. There she was, practically in the altogether. But why should a woman be ashamed of her body?"

My goodness, I thought. What was going on in South Bend? Was Cornelia a suffragist?

Madame says to me in French, "Chanel's clients sell their bodies. Coco does too. Her clothes match her morals."

Madame always understands more English than she admits to. Madame Simone believes in the more-is-better school of dress, and in designs that require controlling undergarments. Often goes on about the scandalous fashions popular after the French Revolution. Women dressing themselves like Roman statues, baring their bosoms. No decorum. No respect.

"When a woman loses her reputation what does she have?" Madame Simone says in her frequent lectures to Georgette and the young seamstresses. "Don't succumb to the sweet words, *ma petite filles*," she tells them.

"Give away your virtue and you lose all chance for a decent life. No home. No children."

"I'm not thinking of *giving* my virtue away," Ursula, the most spirited of the seamstresses, said to me after one of Madame's sermons. "I expect to get a good price."

The French call the seamstresses "milliners" and other women artisans "grisettes"—girls from poor families who made their own way, a hard old life, low wages and no security. Lots of chatter when one of the grisettes, Louise, met a rich man and moved into his apartment on the rue de la Paix. Madame Simone fired her immediately.

"Madame is very moral now," Ursula told me. "She is established, but at the beginning . . ."

It seems Madame Simone once had a patron. A rich man who invested in her shop and in her.

"She thought they would marry," Ursula said. "But when the time came, he wanted to wed a virgin." And then she explained "the rules" to me. "You see, Nora, in Paris the demimonde is its own world, a separate place. Gabrielle Chanel is a grand courtesan, but is not received in society. She's called an *irrégulier*, the mistress of a man who supports her but will never marry her. Such women can fly high but as Madame knows they can crash. At least Madame kept her business. My sister," she shook her head, "fell in love, she called it, with a married man. Ten years of meeting him at odd times, in cheap hotels. Betrayed our family, and when she finally tried to leave, he beat her. She denied it, but I saw the bruises."

"Terrible," I said. "Poor girl." Acting shocked. I know I'm a hypocrite, but I will not—cannot—remember Tim McShane.

And now Madame is unmasking Coco Chanel to Cornelia Wilson.

"What is she saying?" Cornelia finally asks me.

"Well, Madame says Chanel's—uhm, personal life is . . ."

"A kept wo-man. She is," Madame says in clear enough English. "Her clients prostitutes!!"

"Goodness gracious," Cornelia says as we start our tour. "In South Bend a woman like Chanel could never open a shop. No respectable women would buy from her. Too bad. I wouldn't mind letting go of all this whalebone. Still a woman who loses her good name might as well be dead. A dear schoolmate of mine got involved with a married man. He told her his wife had a dread disease, he couldn't leave her, but that she'd die soon enough.

Never happened, of course. The friend had to leave town. South Bend's still talking about her. I'm not judging her, but I do wonder how someone so smart—she got all A's in school—could be so dumb."

I say nothing.

Cornelia's not a Catholic but she's lived under the shadow of Notre Dame University's Golden Dome and insists on seeing the inside of what she calls "the other Notre Dame." She asks about the coincidence of the names.

"Why two Notre Dames?"

"Well, only one Mary the mother of Jesus, but she has hundreds of titles. Tens of thousands, maybe hundreds of thousands of churches and schools dedicated to her," I start.

"Oh," she says, not too interested.

But I continue. "Our Lady, Notre Dame, the Virgin Mary, the Blessed Mother of Jesus . . ." I say as we walk into the cathedral.

So. I've managed not enter a church for six months. Now I'm back in spite of myself. The great space seems oddly familiar. I mean, I'm not comparing St. Bridget's of Bridgeport to the grandeur of this medieval masterpiece and yet, and yet—the votive candles lighting the half darkness, the lingering scent of incense, the feeling of sanctuary.

Altars and statues stuck in every alcove and archway. And there she is, the Lady herself, just to the right of the main altar, not portrayed as a sorrowful mother or remote virgin, but as a young woman with a baby on her hip, head tilted, looking at Him. A crown on her head all right, but more medieval princess than queen of the universe. Mother of God nonetheless.

In front of the statue stands a bouquet of red gladiolus and tall white chrysanthemums, as slender and graceful as she is. Not a particularly compassionate face, I'd say. No easy sentiment. This Our Lady wouldn't tell me, "Ah, dear, you meant no harm. All is forgiven." Couldn't get around her.

I tell the story of the desecration of this cathedral during the Revolution to Cornelia. How a prostitute was installed on the high altar. The cathedral symbolized kings and queens and repression. Smash it. Stefan's interpretation.

No comment from Cornelia. "Which bells did the Hunchback of Notre-Dame ring?" she asks.

"In the tower. You can see it from outside," I say. I start to tell her that the author, Victor Hugo, lived right near me on place des Vosges. Cornelia's not listening. Hadn't read the book. But saw the French movie. Talking about the gypsy girl Esmeralda as she walks toward the door of the catheral. But I can't move. Gabrielle Chanel, the *irréguliers*, prostitutes, and wild gypsy women rise up around me. "You're one of us," they seem to say. But I was a pure young girl once. My body belonged only to me, separate and apart. I had been good. I giggled when Sister Ruth Eileen told us our bodies were the temples of the Holy Spirit, somehow imagining a dove taking up residence inside my chest. But now, standing in this place, looking up at the statue of Mary, I understand what Sister meant. I let Tim McShane have the run of me. Sacrificed my own will to please him. "Take your pleasure like a man," he said. And I traded my very spirit for those sensations. Then so misjudged Tim McShane, I almost let him kill me. And now, Our Lady, so cool and certain, confronts me, judging me by her very remoteness.

"Let's go," Cornelia says.

"I'm staying," I say. "Go on."

"On my own?"

"There's a taxi stand around the corner."

She huffs, but she's already paid my fee. I'll miss the tip that would come over tea at the Ritz, but I can't leave.

Movement on the altar now. Getting ready for Mass. I sit on one of the rush chairs lined up in front of the main altar. No pews in this church, only these flimsy seats, each with a kneeler attached for the person behind.

"*Introibo ad altare Dei,*" the priest says.

The familiar Latin words. The ritual I've known since childhood. The short, thin priest moves briskly along. He gets to the washing of hands in no time. The young altar boy holds up a gold bowl for the priest to dunk his fingers into. I know the English of the prayer. "Cleanse me of my iniquities, wash me of all my sins." If only water and a scrap of linen could purify me, I think. I fully intend to receive Communion as I had in Chicago. I'd given myself permission, reasoning that the hedge of rules around the sacrament were only so much bureaucratic nonsense.

Only now, this time, I can't seem to stand. My feet won't move me forward. Admit it, Honora Bridget Kelly. You gave Tim McShane complete power over you, cooperated in your own degradation.

The Fairy Woman, whom I'd managed to ignore for six months, starts laughing and screeching at me. "I have won! You'll never escape me. Never be a decent woman. No different from the prostitute who lay sprawled out on this high altar. You can't hide from the truth, behind another language, another country, these monuments, this history. No protection against me. You betrayed your faith, your family, and yourself. Shame on you. Shame. Shame. Shame."

Now I have to get out. I stumble over the feet of the woman next to me. She draws back and lets me out. But the lines of communicants moving slowly toward the altar stop me. I step in front of a man.

"*Malade*," I say. "*Malade*," and launch myself into the space between those coming up to receive and those returning to their places.

I weave my way through the slow procession, murmuring, "*Pardon, pardon*," and coughing. I have learned how much the French fear sickness and dread contamination, so even the most pious, with guarded eyes and folded hands, let me through.

Finally I am out into the square in front of the cathedral. Raining now. A gray drizzle veils Paris. Shame. Shame. Shame.

I mean to cross the bridge toward the Right Bank and head for home, but I turn to the left and in few minutes find myself on the boulevard Saint-Michel. Suddenly this isn't just a street name, but more judgment. "Michael the Archangel, defend us in battle. Be our protection from the wickedness and snares of the Devil who roams the world seeking the ruin of souls." Not a prayer. A condemnation.

The Devil. I thought I'd outrun the Devil. But he was in league with the Fairy Woman all along. I gave in. I traded my soul for afternoons in bed with Tim McShane. St. Michael is not about to defend me in battle. I'd run into the snares of the devil willingly. I'm doomed. All my praying and bargaining with our Lady, the saints, even Jesus himself, delusions. I'll never be forgiven.

A glass of wine, nice red wine, to warm you. In a café out of the rain where you can dry off and . . . No! That's her again, the Fairy Woman, the Devil's consort. I keep walking.

Black umbrellas spring up all around me. I can see no faces. Dusk now, and the drizzle turns into a lashing rain. At the top of rue Saint-Jacques the Panthéon rises above me. A place to wait out the storm.

I've taken some of my ladies who wanted an expanded tour here, and read up on the place so I could explain that the structure was first built as a church to honor St. Genevieve, patron of Paris. But after the Revolution the building became a resting place for secular heroes. The street names—Clovis, Clotilde—I say, speak of an earlier Paris and of the rulers St. Genevieve had welcomed into the city after her prayers defeated the Huns. She'd been buried here with the king and queen only to have the revolutionaries sack her tomb and burn her bones in a bonfire. Had they danced around it, I often wondered, celebrating? Heartily sick of virtue and virginity, and a Church that was so rich when they were poor? Such anger. And what had France gotten? More big-shot rulers, an emperor even—a bloody history portrayed on the walls of the Panthéon.

I let the devil take me over just as he'd infected the mob in the streets during the reign of terror. Destroy. Destroy. Only I brought the temple of my body down myself.

Inside I find a place behind a pillar and lean against the stone walls. No crowds of tourists, thank God. Only a group of young students staring up at the dome while an older man speaks to them.

"The burial of St. Genevieve," he says, and the words catch at me. English but not British English, or American either. He speaks with the lilt I know so well—the way Granny Honora spoke and Mam. The sound of the older generation of Bridgeport. Accents I had mimicked and mocked. He must be Irish. One of the students asks a question. Irish, too.

During my six months in Paris, I've met no tourists from Ireland. Americans, yes, and lots of English, and Germans. Russians too, running around the place. But nobody from Ireland.

One of the boys, in his twenties, I'd say, notices me listening and nods toward me. Red-haired. Looks like Ed when he was young. In fact, I could match many of the students' faces to the faces of members of my family or to those of our Bridgeport neighbors. Would I ever see any of them again? No news from home of course. Nobody has my address. One letter from Dolly telling me to stay away.

The speaker, their professor, I guess, is a tall man with a close-cropped beard and a head of tight black curls. The great dome is an engineering marvel, he's saying, the culmination of all the French had learned since the days when the Crusaders had discovered the secrets of the Arab builders.

"Their mosques," he says, "were much bigger than any church built in the West. Open spaces, no forest of pillars. Domes that seemed to float above the interiors, letting in the light. The cathedrals are evidence of those lessons at work. But here in this structure, the architect, Jacques-Germain Souf-flot, surpassed his masters. This dome has three cupolas, one fitted into the next, and see the fresco of St. Genevieve. King Louis XV promised her this church if she cured his illness, and of course she did."

"Sounds like my granny," says the boy who nodded to me. "Always bar-gaining with St. Bridget for something or another."

"Very human that," the professor says. "And who knows, maybe negoti-ating brings its own rewards."

"What do you mean?" a girl asks.

"Well, King Louis thinks St. Genevieve would love a new church so surely she'll hear his prayers. He begins to believe in his own recovery. Sleeps better, eats better, and there you go. He gets better. Didn't Our Lord himself tell the blind man that his faith had saved him? Don't under-estimate what confidence can do. Something we Irish must remember. We are a noble people. Didn't our monks save the old classics of Greece and Rome? Working away in stone huts tucked tight into hills all over Ireland, copying the manuscripts and sharing them with a Europe that was only stumbling out of the Dark Ages?"

"Hard to be confident with England's boot on your neck for eight hun-dred years," the red-haired boy replies.

I see some of the other students nod. I'm right back in our parlor hear-ing Great-Uncle Patrick going on about the Fenian Brotherhood and sing-ing, "'A nation once again, a nation once again, and Ireland long a province be a nation once again.'"

Without meaning to, I say the words aloud, "A nation once again."

And the boy hears me. "Listen to that, Professor Keeley. The American woman has the right idea."

The class laughs.

"Good afternoon, madame," the professor says.

Now, if I could design a man the complete opposite of Tim McShane, there he stands. While Tim was all beef and bluster, this man is slim and wiry with a kind of stillness about him. Very blue eyes. Clear. No drinker. When I bring my ladies to the Panthéon I tell them how Foucault set up his famous pendulum here, and the professor reminds me of that straight, thin line. He even seems to sway a bit in my direction.

"Join us," the boy says.

I can't, I want to say. I'm miserable and probably on my way to hell and not interested in Irish monks or any man at all. The professor seems taken aback by the young fellow's boldness and begins apologizing for the intrusion. Embarrassed. One of those shy men, happier with his books.

"Thank you," I say, "but I don't want to interfere."

"You are most welcome," the professor says. "Not that I have any great knowledge to impart. But it is raining, and we would welcome an American perspective since yours was one of the world's more peaceful revolutions."

"That's nice of you," I say. "And I am glad George Washington and the others didn't cut off anyone's head."

"Did your relatives fight the British?" the boy asks.

"My relatives were probably living next door to yours, in a manner of speaking," I say. "I'm Irish."

"And where are your people from?" the professor asks.

"Galway," I say.

"That's my county," he says. "What town land?"

"Town land?

"Your home place," he says.

"All I know is my granny said she was born on the shores of Galway Bay."

"As was mine," he says. "Out in Connemara. What was your granny called?"

"The same as me, Honora Kelly. Though I'm Nora."

"Lots of Kellys in Galway. And her people?"

"Keeley. She was born Honora Keeley."

He laughs. "My own mother's name. Now you must join us. It's not every day I stumble on a cousin from Amerikay."

"Amerikay," I repeat. "She always said Amerikay."

"Closer to the Irish language," he says. "Come along."

Well, what could I say? That I'm a fallen woman on my way to hell and don't have time for a tour through French history? But those faces looking at me are so like those of my own young cousins. Like my own, really, and that familiar swirl of teasing and laughing pulls me in. I'm sure none of these young girls worry about being *irréguliers* or courtesans or grisettes. More like Rose and Mame and me at St. Xavier's when we were sure of ourselves and ready for anything. Can I go back? Be who I was before Tim McShane? Line up with these students, hear Professor Keeley's discourse? Back in school and able to start again? Even if the hounds of hell are slobbering after me, they're outside in the rain and I am in the Panthéon.

And so I stay, moving with them from painting to painting as Professor Keeley talks about Danton and Robespierre and points out how even the most laudable movements fall into violence and disorder, "until the cure is worse than the disease."

The red-haired boy speaks up, continuing an argument it seems. "But we're not the ones threatening violence," he said. "It's the unionists."

Professor Keeley speaks to me. "Not sure if you follow Irish politics, but this young man . . ."

"James McCarthy," the boy says.

". . . makes a very valid point. Ireland's very close to achieving Home Rule with our own parliament in control of all our domestic affairs but those who wish to keep Ireland united to England, many in the north of our country, say they will take up arms in opposition."

"Which is why we must defend ourselves," James McCarthy says. "Armed Irish volunteers will do more to achieve Home Rule than a hundred speeches in Parliament."

"With the help of the Irish Republican Brotherhood." Another voice speaks up.

"And the Irish Citizen Army," a third says.

Professor Keeley replies, "I'm sure our American cousin is not interested in our military multiplicities."

"Oh, but I am," I say. "My father, his brothers, and his uncle were all part of the Fenian Brotherhood. They even invaded Canada."

"Now that's a tale I'd like to hear," Professor Keeley says. "We're having tea at the Irish College around the corner. Would you care to join us?"

So. I accept. I follow the students down a small diagonal street behind the Panthéon to a honey-colored building.

As I walk with Professor Keeley he tells me the story of the place.

"The college is on rue des Irlandais, but when Lawrence Kelly, a kinsman of yours perhaps, managed to purchase this property in 1769 it was rue du Cheval Vert—green, even then."

"Old," I say.

"The college itself started nearly two hundred years before that in 1578. During the two hundred years of the penal laws—" He stops. Looks at me to see if I know what he's talking about.

"That bastard Cromwell," I say. Always safe to blame Cromwell.

Professor Keeley nods. "No Catholic could own land, vote, serve in the army or the professions. Couldn't be educated. Catholicism itself was out-lawed. Mass forbidden, priests executed," he says.

"Right," I say. A memory pops up in my head. "A price on their heads. Bring in the head of a priest, and you'd be paid twenty pounds."

A bit of history from Uncle Patrick and the vivid picture had stayed with me.

"Correct," the professor says. "So the Irish Church established colleges like this all over Europe. It was Father John Lee who brought six students to study at the University of Paris. The king gave us a building that the Italians had abandoned just around the corner. College of the Lombards, it was called. There are Irish chieftains buried in a chapel there."

I nod. The students are quite a bit ahead of us.

"Sorry. I do go on," Professor Keeley says. He opens two big wooden doors and leads me across the threshold into the courtyard. As happens often in Paris, the rain stops just as the sun begins to set. A last ribbon of light filters through a line of pink clouds and falls onto the stone-flagged floor and the garden beyond.

"Lovely," I say.

"It is," he says, and points to the colonnade. "See, above each arch is the name of a diocese in Ireland. Our seminarians come from all over the country."

"Seminarians?" I say. Understanding. "So this is a college for priests?"

"Of course," he says.

"And you are a priest?" I ask, dreading the answer. Something very lik-able about this fellow but, Jesus Christ, I am not about to start fancying a priest.

"I'm not," he says. "The rector kindly offers me rooms here. I'm sorting out the library for them."

"But the others?" I say, pointing over at the students who followed us into the courtyard.

"Students at the Sorbonne. Some have government scholarships, others have parents with the money to send them away to school. A long and strong relationship between Ireland and France. Have you much Irish his-tory, Madame Kelly?"

"Not as much as I should."

An Irish college in Paris for hundreds of years? I'd never imagined such a thing. This wasn't Auld Ireland, the white-haired sorrowful mother. Who were these people? I smile and say, "It's 'mademoiselle' and I'd like to learn more."

"Ah," he says. "Well, let me just say that in very dire times in Ireland, places like this provided refuge. King James himself and his followers lodged with Irish priests at the College of the Lombards. Many officers of the Irish Brigade . . ." He stopped. "Sorry. This means nothing to you."

"Faugh a Ballagh. Clear the Way and Remember Fontenoy."

"Amazing," he says. "You know about the Irish who fought with the French and defeated the British at the Battle of Fontenoy!"

"I know about the Irish Brigade James Mulligan started in Chicago to fight for the Union. I couldn't forget their motto. My father and my uncles all served in the Brigade or in the Irish Legion."

"Remarkable," he says.

"Yes, well, there were Irish on the other side too. In fact, my cousin married one of the Rebel Sons of Erin, the Tenth Tennessee regiment." I stop. "Which probably means nothing to you."

"Please continue," he says. "But first, our tea."

We go into a parlor—small fireplace, lots of wooden chairs. A young woman student brings out a tray of mugs—crockery, not the delicate china even the Hôtel Jeanne d'Arc offers. No pastries here, but thick slices of brown bread covered with butter and jam. A good feed, like Granny Honora and Mam would've given us after school.

And all that English! I didn't realize how I miss back-and-forth conversation in my own language. Wonderful not to have to strain for meaning, just let myself go along, pulling in the words, no translation needed. I could be sitting with Mam and her friends around the stove in Piper's grocery store, listening to them batting pieces of history at each other, running through the litany of who's got work and who's expecting a baby and who's getting ready to die. How I'd dismissed all their chatter and how good this version sounds to me now. I meet Antoinette from Dublin and Sheila from Limerick. Professor Keeley acts as a kind of ringmaster, bringing in the quiet ones.

"May," he says to a girl, "how is the translation going?" Then to me, "Miss Kelly, meet May Quinlivan from County Tyrone, Carrickmore—the Big Rock. She's putting Victor Hugo's *Les Misérables* into Irish."

"Not the whole thing," May says. "Only passages."

"Well," I say, "I live next door to Victor Hugo's old house. It's a museum now. You could visit it. Get some inspiration from standing in his study. Come by and we'll have tea in my room afterwards." The words jump out of my mouth. I've never asked anyone to my place.

May hesitates, but says, "Thank you. I'd like that."

And then I say, "You'd be very welcome too, Professor."

"Thank you," he says.

And the slobbering hounds pursuing me slope away—for now.

❧

So. They come. May, James McCarthy, and Professor Keeley, who says I should call him Peter. He knows more about Victor Hugo than the woman running the museum.

"A fussy fellow," Professor Keeley says. "Designed and carved all the furniture himself. Imagine!"

Amazed that anyone could care that much about his surroundings.

Not sure if he can come to my room for tea. Shy. James McCarthy whispers to me, "Ask the professor again." I do—twice more. He finally says he'll join us.

"See," James says. "We Irish need multiple invitations. Politeness dictates."

"One room?" Professor Keeley says as he follows the students into my place.

And I very much wish my bed isn't stuck in the alcove. Not quite respectable. But James McCarthy walks right over to the fire, where I've set out a selection of sweets on a small table. I'm ready. Spent two weeks' worth of tips on the pastries and new cups and saucers. A bit worried about the tea.

"I could only find Lipton's," I say as I pour from my new teapot.

"We'll have to get you a supply of Barry's Gold Blend," Peter says.

"My granny's favorite," I say.

He smiles. Relaxing. Good.

"Milk? Sugar?" I ask him.

I spoon a generous mound into his cup but then splash too much milk in and tea overflows, filling the saucer and spilling onto the table.

"Sorry," I say, setting down the milk jug, looking for a cloth.

Now Tim McShane would've yelled "you clumsy" whatever at me and even my brother Mike might've harrumphed but Peter says "No bother," and mops up the mess with his handkerchief.

We laugh.

"Er, I'll have milk and sugar too," James McCarthy says.

"Oh, yes," I say, and pass him the jug. I see James look at May and then back at Peter and me.

"And which is your favorite of Hugo's works?" Peter asks me.

"*The Hunchback*," I say. "Though *Les Misérables* is very good too." Get the titles in fast. Learned that in Sister Veronica's English class. I did read the novels. Well, almost. Turned to the end to see what happened. A lot of dying, just like in the stories of Auld Ireland. But Hugo's famous and lives on my block so I say, "Great writer."

"Interesting how he began as a devout Catholic royalist and ended up an anticlerical republican," Peter says.

"My type of fellow," James McCarthy says.

"You might want to join us for a tour of the Hôtel de Cluny in two weeks," Peter says. "Only a few students with summer coming. But there's a Tudor connection and of course Hugo's play *Marie Tudor* gave a more sympathetic picture of her than the 'Bloody Mary' of Protestant propaganda," Peter says.

"Of course," I say, though I've no idea what he's talking about. But he's invited me. Yippee.

"All the Tudors were pretty bloody to us Irish," James McCarthy is saying.

"The point of my lecture," Peter says.

"The Hôtel de Cluny," I repeat. At least I know enough not to ask if it's a five-star, though why the French want to confuse tourists by calling mansions and public buildings hotels, I don't know.

So. Paris looking well for herself on this June morning as I follow the professor and his students down boulevard Saint-Michel to Hôtel de Cluny. A palace built on Roman ruins, Peter tells us, and now a museum of medieval art. We start in the basement, where Peter shows us the ruins of the Roman baths. He reminds the group that Ireland's name, Hibernia, came from Julius Caesar's plan to use Ireland as winter quarters for soldiers. "Hibernation."

"The Romans never came," Peter says, "but the name stuck."

Peter tells us that Henry VIII's sister Mary Tudor lived here after her husband King Louis XII died. Only a three-month marriage. She was eighteen. He was in his fifties. Henry planned to get hold of the throne of France. But no heir and Mary Tudor defied Henry and married an English soldier in the chapel Peter shows us. He tells us both Boleyn sisters were at the French court. "Having affairs," May whispers to me. It was the Tudors who did Ireland in, I learn. The other invaders—Vikings, Normans—became Irish, but when Henry set up his own Church all Catholics were rebels. Destroyed them and Elizabeth was even worse.

We leave Hôtel de Cluny and start down the boulevard Saint-Michel—the "Boul Mich," as the students call it—heading back toward the college. The students drift off, and I walk with Peter.

But I don't notice until we circle the Panthéon that we are alone.

On the corner of rue des Irlandais, the proprietor of a small restaurant is just opening the doors for lunch.

"Would you have time for a meal?" I ask Peter.

He doesn't answer.

The sign says L'ESTRAPADE, the same name as the street, then CUISINE TRADITIONNEL BASCO BEARNAISE written underneath.

"'Basco'?" I ask.

"Basque," Peter explains. "A section between France and Spain in the Pyrenees with its own very distinct language. Looking for independence, like Ireland."

I steer him inside before he can object.

"Bonjour, Professeur," the owner says as he sits us down at one of just five or six tables.

"Nice fellow," Peter says, "and the prix fixe is very reasonable."

I nod but am already planning how to slip money to the owner to pay for lunch. I begin to tell Peter how grateful I am for the tour and how I realize I've barely scratched the surface of Paris.

"Impossible to do much more than that," he says. "Sampling all of the various cuisines alone would take a lifetime." He shrugs.

I laugh. "Very French, that shrug," I say.

"A variation on our Irish greeting," he says, then cocks his head. "A wag of the head is how we greet each other when passing on the roads."

"And do you miss Ireland?"

"I suppose it's my own homeplace I miss most. My people are fisher-men. Our bit of land hugs the coast of Connemara. We've the Atlantic in our front garden and the next parish is America."

The owner delivers the Basque stew.

"*Xacco*," Peter says and points to the name on the menu. "Basque is a language like Irish. Best to learn the sounds, not puzzle over the orthography."

"The what?"

"The written letters."

Jesus, this fellow's smart, but he wears his knowledge lightly. Asking me questions now about the Irish in Chicago.

"Some of our Keeleys went out there," he says, "but we lost contact."

"So maybe we're related. As I said, my granny was a Keeley."

"From Connemara?"

"I don't know. 'Born on the shores of Galway Bay' is all she said."

He nods.

"Should I claim you as a cousin?" I say.

"Why not?" He laughs.

"A distant one, of course," I say. "I wouldn't want to be too closely re-lated to such a handsome fellow."

Now what was getting into me, teasing the man this way, and him probably married with a family? But he takes no notice, thank God. Here I have a man treating me like a lady, interested in my mind and opinions, and I have to flirt with him. Let's end this now.

"And so your wife stays in Connemara?"

"Oh, I haven't a wife. It's my oldest brother got the farm and the boat and the fishing rights so . . ."

"So?"

"Can't marry without substance," he says. "I thought of following so many others from my village to America but . . ."

He stops.

"I'm writing a book about the historical connections between the French and the Irish," he says. "France is Ireland's oldest ally and yet now the French are so afraid of Germany they've joined Britain in the so-called *entente cordiale* and are opposing Irish self-government. Why it's important to remind them of past connections. The Parisii who founded Paris were

Celts. The River Seine and the Shannon are named for the same goddess—the Old One, the Wisewoman."

He speaks of figures from history as if they were neighbors down the road, going on about Charles Martel and Pepin, and then gets to a name I know—Charlemagne.

"And was he somehow Irish?"

"Not directly," Peter says, "but Irish monks were the most educated fellows going and Charlemagne invited them to his court as teachers. The monks told the French our tales of the Knights of the Red Branch and Fianna. An Englishman heard them and changed the characters into King Arthur and his knights."

"The round table," I finish. "Yes. One of our writers named Mark Twain imagined a Connecticut Yankee transported through time to Arthur's court."

Now, Peter has never heard of Mark Twain but seems really interested. I say, "I must find you a copy of *Huckleberry Finn*."

"Finn," he says. "Interesting."

And we both say, "Irish?" and laugh.

Then I stop. Rose McCabe was the one fond of Mark Twain. I'd been careful not to write to her, sure somehow Tim would confront Rose trying to find out where I was, and somehow show up here. Mad, I know, but fear of Tim still hovers close by, ready to overtake me at any moment. Like now.

Peter notices. "Something wrong?"

"Nothing. No."

How awful if an honorable shy scholar of a fellow knew the kind of woman he is eating *xacco* with and discussing literature.

But he is away into the distant past again. France had Vikings too, who took over a part of the country and named it Normandy—William the Conqueror's people. Thank God I could nod at that name and say, "The Battle of Hastings, 1066. He took over England."

"And his kinsman Strongbow landed in Ireland, our Norman conquest," Peter says.

As he goes on, I think again of how my ladies might very well like to have a distinguished academic take them through French history. Especially the gossipy parts—like Mary Tudor being queen of France and the no–better–than–they–should–be Boleyn girls and their adventures in Paris. And wasn't Mary Queen of Scots in Paris too? I imagine Peter with me and an American lady drinking a glass of wine at Fouquet's. I propose the idea to him, flat out.

"Of course, I'd pay you from what they give me," I say.

He shakes his head as if the very thought offends him. The owner brings two lovely apple tarts to us but Peter stands up, puts a pile of francs on the table, and walks out of the restaurant.

The owner sets the *tartes tatin* in front of me, returns with a bowl of *crème fraîche*, and lands a dollop on top of the caramelized apples as if to say, There—this will make you feel better. I take a spoonful. It's good.

The owner sits down with me, eats the other tart, and consoles me in French for what he sees as a lovers' quarrel. I don't understand it all and finally he resorts to English.

"Professor—good man!" he says.

And I insulted him somehow. In the wrong again.

I show up for next Wednesday's tour determined to apologize to Peter. But Peter waves my words away and leads us down the rue Saint-Jacques. He takes us to Saint-Germain-des-Prés.

"The oldest church in Paris," he says. "Founded as a Benedictine abbey in 558."

He hurries over the first thousand years to get to the tomb of Lord James Douglas, who he said commanded Louis XIII's Scots regiment and that of another Douglas who served Henri IV. He goes on about the close connection between Scotland and France. The "Auld Alliance" he calls it.

"Mary Queen of Scots had a lover called Douglas," May whispers to me.

No tête-à-tête for Peter and me this day. He seems determined to keep the students around him. And then announces the tours are over for the summer. School's out. The students will be going home.

"Professor Keeley seems out of sorts," May says to me as we follow the others along boulevard Saint-Germain.

"I think he's mad at me," I say.

"How?"

"I asked him if he'd help me guide my ladies, give them a bit of history."

"And did you offer him money?"

"Of course. They pay me."

"You offended his dignity," she says.

"I did what I thought was right," I say.

"Father Rector gives the professor room and board and a stipend for his work in the library. Your offer would be like charity. An insult."

So be it, I think. I don't need a touchy fellow in my life. So long, Peter Keeley.

7

JULY 1912

The summer days bring a good run of clients and nice tips though I do wish I could tell my ladies more about the history of the city now that I realize there's stories around every corner.

I do take Jane Poole from Maine to the Hôtel de Cluny but forget what number Louis married Henry VIII's sister. Instead I find myself telling her about this professor and his tours.

"Makes the people who walked these streets down through the centuries very real," I say to her as we sit in Fouquet's watching the crowds promenade down the Champs-Élysées.

"Hire him," she says.

"I tried," I say, and explain how I insulted Peter by offering him money and . . .

"Stop," she says. "You have to be direct. Talk to him straight from the shoulder. He'll accept the job. You'll see."

Straight from the shoulder? Not so easy if you've grown up among people easily offended as I have. Feuds in Bridgeport could start at the drop of a word. Be American, I tell myself. Pretend you don't see any complications. Go to Mass at the Irish College. Find him. I do.

The chapel at the Irish College is a homey space. More of the spirit of my own St. Bridget's here than in the gloomy grandeur of Notre-Dame. Only one stained-glass window: a lamb in a green meadow. Ireland? The wooden walls glow, painted with interwoven circles and spirals.

A few students who are staying on through the summer come in. May sits beside me. A line of priests in black cassocks file in and take places facing each other across the center aisle.

"Like a monks' choir," May whispers to me.

Peter doesn't enter with the procession of priests and I wonder is he coming at all, but then just as the bell signaling the start of Mass rings, he slips into a pew behind the choir, diagonally across from us.

The whole congregation—maybe fifty laypeople and the twenty or so priests—stands as the celebrant enters. He wears the green vestments of the Sundays after Pentecost, ordinary time.

"Introibo ad altare Dei." A lilt in the phrase. The priest's hair is white. When he turns to us, his eyes are that particular shade of blue I know from my own father and brothers. In fact, half the older generation of Bridgeport look like this fellow.

"That's Father Kevin," May whispers.

He has just started the Kyrie when two latecomers stroll in, not ducking into the seats as I'd have expected but taking their places in a front row as if telling us, Now the ceremony can really begin. The man is tall and fair-haired, dressed in a beautifully cut gray suit, very grand. Not Irish, I think, though not French either. But the woman with him could only be Parisian. Small and dark-haired, she wears an elegantly simple black hat with one white feather that makes me want to rip off the bunch of grapes I've sewn on my own bonnet. Her skirt and jacket, the same color of gray as her companion's suit, drape her slim frame. No corset.

I poke May. "Who?"

"Arthur Capel," she whispers. "English, but Catholic. And that's, well, that's Gabrielle Chanel."

"Oh," I say, right out loud. Of course.

"Kyrie eleison," the priest starts, and the Mass continues.

"Why are they here?" I whisper to May.

"Friends of Father Kevin's probably. He knows the oddest people."

Father Kevin steps up into the pulpit. "The Gospel according to Matthew," he says, and makes the sign of the cross on his lips. We all do the same. But then the words rush out in a stream of sounds I don't recognize. I look at May.

"Irish. Gaelic," May says to me.

The language of my ancestors, of my own mother and grandmother. Foreign to me.

And now the priest finishes the Gospel and preaches a sermon in Irish that gets quite a few laughs and nods from the congregation. I recognize a word or two. I see Arthur Capel bend down to Gabrielle Chanel. She closes her eyes.

Communion time and I can't be a hypocrite here I think. I can't receive Communion. I either have to go to confession or stop being a Catholic altogether.

Only Gabrielle Chanel and I wait in the pews while the rest go up to the rail. Peter must notice that I've stayed at my place. Please let him think I broke my fast with water, not that I'm in mortal sin, or worse that I'm secretly a Protestant or have fallen away entirely.

As it is, Peter says little to me as we gather in the parlor for cups of very strong tea and baguettes, covered with delicious butter.

"From Kerry. Danny Sullivan's farm," May explains. She points to a stout fellow talking away to Arthur Capel as Gabrielle Chanel stands looking around the room. "Thick as two planks but he's got acres and acres," May says. "Raises horses. That's what they're talking about. Probably horse-mad, both of them."

James McCarthy comes over to us. "Welcome," he says, "to the two hours a week about which I am able to write home to my mother."

May shakes her head. "He's from rebel Cork and likes to make out he's a wild man, but he's really a decent fellow."

James laughs as Father Kevin joins us, and May introduces me.

"Nora," he says. "A lovely name. Originally Honora. Always nice to have visitors. Hospitality is the great virtue of the Irish."

"I see we're even entertaining the enemy," James says, pointing to Capel.

"Ah well, don't be too hard on the fellow. His mother's French, his grandmother's Irish."

"I wonder does he write to tell her he's been to Mass?" James says.

"And his companion," May is saying, "is famous, Father."

"Really? For what?" James asks.

"She's a fashion designer," I say.

"Not a subject I'm *au courant* with," Father Kevin says. "She seems a bit lost, listening to all that talk of withers and fetters. Shall we?"

And he leads us over to the three of them.

"Good morning, Father," Capel says.

"Good morning, Arthur," Father Kevin says.

And then in French he welcomes Gabrielle, who only nods. Ill-at-ease, certainly.

I speak up, telling her I'm a friend of Madame Simone and interested in fashion.

"Fashion," she says to me in rapid French. "Fashion fades. Only style remains. It takes courage to distinguish between the two." She looks at my jacket and shrugs.

Oops. I'm not stylish enough for Mademoiselle Chanel and not holy enough for the Irish College.

A silence.

And then Father Kevin says, "All is transitory but God has put the eternal in our hearts. Though he does clothe our spirits in flesh."

"Some more than others," Dan Sullivan the farmer says, patting his paunch.

We all laugh except for Mademoiselle Chanel. What a pill, I think. I'm glad Madame Simone doesn't let me bring my ladies to her. She'd just insult them.

Then May speaks. "Nora gives wonderful tours of Paris for American women interested in the arts," she looks at me, "and shopping."

This gets Capel's attention. "Must bring them around to Gabrielle's shop. We need all the customers we can get. Right, Coco?"

She doesn't reply. He nudges her.

"*Oui*," she says.

"English, Coco," he says.

She tries, making French words into English. "You *plaît*," she gets out.

"Please," he corrects.

"*Visitez*," she says.

"Visit," he says. "She's a slow learner," he adds.

Coco looks down at the ground.

A bully, I think. Hearty and all but a bit of Tim McShane under that polished exterior.

At that moment Peter walks up, his tweed jacket rumpled, his white shirt frayed at the collar yet somehow more elegant in his very spareness than Arthur Capel. He doesn't acknowledge me.

"Any luck finding the manuscript, Keeley?" Capel says to Peter before he can even greet us.

"You're pursuing a fantasy, Capel," Peter says. And then to the rest of us, "He's convinced that a seventeenth-century ancestor of his spent time at the college and left behind a priceless manuscript."

"My uncle, Monsignor Thomas Capel, told me."

"Oh, you have an uncle who's a priest," I say. "In England?"

"In America," he says.

"Really? Not Chicago by any chance?"

"I'm not in touch with him," Capel says, and turns back to Peter. "We had a nobleman ancestor in King James's army. He was with the king at Trinity College and rescued an Irish manuscript. I believe it's here. The family fell on rather hard times and my own father's family came from, well, humble circumstances though he was blessed with a talent for business. But now I'd like to claim my heritage."

"Of course there was Arthur Capel, Earl of Essex," Peter says. "But he killed St. Oliver Plunkett so not a good man to be related to."

Gabrielle speaks to Capel in French, and I catch *"mal du têtê."*

"My companion's not feeling well," Capel says. "We'll be on our way. Keep looking, Keeley. I want to purchase that manuscript. Price is no object."

"Not enough for the fellow to be rich. He wants to be noble too," Peter says.

"Well he does have a priest uncle," I say.

"Unfortunate story," Father Kevin says. "Father Thomas Capel was a very popular priest in London. Lots of converts from the upper classes. Made a monsignor. A favorite of titled ladies. He was rather too devoted to them. Accusations of, well, bad behavior came from their husbands. Thomas called it a campaign against him and denied the accusations, anti-Catholic slurs, he said. Who knows? But Cardinal Manning sent him off to America. Thomas plays down his Irish roots. Though I believe he was born in Ireland as was Arthur's father, I suspect, but the son's an Englishman now and has enough money to be an aristocrat. Harmless, I suppose. Thomas had the same need for grandeur. Fancied himself a Renaissance bishop. There are times when I think we should return to a married clergy. A wife would have kept Thomas in line," Father Kevin finishes.

"Where is he in America?" I ask.

"California, I believe."

"Never been," I say. "Chicago is my home."

"Chicago?" Father Kevin says. "Some of my father's people went there from Cork."

Oh no. Lots of Cork people in Kilgubbin who could send him all the gossip about Nora Kelly by return mail.

"We lost touch with them a generation ago," he says.

I feel my shoulders relax. Anyway, surely other scandals have replaced mine by now.

Father Kevin asks have I seen the gardens and starts walking.

Peter has still not spoken to me. So I follow the priest, still clutching my mug of tea.

We sit down on a bench under the trees in the back garden.

"So" is all he says to me. Nothing more.

I try to find a last sip of tea in the bottom of my cup.

"You didn't seem pleased when I mentioned my Chicago connections."

"Oh no, I think it's great. It's just—well I'm not in touch with Chicago these days."

I keep looking down into my cup.

"So," he says again after a pause. "And you came to Mass today because . . . ?"

"Well, I had been going on Professor Keeley's walking tours and . . ."

"Really? When he came up to us he didn't seem to know you. I was going to introduce you but . . ."

"Look, Father, here's what happened. I tried to hire Professor Keeley and May said I'd insulted him. But I want to straighten things out with him."

"Well, that's direct enough. I envy the way you Americans go straight to the point. We Irish tend to meander."

"I'm Irish, Father."

"Well, shall we say you grew up differently. And what is the position you offered Peter?"

"I only want him to talk about Paris to the ladies I guide around the city."

"Why?"

"Because he knows so much, and I'm only showing them the tourist bits."

"And they want more."

"I don't know, but they should."

"Because you want more too. More than sitting in the back of the chapel or nibbling away at the edges of the Irish community here."

"Yes," I say. "I do."

"Lonely, are you, Honora?" Using Granny's name for me.

"Well, of course I miss home and my family, but . . ."

"I mean, are you lonely for yourself?"

"If you're asking, do I miss the woman I was in Chicago, no. She, well . . . Not something I want to talk about, Father. Especially out here."

"Matter for confession?" he says, and smiles at me.

Smiles! And I smile back. Couldn't help it.

"I suppose," I say. "Didn't see any confessionals in the chapel."

"We don't have those boxes," he says. "Can't imagine Jesus asking people to mumble into the darkness in order to have their sins forgiven. Such a lover of nature, our Lord. 'Consider the lilies of the field . . . The sower and his seed . . . My eye is on the sparrow . . .' It was the parables helped Patrick to win the Irish. Those early monks loved the landscape of Ireland, so bleak and yet so beautiful. Now, Honora, I suppose it was a man."

I nod.

"Who was not your husband?"

"I never married."

"Was he someone else's husband?"

"Not formally . . . In a relationship a bit like Capel and Mademoiselle Chanel. Only the woman had the money."

"And you cared for the fellow?"

"I thought so. I was wrong. But I couldn't stop. I didn't dare tell anyone and when I tried to break it off . . ." I stop.

"Violent?" he asks.

I nod. "I ran."

"Good for you," he says.

And it all comes out. How afraid I still feel. How I blame myself for getting involved. How I regret all the years of lying. Why I hadn't been to Mass. Father Kevin utters not a syllable, only keeps those blue eyes on me. And no one disturbs us. All by ourselves at the tip of the garden as I finish telling him how I am convinced that Tim would somehow find me if I wrote home, and now I say what I didn't even know I was thinking.

"I'm afraid he'll kill me, and in a way, I'll deserve to die. There's nothing I can do to escape. Sometimes I think I should just, well, save him the trouble. Get it over with."

After a long silence Father Kevin speaks. "Generations of your ancestors stood against the oppressors and refused to die, Honora, so that you could live."

I nod. "My grandmother would say, 'We wouldn't die, and that annoyed them.'"

"Well put! Can't let guilt tear from you what they struggled to win."

"Oh, I suppose I'd never really . . . though . . ."

"'Half in love with easeful death'? I've always thought that was an aristocratic notion. Only someone who thinks death wouldn't dare impinge on his comfort could write those words. The English might romanticize death, but we Irish know him too well. An ugly fellow who creeps up on children, turns their limbs black, makes them swell up, who uses poverty and war for help in destruction. We stand against death, Honora. Do you know that in ancient times, Irish kings were judged not by how many enemies they killed but by how well their people lived? A rollicking party was more admired than a well-fought battle. But I'm wandering. . . . You mustn't lacerate yourself anymore. I apologize to you, Honora, on behalf of the priests who made Catholicism seem a religion that condemns us to guilt and shame."

"You apologize to me?" I don't know what to say.

I hear voices. The students are leaving. Very quiet in the courtyard. I start to stand.

"Must you leave?" Father Kevin says.

"I don't want to keep you from your work," I say.

He smiles. "Nothing more important than one of God's children."

Me, important? And he was sorry I felt shame?

Never met a priest like Father Kevin.

I sit down. Now he seems to be almost talking to himself.

"How sexual morality became the be-all and end-all of so much of

Catholicism I don't know. It's been made more important than kindness or honesty or mercy. I remember my first pastor told me to get a good stout blackthorn stick and patrol the hedges. Find a young couple courting there and hit the fellow a good whack and that'll terrorize the rest of them. Terrorize! Instilling fear was the mark of a good pastor. Sad that, when 'pastor' really means 'shepherd.' Imagine the Good Shepherd using his staff to beat his people.

"Our people love celebration—Christmas, saints' days when the old traditions come alive again. But that pastor of mine saw our parishioners as pagans—partially subdued but ready to revolt at any moment. He forbade the ceremonies held each year on the Feast of St. Colmcille. Nonsense, he called them. The custom was to circle in procession the ancient carved stones that lined the path that led to the holy well. Walk around three times in the direction of the sun," Father Kevin says, which does sound a bit pagan but I'm deep into the story now and don't want him to stop.

"Then each person would pick up three small pebbles and the procession would move up the mountain toward the well. There was a huge cairn of stones at the top. Centuries' worth, a memorial to those hundreds of years when Catholicism was forbidden and our people kept the faith alive with such practices. The procession would begin at midnight and slowly move upward following the flickering lights of two lanterns. Very beautiful, though eerie."

"Sounds wonderful," I say.

"If the truth be told, long before Jesus was born we were worshipping at holy wells and climbing sacred mountains. When Christianity came to ancient Ireland, nobody martyred those first converts. St. Patrick never condemned the old beliefs. He simply brought them into the new religion. The early monks, who were probably druids themselves, knew they couldn't suppress the old tales, so they gave them a kind of Christian veneer.

"I joined the people in the Colmcille procession. We circled the cairn three times casting one of our pebbles on the great pile on every round. Each one represented some guilt or sin. Then we cupped our hands and dipped into St. Colmcille's spring and drank the clear water. And then headed for the crossroads where we planned to dance until dawn. Very sound psychology. Really.

"Of course I knew the pastor objected. Hated every minute of it but I never thought . . .

"Well that night he was waiting by the side of the road for the pilgrims to pass. They came down the narrow path, laughing and talking, and didn't the pastor jump out at them, swinging his stick and shouting that they were all going to hell. I stepped forward and grabbed for his arm. He hit me a clout, which in a way turned out to be a good thing. Bishops might be expert at turning a blind eye, but they can't allow pastors to break a curate's arm. Bad for vocations. Well, that old pastor started roaring and shouting about how God would punish them all. The blight would come again. God would show them. Now, this was one of his favorite themes—the Great Starvation as retribution. The Almighty killing one million to wean people away from their pagan ways."

"Horrible," I say.

"I agree, and yet such preaching wasn't uncommon. Pure power politics. Remember, before the Great Starvation there were not that many priests in Ireland. We were only beginning to recover from penal days when merely being a Catholic was a crime.

"Just as the worst of the penal laws were lifted came the Great Starvation. After that less people, more priests. The Church wanted control. Always so complicated. Plenty of priests died helping our people through the worst of the Great Starvation, but still money was sent to Rome every year which could have fed . . . Now we're all Catholics in our very bones but I wonder, did Jesus really want us to become such a bureaucracy? The Great Starvation tore the heart out of the Irish people. The very land had turned against us. For all the prayers and entreaties, a million had died. Two million more gone forever to America, England, Australia and millions more following that path year after year, decade after decade. It was a lucky Irish woman ever saw her own grandchildren. Maybe in some ways it was easier to think we somehow brought it on ourselves. A kind of explanation. And a way out. Because if being bad caused the horror, then maybe being good would keep disaster away. Lots of sins committed in the service of being good.

"And now here is this mad priest, their pastor, ready to beat the body to save the soul. Only God knows what went on inside his head. A farmer's son himself and maybe not a man to be set apart and made to believe he alone had the answer to everything. Well, the other men moved in and subdued him and we brought him to the parish house. His sister was his housekeeper. A decent enough woman, though afraid of him too. 'Drink,' she said. 'He was driven to it. Couldn't help himself. It was the drink.'

"Now, I know for a fact he was a teetotaler and proud of it. But a man done in by drink gets sympathy in Ireland. Who of us hasn't had one too many? The bishop sent the pastor away for a rest and found someone for Glencolmcille who understood the old ways. A decent fellow."

"Why didn't you become pastor?"

"Me? No. I was marked too. The bishops said I'd encouraged the people in their disobedience. But my own family are not short of a few shillings and very generous to the Church. So I was sent to Paris and the Irish College. Providence looking out for me after all."

A bell rang. Two o'clock.

"Now, that was a longer story than I meant to tell. Sorry for boring you."

"You didn't . . . I mean, thank you. I think I'm . . ."

But he interrupts me. "Here's Peter on his way toward us. Quick, Honora, are you sorry for anything you've done to separate yourself from Divine Love?"

I nod.

"Then, *ego te absolvo* in the name of the Father, Son, and Holy Ghost. You're forgiven."

"Just like that?"

"Just like that. Grace flows; it doesn't drip-and-drop."

And I do feel an ease, as if I'd been keeping my body clenched and could now let go. I start laughing and can't stop. Father Kevin joins me. When Peter comes up, he looks at us as if we'd lost our minds.

"Sit down, lad," Father Kevin says. "This friend of yours from Chicago has a fair way of listening to a yarn."

"Is that right?" Peter says. "I didn't know."

"And a great benefactor of the college," Father Kevin says. "She wondered would you help her out with a bit of guiding and I said of course you would. Not putting words in your mouth, I hope."

"Peter," I say, "I would so appreciate your help."

"Ah, the Lord loves a cheerful giver," Father Kevin says. "Now, let me tell you the one about the Cavan man borrowed a bull to service his cows. Weeks went by. Finally the owner went looking for his animal only to find the bull pulling a plow through the field and the Cavan man urging him on with a whip. 'I'll teach you there's more to life than romance!'" Father Kevin is laughing before he's finished the joke.

Peter looks at me, shrugs, and laughs too. So do I. Couldn't resist the joy Father Kevin took in his own humor.

My spirit lightens. *Ego te absolvo*. Words offered by this cheerful little priest. As he said, "We're Catholic to our bones." I am restored. A good woman again. Not an *irrégulier*.

Father Kevin and Peter are talking about Arthur Capel and Gabrielle Chanel.

"Capel told me she was brought up in an orphanage. Kind enough women, the nuns, but I'm sure the life in an institution's not easy for a child," Father Kevin says.

"Not easy for anyone," I say, and then realize that the Irish College itself is an institution. All right for Father Kevin and the other priests, I think. But doesn't Peter want a real home?

"And I doubt if Capel will ever marry Mademoiselle," Father Kevin says. "When the time comes, he'll choose the daughter of an English nobleman, put his Irish heritage aside once and for all."

"Who would ever choose not to be Irish?" I say. "In Chicago we brag about our Irish roots. I'm one hundred percent."

Suddenly I want to assert my claim to all of this heritage.

"England's a long way from Chicago," Father Kevin says.

Peter nods. "And this fantasy about a noble ancestor fighting with King James in Ireland. He got hold of the story of Fitzgerald, who was with James and did save *The Great Book of Lecan* when the library at Trinity College was attacked. He brought it here. Capel has turned the incident into a family history."

"Sounds like Monsignor Thomas," Father Kevin says.

"I suppose we all make up identities for ourselves, one way or another," Peter says.

Do I imagine it, or is he looking at me? Well, I know now who I am going to be—a virtuous Catholic woman earning my own way. Chaste and a bit of an intellectual.

"Still, the manuscripts in our library have proved the pedigree of many of our Gaelic nobles," Father Kevin says. "Allowed them to receive French titles. Look at Patrice de Mac-Mahon, once president of France. Because his grandfather was a chieftain of the O'Brien clan Louis XV named him a marquis. His son fought in your American Revolution, Nora."

"I'd like to see those manuscripts," I say to Father Kevin.

"I'm sure Peter would be glad to show them to you. As a Kelly, *The Great Book of Lecan* would have interested you."

"Why?" I ask Peter.

"It contains the genealogy of the Kellys going back to your earliest recorded ancestor, Máine Mor," he says. "The manuscript was returned to Dublin but we have John O'Donovan's 1843 translation of the Kelly material published under the title *The Tribes and Customs of Hy-Many*. The O'Kellys. Hy-Many is the English version of uí Máine—the descendants of Máine."

"We are in an ancient manuscript?!"

"You are indeed," he says.

Well, I think of Gabrielle Chanel—Coco—and Arthur Capel manufacturing themselves. I don't have to do that. I am a Kelly. How could I have forgotten? I've stumbled into a place with people who could help me understand that.

Oh, Granny Honora, I'm so sorry I didn't listen harder to your stories, didn't pay attention when you tried to teach me the Irish language. Busy. I've always been so busy. But here in this sunlit space I have another chance. The woman who gave her body away in that room on North State Street could never have turned the pages of manuscripts that celebrated her ancestors. But I will.

What a relief to step away from the tangle of attraction and humiliation I'd experienced with Tim McShane. What was sex anyway but a quick surge of sensation? Couldn't a beautiful sunrise, a bit of learning, a delicious beef bourguignonne give me the same satisfaction?

And here I have the perfect companion on my explorations—Peter Keeley, a man of high purpose, not tempted by the things of the flesh. I'll live the way he does. A simple existence. I'll be nunlike in my devotion to my studies. An example to young women like May, Antoinette, and Sheila. I'll show them that women do not have to marry to be happy. Or become an *irrégulier* like Mademoiselle Chanel, dependent on a man for her success. I will create a clean, chaste life for myself—the place des Vosges, rue de Rivoli, and the Irish College the three edges of my triangle.

I smile at Father Kevin. He grins back.

I am Honora Bridget Kelly, a businesswoman and a patron of the arts and a self-deluding fool, I know. But on that summer afternoon I think I am calling the piper's tune.

Kellys *abú*!

8

DECEMBER 12, 1912

"Of course I bought all *my* Christmas cards in London," Mrs. Adams, my client, says to me. "So clever of the English to design a way to contact friends without having to write to them."

She's rejecting the cards on offer at a stall tended by a women in the native costume of Alsace. Part of the Christmas market spread across four blocks of the Champs-Élysées. Mrs. Adams spent the last month in London, which is very like her native Boston, she's told me, and vastly superior to Paris. Not impressed with the French is Mrs. Adams. But how can she resist this magic space decorated with pine boughs, red berries, mistletoe? Candles prick the darkness of the December afternoon. An accordion player squeezes out an unusually cheerful "The First Noel." The crowds alone should enchant—ladies and gentlemen of fashion, families with their red-cheeked, big-eyed children all bundled up staying close to their mothers, the fathers walking slightly ahead. Some of the men wear heavy overcoats and tall hats, the uniform of the bourgeoisie (as I have learned to call them), others have on short jackets and soft caps—workingmen. More distinctions are made here than exist in Chicago. But Christmas pulls everyone together.

"Wonderful isn't it," I say to her now.

"I find all this cheap and showy," Mrs. Adams says. "It's Thursday. These people should be at work. And that smell. Terrible."

I sniff. "But that's mulled wine," I say.

"Exactly! I oppose all forms of alcohol!" she says. "Drink destroys the lower classes. Why the drunken Irish are ruining Boston!"

Oh, Lord. Here we go again. I'll ignore her.

Mrs. Adams actually shuddered when Madame Simone introduced me to her in the studio a few hours before.

"Nora *Kelly*? But you're Irish!" she said, and immediately asked Madame Simone to find her another guide. Comical to watch Mrs. Adams try to explain in her clumsy French why an Irish woman could not possibly show her the cultural sights of Paris.

Madame Simone had no idea what Mrs. Adams was going on about and looked to me to explain. Was I going to tell her that Mrs. Adams thought the Irish were ignorant savages bound to superstition and whiskey? Not me. I only smiled as Mrs. Adams sputtered into silence. She had one afternoon to shop and see Paris while her husband finished some business meeting at the Bourse. Madame Simone told her, "Nora, très good."

"And you speak French, real French?" she asked me. Incredulous.

"I do," I'd said, and reeled off a spiel about Mrs. Adams that started Georgette giggling.

Then I quoted twice my usual fee to Mrs. Adams. But what choice had she? She'd spent the afternoon slagging the French *and* the Irish. Annoying.

"It's twelve-twelve-twelve," I say to distract her. December 12, 1912— one year, one month, and one day since Mike and Mame's wedding started me running from Tim McShane and Chicago. Though I wonder now wasn't I on my way out much earlier?

But Mrs. Adams waves a card at me. "This card is in German." Indignant.

"That's Alsatian—a dialect," I say. "It's like German but the people are French. Lots of Christmas customs in France come from Alsace."

"But didn't France let Germany take it away from them in one of those wars not too long ago?" she asks.

I clear my throat. "The Franco-Prussian War, 1870 to 1871," I say, trying to imitate Peter Keeley. He's been joining my tours every Friday throughout the fall, ladling out French history to my ladies though not staying for the glass of wine at Fouquet's as I pictured. Wouldn't take money from me directly. Had to give the envelope with ten francs in it to Father Kevin on Sundays.

"Very nice-looking, your professor," Mrs. Barrington from New Jersey said to me one Friday in October, "and what's your connection to him?"

"His student," I said. Peter's always very formal with the ladies and me though he'll often slip in a comment that makes us laugh.

"Louis began wearing a wig to cover his baldness," he'd said. "His courtiers followed suit. For two hundred years men cut off their own healthy hair to cover their head with heavy, unhygienic imitations. What men will suffer for fashion."

No joking around with Mrs. Adams. "Madame Simone was born in Alsace, in Strasbourg," I tell her.

She pays no attention, rattling on to the Alsatian women in English. Madame Simone told me her family left when the Germans took over, and she still fears Germany.

"The Boche have the biggest army in Europe and one of these days they'll use it," she's said to me many times. Always showing me articles in the French newspapers about reclaiming Alsace-Lorraine. Kick out the Boche.

That's Europe. Can't buy a Christmas card without tripping over history. The Alsatian woman backs away from Mrs. Adams, then looks at me. I take out a franc and buy a small wooden nativity set. The Alsatian woman smiles.

"*Danke,*" she says.

"Those Germans," Mrs. Adams fumes as we move through the fair. "They want to push England out of world markets. They'd love to get their hands on the English colonies in Africa," repeating what her husband says, I think.

All probably true, but I feel I should speak up for Germans if only because of Milwaukee and beer and my cousin Ed's mother, Aunt Nelly and her sister Aunt Kate and their German father. As a little girl I'd listen to him play "Silent Night" on his violin when we gathered at Aunt Nelly's and Uncle Steve's for Christmas Day. The whole clan of us, dozens of Kellys, dancing in their parlor under a huge tree—a pine from the North Woods of Wisconsin covered with the ropes of popcorn and cranberries that I'd helped string. Candles on the branches and Henrietta fussing about the dangers of fire. Can't think about home now. Too sad.

So I tell Mrs. Adams that Queen Victoria's husband Prince Albert, a

German, brought Christmas trees to England and surely she knew some Germans in Boston who weren't dying to wreak havoc.

But she doesn't hear me. Looking at two bundled up little Parisiennes. "Do these children have some kind of disease? Their cheeks are so red."

Geeze Louise.

The next stall displays hand-painted Joyeux Noël greetings. I stop.

Still afraid to write home. Tim McShane could be haunting Rose and Mame. Best if they can honestly say they hadn't heard from me. Still I buy five cards.

Mrs. Adams watches me as, over tea at the Ritz, I scribble a message on each. Glad I remember the addresses. Mame and Mike, Rose and John, Ed and his family, Mary and the family in Bridgeport. On the last I write "Agnella Kelly, care of The Motherhouse, Sisters of Charity BVM Dubuque, Iowa," though Ag's probably got a religious name by now.

I ask Mrs. Adams to post my cards from Boston. Safer. No Paris postmark. No return address.

"All right," she says, flipping through the envelopes. "Oh," she says.

She stops. "My goodness," she says, "this one's going to a convent! Well, I suppose I can take them to the main post office."

"Where no one knows you?"

"Yes."

Mrs. Adams gets very chummy now, telling me about her maid, Bridey, not typical Irish oh, my, no. Very clean. A hard worker! Bought a house at Whiskey Point in Brookline for her family, but still lives in. "Has a load of children, I think, but understands her duty to me comes first. I let her visit them on Sundays," Mrs. Adams says.

Very glad to finally get away from Mrs. Adams at five o'clock. Full dark now. Too late to go back to Madame Simone's studio and give her a share of the twenty francs I got from Mrs. Adams. Then I remember Father Kevin's cold. Sneezing and coughing something terrible at Mass last Sunday. I'll bring him a little treat, and if I do happen to run into Peter Keeley, well . . .

"Thank you, Nora," Father Kevin says to me as we sit in the formal parlor off the entrance eating the madeleines I brought and drinking Barry's tea, sent over from Ireland. Definitely better than Lipton's. Peter promised me a tin but it was May who gave me the tea. Peter was so much friendlier those first days and now . . . I wonder can I talk to Father Kevin about Peter?

"Good stuff," Father Kevin says. "The Lord may want us to forgo wives, but he couldn't expect a man to give up a decent cup of tea."

He pokes at the small coal fire. "Doesn't really heat the place. These stone walls," he says. "Makes me wonder. Jesus, Abraham, and Muhammad were all desert fellows from sunny climates. Think it's easier to be spiritual if you're warm?" he asks.

I laugh. "I don't know. Chicago's colder than here," I say. "Probably buried under a foot of snow right now."

"Not all that much snow in Ireland," he says. "But the damp! What we need here is a good big load of turf. Nothing like the smell of a turf fire, the taste of the smoke baked into a slice of wheaten bread running with butter."

"You miss Ireland," I say.

"I miss Donegal," he says. "And do you miss Chicago?"

I nod.

"Hard at this time of year. Christmas," I say.

"You must join us for midnight Mass and the collation afterward," he says.

"Thank you. I'd like that."

"Now," he says, "there seem to be some extra pastries here."

"For the others," I say.

"Peter Keeley's working away in the library. Perhaps he'd like one." He pauses. "If that's all right."

"Fine," I say.

Sees right through me, does Father Kevin.

I follow him down a dim hallway. The college does have the electric but only few unshaded bulbs here. We turn the corner. Hear the swish of a soutane, see a long shadow coming torward us.

"Good Evening, Father Rector," Father Kevin says.

A well-set-up man, the rector. A bit younger than Father Kevin, square face, furrows in his gray hair. Looks more like a farmer than a scholar. Never spoken to him. He doesn't come to tea in the parlor after Mass.

"Have you met Nora Kelly, Father?" Father Kevin says. "One of our Sunday congregation."

The rector nods at me, then says to Father Kevin, "Don't we entertain our visitors in the parlor, Father?"

"We're on our way to the library. Too cold to take the outside route," Father Kevin says.

The rector looks at the open box of madeleines in my hands. "Food in the library?" he says.

"A collation for Professor Keeley," Father Kevin says.

"Is this that woman? I spoke to Keeley about her," the rector says, then turns to me. "Professor Keeley must not allow himself to be distracted by outside influences. We have committed a portion of our limited resources to him and . . ."

Get me out of here, I think as the rector goes on. No wonder Peter's so guarded. Warned off me by his boss. Amazing he'd shown up for my tours at all.

"I should be going, Father Kevin," I say. But he takes my arm.

"Ah, now Father Rector. Not your usual gracious self. And Nora one of our benefactors. Proof of what you often say about reaching out to the Irish in America. How did you put it? Get our snouts into the trough. A metaphor from your youth. I suppose."

Well that sends Father Rector on his way, but I hesitate.

"The last thing I want to do is get Peter in trouble," I say.

"Don't mind Father Rector and his auld rules. A man of limited imagination as bureaucrats so often are," Father Kevin says.

I follow him into the library, where leather-bound books crowd together on floor-to-ceiling shelves.

"Our patrimony," Father Kevin says. "Ireland's gift to the world."

Peter's not in the library but Father Kevin points to a bright line under the door between two bookcases.

"He's in the vault," he says.

At first I only see Peter in outline. Just two candles set in hurricane lamps on top of the table in front of him for light.

He turns. "Oh," he says, and shakes his head.

"We're disturbing you," I say. "Sorry . . ."

"It's just—well, I'm about a thousand years from here. I think I've made an incredible discovery. Look."

We move closer to him. He slides a piece of parchment toward us.

"I found this sewn into the cover of an edition of *The Annals of the Four Masters*," he says. "I noticed a bulge. I think it's a page from *The Book of Uí-Máine*, the original manuscript."

"That's your book, Nora," Father Kevin says.

"The history of the O'Kelly family commissioned by a Kelly bishop, one of your clan," Peter tells me.

"When, Peter?" Father Kevin asks.

"About 1400," Peter says. "A time when great families hired scribes— monks—to record their genealogy," Peter says. "And to copy material from earlier manuscripts so the clan would have its own Book of Ireland."

"And we were a great family?" I ask.

"One of the greatest," Father Kevin says.

"Gee whiz," I say.

"The scribes added bits from the earlier Books of Ireland, which were themselves compilations of manuscripts as old as the eighth century," Peter says. "And, of course, the original material comes from oral sources going back thousands of years."

I guess I look confused because Peter says, "A lot to take it in, I know, but you'll be really interested in this page because it's from 'An Banshenchas.'"

"'In Praise of Famous Women,'" Father Kevin says. "A list of the heroines of the Kelly clan."

"Virgins and martyrs, I suppose," I say.

"Not at all," Father Kevin says. "These are Irish women, not saints chosen by the Roman Church."

"They're the wives of chieftains mostly," Peter says. "Some married more than one chief."

"And then were widowed and joined the convent?" I ask.

"They didn't," Father Kevin says. "Great respect for independent women in the early Irish Church, which some present-day clerics should remember."

Peter's not listening. He pushes the page toward me.

The letters seem drawn rather than written and some are decorated with the heads of animals. Lots of circles and spirals, interweaving lines.

"I saw something like this in the Irish Village at the Chicago World's Fair," I say. "My granny Honora took us to see a page protected by glass. Supposed to be very valuable. I'm afraid I didn't look too closely. In a hurry to get on the Ferris wheel."

Peter moves the candle closer so I can see. "Just this page is worth a fortune," he says.

"So beautiful," I say.

I hold my hands over the names of these Kelly women. My fingers prickle. I gently tap one of the names.

"And these are my many great-grandmothers?" I say.

"In a manner of speaking," Peter says.

"I wish Mrs. Adams could see this," I say, and try to tell them about my afternoon with her.

I don't have to say much.

"Ah, well. The English must see us as ignorant savages. It justifies them stealing our land and murdering us by the tens of thousands," Father Kevin says.

"By the millions if you include the Great Starvation," Peter says.

"Which we must, of course," Father Kevin says.

"And yet here we are," I say.

"Pushed to the edge of extinction though," Peter says. "And the battle not over yet."

He picks up the page with both hands.

"When the chieftain led his clan against the enemy the sacred book of the tribe was held aloft as a kind of battle flag," he says. "Sometimes a crozier might become the standard."

"Yes, yes," I say. "I know! My uncle Patrick had a golden staff. Wait. It belonged to a Kelly saint. Grellan, I think. Patrick carried it into battle after the Civil War when the Fenians invaded Canada."

Peter jumps up. "Grellan's Crozier? But that was lost," he says.

"Well, it's in Old St. Pat's now. On Des Plaines and . . ." I stop and start to laugh. ". . . Adams. That church is on Adams in Chicago. I should have told her, Mrs. Adams, about St. Pat's stained-glass windows, and walls decorated with"—and I point to the page—"designs like this."

I reach over and grab Peter's hand, pull him down to his chair.

"You have to teach me. Please," I say. I touch the page. "This is my heritage, too."

Peter pulls away.

Damn. I've made a fool of myself! Peter's appalled. He's nervous enough around me with all Father Rector said and now I've leapt at him, but I do so want to learn, to reclaim what I've lost.

But Father Kevin says, "Your heritage, surely. And it's a long, quiet run of days until Christmas. Peter will tutor you, won't you, Professor?"

Here? In the library? Father Rector will never agree, I think.

But miracle of miracles, Peter nods. "We can start Monday," he says.

Father Kevin says, "Good. And now to the parlor for tea—or better yet some hot whiskeys. *Uisce beatha*—the water of life—to toast the Kellys." And we do.

I offer to pay Peter but he waves me silent before I can finish. Thank God because I've just enough money to pay my rent, which is seventy-five francs, and buy food and coal for the month, another thirty-five.

Peter brings some books to the parlor: translations of the *Táin*, Ireland's *Iliad* and *Odyssey*, he tells me. Only the hero is a woman—Queen Maeve, who leads armies and takes lovers. Didn't learn about her at St. Xavier's. Peter tells me the epic concerns a cattle raid; Maeve needs a bull so her possessions match her husband's. The bull's in Ulster. Peter starts striding around the place as he describes the powerful Maeve in her war chariot leading her army. Even chants a few of the lines. I can't help myself, I applaud. Peter stops. "Okay, see you tomorrow," I say, take the books and leave.

That night I settle in with my books and Beaujolais and a decent enough fire in my cozy room overlooking the place des Vosges. No reason why a scholar can't have a bit of comfort is there? Maybe I'll bring a bottle of wine to share with Peter tomorrow. Now to the reading.

I start with Winifred Faraday's translation of the *Táin*. Except the stories are hard to follow. Not as exciting as when Peter was striding around chanting and expostulating. Surprising the fire in the fellow.

Guided by Winifred, I follow Maeve and her army as they cross into Ulster going after a bull. And then, here come the men of Ulster. Except these armies don't go at each other in pitched battle. Each selects a warrior to fight in single combat. Civilized. Though this one fellow, Cuchulainn, becomes possessed by a "battle rage" and demolishes every opponent.

I turn to the last pages to see how the tale ends. In the final combat Cuchulainn fights his foster brother, Ferdia. Winifred provides a note explaining that noble families in Ireland sent their children to be raised by other high-ranking families to create alliances.

They battle to the death—Ferdia's. And then comes the verse after the verse where Cuchulainn laments the death of his foster brother. Sad.

I close the book. I wonder would Tim McShane have been sorry and crying over my body after his rage had passed. This story's from how many thousands of years ago? And now? The king of England, the kaiser of Germany, and the czar of Russia are all cousins. Will they be at each other's throats soon like Cuchulainn and Ferdia?

At our session Peter has the Kelly fragment out again.

Peter is good-looking, no question. I can watch him without him noticing, so intent is he on the manuscript page. I move my hand closer to his.

"Nora, pay attention," he says.

The humpbacked letters in the manuscript stand so companionably together. For a moment I'm back in Sister Mary Matthew's first-grade class trying to write a row of "A"s—capital and small—followed by "B"s and "C"s down through the alphabet. But they are people to me—alive. The tall "A" is the father, the round "B" is the mother, and the little "a"s and "b"s their children, and so I put them all together and then invite the "C" and "D" cousins, the "E" and "F" neighbors over until my paper's a real hodgepodge.

Sister Mary Matthew's annoyed. How can a girl as bright as I am be so disorganized? By third grade I see that the letters have to give up their personalities for the sake of the word, obey the rules, fit in, and the words must serve the story.

But here the letters are free and alive—not uniform at all. I imagine a scribe drawing them, making each unique.

I say as much to Peter and point to the serpent curled around a capital "P."

"Good observation," he says. "Each scribe had an individual style. Some wrote notes in the margins, comments on the weather. There are verses even."

He tells me he visited an abbey in Austria and examined an ancient Latin manuscript that contained a poem in old Irish. Some ninth century monk wrote about his cat Pangur Bán.

"The cat catches mice the way the monk catches words," Peter says. He lifts his hand, grabs an imaginary mouse, then closes his fist. The moves are so quick and unexpected that I actually cry out.

"Didn't mean to startle you," he says.

I pat his arm.

"I'm fine," I say, and I swear he looks down at my hand in a way that makes me want to keep my fingers there. I lift my hand. Muscles in that arm.

"Another monk drew a dog," he says.

"What?" I think of how strong he must be, slender as he is.

"In your Kelly manuscript there's a very realistic sketch of a dog with a long tail."

"Where," I say, bending so close to the piece of vellum my shoulder touches his.

"Not here," Peter says. "*The Book of Uí-Máine, The Book of the O'Kellys* is in the Royal Irish Academy in Dublin. I was allowed to examine it once."

"Once! Jesus. I'd think you'd want to pore over the thing."

"Of course I would. But I'm not a member—and can't be."

"Why not?"

"Costs too much and they don't welcome Catholics."

"What? Who's 'they'?"

"The administration. Headed by Lord Somebody-or-other."

"But that's outrageous! That's a Kelly book."

"It's the same with all the ancient manuscripts. *The Book of Kells* is astounding, one of the world's great masterpieces—I've only ever been able to see one page."

"But Peter, wasn't it Catholic monks wrote the damn things?"

Now I've offended him with my language.

But he only shakes his head and then nods.

"They did indeed."

"Well then?"

"Most of the great books of Ireland were destroyed. Cromwell's soldiers cleaned their boots with the pages. The monks and families like yours risked their lives to save some. Others were stolen, but at least the thieves were intelligent enough to sell them to places like the British Museum or the Royal Irish Academy, but they're still kept from the people."

"I wonder why nobody railed on about this at the Clan na Gael picnics. I never heard my Uncle Patrick talk about stolen manuscripts and he had chapter and verse on the English atrocities," I say.

"If you consider that Cromwell slaughtered all but three hundred thousand of the Irish population and a million starved to death during the Great Starvation, stealing a manuscript doesn't count for much," Peter says.

"You don't believe that," I say.

He takes a breath. "I don't. They tried to erase our very identity, to stamp out who we really are." And he pounds his fist on the table. "But they failed and these very manuscripts might help defeat them," he says.

"Right," I say. "Change our notion of who we Irish are. Why, just meeting Maeve makes me think of myself differently. And . . ."

But Peter cuts me off. "A more direct role for this page. The cause needs money. The new Home Rule Bill is being moved through Parliament right now. And this time we have the votes to pass it. But the Protestant unionists in Belfast are pressuring the British government to stop the bill. An MP called Edward Carson got five hundred thousand unionists to sign a covenant saying they'll resist Home Rule by any means necessary. He's that organized. The Ulster Volunteers say they'll take up arms to stop Home Rule. And they have the money to buy weapons."

What James McCarthy said that first day at the Panthéon.

"Dear God," I say. "The men of Ireland against the men of Ulster."

"And Carson's not even from the North. Born and raised in Dublin. Held the Trinity University seat in Parliament. Worse, his mother's family are from Galway," says Peter. "Carson spent his summers there. Funny about these big-house families. Some get to know the country people and become nationalists. Carson's cousin from down the road, Edward Martyn, works for the Cause. But others . . ."

Now, this is when I start to see the web of connecting families woven through Ireland. In many ways so like Bridgeport, where every conversation starts with whose cousin married whom, what childhood friends have wed.

"Now if the British think that we have a counterforce that's armed too, that'll make them think twice," he explains. "The Ulster Volunteers are buying guns from Germany, where the best weapons are produced," Peter says. "And there are German universities eager to buy Celtic manuscripts." He explains that professors from Germany had been coming to Ireland for years to study the Irish language and translate the manuscripts, more or less shaming the British into valuing this heritage. "So, do I have your permission?" he asks.

"What?"

"Providential, really, that a member of the Kelly clan appears just as I discover this fragment that can become a real weapon. But . . ."

"Wait," I say. "Are you asking me if you can sell it?" I touch the page. He nods. "And Father Rector agrees?"

"Father Kevin doesn't think he needs to know," Peter says.

And here comes Father Kevin through the door and talking as he walks over to us. Waiting to make his entrance, I guess.

"We have this wonderful concept in religious life called 'interpeting permission'—acting first and telling the superior later," he says.

"Useful," I say.

"Pages of Irish manuscripts like your Kelly book are scattered all over the world," Father Kevin says. "We'll never know where most of them are, let alone ever get them back. And if any do turn up, the British will claim them in the name of the United Kingdoms of Britain and Ireland. What do you say, Nora?"

"I say yes. You have my permission on behalf of, well, the Kellys."

Peter stands up. So do I. Father Kevin shakes my hand then and Peter does the same. Do I imagine he holds on for a few extra seconds? We smile. Comrades. Conspirators.

"Now, Nora," Father Kevin says, "you won't mention the Kelly fragment to anyone, will you?"

"No."

"Good," he says. "Don't tell a soul."

"Why? Are there British agents around?" And I laugh. But they don't.

Father Kevin lowers his voice. "Not a joke, Nora," he says. "We are watched. The British know Paris has been a refuge for Irish patriots for centuries. The government would just confiscate the page, and if they found out what we planned, well . . ."

"But surely you are safe enough in Paris."

Father Kevin shakes his head. "Last year a young Irish student was arrested by the French police. He was accused of spying for Germany because he'd traveled back and forth to Berlin studying with a professor of Celtic languages there. Deported and we knew the Special Branch would be waiting for him in Dublin," Father Kevin says.

"Gosh, poor kid. What happened to him?"

"We managed to get him on a ship to America. Of course, he is in exile now and can never return to Ireland."

"But if he becomes an American citizen, he can come and go as he pleases," I say.

"The British don't recognize naturalized American citizens. If you're born in Ireland, you are their subject forever," Peter says.

"But that's not fair," I say.

"Like so many things, Nora," Father Kevin says.

I must admit I do look behind me a time or two as I walk home and even cross the street so as not to pass the Palais de Justice. Though a part of me hears Sister Veronica's reprimand, "You exaggerate to make yourself important, Nora Kelly," after I explained that I couldn't help being late because a horse cart had collided with a delivery wagon on Archer Avenue.

In Chicago maybe we didn't have the grandeur of Paris but at least there we Irish *are* the police.

And then it's Christmas Eve.

DECEMBER 24, 1912

A light snow falling as I walk to midnight Mass at the Irish College. A small congregation. I check the pews for strangers. What better place for an agent. But I recognize all the faces.

A few French families make the college chapel their parish church, and they go off after Mass for their big Christmas dinner. The *réveillon*, you call it. Have to admire the French for serving up a huge meal at one o'clock in the morning. Well, the priests are too Irish for that. I eat brown bread thick with butter and sip hot whiskey with Father Kevin and Peter in the parlor. The other priests go to the refectory.

I start to ask about the Kelly page, but Father Kevin puts his finger to his lips and Peter says, "I'll walk you home, Nora. We can talk on the way."

Peter and I stop in the courtyard to watch snow falling on the frozen garden.

"Won't stick," I say. "Never get a real Chicago pileup here. Paris is too temperate."

"Ireland's the same," Peter says.

We start walking along the empty snow-silent streets of Paris. Only a scattering of flakes left as we cross the Seine. The moon slides out from the clouds, bounces on the water. We pause on the bridge. I take my hands out of my muff and spread them on the stone parapet.

Peter looks down.

I wish he'd cover my hand with his. I wish . . .

But he only says, "Be careful, Nora. Chillbains are easy got and hard to get rid of."

"Like so many things," I say. "Peter, about these British agents, I've been thinking." But he puts his finger on my lips . . . then takes it away.

"Oh, come on," I say. "No one's around!"

"Such a beautiful night. I want to forget everything else," he says.

Well. That's promising.

The moonlight shines on the snowdrifts along the rue de Rivoli.

"'The moon on the breast of the new-fallen snow gave the luster of mid-day to objects below,'" I say.

Peter stops.

"It's a poem, Peter," I say. "About the visit of a wise old man on the night before Christmas."

"Who's the author?"

"A fellow called Moore," I say.

"Irish," he says, and smiles. "I must look it up."

"Do that," I say.

Wait until he comes to the reindeer. What are they called?

Oh, yes. "Watch for Donner and Blitzen," I say.

"They sound like German scholars," he says

"Not exactly," I say. "Though I do believe they did come from quite far north." And I stand there and begin reciting:

"'Twas the night before Christmas'" . . . full out, very serious and I get each word right; naming every reindeer. I finish with a flourish.

"'And I heard him exclaim as he rode out of sight, "Merry Christmas to all. And to all a good night."'"

Well, if ever a man's struck dumb, it's Peter Keeley. And then he laughs. I mean, the bending-over-tears-on-his-face kind of laughing. Then he hugs me. He throws his arms around me as if I am an old friend coming home from a long journey.

Then steps back away from me. "You are such an American, Nora Kelly."

"Me? But I'm one hundred percent Irish."

"You are that, too. Makes me sorry that . . ." He stops.

"I'm going away," he says.

"To sell the Kelly fragment?"

"Eventually. Father Rector has decided to send me to the Irish College at Louvain in Belgium, to help catalog their library."

"Louvain," I say. "Is it because of me?"

I can hardly get the words out.

He looks away.

"Might be for the best," he says. Here it comes. A nicer version of Father Rector's "you're a distraction" speech. Winifred's book had a story about Grania, who'd taken a fellow by the two ears as if he were a calf and told him they were in love. I'd grab Peter's face. Tell him I loved him. Except he'd drop dead on the spot.

"Won't have to worry as much about British agents in Belgium," Peter says. So. Not even thinking about me. The Cause comes first. Uncle Patrick all over again.

"And then there's the other colleges, one in Rome, two in Spain, one in Lisbon. I'm to investigate them all."

"So, a long trip," I say.

At least I can invite him to my room, say a proper good-bye, one he'll remember. There's another bottle of Beaujolais and . . .

The Fairy Woman! Trying to take me over this early on a Christmas morning! Haranguing me as Peter and I cross the place des Vosges to reach the doorway of my building.

I stick out my hand.

"Good luck," I say.

He shakes my hand and says, "I'll be back in the spring."

"Will you write?"

"Safer not to," he says.

"Okay. So long," I say.

"What?"

"So long," I repeat. "It means good-bye."

"Strange," he says. "I thought you said 'Slán,' Irish for good-bye—well, really 'safe.' We say 'Slán abhaile'—safe home."

"Slán abhaile," I repeat. He stands there as I open the door and walk up the stairs.

9

APRIL 1913

April. As I walk up the rue de Rivoli the sun warms my shoulders. Now is the winter past, thank God. Somehow spring always does come. Will Peter be returning soon?

Father Kevin says he doesn't know. I've been going to Mass every Sunday at the Irish College. Back in Mother Church's bosom again. Part of the tribe. Avoiding Father Rector though and hoping for news of Peter. "Professor Keeley has taken on a big job," Father Kevin told me. "The library at Louvain alone has three hundred thousand volumes." And Father Rector will make him check every one.

I miss Peter, no question, but I'll soon be thirty-four, too old to be lovesick over a fellow with no interest in me. I've seen May and the other students at Mass but they're all occupied with their own work. So is Father Kevin. He's writing a book about his fellow Donegal man, St. Colmcille, and the young people are studying and having parties, I suppose, though I am not invited. They wouldn't think of asking me, I guess. Too old. Not that I mind. I'm busy enough myself at Madame Simone's.

During the winter when tourists were few I found my métier—stealing still, but not from the couturiers. It was Miss Hail Britannia did me in.

I'd taken a chance and attended Paul Poiret's February fashion show.

All settled in the press section, pad ready, when here she comes screaming, "*Voleur! Voleur!* Thief! Thief!"

Well, that, as Aunt Máire would say, put the tin hat on it. I ran out of the place as Miss British Lion was telling the newsmen that I was a fraud, a Boche spy probably trying to destroy France's greatest industry . . . couture.

So. I was *desolée* and didn't dare go back to Madame Simone's with nothing. Cold and raining and there was the Louvre—solid, so solid. Warm probably. I really should go in one of these days, I thought—like now.

"*Où est la* Mona Lisa?" I asked. Confusing when the guard directed me to *La Joconde*. "It means 'joke,'" he said in English.

Not sure what I thought of her. Bit of a receding hairline. Wouldn't have been considered a beauty in Bridgeport. Not with that nose. But a lovely smile, no question.

A cluster of art students around her sketching away. I took out my pad. Why not? Except it was her sleeves attracted me. Satin, I thought. I liked the folds. I wonder, I said to myself, as I quickly filled in the scoop-necked dress and added a full skirt. The guard was suddenly standing behind me looking at my pad. He told me he never saw anyone draw the dress and not the face. I explained to him that I was interested in clothes.

The guard took me to see Ingres's portrait of Caroline Rivière and her mother. We could make their gowns in four colors, I thought. When the guard showed me Ingres's sketches I got four more ensembles. And then, God forgive me, I even used the artist's portrait of St. Joan. Her skirted armor became a gown flaring out at the hips. The guard took my five-franc tip with a dignified bow. Elegant in his uniform, a bit of a dandy himself, he told me Ingres's greatest portrait—that of the princesse de Broglie— was not on display anywhere. Kept by the family, who still mourned her death at only thirty-six. "They say that gown is exquisite. Of course the family is one of the greatest in France and the prince served as premier under President Patrice de Mac-Mahon not so many years ago." Mac-Mahon. The Irish are everywhere.

Madame Simone and I also "do" Delacroix and Titian and even Raphael. Madonnas, I know, but we copy the pleating. Madame Simone advertises the gowns as her Old Masters Collection, and the clients love them. We add Monet, Manet, and Renoir. I must say I'm relieved not to be borrowing from the real couturiers. I went to the Hôtel Jeanne D'Arc to tell

Stefan, but he's gone. The new desk clerk said Stefan was in Russia. So. A true Bolshevik, I guess.

I am diligent all that winter. Working, the Bridgeport cure for everything. Still not able to interest Madame in my designs but *c'est la vie*.

One afternoon in the Louvre I heard a woman lecturing a group near a Vermeer painting. Americans. She was easily in her sixties. Is that me in thirty years? I thought. Hope not. "He paints with light," she said. Haven't dared pass myself off as an art expert on my tours. We mostly stroll by the famous paintings.

My guard friend asked if I wanted to meet my countrywoman.

"Sure," I said.

Well, who was it? Only Madame Clemenceau. Wife of the fellow put France in bed with England. "I was Mary Elizabeth Plummer," she told me, "from Wisconsin originally."

"I'm Nora Kelly from Chicago. A neighbor," I said.

"My grandmother was Susan Kelly," she said.

A romantic story, with a sad ending, the guard told me later. Clemenceau had to leave France as a young man. Taught at a girls' school in Connecticut. Fell in love with Mary Elizabeth his student, who was only seventeen. Married her. Brought her to France. Clemenceau had many mistresses, the guard had said. But when his wife was rumored to be having an affair, he divorced her, took the three children, and refused to support her. She earned her living giving tours. "Terrible," I said. Just the kind of fellow who'd cozy up to John Bull, I thought.

Now it's the first of April, "Poissons d'Avril," a kind of French April Fools, celebrated with fish-shaped candy. And I've splurged on two pounds of chocolate fish at Lilac's to give to Madame, Georgette, and all the seamstresses. Madame Simone can't explain the custom to me, but she accepts the gift.

"A business expense," she says. I enter the five francs in the red leather account book she's given me. Madame Simone has me write down every franc I make, every sous I spend. A businesswoman. Me, who always just turned half my pay over to Henrietta and never thought about the cost of food or rent. Left those concerns first to Mam and then to her. Spent the rest on clothes and treats. And now I'm supporting myself.

Not much left in savings, but Madame says I must buy a new ensemble for the spring season. Important to be well dressed. I'll purchase it from her, of course, at a discount. Pay her when I can.

"Thank you," I say. Lucky to have made such a friend. Though I am tempted to buy one of Gabrielle Chanel's spring suits. Black skirt and jacket with a white blouse. Very like my school uniform at St. Xavier's. But wearing Chanel would be a knife in Madame Simone's heart. So, I'll dress in robin's-egg blue and be grateful. Never seen Chanel or Capel at Mass again. Must ask Father Kevin.

Madame Simone, the seamstresses, and I are just about to sample the chocolate fish when a dog—a little yapping thing—comes racing into Madame Simone's studio, runs around in circles, and then jumps up at a dressmaking form.

"Georgette," Madame Simone says, "take him out."

"Now, Simone, you love Basket!" The voice comes from a tall, heavyset woman who enters the studio, sandals flapping on the wooden floor.

"Where are my new ensembles?" she says. "I must have them by this Saturday. A special guest is coming to the salon; a friend of Pablo's from Spain."

She brushes the front of a garment which looks exactly like the habit the Carmelite priests at Mount Carmel High School wear. Except it's browner and more billowy.

"This thing has lost its shape," she says. Then notices me.

"Bonjour," she says, *"je m'appelle Gertrude Stein. Qui êtes vous?"*

"Me? I'm Nora Kelly," I say.

Another woman enters. She's dressed like a gypsy. Long skirt, dangling earrings.

"Hello," she says. "I'm Alice. Alice B. Toklas, if we're being formal."

"Are we?" I ask.

Alice Toklas eases her way between Gertrude Stein and me.

"You're American?" she asks.

"Yes," I say. "I'm from Chicago."

"Pity," she says. "We're from Baltimore. I'm always hoping to meet someone from home."

"We are home," Gertrude Stein says. "America may be our country but Paris is our hometown." Then to me: "You're touring Europe?"

"Well, no. I'm working here in Paris." Why not, say it? "Studying at the Irish College."

But she doesn't take that in. Instead she says, "Working for Simone? An American secretary," she says to Madame Simone. "How clever of you."

"I'm not her secretary," I start.

But Gertrude Stein has moved away from us and is looking at herself in Madame's full-length mirror. She lifts her skirt and lets it fall.

"See how it droops?" she says to Madame Simone.

"Perhaps your laundress wasn't careful," Madame says. "Maybe she used the wrong soap." All this said in a French I can follow.

"Certainly not," Miss Toklas answers in English. "Her other costumes are perfectly fine and I washed them the same way."

"Be that as it may," Gertrude Stein says. "I have to have my ensembles now. Are they ready?"

"They are," Madame says. "I sent you a note inviting you to come in for a fitting."

"A note? We received a note, Alice?" Gertrude Stein is not pleased.

"I told you we did, dear. That's why we're here."

"I thought we were just walking Basket," Gertrude Stein says.

"No, Gertrude. I quite deliberately led us this way."

"You should have told me, Alice."

"I did," she says.

Madame Simone clears her throat. "You are here now and if you'd like to step into to the dressing room, Gertrude, I will bring you your garment."

"I design them myself," Gertrude says to me. "Comfortable and elegant. Madame Simone executes my design."

"I see," I say.

Georgette leads her away.

Alice glides over to one of the small gilded chairs and sits down.

"Chicago," she says. "I don't believe I know anyone in Chicago but I think some of the Hopkinses went to the university there. You have a university, don't you?"

"We have a few," I say. "But I don't suppose you mean Loyola or De Paul."

She shakes her head. "Doesn't sound familiar."

"University of Chicago?" I say.

"That's it," she says.

Gertrude Stein returns, followed by Georgette. Madame Simone helps her onto the wooden platform in front of the mirror.

"See, Simone, I told you corduroy would work," Gertrude Stein says.

"It's light and yet sturdy. Better than that jersey Gabrielle Chanel tried to pass off on me—too clingy. Corduroy stands away from the body."

"Slimming," Alice says.

"I'm not a sylph and wouldn't want to be," Gertrude Stein says. "No one ever criticizes a portly man, but let a woman have a bit of heft . . . Renoir's subjects were nicely padded and look at Rubens."

"Gertrude collects paintings," Madame Simone says to me.

"She's a great art connoisseur," Alice says. "A *patrone* like the Medici. Perhaps you've read about Gertrude in the newspaper," she says to me. "That writer, Harry McBride, called the Stein collection 'a museum in miniature.'"

"Not a museum, Alice," Gertrude Stein says. "That sounds far too stodgy. We support the new. Cézanne, Matisse, Juan Gris, and, of course, the greatest . . . Picasso."

"*Pas cher, les nouveaux,*" Madame Simone says to me.

Gertrude Stein hears her.

"Well, Simone, the paintings Leo and I bought years ago are now worth over ten times what we paid for them," she says.

Georgette has finished pinning the hem. Gertrude Stein turns from side to side. "Don't cover my sandals. They're my signature."

"I wouldn't dare," Madame Simone says. "Now, tea. We'll have your garments ready in an hour."

"An hour?" Alice says. "We can't wait an hour. I'm making a cassoulet for dinner and I can't spare an hour."

Madame Simone looks at her. "Perhaps you could go ahead while Gertrude waits."

But Alice shakes her head, stands up. "Really Gertrude, we must go."

"Simone, perhaps your secretary can deliver my gown," Gertrude Stein says.

"She's not my . . ." Madame Simone starts.

But I interrupt. "An excellent idea," I say.

So that's why an hour later I stand at the tall door of 27 rue de Fleurus, not far from the Jardin du Luxembourg. I can see the Panthéon brooding over the neighborhood. I go through a courtyard to the apartment building. Some kind of garden shed seems to be attached on ground level.

Alice Toklas opens the door. We stand in a small entrance. I can smell her cassoulet so I sniff and say, "Wonderful!"

"A bit of an experiment," she says. "I'm writing a cookbook. Of course, Gertrude is the real writer, but so many have urged me to collect my recipes."

"What does Mademoiselle Stein write?" I ask.

"Surely, you've heard of Gertrude's work," she says.

"Well, I've just come to Paris and . . ."

"But she's famous!"

"I am from Chicago, remember?" I say.

"Oh, yes," she says. "I forgot. Well, I'll take the package," and she reaches for it.

"Madame Simone has a few things she wanted Miss Stein to check. I thought I'd wait until . . ."

"You want to see the pictures, I suppose."

"I do."

Madame Simone had told me to be sure to get into the atelier that adjoins the apartment.

"Everyone wants to see the pictures," Alice says. "But Leo and Gertrude have strict rules about who can see them. I mean they're really valuable. Chicago, after all is a place where . . ." She stops.

"I'm not casing the joint for a heist, Alice," I say. "Don't worry."

"What's this?" a voice says, and a man comes into the hallway. The brother Madame Simone told me about. He wears sandals too and a brown Carmelite-looking outfit. But his is made from rough wool. Scratchy, I think. He's tall with a long red beard.

"I'm Nora Kelly," I say, "bringing a package for Mademoiselle Stein."

"American," he says.

"Chicago," I say. "I don't know anyone from Baltimore."

"Baltimore?"

"Where you're from," I answer.

"Actually, the Steins are a Pittsburgh family. Allegheny, really, but it has become part of the city now."

Pittsburgh, I think. I'm not about to be intimidated by somebody from Pittsburgh. Chicago has it all over Pittsburgh.

Leo's going on. "My father was in the railroad business; traveled often to Chicago."

"He would have to," I say.

"Well, come in, come in. I suppose you want to see the pictures."

"I told her she couldn't," Alice says.

"Not really your decision, Alice." He sniffs. "I think you're burning dinner again."

"Oh my!" She hurries away.

"Well, now," he says. "Gertrude may still be writing but like all writers she welcomes interruptions."

"Are you a writer?" I ask.

"No, I'm a painter," he says. "I'm studying with Henri Matisse. You know his work?"

"I don't, but I've been visiting the Louvre. So maybe I'll come across his paintings."

He laughs. "You won't find Henri in the Louvre, my dear."

He leads me into what I thought was the shed—really a two-storied room, the atelier.

Almost sunset and a kind of rosy light pours through the windows of the small space we step into.

Suddenly I'm surrounded by paintings hanging from floor to ceiling. The frames fit so tightly against each other that the walls seem to jump with color. Hard to separate one picture from the next or to see what they depict. Wait—aren't those apples?

"I like this one," I say.

"Cézanne," Leo says. "My favorite. You've good taste, Miss Kelly."

"And this," I say, walking over to a painting of a woman playing the piano.

"Renoir," Leo tells me.

"I thought so. Some of his work was shown at the World's Fair," I say.

I go closer to a portrait of a woman in a hat. Her face is green. Odd. Yet she seems so alive. A woman I'd like to meet. I turn to Leo.

"The one's . . . well, it's . . ." I stop.

He laughs. "Yes, it is," he says. "So what do you think of our collection?"

"I can't find the words," I start. I hadn't noticed Gertrude sitting in the corner at a wide table, a pile of papers around her. She's heard the exchange.

"You're right, there. No words for them," she says. "That's why I'm reinventing language. My writing is like their art. I take words apart and rearrange them in ways never known before."

She starts to explain to me how she had studied the workings of the mind as a medical student at John Hopkins and now is capturing the randomness of thought. Hard to listen to her with so much to look at. The green-faced woman draws me to her. I walk closer.

"Is it somebody?" I ask.

"Henri's wife," Leo says. "She's a very nice woman, good friend of my brother Mike and his wife, Sally. We all collect Matisse."

"Matisse," I repeat as Leo points out other paintings. All bright colors and odd shapes.

"Are you overwhelmed?" Leo asks.

"I am."

"Good. Though one of his masterpieces isn't there, we sent the *Blue Nude* to the Armory Show in New York. Created quite a sensation." He chuckles. Sharing a joke with me. I nod and smile.

What is he talking about?

"You probably know the Irishman who helped put it together—John Quinn," he says.

"I do," I say, which isn't a lie since I know dozens of John Quinns. I gather from what Leo says that this John Quinn has his finger in every pie going. Lives in New York but from some small town in Ohio. A big-shot lawyer and a power in the Democratic Party, Leo tells me.

Now Gertrude comes over to us.

"All the pictures are wonderful, of course, but here are true works of genius," she says, and turns me toward the back wall full of distorted images.

"Pablo Picasso," she says to me. "Surely you've heard of *him*."

"Sorry, I haven't."

"She's from Chicago, Gertrude," he says.

"Some day all the world will know his name," Gertrude Stein says. "Even Chicago!"

"Well, if he gets famous enough we'll have something of his in Chicago," I say.

Alice comes in and crosses over to a large canvas. "That's Pablo's portrait of Gertrude," she says.

The woman in the painting wears brown all right, and the hair's pulled back, but the face . . .

"You don't think it captures me," Gertrude Stein says.

"I don't," I say.

"Leo told Pablo I didn't really look like the portrait. 'She will,' Pablo told him. He was right. I'm growing to resemble the painting more every day," she says. Pleased with herself.

"Dorian Gray in reverse," I say.

"So," Gertrude says, "you do have some education. The University of Chicago?"

"Sister Veronica's English class," I say. "St. Xavier's High School. And now I've been studying at the Irish College and . . ."

"Dinner is ready," Alice Toklas says.

"I better go," I say. "Thank you for showing me these."

"Stay! Share our meal, Miss Kelly," Leo says.

"Impossible," Alice says. "I made no allowance for guests. Really, Gertrude, tell him!"

"Easy, Alice." Gertrude walks over and touches Alice's shoulder. "I'm sorry, Miss Kelly. But you must come at another time. Perhaps one of our Saturday night salons?"

"I don't think she'd enjoy those evenings," Alice says, then turns to me. "Intellectuals attend, you see, writers and painters. You'd be very uncomfortable. We've never invited Madame Simone."

"I issue the invitations, Alice," Leo says. "I began the collection, and I'm the one who decides who views it."

"Do you see how he speaks to me, Gertrude?" Alice asks. "When all I'm trying to do is make a home here for us."

"Really, Leo," Gertrude says. "You know how sensitive Alice is. Apologize right now."

"Apologize? Why should I?" he says.

"Excuse me," I say. "I'll see myself out."

But Leo walks over to Gertrude's desk, takes her pen, and writes something down on a piece of paper. "My brother Mike's address. Go by and see their Matisses. A most hospitable woman his wife Sally. She'll offer tea or invite you for a meal."

"Listen to him," Alice says. "Compares me to Sarah Stein, who has a maid and a cook. How can he . . ."

"Now Alice, he didn't mean . . ."

I hear them arguing as I practically run out the front door.

I think of Henrietta and me bickering and poor Mike trying to get a moment's peace. Do brothers and sisters ever grow beyond the battles of childhood? And then to add someone like Alice. But the paintings! Dear

God, worth a bit of contention to see those paintings. And more by Matisse at this other place. Somehow I feel like I did when I touched the page from the O'Kelly manuscript. Another world inviting me in.

"Can we really just go up and knock on their door?" I ask Madame Simone two weeks later as we eat dinner at L'Impasse.

"Of course," Madame Simone says.

Neither Madame Simone nor I cook much. I live on omelettes, cheese, and bread. So two or three times a week we come here for a proper meal. Tonight Monsieur Collard serves us a salad of early greens and then a pot-au-feu. I've slimmed down. Tim McShane couldn't pinch a roll of fat on me now. I push the thought of him from my mind. And then I think of Peter Keeley. Not a word from him. Stop dwelling on the fellow, I tell myself. He's forgotten you

"The Steins promote painters," Madame Simone is saying. "They are determined to make their favorites famous. So, yes, they are generous and enthusiastic but the more well known the artist, the more valuable the paintings. So they will welcome our visit. We will tell people who will tell people."

"I didn't think of that."

"You wouldn't."

"Please don't say because I'm from Chicago."

"No, because you are not yet a true businesswoman."

So that next Saturday, we set off. The Steins live on rue Madame only a few blocks from rue de Fleurus. Madame Simone insists we take the métro to the Rennes station. Now, I am still leery of the métro. Just riding under the ground is bad enough, but what if I go by my stop and end up who knows where? Better to stick to rue de Rivoli and stay above ground. But not a bother on Madame Simone. I suppose the métro's really trams, after all, if you forget the tons and tons of earth overhead. I'll say this for the Parisians. They can decorate anything. The stations are handsome and even the letters spelling "Métropolitain" are lovely.

I had seen New York subway stations when I waited for the S.S. *Chicago* to leave. Very plain altogether.

"Here," Madame Simone says, and we're out of the train, up the stairs, and on the rue Madame.

I follow her along the narrow street. At first, we think we've made a mistake because 58 rue Madame is a church. Not as grand as a Catholic church, but a place of worship nonetheless.

"Église Réformée," Madame Simone says. "Protestant. Must be the wrong place."

"I'm sorry," I say, "I thought . . ."

I get the piece of paper Leo gave me from my pocket. Yes, 58 rue Madame.

I show it to Madame Simone. She shrugs. Next to the church is what would be the rectory if this were a Catholic church. Big, with arched windows. I guess the minister of the Église Réformée wants to live as well as Catholic priests do. Maybe he'll know something about the Steins.

We knock at the door and a woman opens it. The minister's wife?

"Welcome. Welcome, I'm Sally Stein," she says.

"Oh," I say. "I thought . . ."

She laughs. "We bought the parish house. The church was glad of the money. They send missionaries to Africa. Though the Africans have perfectly good religions of their own . . . but come in, come in. Leo said to expect you."

Smiling, dark-haired, a pleasant face and conventionally dressed. No Carmelite habit for this woman or for her husband either. "Call me Mike," he says.

A teenaged boy stands just behind them. "And this is Danny." Mike, Sally, and Danny—Bridgeport names. In fact, the Harringtons had a Sally, a Mike, and a Danny. But this Mike has a trim Vandyke beard. Not much like his brother Leo.

Madame Simone and I introduce ourselves. "Leo said you're from Chicago, Nora," Sally says.

"Yes." Here we go.

"Such a shame," she says.

"Now wait," I start. I've had enough of this insulting of Chicago.

"Unconscionable," she says, "for students to burn paintings."

"I'm afraid I don't know what you're talking about."

Well, both Steins trip over themselves to explain that when the New York Armory Show moved to the Art Institute of Chicago there were ructions.

"Some of the New York critics were dismissive, but in Chicago . . ." Sally says. "Students from the Art Institute staged a mock trial of Henri Matisse, accusing him of committing crimes against Art, called him Monsieur Hairy Mattress," she says.

Don't laugh, I tell myself. Do not laugh.

"And then burned three paintings!"

"No," I say. Now, that is bad.

"They were only copies, Sally," Mike puts in.

"But still," Sally says.

"Copies?" I ask.

"Yes, by some students," she says.

"Pretty good ones from the photos in the paper," Mike says.

"So no real harm," I say.

"No harm?!" Sally is furious.

"You have to understand," I say. "Chicago's, well, a kind of meat-and-potatoes town."

"Sally," Mike says. "Nora's our guest. I don't think she is responsible."

But Sally continues. "The ignorance, the bad manners."

Finally Mike intervenes. "Chicago," he said, "is a fine city. Industrious. I've invested in companies there. My father was a streetcar man, not on the scale of your Yerkes of course."

"Not my Yerkes and *not* very popular in Chicago," I say.

"Pioneers never are," he says.

"Qu'est-ce que c'est?" Madame Simone asks, but I'm not about to describe fights about Chicago transportation. Ed used to go on about how the city would never move forward until there was some kind of unified transit authority instead of a scramble of different competing companies. But try to put that in French.

Sally has calmed down now and Mike urges us toward their atelier.

Now where Leo and Gertrude's collection contained different artists' work, the paintings on these walls are all by Matisse. Exuberant, I think, the colors so bright and vivid.

"They make me smile," I say to Sally, who nods her head. She runs her hand over a frame the way a mother might stroke her child's shoulders. And, in fact, the painting is of a young boy holding a butterfly net.

"You?" I say to Danny, who stands in the doorway.

"So they say." Nearly a man now. How does he feel about this younger self on display? Next to the painting is a photograph. I look back at Danny.

"You too?" I ask.

"Yes," he answers. Beautiful lighting, very different than the wedding photos displayed in Chicago parlors where the bride and groom are always stiff and staring.

Mike comes up to me. "My uncle David Bachrach has a photography studio in Baltimore." We stand looking at the portrait.

"I guess there's no point in painting realistically if a camera can give us this," I say.

"Exactly. Well said, Miss Kelly. The camera captures reality. Matisse paints the soul of an object, of a person."

"Très grand, Michel," a voice says. A tall man enters the room and comes over to us.

"The master," Mike says to me. "Henri Matisse."

I don't know what I expected. But Matisse looks no different than most of the French men I pass on the rue de Rivoli; nondescript suit, neat beard.

I look from him to his creations. You never know. In fact the fellow following him in, who wears blue overalls and has long hair, more closely matches my image of an artist. Except he carries a load of wood and turns out to be the carpenter come to build crates for the paintings.

"You came just in time," Sally says to me. "Fritz Gurlitt's gallery in Berlin plans a Matisse show. So exciting. I'm sure the Germans will be more accepting of the master's work."

"Than the people of Chicago," I finish.

She laughs.

And Matisse smiles. He repeats—"Chi-ca-go"—and chuckles. "Hairy Mattress," Matisse says.

Very funny, I think. Then Madame Simone says that if the Germans don't like Matisse they'll burn the real thing. Matisse says something to her in too-rapid French, but she responds slowly so all can understand, "They will attack France," and starts on about the war in Les Balkans.

"You are wrong, Madame," Sally says. "Berlin is full of cultured people, forward-looking. We have many relatives there."

All the while the carpenter sets out the wood and his tools.

Sally speaks a mix of French and English I can follow. Convincing herself her pictures will be safe.

Matisse takes off his coat, walks over, and lifts a painting off the wall. He holds it up for us to see.

"Oh no, Henri," Sally says, "Don't send *Le Luxe*."

The canvas shows three figures. One, a man, I guess, bows before the two women. Nice colors. Blues and browns that match the pattern in the window drapes. Does Sally want to keep the canvas because it complements her décor?

But Matisse waves her objections away.

"It will return to you worth many times more. Fritz is not selling, only showing." And he hands the painting to the carpenter.

I move to a large canvas almost as tall as me.

A windowsill with pots of flowers and beyond the outline of a building. And that green smudge—a tree?

"And this is . . . ?" I ask Matisse.

"A painting," he says, and smiles.

Oh great. A comedian. I turn away but he takes my shoulder and turns me back. In slow French he explains how he was looking out the window of his hotel room in Morocco and wanted to present the view as blocks of paint so the colors themselves, the shapes, could engage the viewer.

"And are you engaged?" he asks me. And funnily enough, I am feeling something, though what I'm not sure.

"You experience the picture directly," he says. "You see?"

And I do kind of.

"I go inside the picture," I say.

"Oui! Oui!" he says. "You wish to study with me? My fee is pas cher."

"No, no. I'm a guide really. I take women around Paris to see the sights and shop."

"And you are from Chicago?"

"Yes." Here we go.

"My friend Jean Renoir tells me in his family a really big meal is called 'un repas Chicago' because after the ladies from Chicago bought his father's paintings they had money." he says.

"Here." He gives me a calling card. "My studio. You may like to see me paint. And your clients too."

Not so hard to enter this world after all.

We do not get invited for a meal, and there is no salon that night. The pictures must be shipped.

"They are very naive," Madame Simone says as we walk back to the métro. She tells me she feels war with Germany coming in her bones—the way people with arthritis anticipate rain. Maybe not this year, she says, but soon. It will be terrible, beyond anything we have ever known. And I think how sad that she always seems to expect the worst. Europeans!

"The Steins will never see their paintings again," she says. She predicts Gertrude and Leo's collection will be broken up, too. Not by war but by the conflict between Leo and Alice.

A month later Madame Simone tells me Leo Stein has moved out. He took half the paintings with him. "He claimed Cézanne's *Apples*," she says. "Gertrude will never forgive him for that. He left her the Picassos, which he said will never be worth much."

"I guess I'll never be invited to the Saturday salon," I say.

And I wasn't.

Still I'd met a real, living artist. No fashions to copy in Matisse's paintings though. I wonder is Peter Keeley interested in painting?

❧

Belinda Lawrence has plenty of money. Happy to order three "Old Master" ensembles from Madame Simone and set out to discover Paris with me.

I take her to Ambroise Vollard's gallery on rue Lafitte and point out the Matisses. Doing my bit to make up for that Hairy Mattress upset in Chicago. Belinda's not interested. A quick stop at the Louvre for the *Mona Lisa* and then shopping, shopping, shopping. Hats and silk hose, and toys from Au Nain Bleu.

"I have three grandchildren," she says.

We stop for afternoon tea with the most expensive pastries the Ritz offers.

"We weren't always rich," Belinda says after eating her third éclair.

"Bartholomew started as a shoemaker with a little shop but then . . ."

She tells me about how her husband opened a shoe factory that "just boomed." They moved to Brookline.

"I'm actually rather afraid of Mrs. Adams and the others. I was surprised she recommended you."

"Really? Why?"

"Well, Irish," she says. "Not that I have anything against the Irish. Oh no. I don't know what I'd do without my Maggie."

"Your maid I suppose?"

"Housekeeper really. She worked for one of the old Yankee families on Beacon Hill and keeps me right when I entertain."

"Where is she from?"

"Charlestown, I suppose."

"No, where in Ireland? What county?"

"Oh, I don't know."

"You wouldn't," I say as she takes another éclair.

I should take her by the arm and march her to the library of the Irish College and have Father Kevin instruct her on the thousands of years of knowledge contained in those leather-bound volumes and ancient manuscripts, and say, "Here is the heritage of your Maggie, Belinda Lawrence." But I don't. I consider my account ledger and ask her if she would like to have her picture taken in front of the Eiffel Tower. The climax of my Parisian tour.

"Oh, yes," she says.

Now, I have a favorite street photographer, Louis DuBois, who stations himself at the Eiffel Tower ready to dash up to any tourist who comes to stare at Paris's most popular attraction.

In seconds he plants his tripod in front of them, sets the camera on top, and then pulls out an accordion folder of photographs.

"At your hotel this very evening," he promises.

We have a routine, Louis and I. He makes his pitch and quotes an outrageous price. I bargain with him until even the most reluctant client is swept into the joy of getting a good deal.

Soon after my visit to Mike and Sally Stein's I went with him to his studio on the rue Saint-Saëns, a small street near the Eiffel Tower. He was teaching me how to develop prints. I was thinking of that wonderful portrait of Danny Stein when I asked him if he'd ever thought of adjusting his straight-on process to add shades and shadows—make the tower loom a bit or dance with light.

He wasn't interested but let me play around a bit.

Louis hated my experiments. "Confusing," he said.

But he did teach me how to load the plates into the camera, how to focus, and how to open and close the shutter to control the light. Then he let me take a few pictures of him in front of his building.

"You're quick," he said. "You have an eye and a sense of the camera which can't be taught. But no funny business. The camera's meant to record what's there."

But today Louis isn't at the tower. And Belinda wants five different poses. Fifty francs—almost a month's rent.

Nothing to do but rouse Louis out of his studio.

"It's close," I tell Belinda as she follows me.

"Impossible," Louis tells me. He's developing three sets of photographs that must be delivered to the Georges V that night. "Take the camera. Do it yourself," he says.

I lift the tripod onto my shoulder and almost go down under the weight. Mrs. Lawrence tries to pick up the camera and can't. "I'm not accustomed to heavy weights," she says.

"Wait," I say. The woman downstairs takes in washing. She has a cart. Three francs and the cart is ours for two hours. So we set out—pushing the cart with the camera and tripod in front of us.

Now, the Parisians won't lower themselves to laugh out loud, but plenty of them snicker at us as we bump along the cobblestones. I'm afraid Mrs. Lawrence will be horrified but when we arrive she actually offers to help me to set up the camera, and we both lift the tripod off the cart.

"*Arrêtez! Arrêtez!* Stop!" one of the regular photographers starts shouting at us. I know him. His name's Claude. Louis calls him "*tyran*—the bully." He practically threatens any reluctant tourist.

Another Tim McShane.

Claude rushes toward us and knocks the tripod over. "Oh, let's go," Belinda Lawrence says.

But I am not the frightened woman who went running through Chicago's frozen streets a year and a half ago. I live in Paris. I order my dinner in French. I've met an avant-garde painter.

So I shout right back at Claude, using French curses I didn't know I'd absorbed. Startle him.

I stop him just long enough for the other three photographers to start laughing. One comes over and tells Claude to calm down. He says that I'm "*la femme de Louis.*" "*Je ne . . .*" I start, but what the heck? I'll be Louis's woman long enough to take Belinda's pictures. And now the Eiffel Tower attendant who has been watching with great amusement says, "Why don't you both come up on the platform? Take a picture of the lady with all of Paris at her feet?"

Why not, indeed? The fellow helps me put the camera and tripod on the lift, and we go up to the second platform, where I photograph Mrs. Lawrence against a lovely pink sunset-stained Paris sky. Then I go up to the next level and shoot her from above with the city spread out below.

Louis hates the photographs. "Fussy," he tells me when I bring them back and ask him to develop them.

But Belinda Lawrence loves the pictures. She pays me one hundred francs (twice the usual fee). I give Louis fifty, which astounds him.

"Americans!" he says. But then he agrees to lend me his equipment. All that spring and summer I'm up and out with the camera and tripod on Madame Celeste's laundry cart, photographing my favorite buildings.

Louis thinks I'm mad.

"The most important thing to focus on in the frame is the franc," he says.

I take photographs of Notre-Dame as first light transforms the cathedral, shooting from every angle, catching pieces of the façade.

"Hopeless," Louis says.

I begin to feel as if I'm rearranging reality too. Following the Hairy Mattress's example. I convince Louis to teach me how to enlarge my cathedral photos and then hang them on the walls of my room. An atelier at last.

When Father Kevin tells me after Mass on the last Sunday in September that Professsor Keeley will be back at Christmas, I imagine taking Peter to my room to see my creations. A very high-minded conversation served with wine. A *salon de deux*.

What's wrong with that?

10

CHRISTMAS 1913

Peter Keeley will come walking in behind the last priest in the procession, I tell myself. I'm kneeling very straight in one of the side pews near the entrance that Peter always favored, waiting for Midnight Mass to begin.

Come on, God. I've been so good. Haven't let myself think of Peter more than once a day and then only as a friend, a teacher. No response from God. Father Rector sits on a kind of throne on the altar. I swear he's staring at me. Hates that I'm at Mass every week but what can he do? I'm back in the fold. I glance up at the Lamb of God in the stained-glass window. "I am the Good Shepherd. I know mine and mine know me." A year of the Gospel according to Father Kevin and I don't feel myself such a sinner.

I catch Father Rector's eye. Gaze right at him. He still suspects me of trying to tempt Peter away from a life of celibate scholarship, which isn't exactly true. I just want to see him, be with him, and . . . And, well, I am not sure what Peter wants.

Four weeks ago, the first Sunday of the advent, after Mass, over tea and brown bread, Father Kevin whispered to me that a delegation of Irish Americans had come to Louvain to meet Peter and "some other Irish patriots."

"One of them, a lawyer, collects old manuscripts," Father Kevin said, "and might be interested in purchasing the Kelly fragment. He's a fellow buys paintings too. The modern stuff. Not short of a few bob."

"Do you mean John Quinn?" I asked, which surprised him. And then I made a bit of a story of my visit to the Steins and meeting Henri Matisse. "Quinn buys his work," I said, and then told Father Kevin how I'd taken a client to Matisse's studio. A disaster altogether. Mrs. Fraser from Rhode Island told Matisse his prices were outrageous and that while her husband had said she could get a few pictures to take home as souvenirs of Paris she'd never waste his hard-earned money on blobs of paint.

I thought Matisse would blow his stack but he'd only laughed. And then in quick French she couldn't follow he'd told me women without husbands, like the Cone sisters from Baltimore, tended to be his best customers. Mrs. Fraser had interrupted and pointed to a half-finished painting on an easel next to a window that looked across at Notre-Dame.

"For heaven's sake," she said. "Is this supposed to be the church? I could paint a better likeness!"

Matisse didn't laugh that time. I'd started apologizing away in French and English, saying that though my funds were limited I'd be honored to purchase something—a sketch, maybe, or . . .

And thank God he'd shrugged, rummaged through some papers, and pulled out a charcoal drawing of a flower, all spiky lines.

"*Un cadeaux pour vous*," he'd said as he signed his name at the bottom, then wrapped the sketch in a newspaper and given it to me with a bow.

I'd "*merci*"ed all over the place and should have stopped there but I had to go on and tell him that I'd been photographing the cathedral and would love to give him one of my photographs in return.

He'd waved away the offer. "I prefer to keep my vision pure," he'd said, but told me that if I'd like to photograph his work that could be arranged. I said I'd be honored. Then pictured myself lugging all that equipment up the stairs and knew I'd never come back.

Mrs. Fraser had become impatient. Annoyed with me.

"You're only encouraging bad art," she'd said when we crossed the Pont Sully. She'd bought a watercolor study of Notre-Dame at a souvenir shop on the Île Saint-Louis. I'd never returned to Matisse's studio and not another word from the Steins.

Father Kevin said maybe this John Quinn will come to Paris with Peter.

I imagine him greeting me as a fellow Irish American. We'd go together to Matisse's studio. Wouldn't Gertrude and Alice be surprised.

Father Kevin told me not to mention John Quinn's visit to Louvain to anyone.

Secrets. But Father Kevin says we can't be too careful with so much anti-German propaganda in the French and British papers and the British ready to see the Irish in league with Germany now that the world seems rumbling toward war.

Madame Simone is keeping her eyes on the Balkans. Delighted that some treaty let Serbia take a big bite from the Austrian Empire. But wary too. Germany's in league with Austria and Hungary.

"The Boche won't like that. They'll retaliate."

She's watching Alsace too. In November, the people started rioting to a fare-thee-well because some nineteen-year-old German lieutenant offered his soldiers a bounty for stabbing any "Wackes," a rude name for Alsatians.

"The German army is beating the demonstrators," Madame Simone had said. "The French will have to move in to protect the people and then, war."

The French don't. But the Alsatian woman vendor is not at the Christmas market. The border between France and Germany as good as closed. A standoff. I don't send cards home this year. Don't want to mail them directly from Paris.

The bells start ringing. Father Rector stands. He's the celebrant. Father Kevin at his side. Splendid in gold vestments. And I pray, "Please. Peter. Please," with closed eyes. But Peter doesn't come.

Father Kevin preaches the sermon in English. Father Rector knows people come to hear Father Kevin and he wants a big, generous congregation. "No room in the inn," Father Kevin begins, and then goes on to talk about how right now in Dublin people are starving because employers have locked out striking workers. "Fathers can't feed their children. Mothers can't keep their babies warm. These are holy families, too. And there is no room for them in their own country."

I don't really understand all he's saying but I certainly know about what happens during strikes—hadn't Mam fed the O'Briens, who lived below us, for months while Joe O'Brien walked the picket line with the railroad fellows?

Father Rector's whispering to the priest next to him. Not pleased. I remember the story of how St. Bridget's Father Sullivan got into trouble with the cardinal for preaching a sermon supporting the strike.

During the Offertory the priests sing "Adeste Fideles," "Come All Ye Faithful." I close my eyes. Peter's been delayed but he'll arrive any minute. Come on, Jesus. It's your birthday. Be generous. Then, footsteps. I sense someone slipping into the pew beside me.

Thank you, thank you, God. I turn, my smile ready. But it's a very tall woman who's settling herself in the pew. A girl takes the place next to her, pulling a little boy along. An older woman piles in behind them. The tall woman smiles at me. A beauty, no question. Older than I am. Plenty of gray in the blond hair that's piled up in curls topped by a hat that could be Chanel. Unusual eyes, not brown exactly, a kind of golden color. Wait a minute, I know her. Maud Gonne. Why, she's famous. Ireland's Joan of Arc, the papers called her when she came to Chicago with Major John MacBride to raise money for the Cause. And now here she is. Next to me at Mass and very devout. Theatrical almost. She bows very low at the Con-secration, keeping her eyes closed. Then lifts her chin up high as the host is raised. Gazing at the white circle Father Kevin holds between his fin-gers, the body of Christ. The little boy kicks his feet against the pew. The older woman grabs his feet. I look over and wink at him. He laughs and so do I. Maud's son with John MacBride. Some Gaelic name. Seán, I think. Yes, Seán MacBride.

The little fellow becomes very prayerful, as he leads the three women up to the Communion rail. Probably just made his First Communion and feel-ing holy. Sister Ruth Eileen told us in religion class that Napoleon said the day he received his First Communion was the happiest in his life. And he had quite a life, I think, as I walk behind them. I see the nudges and nods in the congregation as the little group passes.

Whispers. "It's her. It's Maud Gonne."

Back in the pew, I put my head in my hands. Not praying really but remembering the stir Maud caused in Chicago. Ten years ago now. A big crowd turned out in St. Bridget's hall to see her and Major John Mac-Bride, who fought the British in the Boer War. She was as tall as he was when they took the stage. More women than usual at the meeting. All of us interested in what Maud was wearing. And a lovely outfit it was. A deep blue velvet gown.

Mike and Ed and John Larney had taken Mame and Rose and me. Very impatient with our chatter about Maud's dress.

"I'm here to see Major MacBride. He formed his own Irish regiment to fight the British in South Africa," Mike whispered to us. "A load of Chicago fellows were in it with him. Like our Irish Brigade in the Civil War." The Chicago *Citizen,* our Irish paper, had kept an eagle eye on the Boer War, reporting on the brutality of the British who'd forced women and children, both Boers and Africans, into camps where many died of starvation. The British army then destroyed their farms, salted the land. Determined to claim the gold and diamond mines. Acting in South Africa as they had in Ireland for centuries.

But we girls wanted to get a good look at the woman who'd inspired the poetry of William Butler Yeats. Sister Veronica, our literature teacher at St. Xavier's, loved William Butler Yeats; always used his full name, and wanted us to revere him also.

"Maud Gonne is his muse, girls," she'd said, and explained that a muse is a spiritual companion, a relationship apart from ordinary life. I'd wondered would Sister Veronica have liked to be someone's muse?

"William Butler Yeats dedicated his *Countess Cathleen* to her," Sister had said.

We'd read that long verse drama out loud in class, using parts copied from a book a relative of Sister's had sent her from Dublin.

"My aunt is a member of the Gaelic League and studies the Irish language," Sister had explained.

Well, that sounded revolutionary enough.

I listened to Maud Gonne that night at St. Bridget's as she thundered against "The Famine Queen" Victoria, who had murdered more than a million Irish people and now "grasping the shamrock in her withered hands has come to Ireland daring to ask for soldiers—men to enlist to fight for the exterminators of their race! But no more Irishmen will wear the red shame of her livery!" Maud said.

We the Irish Americans were Ireland's hope. She told us that though we had found good homes and comfort in America we still loved Ireland and we who were driven out now had the power to raise our home country to a position of honor. "Twenty million Americans of Irish blood—surely enough to free Ireland," she said, her voice loud and strong.

How we cheered her, clapping and hooting. Her companion, Major

MacBride, applauded too, gazing at her. This tough-looking fellow, with his dark hair and eyes and straight back, was a soldier all right. But smitten with Maud, I saw. Not hiding his feelings.

Sister Veronica had gone on about the chaste love between Yeats and Maud Gonne, which to me, at sixteen, sounded very romantic and safe, but MacBride did not seem a man who'd love from afar, I'd thought. Poor William Butler Yeats; his muse might have other fish to fry.

Because Mike knew one of the loads of cousins MacBride had in Chicago, we went to a special reception in the rectory. Maud stood next to the major, greeting each of us. I said to Maud, "I've come to know you through the poems of William Butler Yeats and I . . ." But she interrupted me. Shook her head as if to say don't talk about Yeats and said, "Wouldn't you like to meet Major MacBride?" As she introduced us the major took her hand and squeezed it. I wonder, is he jealous of her?

They married the next year. Headlines in the Chicago *Citizen*. The editor, John Finerty, was ecstatic, and then when their son was born the announcement actually called him "The Prince of Ireland, Seaghan (Seán) MacBride." Only a paragraph on their separation a year later, though I think there was some scandal.

And here they are. Maud herself and their blond curly-headed son. Ireland's prince kicking the pew.

I lean back, look at him, and cross my eyes. He crosses his own. I do miss kids. None in my life here. Ed's boy must be running around now and I suppose Mame and Rose have babies. Ah, well.

I wonder will Maud Gonne and her troupe stay for the hot whiskeys after Midnight Mass. Probably not. But there they are, standing with Father Kevin. I'm in the doorway and see Father Rector and that priest he was whispering to in church watching. Father Kevin looks up, beckons them over. Father Rector doesn't budge. Rude. And on Christmas.

Maud's little son comes running up to me.

"Vous êtes la femme drôle," he says. The older woman is right behind him apologizing in French.

"It's all right," I say in English. "We met in church. Merry Christmas."

And the woman says, "I'm Barry Delaney and I want to apologize for Seán's bad manners."

"But I am a funny lady," I say, and cross my eyes again, which makes Seán laugh so loud Maud hears and turns her head, then comes over to us.

She begins to apologize in French again but I say, "Never mind. He's a fine boy and I enjoy trading funny faces with him."

"Introduce yourself," she tells him.

"I am Seán MacBride," he says. "My father's a soldier for Ireland."

"Oh," I say. And then I remember. While the Chicago *Citizen* had maintained a respectful silence, the *Tribune* had reported the court case between Maud and John MacBride. Fighting over custody of this child. Some nasty accusations against MacBride. A newspaper put out by Protestants glad to slander Irish patriots, we thought, and yet I remembered that flash of possessiveness at St. Bridget's hall and wondered.

I realize I've been quiet too long. So I say, "Nice to meet you, Seán. I know your mother," and smile up at Maud. She is tall. "We met in Chicago. My brother Mike's a friend of Major MacBride's cousin Pat."

"I don't recall," she says.

Now why did I mention MacBride? Damn.

"A grand occasion," I say. "You were wonderful. But you must meet so many people." Chattering.

"We did get good crowds, didn't we?" she says. "And I remember . . . a lake," she says, pleased with herself.

"Lake Michigan," I say. "And you spoke at St. Bridget's hall."

"I believe we collected a very substantial amount that night," she says. "Bridget's always been lucky for me. She is the patron of the Daughters of Erin."

Father Kevin comes up and slips between us. "Maud, this is Nora Kelly."

"Hello, Nora," she says. Then nods at the girl, who's eighteen or nineteen. "May I present my cousin, Iseult."

"Nora did some work in our library with Peter Keeley," he says. "Translating the old manuscripts."

"Oh, you know Irish, Miss Kelly? I'm envious," she says.

"I don't exactly . . ."

But she's going on.

"One of the sorrows in my life is that I don't know the language of our ancestors. I adore the stories of ancient Ireland but must come to them through translation. Though I do communicate spiritually with the great god Lugh. I'm under his protection."

Now, what do I say to that?

Only, "That's nice."

"Peter Keeley's such a genius," she goes on. And she looks across and drops her voice. "I understand his mission will meet with great success. I had a note from John Quinn, who's committed to the purchase. With funds from our friends in Ireland we should be able to . . ."

Father Kevin raises his hand and stops her. "Not here, Maud."

"But I assume Miss Kelly's one of us," she says.

Father Kevin only smiles. Shakes his head.

He doesn't trust me, I think. For God's sake. He gives her information about Peter and keeps it from me?

"I better be going," I say. I'd stomp my feet, but we're only yards from the chapel and I still have part of the Communion wafer stuck to the roof of my mouth.

"Easy, Nora," Father Kevin says. "Stay for a bit."

"Have to get home. I'm going away tomorrow," I say, a lie.

"But surely you'll be back for my *Nollaig na mBan*," Maud says.

"The Women's Christmas," Father Kevin supplies. "In Ireland, after the Christmas festivities are over, the women gather for their own celebration on the Epiphany, little Christmas."

Seán is pulling at Maud's skirt. "You will come," Maud says. "Bring any friends. As long as they're female. A grand open house."

"Well . . ." But Maud and her tribe are gone. I start out the door, too.

"Wait, Nora," Father says. "I didn't tell Maud about Peter, she has her own sources. And now you're angry."

"Not at all," I say, though I'm clenching my teeth.

"You think I don't trust you but that's not it. You're an American. You've not been born into our history."

"And she has? Wasn't her father a colonel in the British army?"

"Maud's traveled a long way. I first met her almost twenty years ago in Donegal—going from village to village with her fine clothes and posh accent. Intimidating the judges and bailiffs. Saved a good few of our people from eviction. Gave a fellow in my parish a diamond necklace to pay his rent. She's a patriot, Nora. She's . . ."

"I don't care what she is. I'm Irish, Father Kevin. My own granny had to run for her life because of the families of people like Maud Gonne and Mr. Poet Yeats. So don't patronize me." I've never spoken this way to a priest before.

But Father Kevin only smiles, takes my elbow, and moves me away to a quieter place.

"Easy, Nora," he says again. "It's not you. I didn't want us overheard. Father Rector and many of the other priests are not sympathetic. Most of the bishops want continued union with Britain. Even the Pope thinks we should stay close to the English to reconvert them."

"Fiddlesticks," I say, which makes him laugh.

"Go to Maud's party," he says. "She could use your friendship."

"Mine?"

"The strain's telling on her. She's a target, Nora. British and French agents follow her. The French might arrest her as a German agent to please their British allies. Keep Maud from lecturing on 'perfidious Albion' and writing in French papers about evictions and starvation in Ireland."

"All right," I say. "I'll go to the party."

I have Christmas dinner with Madame Simone at L'Impasse and spend the next two weeks sketching at the Louvre. Madame Simone buys ten for the Old Masters Collection. Entering fifty francs in my book makes me feel better.

JANUARY 6, 1914

NOON

RUE DE L'ANNONCIATION

I'm walking toward 17 rue de l'Annonciation in Passy, an area I don't know. I take my faithful rue de Rivoli to the place de la Concorde, walk along the Seine's right bank to the Trocadero. Cold enough but I'm keeping up a good pace. I stop to nod at the Tour Eiffel. Taking the day off, I tell it. Not sure what avenue to follow, but a woman walking a small dog—a poodle, would you believe—chops the air and then makes her hand a snake. I think I understand.

Here's rue de l'Annonciation. A narrow street, curved. No cobblestones. Not too interesting, though I see a cross and a spire. Must be the Church of the Annunciation. It's not. Notre Dame de Grâce de Passy, I read in the vestibule. I light a candle and resolve to give Maud a chance. Besides, if she does have news of Peter why bite off my nose to spite my face?

The church doesn't feel as old as most in Paris. Madam Simone told me Passy was built by the nouveau riche less than a hundred years ago. Yesterday as this city measures time. I wonder, was there a convent here once? An abbey? Not a spot I could imagine the Angel of the Lord declaring unto Mary. Bourgeois. I'd have thought Maud would live on the bohemian Left Bank.

She must have money from somewhere, I think, when Barry Delaney opens the door and shows me into a beautifully decorated drawing room. As Maud walks over to me I see she has no notion of who I am.

"Nora Kelly," I say. "Father Kevin's friend."

Still no recognition.

"Midnight Mass. Chicago."

"Oh, yes. The lake. And Peter Keeley. Welcome."

"Thank you," I say. I'm tempted to add, "Don't worry, I wasn't followed." But the hard-edged January sunshine filling the room makes conspiracy unreal.

"Sorry," I say, "about, well, I mean Major MacBride and everything."

"Everything," she repeats, and gestures me farther into a room full of women's voices speaking French. I see Antoinette and Sheila, the two students I'd met on Peter's tours last year. May and the rest are home for Christmas. I wonder why these two aren't? I walk over to Antoinette, who remembers me. Thank God. A small redhead, pretty with a quick step and smile. She leads me over to the sofa where two very grand older women dressed in brocade gowns, their diamonds flashing, invisible tiaras on their heads, sit talking to Sheila, a lovely blonde who stands in front of them.

Antoinette speaks to the women in rapid French and then says, "Mademoiselle Nora Kelly."

I almost curtsy to these ladies, both of them with white, very coiffed hair. Easy to imagine them at the court of Versailles. The smaller woman's round face reminds me of Mike's wife, Mary Chambers. Except Antoinette introduces her as Duchess de a-string-of-French-place-names.

"Je suis enchanté," I say. As often happens when I speak French, the response comes in English.

"Good afternoon, mademoiselle," she says. And then adds, *"Nollaig shona duit."* Irish words I recognize from childhood.

"Merry Christmas to you, too," I say. "I'm sorry, I don't know Irish."

"C'est dommage," the taller woman says. A noblewoman too, I'd say, who

actually lifts her lorgnette, looks at me through it, then lowers the glass. She says something in a rush of French to the duchess, who smiles at me. "My friend the countess does not like to speak English," she says. "But I remind her we are *entente* with the Saxons now."

Did I imagine it, or does her English have a lilt? Not a brogue exactly, but something.

"I do however enjoy *la langue anglaise* and appreciate the chance of practice with petite mademoiselles Antoinette and Sheila," the duchess says.

Both the girls smile at this. "We're their companions," Antoinette whispers to me. The taller woman lets out another spate of French. I hear *"Napoléon"* and *"le gloire."* Antoinette translates. Very freely, I'd say.

"Madame la Contesse wants you to know that her great-great-grandfather was an O'Cahan, that's O'Kane, a chieftain of the O'Neills, and left Ireland in the Flight of the Earls, 1607. Since that time, her family has given officers to the armies of the king of France and Emperor Napoleon, too. But only because, well, the emperor made it worth their while—that's the gist of it."

"Close enough," I say.

More French.

"We have all served," the other woman, the duchess, says, speaking in English. "I am glad to meet an American. My great-grandfather journeyed to your country."

"Really?" I say. "To New Orleans? My family came to America through New Orleans."

"Non," she says. "He served with the marquis de Lafayette in your revolution and then died in France defending his king."

"With Lafayette?" I say. "Well, thank you. We appreciate his help. Of course, my family wasn't in America yet. Still, plenty of Irish in Washington's army. Generals too."

She nods. The duchess says, "Ah," as a woman older than either of them moves toward us, being helped by a girl about twenty-one. I get up, find two chairs, and set them in front of the others. Where's Maud, I wonder. Can't imagine she's finishing up the cooking.

"May I present the Élisabeth de Meaux," the duchess says to me.

"Bonjour," I say.

"Good afternoon," she replies. And her English too has a definite brogue. I wonder from which of the Irish Wild Geese she is descended. I take a stab.

"And did your great-grandfather leave Ireland with O'Neill, too?" I asked.

"Oh, no. I am French, only French."

"But you sound . . . your accent . . ."

"My tutors were Irish. You see, my father," and she straightens her back, "Charles Forbes René de Montalembert, was a dear friend of Daniel O'Connell, the Liberator."

The other two titled ladies nod but I am completely and totally confused. I know the name O'Connell. Granny Honora would speak of the bold Daniel.

"We all admired him," the duchess says.

"He came often to our house," Élisabeth goes on. "I remember as a little girl standing with all the household to bid him *adieu* in 1847, the year of my tenth birthday."

Granny Honora's Black '47—the worst year of the Great Starvation. So this woman is what—I did the calculation—seventy-nine.

"A few weeks later," she says, "I found my mother sobbing. '*Monsieur O'Connell est mort*,' she said. "Our families were very close. My great-grandfather served with Daniel's uncle, the Count O'Connell, in the Irish Brigade, fighting with our French king against the English. And then went with him to serve in the British army."

"What?" I couldn't conceal my astonishment.

"The revolution," the sweet-faced duchess says.

"Wait a minute," I say, "so they fought against the British then for them?"

"Even the Liberator was a royalist after all. He wanted a free Ireland with Victoria as queen," the countess replies.

The young woman with Élisabeth de Meaux speaks up. "Don't try to sort it out," she says to me. "We Irish have a way of fighting for all sides. I'm Mary O'Connell Bianconi."

"And are you related?"

"I am Daniel O'Connell's great-granddaughter."

"The de Montalemberts have always been great friends of the Bianconi family, too," Élisabeth says.

"I'm staying with them," the girl adds.

Bianconi? That's a name I've heard too.

"My other great-grandfather brought public transportation to Ireland with his coaches," she says.

"Wait!" I say. "My grandmother spoke of the Bianconi coaches. My grandfather got a job as a blacksmith with the company during the Great Starvation. The work saved them," I say. "They would have died without . . . Here we are with our families' histories intertwined. Meeting like this. Amazing."

"It is," Mary says. "But such connections often happen with we Irish."

We Irish. I like that. "And you live in Paris?" I ask.

"I do. I'm a nurse. You come from America?"

"Yes, I've been here two years." But before I can explain, Maud Gonne comes swinging toward us, arm in arm with a woman almost as tall as she is. A bit older though. Gray curls showing under the brim of a very military-looking hat. The skirt and jacket she wears are made of a dark green wool. And a leather belt is crossed over her chest. She's in some kind of a uniform. Another Joan of Arc? I wonder.

"Ladies, may I present my dear friend Constance, Countess Markievicz," Maud says. "And an officer in James Connolly's Irish Citizen Army."

I stand up and half bow. But she puts out her hand. I grasp it and we pump away for a few minutes. I'm not about to salute her.

"Isn't shaking hands the American way?" she asks, her voice very like Maud's, the same accent. And I think, I know her. Know her story. Hadn't the Chicago *Citizen* written about the Gore-Booth sisters? Daughters of the gentry, but working for the Cause. Sister Veronica said Constance had married a Polish nobleman but now it looks like she's enlisted in some army herself. Very chummy with the titled ladies, as she speaks to them in perfect French.

"I could murder a cup of tea," Constance Markievicz says to Maud.

"Good," Maud says. "Shall we, ladies?"

We move into the dining room, where cakes and cut sandwiches are piled high on china platters. The lovely young woman from midnight Mass stands behind a large silver teapot.

"Iseult, my cousin," Maud had said.

About twenty I think, and this close I notice what I'd missed at church: She's the image of Maud.

Antoinette, Sheila, and Mary Bianconi help the duchess, the countess, and Élisabeth de Meaux to the table. I stand next to Constance Markievicz, ready to explain who I am and ask her if she knows Peter. But before I can speak, she does indeed murder her cup of tea, drinking it down in one long swallow.

As soon as she finishes, I start. "Uhm, Countess, er Maud may have mentioned that I know Peter Keeley. And . . ." But loud noises coming from the other room interrupt me. Someone pounding on the front door. English agents? French police arresting a nest of German spies?

I look at all these well-dressed women, frightened now. Should we run out the back? How do you say "Cheese it, the cops" in French?

Young Iseult moves away from the table, runs to Maud. "It's him. It's him. Breaking in."

Maud puts her arm around her. "Don't be afraid."

Barry Delaney comes up. "How dare MacBride come here!" she says.

So not the police. The major.

"He dares because the court gave him the right," Maud says to Barry. "Take Iseult. Go to Seán's room."

She half pushes them in front of her down the hall.

"Maud could only get a separation, not a divorce," Constance Markievicz says to me in a soft voice. "Some complications of international law. Neither she nor MacBride are French citizens. Maud accused him of violence against her and Iseult but the court found him guilty of only one count of drunkenness and gave MacBride the right to visit Seán. Maud's terrified MacBride will grab Seán and take him to Ireland, where the courts will give him custody."

Tough. What if I'd married Tim McShane? Had a child? Tied to him forever! Horrible to think of having to go to court to get free. God, the scandal of it. Our family disgraced. Or worse. I can still feel Tim's hands on my throat. Men murder their wives, the mothers of their children, all the time. I understand Iseult's panic, the fear behind Maud's reassuring words.

More noise at the front door.

Maud's back.

"Constance, come with me to the door."

"No, I'll go," I say. "Better if he sees someone he doesn't know." Funny how men who abuse their wives don't strike out at random women.

"Tell him we're not here," Maud says. "We'll go down the back stairs."

I imagine myself saying, "Oh, Major MacBride, I so enjoyed your speech in Chicago." Sweet-talking him until the others could get away.

Maud and Constance. Fierce women, all together, willing to take on the British Empire. Scared of this fellow because as Maud's husband he can march in here and wreak havoc. His right. Dear God, what about her right? England invading Ireland. John Bull abusing Erin. Ireland's a woman, God help her.

Antoinette and Sheila stand like bodyguards in front of the three titled French ladies. But Mary O'Connell Bianconi, the nurse, steps forward.

"I'll come too," she says.

As we get closer to the front door the pounding gets louder. I take a breath, draw myself up, look at Mary, and say, "Who is it?"

But no male bellows back at me. Instead, I hear women's voices, all talking at once. And then laughter. Whew.

I open the door.

"You," I say.

Because who's there surrounded by five other women? Only Gabrielle Chanel. They surge into the room.

"Tell Maud it's all right," I say to Henrietta. I step back to let the group in.

Gabrielle Chanel thinks I'm the maid.

"Où est Madame?" she asks me.

And then here comes Maud, all smiles, with Constance.

"Coco, you came. And brought your friends! Wonderful."

The women with Gabrielle, clients, I'd say, all uncorseted and wearing the jersey dresses she's becoming known for, surround the French countess, the duchess, and Élisabeth de Meaux.

Maud's trying to sort out names and introduce the women.

Some of the group with Chanel reply to Maud in English. Not just any English, but my English. These women are Americans. They are about my age, thirty-five or so. Younger than Maud Gonne and Constance the countess, who must be near fifty, but sticking it well, as my uncle Patrick might say. Of course, the French duchess and countess had long ago placed themselves out of time. Friendly to me, these women.

"I'm Natalie Barney," the tall dark-haired woman announces.

"Barney," I say. "Irish?"

She laughs. "Perhaps somewhere far back. Most people know me in Paris as 'l'Amazon'"—she strikes a pose.

"Sorry. I don't know you," I say. "I'm from Chicago."

"Chicago?" she says. "And here how long?"

"Two years."

"Oh, my petite, you have not begun to—what is that phrase in English?—scratch the surface."

"Obviously," I say. "And you've been in Paris . . ."

"Forever," she says. "In Paris when I was a child. My sister and I went to school at Les Ruches, taught by Marie Souvestre herself. Surely you've heard of her!"

"I haven't," I say.

"Well you must know about her famous student, Eleanor Roosevelt," she says.

"Don't know her, but then I'm from Chicago," I say.

"Stop saying that," she says. "What difference where you're from? I'm from Dayton."

The January sun withdraws and Maud lights the gas lamps. Groups form and re-form. Only the French noblewomen remain seated, the center of this kaleidoscope, as more women arrive throughout the afternoon and into the early evening. We eat the cakes, drink the tea, and talk and talk and talk. Natalie tells me her father made his money selling railroad parts to George Pullman in Chicago.

"Oh, Pullman," I say. "I had a cousin who worked there, lived in Pullman, until he couldn't stand it anymore. So many rules. The company owned the workers' houses and told them how to behave. My cousin joined the strikers and said Pullman was a bloodsucker and . . ." My voice trails off. "Sorry. I forgot about your father."

Natalie shrugs. "Pullman was a horrible capitalist exploiter and my father a bigoted class-obsessed tyrant. The best thing my father did for my mother and me was to die young and make us rich. I'm spending his money to create a beautiful life for myself and my friends, support the arts. You must come to see us at the Temple des Amis," she says.

"The Temple of Friendship," I say. "That sounds nice."

"Maud has never joined us there," she says. "Afraid, I suppose. Can't risk scandal because of MacBride and the court."

I nod, though I'm not sure why visiting Natalie would damage Maud's case against the major.

"Men," she says. "Allow them in your life and they'll control you. Liane could never see that she was shackled, even though she was the most sought-after courtesan in France."

What is she talking about? Liane? Courtesan? If only Madame Simone had come. But even she would have been flummoxed by the next woman who comes up to us. Very stern-looking, wearing a man's suit.

"The great painter Romaine Books," Natalie says. Again the pause for recognition. Again I nod but think, who are these women?

"And this is the Duchess de Cleremont-Tonnerre."

"Elisabeth," the duchess says.

"She's a real Frenchwoman," Natalie says. "Not a rich American who snagged a nobleman."

All in all, it's quite an afternoon.

At about five o'clock I think all we need now is for Gertrude Stein to march in with Alice B. Toklas. And guess what? They do. And very surprised to see me.

"What are you doing here?" Alice says. "We heard this is a gathering of the most distinguished women in Paris."

"You heard right," I say. "Would you like to meet our hostess? I'm sure she won't mind you crashing her party."

"Friends from Chicago?" Maud asks me when I bring them over.

"Pittsburgh," I say.

"Was I there?" she asks.

"You could have been. You might not remember. No lake."

"But rivers," Gertrude says. "Three of them."

"Pardon me," Alice says to Maud. "This is Gertrude Stein. Gertrude Stein, the famous writer and collector."

"Of course," Maud says. "John Quinn speaks of you."

Alice smiles. I leave them chatting and go over to the woman standing with Élisabeth de Meaux.

"Ah, Miss Kelly," she says. "Come meet Sylvia Beach. I knew her when she was a child. Her father was the pastor of the American Church in Paris."

"He took us back to New Jersey, but I couldn't wait to grow up and return to Paris," Sylvia says.

"My grandmother was a Presbyterian," Élisabeth de Meaux says. "She converted to Catholicism, of course. But my father supported the American church out of devotion to her." Nice of her to explain things to me since everyone else expects me to know exactly what they're talking about.

She turns to Sylvia. "But wasn't your name Nancy then?"

"Yes. I changed it to Sylvia to honor my father, Sylvester."

"And he's the Presbyterian minister?" I ask.

She nods. I wonder what Natalie Barney thinks of this father worship.

There's a Frenchwoman with Sylvia who tells me her name is Adrienne Monnier. Plainly dressed in wide skirt, white blouse, and vest. She talks to me about her plan to open a bookshop. She wants to call it La Maison des Amis des Livres and has her eye on a place at 7 rue de l'Odeon.

"But women in France cannot open businesses in their own name," she says. "I will find a male partner—who feels the same about literature." Not so easy to escape men.

Sylvia says she wants to start a bookshop too. Only hers will be for English speakers and she'll import books from America.

"I'm going to call it Shakespeare and Company."

Not very original, I think. But I say, "Wonderful. That'd be great. I can't even get a copy of the latest Edith Wharton here."

"Perhaps you can ask her for one," Sylvia says, and points to an older woman who resembles the French-Irish countess and duchess. She's dressed in shades of plum velvet, corseted and crinolined, and has seated herself between the noblewomen on the sofa, where they've spent the entire party.

"That's Edith Wharton," Sylvia says.

I start over to her just as she stands and bows her good-byes to the countess and the duchess and heads for the door. I start to follow her but Gertrude Stein steps right in front of her. A short conversation. Very short and Edith Wharton is gone.

Gertrude Stein sees me standing behind her.

"I tried to tell her I studied with the brother of her great friend Henry James," Gertrude says to me. "William James is the foremost philosopher and religious thinker of our time."

"Oh, sure," I say.

She turns now to the other women.

"William James and I researched the unconscious. A great influence on my writing," Gertrude Stein says loudly.

"The James family—Cavan people," Countess Markievicz says. She's joined us now. "From Bailieborough. The grandfather left for America during the United Irishmen uprising. He was much the rebel," she says. "Cousins of mine in Cabra Castle knew them."

"Bailieborough," I say. "Why, my friend's mother's family are from there. She was a Lynch and married a McCabe. Funny to think her ancestors might have known the James family."

Gertrude Stein nods. "Could have been servants in the James household," she says. "We had a very good Irish housemaid in Pittsburgh."

Natalie Barney and Duchess Call-Me-Elisabeth hear our conversation.

"Oh, yes," Natalie says. "So did we. And the most darling cook from Kerry."

The duchess says something in French. *"Né"* and *"domestique,"* I hear.

"Is she saying the Irish are born to be servants?" I ask.

"No, no," Natalie says. "Only that some races are more suited to serve. The Irish personality. Their loyalty and kindness," she goes on, smiling as she explains to everyone in the circle why the American and English upper classes treasure their Irish help. "We snap up any new stock"—she says "stock" as if speaking of cattle—"from Ireland."

I want to strangle her.

Everyone is listening now. I glance over at Antoinette and Sheila, so gently tending to their ancient noble ladies. True enough, these girls are kind and efficient, able to speak words of comfort. But nothing servile about them. A way to earn money during their student days.

But I'd heard Aunt Máire's stories from her time in the landlord's house in Ireland. Maud and Constance know very well why the Irish work in the Big Houses and what happens to them.

Why do neither of Ireland's Joan of Arcs speak up?

"Listen," I say. "Irish women became maids in America to feed their families when the men faced 'Irish need not apply' signs. But earning your own living's something you ladies would not understand."

They stare at me. Silent all of them.

"For God's sake, Constance," I tell her, "say something."

"Well, Nora," she says. "Of course, you're right in principle. But I'm not sure if you understand as an American, the bonds between a family and its, well . . ."

"Faithful retainers?" I say. "Geeze Louise." I walk over to her.

"Wake up, Constance," I say. "My great-aunt Máire was forced to serve in the landlord's house in Ireland. Abused something terrible by the family. The Scoundrel Pykes, she called them. She put the best face on her time there for her children because their father was Pyke's son but believe me, there are young girls being raped by their employers right now," I say.

"Please," Gertrude Stein says. "If you're referring to droit du seigneur, such behavior hasn't happened since the Middle Ages."

"No." Maud speaks up. "Nora is right. Maids are still vulnerable. Landlords own their tenants body and soul. And really, I must disagree, Natalie. It's necessity forces Irish people to become servants, not some special penchant. In the free Ireland, everyone will choose the work they want to do."

"Choose?" I say. "Only if there are jobs! My older sister worked as a maid—twelve to fourteen hours a day. Making less money in a month than her employers spent on food for one fancy dinner party. And I would have done the same except I was the youngest. The money the others earned let me stay in school, graduate from St. Xavier's at a time when there were finally other jobs for women."

No one says anything until Sylvia Beach speaks. "Most of us here live on funds from our family. Our father's money, really. What would we do if we had to earn our living?" she says.

"What indeed," Maud says. "When I started the Daughters of Erin, we condemned the Dublin streetwalkers. Said how could any Irishwoman sell herself to a British soldier. But I didn't realize that these women were desperate to feed their children and took the only way open to earn money for them. Terrible. I apologized to them."

Mary O'Connell Bianconi speaks up. "At least nurses are paid. Not great sums of money, but earning it for ourselves."

Now, I hadn't meant to start a fight. But had any of these women spent even fifteen minutes in the real world? And I say that, repeating "real world" very loud.

"It's because we've all been wounded by the real world that we prefer to create our own," Natalie says. "And Paris gives us that chance." She goes over to the two French noblewomen who are standing now, hands on the arms of the young Irish students, ready to leave.

Natalie says to them in French, "For which we are very grateful." She curtsies very deeply. She looks up at the countess. "I meant no disrespect to your heritage."

And the countess says, "Stand up, my dear. You bow to me and yet for

OF IRISH BLOOD ─── 197

all you know some distant cousin of mine may have worked in your American household." She smiles at me. "You must continue to instruct your countrywomen, Nora," she says. "They seek to make distinctions among us. They don't realize you and me, Maud, Constance, the James family, our people scattered across every continent share an essential bond. We are all of Irish blood. A strong inheritance carried in every drop—never completely diluted. You have much to learn about us Irish," she says to Natalie. "I hope you will."

And then, she, Antoinette, Sheila, and the duchess process—no other word for it—out of the door.

"Well," Natalie says to me. "Lesson one. I apologize if I insulted you. Truly, I am sorry."

Well, what could I say. Only, "I'm sorry, too. I didn't mean to get so hot under the collar. It's just that . . ."

"We know," Gertrude Stein says. "You're from Chicago."

And we all laugh.

"And I'm proud of being from Chicago," I say.

"Except you left," Natalie says.

"Haven't we all," Gertrude says.

11

So—the others are gone by seven o'clock, but Maud asks me to stay. She brings out a bottle of red wine and glasses as the countess, who tells me to call her Constance, and I pull up three chairs close to the fire.

"That was some crowd you assembled, Maud," Constance says.

"Father Kevin asked me to invite Coco Chanel," she says.

"And the others?"

"Not sure where some of those came from. But that's Paris," Maud says. "I'm always running into people who studied painting at Julian's when I did, some quite well known now."

Maud fills our glasses.

And I have to ask, "Julian's?"

"Académie Julian. First place to accept women. I studied there, too. Why I came to Paris," Constance says. "Many years ago. Seems another lifetime. A respectable thing for a young woman, or not so young woman, who wasn't married, to do. Very shocking to some in Sligo. But, of course, most of them had given up on the Gore-Booth girls by then." She takes a lazy swallow. "Do you have a sister?" she asks me.

"I have a few," I say.

"And are you close?"

"Well . . ." I start, then stop. The countess isn't listening.

Caught by memories, she stretches her legs out. I guess those are riding boots she's wearing. Part of the uniform? No explanation for the outfit and I'm not asking. Beautiful leather, those boots. Awfully close to the fire. Constance takes no notice.

"This afternoon reminded me of the talks Eva and I used to have. She's the one who was the crusader then. 'Women must vote. We will never be equal until there is universal suffrage,' she'd tell me over and over."

"She's right," I say. "I have two friends in Chicago who are as close to me as sisters. We marched with the suffragists."

"So did we. Eva organized a campaign in England, kept that awful fellow Winston Churchill from winning a seat in Parliament," Constance goes on.

"But he got it in the end," Maud says.

"Well, we humbled him a bit," Constance says.

Maud pours more wine. "I want women to vote too, of course," she says. "But we can't be distracted from our objective: Ireland's freedom."

"I'd say they go hand in hand," I put in.

Constance smiles. "Well said, Nora. Maud tells me that you're studying with Professor Keeley."

"Studying might be an exaggeration," I say. "But I did have a few sessions with him in the library before he left for Louvain." I tell her about the excitement I felt touching the Kelly page, learning about the heroines of Ireland. "Maeve, especially," I say.

"Oh, Maeve. I named my daughter Maeve," Constance says. "She's with my parents at Lissadell. Almost fifteen now. Thinks her mother is mad."

Maud closes her eyes and speaks in a kind of drone. "I am Maeve and Willie is Aillil on the Astroplane."

Silence. What do I say to that? Constance winks at me. "That's nice," I try.

"Has Willie asked you to marry him lately, Maud?" Constance says.

"Pressing me to get a divorce, as if I could. Hard enough to have the courts allow a separation. Augusta Gregory thinks Iseult should marry Willie."

"But isn't he nearly fifty?" I say. "And what is she? Twenty?"

Maud nods. "Augusta says her husband was thirty years older and they had a satisfactory marriage."

"Well, Queen Maeve wouldn't have settled for an old man," I say, and we all laugh.

"I took the name Maeve," Maud says, "when we began the Daughters of Erin. Inspiring those tales."

"It's the old stories that woke all of us," Constance says. And she begins to tell me how she grew up feeling a certain connection to the country people on her father's estate. "He was as good a landlord as he knew how to be," she says. "Trying to make up for the past."

She drinks some wine.

"You have to remember those were difficult times, Nora. And, well, I mean what do you do when millions are starving? My grandfather really believed his tenants would be better off in Canada."

She stops.

"He couldn't know what would happen, Constance," Maud says.

"Still," Constance says.

"Constance, you mean during the Great Starvation your grandfather . . ."

"Paid the passage for his tenants to go to Canada," she says.

"Evicted them," I say.

"I suppose," she says. "Though he thought it was for the best. The only way to save the estate. He didn't know that the ships were derelict."

"Coffin ships," I say.

She sighs. "Hard to explain to you. The people were a faceless mass to my grandfather. He'd already cleared a whole area, the Seven Cartrons—wanted the land to graze cattle. More economical. Eighteen thirty-four it was. Loaded the ship with tenants. It sank within sight of land. All were lost."

"And these were the ancestors of the country people you felt so connected to," I say.

Monsters those landlords. And now here's their descendant dressed up in green?

"I know," Constance says. "It must seem such a contradiction to you. But, Nora, I wish I could make you understand how I grew up. Such a contained world—balls and hunts and horses . . ."

She stands, pacing.

"Nora," Maud says, "we need your help!"

"Mine?" I say.

"You're an American, an innocent, one step up from a tourist. Not watched, not suspected."

They both lean forward. "So . . ." But just then, Iseult comes into the room holding the hand of the little boy from church, Seán.

"He woke up, Maman," she says.

Maman? I thought Iseult was Maud's cousin.

Seán runs over to me.

"The funny lady," he says.

And I think, with all the odd women who have trooped in and out of this apartment today, I'm the funny lady?

But I look straight at him, cross my eyes, and stick out my tongue. He laughs. Maud reaches out and draws the boy to herself.

"I want my supper, Mama," he says, first in English then in French.

"Let's see what Cook has in the kitchen, Bichon," she says, and runs her hand through his curls. "Isn't he just like a little puppy?"

Maud turns to me. "Let me get him settled and we'll talk more."

And the four leave the room.

"Maud's little tribe," Constance says after they've gone. "I admire her for keeping her children with her."

"So Iseult is her daughter. I thought so. They look so alike," I say.

Constance nods. "Everyone knows but we all pretend we don't. Makes it easier in Dublin. *Ná habair tada*," she says.

"I know that phrase," I said. "Whatever you say, say nothing."

"Exactly. Iseult's father is a French politician. Maud met him when she was twenty. Married. But he and his wife, well, they had an understanding."

"Mmmm," I say.

"Maud gave birth to a little boy here in Paris. A great secret. The child got very sick a year later when Maud was in Dublin. She got back just before he died. She blamed herself. Iseult was born to reincarnate little George's spirit."

I say "Mmmm" again.

"Don't judge her, Nora. Her mother died when Maud was a child. Her father did his best to raise her and her sister. Then he died suddenly. Maud adored her father. But after he died, she discovered her father had put his brother in charge of them and of the family's money which had originally come from Maud's mother. The uncle told the girls there was very little money left, made them move into his house in England. A real tyrant but Maud," and now Constance laughs, "found work as an actress. As soon as the uncle saw the poster with the Gonne name writ large he admitted there was money after all.

"So a small but steady enough income for her. Always generous though. It seems her father had a mistress who gave birth to a baby daughter right before he died. The woman came to Maud's uncle's house asking for help. The uncle threw the woman out. But Maud found her and helped her. Later she arranged a job for her with a family traveling to Russia and Maud took the girl in. Eileen, you call her, lived with Maud and Mac-Bride until one night . . ." Constance lowers her voice. "Maud doesn't talk about it but soon after the incident, Eileen married MacBride's brother, much older than she but a solution. I believe the marriage is happy."

"Sounds awful," I say.

"Life doesn't always follow the patterns we would wish," Constance says. "When I met my husband, he was married. His wife died, but if she hadn't." She shrugs.

"Oh, Constance, believe me I'm in no position to judge anyone. I . . ." Ready to spill the whole Tim McShane story only Maud comes back.

"Time for me to go," Constance says.

"We'll talk more," Maud says. "After Mass on Sunday, Nora," she tells me as she walks us to the door.

"Nora hasn't said she wants to join us," Constance says.

"Of course, she does," Maud says. "She is of Irish blood."

"Well," I say.

I want to say, "Yes, yes, I'm with you," but I don't. Not sure what I'm thinking or feeling really. Who would after such an afternoon?

Constance says she's staying with relatives of her husband. He's in the Ukraine, she tells me very matter-of-factly, as if husbands usually are separated by thousands of miles from their wives.

"The apartment's being watched, of course," she says. "My minder followed me here but I hope he didn't bother to wait. British Secret Service will probably get all the information of what happened this afternoon by questioning one of those women."

"Not me!" I say.

"We don't suspect you, Nora. You're not the type," Constance says. "Too naive."

Should I be insulted?

"That's why we want you," Constance says. "Would you like to have a coffee with me?"

"Now?" I say.

"Why not?" Constance says.

Constance tells me to go to the café at the end of rue de l'Annonciation and wait. She'll look for me there. If someone is following her, she'll go past, she says.

Maud looks out the window. "The British sometimes use French police. Then it's hard to tell. I found that my former maid was copying my correspondence and sending it to Clemenceau's people when he was in power."

Constance nods.

"The French have joined the hereditary enemy. Too bad. My minder's a very English-looking officer. A rugby type. Probably one of General Henry Wilson's fellows. Wilson grew up in our world, Nora, but he never woke up. For him, Irish people are 'the natives,' bound to serve the British Empire and him," Maud says.

"Just our hard luck that so many officers in the British army are Irish unionists," Constance says.

"Hard luck for the world," Maud says. "Wilson and the others will do anything to prevent Home Rule for Ireland including pushing the world into war."

Now that is too dramatic for me.

"Come on, Maud," I say. "I don't think what happens in Ireland makes that much difference to the rest of the world."

"Listen, Nora. I know what's going on in the French cabinet. Prime Minister Viviani doesn't want to go to war against the Germans and the Austrian Empire. He's a socialist and wants peace. But Poincaré . . ."

"He's the president, right?" I say.

"The president, of course. He thinks if France and Russia unite, they can pick up some territory from the Ottoman Empire, which is falling apart. And even push the Austro-Hungarian Empire over the edge. Lots of territory to occupy then," Maud says.

"All right," I say. "I can follow that."

"But France and Russia won't take on Germany unless England will support them," Constance says. "And there's a war party in the British Parliament ready to sign on for the fight."

"Oh, well," I say. "I suppose the British want territory, too."

"Perhaps. But most of the British cabinet want to stay out of Europe. Why fight so France and Russia can get rich? Better to stand aside. Let the European nations have a go at each other and then move in. Pick up the pieces. Get new colonies at bargain prices, as it were," Maud says.

"Which sounds sensible," I say.

"Except the army and the Conservative Party told Asquith—"

"The British prime minister," I say.

I want them to know I'm somewhat informed.

"Very good," Constance says.

If she's being sarcastic, I don't care. Difficult to keep all this straight in my head.

"So they told him that the army cannot both enforce Home Rule in Ireland and intervene in Europe," Constance goes on.

"There are two hundred and fifty thousand men in Ulster pledged to oppose with arms any move towards Irish self-rule," Maud puts in.

"The Ulster Volunteers?" I say. "Peter, er, Professor Keeley and Father Kevin mentioned them to me."

"That's right," Maud says.

"The leader of the Conservative Party, Bonar Law, is encouraging them to fight against their own government. He himself has Ulster roots though he was born in Canada and should know better," Constance says.

"Wilson's got the French believing that the English will join them which the French have told the Russians," Maud says. "So, of course, the Germans and the Austrians found out that the British are getting ready for war and now they're mobilizing. The unionists know if Britain goes to war in Europe, that's the end of Home Rule."

Now that's a lot to take in. But I manage to work out the conclusion.

"Wait, you mean the Irish Unionists will push England into a war to keep Ireland . . . down?"

"Exactly. They're terrified that Catholics will get power. The Protestant minority in Ireland will no longer be in control," Maud says. "Half the aristocrats in England live off rent from their Irish estates. That money supports the Big Houses full of underpaid servants, the tennis parties and hunt balls and well, the world we grew up in. Rotten to the core."

"So you see why you must help us," Maud says. "We have to show the British we nationalists can defend ourselves. Only way to stop Wilson."

"And save the world from war," I say, and can't help laughing. But I do agree to meet Constance at the café.

They're both nuts, I think as I walk down rue de l'Annonciation. Imagining things. But I do as Constance says; turn in to La Mirabelle and take a table by the door and wait.

Countess Markievicz, looking very prosperous and Russian in her full-length sable coat and fur hat, strides by the café without looking at me and, Jesus Christ, if a few minutes later a fellow doesn't come after her. Probably just a man out to buy cigarettes, I think. But he's tall for a Frenchman, and broad-shouldered, wearing a gray overcoat that doesn't fit him very well. Officer? Rugby?

I pull back from the window. The waiter is watching me. Suspicious. Is he an agent too? Placed here to see who goes into Maud's house? But then the waiter asks if I'm going to order something or not.

"Not," I say, and get up.

He shrugs. A Parisian waiter, no questions.

I go straight to Madame Simone's apartment. Only been there a few times. French people, she explained to me, prefer to meet friends in cafés, brasseries, and restaurants. Why there are so many such establishments, I guess. She lives on the Île Saint-Louis right in the middle of the Seine with bridges to everywhere—Notre-Dame Cathedral, Right Bank, Left Bank. Her gray stone building has tall windows. "For the view," she'd told me. A big rambling place where she's lived all her life. Her parents had died years before but I'd say the furniture was theirs. Comfortable armchairs that I want to sink into right now.

She lets me in and leads me to the kitchen, where she brews coffee while I try to sort out what's happened. I start by telling her about the French-Irish noblewomen, which interests her. And she likes the countess part of Constance Markievicz's story and isn't a bit surprised that Maud's passing off her daughter as her cousin or that her marriage to MacBride failed so spectacularly.

"I think she married him for respectability," she says.

"But he's a revolutionary. A fugitive practically," I say.

"So? He's a husband and now she's a matron with a son."

We move into the main room, which I can see she uses instead of keeping it only for guests as we did our parlor in Bridgeport. There's a fire in the grate. We sit down. I set our cups on a table between the chairs, which are every bit as comfortable as they look.

"A separated matron," I say, "living in fear of . . ."

And I tell her how terrified Iseult had been when Coco Chanel and her group arrived because she thought it was MacBride.

But Madame Simone hears only one word. "Chanel? She was there?"

"With an entourage," I say, and start describing the other women. She laughs when I tell her how surprised Gertrude Stein was to see me there but stops me when I mention Natalie Barney's name.

"I know her. At least, of her," Madam Simone says. "Her affair with Liane de Pougy was the sensation of Paris one season. But Liane could not give up men," Madame Simone says. "After all, they support her."

"Of course," I say.

And Madame Simone says, "You have no idea, do you Nora?"

And I don't know what I have no idea about so I say, "Well . . ."

"The women you met today prefer to love other women. Gertrude and Alice are married to each other. Gertrude's the husband, Alice the wife. And Natalie, well, she's freer, has many partners but I think she and that painter . . ."

"Brooks?" I say. "Romaine Brooks? The one who dresses like a man?"

"Yes. They are together."

Now, I am pairing them off in my mind. Sylvia and Adrienne. Natalie and Romaine.

"Was Elisabeth, the Duchess de Cleremont-Tonnerre there?" Madame Simone asks.

"She was."

"Ah, you met the *crème de la crème* of *les femmes de Lesbos*."

And Madame Simone explains to me how in ancient Greece Lesbos was the name of an island where a poet named Sappho wrote and lived with a community of women.

"She composed poems about their love for each other," Madame says, and tells me that Natalie Barney wants to re-create that community within her circle in Paris.

And I think, Love? What kind of love? And ask, "Do they . . . ?"

"They do . . ." Madame Simone answers. She sighs. "Sometimes, I wish I were attracted to women. It would have saved me a great deal of trouble."

"Me, too," I say. And we laugh. Paris.

Almost midnight now and Madame Simone's yawning, half asleep when I start telling her about Maud and Constance's battle against the English. I think she's not listening.

"And I thought Countess Markievicz was just crazy, talking about being watched and followed by the police. But then, I saw somebody who I think was a policeman."

That woke her. "Police? What police?"

"A British agent I think but I suppose if the French suspect that Maud and Constance are agents for Germany . . ."

"Your friends are spying for the Boche?"

"No, no, they're not. I don't think so, at least. All they care about is Ireland, though if Germany would help Ireland . . ."

"You are not to see these people again. I forbid it." Madame Simone slaps the table. Our coffee cups rattle. "I am your employer. I give you clients. And you betray me?"

Then she stands up. "Go, go!" Takes the cup out of my hand. "Go, go!"

"Wait, wait, I'm not spying for Germany and neither are they. Please, Madame Simone, please!"

I manage to calm her down with the help of a glass of brandy from a bottle I see in a cabinet near the fireplace.

"You are so naive, Nora. Do you know what French mothers tell their children? Not 'Be good' like the English do but 'Soyez sage,' 'Be wise.' So I tell you: Be wise. War is coming. And the police will not think it amusing if an American woman involves herself in such intrigue. They will deport you, Nora, and be right to do so."

I'm an Irish woman too, I want to tell her. But I don't. Instead I promise not to see Maud and Constance again and head for my apartment.

The rue Saint-Antoine's quiet but I walk as fast as I can home. No rugby player follows me as I start across the place des Vosges desperate to get to my room.

How old this square is. All of Paris really. Peter told me the place des Vosges was once the place Royale. For centuries kings lived and died right where I'm standing. Some fell in battle. Others were murdered, by a relative, as often as not, who wanted the throne. One fellow, Henri II in the sixteenth century or so, got himself killed in a jousting tournament. Wouldn't you think the other fellow would have been more careful of the king? Peter says when the English took Paris in fourteen hundred and something, the duke of Bedford claimed the square, planted a garden. His brother was one of the Henrys of England. History is like breathing to Peter and he's good at pointing out how England has been trying to take over France forever.

The hereditary enemy. Except now Madame Simone's siding with the English because she's so afraid of the Germans.

The gates of the park are open so I cross to the center of the place des Vosges and stop. Not cold by Chicago standards. I sit down on a bench. A bright moon tonight, casting shadows into the arcades. Ghosts under those arches. All those kings and queens and dukes and their mistresses and servants and good old Victor Hugo. I wish I were standing on a swath of Lake Michigan beach when the wind sweeps over the water and the waves smooth the sand.

But I am in Europe, where the old quarrels never get settled until somebody makes war on somebody else. What had Peter told me? Oh yes, the wife of the king who was killed in that tournament, Catherine de' Medici, leveled this whole place after he died. Knocked down every building. Was that about to happen again?

I want nothing to do with their war, I think. And I must not be deported. Can't face Tim and my family. If he doesn't kill me, the questions and recriminations will. Henrietta'd be delighted that I'd completely disgraced myself. Brought home in handcuffs. No. I'll be what Sister Ruth Eileen said a good Christian is, "in the world but not of it." That's me. An Irish American in Paris but not of it.

❧

". . . so I just can't get involved," I say.

I've led Maud and the countess upstairs to the library of the Irish College after Mass. We stand next to the shelf of leather-bound books near the door to the little room where Peter and I worked.

Maud and Constance wait. Very still, these two tall women so smartly dressed. Maud wears a dark red hobble skirt and a tunic and Constance is in a very finely woven tweed jacket and gored shirt, yet they are making themselves criminals.

Constance puts her cup down on the library table. "No need to explain. But Nora, you must be silent about us and Peter Keeley and Father Kevin."

"Of course," I say. "Jesus Christ, the Kellys are not informers. My uncle Patrick was a Fenian when your ancestors were confiscating my ancestors' crops and evicting them. . . ."

Maud steps closer to me. "So that's it? We're still the gentry to you and not to be trusted?"

"No, no. I'm not judging you. It's just . . . Dear God, Maud, I don't want to be a secret agent spying for the Germans and you shouldn't be one either."

Now Maud sets her cup down with a definite crash. "Who have you been talking to? Some Englishman?"

"Have you betrayed us already?" Constance says. "And Peter Keeley. Did you give his name?"

They are nuts, I think.

"I haven't talked to anyone except a French woman who is sure the Germans are planning to invade France. I don't know if she's right, but I certainly don't want to help them."

Maud looks at me. "You'd understand us better if you'd ever stood on Irish soil, seen the spring come—snowdrops and primroses, the baby lambs and yellow whin bushes against the green hills," she says. "You'd feel a connection, a love that . . ." And that gets me. *She's* lecturing *me*?

"Don't talk to me about loving Ireland, Maud," I say. "I'm of Irish blood! One hundred percent!"

Maud shakes her head. "Blood that runs very cold," she says.

"I'm also an American, Maud. I'm not sure you understand what that means. We've put these European quarrels behind us. I want Ireland to be free. But I'm not getting myself arrested and deported. Maybe you don't care about your family but to be a Kelly of Bridgeport means something in Chicago. And I'm, well, I'm not going to disgrace myself or them."

I leave, walk out of the library through the tall wooden doors onto rue des Irlandais. Done. There. The right thing.

12

JANUARY 1914

So.

No Maud Gonne, no countess. I'm back at Madame Simone's that Monday. I tell her I'm heeding her advice. She starts again about Alsace and *"la revanche,"* I give her my "I'm an American" speech. I looked up *"revanche,"* which I thought meant revenge. In my dictionary the word also means rematch, as in soccer. Jesus Christ, a game. All of it a game. And Maud and Constance in over their heads. Well, not me.

I suppose it was Father Kevin who gave Maud my address because a week later, she's knocking at the door. Herself alone. No Barry or Constance. I almost don't let her in. But it's so cold in the hallway, and the fire glows just behind me, heating my room. She's coughing, hacking away, not looking well. She's still beautiful, of course; those cheekbones and gold brown eyes can withstand anything. But she's pale and thin and I don't know . . . diminished.

"Come in, come in," I say, and make us tea.

She sits down by the fire and sips from my best cup while looking around. "So, you eat, sleep, and entertain in this one room?" She can't hide her surprise.

"I do."

"Very charming," she says.

"I do like it. There's enough space for me," I say. Not about to apologize.

I can see she's getting herself ready to talk and I stop her. "Look, Maud. If you came her to try to convince me to . . ."

She interrupts me. "I've been thinking of what you said. That I don't understand what it is to be an American. You're right. I often marvel at John Quinn. Born into a very modest family in the middle of nowhere."

"Ohio, I think," I say.

"Yes, somewhere like that. He's not even sure where his family came from in Ireland, and yet he goes to New York, makes his way into society, and gets rich. Wealthy and accomplished in spite of his background."

"Maud, he's an Irish American. There are millions like him. My brother Mike, my cousin Ed, all doing well for themselves and proud of being Irish."

She's coughing again.

"Have you seen the doctor, Maud?"

"Ah, my chest. An old problem," she says. "I'll recover."

"Well, then, thank you for stopping by." I reach out for her empty cup.

"Nora, come to dinner with me," she says.

"That's very nice of you, but it's cold and I've eaten."

A lie. A bit of cheese and half a baguette would be my meal.

"Please, Nora. Barry and Iseult think I'm in bed. But I'm leaving for Dublin soon, and there's somewhere I want to take you and someone I want you to meet."

She stands up, putting on her coat.

"Someone?" I say. Peter, I think. It's Peter. Suddenly I'm sure of it. He's waiting, hiding. She's afraid to say his name out loud.

I get my coat and hurry down the stairs after her. There's a taxi waiting outside.

"Jesus, Maud," I say. "If I knew you left the meter running, we could have skipped the tea and I would have let you convince me much faster."

We cross the Seine on the Petit Pont, which is actually the widest of the bridges. Plenty of traffic, though it's nine o'clock at night. New floodlights shine on Notre-Dame and illuminate the Fontaine Saint-Michel, where the archangel himself, wings spread, soars aloft.

The taxi turns off the boulevard onto a crooked street. One of those old rues that twists around this, the most ancient part of the city.

"Here," she says to the taxi driver. And we get out in front of a four-story building.

Lights in the windows of the first floor. I can see people eating. A rather grand entrance with a marble staircase into the restaurant. When the maître d' approaches us, Maud puts on her grande dame self. He leads us to a banquette by the window. Lots of red velvet and gilt.

"Here," she says. "Right here."

And spreads her hands as if giving me a gift.

"I'm sorry," I say. "I don't know what you're talking about."

"This restaurant is called Le Procope. It's two hundred and fifty years old. This is where your countrymen Benjamin Franklin, Thomas Jefferson, and John Adams plotted the American Revolution. They met here with the French who would help you defeat England. Lafayette came. He was only twenty years old. And Thomas Conway, an Irishman who'd fought in the French army but then enlisted in yours. He was the one who convinced the king to send money and troops to America. Poor Louis risked everything. Bankrupted the country. The start of his troubles."

"What are you saying? That aiding the United States sent Louis XIV to the guillotine?"

"It didn't help," she says.

Maud seems to be watching the doorway. She half stands, looks toward the entrance.

And sure enough, before we can even order, a man comes in and walks right over to us. French, no question. Sixty, maybe. Bald, but with an impressive mustache. The maître d' runs behind him, pulling out a chair, calls the fellow "Monsieur le Deputy."

"Nora," Maud says, "may I present Lucien Millevoye."

Millevoye. Iseult's father?

"Lucien's a great student of French history and I thought he might be able to tell you more about how his country aided yours. Only a dream of revolution when those Americans sat in this place."

Oh, great. Does she think I'll help her from some sense of guilt or gratitude? France supported us so I aid Ireland?

"The Kellys were farming in Galway during the American Revolution," I say. "Why . . ."

Millevoye leans forward, speaks to me in an English I more or less can follow. I expect to hear about Lafayette, but he wants to know about me. Am I friend of the American ambassador? Do I know any senators or congressmen in the États-Unis? Does my family have influence?

Maud shakes her head. "Don't interrogate her. Not very gracious, Lucien," she says. "You told me you would tell Nora about the glorious relationship between France and the United States at her country's beginning."

He flicks his hand at her. Leans toward me. His eyes protrude. Some disease?

"America must not remain neutral," Millevoye says. "You must stop supplying Germany. Must . . ."

"Wait a minute, Lucien," Maud says.

"And you, Maud, no more foolishness about Ireland. War is coming. The British have agreed to aid France. *Vive la revanche!*"

"*Vive,* indeed." The voice comes from a tall man standing with the maître d'. A stringbean of a fellow dressed in a military uniform with a scar that seems to go right across his eye. Another bald man with plenty of mustache. The fellow with him looks familiar. Arthur Capel, Coco Chanel's friend. What is going on? Are they dining here, too? Chairs are pulled out for them. The two men sit down.

Maud stands.

"How dare you, Lucien?" she says to Millevoye. Loud. The older couple, at the next table, looks toward us.

Millevoye grabs Maud's arm. "Sit down, Maud. General Wilson wishes to talk to you." And then he looks at me. "And you, too."

"Lucien, what have you done?" Maud says. "Henry Wilson is my enemy."

Wilson, I think. The man who'd rather have a European war than Home Rule for Ireland.

Maud is speaking French very rapidly. And I realize she moderates her Gallicness for me because now her hands, her shoulders, her face all are *très, très parisienne.* She reminds me of the woman I saw in the bird market yesterday. A fellow was poking his fingers into the cage of one of her canaries when she turned on him.

"*Cochon! Cochon!*" she'd screamed, and her hands said worse things. Now Maud's showering Wilson and Millevoye with "*Cochon*"s, her fingers stiff and quick as she points at each one of the men.

I think Wilson doesn't understand until he starts to laugh, shakes his head, takes out his handkerchief, wipes his eyes as though Maud is overwhelmingly humorous. And now he's batting French back at her. As dramatic as she is. Hands chopping the space between them. A lot of spaces between the French words, which he pronounces with a decidedly English accent. I recognize *"femme dérangée."* Then he throws a litany of *"votre père"*'s at Maud that shocks her into silence.

He turns to me and says in English, "I am assuming that you are merely stupid and don't understand you are playing games with murderers."

Maud rallies at this.

"It's your lot who's ready to march against the British government, not us. Those fanatics in Ulster can't bear to see justice being done in Ireland. They refuse to abide by a law passed constitutionally."

And now Wilson brays out his laugh again.

"Laws? Constitution? Remember, madame, King James had all the lawyers on his side. Everything all very legal with those Stuarts. But words written on paper didn't stop King William from saving the English people. Wilsons marched with King Billy into Ulster, and my people have protected the Glorious Revolution ever since. Do you think I'll see Ireland turned over to a bunch of priests and deluded poets? Might as well let the Hindus run India, or the Fuzzy Wuzzys Africa, or the idiot suffragettes take over Britain. Do you think we'll risk the empire by letting politicians in frock suits call the tune? The army will not take orders from Johnny Redmond. Never. No Home Rule ever. Never. Never. Never. No surrender."

"You can't stop the bill," Maud says. "The House of Lords can't veto it anymore. Home Rule will pass."

"There are two hundred and fifty thousand Ulster Volunteers who will rise up against it," Wilson says. "We'll take over Belfast City Hall and then march on Dublin."

"You're talking civil war," Maud says. "Do you think the government will allow you to . . ."

He interrupts. "How will they stop us? You think that the British army will move against the Ulster Volunteers when half of the officers' corps and most of the leaders of the Conservative Party are Ulster men themselves?"

Oh, God, I think. It's happening. The *Tain* all over again. The men of Ulster against the men of Ireland. But this time, Ulster's got the guns.

Now Maud's laughing. "You throw my father up at me? And, all right, perhaps he had certain weaknesses. But he was a soldier's soldier. And I've heard him say over and over: 'A soldier's glory is that he obeys his orders.' Are you telling me officers would mutiny? Sacrifice their honor, destroy their careers? Never."

And now Millevoye, who'd been watching the argument like a spectator at a boxing match, speaks up in English.

"Honor? General Wilson is the only man of honor on the British side. He's committed himself to France, promised his government to join us in driving the Germans from Alsace."

"Oh, Lucien," Maud says. "He's spinning you fairy tales. Telling you what he wants to be true. Plenty in the cabinet will refuse to risk Britain for France or any European country. You'll see. If war does come, the British will sit on the sidelines selling arms to all sides and pick up the pieces when it's all over as they've always done."

"You're very cynical about the country your father served," Capel says, speaking for the first time.

"It's not my country," Maud says. "Ireland is my country."

"Ireland's not a country," Wilson says. "It's a province of the British Empire for which all sensible Irishmen thank God every day. And you're quite wrong about our commitment to France. True enough, there's plenty of politicians blathering on about peace. Frocks, I call them. In league with the ancient admirals who think the creaky old British navy can defend our island and see the army as nothing more than a glorified police force. I'm on my way to London now. I've just come back from a mission for the war department. I'm going to report on what I've seen: Germany and the Austrians are getting ready for war. Russia will fight with France. I'll scare the frocks out of their fancy pants with stories of great armies gathering and poor France, at the mercy of these bullying . . ."

"Wait, monsieur," Millevoye says. "France is strong, too. We'll be ready for the Boche this time. *Attaque,* as Joffre says. We Frenchmen have an '*élan vital*' no other nation can match. We failed in the past because timid generals fought a defensive war. The French temperament is more suited to offense. Boulanger knew that, and now we have generals with spirit leading our army."

"General Boulanger," Maud says to me, "Lucien's hero. He was to restore France's honor. Bring back the monarchy. Instead he let them all down. Committed suicide on his mistress's grave." She turns to Millevoye. "Wake up, Lucien! If war does come, the Germans will roll over you. What help will the British give you? Not much I'd say." Maud hits the table with her palm. The glasses rattle. . . .

I wonder if we're going to order dinner at all. Not the time to bring it up.

"The French are not beggars," Millevoye says. "Our army is bigger than England's. But promises of British support will reassure Russia."

This fellow's saying what Constance said. They sound like kids. Tell your mother my mother said yes, and then your mother will agree. Geeze Louise!

"Ah, Lucien, no need to tip your hand," Wilson says. "Better for France to be the victim at this point. The nation Britain must defend."

"This is all such poppycock," Maud says. "The Russians are getting ready to fight because they think the Germans are preparing for war. The Hungarians are afraid of the little Serbians. France, obsessed with the 'revanche,' will go to war because they think Britain will fight with them. But Britain's army is small . . ."

"There will be conscription in Britain," Wilson says. "And in Ireland, too. Our army will number in the millions."

"Millions," I say.

"All needed to fight in Europe, Miss Kelly. No one available to pacify Ireland," Wilson says.

"Wait a minute," I say. "You would really push England to war to keep Ireland subjected?"

"I'd do a lot more than that. And now, I have a message for you and all those Fenian murderers hiding in the United States. Fingers will be pointed. They will be labeled German agents. The newspapers will print stories about the Irish collaborating with anarchists and Bolsheviks, trying to drag America into a foreign war. And some may meet with unfortunate accidents. You, yourself, should perhaps be concerned."

"Me? But I'm not political. I don't understand half of what you're talking about except that my father fought in the Union Army during the Civil War and Mam said he regretted it until the day he died. Hated killing other men. Told her wars are easy to start and hard to end. And my aunt

Máire once said to me that the fellows who push for war never fight themselves. No point in threatening me."

He stares at me; the scar swelling, red, getting brighter.

"And you know, General, I've got brothers in Chicago who'd be awfully
mad if something happens to me. My cousin Ed's a big noise in the Democratic Party and has a lot of pals in Congress and the Sanitary District. So
I wouldn't suggest picking on me or Maud either. You might need America sooner or later."

Maud and I stand up and stomp out.

Arthur Capel catches up with us as we turn onto boulevard Saint-Michel.
He takes Maud's arm and steers her toward the fountain, where the archangel Michael is still waiting, sword raised.

"Defend us in battle," I say to myself. The prayer comes to me, the words
registering as never before. "Be our protection against the wickedness and
snares of the devil." Something of the devil in that fellow Wilson, no question. Easy to imagine his gaunt figure as a confident Satan laughing at his
own cleverness, setting the traps that will lead to war. Seeing himself as
Ireland's savior crushing the rebels and Redmond. What had he said? The
army wouldn't take orders from Johnny Redmond. Weren't Redmond and
his supporters elected representatives? And hadn't they argued the case for
Irish Home Rule over decades until they finally convinced a majority of
the British Parliament that Ireland should have some control over its own
destiny? For God's sake, all the Irish want is to be Canada. What's the big
deal? Would Wilson really start a civil war to keep Catholics in their place?
"Croppies lie down."

"Listen," Capel is saying. "You've got to understand a fellow like Wilson,
not really out of the top drawer. You heard him bragging about his ancestors
marching into Ireland with King Billy? Not true. The Wilsons were lowland
Scots, cleared off their lands and planted in Ulster to pacify the Irish. Some
grandfather of his made money in trade. The Wilsons bought an estate in
Longford from a family who went bust. See themselves as landed gentry but
have never been accepted by the best people. But now he's a golden boy in
all the Big Houses. Lord Londonderry, Baron Inchquin, and the Earl of
Drogheda invite him and his dumpy wife into places they never would have
gotten inside. Not as popular with his fellow soldiers. See him as a conniver,
a bit of a coward, too. He manages to avoid the battlefield. I had a fellow ask
me how I could bear spending time with that snake Wilson."

"How can you?" I ask.

"He loves France," Capel says, "as I do. It's my mama's country. And, I have all my money invested here."

"And there's Coco," I say.

"Of course. Mademoiselle Chanel has quite wisely set up a shop in Biaritz and will be away from Paris during the coming unpleasantness."

"So there will be a war?" I ask.

"You heard Wilson. Plenty of generals on the French side just like him ready for 'Attaque.' Viviani's trying to put on the brakes, but Wilson's got them all convinced England will stand with France if she takes a swing at the Boche. And so they will, my dears. So they will."

Maud's been silent, staring at the fountain, water shooting up from the angel's feet into the light. Darkness all around us.

"So Wilson's a snob," she finally says.

"A snob with very little money," he says. "The worst kind. My papa made so much lovely lucre in trade I can be as noble as I want to be. And if poor old Peter Keeley does turn up proof of my pedigree, then as you Americans say, 'Katie, bar the door!'"

"Will you fight if there is war?" I ask him.

"Oh, I'll buy myself into a good regiment. I can afford the best. The fight will last a few months at most, enough time for me to be mentioned in dispatches. Good for business. But Monsieur Wilson. Ah, he's different. He wants to become a field marshal, stand at the tippy top. Master of all he surveys. Not possible to advance like that in peacetime."

Maud is pacing. "Tommy used to talk about fellows like Wilson who could not really afford to be officers."

"Afford?" I say. "But doesn't your army pay its soldiers?"

"A pittance," Maud says. "An officer needs a private income to live. Uniforms alone cost a fortune. And then there's swords and horses and houses for entertaining. It's possible to scrimp, of course. But, well, not the done thing."

"Wilson found a way," Capel says. "Got himself appointed to the staff college. Cheap housing."

Maud's not listening. "Tommy always said fellows without enough money have a chip on their shoulders. More concerned about their careers than their country. And now Wilson will be the big man on the horse, conspiring with Bonar Law and all those other climbers. Desperate to be Sir Henry Wilson, I suppose. The Earl of something or another," she says to Capel.

"Positively salivating for it, my dear," he says. "Never a good idea to get between a hungry dog and his bone. Well, I'm off. Did my bit pro patria. Both patrias really. That's my job now, helping out Clemenceau and the boys. Good evening, Mrs. MacBride. I'm having a late drink at the Ritz with an old pal of mine and his wife . . . somebody I believe you know. Percy Wynham. He's a half brother of the Duke of Westminster and his wife is Lord Ribbesau's daughter."

Maud nods. "I was presented at court with her."

What is it with these people and their titles? I think as Capel walks away onto the street under the lamps of boulevard Saint-Michel. Handsome, no question, but how can Chanel bear all that blabber about who's related to whom?

I say as much to Maud as we walk up to rue Jacob toward the Panthéon and the Irish College. We both need a dose of Father Kevin. Nearly eleven o'clock. I hope he's still up.

"It's why men like Wilson hate Constance and me," Maud is saying. "We're the real thing."

"I am, too, Maud. A real Irish American."

Maud tells the seminarian on porter duty we must see Father Kevin. He lets us in. Probably thinks we're desperate to confess our sins.

When Father Kevin comes down he takes us into the cold parlor and Maud relates our encounter with Wilson.

"He threatened Nora," she says.

"Wilson is all bluster and bullying," Father Kevin says to me. "He can do nothing to you, Nora. You're an American citizen and, besides, you've decided not to get involved with us."

"Well," I say, and look over at Maud. "George Washington and Lafayette and my uncle Patrick fought against men like Wilson. I am not going to disgrace them."

"So, you'll help us?"

"I will."

"You'll be a Daughter of Erin!" Maud says.

"Jesus, Mary, and Joseph, Maud, haven't I always been?"

JANUARY 12, 1914

I don't know what I expected. That I'd be initiated? Swear a blood oath? Learn secret handshakes? Maud has said that her investiture into the Golden Dawn, the esoteric society Yeats belonged to, was so disappointing she quit the next week. "Found out they simply ginned up Masonic rituals," she said. "Silly, really. And such drab people."

Maud and her friends had started the Daughters of Erin to teach Irish culture to poor children in the Dublin slums and feed the kids too.

What ceremony would they offer?

When I get a note inviting me to Maud's apartment the next evening, I'm not sure what to wear. Something green, I suppose. I do have a bright green scarf and a small marcasite harp I found in the flea market.

I'm surprised when Father Kevin opens the door to Maud's apartment. Shouldn't the Daughters of Erin ceremony be women only?

Maud still has that same cough, but she's excited as she greets me and brings me into her drawing room, where Constance is fussing over a dark-haired woman sitting close to the fire. She resembles pictures I've seen of Susan B. Anthony, the suffragist.

"Molly," Father Kevin says, "may I present a fellow American, Nora Kelly?"

The woman stretches her hand out and I reach down. We shake. She has a strong grip.

"I'm Molly Childers," she says. "From Boston originally. And this is Mademoiselle Barton, my husband's cousin."

"*Bonjour,*" says Mademoiselle.

Younger than Molly. About twenty-five I'd say. Her clothes, her accent . . .

"You're really French," I say.

"*Je suis une femme d'Irlande aussi,*" she says.

I wait for her pedigree, but she only smiles.

"The Bartons have produced great wine in France for generations," Father Kevin says. "But they are Irish."

"And I'm Mary," the third woman says. Older than the other two, gray-haired, wearing a modest dress. Their maid, I suppose.

Now Molly Childers's gesture brings us all close to her.

"My dears," she says, "the greatest news. The *Asgard* will be able to carry two thousand rifles."

Rifles? What are they talking about? No one is paying a bit of attention to me—the latest Daughter of Erin. All eyes on Molly.

"We'll be able to sail from Hamburg right to Howth. Erskine says the weather will be suitable in April or May so we have four months to raise the money for the rifles."

"But, Molly, is the *Asgard* big enough?" Constance asks.

"We're having the *Asgard* refitted in the same boatyard in Norway where it was built. When my father gave us the yacht as a wedding present, a very clever craftsman made a harness that will hold me securely on the deck."

She smiles at me.

"I've a bit of bother with my legs, Nora," she says, "but we American women are tough, aren't we? When Maud told me a countrywoman of mine had joined us, I was delighted."

"Oh, right. Yes."

Rifles? What are these women planning? My God, I can just imagine what will happen if that awful General Wilson hears about this.

"*Asgard*," Maud is saying. "Isn't that the name of the Norse heaven?"

"Yes," Molly says. "Such a good omen. What could be better than sailing in to save Ireland in a boat named for the home place of the Vikings."

"But didn't the Vikings invade Ireland? Rape and pillage and destroy the monasteries, and . . ." I say.

Molly waves away centuries. "At the start," she says, "but the Norsemen married Irish women and settled in nicely. Why, some of our finest families have Viking roots. The McAuleys and the McAuliffes were originally Mac Olaf, son of Olaf. And friends of ours from Westmeath are called McKissick, which was MacIsaac, and, of course, all the Normans were once Norsemen. So . . ."

Irish history again. I know Maud and Constance are, well, fanciful, but for this hardheaded American Yankee to be seeking signs and omens . . . Maybe some combination of Yeats's Golden Dawn, Maud's ornate Catholicism shot through with Celtic mythology, and St. Bridget's parish novenas will get a higher power to work for Ireland. I hope.

"You believe in Norse gods, too," I say to Maud.

"What does it matter if we call these messengers archangels or emanations or Krishna or the great god Lugh?" Maud says. "The spirit is moving through the Irish people, and it will not be denied."

Constance, who has been very quiet during all this, now says, "In the material world we'll need money to buy the rifles."

"The Daughters of Erin are making flags to sell," Maud says.

"Maybe they can bake cakes, too," I say. I mean, come on. They sound like the Altar and Rosary Society at St. Bridget's planning the spring fundraiser.

"Good idea," Molly says. Even she doesn't see the absurdity.

The third woman has been very quiet.

"What about you, Mary?" I say. "Do you think it's a good idea? After all, you're like me—one of 'the people' that this crew wants to liberate."

She looks at Molly but doesn't reply.

"Shouldn't even a maid be able to speak her mind?" I say.

All the women and Father Kevin laugh.

"Oh, my dear, Mary is Mary Spring Rice," Molly says. "Lord Monteagle's daughter."

"Is your family descended from one of the Gaelic chieftains?" I ask.

"Not really," Mary says. "The queen gave my grandfather the title for service to the state."

"Aren't you related to the O'Briens and the de Vere de Veres?" Maud asks Mary, who nods.

De Vere de Vere? I think Maud's having me on, but no; she goes on about Aubrey de Vere de Vere, a well-known poet—though not to me.

"He's converted to Rome, hasn't he?" Maud asks.

Again Mary nods.

"Soon all the best people will be in the Church, Father Kevin," Maud says.

The best people?

The women chat away about who is married to whom, and I move closer to Father Kevin and ask in a soft voice, "Aren't there any regular Catholic women in this group?"

But Maud hears me. "All the Sheehy sisters are born Catholics," she says.

"Their father, David Sheehy, and I studied together right here in this very college as seminarians," Father Kevin says. "He went home for a visit, fell in love with Bessie McCoy. They eloped. Now they have six grown children."

"Good for them," I say, and then realize how that sounds.

"Oh, sorry Father Kevin. I didn't mean that. And, of course, you are doing great work for Ireland, and he's probably a clerk in a bank or . . ."

"Not at all, Nora. David joined the Irish Republican Brotherhood, worked with the Land League, was jailed by the British and then elected to Parliament, served twenty years as part of the Irish Party at Westminster. And has a son a priest! I've met his daughters, lovely women—all four made good matches," Father Kevin says.

"To husbands who are for the Cause too," Maud adds.

I feel like I'm back in Bridgeport as Maud asks Mary Spring Rice if the O'Brien Kathleen Sheehy married is one of her O'Brien connections, and they go off tracing relations.

"That reminds me," Mary says, "my cousin Conor's willing to help us sail the *Asgard* from Germany."

And I wonder is the Irish Revolution only a web of sisters and sisters-in-law and cousins and school friends? But then, I think, isn't the Democratic Party in Chicago a similar kind of conspiracy of families and friends? In fact, having a lot of relations is almost a requirement for running for office. Who else would get out and knock on doors for you? Where else could you find an inner circle of people you could trust?

"Plenty of Catholic women in Inghinidhe na hÉireann, the Daughters of Erin, and the Cumann na mBan's simply overrun with them," Constance says.

"The what?"

Hard to join a movement when you can't pronounce the names of half the organizations. Oh, why didn't I listen to Granny Honora and hold on to some of the Irish she and Mam and Aunt Máire spoke so easily? I used to get the occasional word, but after a while, even that floated away.

Maud translates for me. "The women's auxiliary of the Irish Volunteers. Kathleen Kelly called them together in a great meeting in Wynn's Hotel."

"They're raising funds, too, making flags to sell," Constance says.

And baking cookies, I suppose.

"But the money must be smuggled out of Ireland and then converted into dollars," Constance says.

"German agents demand payment in American currency," Father Kevin says.

"That's where you come in, Nora," Maud says. "We need someone with a dollar bank account."

"Like me?" I ask.

"Like you," Constance says. "Think of it, Nora, women and men marching together. Rifles on their shoulders."

"I'm not wearing a uniform," I say. "Not unless Coco Chanel designs it." They laugh.

"So am I an Ingh, whatever, Daughter of Erin now?"

"As you've always been," Maud says.

13

FEBRUARY 1914

And then nothing. Here I am ready to march into battle, defy old General Henry Wilson and the whole British army, and my comrades disappear. Molly Childers, Mademoiselle Barton, and Mary Spring Rice have gone to the Barton estate in Burgundy. Constance Markievicz is in Ireland. Maud was to go with the countess but bronchitis delayed her. Not in the greatest health is Maud. Still she manages to get over to Ireland in time to prepare for the massive demonstration. British trade unionists will come to Dublin to join the Irish strikers.

"When they all march up Sackville Street, the employers will give in. Negotiate with the unions," Father Kevin says to me. Only the two of us in that cold parlor. He's not looking well, coughing away. Never talks about his age but Father Kevin's well into his seventies, I know, and has a weak chest.

"I'm worried about you, Father," I say.

"Nothing a hot whiskey won't cure," he says as he pours boiling water and a good shot of whiskey into a cup, squeezes a lemon into the mixture, adds sugar and cloves.

"Medicinal," he says, and smiles. "You'll join me?"

"I will."

He makes a second drink.

As I take that first warm sip of the mixture he brews for me, I think, Why am I sitting in the Irish College instead of setting out on some mission for the Cause? Am I going to be like those fellows who arrive in Chicago full of stories about defying the Sassenach in Ireland but never give any proof of what they themselves actually did? "Another man who gave his life for Ireland and lived to tell the tale," my uncle Patrick would say. I even wonder about Maud and Constance's efforts. What real difference does serving soup to the strikers make?

I say as much to Father Kevin but he assures me the battle for Ireland is being fought in the streets of Dublin right now. Father Kevin explains that Dublin tramcar drivers work as much as seventeen hours a day for buttons.

"Can't support their families. Shocking, the poverty in Dublin," he says. "More babies die at birth than in any other European city. And the wee ones who do live are malnourished and . . ."

"Wait," I say. "These are the kids taking Irish dancing lessons from Maud? How does that help?" I say.

"Ah now, Nora, take that derision out of your voice. A child who learns to hold up his head and move his feet to a *bodhrán* drum is more likely to stand up against oppression."

And the workers had found the courage to strike. He tells me about the leaders, James Connolly and Big Jim Larkin. Both men born to poor Irish Catholic families—Larkin in Liverpool, Connolly in Edinburgh. Hardscrabble lives. Worked as laborers. Very Chicago-sounding both of them. Not big house patriots. These fellows were union organizers who I could imagine talking to railroad workers in Bridgeport.

"Driving the Protestant owners crazy I suppose," I say.

But Father Kevin shakes his head.

"Sad to say, it's one of our own leading the bosses against the workers. The owner of the tram system is a good Catholic called William Martin Murphy, a Belvedere boy, educated by the Jesuits but rich now and terrified he'll lose his money. He locked out his workers and got other employers to do the same. Convinced them it was the only way to stop the Bolsheviks from taking over Dublin and putting Larkin and Connolly over them all."

"James Connolly," I say. "He's the countess's friend." I tell Father Kevin about her uniform and laugh. The outfit seemed to me an affectation, like Romaine Brooks wearing a man's suit.

Father Kevin reprimands me.

"Don't be mocking the Irish Citizen Army, Nora," he says. "It's no joke. At the end of August the police charged a meeting of strikers and killed two of them. Then a crowd of strikebreakers hired by Murphy murdered a woman named Alice Brady who was carrying food to her family. Imagine the hate that drives a man to murder a woman," he says.

Not hard to imagine. Hadn't Tim McShane been ready to strangle me? For what? For standing up to him.

"So now, the Irish Citizen Army acts as bodyguards for the strikers," Father Kevin says. "A defensive force, really like the Irish Volunteers."

Tens of thousands joined the Irish Volunteers to counter the 250,000 Ulster Volunteers and defend implementation of the Home Rule Bill, he tells me.

I get excited.

"That ugly fellow Wilson talked about them, the Ulster Volunteers. Hard to believe that the Protestants would fight against a lawful order of the British government while the Catholics are ready to fight for it!" I say.

I mean this stuff is confusing.

"Strange isn't it?" he says. "Officers from Ulster in the British army are threatening to mutiny rather than enforce Home Rule. We've learned that the Ulster Volunteers have raised almost a million pounds and are negotiating with a German arms dealer to buy guns."

"German? Do the British know?"

"They're turning a blind eye. All right for Ulster men to arm themselves but the government won't tolerate nationalists getting weapons. Which is why we need you, Nora. It's time to act."

Oops. Here it is. My orders. And suddenly I'm very nervous.

"Listen, Father Kevin. I don't think I'm ready to carry a gun for Ireland," I say.

"Oh, we wouldn't expect that, Nora."

He leans toward me, lowers his voice.

"As I told you the Germans want payment in dollars. We're asking you to lodge the funds the Daughters of Erin collect in Ireland into your account. The British watch Maud's bank account and monitor anyone they think is sympathetic. They'd even question any large sums paid into the college's account. But you can hold the money then get a dollar draft from your bank. Say you're sending money home."

"Not very believable for me to deposit loads of money of any kind in my account," I say. "I just manage to cover my expenses."

"But what if you have a run of generous clients—women grateful to you for showing them Paris and able to pay you well?"

"Is this a prediction?" I say.

"A certainty," he says.

But a whole month goes by. Maud's still in Dublin. The strike's over. The employers won. The British workers never came to support the Dublin strikers. The Irishmen had to crawl back. Could only get jobs if they promised not to join a union. Father Kevin tells me Maud wrote to him saying John Quinn had sent money for the strikers' families and she's distributing it so families can redeem their possessions from pawnshops.

"The gombeen man does well from tragedy," Father Kevin says. "Very sad."

I'm spending time in the Louvre copying any likely gown and learning about painters, though no more visits to Gertrude Stein. Still smarting from her servant crack.

Then at Mass Father Kevin tells me I'll meet my clients at Madame Simone's that next day.

FEBRUARY 18, 1914

Molly Childers, Mademoiselle Barton, and an older woman called Alice Stopford Green wait for me in front of Madame Simone's studio. Mary Spring Rice is back in Ireland, Molly tells me.

I help Molly Childers struggle up the steps. Her fists are tight around the railings. I guide her from the back while Mademoiselle Barton helps from the front. A brave woman, Molly Childers.

I look for something to say to ease our slow way up the stairs.

"Did you know Madame Geoffrin lived in this building and held her famous salon here?" I ask, acting as if I knew all about the woman who'd hosted famous figures from the French Enlightenment though I'd never heard of her or it until Madame Simone instructed me on the history of the building. No place in Paris without some kind of tale.

But Mademoiselle Barton really does know all about Madame Geoffrin. "I believe my great-grandfather 'Irish' Tom Barton came to her Wednesday dinners whenever he was in Paris. He saw Madame de Pompadour here once. Though he was better acquainted with Louis XV's younger mistress, Marie-Louise O'Murphy, whose father was an Irish soldier."

"Oh," I say. My God—she's talking about people who lived over a hundred and fifty years ago as if they were neighbors. These families have long memories!

Molly finally reaches the top landing.

"I wouldn't fancy being a royal mistress or a royal anything," she says. "We Americans were right to put all that nonsense behind us. Weren't we, Nora?"

"We were," I say, thinking of all those French aristocrats climbing the steps to the guillotine.

There's revolutions and then there's revolutions. Though for all I know English agents followed Martha Washington. I think of the fellow who was trailing after Constance Markievicz, Maud's story of minders, and General Wilson's threats. I'm a bit worried that these women, known to be sympathetic to the Cause, will attract attention from the British government. Surely if they smuggle money out of Ireland the government will notice.

But Father Kevin says that the British know these women are the kind who buy new clothes in Paris.

"And you're simply their guide. Besides, we have a contact at Dublin Castle," he said. "You're not suspected by British Intelligence. Wilson was only blustering at you."

Which is good, I guess. A bit disappointing to be so easily dismissed, though.

How will I explain these women to Madame Simone, I wonder as Georgette ushers us in. I'd promised to avoid Maud and Constance. But these three look so absolutely respectable that she asks no questions, especially when each tells Madame Simone that she wants a day dress and coat and is willing to let her choose a design from the Old Masters Collection.

Madame Simone begins with Mademoiselle Barton. "A revered name, Mademoiselle," she says to her. "I myself enjoy the wine of your vineyards."

"We must send you a case," Mademoiselle Barton says, which helps.

Madame Simone and Georgette practically curtsy to Mademoiselle

Barton as they lead her to the dressing room to take her measurements and show her various materials. Alice, Molly, and I talk quietly in English, general conversation, careful to say nothing about our mission. Molly mentions Alice's book *The Making of Ireland and Its Undoing*, surprised I haven't read it.

"But it's an excellent history. Gives a picture of Ireland under the great Gaelic families—the wonderful music and literature the Tudors destroyed," Molly says.

"Sounds like *The Annals of the Four Masters*," I say. Let these women see that I have some knowledge of my heritage.

"Well, thank you, Nora," Alice says. "That's a lovely compliment. I did refer to the old manuscripts while writing." She tells me she grew up in Kells and naturally was interested in . . .

And I finish her sentence. "*The Book of Kells*, Colmcille's Gospels."

And again, she nods.

"My grandfather was the bishop of Meath, Church of Ireland," she says.

"Let's hope so," I say. Hate to think of an Irish Catholic bishop having grandchildren.

"We lived right across from Colmcille's house, an ancient tower where the monks worked on the masterpiece. That sparked my interest," Alice says.

"And then she married a famous historian," Molly says.

"And he's where?" I ask, expecting to hear that he's living in the South Seas or somewhere.

"Passed away," Alice says. These women do get free of their husbands one way or another. Except for Molly, who starts going on about her fellow, Erskine (odd name that), and how he'd swept her off her feet in Boston.

"Didn't seem to mind that my legs don't work so well," she says. "I was injured in a skating accident when I was only three years old. We were married six months after we met. He was with the Royal Artillery unit of the British army."

"But wait," I say, and lower my voice. "Aren't you helping to buy guns in Germany and bring them to Ireland to help in the revolution against the British?"

She nods but puts her finger to her lips.

"And your husband was in the British army?" I whisper.

"Oh, yes."

I swear she doesn't see the contradiction. Oh, well.

Alice goes to be fitted next, saying "I want something very serviceable" to Madame.

When Alice returns, Molly says to me, "You must go to Ireland," then tells Alice, "Nora's never been to Ireland."

"Oh, my dear, that's terrible! Why, it's only a boat trip away. And the fares are very reasonable," Alice says.

"Hmm," I say. I can't explain to them why I haven't gone there. I don't know myself. Ireland's a dream to me, made up of Mam's and Granny Honora's memories, full of myths and music, not a real place you can go to. And through all the gauzy images floating around in my mind, I sometimes hear Aunt Máire's voice: "They don't write songs about children starved down to their bones, and bodies piled in ditches. You want to touch the best of Ireland go look at the stained-glass windows at St. Patrick's Church here in Chicago."

Now Madame Simone and Georgette come in and measure Molly in the gilt chair where she sits.

"Please don't make the skirt too heavy, Madame."

Molly goes on to tell Madame that she rides horses and helps dear Erskine sail their yacht.

"It's walking that's difficult. But I live quite a normal life," she says, "with three children to keep me busy."

And the revolution, I think.

Now the tour of Paris.

We bundle Molly into a taxi, which Alice Stopford Green tells me is called a fiacre, after an Irish monk, who's the patron saint of taxi drivers.

"Why?" I say.

"That no one knows."

A warm enough day for February. We start at the Tour Eiffel, where Louis lets me take their pictures in front of the tower. This impresses Molly.

"So you're a photographer? I do enjoy artists," Molly says. "They see the world in new ways. Am I correct, Nora?"

"Well, I do look at light differently," I say, as I watch the reflected glow of sunset soften their faces. Who wouldn't believe they are three well-born and fashionable ladies enjoying an afternoon in Paris with no worries except how their husbands will react to the money they've spent?

We keep the taxi, circle the obelisk on the place de la Concorde, ride up the Champs-Élysées, and then join the autos surging around the Arc de Triomphe. So innocent. Above suspicion.

Except when we settle in for tea at Fouquet's, which they prefer to the Ritz, a heavyset man comes in and sits at a table near us. Not the type of fellow who whiles away an hour watching the crowds promenade on the Champs-Élysées. It's the fellow I think of as the rugby player who followed Constance Markievicz. Molly looks at him, nods at me, and loudly leads us in analyzing Madame Simone's designs. Will the bodices be pin-tucked or plain? Will Madame employ pleats? Should they purchase new petticoats? That drives him away.

"You really think he was spying on us?" I ask. Father Kevin had been so sure we wouldn't be suspected.

"You can't be too careful," Alice says.

She hands me a thick envelope.

"We can thank Alice for a large portion of this," Molly whispers to me. Alice shrugs.

"Thanks," I say. We order more tea and so my career as a secret agent begins.

The three are staying at Le Grand Hôtel near the Opéra. No shabby Left Bank two-star for them and certainly not Le Grand Hôtel Jeanne d'Arc.

We help Molly up the steps into the huge lobby, once an open courtyard. Horse-drawn carriages turned around in this space during the reign of Louis Napoleon. Now a skylight covers a lobby full of overstuffed chairs and small marble tables where guests—very elegant—sit and chat. I think Molly sees judgment on my face, because she says "Luxury can be a protection" to me as I stick my toes into the thick carpet.

"Regardez," Mademoiselle Barton says, and nods toward a corner where Monsieur Rugby sits slumped in an armchair. Not even trying to blend in.

"Let's go!" I say, but Molly steers us right toward the man.

"Hello," she says. "You look very familiar. Are you a friend of my husband Erskine?"

"The famous author," Alice Stopford Green puts in. "He wrote 'The Riddle of the Sands,' a story of espionage."

The man looks down. Says nothing.

"Aren't you feeling well?" Molly asks. "Gentlemen usually rise when a lady addresses them."

Oh, great. Make him mad. The absolutely worst way to deal with a cop.

"Perhaps he doesn't understand English," Mademoiselle Barton says, and addresses him in French.

The rugby man doesn't respond but does kind of stumble up onto his feet.

"Are you staying in this hotel? Louis Napoleon was its patron, you know," Molly says.

Now Alice Stopford Green speaks up. "He was a pal of my husband's grandfather. Louis 'Nap' he called him. The emperor lived in England at the time and would come to call. A bit embarrassing because Queen Marie-Amélie, the wife of Louis-Philippe who the emperor deposed as king, sometimes visited my husband's grandmother. Always worried the two might meet!"

The three laugh. Fluty and phony-sounding but I join in heartily. Overdoing it but we do manage to flummox the fellow. He wants out, I think.

"Well, nice chatting with you," Molly says. "We're going into the Café de la Paix right through that doorway for an apéritif if you'd care to join us?"

I make a sweeping motion with my hand like a matador waving a cape at a bull. The rugby player takes off.

Now we do laugh.

"Let's not settle for an aperitif," Molly says, as we look over the menus at Café de la Paix. "Let's order glorious *pêches Melba*."

We do.

"Well done girls," I say, as I get just the right combination of peach, ice cream, and raspberry topping onto my spoon.

"Maud told me to always confront the watchers," Molly says. "One of them followed her into the Brown Thomas store in Dublin. Maud led the fellow right into the corset section, then complained to the floorwalker that this unsavory and obviously perverted man was annoying her. They threw the fellow out and he was a Special Branch detective."

Efficient, I think. Maybe revolutions do need highborn ladies.

The next day I'm back at Madame's studio. Now I hate not being able to tell Madame Simone the story of our rout of Monsieur Rugby and even sorrier that I have to lie to my red leather book.

"They only gave you twenty-five francs?" Madame Simone says. "Terrible. I will give you a share of the two hundred francs they paid me," she offers.

I assure her that I am satisfied. "They are my Irish countrywomen," I say, as I open the red ledger and make an entry.

She shakes her head. "You are not like them," she says.

I know she's about to tell me why.

But Georgette comes in.

"A client, Madame," Georgette says. "With no appointment."

Strange. Madame's doesn't attract casual shoppers. But she has Georgette show the woman in. Not our usual customer. About forty and dressed a bit flamboyantly.

Georgette says, "Here is Madame LaSalle," and stands behind the woman instead of leaving as she usually does.

Madame LaSalle wants a new dress, she tells Madame, who then asks the woman if she understands the cost of a Madame Simone creation. She nods, takes out a wad of francs from a pocket in her dress, and puts them on the table.

Madame sends Georgette for the tape measure and Madame LaSalle turns to me. "From where you come?" she asks in English, and seems surprised when I say America, Chicago.

"Ne pas Irlande?" she says to Madame, and then lets out a long run of French.

"This one's telling me that some Irish women she knows recommended me," Madame Simone says to me. "Your friends. She wonders if they're still in Paris and will they be returning here and also she wants you to take her on a tour too."

The woman listens very intently, maybe she understands English better than she speaks it. Like me and French.

"Those Irish women?" I say to Madame in English. "Gee whiz. I don't really know them at all. The concierge at Le Grand Hôtel put them in touch with me. But sure, I'd be happy to take Madame LaSalle on the tour. We'll start at the Eiffel Tower. I'll take her photograph and then . . ."

"Photograph?" The woman picks out the word, repeats it, and then speaks to Madame with many gestures.

"The lady doesn't want a photograph taken," Madame says to me.

I turn to the woman and tell her in careful French that I can even get her picture into the newspaper. A grand surprise for her friends—and what's her full name for the caption, Madame What LaSalle?

Well, she panics, tells Madame Simone she's changed her mind, turns, hurries out. Madame Simone stands up, walks over to where I'm sitting with the red ledger open, and looks down at me. Angry.

"She came from the police," she says. "I told you not to become entangled"—her word, and believe me it sounds worse in French, like being pulled underwater by the tentacles of an octopus. Madame goes on and on. I don't say anything. Georgette comes in.

"Not police or at least not French police," she says. "I followed Madame LaSalle"—drawing out the "Madame"—"to the place Vendôme where a big man waited under the column. I saw her take money from him. Heard them speak in English."

"The rugby player," I say. "Damn!"

They both look at me. *"Comment?"* Madame Simone says.

So what do I tell this woman who befriended me, made my life in Paris possible? I can't lie to her. But I do. I'm surprised at how easily the words come.

"He must be a private detective. The husband of Molly Childers is considering a divorce action." Forgive me Molly and your oddly named husband. "He may suspect she met a lover here."

"Ah," says Madame Simone. She sits down. Georgette laughs.

"Not the first lady to use our premises for a tête-à-tête!" Georgette says.

"Georgette!" Madame says, but then smiles too. "I suppose *amour* is in the very walls here. Madame Geoffrin was most tolerant."

I make that noise with my mouth French women use to mean *"C'est la vie."* Whew.

Two weeks later, my next client comes in. We meet at the Panthéon. Best to stay away from Madame Simone's.

"Good afternoon, I'm Alice Milligan," she says.

Alice doesn't want to linger in the Panthéon.

"There's a church not far from here I would like to visit. On the rue des Carmes."

"I know it," I say. Hadn't Peter taken us there on one of the student tours? "The church was originally a chapel of the Irish College," I say.

"Then you can see why I want to visit it," Alice says. "You see, I'm from Tyrone. 'Tír Owen,' the land of the Chieftain Owen."

"Of course," I say, though I'm not sure what she means. Peter had told us something about the church being a place where the exiled Irish chieftains and their followers worshipped, but I didn't really listen. Too busy whispering with May Quinlivan in the back.

Now Alice Milligan tells me she believes two members of the chieftains' clans, an O'Neill and an O'Donnell, are buried in this small church. St. Ephrem's it's called now and belongs to the Syrian Catholics. She says that a very conservative Catholic organization meets here. "Royalists," she says.

"Do French people really think they'll get a king back?" I ask.

She shrugs and I think of Millevoye.

No meeting here today. The church is empty. A vague light comes through the dusty glass skylight. Very plain altogether.

I guess the Irish priests took the good stuff, like the Lamb of God stained-glass window, to the new chapel. Alice grabs my hand and leads me to the far side of the sanctuary, where two stone slabs stick out from the wall.

"These are their graves," Alice says. She kneels down, puts her two hands flat against one of the graves. In the half-light I can see Gaelic script, the letters worn into the stone. She closes her eyes.

"Imagine them leaving all they love behind them. Couldn't even lay their bones in the Irish earth. Pray for us, Nora. Pray we succeed. Ireland can't bear any more exiles."

She stays still for a long time and I think, This one's a different kettle of fish altogether from the other Irish revolutionary women. None of Maud's theatricality or Constance Markievicz's bold ways. Nor does Alice have the kind of born-to-money confidence of Molly Childers or a sense of worldly accomplishment that Alice Stopford Green shows. She sent me a signed copy of her book, *The Making of Ireland and Its Undoing*, with a note. "As you can see my publisher is Macmillan, the same house that publishes both Thomas Hardy and Lewis Carroll—a happy range of interests," she'd written. "The Macmillan brothers are from the Aran Islands in Scotland. So kindred spirits!"

I wondered if that formidable Alice Stopford Green was connecting herself to Alice in Wonderland. Showing a sense of humor? Good.

This Alice isn't laughing as we finally leave the church and walk down the rue des Carmes. She reminds me of someone. Who? She's from Tyrone like May Quinlivan and both have a kind of quiet flintiness. Women of Ulster. But May's more well, normal. Catholic of course. This Alice told me her father was a Methodist minister.

I keep sneaking looks at Alice Milligan. Her small features, the decorous hairstyle, subdued clothes, Protestant clergymen background. And I get it. "Jane Eyre," I say out loud, which stops Alice.

"Pardon me?" she says.

"Er, I was wondering if you've read *Jane Eyre*," I say.

"Of course," she says.

"Oh, I did too," I say.

And she looks at me. Who is this crazy woman, I imagine her thinking. But now the connection seems so obvious, she's Jane Eyre after Rochester died. I loved that book. Not one we read in Sister Veronica's English class but something Rose and Mame and I found and shared. And we adored the movie. Such an adventure to go to the cinema anyway but even more exciting to see a story we knew up there on the screen. I sometimes wonder if I didn't fall for Tim McShane because I pictured him as Mr. Rochester. In that dark theater, I wished for Tim to be blinded and lose a hand so that we could be happy together.

Alice Milligan does not look so much like the young Jane, but resembles the older woman she would have become. And now she was talking about the Brontës.

"Their people are from County Down," she said. "Ulster women in their blood. Their father, Patrick, was involved with the United Irishmen in 1798."

Oh God, I think, which group is this? The Irish Citizen Army, the Irish Volunteers, the Irish Revolutionary Brotherhood, the Fenian Brotherhood? I don't want to ask.

But she's explaining. "Many Northerners were involved in the uprising because of the Presbyterian leadership," she says.

Uprising. That should tell me something. But so many waves of uprisings had swept over Ireland. I knew them from the Clan na Gael picnics and Uncle Patrick's stories. Beaten back. Betrayed. But ever returning.

Alice is going on. "Their newspaper, the *Northern Star*, inspired Anna Johnson and me to start the *Northern Patriot* and then the *Shan Van Vocht*."

And now she's lost me entirely. So finally I just have to say, "You have all of the Irish history at your fingertips. But I, I don't."

And then she becomes the governess I pictured. "Let's find a café or restaurant and I'll explain."

"Here!" I say, and lead her onto rue de Lanneau, a narrow street. Empty now—early afternoon, *déjeuner* over. No one is following us. Thank God.

And now I parrot a bit of what I remember from Peter's tour. "This was the rue Mont-Saint-Hilaire," I tell Alice. "Fourteen bookstores on this street five hundred years ago. There was a medieval abbey. Peter—er—Professor

Keeley thinks this restaurant stands on the site of an old Roman bath," I say as we go into the stone town house.

Of course she's thrilled and wonders if maybe O'Neill himself drank in this *cave à vin* as we settle ourselves next to a giant stone fireplace.

"My goodness," she says. "I'd say this hearth is thirteenth century." The waiter explains that the restaurant has just been bought by a trio of actors.

It had been Puit Certain—Certain's well, named for the abbot of the abbey, the waiter explains.

"But we're calling it Le Coupe Chou," he says.

He sees we don't understand.

"The name for the barber's razor."

He mimes shaving.

"A cabbage cutter," he says. "A medieval barber had his shop here. Though there are rumors he sometimes"—and the waiter draws an imaginary straight razor across his throat.

"They say some of his clients' bodies were sent to the butcher across the way as material for sausages. But then these stories are told of many barbers," he finishes.

"Yikes," I say.

I suppose it's a tribute to Alice's revolutionary spirit or her shaky French that she doesn't flinch. The waiter agrees to serve us café crèmes and napoleons and she starts my lesson. I keep my eye on the door but no one comes in.

"The United Irishmen," she says, "were begun by Wolfe Tone."

Thank God I could truthfully say, "I know about him."

"They fought for Catholic emancipation though Tone was Church of Ireland and the other leaders were Northern Presbyterians. And Methodists, too," she says, "as my family is."

"And were Catholics involved?" I ask.

"Of course. The Defenders were a secret society of Catholic farmworkers who joined with the others. The French Revolution and your American War of Independence inspired them all. 'Why shouldn't Ireland have a revolution?' they said. Napoleon was to send troops to support us."

"Wait," I say, "I know this part. I've heard my uncle Patrick go on about the 'Year of the French,' the landings in Mayo. 'Too little, too late,' he'd say."

"He was right," she says. "The countryside rose up in rebellion but the

French were few enough and then masses of British soldiers descended. The French were sent home, but the Irish were hanged from every tree."

I nod, sigh, and we each take a bite of our napoleon.

"So another failure," I say, "like the strike in Dublin."

"Yet their bravery continues to inspire." She starts to sing in a soft soprano:

> "Who fears to speak of Ninety-Eight?
> Who blushes at the name?
> When cowards mock the patriot's fate
> Who hangs his head for shame?
> He's all a knave, or half a slave,
> Who slights his country thus."

And I join her. I know the song and wasn't I the best alto in St. Xavier's Glee Club? I harmonize on the words "But a true man, like you, man, will fill your glass with us."

"That song's a favorite," I say, "at the Clan na Gael picnic. I like the last verse:

> "Then here's their memory—may it be
> For us a guiding light,
> To cheer our strife for liberty
> And teach us to unite.
> Though good and ill, be Ireland's still
> Though sad as theirs your fate;
> Yet true men, be you, men,
> Like those of Ninety-Eight."

"It's a grand song," she says, and sips the café crème.

"We should be drinking Jameson's," I say.

"Or Bushmills," she adds. Not so much Jane Eyre after all.

"Well, our rebellions may falter but our songs are strong. Like the one about Roddy McCorley," I say, and sing a bit of it. "'And Roddy McCorley goes to die at the bridge of Toome today.'"

The waiter and maître d' are watching us from behind a very old wooden counter.

"Un autre napoléon, s'il vous plaît," I call out to them. And then say to Alice, "Too bad the Emperor Napoleon wasn't as satisfying as these pastries," and laugh.

But she doesn't see the joke. "I remember when Anna wrote that song about Roddy McCorley," she says.

"Anna? The woman who started newspapers with you?"

She nods.

"The people took to it immediately. Anna and Maud and I traveled all over Ireland, a 1798 centenary tour in 1898."

The waiter sets down our pastries.

"We went from village to village, lecturing on the '98 Rebellion, trying to make people struggling against eviction and starvation see that things were not as hopeless as they seemed. Our ancestors had fought the Sassenach and we could too. We were together, Anna a Belfast Catholic, and Maud a member of the Church of Ireland then, and me a Methodist. Protestant, Catholic, and Dissenter united just as Tone and the others had hoped. We had some great times in Donegal. The people had nothing, yet they offered us feeds of boxty and potato cakes. And such quick learners; they picked up the tune right away. Anna would sing a line to the crowds and they would echo it."

Alice sang softly.

> *"Oh Ireland, Mother Ireland,*
> *You love them still the best,*
> *The fearless brave who fighting fall*
> *Upon your hapless breast;*
> *But never a one of all your dead*
> *More bravely fell in fray*
> *Than he who marches to his fate*
> *On the Bridge of Toome today."*

"Lovely," I say, "and so sad like Mr. Rochester, burned and blind."

"Except Roddy McCorley was real; only nineteen when he fought with the United Irishmen," she says.

"Such a young fellow," I say.

She says, "He almost escaped to America, but he was betrayed."

"Too bad," I say.

And think to myself, I wish to God all the rebels had escaped to America. I wish the song was "And young Roddy McCorley came to Bridgeport and raised a family."

Oh, Ireland, Mother Ireland, I think, don't you want to be a grandmother? Why must you always be pictured holding your dead child? Uncle Patrick probably would have been hanged like Roddy McCorley if he hadn't gotten out and come to Chicago. "He left to save us," Granny Honora had told me. "The money he made digging the I and M Canal meant Máire and I could leave and bring your Da and your aunts and uncles with us. All of us alive because of him. And he's why you're living, Honora. You and your cousins and all their children down the generations." And I'd said, "Gee whiz. I'm glad he got away!"

Now Alice is telling me about the effect the poems published in their newspaper, the *Shan Van Vocht*, had.

"'Shan van vocht' means 'the old woman,' right?" I say. "And Ireland's the shan van vocht."

Want to show her I'm not a complete dunce.

"Same name as the Seine River, another goddess figure," I finish. Peter Keeley told me about the connection. I do miss him. Father Kevin's had no word from him at all.

"Yes," Alice is saying. "The goddess is often associated with a lake or spring or well. All portals to the other world. And in the same way, the poems and song we published offered an entrance through imagination to another dimension for our people. Important for the Irish to know we have a glorious past; that we have always fought against the oppressors."

"And lost," I say.

"Different now. We are truly united. Protestant, Catholic, and Dissenter, the theme of so many of Anna's poems. You probably know her as Ethna Carbery."

"Oh, that's why I didn't recognize her name." Making it up.

"After she married Seamus MacManus, she took a pen name. He was a poet, too. She was afraid they'd be confused."

Good, I think. A married revolutionary. Holy woman, neither virgin nor martyr.

But Alice lowers her eyes. "So sad. She died a year after their marriage."

Oh, great. "In childbirth?" I say.

"No, a gastric problem I believe. Almost ten years now but Seamus keeps the flame burning. Do you know the book he published of her poems? *The Four Winds of Eirinn?*"

"I don't," I say.

"I must send you a copy. Very successful. I wonder, does any other country love poetry the way we do in Ireland?"

"And are all the poems patriotic?" I ask. If Ethna loved this fellow Mac-Manus, maybe she wrote some romantic verses, something I could quote to myself when I'm thinking of Peter. So I ask, "Any love poems?"

"I don't recall any," Alice says. "Remember, Maud and she and I, all the Daughters of Erin, we see the arts as a way to encourage people. I'm experimenting with using magic lantern slides to tell our history and have music playing behind them."

"Like cinema," I say.

"Yes," she says.

"Wow!" I say. "I might be a help there. I'm a photographer." And I realize, I've never said that before. "I'm a photographer."

"Splendid!" she says. "I need beautiful landscapes. When are you planning to come to Ireland?"

"Soon," I say. And I mean it as I take the envelope of money from her.

But Father Kevin says absolutely no trips to Ireland for me. "You're an innocent American. You have to stay that way."

An innocent American, I think, with a growing bank account. Forty thousand francs—about eight thousand dollars.

"How many rifles can we get for that?" I ask Father Kevin.

"Erskine Childers is over in Hamburg negotiating for us right now," he says.

And then I ask the question I just couldn't put to the dignified ladies. "Does it bother you, Father, that these weapons can, well, kill people?"

"But they won't, Nora. That's the point. When Home Rule is voted into law, the British will see that we're armed and a match for the Ulster Volunteers and then . . ."

"They'll enforce their own laws."

"Exactly," he says. "Now, the two last women are coming next week—one on Monday, the other on Wednesday."

"More poets?" I say. I'm joking. I mean, how many more could there be over there?

But Father Kevin only nods, smiles. "They are. Katharine Tynan and

Alice Furlong. And speaking of poets, you must ask Katharine to tell you about her friend Hopkins."

"Who?"

"Gerard Manley Hopkins, the Jesuit, the poet," he says.

"Who wrote patriotic verse?" I ask.

"Not at all. Taught at University College Dublin. Not very happy in Ireland I'm afraid. He was a convert, you know. Never found his footing in Dublin. Still, Katharine tells me he did love excursions into the country-side. She sent me a lovely verse of his. I often repeat the first line to myself: 'Glory be to God for dappled things.' Hopkins was one of the family for Katharine and her husband."

"She has a husband?" I say.

"She does."

"And he's alive?"

"He is," Father Kevin says. "Nice fellow, a barrister. She chose him over Willie Yeats."

"But I thought Yeats has been in love with Maud his whole life."

"He has. But he's practical, too. Tried for other women when Maud married but he'll be coming around again now that MacBride's out of the picture."

God, these people live complicated lives, I think.

Katharine Tynan and Alice Furlong come one after another during the first two weeks of March. I take each one separately on my standard tour. The Panthéon, the Louvre, tea at Fouquet's, and photographs at the Eiffel Tower. Even being a secret agent can become routine, I think.

Katharine won't be drawn into any gossip about her proposal from Yeats, but offers to send me a book of poems by Hopkins.

Alice Furlong is the third Alice I've had. She tells me she's published dozens of books.

"They're popular, thank goodness. I live on the royalties."

It's impressive to think that these women not only write books but sell them. I wonder, would anyone buy one of my photographs? I think of Matisse, so obviously anxious to turn his canvases into cash. As much for the approval as for the money, I suppose. But of course, these Irishwomen want to rile up their audience, not just profit from them. Still nice to earn something from your work.

Imagine having one of your books on the shelf in some stranger's house.

Or a painting on the wall, or even a photograph. I try to say this to Alice Furlong and she understands.

"A great feeling altogether," she says. "As soon as I finish one book, I start writing the next one. My audience expects a steady stream from me."

"Great," I say. "But I have to ask you one thing. Why are so many Irish women called Alice?"

"Well, for myself, my mother admired Queen Victoria's daughter Princess Alice."

"Oh," I say. "But I thought Irish people want to get rid of royalty."

"Oh, not necessarily. And Alice was special. Then she had to go and marry some German. All those princesses seem to do that. But she worked with Florence Nightingale and even questioned the Victorian version of Jesus."

"You sound as if you admire her, too," I say.

"I do. Yet I helped Maud stage demonstrations against her mother, Queen Victoria, when she came to Ireland."

She's smiling at the memory. "You see the government had organized an outing for Dublin children in the park to meet the queen and eat sweets. They were sure all the little Dubs could be bribed into bowing to Her Majesty. But Maud and I and the rest of the Daughters of Erin put on our own children's picnic. And thirty thousand children came. Many more than the governments could coerce. A great show and one on the eye for the British."

She laughs.

"Do they serve Irish whiskey in this place?" she asks me as we enter Fouquet's.

"Fouquet's serves whatever you want," I say. A bit flighty, this Alice. And I'd bet that's rouge on her cheeks. Attractive in a tweedy kind of way. And the waiter does find a bottle of Jameson's and brings it to us. We'll be singing before the evening's over, I think. I almost wish Monsieur Rugby were here so we could stand up to him, but I haven't seen him again since that woman who called herself Madame LaSalle came to Madame Simone's. Father Kevin was very relieved that he hadn't appeared again.

"They must be convinced you're innocent," he said.

Now Alice is sipping her whiskey and telling me, "You know Daniel O'Connell himself could never believe that 'the little queen' was cold-hearted enough to let millions of Irish people starve. 'She didn't know,' he said. You have to understand, Nora, the Irish people see the royal family as a kind of drama. All the display and plenty of tragedy. Two of Alice's children died of the blood disease Victoria's children all seem to have. Odd, isn't it? That their prized royal blood destroys them. Alice was only thirty-five when she died and it's her daughter that's married to the czar of Russia. Their son has the disease."

"Oh," I say. "Too bad."

"And then there's her niece, Alice, the Countess of Athlone . . ."

"Irish?"

"No. The royals make up titles for themselves and their friends. Dish them out as rewards. The Baron of Killarney, the Duke of Cavan, the Countess of Donaghmore."

"And Irish people don't mind?"

"It infuriates many of us, but for lots of ordinary folk the royals are characters in storybooks who exist in the newspapers and in the songs that are written about them. And the gossip. Rumors about Victoria's mother and the Irish soldier who ran her household. Maybe the Famine Queen's not so royal after all. Anyway they're our time's versions of Bread and Circuses," she says. "I suppose you can't understand as an American."

"Well, we had our own Alice," I say, "Theodore Roosevelt's daughter. And there was a song about her. 'In my lovely new Alice blue gown.'" I don't sing it.

It's after her third whiskey that Alice asks me a whole string of questions about John Quinn. I tell her I've never met the man.

"But I thought you were one of his women," she says.

"What?"

And she tells me this long rambling story about how when John Quinn came to Dublin ten years before he'd charmed them all.

"Even Lady Gregory," she says. "And I believe he and she had, well, a liaison when she visited New York."

She takes another sip. "Hard to believe. But Augusta is a woman after all. Maud never succumbed. Maybe she's so good at keeping men at arm's length because she's very tall."

Alice giggles.

"A funny picture that." And she stretches out her arm as if holding a fellow at bay.

"But me," she says, "I—well I wasn't the only one he courted. Mae Morris is another. I understand she is besotted with him—and her an Englishwoman with that famous father. And then he brought his American mistress with him to Ireland. Yeats flirted with her. Caused an awful row. John writes to me but then he writes to us all. Dictates the letters to his secretary."

"And you thought because I'm an American I was another one of his . . ." I stop. "For God's sake, Alice, I'm a suffragist!"

"So am I," she says. "It doesn't help." She finishes off the whiskey.

"Ah well. A broken heart's not a bad thing for a writer," she says. "I even sent him a poem."

She holds up her glass.

"Fueled by this."

And doesn't she recite the last verse to me:

> *"I know you not, I never knew you,*
> *And yet unto you all my heart goes forth,*
> *As the sun-kissed needle seeketh the black north!"*

I don't know what to say. But now this Alice is away with the fairies. Tipsy, Aunt Máire would say.

Sober enough to hand me an envelope of money and a signed copy of her book.

Later that night, I page through her *Heroes and Queens* hoping for a chapter on Maeve and then I think, why not forget the whole idea of royalty? Old Irish nobles or new. Americans don't miss kings and queens at all. If we want storybook figures, we go to the movies. I think of Maud playing the Countess Cathleen, Ireland as a queen. Why not portray her as a regular woman? And John Quinn. Where does he fit in? All these women have too much imagination. But quite a collection!

Well, that's it. I'm done. I lodge the last ten thousand francs into my account and ask for a balance. I expect the manager to congratulate me but he just opens a file drawer and takes out a sheet of paper. "Fifty thousand and one hundred forty-nine francs," he says. And now the hard part.

"I'd like a draft in dollars please," I say, and begin to explain how I'm buying a house in Chicago and need to send a dollar check but he's not listening, only smiles, calls in his secretary, and in ten minutes I have the bank draft—ten thousand dollars! Incredible.

But isn't the Fairy Woman waiting outside. A blustery day and the rue Saint-Honoré jammed with umbrellas.

"Why not just go," she says. "Leave all this nonsense behind. Italy would be full of sun—or Spain. Haven't you always wanted to see Granada?"

But I turn away from her. Me, betray the Cause? Never! I'm one of the Women of the Revolution. And I'm delighted with myself when I hand the draft to Father Kevin.

"There," I say. "I've completed my mission."

"Wonderful!" Father Kevin says. "And with what Peter brings, we should have more than enough."

"He's sold the fragment," I say. "He's coming back?"

"Nothing confirmed, but I had a note from one of the priests in Louvain. Very short. Prepare the professor's room. It should be freshened up."

"I'll do that," I say.

"You won't, Nora. No women are allowed on the upper floors except the maids," he says.

"Oh," I say. I guess poetry can't ferry women across some boundaries.

"Now the money needs to be taken to an agent in Strasbourg."

"Oh," I say.

"And Strasbourg's a place where American tourists often visit," he says. "A place someone like you would want to see."

"Yes, I'd love to see Strasbourg. It's Madame Simone's home . . ." I stop. "You mean you want me to deliver the money?"

"I do," he says. "Maud's back. She came here last night. Delighted with all you've done. She thought you could be the courier and . . ."

"She did? Well she can think again. Absolutely not," I say. Smuggling money across borders and meeting a German agent? Me who doesn't even have a proper passport. Judge Craig's letter works well enough in Paris, but at the border?

"I'm sorry, Father Kevin. No." What if I got arrested? I tell him that my family would be devastated. Henrietta would die of shame. And Madame Simone? Me working for the Boche? I could just imagine the *Tribune*'s headline. "Nora Kelly of Bridgeport Arrested as a Spy." Or worse. "Executed!" Devastating for the family. And Rose and Mame, with her winning patriotic essay. And Ed? My God. "Cousin of Chicago Official Is German Agent."

I babble through all this to Father Kevin, even tell him about my very temporary passport. He seems a bit dazed as I finish with "I'm sorry but I can't."

"Don't be sorry," he says. "You've done your part. We'll find someone. I'd do it myself but I have no reason to go. Don't want to raise suspicions."

"I hope you're not angry with me."

"Not at all. I appreciate what you've done. Forget it, forget it. Just remember that Peter Keeley's coming home and you can start your studies again. But Nora, you should get a proper passport. Britain requires them now, so does Russia. France will soon enough."

"I will," I say.

But as I walk into the almost spring of Paris, it's Peter I'm thinking about. I've done my duty for Ireland. Peter'll be proud. I imagine the two of us married and on our way home to Chicago. Fantastic? Not when I'm walking through the Tuileries with the chestnut trees ready to pop into green and the sun warm on my back.

Peter'll say, "Thank God you didn't agree to go to Strasbourg. Much too dangerous for a couple about to become man and wife. We have to think of our future children."

And I'll respond, "We do, Peter. We do." I go to the American embassy that very day and get my temporary passport made permanent.

14

MARCH 31, 1914

A miserable afternoon. Spring has stalled. Rain floods the streets. I leave wet footprints on the steps as I climb up to Madame Simone's studio. Quiet; no clients today. Madame Simone seems to have forgotten about Molly Childers and the "femmes irlandaise." She has convinced herself that such respectable women could never plot against the government of France.

I haven't seen Maud since the special St. Patrick's Day Mass sponsored by l'Association de Saint Patrice at Notre-Dame-des-Victoires. I stood with her on the steps of the church as she pointed out le Comte d'Alton O'Shea and Capitaine Patrice de Mac-Mahon—the countess and duchess were there too, dressed in emerald green gowns.

The assembly processed through the great doors followed by a crush of students, seminarians, and young women clutching shawls around them. "Irish servant girls," Maud explained to me after Mass. Later they were the ones who came up to Maud offering her coins "for the Cause."

"Only we Irish could assemble such a strange collection of royalists and republicans," Maud said. "Still we're all of Irish blood and in agreement on one thing—the Home Rule Bill. It's not everything we want. But it's something. We need a victory after the horrors of the lockout."

She and Father Kevin moved among the groups chatting in front of the gray stone church with me trailing behind hearing "The bill is moving through Parliament—keep the pressure on." "Write to anyone you know."

Maud explained to me that Asquith needed the Irish Party's votes to stay in power. The party leader, Redmond, was sure Ireland would finally have her own government, Home Rule, and would be in charge of all domestic affairs.

"But still within the empire," I said.

"For now," she said.

I'm glad Maud's not angry at me anymore for refusing to carry the money to Strasbourg, I think as I sit down with Madame Simone at her desk. I present the red ledger. Very few tourists. I need money. Time for another visit to the Louvre, a regular thing now. Thank God there's so many paintings.

Madame hands me an envelope. A letter—but no one knows where I am except . . .

"From Dolly McKee," she says.

But Dolly shouldn't have written. What if Tim McShane had seen the address?

I open it. A clipping from the Chicago *Tribune* falls out.

"Honora Kelly, 34. Reported Dead" reads the headline.

The letters blur.

"Bad news?" Madame asks.

I translate the headline.

"Mort?" Madame Simone says. "But you are alive. A mistake?"

"Must be," I say.

But the article quotes the victim's sister, Henrietta Kelly.

> "Nora has been working and traveling in Europe. She wrote to us to say she planned a trip to Australia where we have family and would be sailing on the *Volterra*. So when the ship went down with no survivors, we were concerned. We just received notice from friends of hers in Paris that Nora did sail on that ship. She's most certainly dead. Her family and friends mourn her." Miss Kelly is survived by brothers Michael, Martin and Edward Kelly, sisters Henrietta and Anne. She is a first cousin of South Park Commissioner Edward J. Kelly, who commented, "We all love Nonnie. She'll be missed."

"What? This is awful," I say to Madame Simone. "Someone fed my family a load of lies. Sent a forged letter to them Why?"

Maud Gonne, Miss Joan of Arc. She did this. Probably used John Quinn to find my family in Chicago. Wrote and told them that I was dead. What better way to keep me tied to their plots. Easier to convince me to carry the money if I were a single woman with no family. Next they'll have me assassinating somebody or planting a bomb or . . . I know, I know, this sounds crazy and far-fetched but try reading your own obituary some day, complete with a quote from your sister.

"What will you do?" Madame Simone asks me.

"I'll have to write to my family right away, tell them I'm alive. They'll be so happy." And then I'll settle things with Maud "All for Ireland" Gonne.

"But, look, there are two other letters here," Madame Simone says.

I hadn't noticed the folded papers. I open the first. Henrietta's signature is at the bottom.

Dear Nora,

As you can see from the enclosed clipping you are now dead to us and to Chicago.

You don't know or care what's been going on here for the last two years. That gangster, Tim McShane, comes around at all hours of the night and pounds his fists on the front door and yells 'Where's that whore?' Every window on Hillock opens, the neighbors eager to catch every word, and then full of false condolences the next morning. 'Hard on you, Henrietta,' they say. 'The fellow is obviously mad.'

Long faces but I know they are laughing at me. Especially that Annie McFadden. She even asked me had I consulted Father Sullivan about my problem. All because I did my duty and told Father her slut of a daughter was pregnant and should be read out from the altar. And then Jack Farrell has the nerve to ask if I'd called the police. Snide. Not a bit grateful to me for making Mart press charges against his son, Johnny, after he stole those bullseyes from Mart's candy store. That juvenile home did the boy a world of good and so what if Lucy Farrell doesn't speak to me.

The idiot, of course I'd called the police. Dozens of times. Little enough they do.

John Larney tells me unless McShane does me physical harm, they can't arrest him. And Mart! Mart had the nerve to take McShane for a drink at McKenna's last month. McShane was coming around every single night. I finally shouted at him 'She's in Paris, France.' Figured that from those strange Christmas cards you sent.

Oh, dear God, she told him I was in Paris?

The only one with any sympathy for me was Dolly McKee. I went to her. I had to. The sinking of the Volterra was in the news. And I said to Dolly, 'Too bad Nora wasn't on that ship.' And Dolly said to me maybe Nora could be.

She's the one called the newspaper for me. But I arranged your funeral. You'll be happy to know Father Sullivan said a lovely mass for you at St. Bridget's. The whole family came and a good few of your friends. Mike insisted on buying you a grave at Mount Carmel. Though I said why bother when there's nobody in it. Wouldn't do as much for me. Probably just dump me in with Mam and Da when my time comes. But you've got your own headstone with some silly verse Mame came up with.

You should be grateful to me, Nora. I have restored your good name. You've always been selfish with no regard for me or anyone else in the family. Now show us some consideration and stay dead. No more fancy foreign cards. Believe me, Nora, the family is relieved. Poor Mike turned himself inside out trying to find you. Mame putting him up to it, no doubt. He wrote to the Embassy in Paris. And Ed went to Dunne the Governor! Now, they'll have some peace.

Of course, the embassy didn't have my address. Only went there recently for my passport. Probably told Mike no Nora Kelly in their records.

If I know you, you've got some man in your life. Another gangster, I suppose. Agnella's having masses said for you at her convent. Don't embarrass her, please. Forget yourself, for once, and think of your family.

I pray that God will forgive you, Nora.

Your sister,
Henrietta

The second letter from Dolly is much shorter.

Dear Nora,

When Tim's drinking, he goes on about you to me. He insists that he'll find you and make you pay. For what I'm not sure. Tim used to forget all about his raging the next morning but after your fool sister told him you were in Paris, he went mad. The next thing I knew, he was down at the concierge desk at the Palmer House, buying a ticket on ship to France. Charging it to my account. They called me. I stopped him this time. But I don't know how much longer I can control him.

Tim has even threatened me. He thinks I know where you are. He knows I buy clothes from Madame Simone. If he puts two and two together you're not safe. Nora, I think you should take this chance for a new life. I've been dead to my hometown and my family for years. Best for everyone.

Good-bye,
Dolly McKee

I put her letter down and just stare at the words. Had I understood? Both Henrietta and Dolly want me to erase myself? Would Mame and Rose and Ed and Agnella really be better off without me? And yet, dear God, if Tim McShane did start searching around in Paris, it wouldn't take him long to track me down.

Madame Simone's waiting for me to explain. She'd be in danger, too. Tim might go to the police, start them asking questions. God, they'd look more closely at me. Ask questions about the Irish women, investigate Maud too. How would I explain that money in my account? Maybe Nora

Kelly should die. Maybe she's dead already. I think of Natalie Barney. Was she alive to anyone in Dayton? Or Sylvia Beach to her family in Princeton? I doubt it. I say nothing for a few minutes, but then explain the letters to Madame Simone, who nods as she listens, and when I finish, she puts her hands over mine.

"The past is ashes," she says. "Gone for all of us. Only regrets linger and the longing for what can't be. My father never stopped mourning our lives in Strasbourg, hoping for *la revanche* when France would reclaim Alsace. Perhaps now he will have his wish. But at what cost?"

"I have to think," I say, and let the rue de Rivoli move me to the place des Vosges.

A dozen children chase each other around the wet green park. I think of Ed's kids, Mike's. Henrietta would condemn me to never ever seeing my nieces and nephews?

And Ag. Dear God, Agnella. She must be heartbroken. Loved me as much if not more than she loved her own mother. I imagine the nuns in her convent, so sympathetic. They'll say, "Only thirty-four? Not very old. But not young either. Enough time to earn her eternal reward. Perpetual light shine upon her. May she rest in peace."

Peace. My gift to Agnella. A relief from her mother's complaints about me. Always did try to turn Ag against me. Hated how close we were. How Henrietta must have enjoyed telling Ag about Tim's rants. Probably played up how terrified they made her. Let Agnella say a word in my favor Henrietta would blast her no question. Well Ag won't have to fight Henrietta anymore.

And what about Mike and Mame, or John and Rose? Dear God—they all know about me and Tim McShane. Oh. A groan comes out of me. Is all of Bridgeport talking about my disgrace? I can only imagine how Henrietta's tormented them with her fears of McShane. Will even they think maybe it's all for the best that Nonie's gone? And Ed. Easier for a politician to have a dramatically drowned cousin then one connected with a living scandal. Because if I write to the family and tell them the truth the Kellys will be shamed down through the generations. "Aren't they the family whose sister was no better than she should be and pretended to be dead only to come back alive? Probably looking for money." Oh, yes, I'd be the one blamed. What future for me then? Tim McShane killing me might be the best I could hope for. Go back to Chicago and I'll always be that odd old maid who disgraced her family.

I look around the square. The rain has stopped. The leaves on the linden trees are opening toward the sun that finally seems serious. Spring. Here. I'm in Paris. Living. Working. Conspiring. Maybe the Nonie Kelly who lived at 2703 South Hillock has already faded away. Gone. And before I know it, I'm singing to myself.

"Has anybody here seen Kelly?
K-E-double-L-Y
Has anybody here seen Kelly?
Have you see her smile?
Oh, her hair is red and her eyes are blue
And she's Irish through and through
Has anybody here seen Kelly?
Kelly from the Emerald Isle!"

No. Nobody can see Kelly. She's invisible now. She's free. And, you know, I hum the song all the way up to my room, my own room, my home.

"I'll do it, Maud. Take the money to Strasbourg," I say. We're in her apartment the next morning. She's packing. Going to spend Easter in Florence.

"But why?" she says. "You were so sure you wouldn't, couldn't deliver the payment."

"But now I'm dead," I say, and explain.

"Not dead," she says, "but risen. A new life. And so near Easter. Very few have the chance to be reincarnated into their next life without the bother of dying," she says as we sit down by the fire. Barry brings us glasses of sherry.

"Harvey's Bristol Cream," Maud says. "Quite a story there. Harvey was the Church of Ireland bishop in Derry and . . ."

But I interrupt her. "Please Maud, I don't think I can absorb any Irish history today."

She leans forward. "Sorry, Nora. But isn't it true if this bastard who tormented you believes you are dead, he will go away."

"Yes," I say.

"I wish I could solve my troubles with MacBride so neatly," she says. "I would adore disappearing and starting again." She sighs. "But of course, I'd have to take Iseult and Seán and Barry and Dagda, and he's such a large dog. And then there's Ireland."

I start laughing. "I'm afraid you're stuck, Maud," I say.

We go to see Father Kevin.

"Terrible news," he says, and I somehow think he's talking about my so-called demise. But of course he doesn't know about it. He has bigger worries than my deranged sister's revenge.

"The Ulster Volunteers unloaded twenty thousand rifles at Larne," he says. "Marching through every town and village in the North with guns on their shoulders. Singing 'Croppies Lie Down,' daring the British army to intervene."

"Which they won't," Maud says.

"Not at all," says Father Kevin. "I've heard that fifty or so British officers stationed at the Curragh have resigned their commissions, said they wouldn't move against the Ulster Volunteers, or accept the Home Rule Bill. Carson's setting up his own government—one for the six counties, has retired British generals training his army, and the Conservative Party leader, Bonar Law, is supporting them."

"I didn't believe Wilson," Maud says. "Didn't think soldiers would violate their oath to the king."

"I bet Henry Wilson's stirring them up," I say.

"The Ulstermen are threatening to occupy Belfast City Hall," Father Kevin says, "and then move on Dublin, take over the castle and government buildings."

"That's crazy," I say.

"Who's to stop them? You heard Wilson," Maud says. "The Unionists are determined to bring down Asquith, put in Bonar Law—start a civil war if necessary."

"All to keep Ireland from being Canada? I don't understand," I say.

But they're not listening. "We have to make our own show of strength," Father Kevin says. "Arm our volunteers! And here I am with ten thousand dollars and the agent in Strasbourg waiting."

"But I'm taking the money," I say.

I tell him the story of what Henrietta has done. He doesn't take my death as lightly as Maud did.

"A very unhappy woman, your sister," Father Kevin says.

He thinks I should write to my family, tell them the truth. But, you know, I'm already a different Nora. No ties. Not woven into the web of Chicago. No family to disgrace; no neighbors to judge me.

"I'm going," I say.

They insist that I take the Orient Express—a quick run to Strasbourg in the company of other rich travelers going farther east. An overnight trip.

"Maybe I'll stay on board and make a new life for myself in Istanbul," I say, joking of course, but they don't laugh.

"You wouldn't be the first to steal from the Cause," Maud says.

She takes me back to rue de l'Annonciation. I'll carry her Louis Vuitton train case and wear her Paul Poiret traveling gown, she decides. I'm a wealthy American tourist seeing the sights of Europe. She insists I take a parasol. The final touch. To protect my ensemble from flying cinders from the engine as great ladies do.

"Conductors and border officials always defer to the rich and titled," Maud says. "I called myself Lady Gonne when I smuggled papers to Russia for General Boulanger. A story I've told for years. Always gets a good response. A woman in danger. The best of all plots."

APRIL 12, 1914
HOLY SATURDAY
GARE DE L'EST

"Well, here I go," I say to myself. I expect to be watched but no one seems a bit interested in me as I get out of the taxi in front of the station. The driver saw me turning to look at the traffic behind us.

"No one following us," he said. "A little holiday for Madame without her husband," he added while grinning at me in the rearview mirror.

I'm not an adulterous wife, I wanted to say. I'm a secret agent. I mean, is everything about *l'amour* in this city?

But not one of the men rushing out of the station even glances at me, though Maud's Paul Poiret dress is very becoming and I carry the parasol with a certain flair if I do say so myself. I guess it's *bonjour* to *l'amour* these days.

I look up at the statues that sit on the roof of the station. Two female figures. One represents the city of Verdun, the other Strasbourg.

Very formidable women both of them. No dalliances for them. Look at the arms on the one labeled Strasbourg. Not happy that the Boche hold her city. She'd like to go into battle herself instead of having to wait to be rescued.

Well, lady, I say to her, here's one of your own sex ready to fight. And it's with a distinctly martial tread that I enter the train station.

Crowds of people coming at me—all of them seem to be coming from the direction I'm heading, getting off trains from Berlin, Budapest, Belgrade, and Istanbul too, judging from the fellow with the fez who walks toward me trailing women and children and porters carrying suitcases and baskets and long wrapped packages. And he's not the most laden.

Dozens of family stand surrounded by boxes and trunks. Fathers shout in bad French. I don't need Madame Simone's bones to feel war approaching. The French papers keep saying if Germany declares war, the army will attack the Germans on all fronts. Stop the Boche and do it fast. The crowds at the Gare de l'Est don't seem to agree.

The Orient Express lives up to Maud's description. I feel as if I'm entering the lobby of the Palmer House, only it's on wheels.

I find a porter and stand in the corridor rattling on to him in English about how lovely the train is and I'm so glad I bought a first-class ticket. Two men in dark overcoats walk past me speaking to each other in German. *"Amerikanische,"* I hear. Very disdainful. Good. I hope any other German agents or English spies on the train see me as a featherbrained American woman who has no idea she's heading into a Europe that's on the brink of mobilizing for war.

"Mobilize."

Abstract to me until the train reaches the French-German border. Through the window I see a troop of about, I don't know, a thousand German soldiers, marching along the railway tracks behind ten officers on horseback who wear helmets with pointed spikes on the top.

Are they meeting the train? I wonder. Following it?

The German police board the train and walk from compartment to compartment. I'm glad I had the sense to sit with two of the few women on the train. Mother and daughter, I'd say, and not short of money from the look of their clothes. They too have Louis Vuitton hand luggage and parasols. I'd kind of shaken Maud's train case and parasol at them as I came into the compartment. The older woman nodded me into their space but hadn't spoken to me.

The policeman who stands in the doorway of our compartment is a tubby fellow, barely able to button his uniform tunic. Not very fearsome until he looks through the window at the troop of soldiers who've stopped on the road across from the platform, then back at us and smiles. Jesus.

The policeman bows to the older woman. She hands him her passport and he takes it in both of his hands. *"Danke, danke,"* I hear.

I pick out "Baroness" from the policeman's jumble of German. I try to give the impression that I'm traveling with the women, catching the girl's eye and smiling as the policeman *"danke"*'s her mother again, hands back the passport, and turns. It doesn't work. Very stern and correct with me the policeman is, and again jerks his head toward the army troop outside. He ignores my outstretched passport. I thank God I have a proper document. This fellow would disdain Judge Craig's letter. The policeman starts asking me questions in German. Of course, I don't understand a word of it. I keep repeating "I'm going to Strasbourg for Easter" in English, but he only talks over me; then he waves away my passport.

"He wants to know where you are going," the baroness says in English.

"I told him, to Strasbourg for Easter."

Another question.

"Where do you come from?" she translates.

"Paris," I say.

Which seems to annoy him.

"Is that your birthplace?" the woman says.

"Oh dear God no, America," I say, "born and raised." Again I try to hand my passport to the policeman.

Finally, he takes it, turns the pages over, holds up the photograph, looks at me.

"American," I say again.

"Tell him what city," the woman says.

"Chicago," I say.

Another rush of German from the policeman. But finally I hear a word I recognize: Milwaukee. And then, am I hallucinating? Schlitz Beer.

"He says . . ." the baroness begins.

"It's okay, I understand."

I point to the policeman and say, "Milwaukee?" And then point to myself: "Close to Chicago, my home." Nice and slow and loud.

"He doesn't understand English," the baroness says. "No matter if you screech at him or drag out your words."

Screech? That's a little harsh, I think. But the baroness takes over and before long I find out that this fellow's brother does indeed live in Milwaukee and works as a brewer at Schlitz. The policeman gives me back my passport and he's gone. The train moves away, the army troop doesn't.

It's a good fifteen minutes before I thank the baroness.

"At first, he thought you were English. Not good to be English in Germany now," she says.

"Oh," I say. "But you speak English so well."

"I had a British governess. A most bossy woman. Typical of her countrymen. You know it's the English who are pushing the Russians to make war on us," she says.

"Oh," I repeat. Seems the safest response.

"Very disappointing," she says. "England should be our natural ally, two Saxon nations, but they feel entitled to rule the world so stir up the Russians. Of course, the French already see a Boche under every bed and if they can count on the British army, well, who knows what the fools will do!"

The young woman says something to her mother.

"She wants to know what America is like," the baroness says.

"Well, policemen don't get on trains and check your papers and scare the life out of you, I can tell you that."

And yet if that fellow worked alongside his brother at Schlitz, he'd probably be a perfectly nice man. The baroness tells me I will enjoy Strasbourg and to be sure to have a meal of *Flammekueche*, sauerkraut, and *Gerwürztraminer* wine. She has me write down the words.

"I'm extra grateful," I say, and do a little bowing and scraping myself as I leave the compartment of the train.

More soldiers at the station. I note two of the pointy-hat fellows watching the passengers as they present their tickets. But they don't stop me. Good. Step one.

Maud has made a reservation for me at a small hotel. It must be a very old part of the city because all the buildings are half-timbered like paintings of England in Shakespeare's times.

The desk clerk speaks to me in French, which suddenly sounds wonderfully familiar. "I'm just staying overnight," I say. "Going to the eleven o'clock Easter Mass."

That's where I'm to meet the agent, a shivery word, in front of the astrological clock near the Tower of the Angels, at 12:30.

I tell the clerk I'd like to find a restaurant that serves, and I read from my paper, "*Flammekueche,* sauerkraut, and *Gerwürztraminer.*"

"You mean *tart flambé,*" he says, "and *choucroute.*"

"I do?"

He tells me that Alsatian food is delicious but I cannot go out to dinner here if I am alone.

He's speaking quick French, but I get the gist. Any restaurant I go to will be full of German soldiers eating and drinking. Wouldn't I like a tray in my room with all the Alsatian specialties?

I mention the tour boat I saw offering a ride on the canals surrounding the city.

"*Non,*" he says, "*Non. Non. Beaucoup le Boche.*"

So all I see of Strasbourg is the view from my window. Even Matisse would have a hard time making something from the wall I'm facing. But the food is good.

Hard to fall asleep with the envelope with the ten-thousand-dollar draft under my pillow. But I finish the *Gewürztraminer* and that makes me nicely drowsy. Another reason to stay dead in France, I think. No wine in Chicago.

I'm up and out early. The sun is bright on the white buildings all crisscrossed with dark wooden braces. I understand why the French want this city. It is beautiful. I find the cathedral, which looks very like Notre-Dame. The same rose window, gothic arches, and the spires. But this cathedral's made of a pinky stone that seems to glow this Easter morning. Dim inside except for the paschal candle's pinpoint of flame near the altar.

Very fancy vestments on the whole load of priests who process onto the altar as the service begins. *Introibo ad altare Dei.* The Latin of the Mass is familiar but one vigorous-looking priest preaches the sermon in German. Lots of German soldiers in uniform throughout the congregation. They stare up at him. Something martial in the words booming down from the pulpit. I imagine the French military men attending Mass in Notre-Dame de Paris at this moment. Praying for peace? Probably not. Victory, whatever that means.

A crowd gathers in front of the famous astrological clock after Mass. What a stupid place to meet my contact, I think. And so typically Maud— always overly theatrical. Why not one of the dark corners in the back? No one in Strasbourg has taken the least notice of me since I left the train, but what if someone in this crowd sees an odd exchange between two strangers? Plenty of Boche soldiers around me right now. Are they looking at me? "The Germans are convinced every British tourist is a spy because, well, German tourists often do collect intelligence," Maud had told me. "They might suspect Americans too."

"So being an innocent traveler won't protect me if I'm caught?" I asked her.

"Don't get caught," she said.

So I'm very alert and determined not to be distracted by the mechanical show.

But once the figures start moving, I'm transfixed.

First an elaborately painted angel rings a bell, which makes a second angel appear. Then Death moves forward to observe a parade representing the span of life—a child, a young man, an adult, and old man pass by. After them, all twelve apostles assemble in front of Christ. The crowd claps. No one else hears the woman next to me say in careful English, "It took over two hundred and fifty years to build this cathedral." The code phrase.

"My country's not even two hundred years old yet," I say.

She hands me a guidebook.

"Perhaps you'd like to read more."

I take the book and sit down on a rush seat to look at it. She wears a hat with a veil over her face. She's older than I am, I'd say, and screens me with her body as I slip the envelope with the check into the book, close it, and hand it back to her.

"Thank you," I say. "Fascinating."

She is putting the book into her bag when I feel a tap on my shoulder. Damn. A German soldier. Officer I'd say from all the gold braid on the sleeve of his uniform.

"You are English?" Gargling the words. Not a linguist, this fellow. He carries one of those spiky helmets. Tall, not bad-looking in a stiff, stone-faced kind of way with gray hair. Too old to be just flirting with me. Trouble.

"English? Me? Good lord, no. I'm an American, General, from Milwaukee, Wisconsin. Now, don't tell me. You have a cousin in Milwaukee, right? One of the Schlitzes maybe or Pabsts? Haven't had a chance to try your beer yet, but that *Gerwürztraminer* packs quite a kick and . . ."

Of course he hasn't the slightest notion what I'm going on about but "*Gerwürztraminer*" registers. "You drink wine?" he says.

"That's why I'm in Strasbourg. Go to Mass, drink, eat *flammekueche* and sauerkraut. That's me."

Oh dear God what am I doing? Answering questions he hasn't even asked me. Making him suspicious. Which he is.

"Show me your papers! Passport, train tickets!"

Great. Well, God forgive me, but I put my hand right on his decorated sleeve and look up into his eyes and say, "Oh General, I left all my documents at the hotel! I'm such a birdbrain, I was afraid I'd lose them." Smiling like a fool.

But I can see that the woman in the veiled hat, my contact, is well away now. I squeeze his other arm, the one he's got wrapped around the spiky helmet. Am I overdoing it? He calls over another soldier. Again I play the idiot woman. This man's English is better. He repeats, "Birdbrain. What is that?" I shrug my shoulder, point to my head. "Flighty," I say.

They confer.

"You will take me to your hotel," the general says.

"Wonderful," I say, "you can look over my papers while we drink *Gerwürztraminer*."

So now I'm walking through Strasbourg on the arm of a Boche officer. The clerk at my hotel does not approve.

Mein Herr is all ready to accompany me up to my room, but I manage to settle him down at a table in the lobby.

I go up to the clerk. "Wine for the general," I say loudly. The clerk only stares.

"I'm in trouble," I whisper in French. "Got to get this fellow drunk."

The clerk nods.

"I'll be right back," I say to the general and hurry to my room.

I throw my things into Maud's train case. The Orient Express leaves at 4:00 p.m., it's 2:00 now. Have to distract this fellow and then give him the slip. How far does a Daughter of Erin have to go?

A tall silver bucket on the table, linen napkins, two glasses. The clerk's French, after all, can't keep himself from setting a lovely table.

I sit down and hand my passport to the general. The way he stares at the open page I can tell he can't read a word but he recognizes the ticket folder that says Orient Express.

"I am going to Berlin," I say, "to visit Baroness Von Stuben, perhaps you know her?" Now he's only getting every third word but the "Von" helps. And the *Gewürztraminer*, too.

He sets the helmet down and takes my hand across the table and lets out a burst of German.

"He wants to go up to your room," the desk clerk says.

"Tell him that I checked out, that my train is leaving," which the clerk does. Fluent enough German when he wants.

"But," I whisper to the general, "I have a sleeping compartment on the Orient Express. A wagon-lits privee," I say "Bed."

He understands.

Annoying that he assumes I'm a loose woman, but helpful too. He hands me back my passport.

"We go," he says.

He is surprised all I have is the train case but I tell him the rest of my luggage is on the Orient Express. He actually clicks his heels and grabs the case. I raise the parasol.

The train station is surprisingly busy for an Easter afternoon but again most travelers seem to be arriving from the east not heading there. How can I get away from this fellow?

Two Orient Express trains. One under a sign that says DEPARTURE: 17:00: BERLIN. The other 16:00: PARIS. We move toward the Berlin train.

Now the German is shouting at a conductor something to the effect that Madame, me, insists on boarding the train now. After all, it is here and so are we. But the conductor's arrogance matches the general's.

"Ah, well. *Gewürztraminer*," I say to the general, and lead him to a café. Now what? I'll have to board that Berlin train. And then . . .

"You must come with me to the baroness's home," I say, speaking very slowly. "She knows everyone. Probably even you or your wife."

I give him a pencil and paper from my bag and say, "Please write your name."

That slows him down a bit. However loose he thinks I am, he doesn't want me blabbing to some baroness with who knows what connections. He downs the wine and orders another and another and another. Now he's holding my hand as I watch the Paris train leave the station. Damn. But what could I do? Hit him with the parasol and run? Not really.

By the time "All aboard" sounds for the Berlin train he's well and truly drunk and I'm not doing so well myself. We barely make it to the train. Any thought of using my privee wagon lits is gone.

The general hands me over to the conductor, who's happy to deposit me in an empty compartment without checking my ticket.

It's two hours and a nap later that I face the music.

The conductor assumes that I'm a stupid woman too tipsy to board the right train. He puts me off at Lucenay, and I doze in the waiting room until the Paris-bound night train puffs in.

Still enough *Gewürztraminer* on my breath to make my story of getting on the wrong train convincing and the conductor takes my ticket and says something like "Sleep it off, lady" in French.

Almost dawn when we arrive back in the Gare de l'Est, drizzling onto Madame Strasbourg atop the station.

"I did it," I tell her. And saved my virtue though I have a terrible hangover. Not the first one to drink for Ireland I think.

Maud's away in Florence so I go to the Irish College. Father Kevin is delighted with me. "And just in the nick of time, Nora. England's forbidden the importation of any weapons into Ireland. Typical, they let our enemies arm themselves and make it illegal for us to defend ourselves. Thank God, you got the money there on time. The deal will be done, the guns bought. Now, to get them to Ireland."

"Don't look at me," I say. "I've hung up my parasol."

He laughs. "The *Asgard* is ready. But they're going to have to evade the British navy."

Oh, great, I think. I've taken all this risk and now the whole mission depends on a crippled woman in a sailboat. Well, at least Peter will be pleased I think.

"When will Professor Keeley arrive?" I ask.

"Postponed again, I'm afraid. Had a wire from Louvain. Professor Keeley's helping the university secure their library and move the most valuable books and manuscripts. When war comes, looting will be the real danger."

When war comes, not "if" anymore. But when.

I can't resist telling Madame Simone that I've visited Strasbourg. "I wanted to be in the cathedral on Easter," I say. I tell her how beautiful it was, lovely singing, the music, the pink stone.

"Now you understand *la revanche*," she says.

Very few tourists come to Paris throughout the rest of that spring, afraid of marching armies.

Maud's away for the whole month of May and there's no sign of Peter Keeley. Father Kevin tells me "patience is a virtue" when I see him at Mass, which I find annoying. "Old cultures know how to wait," he says. "While you Americans . . ."

I interrupt him.

"Get to work."

I do.

Madame Simone has no clients, but I'll solicit some of my own, I think. I station myself with Louis at the Eiffel Tower. A gray-haired fellow with a bulging stomach approaches me and says he'd like a very special tour of Paris and winks. The German general all over again. I tell the fellow to get lost, which makes Louis laugh.

I decide to try to get work as a clerk in a bookshop and contact first Adrienne Monnier and then Sylvia Beach. But neither one has been able to open her shop.

"Want a secretarial position?" Sylvia asks me. "Edith Wharton is looking for someone."

And so I go to see the famous Edith Wharton, despite the fact that I can't type or take shorthand. If only Mame were here. A whiz on the typewriter, I think, and feel a kind of pinch in my heart. Awful that I'll never see any of them again. Last week, I dreamed we were sitting on Aunt Kate Larney's porch sipping lemonade while the boys drank their beer, just as it was the night of Tim McShane. Only in the dream, his Oldsmobile just drives by. I never take up with him. I woke up wishing the dream were the reality.

Edith Wharton lives in a grand apartment off the Faubourg Saint-Germain. Very classy altogether, but then she has family money. Couldn't live like this from selling books. Now here's a woman who has arranged life to suit herself, not derailed by passion, I think as her maid shows me into a sitting room.

I seat myself on what's certainly an antique sofa, from one of the King Louis periods, I'd say. I pop up when Edith Wharton enters. Pleasant enough to me though a bit stiff and not pleased at all when I tell her I can't type but am willing to learn.

She shakes her head and asks how do I plan to stay in Paris if I can't support myself. I say I have to find some way because I don't want to go home.

"None of us do," she says, and then out of the blue tells me she's managed to settle her husband in Boston and is going to live here on her own forever.

"I think, Nora, life can be a tightrope or a feather bed. I chose the tightrope."

"Well," I say, "that gives us something in common."

I report back to Sylvia, who tells me Edith has just taken a lover at age forty-nine, probably her first real sexual experience.

"Who?" I ask.

"Some friend of Henry James," she says.

Never too late, I think, and wonder if Peter Keeley will ever return.

15

JUNE 1914

"I have an opportunity for you," Madame Simone says to me.

June now. I'm really worried. My savings are almost gone. No clients are coming to Madame Simone and fewer tourists are on the streets of Paris. The whole world seems to be holding its breath, listening for the first heavy treads of marching armies.

"Jeanne Paquin," she says.

Madame Simone approves of Jeanne Paquin. Unlike Chanel, she is a designer in the grand manner, like Poiret and Charles Worth. I admire her fashions, too. The elaborate gowns are just simple enough to be beautiful. She and Madame Simone worked together as dressmakers at the House of Rouff as young women.

"I saw Jeanne yesterday. She wants photographs of her clothes to appear in *La Gazette du Bon Ton*," Madame Simone says.

I know the magazine. Very fancy, very expensive, with color illustrations. And now, photographs.

"She wants to hire a photographer. I recommended you."

"Thank you, Madame, but I'm not a good enough to . . . I mean, I'm only starting, I . . ."

"Make that your asset," she says. "Say you have a fresh eye, new ideas.

Besides, all the men will be fighting soon. Not bad to have a woman re-
placement handy."

Fresh eye, new ideas, I repeat to myself as I walk to the House of Paquin
on the rue de la Paix. Her shop is right next to the big boys'. No nonsense
about Jeanne Paquin, Madame told me. And no small talk either.

"Be very direct with her," she says. "Be American."

That achingly blue sky blesses Paris only in early summer. Like Chicago's short sweet season before the heat and humidity of July and August
muffle the city. No Lake Michigan here, of course, so no cool breezes.
Stop, Nora. I must not let myself dream about a city that I'll never see
again. What did Gertrude Stein say? "America is my country but Paris is
my hometown." Me too, Gertrude.

"Both she and Alice have gone to Spain, packed away their pictures,"
Madame Simone said. "They think the Boche will not bother Spain." So
much for defending the old hometown. But then, lots of French people
have left Paris, beginning the long *vacance* early enough to avoid the Germans. Gabrielle Chanel is waiting for the vacationers in Biarritz. I suppose
even during a war the rich will still want new clothes.

I follow a maid up a stairway past the hushed rooms where clients view
Madame Paquin's creations. Polished marble floors here, Oriental carpets,
and on the walls, enlarged illustrations of Madame Paquin's designs. Farther up the staircase, elegance turns utilitarian. Women bend over sewing
machines, their feet ride the treadles, marching in place. Madame's office
is on the top floor. A skylight lets in that blue sky. Even here, in the outer
waiting room, I can see the yellow-green tops of chestnut trees.

I don't wait long. Madame Paquin has strong features. Her dark hair's
dressed in elaborate curls. She sits at a desk that might have come from
Versailles, wearing a dove gray jacket with tucks along a bodice that even
Madame Simone couldn't copy.

And she's not alone. A fellow sits on a settee across from her against the
wall. He stands when I come in. A French gentleman, I think. Though his
suit's a bit big on him. And when I look down at his shoes, I wonder. Madame Simone says shoes tell all. His shoes are wingtips like my brother
Mike wears. But I'm not going to start thinking of Mike now.

"Sit down, sit down," Jeanne Paquin says. "Now, Madame Simone tells
me you are her client's photographer and that you have a sense of women
and clothes."

"Well," I say, "I have been taking pictures of her clients in her designs."

Jeanne Paquin stops me. "I do not wish to talk about Esther's 'designs.'"

I have to speak up. "Madame Simone doesn't copy you. You are a great couturier who inspires her and . . ."

"Didn't you hear me? We are not talking about Esther. I understand but I do not applaud."

The young man pretends he's not listening. Polite, well-bred, despite his shoes.

Jeanne Paquin points to a magazine open on her desk. It's *Art et Décoration*, another very fancy French publication. She pushes the magazine over to me. I see a full-page photograph, very dramatic, of a woman in a gown by Paul Poiret.

"What do you think?"

"It's wonderful," I say. "A famous photograph. The lighting, the placement of the woman makes it look like a painting. And did you know the photographer's an American?"

I stop. Of course, she knows.

"I'd like pictures of my collection *comme ça*," Jeanne Paquin says.

"Then hire the photographer. He lives in Paris, though I've never met him," I say.

"I have offered him," Madame Paquin says, "and have been refused." She looks at the fellow sitting on the settee, who speaks to me.

"I told her I just can't. I'm getting frantic letters from my mother, terrified about the war. Everybody in Milwaukee's afraid their neighbors will turn on them if there is war with Germany. Even though we're from Luxembourg, everyone assumes we're German."

"Milwaukee?" I say. "So you're . . ."

He sticks out his hand.

"Eddie Steichen. Nice to meet you. I didn't get your name."

"I'm . . ." But who am I? Nora Kelly from Chicago? Not anymore. If this fellow's going home to Milwaukee, he'll be passing through Chicago. Who knows who he knows?

"I'm Kelly," I say. "I only use the one name professionally." Sounds lame, even to me, but he smiles.

"And from Chicago," he says.

Oh, dear God, he knows.

"I can tell from your accent. Nobody flattens those 'a's quite the same way."

I smile. After all, there are thousands and thousands of Kellys in Chicago.

"And you're staying here?"

"Yes, I am," I say.

"But won't your family be concerned? Looking for you?"

And then doesn't he stand up and sing the first line of my song? "Has anybody here seen Kelly?"

Flummoxed altogether is Jeanne Paquin, especially when I get up and join in "K-E-double-L-Y. Has anybody here seen Kelly? / Have you seen her smile." We sing together:

"Oh, her hair is red and her eyes are blue. / And she's Irish through and through. / Has anybody here seen Kelly? Kelly from the Emerald Isle."

We laugh and applaud each other. I do love Americans, I think. I'm sure Jeanne Paquin is going to throw out both of us, but she more or less pretends nothing's happened, and we sit down.

I say to Eddie, "You know I can't replicate that," pointing to the magazine. "I mean, you're a real artist."

"Show us some examples of your work," Madame Jeanne says.

"I couldn't, I'm . . ."

"Come on, Kelly, an artist can't be humble," Eddie says.

I open the envelope that I've been clutching and take out some of the shots of my ladies taken at the Eiffel Tower. The Distortions, as Louis calls them.

Ed picks up the photo where Mrs. Lawrence seems to have Paris at her feet, and walks over to the window. Damn, he thinks they're only snapshots made with one of those Brownie box cameras that every American seems to have now.

"What was your light source?" he asks.

"The sun," I say.

"No fill, no reflectors?"

I shake my head.

"Well, Kelly, you have an eye and imagination."

I wait for the "but" as Jeanne Paquin grabs the photographs.

"Impossible," she says. "I don't even see the dress. I do not wish to sell the Tour Eiffel."

"Oh, I like Kelly's photographs," Eddie says. "See? This woman is having an adventure, flying high before she settles down in Utica."

"Boston," I say.

"Look how relaxed she is. Not easy to get that natural look. What other photographs do you have?"

"Well, I did a series of shots of Notre-Dame. Took them at all different times of day. Got some great shadows."

He doesn't say anything.

"You don't like cathedrals?"

"I love cathedrals," he says. "But I'd say your strength is people, regular people, women probably. Show the faces that others ignore."

Now we're speaking English but Jeanne Paquin seems to follow us. She knows "ignore."

"Ignore?" she says. "I do not want my fashions ignored."

And he tries to explain but within minutes, the interview is over.

"So, I'd better learn to type," I say to Eddie Steichen as we walk down the rue de la Paix. "At least I could get some kind of a job."

"Don't give up on photography," he says.

"But no one will pay for pictures of ordinary people. Even the most fashionable outfit has to be worn by a famous actress to make it into a magazine," I say. "That's why Maud portrays ancient queens."

Of course, he doesn't understand what I'm talking about.

"It seems to me all these Europeans, even the Irish, assume that only the upper classes have any real value. They worship noble families with royalty at the top of the heap. Even some so-called republicans," I say.

"Oh, come on, Kelly," Eddie says, "Frenchmen killed each other for equality, fraternity, and liberty."

"And now, in the very place where that happened, is a whole industry caters to the elite and makes them the models for all women," I say. Quoting Stefan, wherever he is.

Eddie doesn't reply.

"You know what should happen, Eddie? These designers should make clothes the way Henry Ford turns out cars. Hundreds of thousands of dresses, cheap enough so that regular women can afford them. That's equality, liberty, and sorority."

"But women's clothes are mass-produced now," he says.

"Cheap stuff," I say. "Inferior fabrics, bad fit. No, I mean beautiful clothes, designed for American women who don't think you have to be a blue blood to want to look nice." I stop. "Then again, maybe women should just wear some kind of a uniform, like Gertrude Stein's brown habit. Forget fashion entirely."

Now I have lost him. But a nice well-brought-up Milwaukee boy is Eddie Steichen. So he offers to buy me a coffee or a glass of wine.

I tell him, "No, I have to report to Madame Simone on the interview with Jeanne Paquin."

"Well, at least stop by my studio and see some of my work. I'm packing up to leave."

And now I wonder just how well-brought up he is. So I say, "And is your wife in Paris with you? I'd love to meet her."

But he laughs. "Don't worry, I really do have something to show you."

And he does. His studio is one large room off the boulevard Saint-Germain. He hands me a copy of a magazine called *Camera Work*. Pages and pages of wonderful photographs, many of ordinary people.

"I thought you'd like this one," he says, pointing to a photograph. "It's Gertrude Käsebier's work."

"Gee whiz" is all I can think of to say as I look at the Indian who is staring back at me. Talk about getting beyond appearances into the soul.

"Gertrude did portraits of the Sioux Indians in Buffalo Bill's Wild West show when they were at the World's Fair in Chicago," he says.

"But I was there," I say. "I'll never forget looking down at the tepees from the Ferris wheel."

"Me either," he says. "Funny how many of us used a camera for the first time there at the Fair."

"Yes," I say, "I remember my brother Mike rented a Kodak camera to take our pictures."

"And look how far we've come," he says. "A gallery in New York's exhibiting our work and even manages to sell the photos. Gertrude got a hundred dollars for one of hers."

"This one, maybe?" I say, and push the magazine over to him. Two oxen turn their faces toward the camera. One has a yoke and the other, a muzzle. The photo is entitled "Marriage."

He laughs.

"Actually it was another shot. This one, 'Manger.' Religion still sells. Even in the twentieth century."

"Come on, Eddie. Think of Michelangelo, da Vinci, all of the masters—saints and the Bible were their bread and butter."

"Stieglitz hates her for becoming commercial."

"Who's he?" I ask.

"A fellow who's determined to have photographers accepted as fine artists," Eddie says.

Fine artists. Titled ladies. Noble families.

"That's not for me," I say. "I'm a regular girl from Chicago. I'd like to take pictures but . . ."

"Oh, come on, we're all from somewhere. How many regular girls are living in Paris and trying to be artists?"

"An artist. Me? No. I just need to earn money," I say.

"So did Gertrude Käsebier. And she does. Turn back to the Indian. Look at his face. See the way he stares at the camera? Can't you hear him thinking, 'I fought the whole United States cavalry and now I'm reduced to being a show business Indian pretending to attack the stagecoach so the palefaces can scare themselves'?"

"Yes, I see that," I say. "But something else, too. He's chuckling to himself. 'They're paying me.'"

Eddie turns a page. "Gertrude relaxes her subjects the way you do. See that mother and daughter? The family at the window? Nothing stiff or contrived there."

"Is that what art does?" I ask. "Makes people see something in a different way?"

"I'd say so," he says.

"Henri Matisse told me something like that," I say.

"You know Henri?" he says.

I tell him about our meeting at the Steins'. And he says that Matisse shows his work in the same gallery where Gertrude's photos are displayed.

"And he doesn't mind his paintings mixing with photographs?"

"He's delighted," Eddie said.

I tell him about the "Hairy Mattress" incident in Chicago and he laughs.

"When artists can't laugh at themselves, we're done. Now, show me more of your photographs," he says.

I spread out the ones that I've taken of Molly Childers, of Alice Milligan and Alice Stopford Green and the other conspirators.

"Now, these faces are very interesting. Something going on in these women, some purpose. These aren't casual tourists."

I fan my photos in front of him.

"Yes, my first impression is correct. You have a special talent. Wait a minute."

Eddie goes into a closet and comes out carrying a box. He sets it down on the table in front of me. There's a drawing of an Indian chief on the top.

"More Buffalo Bill?" I say.

"Not exactly."

He lifts out a camera. First, I think it's a Kodak box camera. Oh, great, I think, all I am to him is an amateur. But then he pulls the camera apart and shows me the accordion-like center.

"It's a Seneca," he says, "made by a company in Rochester that was once part of Kodak. But now they're independent. They manufacture amateur cameras, but this one's for professionals. It's got a good lens and the film's light-sensitive. It'd be good for you."

"Hmmm," I say. "And are they expensive?"

How much can I come up with?

"This one isn't," he says. "I'd like to give it to you."

"Oh, thanks. But I can't."

"Take it," he says, and thrusts it into my hands.

So light. I could carry this anywhere.

"I have too much stuff already," Eddie says. "And I can get another one in New York. Just got their latest catalog. New models coming out."

He turns around, opens a drawer, and holds out a thick paper catalog to me. I set the camera down to look. The cover shows an Indian chief holding the Seneca camera. Inside, more braves and Indian princesses urge photographers to give this camera a try.

"Why Indians?" I say to Eddie.

"Why not?" he says. "Photography's still a novelty. I suppose, the noble savage is as good a pitch man as any."

"The noble savage," I say. That's how the English see the Irish. Do leprechauns advertise British tea? I wonder. Insulting. But what the heck? I do like this camera. If I had this, I could have taken much more interesting photographs of Molly Childers and the three Alices. Dear God, Maud would love to pose for me. No end to what she'd come up with.

"The best thing about this camera is that you can catch your subjects unaware," Eddie says. I think of the moments I have observed—Maud stroking Iseult's hair; Seán crossing his eyes; Peter Keeley bent over a manuscript; Father Kevin stretching his legs out to the fire. Revealing. But, is there money to be made from the ordinary?

Eddie puts the camera back into the box. "Somebody needs to photograph what's going to be happening in Paris during the next few years, when this war really gets going."

When again. Not if.

"The city deserves to be remembered as it was," he says.

"Oh God, Eddie, you sound so glum."

"I am," he says.

"No job," I say to Madame Simone. I get back to her studio just as she's closing up. "But I do have my very own camera."

I start to show it to her when we hear shouting from the street. We open the window. A newspaper boy calls out: *"Archduke Ferdinand assassiné. Austria et Serbia en guerre."*

I run down and buy a paper and bring it up to Madame Simone.

"Imbeciles!" she says. She tells me a Serbian student has killed the crown prince of the Austro-Hungarian Empire.

"And what does he accomplish?" she says. "Only war."

And I remember how Maud told me that she and MacBride had gone on their honeymoon to Gibraltar because King Edward was going to be there.

"We planned to shoot him and then die together," she told me.

"A great way to start a marriage," I said to her.

And what if they had succeeded? I imagine the British army punishing Ireland the way Austria will punish Serbia.

"Serbia can't really fight long," I say. "A short war, maybe."

"Russia is allied with Serbia," Madame Simone says. "And France with Russia. And the Germans with Austria."

"But really, Madame, won't they all see this is the action of one crazy student? Look at us Americans, when John Wilkes Booth killed Lincoln, we didn't restart the Civil War. Surely, some of these politicians have sense."

"The Boche," she says. "The Boche will march. You will see."

Now I'm devouring the newspapers like everyone else, parsing the French as best I can. Surely, the whole world won't go to war because a nineteen-year-old student goes a little nuts. Lots of negotiations happening and much speculation about the outcome. The Serbians are eating humble pie but the Austrians aren't satisfied because the Germans are backing them up. Go ahead, grab Serbia, they've told the Austrians. We'll help you. And if the Russians don't like it, let them try to fight us. So what if the French join in? Our army's strong enough to defeat them all. The German chancellor was heard to say, "Might as well have the war now before the enemy gets any stronger."

❦

Lots of prayers for peace from the altar at the Irish chapel this last Sunday in July. Warm and sticky, one of those days when breathing's an effort. I'm fanning myself with a holy card as I sit in my pew. Still, no Peter, and Father Kevin hasn't heard a word. Great. It doesn't take a military genius to look at a map and see that Belgium is stuck right between France and Germany. I think of the German soldiers in Strasbourg, those spiked helmets on, with Peter at Louvain in their path. One good thing. Father Rector and a number of priests have decided not to return to Paris from their annual leave in Ireland. Father Kevin's in charge.

When I come back from Communion, I hold the wafer in my mouth, shut my eyes, and do some very serious praying. I'll give up sweets, I tell Jesus present inside me. Wine even. What else? Sex? Not much point in giving up something I don't have. OK, I'll forgive Henrietta. I'll stay dead without complaining. As I search for more things to promise, I sense someone slipping into the pew beside me. I half open my eyes. Jesus, Mary, and Joseph. Him. Peter Keeley. I gulp and swallow the host before I can say a proper thank-you.

Talk about the power of prayer. And he smiles at me, right there in church. The reserved Professor Keeley smiles at me.

After Mass, I invite Father Kevin and Peter to have lunch with me at L'Impasse. Please. Please, I say, a celebration. Suddenly, I'm sure God's not going to let war come after all.

We walk along the rue de Rivoli. Banks of rainclouds move slowly over the scene. We need a thunderstorm to cool things off, lighten the heavy air.

As we walk, I'm bursting to tell Peter how I collected money for the rifles then carried it to Strasbourg, and how I outsmarted the German general and . . .

But I know to keep quiet.

I only say, "Have our friends the Childers started their sailing trip yet?"

But neither one replies. Both stare at everyone who passes us, though I doubt if that woman and her son are secret agents.

Finally, Father Kevin says the British navy's blockading German ports. Makes any travel difficult.

I imagine Molly Childers and Mary Spring-Rice stuck with a yacht full of rifles at some dock in Germany. Millions of men and machines mobilizing all over Europe and we're relying on a small yacht sailed by middle-aged women. Is this another Irish uprising dead at birth? I wonder.

Not many in L'Impasse. Most restaurants are already closed for the *grande vacance*.

Monsieur Collard stays open through August to serve the merchants at the Market Saint-Antoine, which never closes. Monsieur's glad to see us. Madame looks up from behind the *caisse*, which takes up one side of the tiny space, and nods. I tell Father Kevin and Peter that the Collards sell fodder, too, and that during the week, horses and wagons crowd the impasse Gué-ménée. But all is quiet this Sunday afternoon. Monsieur Collard leads us to a table on the sidewalk under the awning where there is an anemic breeze.

"I never order," I say. "I let Monsieur choose for me," which makes Monsieur Collard smile.

Father Kevin nods.

But Peter asks about the steak *pommes frites*. Monsieur Collard tells him, "Restaurant L'Impasse serves the best in all of Paris and therefore, in the world."

"My mother always had a bit of beef waiting for us on Reek Sunday," Peter says, "after we climbed Croagh Patrick, the Reek."

"Oh," I say.

"You don't know what he means, do you?" Father Kevin says.

"I don't."

"In Ireland, the last Sunday in July is called Reek Sunday, the start of the festival of Lughnasa, the harvest celebration on August first," Father Kevin says.

"Lughnasa," I repeat.

Some vague memory of one of Granny Honora's stories coming back.

"Named for the ancient god Lugh," Peter says.

"Actually, it was Lugh's Mountain where St. Patrick fasted," Father Kevin says.

"Wait, St. Patrick and a pagan god? Together?" I ask.

"On speaking terms at least," Peter says.

Whatever that means.

Just then, Monsieur approaches with the dinner. Perfect cold salmon fillets for Father Kevin and me, plates of vegetables. Peter's steak is piled high with *pommes frites*. Still can't get use to these thin cuts of meat.

"Someday," I say to Peter and Father Kevin, "we'll go to Chicago for a real steak, thick and juicy."

Silence. Peter sets down his knife and fork. Stares at me. What did I say? Can he read my mind?

"Oh. Look, I didn't mean . . ." Jesus. All those daydreams about Peter and me escaping into a life in Chicago, Roddy McCorley and his sweetheart alive and well in Bridgeport, are even more impossible now that I'm officially dead. Though if I did show up with a real Irishman and a patriot to boot, maybe I could explain away my demise.

Father Kevin breaks the silence.

"I'd love to see Chicago," he says. "Half my family's in America somewhere."

Peter doesn't say anything. I wonder, has Father Kevin told him about my sister declaring me dead? Catch yourself on, Honora Bridget Kelly. The man has been away a year and a half. He's no interest in you. He's treating you as if you were a stranger.

Have some pride, I tell myself, and say in a very formal tone, "Father Kevin tells me you found treasures in Louvain. Any of them as valuable as the Kelly fragment?"

And Peter actually puts his fingers to his lips and he shushes me though we're yards away from the French mama and papa and two teenage sons at the table across from us. Strange. No conversation at their table. Maybe they are listening to us. Then I realize these two teenage boys will be called up when the French army does mobilize.

Finally Peter starts talking, telling me about the Catholic University of Louvain's incredible collection of 300,000 books.

"Hundreds of medieval manuscripts," he says, "thousands of incunabula."

"Which are?" I ask.

"Books published before Gutenberg's printing press," Father Kevin puts in.

"Rare?" I ask.

Peter nods. "Invaluable."

And I blurt out, "Oh gosh, Peter, what will happen to the books if the German army marches through Belguim?"

"I can't see them attacking a library," Peter says. "The Germans respect scholarship. Remember, I knew them in Dublin."

"But it won't be professors in the ranks. If those books are valuable, better get them out of there," I say.

"Some we have sent away. But as I said, there's hundreds of thousands."

Monsieur Collard approaches, carrying a wine bucket. He sets it on the table.

"Rose from Provence," he says.

"Grand," says Father Kevin.

Monsieur Collard pours the wine in Father Kevin's glass. Waits. But Father Kevin says, "I'm sure it's delicious."

"Perfect to toast your return, Peter," he says as Monsieur Collard fills our glasses.

What do I do?

I can't break a vow that's only an hour old. But Father Kevin is raising his glass and gestures for us to do the same.

"As Belloc says, 'Wherever the Catholic sun doth shine, There's always laughter and good red wine. At least I've always found it so. *Benedicamus Domino!*' Let's drink to friendship, to Lugh and St. Patrick and that sense will prevail."

What can I do? I raise my glass, touch his. "Amen," I say.

"*Sláinte,*" says Peter.

He reaches across and our three glasses are joined. We drink. God will understand, I think. And I definitely won't have dessert.

Father Kevin keeps going on about Belloc. Peter smiles and turns to me. "Another of Father Kevin's friends."

"Interesting man," Father Kevin says. "French father, English mother, who was converted to Catholicism by Cardinal Manning. Very much the English gentleman but a true Catholic; a bit like Arthur Capel. A good fellow, comes to college when he's in Paris; brought that friend of his, Chesterton, one time, who told me that he's thinking of coming over to Rome."

Peter clears his throat.

"You don't approve, Peter?" Father Kevin says.

"I don't have much patience with English Catholics who think religion's all about building private chapels and kissing bishops' rings. No sense of how we Irish held on to the faith through generations of persecution by the English."

Not worried about that French family hearing this now.

"Be fair Peter, Belloc and Chesterton both spoke up for Home Rule and Parliament did pass it."

"And will never implement it," he says.

They're talking louder now and one of the French boys looks over, probably thinks we're English tourists. Father Kevin notices and smiles at him.

"Poor fellow," he says to us. "God only knows what's in store for them. I performed three marriages yesterday. Every Frenchman between eighteen and forty can be conscripted."

"Well, at least they'll have a wife at home, writing to them, praying for them," I say.

"A very strong impulse to marry. Ever hear of why the famous St. Valentine was martyred?" Father Kevin asks.

Peter and I shake our heads.

"The emperor had forbidden any of his soldiers to wed and Valentine was secretly performing marriages. He died so that others could have love."

A very romantic interpretation. "I think it's selfish for a man going to war to tie a woman down like that," Peter says.

"I disagree," Father Kevin says. And then to me, "Peter and I have been arguing about marriage this morning."

"Now, Kevin, stop," Peter says.

"Please," Father Kevin says, "I'd like Nora's opinion." He leans toward me.

"Peter thinks a man can't propose marriage unless he's well fixed financially. And I say that nowadays, with women working, marriage is much more of a partnership. Look at a woman like you. You can earn a living. Love finds a way. Even Valentine himself fell in love with the daughter of his jailer, left her a note when he was killed. 'Love, Your Valentine.' Remember, priests could marry in those days, which would still be a good idea. Valentine's buried in Ireland, you know," he says.

Why am I not surprised?

"And then there's the Brehon laws," Father Kevin says.

"Easy now, Kevin," Peter says. "Don't drag in laws that are a thousand years old and only applied to noble families."

"But sound principles in them," Father Kevin says. "Perfectly fine for a man with little substance to marry a woman with more. We've never been a materialistic people, really. Even old Gerald of Wales, no fan of ours, observed that for the Irish 'the greatest wealth is to enjoy liberty.'"

Wait a minute, is he talking about Peter and me? I look down and start shoveling in the salmon, take a swig of wine, kick Father Kevin under the table, but he won't stop.

"I come from a family of matchmakers. *'Basadóir'* in Irish," he says. "Sometimes, unlikely couples need a bit of a push especially in these desperate times. Important for a man and woman who love each other to declare it."

Now he's going too far.

Peter pushes his plate away. "I really must get back. I'm expecting a cable." He takes a few bills from his pocket.

"No, no, Peter. I want to pay," I say.

But he puts the money on the table and walks out.

"I'm sorry, Nora. I thought . . ." Father Kevin starts. But I shake my head and I finish my meal. I don't eat the profiteroles.

A flash of lightning, followed seconds later by thunder, as Father Kevin and I cross the Petit Pont, hurrying, trying to beat the rain. I've never let myself be angry at a priest before but, Jesus Christ, I'm mad now. Father Kevin's ruined any chance I have even to be Peter's friend. I would have stomped off, but I have the only umbrella and I can't let a seventy-something man get drenched.

We're at the Panthéon now and turning in to rue des Irlandais when the first drops hit. I get the umbrella up and hold it over the two of us. Not far to go, but then a strong gust of wind blows against the umbrella. I can't hold the handle. Father Kevin reaches up to help me but a second blast gets between us and turns the umbrella inside out just as the deluge begins. We're soaked in seconds. My hat melts around my face. My skirt and blouse are plastered against me. Even my shift's wet. Father Kevin's cassock hangs on him, water dripping from it.

"We have to run for it," he says, and takes off up the street to the college entrance faster than a man his age should be able to move with me right behind him. He swings open the wooden doors and we're in the hallway.

I start laughing. Hard to stay mad. The young priest on porter duty steps out, looks at us.

"What the . . . ?"

"All's well, Father James," Father Kevin says. "We'll be in the visitors' parlor."

Not many priests around. Most of them still in Ireland for the summer. Only a few of the youngest seminarians.

"There's a message for you, Father Kevin," Father James says. "Professor Keeley wants to see you as soon as you return. Urgent."

Father Kevin goes off and I head for the parlor.

No fire in the little room today and I'm not about to lower my soaking self onto one of their fancy chairs. Hope Father Kevin finds some kind of nonclerical towel around here somewhere. But it's not Father Kevin who comes into the parlor but Peter Keeley, who strides over to me and takes my two hands.

"Oh, Nora, we did it! We did it! The guns, they landed them at Howth this afternoon. The volunteers unloaded them. The countess was there and her Fianna. They set those rifles on their shoulders and marched into Dublin. And no one stopped them. The army came out but could do nothing. Stand up to a bully and he backs down."

"Gee whiz," I say. "Great! Wonderful!"

And then Peter hugs me, grabs the whole wet mess and pulls me close. He'd have kissed me too if Father Kevin hadn't come in at that moment.

"Peter told you then?" Father Kevin says.

"He did."

"Imagine! The Childerses and Mary Spring-Rice sailed that boat in with the help of two Donegal sailors. As they approached the shore, it was Molly herself at the wheel of the *Asgard*, strapped in and holding firm."

The Irish navy and Boy Scouts the army of Ireland. Great.

I think of those helmeted German troops and imagine those boys at L'Impasse, the hundreds of thousands of other French conscripts, the millions

of men of the Russian army, and regiment upon regiment of British soldiers. All of Europe massed for war. What chance for the Irish? And yet,
and yet, we'd gotten through the blockade, defied the British government
and armed at least nine hundred of the volunteers.

"Hurrah," I say to Peter, "Hurrah for Molly and the Alices and Mary
Spring-Rice and Maud and Constance and you and Father Kevin and me,
too. Hurrah, hurrah!"

I reach out for Peter's and Father Kevin's hands. I sing a bit of Uncle
Patrick's song: "'A nation once again. A nation once again.'" The two men
join me. "'And Ireland, long a province, be a nation once again!'"

"Amen," Father Kevin says. "Amen." And only then does he hand me
the towel and a bundle. "Here, dry off. Change in the cloakroom there."

Now I'm shivering, my teeth chattering. In the cloakroom, I take off my
wet clothes and rub myself dry, then open the bundle. What? I shake out
the garment. Jesus Christ. I can't wear this. But I do. I step into the black
cassock and button it up. A bit tight over my bosom but it covers me well
enough. The soft serge feels good against my skin. And I'm not about to
put my soaked shirt and blouse back on.

I walk into the parlor, where Peter is alone, crouched down trying to
start a fire.

"Father Kevin went to find us a drink," he says, then turns around.
"Dear God," he says.

I trace a sign of the cross in the air. *Dominus vobiscum,* I say to Peter.

He stands up and stares at me.

"Now, don't be offended," I say. "It's Father Kevin who gave it to me.
And it's a skirt after all."

"I'm not offended," he says. "I'm . . ."

Quiet now, he speaks not much above a whisper.

"Here we are," Father Kevin says, carrying a bottle of Jameson and three
glasses.

"You look very nice, Nora," he says to me. "You'd make a lovely priest."

"Well," I say, "after we get the vote and straighten out the governments,
why not women priests?"

But if truth be told, I'm not feeling one bit priestly. I'm still hearing
Peter's voice: "I'm not offended, I'm . . ."

I'm . . . what?

A wonderful giggly evening. With most of the priests away, there are no formal meals and the three of us eat bread and cheese. I toast the slices over the fire. Easy to bend down, feeling very unbound in this cassock, no corset, no underclothes. My clothes dry near the fire. Feels good to be so unconfined. No wonder Gertrude Stein likes to dress as a Carmelite. I wonder, could I interest Gabrielle Chanel in a vestment collection? I say this out loud to Father Kevin and Peter.

"Maybe a surplice for evening wear," Father Kevin says.

I find that hilarious and even Peter contributes.

"A soutane around the waist," he says.

Which stops me laughing, surprised he even knows I have a waist. We spend the rest of the time convincing ourselves that there will be no war and that the British will keep faith and enforce Home Rule.

I say to them, "The armies will all line up at the borders and the generals will send planes up to observe and they'll see acres and acres of armed men and they'll all report that the soldiers will just bump in to each other and go nowhere. So what's the point?"

Now, I've had a few whiskeys. Glad I'd promised no wine to God and left spirits out of the bargain. Sure He won't mind. Not on the day Ireland faced down England. Everything does seem possible. Ireland free. The world at peace. And Peter and me . . . married? Well, why not? With Father Kevin pushing us along, our own personal cupid. I imagine Father Kevin, his face on a cherub's body with a bow and arrow, like the image decorating a Valentine's Day card, and I start laughing so hard, Peter hits me on the back, thinking I'm choking. His hand feels so solid. The rest of the world goes away.

Almost nine o'clock when the rain stops. My clothes are dry enough and me sober enough after plenty of cups of strong tea to go back into the cloakroom and reassemble myself.

We walk out into the hallway together and I'm sure Peter will offer to see me home. But as the three of us stand there, there's a knock at the hall door. No porters, so Peter pulls on the iron handle.

A messenger stands there. "Cable," he says.

Sunday-night delivery. Somebody's paid a fortune, I think, as Peter hands the boy a franc.

"For me." Peter says.

"More news?" asks Father Kevin.

Peter nods.

"Casualties," he says, and hands the cable to Father Kevin.

"The soldiers who let the volunteers pass were the King's Own Scottish Borderers," Peter says to me. "They met a crowd of Dublin people at Bachelors Walk who started to jeer at the Tommies. The soldiers shot into the crowd. They killed a woman and two men, wounded thirty-eight right in the center of Dublin. These weren't Irish Volunteers or members of the Citizen Army, only regular Dubliners."

"Damn," I say. "Damn, damn, damn."

I put on my damp clothes and leave. Father Kevin and Peter don't seem to notice.

Two days later Austria declares war on Serbia. Russia mobilizes. Germany calls up its troops and on the first of August declares war on Russia. The German army moves into Luxembourg and, on August 3rd, Germany declares war on France.

Bands of young fellows head for the Gare l'Est singing the Marseillaise "Marchons, Marchons," a great song for making fighting seem glorious, fun almost. I run into a group of them as I'm on my way to the Irish College.

One tall young man is waving his necktie like a flag. I want to reach out and grab his sleeve: "Don't go. Don't make your mother walk up and down through rows of graves looking for yours." He feels me staring at him and stops. Now, tell him. But I don't. Instead, I take the Seneca out of my bag and ask if I can take a picture of him.

And he's only too delighted, calls out for his friends to wait. They cluster together. A soccer team posing for the victory photo.

"I'll send it to your mother," I say.

But they're gone, singing, *Aux armes, citoyens, Formez vos bataillons, Marchons, marchons!*

Some of those boys I just photographed will die, I think. But I'm alive, Peter Keeley's alive. Now I understand the urgency of those couples that have come to Father Kevin to be married. I know why St. Valentine was willing to perform marriages even though it meant martyrdom. Life against death.

Marchons, huh? Well, I'll march too, right up to Peter Keeley's door and pound on it. And I don't care about ceremonies or Brehon laws or fallen women. I'm going to take him and go back to my apartment and we'll make love all night. Tomorrow morning. I'll book passage on the first ship heading for New York. Borrow money from Madame Simone if I have to, and when I get back to Chicago and he's with me, I'll tell everyone something. That I was saved and have been living on an island. That I had amnesia. Peter and I will handle Tim McShane together. I'm going home, he's coming with me, and that's it.

But when I get there Peter isn't at the Irish College. He's gone back to Louvain.

16

THE GREAT WAR 1914–1918

AUGUST 1914

During those first few days of war, what complete idiots we all are . . . me, Madame Simone, even Father Kevin. Part of it is the newspapers. Story after story about the brave French soldiers and the success of *"l'Offensive à outrance."* The generals had learned from the failures of the last war. The army is attacking this time, not merely defending. Alsace is the first target. Me, as foolish as everybody else. *Le Monde* buys my photo of the young students who'd gone off singing to enlist. They use it big on the front page with the headline "Esprit de Corps." The caption says that the students embody *"Victoire c'est la volonté,"* the will to win, which will bring victory.

"Strasbourg will be free," Madame Simone says to me. Thursday now, August 6. "The people will rise up in support of their French liberators. Look." She shows me an article quoting a French general who promises "a quick strike, few casualties."

A week later, the real news comes. The French army is defeated. Casualties: 250,000. Jesus, not a month into the war and 250,000 gone already. A third of the French army lost and the rest are skedaddling toward Paris with the Germans rushing at us and cutting down the

Belgian army as they come. And Peter Keeley at the center of it all in Louvain.

But that Sunday, August 9, Father Kevin is reassuring, telling me after Mass he'd gotten word from a priest at Louvain that the Belgian army was occupying a fort near the city from which they would stop the German army. Even if the Germans reached Louvain, they would not attack the college or the library.

"The Germans aren't barbarians," Father Kevin says. "They won't hurt civilians. Peter will be safe." He squeezes my hand.

"The Brits are in it now," Father Kevin tells me. "Half of the army are *Irish*. Good fighters. Stalemate, that's what we want, Nora, a quick peace treaty. There might be some good come from this. England's trumpeting Belgium's sovereignty and the rights of small nations. And what's Ireland but a small nation that deserves sovereignty."

We're sitting in the one shady part of the courtyard. Only two weeks since the celebration of the landing of the guns at Howth and our silly, rain-drenched afternoon. Are we even the same people? Father Kevin is saying England has to go forward with Home Rule for Ireland or look like a complete hypocrite.

"But haven't they suspended the implementation?" I ask.

"An emergency measure," he says. "And now, with the Irish Volunteers enlisting into the British army, Redmond's hands will be strengthened. We'll get even more . . ."

"Wait a minute," I say. "What are you talking about? The Irish Volunteers are enlisting in the British army? The same Volunteers that armed themselves with rifles two weeks ago? The rebels?"

Just when I think I'm getting some grasp of Irish politics, I realize I haven't a notion. My brain flinches. I feel like I did in Chicago trying to follow Mike and Ed through some complicated strategy during a primary fight in the Sixth Ward.

"It's true that half of the Volunteers did refuse Redmond's directive to join the Brits. 'Why help England?' they said. 'England's difficulty is Ireland's opportunity.' And I see their point. But a long war serves nobody. Tom Kettle plans to join the Dublin Fusiliers, and Childers has been commissioned a naval officer . . ."

I stop him.

"Childers? The fellow who sailed the guns in?"

I am confused and wish Maud were in Paris. Which side would the colonel's daughter take? Or, Constance, for that matter, with Poland at risk of invasion by Germany and her Markievicz family in jeopardy.

And what do I think? Peter and I should get out of here. Go home. I'll find some way to resurrect myself. The United States has too much sense to get caught up in this maneuvering. We fought our revolution, suffered the Civil War, done and dusted. Get out.

But on the last Sunday in August, Peter is not back. The Belgian army is finished, and the British have failed to stop the Germans.

Father Kevin is beside himself.

"That fool general *Sir* John French! So full of his own importance. He should be court marshaled. He lost the Battle of Mons through sheer stupidity."

My Donegal scholar has become a military expert all of a sudden. We're in the courtyard with a map held between us. He points to the area that the British were supposed to defend—their portion of the line. Their army has fallen back.

"Criminal," he says. "They wouldn't support the French army. It's that pigheaded English sense of superiority. Won't even cooperate with their own allies."

I didn't point out to him that last week, the British army was going to save us all. And I say to him, "Father, I've been thinking. It might be time for me to go home. As soon as Peter gets here, I'm going to make him go with me."

But Father Kevin lifts the map, shakes his head. "Nothing to hold the Germans back, Nora. They've already taken most of northern France. Impossible to travel, I'm afraid. You've left it too late."

"And Peter?"

"All the railroads between here and Louvain have been commandeered by the various armies. The Belgian, the British, and the French soldiers are retreating. The Germans are moving forward. I'm afraid he's stuck there."

"Trapped," I say.

"I'm sorry, Nora," Father Kevin says. "You could've gotten out. It's me and my matchmaking that stopped you. But when Peter told me . . ."

He stops.

"What?"

"He does love you, Nora. But pride and custom keep him silent. He's poor and his older brother holds the lease to their farm and the fishing rights."

"But we'd find some way. I'm making money with my photographs."

"A man who depends on a woman for his living is held in very low esteem where Peter comes from."

"That's . . . that's bollocks," I say.

"Nora, that is a word no lady uses," Father Kevin says.

"I'm not a lady, Father Kevin, and I'm angry. If Peter feels that way, why won't he speak up?"

"Oh, Nora, you are so American."

"Damn right," I say, and stand up.

"Don't leave," he says. "It's my fault. Peter had accepted his life as I've accepted mine. But I'm close to eighty and Peter's half my age. He still has a chance to have a wife and a child."

"Oh, Lord, Father Kevin," I say. "Did you want a family?"

"I didn't, Nora, not at the start. God was calling me. And if I had to sacrifice the ordinary joys of life, well, that was the price. I was a priest, father to hundreds, thousands even instead of only a few. And to be honest, I thought myself a bit above the kind of labor a man has to do to support a family. My father was a schoolmaster, very well respected. But earning a pittance, really, and always concerned about money and staying on the right side of the parish priest. Priests are in charge of the schools in Ireland, and pretty much everything else."

He shrugs.

"So, I made my choice. And then, I'm in the seminary. I entered that other world of books and great thinkers. I missed my studies when I was assigned to a parish though I told you I did enjoy the people. But my battles with the parish priest ended that. Probably for the best. I always liked the Irish word—'*léann.*' A bit of a mystical charge on that word, memories of the druids. '*Léann*' means 'study,' but shift the *fada* and add '*nán*' and the word becomes '*leannàn,*' 'lover' or 'darling.' Also the root of 'faithfulness' and 'continuity.'"

Father Kevin can go on like this sometimes, covering what I think I hear him say, so I interrupt him.

"Wait—do you wish you'd married and had children? And you don't want Peter and me to miss that chance?" I ask.

Father Kevin leans back. "That's putting it a bit baldly. I'd layer some nuance around those words, but I suppose I do. I wish it for you."

"For God's sake, Father Kevin, can't you just say 'yes'?"

He laughs. "No word for yes or no in the Irish language. Entirely too diametrical for us, and I think Providence shapes us and knows what's best. So my path . . ."

"Yeah? Well, I am an American and we believe in giving Providence a helping hand." And my prayer is, Just get Peter here, God, and I'll take care of the rest.

During those last frantic days of August, I watch every Parisian left in the city who can afford to get out head for the hills or the mountains, or the seashore. On the rue de Rivoli bourgeois fathers drive Renaults loaded with family and suitcases, chauffeured limousines with shaded windows pass horse carts jammed with children and bundles. Madame Simone does not go.

"The French army will make a stand," she says. "They will not let the Boche into Paris."

But when I hear the pounding on my door just after midnight on the last day in August, I think it's Madame Simone. She has some news. Time to get out. I don't bother with a dressing gown but run to the door in the wisp of shift I wear on this hot night. I turn the lock and pull on the heavy brass knob. Open the door.

And there stands Peter Keeley, the collar of his shirt undone, his hair matted, unshaven. His coat's open; his shirt's hanging out of his pants.

"You're a mess," I say.

"I am," he says, "and wounded. I'm afraid."

"Dear God, come in. What happened?"

"The Germans burned the library, Nora. Three hundred thousand books and manuscripts put to the torch. I tried to stop them. A thousand years of knowledge, gone overnight. No military reason. A show of force. Evil."

I open my arms and Peter steps into them and we hold on to each other. A still point in this brutal nightmare. Comrades protecting each other except I'm more or less naked with only my silk shift between him and me. I should pull away, but I press closer to him and begin patting his back. I look up. He's closed his eyes, and I feel each of his breaths.

"Peter," I say, "Peter, it's all right. You're here. You're safe. It's all right."

He opens his eyes, looks at me.

"I am here, aren't I?" He steps back. "Strange, all the time at Louvain, on the road, when the soldiers beat me, I imagined myself here with you, and now, I am." He touches my shoulder. "Oh, Nora, I'm sorry."

"Don't be. I'm glad you came."

But he's pointing down and I see that his blood has smeared the front of my shift. I take his hand. He starts for the chair, but I steer him to the bed, where he collapses.

"I haven't slept for days," he says. He tries to sit up. "I don't want to bleed on your bed," he says.

"Oh, for God's sake," I say, "let me see."

I unbutton the shirt. A gauze bandage is wrapped around his chest, but blood is seeping through it.

"We'll replace this," I say, astounding myself. What do I know about wounds? I unwrap the bloody bandage.

"The blade didn't pierce my chest," he says. "The sword slashed me. The cuts were healing I think until . . ."

"Whist," I say to him.

Soap and water never hurt anything, Mam would say. I remember her doctoring my brothers when their gang the Hickory boys mixed it up with fellows from Canaryville. So I bring my rose glycerin soap, hot water, and a cloth, and dab at the cuts on his chest. Peter relaxes, takes my hand.

I want nothing more than to put it against my heart. But he lets go, closes his eyes.

"I should get dressed," I say.

And in a few minutes, I'm back corseted, gowned, and wrapping his chest with strips torn from a tablecloth. "You should sleep," I say.

He nods. "Could I have a cup of tea first?"

"Oh, yes, of course. Sorry." Of course he wants a cup of tea and food too probably. "Are you hungry?"

He smiles and says, "It has been a few days."

Thank God I have half a baguette, a lump of cheese, and a few apples. I make tea for Peter, coffee for myself, and bring the tray to the bed. Peter's eyes are closed, asleep already. But no, he sits up, takes the tea and sips.

"Milk and one sugar," I say, "as you like it."

He smiles. "I pictured this, you and me, having a meal here. You remember that Christmas Eve when I walked you home?"

"I do."

"I stood below waiting, looking for the light to go on so I'd know which windows were yours, wishing I had the courage to come up to you. Afraid you'd be shocked, offended. A respectable woman."

"If only you knew," I say. But he doesn't seem to hear. Away with the fairies, as Granny Honora would say.

"Eat, Peter," I say, and hand him a chunk of bread with some cheese, which he eats.

"The shops will be open soon, I'll go out and get us some real food," I say.

"Don't, don't leave. I'm afraid that when I sleep I'll see it all again. The flames . . ." He stops.

"Do you want to tell me?" I say. "You don't have to."

"Please," he says, takes my hand again. I sit down on the edge of the bed.

As Peter talks, I see he's trying to put sense on what he saw to make himself believe that it had really happened.

"At first, the priests at the college and I thought the Germans would just pass through Louvain," he says. "No question Paris was their goal. We watched them march through the streets, with those pointed helmets, moving at a good clip. The wagons following them had signs on the sides. *'Nach Paris'*—'Next stop Paris.'

"The Belgian army had retreated but some snipers stayed behind to harass the Germans, and a few students in Louvain, armed with hunting rifles, joined them. Good shots, those fellows. The Germans had left a small force to secure the city. The day after they marched in, an officer came to call on us at the college. A captain, I think, uber-something. Very pleasant and polite. He told us that they were in the city to keep order.

'Life will go on as before,' he said. 'You might find we're much more efficient than the Belgians—too much *'Froschfresser'* in them.'

"That's what the Germans call the French—frog eater," Peter says.

"The captain went on about how the Gallic temperament just isn't suited to government and that the preening French had forced this war, along with the brutal Cossacks and the brutish Slavs. The money-grabbing Jews behind it all, drawing the British in when King George, the kaiser's cousin, wanted a German-British alliance.

"'Europe will thank us,' he said. 'The Bolsheviks and their Jew partners want to destroy everything. We are the builders.'

"And then, he asked for a tour of the library. The uber-captain told me he had studied the classics at Tubingen University, and was especially interested in medieval manuscripts, especially any copies of Plato's work. And then, he went through a whole meander about how the platonic ideals need the manly Aryan virtues to become a reality. He'd written a paper on how the French had debased Plato by using the term 'Republic' for a government run by a violent rabble. Talking on as we strolled along the shelves.

"I said that we did have a manuscript copy of the *Republic* created by Irish monks.

"I told him that we'd saved the classics when the Teutonic tribes had employed their manly virtues to sack Rome and destroy learning.

"But he only laughed.

"'My dear professor, you're not going to go on about all that nonsense about the Dark Ages, are you? Haven't you read your own scientists, Darwin, Spencer? Nature is engaged in a battle for the survival of the fittest. Societies, too. Rome was weak and corrupt. My ancestors cleansed it. The blood sacrifice was necessary. The strong culling the herd, eliminating the weak. You English with your Anglo-Saxon common sense, know that. That's why we should be allies, not enemies.'

"And then I lost the run of myself, told him I was not English but Irish. And one million of my people were murdered by fellows culling the herd during the Great Starvation.

"'Do you mean the potato famine?' he said. 'But Professor, that makes my point. Nature doing its job. Famine, pestilence, war . . . all needed from time to time to rid us of the undesirables who weigh humanity down, keep us from reaching the heights.'"

"What did you say?" I ask Peter.

"Bollocks," he says.

"And the uber-captain wasn't pleased. But then, he made a great joke out of my response and of me, too. And I realized I was just one of the weak to him. And I thought again of those German scholars who'd come to Ireland because they valued our literature. And hadn't we just done a deal with the merchant in Hamburg to buy those rifles?

"But this man, so confident, so arrogant and so full of casual hate, shook me. The way he looked at me. I'd seen that same expression on the face of the agent who'd demand the rent from my father. The landlord and his friends would race their horses through our village not even seeing the children trying to dodge those death-dealing hooves. This captain had that same disdain for me and the priests.

"And I'd thought, We're going to have to tug the forelock until these bullyboys move on."

Peter stopped.

"Thinking subservience would save us."

He went quiet.

"Leave it, Peter. That's all right."

But he had to talk.

"Then, some of the Belgians had the audacity to defend themselves. Those fellows with rifles, *franc-tireurs*, the people called them, took on the Germans. Really very limited. A few shots from apartment windows, rooftops. But the German soldiers went mad. How dare this scum resist? Next thing I know, the captain's at our door, orders us all out. Brings in barrels of gasoline, the soldiers ready with torches in their hands. They douse the interior of the library with the fuel. The rector stepped forward to speak to the captain.

"'Shoot him,' the captain said and the soldier did. Through the heart. Couldn't believe it. 'Stop this!' I said to the captain. 'You are not a monster.' He laughed. He ordered two of the soldiers to hold me while the third, the one who'd shot the rector, picks up his bayonet and slashes my chest."

I reach out and touch the space above Peter's bandage very gently.

"I felt so helpless," he says. "Then another priest tried to help. The captain shot him, called him a pimp for the whore of Babylon, the Pope. Not fond of Catholic priests are stout German soldiers. The other priests ran, thank God. The captain tied me to the wheel of one of the carts so I had to watch them burn the library.

"Something strange about the fire, Nora," he says. "The colors. Maybe because of the leather covers of the books, the age of the paper, the ink. Some of the inks were made from jewels, lapis lazuli for blue—anyway the flames turned the most beautiful colors . . . shades of indigo, purple, then crimson, vivid orange. The captain commented on it. 'Magnificent,' he said. They let me go finally. I longed to tell him that I'd sent away some of the most valuable volumes already."

"I hope you kept your mouth shut," I say to Peter.

"I did," he says. "Started walking out of town and soon I had plenty of company. The Germans expelled the whole population of Louvain. Ten thousand people on the roads, automobiles with twenty or thirty people inside, trucks, farm carts, whole families walking, even the children carrying bundles. And I joined them. A Red Cross truck was parked at a roadside and a nurse dressed my wound. Antwerp was still held by theBelgian army so most were headed there. But I took a turn toward Paris.

"And then, I thought I had great luck. I found a French army unit but I almost got shot again. They weren't sure whether I was a deserting German or a spy. I kept saying *'irlandais'* until someone understood. They decided to send me across to a British unit only a half mile away. I never thought I'd be glad to meet an English officer.

"'I'm Irish,' I said to him and started to tell him about Louvain. But, would you believe it, Nora? He went mental, started shouting about the Micks and Paddys disloyal to king and country. And that we were no better than the Huns.

"Had a soldier pull the bandage off and then whacked me across the chest with his swagger stick.

"He told me that they hanged spies on the spot and that was what was going to happen to me. But thank God another officer came walking by.

"'Here's one of your own,' the first officer said to him. 'Weren't you born in Dublin?' And the man said, 'Yes but like Wellington said, being born in a stable doesn't make me a horse.'

"But I named some Trinity professors. Even, God help me, talked about Lord Lucan, my landlord.

"'He's only a fool,' the officer from Dublin told the other one, 'a type they breed in Ireland. Not a threat.'"

"Did you want to slap him?" I said.

"I did. But I said 'thank you' and they let me go," says Peter.

"Showed some sense," I say.

"Not proud of myself, Nora."

"Go to sleep, Peter. I'll tell Father Kevin you're here and be back with food. Don't leave."

But he's already asleep.

I go to the Irish College.

"You can't come in, Nora," Father Kevin whispers to me as we stand on the porter's hall. "The French police are here. The British have them thinking we're a den of German spies and they somehow found out that Peter was at Louvain, and some idiot of a priest told the authorities that Peter

Keeley had been very friendly with the Germans, showed them around the library and then Father Rector was shot. So Peter's some kind of German collaborator because he's Irish."

I tell him that Peter was battered by the Germans, French, and British.

"Leave it to the Irish to be at odds with the whole shebang," Father Kevin says.

"So, you'll be here with me for a while," I say to Peter when I come back to my room. "Father Kevin thinks he can get you sorted. He's not without influence with the French police. But for now . . ."

I'd bought a razor, underwear, and a shirt and overalls like the fellows in the market wear. He takes the lot, washes himself and dresses. The clothes suit him. Peter has the build of a workingman, muscles in his arms and shoulders.

Over a dinner of ham and cheese, I tell him what Father Kevin said. Peter's silent. I wonder if he takes in my words. I tell him I couldn't get much food. The shops are empty, the streets quiet. The Parisians are preparing for a siege, staying home. The French army's in retreat. The Boche are closing in. Again, no reaction from Peter.

"Strange to be here alone with you like this," he says. "I've not had much experience with women. There was a girl in Carna. We courted, some kisses, but . . ." He stops.

"But what?"

He's not saying.

"She left?" I say. "Went to America? Happened a lot, Peter. No reflection on you or your kisses."

"She died," he says, "when we were eighteen. The next year I got the chance to go to university. Our parish priest organized it. Sure I had a vocation, but I knew I could never be a priest."

He smiles.

"Those were powerful kisses, there's been no one else."

"Why?" I ask. He lists all the things Father Kevin mentioned—no home, no money. "I love my work, but it doesn't pay enough for a man to support a wife and children. And now, well, I thought I was past it, glad really. Until you came into the Panthéon dripping with rain. I was glad when I was sent to Louvain. I planned to stay there forever. But now . . ."

"You're trying to tell me something Peter. Say it."

He doesn't. But he leans over the table and kisses me. Powerful indeed.

So, lovely how one thing can lead to another. At first I wonder if I will even remember how to make love. But I suppose once you get the knack of it, you don't forget. And Peter's very willing. I even forgive Tim McShane a little, understanding now the joy of unlocking someone, seeing Peter experience pleasure, connection. And neither of us are worrying about mortal sin or anything else. During the three days we spend in my room above the place des Vosges, we hear the sound of big guns coming closer. But we're alive. Surely God wants us to be happy. I know Father Kevin does.

SEPTEMBER 2, 1914

"The Germans burned the library in Louvain to terrorize the world," Peter says. "Show that resistance accomplishes nothing."

We are at the Irish College. Father Kevin thinks Peter's safe enough. The Paris police too busy to concern themselves with him. I've brought bolts of material from Madame Simone. Peter, Father Kevin, and I are wrapping books and manuscripts and setting them into wooden crates.

"Madame Simone says the Germans are only a few days' march away," I say.

"Surely they won't want to destroy Paris," Father Kevin says. "It's their prize after all. The newspapers are saying the government will declare Paris an Open City. Not defend it against the Germans."

I pull the green velvet tight, trying not to damage the edges of the manuscript, but flakes of vellum fall into my lap.

"It's disintegrating," I say to Peter.

"Almost a thousand years old," he says.

He looks over to Father Kevin. "The Germans decided to burn the Louvain library. Calculation, a demonstration. Why not do the same thing to Paris?"

"Joan of Arc will never let the Germans destroy Paris," I say.

Peter smiles at me. On the way from my room I made him stop at the statue of Joan facing the Louvre. We weren't the only ones gathered there to ask for her help. A crowd—women mostly, some on their knees, but a good few men and a scattering of soldiers.

"Never wise to rule out miracles," Father Kevin says.

We're waiting for Myron Herrick to arrive. He's supposed to come at

noon. The American ambassador to France, from Ohio, a Republican politician but a friend of John Quinn who has agreed to take some of the
books and manuscripts to the American embassy for safekeeping. Almost
three o'clock when he arrives. "A busy day," he says. "Never been here before." He's looking at the half-empty shelves. "Quite a place."

"Ours for over three hundred years," Father Kevin says. "Endured many
wars and occupations."

"None like this war, I'm afraid," Herrick says. "I was standing outside
the embassy and an airplane dropped a bomb only a few feet from me.
Airplanes—that's new. And the German artillery. They have a howitzer can
send a mortar shell through concrete. Big Bertha, the troops have started
calling it. The gun can hit a target eight miles away. Destroyed the Belgian
forts. It's headed our way, I'm afraid," he says.

"A gun that can shoot eight miles? Horrible," I say.

"Think that's bad?" Herrick says. "Krupp's developing a gun that can hit
targets eighty miles away. Modern warfare. Imagine what a gun that can
destroy concrete does to the human body. The French government thinks
the Germans could be here by the end of the week. Poincaré is moving the
whole administration to Bordeaux."

"Abandoning us? That's awful," I say.

Herrick shrugs. "I told them I'd fly the American flag over the Louvre
and Notre-Dame, and put the museums under the protection of the United
States," he says.

"We're very grateful to you for taking these, Ambassador," Father Kevin
says. "They're priceless."

"So John Quinn says." He points at the crates. "I can't take them all," he
says, "or guarantee their safety. I'm hoping the Germans respect our neu-
trality, but I just got a note from the German foreign minister objecting to
us treating wounded French soldiers in the American hospital at Neuilly."

"Surely caring for the sick isn't an act of war," Father Kevin says.

"Well, the Germans maintain that because the French government gave
us a building to use as an annex to our hospital, we are collaborating with
the enemy. Collaborating! We're not even opened for business yet. Dr.
Gros got the place started. Been here so long he knows most of the Americans in Paris. Many out there cleaning, getting ready." He looks at me.
"You're American, aren't you?"

"I am," I say.

"Don't believe we've ever met. You don't attend embassy events?" he asks.

I shake my head. Always a bit worried I might run into someone from Chicago. Awful to have them say, "Nora Kelly? But you're dead!" Of course, now that the world is falling apart, my so-called death doesn't seem as important.

"I'm from Chicago," I say. I mumble my first name, then add Kelly.

"A Democrat, I suppose," he says. "Well, no divisions these days. We need workers. Get out to Neuilly. Report to Mrs. Vanderbilt. She's in charge of cleaning and outfitting the place. Any supplies we don't have, she goes out and buys."

Peter, Father Kevin, and I carry the crates to Herrick's car.

"Thank you," Father Kevin says. We watch him drive away.

"What about this?" I point to a large manuscript still on the table.

"That's a fourteenth-century copy of a section from *The Book of the Dun Cow* which Peter will take," Father Kevin says.

"Take where?" I say.

"Home," Peter says, "to Ireland."

"No," I say. "You can't try to get through the lines again. Armies all over the place. He was almost killed last week," I say to Father Kevin.

"He can go south," Father Kevin says. "Get a ship from Marseilles."

"I'll have help," Peter says.

"You can't go, Peter. Not after . . ."

"Nora," Peter says. "There is important work waiting for me in Ireland."

"Oh, for God's sake, there are more important things than saving manuscripts. Your life, for one."

"Remember how I told you the O'Donnell chieftains would carry the Cathach—St. Columcille's psalmbook—into battle as a kind of standard?" Peter says.

"I remember. So what? My uncle Patrick led troops with Grellan's Crozier. You're going up against Big Bertha with *The Book of the Dun Cow*?" I say.

"Listen, Nora. England has always turned to Ireland for her soldiers. Ten thousand of our fellows have already enlisted in the British army and are fighting at the front. They think they're saving poor Catholic Belgium. Proving we deserve Home Rule. And now, after Louvain, the recruiters will be appealing to the Irish sense of justice. Tempting them to take the king's shilling, telling them the war will be over by Christmas. I have to stop them enlisting."

"Wait. I don't understand. How can you and the manuscript keep young Irishmen from joining the British army?"

Peter takes my hand. "Nora, in every town and village in Ireland there are groups of young people learning the Irish language, playing ancient music, doing the traditional dances. Athletes are competing in the Old Gaelic games. They're determined to revive our culture to become Gaels again. These groups are the core of our movement."

Peter lifts up the manuscript. Hands it to me.

"When you hold this, Nora, you're touching our ancestors. The kings and queens, saints and scholars who are the real Ireland. A history you can hold. Imagine one of these groups passing this manuscript from hand to hand. What chance would the British recruiter have? What young man who sees himself as the heir to Finn or Red Hugh O'Neill or the O'Kellys could enlist in the Sassenach army? What young woman would allow it?"

I remember my uncle Patrick talking about how he toured the logging camps in the North Woods bringing Grellan's Crozier to the fellows. They'd clutch it and swear the Fenian oath, promising to fight for Ireland.

Peter had Uncle Patrick's firm resolve, and there was no way I could stop him. "But I may not see you ever again." I say.

I turn to Father Kevin. "He's leaving the way those French boys whose weddings you've been performing did. You said St. Valentine was martyred for marrying those Roman soldiers to their sweethearts. So, it's only fair."

Father Kevin and Peter look at each other.

"What are you going on about, Nora?" Father Kevin asks.

"Marry us," I say. "Now."

Peter shakes his head, "Impossible," he says.

"You have to. Only honorable," I say.

"It would be dangerous for you to be my wife," he says. "What if I am arrested? They'll come looking for you."

"Who has to know?" I say. "Come on, Father Kevin. What about all those Brehon laws? I've done a lot for the Cause. Marry me, Peter. It's the least you can do."

"Nora, please," Peter says, but Father Kevin puts a hand on his shoulder.

"Shall we go to the chapel?" he says. What can Peter do?

So, Peter and I stand together while Father Kevin blesses us in Irish, Latin, and English. "Three times the charm," he says.

"And we're married?" I say.

"Marriage is one sacrament the participants give to each other. As the priest, I'm merely the witness," Father Kevin says. "It's up to yourselves."

"So," I say, and kiss Peter. He kisses me back, thank God.

One other person at our wedding. A man who steps in at the end just in time to see the kiss. A fellow whose name I'm not told but who is from Ireland.

Of course, I want to say to Peter, "Don't go. Stay." But I don't. Tens of thousands of women are watching their husbands leave, or worse, getting letters telling them the men will never return. Hundreds of thousands more to come.

"Well, now," Father Kevin says after Peter and his comrade leave. "If he does die, he won't feel he has missed out on loving altogether."

"Is it that dangerous?"

"Peter's about to put his head in the lion's mouth, and I'm afraid he's the type that will pull its tail," Father Kevin says.

So. I leave the college and go to Madame Simone's studio. She's been expecting the Germans to march into Paris for thirty years. At least she'll be prepared.

I find her sitting at her desk, a sword in her lap.

"You going to take on the Boche single-handed?" I say.

She's drinking champagne, an open bottle next to her and five magnums lined up on her desk.

"You need a glass," she says. "Georgette," she calls. Georgette comes from the back carrying two crystal flutes. I know Madame Simone keeps a supply of champagne for her clients. I guess she's emptying the cellar.

"The Boche may loot Paris, but they'll get nothing from me," she says.

I see that the studio is bare. No bolts of material on the shelves, no spools of ribbon, cards of buttons on the counters. The dressmaker dummies are gone. Even the four sewing machines have disappeared.

"We divided everything up," Georgette says. "All the girls took a share. Monique's brother loaded the sewing machines onto his cart. He lives in the country. He'll keep them there. Safe."

Georgette pours a glass of champagne for me and one for herself. "Drink quickly," she says. "We have to finish these. Madame didn't want the girls to be corrupted by wine."

"We have fooled the Boche," Madame Simone says. "When they pound on the door demanding my gowns, they will find nothing."

I can't imagine that the German soldiers I saw in Strasbourg wearing those spiked helmets will be interested in couture. I say as much to Madame Simone.

"I am world-famous," she says. "These brutes have wives, mistresses. They will try to steal from me. And then . . ."

She lifts the sword, whirls it in the air.

"Be careful," I say. Here is the kind of élan the French army could have used.

Now she stands up, grasps a champagne bottle, and slices at it with a sword. Too much élan. But . . .

"*Voilà,*" she says.

And doesn't the cork pop out of the bottle and rocket across the room.

"Big Bertha, Paris style," I say.

"Drink," she says, and fills my glass.

I look at the bubbles jumping around in the clear gold liquid and think, Why not tell her?

"I want to propose a toast. To Mrs. Peter Keeley—me."

Of course, they have no idea what I'm talking about. Hard to explain my marriage in French or in English, but I do get across that a ceremony has occurred and the groom is gone. I tell them nothing will really change including my name. I'll still be Nora Kelly to the world but Honora Keeley, secretly, Granny's family name.

Madame Simone had met Peter when he was acting as a guide on my tours. "*Pas mal,*" she'd said. Not bad.

Neither woman seems especially surprised. They're drunk. I'm married. The Boche are coming.

Of course, less than an hour before I'd assured Father Kevin and Peter that I'd tell no one about the wedding. A secret. But the champagne demands some good news.

So we drink to Peter and me through the rest of that September afternoon.

"I should go," I say. "Get home before dark."

The setting sun fills the studio with a lovely pink light. I wish I had my Seneca. Take a photo of Madame Simone. Didn't even think to shoot a picture of Peter. Some chronicler I'll be. Don't want to photograph the German troops marching up the Champs-Élysées. What if that general from Strasbourg is leading them? Dear God, don't let the Boche win. Joan, where are you?

"Why don't I walk you home?" I say to Madame Simone.

"No. I stay here," Madame Simone says, and swings the sword again.

"Won't you be safer in your apartment? No fighting around Notre-Dame surely."

"No fighting anywhere," Georgette says. "Our army has deserted us. Cowards."

So.

I'm almost at the door when we hear footsteps coming up the staircase.

Madame Simone stands up and extends the sword as if she were a fencer.

"En garde," I say in spite of myself.

The knock seems gentle for a Boche soldier, and the man is speaking French. That voice. Louis!

I open the door. Louis DuBois rushes in.

"Good. You are here. I tried your apartment," he says.

He turns back into the hallway, picks up his tripod and camera, brings them into Madame's studio.

"Hold on to my equipment for me. And here's the key to my place. You know how to use the darkroom. Try to keep the business going until I get back."

Madame Simone and Georgette stare at him. One more mad moment in a crazy day.

"Oh, Louis. The only tourists there'll be in Paris are German soldiers."

"You don't know the news. Ladies, the German army has turned away from Paris," he says.

"What? Why?"

"I suppose the Boche generals plan to surround our army. Destroy it completely and then march to Paris without opposition. Think we're already beaten. But they have given us a chance. We are to fight them on the Marne. I am going to the front now with my Paris unit and . . ." He pauses, throws his hands up in one of those French gestures I can never imitate. "We are traveling the thirty miles to the front by taxi."

Madame Simone, Georgette, and I insist on seeing Louis off. We walk down to the waiting taxi. The driver says that they are first going to Les Invalides, the assembly point.

"Would you like to drive with us and see the great cavalcade?" the driver asks. "Every taxi in Paris has been summoned."

As we approach the imposing building, it seems to stretch for half a mile. I took those of my ladies who wanted to see Napoleon's tomb here. One of them was surprised to see an elderly soldier wandering the hallways. "Built for them," I said. "The 'invalids'—get it?" Nice of the French, I'd thought, to let their old soldiers live right in military headquarters.

"Look, look," the driver says.

We are close enough now to see hundreds of taxis lined up in ranks, bumper-to-bumper, all with their headlights on. Amazing.

Six hundred Paris taxis will transport six thousand soldiers to the Battle of the Marne before dawn, the driver says.

He hurries us out of his taxi. It's a military vehicle now.

Madame Simone, Georgette, and I wave like fools at Louis, who salutes us as his taxi pulls into the line. The drivers start their engines at the same time and pull out in a slow, steady procession. Some have passengers already, some will meet troop trains, but all will bring the reinforcements needed by the French troops who have turned to face the Germans, an old man whose son is going tells us.

I go home with Madame Simone. Georgette joins us. Not a night to be alone.

"La Gloire," Madame says just before she falls asleep.

So. The French with some help from the British do stop the German advance. The Boche do not march into Paris, but it's a close thing. The Allies haven't won the war. They've just kept the Germans from victory.

"A long war now," Father Kevin says to me the next week at the Irish College.

"I guess we'd better head to the American hospital," he says. "Hope they need a chaplain."

"I'm sure they need a cleaner," I say.

Weeks before we know what's being called the "Miracle at the Marne" cost in lives. No official numbers are released, but one of the doctors at the hospital tells Father Kevin there were 250,000 Allied and 220,000 German casualties during the battle. Eighty thousand French soldiers dead. Louis is one of them. Not really a soldier . . . an artist, a boulevardier. No notion of what he'd be facing. But who of those boys marching to the slaughter did? The taxi cavalcade is the last moment of élan. The awful grinding butchery begins.

17

CHRISTMAS EVE 1914

"I want my Mam," the young soldier cries out. Two o'clock in the morning. I am the only one on this ward. Thank God Margaret Kirk's close enough to hear me holler if one of these fellows takes a bad turn. She's always so cool. Not a talker. Intimidating.

Part of the bunch that came over on the U.S.S. *Red Cross*. Doctors, too. Glad Dr. Gros has some help. Though I'm proud enough of what we Americans in Paris did to get the hospital up and running during those first months of war. So many wounded flooding in then. Father Kevin giving the Last Rites to poor fellows dying on stretchers in the hallways. Much better organized now. Even have our own ambulance service thanks to Mrs. Vanderbilt. I do wonder sometimes about the drivers. Boys from the States, lots of them some only eighteen years old. But then the soldiers themselves are not much older.

This lad, John Feeney, nineteen, is in the Dublin Fusiliers. Fought at the Marne, then the Aisne River, wounded at Armentières. Casualties beyond counting in those battles. John's chart says wounded while "advancing against the enemy." Sounds so neat and military. But John told me his squad had been forced to stumble through mud and barbed wire into enemy machine-gun fire. All to gain a few yards of ground the Germans retook the next day. Insane.

John's tall, with long legs, both in plaster held up in traction.

I bend over, take his hand.

"Mam?" he says, and opens his eyes.

"It's me, Nora," I say.

"I was dreaming I was home," he says, "in Galway."

"My family comes from Galway," I say.

"What townland?"

"I don't know."

"You don't? How can you forget where you're from?" he asks.

"My people left a long time ago," I say.

"In Ireland a long time ago's never very far away," he says. "So where is your home?"

"I'm an American from Chicago but have lived in Paris for three years." Sounds simple but then something makes me add, "My husband is from Connemara."

"Husband?" he says, settling back on his pillows. "Didn't figure you for a husband. He in the war?"

"He's in Ireland."

"Well, if your husband is there and your people are Irish, I'd say Ireland is your home place," he says.

Now, I haven't confided in Margaret Kirk or told Maud about my secret marriage to Peter Keeley but here in the middle of the night on Christmas Eve I'm glad to tell this Irish boy.

"Do you have children?" he asks.

"We don't."

"Is it Christmas yet?" John Feeney asks.

"It is," I say.

"War shouldn't be allowed at Christmas," he says.

"Pope Benedict tried to get the governments to agree to a Christmas truce. He said 'At least the guns should fall silent on the night the angels sing.'"

"Angels," he says, and leans closer to me. "I saw a band of angels on the battlefield." He takes my hand. "Not with wings and halos. These angels were my pals, six fellows from my own unit. We all got hit with a blast of artillery after our damn fool lieutenant ordered us forward into no-man's-land. *Amadán!* The seven of us were facedown in the mud when I saw Pat and Jimmy Mac stand up and then float right over the battlefield. The others, Dennis, Danny, and Kevin rose up too. All of them smiling at me, protecting me until the medical fellows got there. Angels. They didn't sing but they saved my life."

He lets go of my hand, leans back on the pillows, closes his eyes.

"You don't believe me, do you?" he says. "The nurse at the field hospital didn't either. Said I was shell-shocked. Hallucinating. A big word for making it up. Is that what you think?"

"I think our minds can create . . ."

He opens his eyes. "You're the same as her. I was hoping you might be a Catholic."

"Of course I'm a Catholic."

"Then you should understand. My mam's got a devotion to St. Bernadette. Wants me to send her water from Lourdes. As if I could take off across the country without a by-your-leave. My mam believes Bernadette had a vision of Our Lady. Why can't you believe I saw my pals become angels?"

"Why not indeed?" I say.

"I want to go back to the front line," he says. "Have to. The boys are waiting for me. They'll make sure no bullets can touch me."

"Shut your gob, Feeney!" This from the fellow in the next bed, Paul O'Toole, a big fair-haired man. No wound but a bad case of pneumonia. Delighted to be here. Showed me the note he carried in his pocket that said, "If wounded take me to the American hospital Neuilly, Paris, France." An operator is Paul.

"If it was possible for a man to give himself pneumonia, I'd say Paul O'Toole managed it," Dr. Gros told me. Paul coughs up a storm when ever Dr. Gros comes around.

"My father had a weak chest and his father before him," he'll tell the doctor, "chronic," and wheeze away. Clear as a bell his voice is now. "Jesus, Mary, and Joseph give it a rest or I'll send you up to see the angels myself."

"Quiet down, Paul," I say to him.

"And a happy Christmas to you too, Nora. And why wasn't I told about this mysterious husband of yours? An Irishman from Connemara? Did you meet him in Paris?"

Someday I'll learn to keep my mouth shut. Someday.

"You're dreaming, Paul," I say. "Must be your fevered state."

Ná habair tada.

"When are you going to take my photograph?" Paul asks.

I'd been bringing my Seneca to the ward, snapping pictures of the men and making prints for them to send home. Reassuring for their families to actually see them. I concentrate on their faces.

"Just take my good bits," one fellow said, turning his head in profile. Shrapnel had shattered the left side of his face.

"Paul," I say now. "I've given you ten prints."

"I need more, for my Mariannes in Armentières," he says. "A very friendly town that."

"Go to sleep, Paul. You too, Johnny," I say.

"You know what, Nora?" Paul says. "This boy wants to go back to the front line so they'll say he's crazy and send him home. Me, I want out, so they'll decide I'm sane and dump me back into the madness. Bonkers the whole setup."

I see Margaret walking toward me.

"It's almost dawn. Try to get a few hours of sleep," I say to them.

Margaret's shaking her head as she walks through the ward. "You can't let them pull you in like that, Nora," she says to me. "Especially that O'Toole. He'd talk the hind leg off of a donkey."

I laugh. "My granny used to say that," I say.

"So did mine," Margaret says.

Good to be with my own again, I think.

Katie McMahon and Sally Blaine take our places while Margaret and I go to the nurses' dormitory for a few hours' sleep.

Have to remember to be careful around Paul O'Toole. Father Kevin's found out he's an informer passing information about the men to the British colonel who sometimes visits the ward. All I need is for him to mention my name to Henry Wilson. Do colonels know generals?

We bring the men to one ward for Christmas Mass that afternoon. A comfort in being together and hearing Father Kevin's lovely brogue read the Christmas Gospel.

"Peace on earth, goodwill to men," he begins his sermon. "I'm sure no one wants peace more than you men who'd been in combat."

Heads nod.

"I'd like to begin with a report from the Western front."

No, Father Kevin, I think. No war news please, not today.

"It's not me who will be speaking to you," Father Kevin says. "Tony has something to tell you."

Tony Hulman, an ambulance driver, only seventeen, stands next to Father Kevin. Margaret and I have made a bit of a pet of this boy from Indiana. "Terre Haute," he told me. "'Terry Hut' we say, but they pronounce it different over here."

I'd said I'd heard of Saint Mary-of-the-Woods. He told me he'd often visited the college and the motherhouse, which were just a few miles from town.

"The Sisters of Providence," he'd said.

I know about the place because the same order of nuns taught Mame and Rose at St. Agnes in Brighton Park. Mame's favorite, Sister Bernice, had been in the side pew at Mame's wedding.

A good lad Tony, but shy. Not the type to give a Christmas sermon. But Father Kevin gestures him forward. "Tell them, Tony," Father Kevin says. Tony clears his throat a few times and then says, "I was on the line near Flanders. I'd heard there were some Americans in one of the French Foreign Legion units nearby and went to see them. There was a guy from Chicago with them called Phil Rader. They even had a colored cook from Alabama. Pretty miserable they were. Water slushing around in the bottom of the trenches. Days of rain. Not much real fighting though. But the Germans were only fifty yards away and each side would shoot at the other the odd time. God help you if you stuck your head too far up. Then yesterday morning it got very cold. The mud in no-man's-land froze. Phil Rader was afraid some bonehead general would order them to charge the German trenches."

He stops, looks at the men.

"Didn't mean to insult your generals, but . . ."

"We know them, lad," Paul O'Toole says. "Bonehead's a compliment."

"Go on, Tony," Father Kevin says.

"Anyway, I decided to stay with them for the night. I had a bottle of brandy and . . ." He stops again.

"That's all right, Tony, go on," Father Kevin says.

"Anyway," Tony says. "The moon came up early. And then snow started falling, covering no-man's-land, filling in the shell holes and piling up on the barbed wires. One of the fellows yelled that there were lights in the German trenches. Flares? What were they up to, we wondered. Phil had binoculars. 'Jesus' he said. 'Those are Christmas trees.'

"Sure enough the Germans had set up three pine trees on top of their trenches and were decorating them with candles, right out in the open. Perfect targets and one of the fellows raised his rifle. 'Merry Christmas, you Hun bastard,' he said. But Phil pushed the gun down. Yelled to the sergeant, who said, 'Hold your fire, men.' Loads of Germans came out, stood on top of the trenches singing 'Silent Night' in German. Well, our boys answered with 'The First Noël' in French, of course. Then Phil started singing 'O Come All Ye Faithful' in Latin. Which the Providence nuns had taught me. 'Adeste Fideles,' we sang. The Germans joined in and we were all singing together. Then a few Germans started walking toward us so our fellows climbed out of the trench. Now the French government had sent these Christmas tins to every soldier. One of the boys near me gave his tin to a German. I was right in the middle of the bunch and saw some Germans get the tins their government had sent and swap them with the French. All of us standing around, talking and the snow falling through the moonlight. Some French soldiers pulled buttons off their uniforms and exchanged them for German buttons. The Negro cook took out a mouth organ and played 'Swing Low Sweet Chariot.' Both sides seemed to know the tune and they hummed along. Then he played 'Watch on the Rhine.' The Germans really bellowed that out, but then afterwards we all started singing 'La Marseillaise.' Quite a singsong. One of their officers came out. Shouted that he wanted to meet with one of our officers. Well, the officers decided there would be no more fighting for the next few days. One of the Germans shouted out in English, 'Any Americans there?' Phil said, 'Over here.' Turns out this guy was born in Milwaukee. Moved back to Berlin when he was a kid. Got drafted. 'This is crazy,' he said. 'This war is not our fault. We're all of us husbands and fathers, sons and brothers. Why are we killing each other?' I drove twelve hours straight so I could tell you what happened."

I look around at the men. Smiling most of them.

"A fine report, Tony," Father Kevin says. "Thank you. So, men, the Pope got his Christmas truce after all. There are reports of these kinds of celebrations all along the line. Some of the British troops even played a game of soccer with the Germans," Father Kevin says.

"Good on them," John Feeney shouts out. "A soldiers' truce." He turns to me. "I told you strange things happen on the battlefield."

We serve a decent Christmas meal thanks to Madame Collard, the St.

Antoine market, and Mrs. Vanderbilt's money. After dinner, Mrs. Vanderbilt visits the ward. I get the fellows to sing a Christmas carol or two for her, but it's Paul O'Toole who really gets the place going. "Here's one for you, Nora," he says.

"Mademoiselle from Armentières. Parley voo," he sings. The others join in. "Mademoiselle from Armentières. Parley voo." Paul takes the next line. "Mademoiselle from Armentières hasn't been kissed for forty years. Inky dinky parley voo."

Margaret can't help laughing.

"Thanks very much, Paul," I say. All the soldiers know the next stanza.

"I had more fun than I can tell. Beneath the sheets with Mademoiselle."

"Let's leave them to it," Father Kevin says.

"If they can stop war for a day, why not end the whole thing?" I ask Father Kevin as we ride back to Paris from Neuilly in the horse and cart he got from somewhere. He drives quite well.

"The governments didn't bring about the cease-fire. Ordinary soldiers did," he says.

Father Kevin drops me at L'Impasse to thank Madame Collard. Nearly ten o'clock. She and Madame Simone are sitting together sipping brandy. I join them. Madame Collard's received no word from Monsieur or her son Henri, both on the front.

"No news is good news," I say. Ridiculous these phrases but a kind of currency these days. I tell them about the Christmas truces. Madame Simone shrugs. "And then they will go back to shooting at each other," she says.

When Madame Collard leaves us, Madame Simone says, "I have some bad news."

"Your nephew?" I say.

She shakes her head. "I have a letter from your sister in Chicago."

Henrietta writing to me? At last! The war. She's worried about my safety. Hasn't forgotten me. She's sorry. She's told the family she'd lied. They're so happy I'm alive. I can go home now. Meet Peter in Ireland and then both of us will go to America. Better stay at the hospital until spring. Everyone says an Allied offensive will end the war, but lots of casualties.

Madame Simone hands me the letter. I open the envelope. Only a newspaper clipping inside. I read the headline aloud. "'Dolly McKee Is Dead.'"

"Oh well," I say to Madame Simone. "She was not young. Anyone these days who dies in bed is lucky."

I read on, stop, look up at her.

"Oh, dear God. She was killed. Murdered. Her maid, too."

I remember that snowy November night three years ago and the two women who had rescued me. Tim McShane. Carrie had always feared Tim McShane. But the newspaper says Dolly was murdered by a burglar who broke into her isolated mansion, stole her jewelry. At least that's the theory put forth by her husband. Husband? And there it is. "The deceased had recently wed her longtime manager, Tim McShane." Married. So he'll get everything, I think. Poor, poor Dolly. I remember Tim's hand around my throat. The burglar's a fiction. The murderer will inherit.

"McShane killed her," I say to Madame Simone. "Look, Henrietta thinks so too." I show her the clipping with Henrietta's scrawl. "This could've been you or me. Stay away," Henrietta's written.

"How horrible," I say. "Worst somehow for it to happen now."

"Why?" Madame Simone says. "Because of the war? Men kill their wives, war or no war. It happens."

"But today the soldiers stopped the slaughter. They refused to fight."

"And if they do the same tomorrow, their own officers will shoot them as cowards. Make an example to the others. I too think that Dolly's death is terrible, but what is one life among so many?" she says.

"But soldiers die randomly," I say. "They're not murdered personally. Tim squeezed the life out of Dolly while he was looking into her face."

"I would prefer that my murderer know me," Madame Simone says. "More terrible to die just because you were born French or German and are a man of military age. Or a Belgian in Louvain or a Russian peasant. But my dear Nora, we should not say such things too loudly. A woman was arrested because she was heard by a neighbor questioning the war. *Soyez sage. Soyez sage.*"

JANUARY 1, 1915

"Of course, this war is ridiculous," Maud is saying to me as we sit with Father Kevin and a fellow from Dublin in the parlor on New Year's Day. "A wind of folly and futility that's driving Germany and France to their ruin. Whether conqueror or conquered both will end up second rate powers, and for this they are sacrificing their strongest and bravest, and no one dare protest. Only England will benefit. Grabbing up everyone else's trade. At least you Americans have resisted and held onto your shipping trade."

She's back from months of nursing soldiers in the Pyrenees. Very thin, with circles under those gold-brown eyes, more gray in her hair.

Father Kevin has developed a bad cold, and Dr. Gros has ordered him to stay away from the hospital. I found him and Maud sitting with this fellow called Thomas Kettle—about my age, I'd say. Father Kevin had introduced him as a barrister and Member of Parliament for the Nationalist Party.

"Tom's married to one of the Sheehy girls," Father Kevin says to me.

"A Daughter of Erin, Maud?" I ask.

"She is. Though what Mary thinks of your views on the war, Tom, I can't imagine," Maud says.

"She supports my decision," he says. "Understands why I'm enlisting."

Maud grunts.

"Redmond thinks," Kettle goes on, "if all Irishmen, North and South, band together to fight Germany, our country will be united. Home Rule will be accepted in the North and . . ."

"Bollocks," Maud says. Both men laugh.

"I tried to get into the Fusiliers," Kettle says, "but they wouldn't take me because of my health. There are a few strings I can pull yet."

"A good number of the Fusiliers at the American hospital where I'm nursing," I say. "They've suffered terrible casualties. I'd say they need replacements."

"Well, I'm ready," he answers.

"You want to fight, to die?" Maud says.

"Well, of course, I hope not to die, but if I do, a grave here in the France I've loved would be no bad thing," Kettle says.

"Death's always a bad thing," I say.

"I agree," Kettle says, "but we must fight for European civilization. If we allow the rights of a small nation like Belgium to be trampled underfoot what chance for Ireland, Home Rule or no Home Rule? We Irishmen are Europeans in our hearts. My brother-in-law Francis agrees that our future is with Europe though he's taken a pacifist stand against the war," Kettle says.

"As has his wife Hanna," Maud says.

"Another Sheehy girl," Father Kevin says. "Francis took her name. They're both Sheehy-Skeffington."

"Hanna is a suffragist and like most of them opposed to the war," Maud says. "Thousands of women from all of the countries fighting signed a Christmas letter appealing for a truce."

"But," Kettle says, "many of the suffragist women do support the government."

"Because they think they'll get something from them," Maud says.

"You're very cynical, Maud," Tom says. "I've tried to put how I feel into the poem I've written for my daughter. Something to explain why I'm willing to die. I've left it with Father Kevin to send to Mary if . . ."

Silence, Dear God, I have to say something.

"Would you ever read some of it to us?" I ask. Finally meeting one of these poetic Irish fellows.

Kettle clears his throat. "I'll just give you the end."

> Know that we fools, now with the foolish dead,
> Died not for flag, nor King, nor Emperor,—
> But for a dream, born in a herdsman's shed,
> And for the secret Scripture of the poor.

Maud stands up. "Tom, Tom, you are deluding yourself. I prefer the line written on the banner James Connolly hung over Liberty Hall, 'We fight for neither king nor emperor.' Why should working men die for capitalism?"

"We may not agree, Maud," Kettle says as he stands, "but I love Ireland as much as you do."

"Hold on, you two. Irish people of goodwill on both sides. We can't let the British divide us," Father Kevin says.

I think of Peter Keeley in the middle of all these ructions, trying to keep Irish fellows out of the British army, and of Woodrow Wilson promising American boys won't die in the conflict. Running for reelection on the one slogan, "He Kept Us Out of War."

Thomas Kettle and Maud manage to be civil to each other talking about mutual friends in Dublin whose sons had died.

"I may be against the war," Maud says, "but I'm not against the soldiers. I admire their bravery. The fellows I nurse are so stoic. They just hope it will be over."

Maud and I walk out of the Irish College together. I ask her if we will be celebrating Women's Christmas this year.

"Oh, I couldn't, Nora," she says.

"Why not come to my place?" I say.

"But you really don't have room to entertain," she says. "Maybe I could have you for the afternoon. Might cheer Barry and Iseult."

"I'd like you to meet the woman who nurses with me," I say.

"And we won't talk about the war," Maud says.

"Her name is Margaret Kirk," I say.

"Kirk," she repeats. "The Scots word for 'church.' An omen. All right, bring her. I suppose a sherry by the fire's one way to poke a stick into the eye of this war."

❦

So. We gather on rue de l'Annonciation. Barry and Iseult take Seán and the dog out to the park; Maud, Margaret Kirk, and I settle in around the fire. Maud declaims a bit, repeating what she'd said about the war to Kettle. Margaret looks over at me, raises an eyebrow.

"You should write an article," I say to Maud.

"I have," she says. "And sent it to John Quinn in New York, but I just got a letter from him warning me not to sound pro-German. He says the Irish in America are making that mistake. Alienating many supporters. It seems America's neutral in favor of the Allies."

"My father was German," Margaret says. "Noll's my maiden name. Plenty of Irish-German marriages."

"Like my aunt Nelly and uncle Steve," I say. "Hard to see her as a Hun, or her sister, my aunt Kate, either."

"Of course not. It's the militarism of Germany, the imperialism of Britain that's pushed the world into war," Maud says. "Poor France didn't really want this."

"Tell Margaret about Henry Wilson who preferred a world war to Home Rule for Ireland," I say.

"Maybe we should give war talk a rest," Margaret says. "Your children are charming, Maud."

"I want to take them to live in Ireland," Maud says. "Sean should go to

Pearse's school, St. Enda's, but I'm afraid if I enroll him there MacBride will snatch him." She looks over at Margaret. "You know the story?" she asks.

"I know your marriage ended," Margaret says.

"At least the war's keeping MacBride in Ireland," Maud says. "He won't be trying to beat down my door."

My very thought about Tim McShane. He might murder Dolly and Carrie, but he wouldn't chance U-boats in the Atlantic to get to me.

"Drink and jealousy drove John MacBride mad," Maud says. "Every single man I knew was my secret lover, according to him. And the questions. Over and over. Why was I so long in the meeting? He'd wake me up in the middle of night, interrogating me. Who was I dreaming about? Searched my writing table, found Willie Yeats's letters to me, years of them. Very drunk that night. Laughing as he read them. 'He calls you Maeve and he's Ailill? Is that what you landlords do? Put on Ireland like a costume? Actors in a pantomime?' he said. Then he found mention of the 'spirit world' and 'piercing the veil.' More fits of laughter. He piled up the letters, set them aflame. And I stood there and watched. That's the shame of it. Me, a soldier's daughter who's faced down bailiffs and constables and put myself in front of battering rams. I did nothing. Frantic that he'd wake Iseult and terrorize her. Only a young girl and he called her the vilest names. Finally, he staggered away and fell asleep. I collected the ashes of the letters. Saved them. I never told Willie that all those words of his had burnt away. And yet the John MacBride I'd met only a few years before was admirable. A soldier, a gentleman. No hint of what he was to become. Was I to blame? Perhaps I brought out the worst in him, challenged him in ways I did not understand."

"Not your fault. Yet I understand."

Maud stops, looks at me. "Perhaps, you do know," she says.

"I do," I say.

And something about the three of us gathered around the glow of Maud's coal fire while the afternoon darkens and a far blacker night falls over Europe starts me talking. I suppose I am still shocked by Dolly's death, because I tell Maud and Margaret about Tim McShane, matching Maud's honesty. I'd never gone into detail with Maud before. All she knows is I too had a MacBride in my life. And Margaret, well, she's so reserved I never thought to confide in her. But now it all comes out.

The years visiting Tim in the State Street Hotel, betraying Dolly. His attempt to kill me. My sister Henrietta's declaring me dead.

"And yet, I really thought I loved him," I say.

"Did McShane and MacBride change? Or did we not see what was really there all along? Mean alcoholics. Bullies," I say.

"In Ireland, drunkenness excuses any behavior," Maud says. "'Sure, isn't the whisky the devil?' Don't hold a man responsible for what he does under the influence." She sighs. "Thank God the French courts see drunkenness differently. Enough to prove intoxicating behavior; didn't have to go into what he did to my sister Eileen or his attempts on Iseult."

Maud pours more sherry into our glasses. "And because I can't get a divorce under Irish law, MacBride still has rights to Seán. The Gonne women are cursed."

She pokes the fire.

"Really, we are. One of my ancestors stole land from the Church. A priest cursed the family. No Gonne woman would have a happy marriage and it's come true."

Margaret's said nothing all afternoon.

Maud turns to her now. "Kirk. There were Kirks at Castle Caulfield. But perhaps your husband's family immigrated directly from Scotland."

"I really don't know," Margaret says. "Benjamin and I were only married a few years when he died."

"I'm sorry," I say to her.

"Thank you," Margaret says. She looks at Maud. "No priest cursed our family but neither my mother nor I were very lucky in our marriages. My first marriage was annulled," she says.

"You must have been very young," Maud says.

"I married my first husband because he had a house," Margaret says.

I take a drink of sherry.

"My mother, Lizzie Burke, was twenty years younger than my father."

"Burke," I say. "So you're Irish?"

"Yes."

"And Catholic?"

"I am."

"Then why don't you . . ." I stop.

Never saw Margaret go to Communion at Father Kevin's Masses.

"Go on, Margaret," Maud says.

"My father only lived long enough to give my mother three children. Dead at forty. We lived in St. Joe, Missouri, about fifty miles from Kansas

City. Mam got a job as a laundress at the World's Hotel. Quite a place in those days.

"Then we went to Kansas City. My mother was a good seamstress and thought she'd find work in a Big House. But there were loads of Irish women with those skills. She got some piecework, sewing dresses for a neighbor who lived on the block named Nelly Donnelly. Not much money. Though now Nelly's doing well. I wanted to help, but Mam wanted me to stay in school. We'd known a family in St. Joe, who were big in politics in Kansas City. They helped people. Without them we wouldn't have survived. And we had no votes in our house, a widow and her children. My mother said she'd be a suffragist two times over, could she mark the ballot for Jim Pendergast."

I nod. "Chicago's the same," I say. "Precinct captain knows when a family needs food or a job, or has a boy in trouble. My brother and cousin are part of all that. We always had an inside track."

"Lucky," Margaret says. "But even with help we were slipping further down, living in one room in a boardinghouse, months behind in our rent. My mother finally let me go to work. I found a job in the stockroom at Sheehan's Dry Goods. I was only sixteen.

"One day who should come in but this fellow Ralph Danenberg. He was twenty-five but seemed like a man to me. Rough-enough-looking, worked in the stockyards and had a bit of money. A loner from Iowa or some farm place, he'd saved up and bought himself a tidy house on Summit—1616 Summit. I remember the number. Irish Hill, they called it. A big step up from The Bottoms where we lived. The other houses on the block had windows hung with lace curtains. Pianos, even, in many a parlor. That's how he proposed—invited Mam and me to see the house. Said there'd be room for my brother and sister, the whole kit and caboodle of us."

Margaret sips her sherry. Her words slip into each other. Not her usual clipped speech. Here is the young Irish girl within the woman I thought I knew.

"So we went up to the cathedral and talked to Father Ross. Now, I was only sixteen but my mother had married at sixteen," she says.

"Mine too," I say.

"And mine," says Maud.

"But I . . . Well, I remember looking up at this fellow whom I'd said not three words to and wondering what will we talk about? Though that wasn't

Father Ross's concern. He kept asking if I was ready to be a mother. Now I've been taking care of my brother and sister since I was four years old, so I knew I could handle a baby, though I had no notion of how I would get this baby. Something to do with kissing, I thought."

Maud refills her glass.

"Something," I say. "When I was a child I thought a golden shaft of light came down from heaven and turned into a baby, like in the pictures of Baby Jesus in the manger."

Margaret smiles. "Ralph had no golden shaft, I'll tell you that. I tried, I did, but I couldn't. I just couldn't."

And Maud is nodding. "I've never enjoyed the physical side of love either," she says.

Margaret's deep in her memories. "He was patient at first but then, well, one day he just forced himself on me."

"Raped you?" I ask.

"A man can't rape his wife. I found that out when I went running to Father Ross. Not against the law for a man to have relations with his wife no matter how he does it. Not even a matter for confession, Father said. Go back to your husband. I think Ralph was sorry when he saw how terrified I was. He stopped trying. Didn't throw us out either. But then, well, he met a girl, a normal girl, he said, and he had our marriage annulled. Went before a judge and swore I'd never been a wife to him. So I was single again. Mam said she didn't blame me but where to go? I wonder how many young girls were just like me. Then they somehow have a child and . . ." She stops.

"As I did," Maud says.

I wonder will Maud tell Margaret about the death of her first child and Iseult. But Maud seems content to listen.

"I met Benjamin Kirk, and he was much older. Really just wanted a cook and a housekeeper, I think," Margaret says.

"As does Willie," Maud says.

"I did tell him I was shy about marital relations and he said it didn't matter. Except he was a Protestant. Father Ross told me I'd be excommunicated if I married Benjamin Kirk unless he signed papers saying our children would be raised Catholic. Benjamin refused. Wouldn't be told what to do by a priest," Margaret says.

"But if he loved you," I say.

And Margaret smiles. "Don't think love came into it. More a business deal for Benjamin. We married and moved to Denver. He traveled a lot. I had a good job buying for the local department store and a nice apartment near the courthouse and I could send money to my mother. I could see the mountains, so clean and pure, holding their own against the prairie and the sky. I thought I'd be happy if I could just look at them every day. Then Benjamin died. He was working out West for the railroad. They didn't even send the body back. Hard to be alone in a place where you don't know many people. The Red Cross came to Denver. Nurses' aides were needed. I thought I could be of use."

"And you are, Margaret. The hospital couldn't run without you," I say. "Are you ever homesick?"

"I do miss the mountains. Something about seeing them rising up against the sky puts things in perspective," Margaret says. "I'd leave the department store and walk over to Murray's to shop. Great coffee. And you'll never guess who worked there—Douglas Fairbanks!"

"No!" I say.

"Yes, he did. Gorgeous-looking. I'd sometimes wonder if I'd met a man looked like that . . . But I'd walk out of the store and the sun would be setting behind the mountains, the clouds all shades of red and purple, and I'd think, if I had a little cabin up there and could sit and watch that show every night, I'd be completely happy."

"Only you in that cabin?"

She nods.

"No room for Douglas Fairbanks even?" Maud asks.

Margaret laughs. "Only me," she says. "And an eagle, maybe."

"Usually a pair of eagles," I say. "At least in Wisconsin."

"Wisconsin? Didn't know Wisconsin had eagles," Margaret says.

"My cousin Ed has a place in a town called Eagle River."

"Eagle River—that's a nice name," Maud says.

"I miss those weeks up there with the family," I say.

"I'd have a cabin too—but in the Wicklow Mountains. Let's make a pledge, girls. When the war is over each of us will find a place of rest," Maud says.

"You'll need room for Iseult and Seán and all your animals and half the revolutionaries in Ireland," I say.

"Well then I'll visit you and Margaret, " Maud says.

"I have a cabin in mind, too," I say. "Except I'm not alone."

And I blurt it all out—Peter Keeley, the ceremony with Father Kevin.

"Oh, a spiritual marriage! Like Willie and I have," Maud says.

"Well not only spiritual, but I never thought I'd meet a man I would really love. You will too, Margaret. Someday. And you, Maud."

"Love," Maud says. "Willie says he's loved me for thirty years. Wants to help me get a real divorce so we can marry, but I wouldn't make him happy. A poet needs unrequited love."

"I'm not sure I've ever really been in love," Margaret says.

"And will you go back to Kansas City?" Maud asks Margaret.

"I don't know. Hard to be that woman, slumped down in the last pew, not going to Communion. Hard enough here when I stand in the back at the hospital during Mass."

"You don't go to Communion?"

"How can I? I married Benjamin Kirk. Father Ross said I was excommunicated."

"Oh, for God's sake, Margaret, you need a good dose of Father Kevin," I say.

Whatever Father Kevin says to Margaret, that Sunday she goes to Communion.

18

MARCH 21, 1915

"Fecking spring," Paul O'Toole says as he hands a wet bedsheet from the laundry basket up to me. I drape the heavy linen over the line then clothespin it down against the first warm breeze of the season.

"I hate it, too," I say.

"'A great day for drying,' me mam back home in Naas would have said. Now, it's a day for dying," he says.

Paul passes another dripping load up to me.

"The spring offensive, they call it. The time when good weather lets them force the fellows out of the trenches with some bollocking battle plan that'll turn out to be fecking useless. Take a few yards one day, lose them the next, and thousands of dead measuring every inch," he says.

"But you won't be fighting, Paul," I say.

"And glad I am Nora, my heart," he says. "Don't try to make me feel guilty."

"I wouldn't dare," I say. Impossible anyway.

Paul's still with us, coughing strategically when Dr. Gros is about.

"How O'Toole got himself assigned to the hospital I'll never fathom," Dr. Gros had said to me. "His father a general something?"

"Something," I said.

British Army Liaison to the American Hospital is Paul O'Toole's very grand title, though he's willing enough to lend a hand around the place.

"A champion chancer," Father Kevin calls him, "and an informer to boot. But better the devil you know," he'd added.

At least no one else is following me now that I'm Paul's assignment.

"I've arranged for a kind of tea today when your friend Mrs. MacBride and that American reporter call around," he says as we hang the last sheet on the line behind the American hospital.

"Thanks," I say, though I can't remember mentioning the meeting to him.

I've stopped asking how Paul rustles up these treats—tarts, madeleines, and napoleon slices he makes appear along with fresh milk and even sugar.

"There'll be five of us—Father Kevin, Margaret, Maud, Carolyn Wilson, and me."

"And what newspaper does this Wilson woman write for?" Paul asks.

"The Chicago *Tribune*," I say as we walk past budding trees and daffodils. Once welcome signs of life renewed, now they're omens of disaster.

Plenty of casualties through the winter, from shells fired into the trenches, and soldiers beyond counting are made sick from living dug into the earth, standing in icy water up to their knees. All weak from dysentery. Paul only laughed at me when I asked how they managed sanitation.

"Shite manages us," he said. "Mixes with the mud and flows through the trenches. That's the Western Front, Nora."

But spring starts the real killing.

"Carolyn Wilson's a fine reporter," I say to Paul. "Been right in the midst of the fighting."

"Better her than me," Paul says.

He puts about as much energy into spying as he did into soldiering, I think. I'm safe enough. The rugby man's at the front, I suppose. Hope he's in an especially wet trench.

Very warm that afternoon and Paul sets a table for us in the backyard of the hospital.

Carolyn Wilson's younger than I expect, just five years out of college, she tells me.

"Wellesley," she says, then asks where I went to school.

"St. Xavier's High School," I say. "Chicago."

Maud and Father Kevin haven't arrived and Margaret's had an emergency, so Carolyn and I are alone. Paul, imitating a French waiter, pours out the tea and presents us with a plate of madeleines.

"Of course I know your city," she says to me. "I had to spend some time there until the Chicago *Tribune* assigned me to Paris just in time for the start of the war. A lucky break."

"Lucky," I repeat.

"Yes, it was," she says, and then picking up on the tone of my voice, adds that of course she'd prefer there was no war.

"Of course," I say. Silence. Why am I being so hard on her? Only doing her job.

"I liked your piece on French women knitting," I finally say.

"Such intensity in those clicking needles," she says. "As if the sweaters, scarves, and socks they make won't just keep their *p'tit plouplou* warm but somehow protect him from bullets and mortar fire."

A bit too poetic, I think, but then she is a college graduate.

"But," she says, "I also want to emphasize how women have taken over men's jobs—managing shops and restaurants, driving ambulances, and even those stuck in more traditional female roles like you nurses have tremendous authority."

Thanks a lot, I think.

Carolyn showed up at the St. Patrick's Day Mass at Notre-Dame-des-Victoires. Ambassador Herrick introduced me to her as a fellow Chicagoan.

Carolyn went on about the American hospital and how she'd like to interview the American nurses but gave herself away when she saw Maud.

"That's her, isn't it, Maud Gonne," she said. "Do you know her?"

"I do."

"Any chance of an introduction? My editors would be very interested in her views on how the war has affected Ireland. Would she be willing to talk to me?" she asked. Maud was delighted. Lots to say always.

Maud suggested the hospital as our meeting place and wanted to do the interview right away. No flies on Madame MacBride, but where is she? Visiting the Irish soldiers in the wards, I suppose, but I wish she'd get here. I don't want Carolyn Wilson to start asking me questions about myself.

I talk about the logistics of running the hospital until even Paul's bored. Carolyn's taking notes.

"At least there's nothing in the story to alarm the censors," she says.

She tells me that both the French and British military authorities insist on reviewing all her dispatches.

"Annoying," she says. "Won't let me report on how terrible condition are at the front or the number of casualties. I'm going back up to Ypres. Supposed to be another battle there, though that's secret."

"Better watch yourself, Miss Wilson," Paul says. "Not a good idea to blab such information."

"You're right," she says. "The French and British see spies everywhere. I had to answer a lot of questions when I registered at the police station as a foreigner living in Paris," she says.

"Margaret Kirk and I did too," I say. "But when we told them we were nursing they became very gallant."

Where is Margaret anyway?

"Paul," I say, "see if you can hunt up Margaret Kirk and look around for Father Kevin and Maud."

Not pleased to be sent away, is Paul. Afraid he'll miss something. Father Kevin says that Paul knows we know he's spying on us. Doesn't expect us to say much in front of him. A kind of game.

"Probably makes up yarns to send to British Intelligence so they'll let him stay at the hospital," Father Kevin said. "And who can blame the poor fellow."

I ask Carolyn if she's interviewed Sylvia Beach or Gertrude Stein. All the *"femmes de Lesbos"* doing their bit—Gertrude back from Spain and driving an ambulance, and Sylvia nursing. Natalie Barney's militantly pacifist.

"Yes, I have," Carolyn begins just as Paul leads Maud, Father Kevin, and Margaret out to the tea table. Paul's chatting away to Maud. Father Kevin's warned her about him, of course, but Paul's caught her up into that Irish dance of "Who do you know?"

For all his talk of "me mam and the humble cottage," Paul's able to pull out the names of a few Kildare families who were friends of Maud's.

"Gentry, of course," Paul says, "and not pals of mine exactly but we're all horse-mad in Kildare, and I've spent time with them at the Punchtown races, which is where we should all be right now."

"A racecourse is the one place all strands of Irish society meet and mingle," Maud says.

"Plenty of foreigners, too," Paul says. "I suppose you would have known loads of Germans, Mrs. MacBride."

And I'm embarrassed for Paul, so obvious. I mean if he's going to be a spy, let him be a good spy.

Maud laughs.

"Put this down, Paul—Miss Gonne refused to be drawn but did however launch into an impassioned denunciation of the war," she says and turns to Carolyn.

"You see, Miss Wilson, I believe both sides in this struggle will end up defeated and weakened," Maud says. "Art, music, literature—all the expressions of the soul that Europeans have developed over the last thousand years are carried in fragile human vessels. Now those bodies are being blown apart, riddled with shrapnel, and for what?"

Maud is in full swing when Barry Delaney comes walking toward us.

"Maud," I say. She turns, sees Barry.

"What, what?" She gets up, goes to Barry. Maud asks, "Something wrong? I know, Seán's sick."

Barry shakes her head.

"Worse, he's dead? My baby? Another one taken? How?" Maud clutches Barry's arm.

"Not Seán," Barry says. "A telegram came from your sister Kathleen. Her son Tom has been killed near Neuve-Chapelle."

Maud slumps forward. Father Kevin and Paul are there, each take one of Maud's arms, holding her up.

"No, no," Maud says. "He's only twenty-one. So charming, so handsome, so alive. Kathleen adores him. How will she bear this? It will kill her."

"Here Maud, sit down," I say. The men help her back into the chair.

"I'll get some brandy," Margaret says.

Carolyn holds her pencil above her notebook.

"What was his full name?" Carolyn asks.

Maud looks up at her.

"Thomas Percy Pilcher," she says. "Lieutenant in the Second Battalion, Rifle Brigade, the Prince Consort's Own."

Maud turns to Paul.

"Put that in your report, Mr. O'Toole," she says. "Now, leave us. Go."

Paul pouts for days. Not speaking to me. When I lug the laundry basket past him, he turns his head.

Maud and Iseult have gone to the military hospital at Paris Pelage Pas-de-Calais, where Maud's sister Kathleen is nursing. They'll work there together.

"Only way to face death is to struggle for life," Maud says to me before she goes.

No time to mourn, I think. These twelve- and fourteen-hour days exhaust all feeling. And then two weeks later, a letter comes from John Feeney. Shipped home and safe, I thought, hoped, but he managed to get himself back in the Dublin Fusiliers. Foolish boy, I think. Foolish. Foolish. I'm angry at John. Can't help it. He was safe, one fellow I didn't have to be afraid for.

> Dear Nora,
>
> Going to a place called Gallipoli, lovely sounding name, isn't it? Were not supposed to know where we're going, but the invasion has been reported in the London newspapers. So we won't be surprising Johnny Turk. Just as well. I'm ready to fight a real battle. My angels have promised to surround us all. My best to your Connemara husband.
>
> Your friend,
> John Feeney

I find Paul.

"I know you're mad at me, but you have to read this. John Feeney's back in the war on his way to Gallipoli."

Paul snatches the letter. He skims it.

"Eejit," he says. "They'll be landing on a beach, so a chance for both the army and the navy to make a balls of it."

"Listen, Paul," I start.

"No need to apologize," he says.

"What? You're the betrayer. What do I have to be sorry about?"

"You well know I'd never report anything really damaging about you or anyone. And for Mrs. MacBride, who I've admired for years, to accuse me like that, as if I wouldn't respect her grief, I'm very offended."

"You mean you didn't send in a report on our meeting with Carolyn Wilson and Tom Pilcher's death?"

"Now, Nora, of course I did. I had to. You were seen. Do you think I'm the only undercover fellow in this hospital? But you came out very well and the colonel's interested in Carolyn Wilson. She could go observe some German troops, her being neutral and all. Then report to the colonel. Nice money in it for her. Would you ask her?"

"Shut up, Paul," I say, and go to find Father Kevin.

"Listen to what Paul proposed," I say, and tell him.

"Watch him, Nora," Father Kevin says. "Not the *amadán* he pretends to be. Say nothing about Peter Keeley to him."

"Of course not," I say.

Father Kevin says, "Conscription's surely coming to England. And the British government will try to draft Irishmen, too. Then Peter will be in the lion's mouth. They'll call keeping the Irish boys out of the British army treason, a capital crime, a hanging offense."

O dear God. Please. I'm doing your work here. Please. Please. Protect Peter.

Almost the end of April when I see Carolyn again. Find her in the yard where the ambulances bring in casualties after taking them from the train station. Not the confident young woman of a few weeks before. Dr. Gros has called all of us nurses out to await a convoy coming from Ypres.

The battle Paul calls a "cock-up."

Young Tony Hulman's driving the first ambulance, moving very slowly for him. He usually roars up, slams on the brakes. Urgent no matter the condition of the patient. But now he parks, gets out, and waves Paul over.

"We'll need you," Tony says.

Paul and another orderly run forward with a stretcher. But Tony's partner, Charlie Kinsolving, a young New Yorker, has already opened the back door and is helping the first soldier step out of the ambulance.

An Arab, I see, one of the French colonial troops. A white gauze bandage is tied around his head covering his eyes. Paul takes his arm, moves him forward to Dr. Gros, who carefully lifts the bandage and examines the soldier. Two more soldiers bandaged in the same way join the first. They stand very still.

"They're all blind," Carolyn says to me. "Gassed. The Germans shot canisters of chlorine gas into the trenches manned by these Algerian troops. Yellow clouds of the stuff fell down over the men. Some ran, some dived into the bottom of the trenches, but they couldn't escape. Hundreds died within ten minutes. I saw the bodies. Survivors told me the gas burned their lungs. They couldn't breathe. They lived or died depending on which way the wind was blowing."

"How many killed?" I ask her.

"Thousands," she says. "And many more blinded like these poor fellows."

Ambulances continue to arrive. And over the next hour we admit almost two hundred patients. More Algerians and then a whole load of Canadians who Carolyn tells me held their position in the line during the gas attack.

"They stood firing back even while they were choking to death," she says.

Dr. Gros tells us there is nothing we can do but wash the fellows down, burn their clothes, and try to make them comfortable.

Margaret starts a bucket brigade and we line up the troops, sponge them down with warm soapy water, and get them into clean nightshirts. Thank God, Mrs. Vanderbilt buys in big quantities.

The men fill every empty bed. We set up cots in the hallways and along the aisles of the ward. About half the soldiers are blind. All have burns on their faces and bodies as well as other wounds. Father Kevin moves from bed to bed hearing the confessions of the Catholics, anointing the fellows in the worst shape, and praying with the Moslems. Carolyn follows him. Some of the fellows are eager to tell her about how terrifying it was to be enveloped in a cloud of chlorine gas. Many thought the Germans had sent out a smokescreen to cover an infantry attack. But as soon as they breathed, they felt their throats close, their eyes burn, and saw the men around them collapse.

"Somehow they think gas is worse than artillery. One Canadian soldier told me, 'It's just not sporting,'" Carolyn says.

Paul brings Carolyn, Margaret, and me into his hidey-hole. Well after midnight as we drink tea braced with brandy. I think of what Maud said. The human body is a fragile vessel. I mean to die from breathing?

"I don't know how much longer I can do this," Carolyn says as she drains her tea. Paul pours straight brandy into her cup.

"Important for the world to know the truth about this war," I say.

"It is. But nothing I write can really make what those fellows endure real. Those bodies. The faces. Lips pulled back, mouths open. They died screaming," Carolyn says.

"I wish America would just come in and end this whole thing," Margaret says. "As much as I hate to see our boys suffering, at least the war would be over."

"Don't be so sure," Paul says. "Your country has a very small army and I've heard the British officers talking. Not much respect for your military. They say that American soldiers are a bunch of cowboys and immigrants. They can't be trained to proper discipline. They won't fight."

"Discipline," I say, "like standing in place while you are choking to death?"

"Listen, Nora," Paul says. "Any normal man dropped onto the middle of a battlefield would run for his life when the guns started to go off. Military training tries to bury the survival instinct. Brainwashes soldiers to stand and fight."

Carolyn shakes her head. "Sometimes there are more direct methods. I saw a British officer aim a pistol at a gassed French soldier and order him back in the line."

"Well, there is that," Paul says. "They shoot you if you run."

"If our fellows come over here, they won't run," I say. But please, God: America will not go to war.

"Lots of Irish fellows among those Canadians," Father Kevin says when he joins us an hour later. "Asking questions about the situation in Ireland. Would we ever get Home Rule? One very knowledgeable fellow. Said his family had been Fenians for generations."

"Which one is that?" Paul wants to know.

"Now that's enough, Paul," Father Kevin says. "We tolerate your little games because no man should have to suffer the hell of the Western Front. But if you start bothering the patients . . ."

"Paul spies on us," I tell Carolyn. "In fact he wants to recruit you. Dispatches from behind the German lines with a little extra for British Intelligence."

"All a cod," Paul says. "You know I'd never do you any real harm."

I would like to meet the soldier who's the Fenian. Odd if his grandfather helped my uncle Patrick invade Canada. Wonder if the fellow wishes his country had left the British Empire altogether and joined the United

States. That had been Uncle Patrick's idea. Then Canadian soldiers wouldn't be lying in a hospital in Paris, blind from a gas attack. Please God, keep America out of this mess.

But only two weeks later, a German U-boat sinks the British liner *Lusitania* off the coast of Ireland. Over a thousand people drowned, a hundred and twenty-eight Americans among them.

"That's it," Paul says to me at the hospital two days after we get the news. "Yous'll be in it now. Can't let the Huns blow innocent souls into kingdom come especially if some of those souls are Americans."

He lowers his voice. "Though the *Lusitania* was carrying weapons and ammunition for the British army, make no mistake about that. And to be fair, the Germans took out ads in the American newspapers warning people not to travel on her. But of course the Brits are always so cocky. Sure the *Lusitania* could outrun any U-boat, though I hear the company had closed down one furnace to save money so the ship wasn't traveling at full speed."

"How do you know these things?" I ask.

"I have my sources," he says.

When the list of the victims comes out, I notice the name Vanderbilt. Some relation I suppose. So when I see Mrs. Vanderbilt in the ward the next week I stop and speak to her. "Sorry for your troubles," I say, and realize I sound like I'm greeting a widow at a Bridgeport wake.

"Thank you," she says.

Anne's her first name. But I never call her anything but Mrs. Vanderbilt. William's second wife, I know, and herself divorced. Plenty of fallen women around Paris I guess. Though I doubt this lady would ever let guilt stalk her or listen to the Fairy Woman's voice.

"I know your face," she says to me. "But not your name."

"Nora Kelly," I say.

"Oh, Irish," she says. And I wait for her to tell me about her beloved nanny from County Cork.

But no, instead she says, "My stepson, William, married an Irish girl. Perhaps you know her—Virginia Graham Fair?"

Now that's a familiar name. One of my uncle Patrick's favorite stories was about the four Irish fellows out West prospecting—no-hopers—who then struck it rich. The Silver Kings he called him. Building mansions all over the place, on top of the world. William Fair was a Tyrone man, I remember, and his daughter became a famous socialite. Pictures in all the papers. Hardly an Irish girl I would have met at dances in Chicago.

"I've heard of Virginia," I say.

"And of course the Irish fishermen in Cork made such valiant efforts to rescue the *Lusitania* passengers," she says.

"They did save more than seven hundred," I say. "And risked their lives doing it."

Mrs. Vanderbilt nods.

"Father Kevin is saying a special Mass for the victims tomorrow morning here at the hospital," I say. "You'd be very welcome."

"Thank you, my dear. But I'm afraid Catholic rituals befuddle me."

"Eternal Rest grant unto the soul of Hugh Lane, Oh Lord," Father Kevin prays at the end of Mass for the Victims of the *Lusitania*.

"And let perpetual light shine upon him," we answer. The words seem to run through my mind continuously these days.

"He was Lady Gregory's nephew," Father Kevin tells us as we help him put the mass vessels into a small cupboard in the broom closet that's become the hospital sacristy.

"A friend of Maud's and Willie Yeats. Of John Quinn, too. A great art collector. He's left his paintings to the Irish nation—the core of a great National Gallery," Father Kevin says.

"When Ireland long a province becomes a nation once again?" I say.

Margaret taps her toe. Impatient with talk of Irish politics, but I feel closer to Peter when Father Kevin and I run over the old phrases. A bit like fingering rosary beads.

"It's the American nation I'm concerned about," Margaret says. "Sat up half the night with the other nurses in the dormitory arguing about whether the U.S. should enter the war or not," she says.

"What do you think?" Father Kevin asks her.

"I don't know," she says.

"Neither do I," I say.

"Not up to us to decide," Margaret says. "I have patients to see. Those Algerian soldiers are so grateful. And have you noticed their teeth? Excellent condition. One fellow told me they use twigs to clean their teeth. An almost religious practice."

"Must feel very far away from home," I say.

NOVEMBER 1915

So. Truly a world war now. African troops, many regiments from India. Then news comes about that place John Feeney was sent. Gallipoli. A terrible defeat for the Allies.

"I told you," Paul says when the newspapers report the failed landings. "Disaster. Criminal. A slaughter."

And long-legged John Feeney dead on that rocky beach, Sulva.

"Better for him to have died beneath an Irish sky fighting for his country's freedom than in such outlandishly foreign places," Maud says when I tell her. Oh Johnny, where were your angels? "And of course the British generals send Australian troops against the Turks' big guns. Don't see the Ulster regiments in these truly hapless battles. No—the Colonials. And of course so many of the Australians and New Zealanders have Irish blood, too."

Maud and I have been to Mass at the Irish College. The first Sunday of Advent.

November now. She and Iseult have returned to Paris after a hard summer's nursing in Paris Plage with her sister Kathleen.

"Some consolation for Kathleen in caring for poor wounded boys," Maud says. "Still can't believe Tom's gone."

Not many in the Irish College chapel. The streets around the university empty. Is there a young Frenchman anywhere not at the Front? Many of the Irish fellows in the British army. Alive or dead, who knows? The young women from Ireland staying home, too. Not easy to travel back and forth to France.

We're waiting for Father Kevin in the parlor. He's got some important visitor and we're drinking up his supply of Barry's tea.

"Kathleen went to London," Maud says. "And was denied permission to travel back here. Had to get a doctor to verify that she was required to go to Switzerland for her health. True enough. Tom's death destroyed her. Heartbreaking to see her try to smile at the soldiers."

"Wonder does anyone count the families of the fallen in the casualties lists," I say. "I mourn every patient in the hospital who dies and I barely know them."

I have a gallery of photographs of soldiers now. Stuck them up in the wall of my room. Put a candle on a table in front of the display of the living and the dead. A kind of memorial. I find myself describing the altar to Maud. She becomes very enthusiastic.

"Yes," she says. "Some material expression is important. I've designed a beautiful gold cross with rays shooting out from the center to place in the church at Neuve-Chappelle as a memorial to Tom. Some comfort for Kathleen," she says.

"Sounds very dramatic," I say.

"It is," she says. Nothing plain for Maud.

"You should publish your photographs," she says to me.

"Carolyn Wilson has used a few of my portraits of the soldiers to illustrate her articles," I say.

"And paid you, I hope," Maud says.

"I don't expect her to and besides I don't want any credit, especially in the Chicago *Tribune*. Remember, I'm officially dead," I say.

"Soldiers die all the time with barely a mention," Maud says. "Amazing now to think you had a whole newspaper article to yourself."

"Something to be grateful for, I guess," I say.

Maud doesn't laugh as Margaret would have. I'm getting used to being around Americans. A different sense of humor.

"And how is Margaret Kirk?" Maud asks.

Had she read my thoughts? Can't underestimate Maud.

"Working hard," I say. "The hospital's capacity is six hundred. We have eight hundred patients. Margaret made me take a few days off," I say. "Most of the Algerian soldiers have left. Back to their homes. Hard to think of them trying to make their way as blind men in some tiny village."

I tell Maud about the photograph I took of the Algerian soldiers down on the floor praying.

"Facing Mecca?" she asks.

"Yes," I say. "Some of the Moslems among the British Indian troops joined them."

"The colonized sacrificing themselves for the colonizer," Maud says. "But not forever. Ireland will be the first to throw off the chains but other countries will follow," she says. "Mark my words."

"Let's get this war over with first," I say.

Father Kevin leads a tall thin man in a very fancy cassock with red piping into the parlor. The fellow could have stepped out of a Renaissance painting of an Italian bishop—that Roman nose, high forehead.

"Ladies, may I introduce Monsignor Pacelli," Father Kevin says. "He's visiting the prison camps for the Pope. Reporting on the conditions. Bringing some aid, too,"

The monsignor inclines his head.

"Monsignor Pacelli tells me Pope Benedict has committed the Vatican treasury and whatever personal money he has to refugee relief," Father Kevin says. "He has kindly given me a donation for the hospital."

Monsignor Pacelli nods at me. A twitchy fellow. Very intense. He's been meeting with the representatives of the belligerent nations, trying to broker a truce, he tells us.

"They are all suspicious of me. Don't believe the Vatican is neutral. Each thinks we favor the other side," he says.

"At least the Pope is trying," Maud says. "The only honorable thing to do now is to work for peace."

Maud kneels in front of Monsignor Pacelli for a very formal blessing and then he's gone.

When Father Kevin returns, he says, "Poor man. A sensitive fellow. Horrified by the conditions in the prison camps. Close to a nervous breakdown, I'd say. Off to stay with the nuns at Lake Constance. They'll put him right."

"Any news from Ireland?" I ask.

"Nothing directly from your friend but the Irish Volunteers are drilling, carrying the rifles you helped obtain, Nora. Members of the Irish Republican Brotherhood with them."

Father Kevin goes to a cabinet—brings out a bottle and fills our teacups with whiskey. "Medicinal," he says.

"I've been having a strange dream," Maud says after a good jolt of whiskey. I take a sip. Very warming.

"Since Samhain. A kind of waking dream, really. Haunted by an air with the rhythm of a reel. I hum it unconsciously and then this morning at Mass I could finally translate into consciousness scraps of the experience I was going through."

I take another slug of whiskey. I may need it. Maud's off and running.

"I remember that I'd heard the tune once before when I'd climbed Slieve Gullion," she says.

"In Donegal," Father Kevin tells me.

Maud nods. "The sound seemed to come out of the mountain and I associated it with an ancient smith. It reminded me of Wagner's song of the sword."

She's lost me but Father Kevin's leaning forward taking in every word so I listen harder.

"I also heard an air like it at a Gaelic League *feis* played for an eight-hand reel," Maud says.

OK. Reels I know.

"So incessant is this air I could hardly keep my feet from dancing," she says.

"In the chapel?" I ask, but Maud doesn't hear me.

In a trance almost.

"During your sermon, Father Kevin, I realized what I've been seeing. Masses of the spirits of those who have been killed in this war. They are being marshaled and drawn together by waves of rhythmic music. It draws them into dances of strange patterns.

"The thousands of Irish soldiers who have been killed dance with a frenzied intensity to this wild reel and they draw others in and the rhythm is so strong they have to dance. And they are all led back to the spiritual Ireland. Both those who went into this war inconsequently and those who died with a definite idea of sacrifice. All brought together through these wonderful patterns into a deep peace, the peace of the Crucified, which is above the currents of nationality, beyond hate. And I know, deeply know, that they will bring Ireland great strength."

"Dear God, I hope so," I say. Sometimes I wish I had Maud's faith as, well, unusual as it is.

Maud and Father Kevin are talking away about how the hard men of the Irish Republican Brotherhood have joined with the more middle-of-the-road Irish Volunteers and what that will mean. Maud says there'll be an uprising within the year. Father Kevin's not so sure.

"What better time to act than when the British army's losing to the Germans? The government will be relieved to let Ireland go," Maud says.

"Oh Maud," I say. "You heard that General Henry Wilson. The British will fight to keep Ireland. And then what? More killing?"

"Better have the battle now and get it over with," she says.

"But does Ireland even have enough men to fight?" I ask.

"We have our Fenian dead, Nora," Maud says. "And the thousands of fallen Irish soldiers who have come together to free their country."

And now I don't know what to say. I'm back in my conversation with Margaret about America entering the war. Stay neutral or send in the marines?

It's Carolyn Wilson who helps me make up my mind that very next week when she brings a whole group of American women who are passing through Paris to the hospital.

Friends of Mrs. Vanderbilt, maybe. Society ladies, I assume. Rich enough to travel and not able to give up a bit of Paris shopping. Madame Simone still getting the occasional American customer in spite of the war.

But when Carolyn arrives with the four I see these women are very different from Madame Simone's clients. They've come in a taxi. Carolyn helps the first woman out. Older. Sixty, I'd guess.

"Nora Kelly," Carolyn says. "I'd like to introduce you to my teacher from Wellesley, Emily Balch. One of the leaders of the WILPF—Women's International League for Peace and Freedom."

Miss Balch shakes my hand. I see a distinctive figure leaving the taxi. Oh, Jesus. Of all people. I recognize her. Nobody living in Chicago who couldn't pick Jane Addams out of a crowd. Hadn't Rose and Mame and I gone to see the Abbey Players at Hull House? Oh, yes, Jane Addams is for all the right things—votes for women, unions, fair wages, does great work in that Westside neighborhood around Hull House. Except, as Ed said to me once, if Jane Addams could bring herself to work with her alderman, she'd do more good. But a powerful woman altogether.

The last two take some time climbing out of the backseat. I move forward to help but Carolyn puts her hand on my arm.

"They can manage," she says.

A white cane comes out first and pokes the ground and then a woman steps out. Blind. The second woman's right behind her wearing dark glasses. The two stand still for a moment, getting their bearings, I suppose.

Wait a minute. I know that face. Jesus, Mary, and Joseph. It's Helen Keller and the other woman must be Annie Sullivan. A famous pair and a great story. The blind-deaf little girl brought out of her darkness by the devoted teacher. What a group of women!

"I'm honored," I say, and then to Carolyn, "Thanks for bringing such distinguished guests. Oh, the soldiers will get a real kick out of meeting them."

I assume the French and British will know about Helen Keller. I mean there was a movie made about her life.

Well, it turns out all four women had been at the big women's peace conference at The Hague. Not too much in the papers here about the meeting. Carolyn tells me over a thousand women including delegates from the countries warring against each other attended. Though the British government wouldn't give women from their country passports so they could go.

"The Peace Conference called for an immediate truce and said when women got the vote they wouldn't let their countries go to war," Carolyn explains to me as we go into the hospital.

As we walk into a ward Jane Addams tells us she's been going from capital city to capital city in Europe trying to make the governments see reason. Stop the War.

"Any luck?" I ask.

"Not much," she says.

Of course Paul O'Toole appears out of somewhere. Not about to miss this. And charms the ladies. Going on about his Sullivan relations to Annie. He somehow knows Helen Keller's a dog lover and launches into a speech praising man or woman's best friend.

Helen wants to meet the blind soldiers right away.

"God works in mysterious ways," she says to me. "Do you know the name George Kessler?" she asks.

"I don't," I say.

"Really? He's the Champagne King."

"French?" I ask.

"American," she says. "One of the passengers on the *Lusitania*."

Well I've been so immersed in Maud's mysticism, I think Helen's going to tell me George appeared to her, popping corks in heaven.

But no, Kessler was rescued. While bobbing around in the Atlantic, he'd promised that if he were saved he'd spend his money doing good. Got in touch with Helen and they have just started the French, English, and Belgian Permanent Blind War Relief Fund.

"I'll show you to the ward," Paul O'Toole says to her.

Emily and Carolyn walk together and Paul's got Annie Sullivan and Helen Keller mesmerized. So it's Jane and me.

"So Miss Addams," I say. "You'd be against America entering the war."

"Absolutely," she says.

"But what if by coming in, we'd help end the fighting?" I ask her.

"Easy to get into a war," she says. "Hard to get out. I told Woodrow that."

So. Quite an afternoon. It's over one of Paul's conjured-up teas that Helen Keller makes the argument against that the war that convinces me.

"Congress won't be going to war to defend the people of the United States. No, they plan to protect the capital of American speculators and investors and benefit the manufacturers of munitions and war machines," she says.

"These are the points I'll make in my speech in Carnegie Hall in January," she tells us. "All modern wars are rooted in exploitation. The present war is being fought to decide who shall exploit the Balkans, Turkey, Egypt, India, China, and Africa. And now America's whetting the sword to scare the victors into sharing the spoils with us. But the workers who will fight and die are not interested in the spoils. They won't get any of them anyway."

I don't know. Maybe because Helen's blind and deaf and her being able to speak at all is a kind of miracle, her words hit me.

She's right, I think. Flags, patriotism, the songs, the drums, all a cod, as Paul would say. Ways to get soldiers to die to make other people rich.

There. I've decided. Nora Kelly, pacifist. Peace now. And I hold on to my commitment through that terrible winter.

19

JANUARY 1916

So.

I suppose I should have become suspicious when Paul O'Toole starts asking me all those questions about Helen Keller and James Addams, but I assumed he was interested in them because they were famous. Nothing secret about their views, after all.

Yet, Paul quizzes me for days after "the peace women," as he calls them, toured the hospital. Still, the penny didn't drop, even when he said to me, "They're socialists, you know." Using a certain tone.

"So what?" I said. "Lots of the patients are too. Working fellows after all."

Since Christmas, the union members among the soldiers have started meeting in the hospital dayroom most afternoons, the French and British soldiers together, and the Scottish, Irish, and English fellows mixing with each other. Unusual that.

I stop by on New Year's Day to wish them health and peace. Tell them about the women's peace march in New York. I repeat Helen Keller's statement, that the war was being fought for capitalism.

"She's right," one Scottish solider says.

"But what odds," says another. "We have to win the thing now. Too many fellows have died to let it all sputter to nothing."

But then a third solider speaks up. "Maybe we should all go on strike. The Christmas truce made permanent."

Paul starts going on about Big Jim Larkin and James Connolly. Tells the fellows he was one of the men locked out in Dublin in 1913.

"But I thought you were from Kildare," I say to him.

"I was working in Dublin," he says, "as a tramcar driver."

Now I haven't forgotten Paul is an informer, but nothing hidden about these meetings. Officers from the other wing of the hospital even attend, the only time they mix with ordinary soldiers. Strange to me this insistence on absolute separation between the officers and the enlisted men, but as Margaret Kirk says, "When in Rome, do as the Romans do." Or in this case, follow the dictates of the British and French armies. Even the prison camps were divided, that Italian monsignor had told us.

I hold a very small Women's Christmas in my room at the place des Voges. Maud isn't easy about the date, January 6, 1916. "Six is an unlucky number," she says, but comes along for a glass of wine with Margaret Kirk, Madame Simone, and me.

No secrets round the fire this year, only sad news. Two of Madame Simone's nephews have been killed. Maud says the French army is suffering greater casualties than the British. Millevoye's son is dead. Maud's convinced the British will try to impose conscription on Ireland.

"British ships are already refusing to carry Irishmen of military age to America," she tells us, "and arresting anyone writing in favor of peace."

Before she leaves, she gives me a book.

"Willie Yeats sent it to me. I didn't like it," she says. "Written by this young fellow Willie is trying to help called James Joyce. Joyce was in Paris years ago, sent me a note asking to call. I wrote back, telling him I was sick. Never heard from him again. Took offense, I suppose."

She shrugs.

"Maybe just as well, this James Joyce has a very sordid imagination. Sees only ugliness in Dublin, and yet he was a friend of Skeffington and Kettle. Spent musical evenings at the Sheehy house, knew all those girls. Such vivid young people, but I'm afraid Joyce is the kind of writer who looks at the stars and sees only bits of tinsel paper."

So why give the book to me, I wonder.

But then she says, "I might be missing something. Read it and tell me what you think, Nora."

During the rest of January, I read a few pages of *A Portrait of the Artist as a Young Man* each night, imagining Peter across from me at the fire, deep in his own book.

I find I like Stephen Dedalus and his friends. They remind me of the fellows I grew up with in Chicago. At least the ones who went on to St. Ignatius, or even Loyola University. Easy to imagine Ed and Mike walking through Dublin with Stephen's crowd.

Odd to find mention of the Litany of Our Lady, the Sodality, and prayers like "Bless us, O Lord, and these thy gifts" in a book. That long sermon that scares Stephen? Redemptorist priests thundered those very words at me, during the yearly mission at St. Bridget's. And I certainly understand Stephen's lightness of spirit after confession. Hadn't Father Kevin given me the grace of a cleansed soul? Must give him the book.

Father Kevin tries to come to the hospital every day. Says Mass here Sunday and marks every holy day. The rituals seems to console the fellows.

I stop him on Ash Wednesday after he's distributed ashes in the wards and ask if the Jesuit school Stephen goes to is a real place. "It is," he says. Father Kevin met James Joyce when the writer came to Paris ten years before, he tells me. "Joyce wanted to be a doctor then," Father Kevin says.

"A prickly fellow, but being very young and short of money does that to you," he says.

"I think he's going to France at the end of the book," I say. "Stephen's mother packs up his new secondhand clothes and prays for him." I read a bit to Father Kevin: "'That I may learn in my own life and away from home and friends what the heart is and what it feels.'

"Exactly what I'm trying to do," I say. "Though the last lines seem to be a little highfalutin for me." They should have pleased Maud. Listen, 'Welcome, O life! I go to encounter for the millionth time the reality of experience and forge in the smithy of my soul the uncreated conscience of my race.'"

"Lovely stuff altogether," Father Kevin says.

Definitely reaching for the stars, not tinsel paper.

The next week I give Margaret Kirk the book to read.

"Glad for anything in English," she says to me.

Not as enthusiastic as I was after she reads *A Portrait of the Artist as a Young Man*.

"I skipped all the religious bits. I had enough of that growing up," she says.

"What about the 'welcome, o life,'" I say, "and 'encountering experience.' Did you like that?"

"Well, we're encountering experience all right," she says.

New casualties are coming in faster than ever. Only February, and yet the fighting has begun in a place called Verdun.

All of us run off our feet, Paul O'Toole working right along beside us all through February and March. The dayroom becomes a ward again, and most of the union fellows are sent back to the front lines.

APRIL 1916

April now, and a load of French soldiers in my ward. I confuse them with my French, I know, but thank God today a wounded French officer comes in to visit who speaks perfect English.

"Prosper Cholet," he says, introducing himself. "I am a lieutenant in the Chasseurs a group like your Marine Corps," he tells me. Handsome though his whole head is bandaged.

"How are you feeling?" I ask.

"I am a lucky man," he says. "I was buried under debris on the battlefield. Only the top of my head sticking up, left for dead. But I was saved by these fellows from my unit." He points to three soldiers propped up in their beds, smiling. They don't understand a word but are happy their officer is telling the story of his rescue, and their heroism.

Lieutenant Cholet's very different from the English officers who inspect the men when they visit by marching past each bed, hardly speaking.

"Nice to see an officer at ease with his men," I say.

"Well, you see," Lieutenant Cholet says, "I have lived in America for years, I am a chemist and worked for the Michelin tire company in New Jersey. Do you know New Jersey?" he asked.

"Heard of it," I say. "But I'm from Chicago. My name is Nora Kelly."

"Irish?" he says.

I get ready. He's had an Irish cook in New Jersey, I suppose. But Lieutenant Cholet takes something out of his pocket, a photograph. He shows me a portrait of a young woman.

"My fiancée," he says. "Mary Caroline Haywood. She gets her beauty from her Irish mother."

"She's lovely," I say. "You must miss her."

"I write to her every day. Even from the trenches."

"Aren't you going to introduce me to the lieutenant," Paul O'Toole says. Sidling up out of nowhere, nosy as always. Lieutenant Cholet becomes very aristocratic and French of all of a sudden.

"I am Lieutenant Prosper Cholet," he says to Paul. "I appreciate the service you are giving my men." And then turns to me. *"Bonsoir, mademoiselle. I will return tomorrow."*

"Toffee-nosed," Paul says.

When the lieutenant comes the next day, he asks me about Paul. "Why is an able-bodied man not fighting at the Front?"

"He is meant to be spying on us," I say. "But he's harmless."

"Soyez sage, mademoiselle," Lieutenant Cholet tells me as he leaves.

Paul comes up to me. "Who does that fellow think he is? Walking around us as if he owns this place? I saw him yesterday, out in the garage, chatting away to Tony and Charlie."

"Well he works for a tire company, maybe he's interested in the ambulances."

"Can't trust those frogs," Paul says.

The next day, Lieutenant Cholet tells me he heard I take photographs, and he would like a picture to send to "my beloved Caroline."

I go to get my Seneca from the nurses' dormitory where I've been sleeping sometimes. He's to meet me in the back garden. I find him posed against a blossoming apple tree. He wears a kepi, which disguises his wound. The brim of the cap diffuses the light, brightening his eyes.

"Very handsome," I say, when I line him up in the lens. "Mary Caroline is a lucky woman."

"Because of her I will survive," he says. "She's praying for me. You Irish are more intensely Catholic than we French."

I ask if he'd care to read James Joyce's book. He finishes it in two days.

"I like the way the boys in the book joke back and forth. That male camaraderie is what armies count on."

As he gives me back the book, I see Paul O'Toole watching us.

"Are you looking for me, Paul?" I ask.

"For His Nibs. He's got visitors. Big shots at the front entrance," Paul says.

Big shots, no question. Not only Mrs. Vanderbilt in her white couture nurse's uniform, but her husband, W.K. himself. A man I've only seen once in the two years I've worked at the hospital. Dr. Gros stands with them, and a man I don't know. Older, bearded, heavyset.

"Prosper," the man says, grabbing Lieutenant Cholet's hand.

"Édouard," he replies.

I intend to just walk past them, but Lieutenant Cholet stops me.

"Please, let me introduce Édouard Michelin, my employer and friend."

Paul's right there, of course. "I could arrange some refreshments, Mrs. Vanderbilt," he says.

"Very kind of you, young man," she says, "but Lieutenant Cholet is dining at our home."

We watch them leave.

"Well, I like that," Paul says. "Who is this fellow anyway?"

Lieutenant Cholet comes to the ward early next morning.

"I am here to say good-bye, mademoiselle, to you and my chasseurs. I have a new assignment. I am to serve with the Americans who are flying for France."

He's filled with enthusiasm, telling me how Dr. Gros has enlisted Mr. Vanderbilt's financial support in starting an American flying unit.

"They have pilots now, and planes, and the French have accepted the unit. The Lafayette Escadrille they are calling it. A fine name, isn't it?"

"You are a pilot?" I ask.

"Not yet," he says. "Few are. But I can help with the mechanics. Mr. Michelin has given land for an air station, and one of your young drivers has already offered to volunteer."

"Charlie Kinsolving, I bet," I say. I'm right.

"Mr. Michelin found out that I had been wounded twice. Told me that is enough for any man. The prayers of my Mary Caroline are answered. I am out of the trenches and up into the air," he says.

Doesn't sound a lot safer to me, I think.

EASTER WEEK 1916

"Glad to see the last of that fellow," Paul says to me.

It's Good Friday, April 20th. Father Kevin is going through the wards for the Veneration of the Cross. I remember how we lined up at St. Bridget's to kiss the crucifix as the choir sang dirgelike hymns. Paul and I accompany Father Kevin. Paul rings a small bell as we enter each ward. I walk next to Father Kevin with a candle as he goes from bed to bed. The men do seem to get some comfort from touching their lips to the wooden figure of Christ.

Paul's still muttering to me about Lieutenant Cholet as we move to the next ward.

"Don't know why you took against him," I whisper.

"He's a show-off," Paul says. "Airplanes? I ask you! And to take a little shite like Charlie Kinsolving and then laugh at me when I volunteer . . ."

"You volunteered?" I say. "To fly?"

"I'm mechanically inclined," he says. "I could work on the planes on the ground. Very nice accommodations for the air units. They live in hotels."

"What's happened, Paul? Someone pressuring you to go back to the Front?" I ask. "Have your superiors finally realized we're no threat?"

"It's that Frenchie who stirred things up," he says.

We move onto the next ward. I think of Maud's vision, what did she call it? The peace of the crucified? I'm voting for Easter.

Maud's in Normandy for the holidays, planting potatoes in her garden, convinced that there will be no food next winter.

A lovely Mass Easter Sunday in the dayroom. In his sermon, Father Kevin tells the soldiers that in Ireland the rooster symbolizes the resurrection.

"The connection originated," he says, "in the story of the Roman soldiers assigned to guard the tomb of Jesus. Pontius Pilate was afraid Jesus's followers would steal his body, so the soldiers rolled a huge stone in front of the sepulcher and went back to the barracks for their dinner. The cook had a fat rooster on the boil. They all sat down. But their captain came in, furious. Why were the soldiers here? They should be on guard, he said. But the sergeant stood up to the captain. 'There's no more chance of that Jesus getting out of his tomb than of that rooster in the pot standing up and crowing.' And at that very moment, the rooster flew out of the pot, his cry in Irish is 'Slán mhic Máire!' 'The son of Mary is safe!' Those soldiers became believers, right then and there. I think Our Lord had a *grá* for sol-diers. He understood the fellows didn't have much choice in what they did. Some had probably enlisted in the army to earn a bit of money to send back to Gaul or Syria. Others had been drafted, and even the ones who were convinced that fighting so Rome could rule the world was a noble thing, probably ended up with some doubts after enough years of service. But Jesus showed great compassion for soldiers. Remember when Peter cut off the ear of the high priest's bodyguard? Jesus rebuked him, and made the soldier whole. He cured the centurion's servant. Be assured that the Risen Christ loves you men and is with you always. But remember too, that the Lord greeted all of His followers after the resurrection with the same words. 'Peace be with you.' May the peace of the Risen Christ be with each of you and may that same peace come to our troubled world."

Dear God, please, I pray.

Late Easter Monday afternoon, I'm scrubbing out the toilets when Paul O'Toole comes in.

"Come outside," he says. "News from Dublin."

Oh no, I think, Peter's dead.

I follow Paul out into the garden.

"Your friends have gone mad all together. They've occupied the GPO. Declared an Irish Republic, if you can imagine, and are shooting it out with the British army."

I just stare at him

"Pearse and that lot," he says. "Daft. The Tommies will mow them down before morning."

I run through the wards looking for Father Kevin. I find him anointing an Irish soldier. The fellow doesn't seem to be conscious. I take a step for-ward, but Father Kevin waves me away from the bedside. I stand back while he dips his finger in oil and makes the sign of the cross on the young fel-low's forehead, hands, and feet. Father Kevin prays not in Latin but in English. "The Lord forgives your sins and will raise you up," and then adds in both Irish and English, "*Slán abhaile*. Safe home."

The young soldier opens his eyes. He looks straight at me. I can't help myself. I step forward and say to him, "They've done it. The Rising. Pearse and the others. Declared an Irish Republic."

Not sure if he has any notion of what I'm talking about, but he smiles, then closes his eyes. I feel for a pulse. Gone.

Father Kevin's not at all pleased with me.

"You should have waited," he tells me when we finally leave the ward.

"But it's happening, Father Kevin," I say. "Right now, finally happening. I thought he'd want to know."

Father Kevin's desperate to get some real news. We find Paul. He learned about the Rising from the British colonel.

"He telephones me from time to time," Paul says, "and I tell him things."

But after the first contact, the officer doesn't call again. Paul hears nothing more. No one does.

"It's like Dublin's cut off from the world," I say to Father Kevin.

All the next week we struggle to get information. The French papers report only that a thousand Irish rebels are concentrated in the center of Dublin and that there's fighting. Maud telegraphs from Normandy. Hoping we have news. We don't.

I go to the Irish College on Thursday. A priest at the college has gotten a call from the archbishop. British naval guns have destroyed whole blocks of Dublin.

It's ten days before Father Kevin gets his hands on a London newspaper. "Irish Rebels Surrender," the headline says. And there's a photograph of Patrick Pearse, in uniform. "The President of the Irish Republic," the caption calls him. He's arrested.

The newspaper story says that Pearse and James Connolly ordered a cease-fire on Saturday, April 29ᵗʰ, to prevent more civilian deaths.

"An unconditional surrender," Father Kevin reads. All the leaders and hundreds more have been arrested. I don't go to the hospital that day. Martial law in Ireland, the papers report. All communication subject to government censorship.

"They're court-martialing the leaders, executing them starting tomorrow," Paul O'Toole says. "What the hell did they expect?"

I'm back at the hospital. The British colonel has stationed himself in the ward, watching the Irish soldiers.

"Afraid of a mutiny," Paul O'Toole tells me.

"From men who can't walk?" I say.

It's all happening so fast. Why doesn't President Wilson speak up? The French? Somebody? But the British accuse the Irish rebels of staging the uprising to aid Germany. The allies are silent.

On May 3rd, Patrick Pearse, Thomas MacDonagh, and Thomas Clarke are shot by a firing squad. The next day, Joseph Plunkett, Willie Pearse, Edward Daly, and Michael O'Hanrahan are executed. May 5th, John MacBride dies. He'd been in Dublin for a wedding, knew nothing about the Rising, but happened upon the force occupying Jacob's biscuit factory and joined the fight. Four more on May 8th, and finally on the 12th Séan Mac Diarmada and James Connolly, who was so badly wounded they shot him while he sat in a chair. Again it's a week before we get the details. I have no way of knowing where Peter is. What's happened to him? Father Kevin says there was fighting in Galway.

"I'm going to Ireland," I say to Father Kevin at the end of May, "I have to."

AUGUST 14, 1916

"No, miss," the young clerk at the British embassy says to me, "your request for permission to travel to Ireland is refused—again."

I know this fellow well. I've been coming to the office once a week since May. Each time this young man passes back my application stamped "NO ENTRY." Won't give me any explanation.

"But did they read the letters I've enclosed from Mrs. Vanderbilt, Dr. Gros, five American nurses, four ambulance drivers?" I ask him, pointing at the thick stack of documents on the counter.

He shakes his head, shoves the papers toward me. Says nothing.

Each time I bring more letters, more testimonials from ever more impressive people, and still I'm refused permission to travel to Ireland.

"I suggest you do not return here, Miss Kelly. You have become a nuisance," he says to me.

"How old are you?" I ask him.

"I can't see why that's any of your business," he says.

"I'd guess you are about twenty-five, very healthy-looking. Though you're getting a bit fat and that high color—too much wine. Odd to see a fellow your age looking so pink and pampered. The men I take care of at the hospital . . ."

He turns away, walks from the counter into a back office.

No news of Peter and no way to get to him.

"Give it up," Margaret says to me when I get back to the hospital that afternoon. "Do you really want the British government to start investigating you?"

"They'd hardly stumble across my obituary in the back issues of the Chicago *Tribune*," I say.

We're standing outside the nurses' dormitory. I'm taking the night shift. Paul O'Toole comes up. Doesn't even pretend he's not listening.

"There's a young fellow here wants to see you," he says. "One of the American ambulance drivers who's been at Verdun."

"And he knows me?" I ask.

"Not you exactly, Nora," Paul says. "But I was chatting with him about Ireland. He's one of those Americans who fancies himself Irish. Keogh you call him. But a very posh given name. Grenville Temple, if you can feature that. Says his own father was born in 'Auld Ireland.' Mentioned Maud Gonne to me, said I hadn't seen Madame around here much lately but her pal would be available. He's in Ward Eight."

Maud was in Paris for May and June. We spent hour after hour with Father Kevin at the Irish College poring over every English newspaper we could get our hands on.

"My friends. My friends. Dead. In prison. Why is no one writing to me with news?" Maud said over and over.

"Censorship," Father Kevin said. "None of the priests here are receiving letters from Dublin either. Now that the government's imposed martial law, the British can do anything to us they want."

Only two pieces of good news. Constance Markievicz's death sentence has been commuted to life imprisonment, and Eamon de Valera, another one of the leaders, was spared execution because, Maud says, he was a citizen of the United States.

"Helps to be a woman or an American," I said to Maud that last afternoon on rue de l'Annonciation as I helped her pack to return to Normandy.

"I have to get back to the sea," she said, "out from under this black cloud. I haven't slept, haven't eaten. I'm frightening the children. I am so very, very sad, Nora, when I think of the friends I have lost but at the same time I'm so proud to belong to the Irish nation that produced them."

"Yes," I said. "Me too."

"At least," she said, "they died fighting for the liberty of their country. Not like the poor Irish soldiers on the Front who fight because they would be shot if they didn't."

"True," I said.

"I've had no letter from John Quinn. I'm hoping American opinion favors Ireland," she said.

"Don't worry about that," I say. "Carolyn Wilson said the newspapers at home are full of condemnations of England. Americans not so ready to fight for England now."

"I sent an article off to the New York *Sun*. I hope they print it. If you would stop by my place every once in a while, Nora, to look for any mail I would appreciate it," she said.

Of course I agreed. But during the last months there'd been no letters from America, though a number from W. B. Yeats, which I had forwarded to Normandy. Courting the Widow MacBride, I thought.

Paul is waiting for me to follow him. We find young Keogh sitting up in bed with the sketch pad on his lap, drawing away. More college football star than artist though. A big smile for me.

"Gosh, Miss Kelly," he says. "You look just like my aunt Annie."

"A favorite aunt, I hope," I say. "And my name is Nora."

"Well, mine's Grenville Temple."

He shrugs.

"Family names from my mother's side of the family. Very proud of her ancestry. Claims we're related to the Bold Robert Emmet."

"Good for her," I say.

"Most of the fellows call me 'Keogh,'" he says.

"Lots of Keoghs in Chicago," I say. "Most of them from Galway."

"My father was born in New Ross, Wexford," young Keogh says. "Came to America at eighteen. Went to Boston first because a family called Kennedy from New Ross was doing very well for themselves there. Helped him. Then he came to New York. Got involved in politics. He's a judge now."

Be careful, Nora, I tell myself. Judge Keogh could very well know Ed Kelly. I take a quick look at the chart. This boy is only nineteen and has been in France over a year and wounded twice.

"Sorry to interrupt," Paul says. "But I brought Nora over because you said you have a message for Maud MacBride."

"A letter, actually from a friend of my father's. John Quinn. He sent it to me here at the hospital because he was afraid her mail might be . . ."

"A wise man," I say.

Young Keogh takes the letter from the back of his sketch pad.

Paul reaches for the letter.

Keogh pulls it back and then hands the letter to me. "Thank you," I say. "Can we see your drawings?" I ask, but I'm really thinking, What is Paul up to now?

"They're only cartoons really," he says. But turns the pad toward me.

I pick it up and turn the pages. Pencil sketches of his fellow ambulance drivers, a French infantry soldier with the weariness of battle in the droop of his shoulders. A number of quick impressions of the people he must have met on the roads. Peasant women, young children, a few very beautiful Mariannes.

"You care a lot about the French," I say.

"Yes," he says. "I'm proud to be doing something for such a brave people. I only hope our fellows will get over here soon."

What do I say to that?

"Lucky I got this letter now because I'm not going back to Verdun," Keogh says. "I am leaving the ambulance service. Transferring to an aviation unit in Macedonia."

"Another flyboy," Paul says. "Only the posh need apply."

"You're wrong there," Keogh says. "A Negro fellow name of Bullard is joining with me."

"Probably an African prince," Paul says.

"Not at all," Keogh says. "I met him here in the hospital. Told me he's from Georgia. Stowed away on a ship from the states. Became a boxer in England and then joined the French Foreign Legion."

"And they took him?" Paul says. He shakes his head.

"Well, good luck to you," I say to Keogh. "And thank you for the letter. I will get it to Maud."

Full dark as Paul and I cross the lawn toward my ward.

"Will every American ambulance driver be headed into the sky?" I say to Paul.

"Probably and me sure to end up on the Somme," he says. Paul holds the door for me and we step into the ward. Quiet. Most of the men asleep. The long night beginning. I relieve Theresa Ryan and say good night to Paul, but he doesn't leave. "Let me see that letter," he says.

"What?"

"The letter to Maud Gonne. Give it to me," Paul says.

"I will not and keep your voice down, you're going to wake up the patients."

"I mean it, Nora. I need that letter. Probably crammed with subversion," Paul says. "Could be just what I need to stay right here in the hospital watching all you rebels."

He makes a grab for the envelope. I stick the letter inside the top of my dress and run down the center aisle of the ward. He comes after me. Grabs my arm. I shake him off.

"Leave me alone or I'll scream. I swear, Paul," I say.

"You won't," he says. We're at the end of the dimly lit ward. He pushes me against the wall. I can hear the patients' labored breathing.

"Stop it. Do you want to wake these poor guys up?" I say. But he's pulling at the top of my dress. I break away and run out the door. If I can get to the nurses' dormitory, I think . . . but Paul steps in front of me.

The look on his face. No trace of the accommodating chap who serves napoleon slices and tea. Or the charming cynic playing both ends against the middle and assuring me that he was only a pretend informer. I can hear Lieutenant Cholet's *"Soyez sage"* and Father Kevin, "Not the *amadán* he pretends to be." I'm back in that room on State Street with Tim McShane's hands around my throat. Dodging the German general in Strasbourg.

"Give him the letter." It's the Fairy Woman. "What do you care about Maud Gonne, the colonel's daughter, with her villa in Normandy? Give it to him."

"Shut up," I say to her. Paul is tearing at the top of my dress, bent over me, straddling my legs. I bring up my knee and connect. Hard. Paul drops his hands, bends over.

"You bloody bitch," he says. But I'm away running across the lawn into the nurses' dormitory and right over to Margaret Kirk's bed.

"Wake up! Wake up! Paul O'Toole's gone mad," I say. We go back to the ward, but Paul's gone.

"Do you want to go home?" Margaret asks me. "I could get one of the ambulance fellows to drive you."

"What if Paul's waiting for me in the garden?" I say to her. "The last thing I want is a scene. I'll take my shift," I tell Margaret. "In the morning I'll . . ." What? Report Paul? I'll take Maud's letter to Father Kevin first, ask him what he thinks I should do.

Margaret stays with me throughout the night. The patients are very quiet. The casualties from the Somme are the most serious we've seen. Most of the fellows in such pain the doctors fill them with morphine or give them opium. Poor, poor boys.

I arrive in time for Father Kevin's morning Mass. Forgot it was the Feast of the Assumption. Where were you last night Blessed Mother, I think.

Warm inside the college so Father Kevin and I go into the courtyard.

"Terrible, terrible," he says when I tell him about Maud's letter and Paul's attack.

"Dangerous to cross a gombeen-man," Father Kevin says. I hand him the letter. He feels the envelope. "Something inside. Probably a bank draft. John Quinn very generous . . ." he says. "We better open it."

"But it's Maud's letter," I say.

"The only protection we have from what O'Toole will say is in this letter is the actual contents."

"You'd give him the letter?"

"Not him," Father Kevin says. "But if O'Toole starts any real trouble there are sympathetic French officials and even some decent men in the British army."

"Arthur Capel?" I ask. I know he comes to see Father Kevin.

Father Kevin opens the letter, takes out a bank draft, shows it to me. It's made out to Maud for five hundred francs.

"A kind man, John Quinn," Father Kevin says. He takes out a folded newspaper clipping. It's the article Maud has written for the New York *Sun*. Wonder if she's seen it. She'll like the headline, "Irish Joan of Arc Comes to Defense of Sinn Fein."

"Now let's see what Quinn has to say," Father Kevin says. "He might know more about events in Ireland than we do. Can't silence the American press." I stand up to read over Father Kevin's shoulder.

So. First of all John Quinn is not at all enthusiastic about what he calls "the outbreak." He writes that it was a "sad, mad and tragic business fore-doomed to failure." But he blames the liberal party in Britain for the disaster. "Words cannot express my rage, contempt and loathing for Asquith. Redmond carried out his part of the bargain and was betrayed," he writes.

"So Quinn supported Redmond?" I ask Father Kevin.

"That American sense of fair play at work," Father Kevin says. "He thought because Redmond recruited soldiers for the British army the government would make good on its promise and grant Ireland Home Rule. Instead we got nothing. Now our young men are being slaughtered on the Somme, in Verdun, at Gallipoli. Redmond's own brother was killed last month."

Father Kevin and I look at each other. What is there for me to say?

Father Kevin picks up the letter again. Quinn writes that he'd worked to save Roger Casement and the leaders of the Uprising. He lists all the influential men he rounded up who had cabled the British asking for clemency. An impressive list. Quinn's got clout no question. Flexing the muscles of his influence but failing. He doesn't like it.

Quinn lays out the argument he presented to the British. Shooting the Irish leaders would cause as much public outrage against them as sinking the *Lusitania* did against the Germans. They hadn't listened. Quinn writes, "It's made it impossible for England to pose as the champion of small nations. It's utterly unthinkable for the United States to go into this War on the side of England. Only France stands as the champion of liberal ideas now."

"Hmmm," Father Kevin says. "That's the position those who want America to get into the war will take. 'Fight for France. *Vive Lafayette.*'"

"But Woodrow Wilson doesn't want war," I say.

"Are you sure?" Father Kevin asks me.

I think of Helen Keller's words. What difference do politicians really make, I wonder, if big-business people are determined to go to war? Quinn spends the next paragraph of the letter warning Maud against being seen as pro-German. He even complains because Victor Herbert chaired a memorial service for the Irish martyrs at Carnegie Hall. "His mother might be Irish," Quinn wrote. "But he's German to his backbone."

"Victor Herbert?" I say. "*Naughty Marietta?* 'Ah, Sweet Mystery of Life'? Never seemed political to me."

Father Kevin has no idea what I'm talking about. He reads on in the letter:

"Quinn writes that too many Irish politicians think statesmanship means hating England," Father Kevin says. "Quinn's right about that."

"He is? How can anyone not despise the English right now?"

"We can't let hate take us over or Britain will win. We'll have to make an accommodation with them eventually. Need to find men on each side who aren't blinded by prejudice."

"Good luck," I say.

"But look here," Father Kevin says, pointing at the letter. "Quinn says the British ambassador to the United States, Spring Rice, tried to help win clemency."

"Some relation to Mary?" I ask.

"He is," Father Kevin says. "Remember there is real feeling for Ireland among that class. After all, Maud and Constance were converted."

"But they're women, Father Kevin," I say. "Men don't give up their power so easily." I'm thinking of the ugly British general Wilson.

The last part of the letter is surprising. Quinn confesses to feeling "wretched and powerless." Not easy for a fellow used to being one of the boys in the know to admit that. Maybe that's why he is so hard on the Irish Americans who encouraged these young men to rebel. "They weren't risking their lives or the lives of their families," Quinn writes.

"He has a point," I say to Father Kevin. "Easy to be brave when you're almost three thousand miles away."

In the letter, Quinn asks Maud why Pearse and Connolly couldn't have waited until the war was over.

"Why didn't they?" I asked Father Kevin.

"The problem is that most of the volunteers did wait," he says. "The order for the Rising was given, then countermanded and then given again."

A cock-up, as Paul O'Toole would say.

I skim the rest of the letter. "He has nice things to say about MacBride," I say to Father Kevin. I read out what Quinn wrote: "'MacBride's finish was a fine one. I understand MacBride refused a blindfold and said 'I have looked into the barrels of guns too often to be afraid of them now. Fire away.' Better to go this way then spending years living in the past, drinking and talking out his life. The fates gave him a fine redemptive end and your boy will bear an honored name.'"

So.

"Nothing really incriminating in this letter," Father Kevin says to me. "But snippets could be taken out—made to seem treasonous."

"But Quinn's so against Germany," I say. "He doesn't even like Viennese operetta."

"Still I'm afraid to post the letter," Father Kevin says. "If only someone could deliver the letter and bank draft directly to Maud."

"Well, don't look at me," I say. "Not the time to desert the hospital."

"True enough," Father Kevin says. "When Capel was here, he told me the British army estimates that it suffered sixty thousand casualties on the first day of the Battle of the Somme. And two-thirds of them died. He said a million men could be killed or wounded with neither side making any real gain."

"I can't even imagine such numbers," I say. "And Verdun's taking the same kind of toll. The worst is that these battles go on and on. I don't know, Father, I'm all for peace. But if America doesn't come into this war, it may never end."

I have to change my clothes. A fresh uniform, clean underwear, a wash will make me feel better, I think as I walk across the place des Vosges. Margaret Kirk waits outside the door of my flat. How nice of her. Worried about me, I think.

"I'm fine, Margaret," I say when I reach her. "It takes more than a bastard like Paul O'Toole to do me in." But she's shaking her head.

"Let's go in," she says.

"A cup of tea, a glass of wine?" I say to her as we walk in. "It's three o'clock now. All right to drink some wine. Sit down," I say.

"Nora," she says, still standing. "Better if you don't come back to the hospital."

"I'm all right really. I . . ."

"You don't understand. Paul O'Toole got in to see Mrs. Vanderbilt this morning. He was very apologetic."

"He admitted he attacked me? I'm surprised," I say.

"That's not what he told her," Margaret says. "He explained how you two had a lovers' quarrel last night. And he hoped none of the patients had been disturbed."

"You're joking, right?" I say. "Even Paul O'Toole wouldn't have the nerve to tell such a lie. Mrs. Vanderbilt would never believe him."

"Well," Margaret says. "That's just it. You know you still hear people talk about nurses being no better than they should be," she says. "Well, I'm afraid that . . ."

"Margaret, for God's sakes!"

"I know. I know. But there are even songs about the fast Red Cross girlies."

"But Mrs. Vanderbilt knows me," I say.

"That's just it. She doesn't, Nora. Couldn't place you. And Paul had

brought this ugly English general along. A ride-to-the hounds Irish Protestant and he blarneyed away in a brogue about naive American women
getting swept up into conspiracies."

"What?"

"Yes, Maud Gonne led you astray."

"So, I'm a spy as well as a whore?" I say.

"Nora, he made you sound like some kind of Bolshevik," Margaret says.

"Henry Wilson," I say. "He hates Irish natives."

"Paul told Mrs. Vanderbilt about the socialist meetings you held and
the tour you gave Helen Keller and Jane Addams. You know the Vander-
bilts want America to get into the war. And Paul made it sound as if you
were a defeatist, spreading enemy propaganda, trying to destroy the soldiers' morale."

"Oh, my God," I say. "So I'm fired?"

"Mrs. Vanderbilt didn't go that far. We were lucky. Her secretary, Louise,
heard what was going on and found me and I got Dr. Gros to come to her
office. And, well, you're on leave." She takes a breath. "For an indefinite
period. And you have to go to the police station and renew your residence
permit. I don't think the French will deport you. But Wilson wasn't pleased
that you weren't fired outright."

"Damn. Damn. Damn," I say. "I'm so sorry, Margaret."

"What do you have to be sorry for? We both knew Paul O'Toole was
a rat. We were foolish to try to tame a predator. Now, why don't you open
that bottle of wine?"

After we both sit down and are drinking the wine, she hands me an
envelope. "Your vacation pay," she says.

"Oh well," I say. "I've been wanting to spend some time with Madame
Simone. I'll get her to make us some new uniforms."

"I wouldn't, Nora," Margaret says. "Wilson mentioned Madame Simone. Probably best to stay away from her for a while. Don't want to get her
in trouble."

"Jesus, Mary, and Joseph," I say. "I guess I'm taking Maud's letter to
Normandy."

"If it's any consolation, Paul O'Toole's headed for the Somme."

20

SEPTEMBER 1916

"I'm so sorry, Maud," I say to her. "John MacBride. I can't find the words . . ." I stop.

She takes my arm, hurries me down the steps of the Deauville train station. Not the nearest station to Colleville but the biggest one. "Busy. You won't be noticed," Father Kevin said as he saw me off on the early train.

The other travelers steal looks at Maud. A good chance they've never seen a woman six feet tall before. Certainly not one dressed all in black, wearing a long veil. Maud's wrapping herself in widowhood, head to toe, I think. I wonder, wasn't she the slightest bit relieved? How I would rejoice if Tim McShane died! To have that shadowy fear removed. I remember that first Women's Christmas, Iseult's panic when she thought MacBride was at the door. Maud's confidences to Margaret and me by the fire. But now MacBride is transformed, a martyr for Auld Ireland.

"Willie Yeats is outside. He hired a car and driver. A day out. We all need one," she says.

"Wait," I say. "I have your letter from John Quinn."

"Thank you. Father Kevin sent me a cryptic telegram. 'Nora coming for rest. Bringing spiritual reading.'"

"Here it is," I say, and hand her the letter. I briefly tell Maud about young Keogh, Paul O'Toole, Henry Wilson, and my enforced leave from the hospital.

"Margaret Kirk got me an official-looking Red Cross document that allowed me to travel," I say.

She's not listening. Opening the envelope. Does she notice the flap has been re-glued? Father Kevin said to tell Maud we'd opened the letter but now does not seem the right moment. Maud takes the bank draft out of the envelope.

"John Quinn is such a good friend," she says. "And he sent along my article. They printed it. Good."

She reads the letter. Standing still, oblivious of the people around her.

"I don't think John Quinn understands the nobility of their sacrifice," Maud says.

She hands me the letter.

"Tell me what you think," she says. I decide not to mention that I've already read it.

"Glad the censor couldn't chew over this," she says. "Kind of you to bring it. Good of John to say that Seán can be proud of his father now. He sacrificed himself for his country, atoned for all."

An actor finally playing the right part in her life, I think. While Tim McShane . . . Poor Dolly. I wonder had she tried to throw him out. He turned on me when I ended our affair. Though "affair" seems a mild word for those years I'd lost. But I could have lost more, I could have lost my life. I had a lucky escape, no question. But the thought of him spending Dolly's money. I wonder what Maud and Willie Yeats would think of me if I said to them . . . "I was the mistress of a violent gangster"?

Maud and I settle into the backseat of a big touring car. William Butler Yeats himself, I think, sitting in front with the driver like any other fellow. Older than I expected. Hair completely gray. Pale. A poet's face no question. Sister Veronica would swoon. But he seems a little, well, brittle's the word comes to me, but he's nice enough as he says, "Welcome."

"Maud tells me you are from Chicago," Yeats says.

"I am."

"I lectured there. Took a tour of the Stock Yards. The stench of the place. Thousands of hooked carcasses moving along on those mechanical belts. The apotheosis of a brutal world," he says.

"I suppose," I say. "But lots of jobs in the Stock Yards—and a strong union. Wouldn't dare to lock out workers like they did in Dublin."

"Are you a socialist, Miss Kelly?" Yeats asks.

"I'm a Democrat," I say. Starting not to like this fellow.

"There is that lovely lake, Willie," Maud says. "I remember when John and I . . ."

She stops, takes a handkerchief from her bag, and touches the corner of her eyes. A graceful gesture. No blubbering for Maud, no red eyes or runny nose. Takes a deep breath. I pat her hand.

"The British consulate has held up my request for permission to go to Ireland. Imagine. Barring me from my own country. Refusing to allow me to pay my respects to my husband's remains." Furious now. "His remains, such as they are. The British pitched the bodies of the men they executed into a mass grave then tossed lime over them. Barbarians. They know that every Irish family longs to have their loved one tucked away in a tidy grave in the churchyard among their ancestors. A place to visit and honor. They denied my husband the dignity they give the most murderous German soldier."

She begins pounding on the seat.

"Maud, Maud," says Yeats from the front seat. He turns around, and reaches across, holding out his hand to her. "Please, dearest."

She stretches out her hand, grasps his. Lets go and falls back against the cushions. I touch her shoulder. She covers my hand with hers. An actress, I think. She can't help it. No less sincere for being dramatic.

Yeats speaks to me. "I've convinced Maud to go on an outing to show you something of the countryside and the towns of Normandy, so full of history. Didn't we decide that, Maud?"

"Good for you, too, Willie," she says. "A day out from writing to replenish your creative energy. We will go to Honfleur, where the Impressionists went to paint. Charming. Then perhaps Bayeux. The tapestry."

"Isn't that splendid, Miss Kelly?" Yeats says.

"I'm Nora," I say. "Wonderful. A famous tapestry? Is it the one with the unicorn?"

"No," Yeats says. "You'll see."

Why hadn't I paid more attention to Sister Veronica's talks on French art?

"Honfleur," Yeats tells the driver.

"Wait. No," Maud says. "First Quillebeuf-sur-Seine. That's where we'll go. Look to our Irish history."

"Quillebeuf?" says Yeats. He speaks to the driver and then turns back to us. "Robert says that's quite a distance; four hours."

"But that is where I'd like to go. It's only ten in the morning," Maud says to him, and then to me, "I want you to see the place Hugh O'Neill and Rory O'Donnell landed. The Flight of the Earls, Nora," she says. "More than three hundred years ago."

"Here we are," Maud says as the car climbs up a hill into the old city of Quillebeuf.

"Can't you just imagine the earls striding through the streets?" Maud says as she leads us past rows of black stone houses, their fronts patterned white pebbles.

"I thought they were headed for Spain," I say.

"Blown off course," Yeats says. "The channel's treacherous anytime and terrible for a small boat in September."

"Fortunate to find a harbor here at the mouth of the Seine," Maud says.

"This is where the O'Cahan harpist played his lament." Maud begins to hum.

"I know that song," I say. "But I thought it was new. May Quinlivan taught me the words." I begin to sing: "'O Danny boy, the pipes, the pipes are calling, from glen to glen and down the mountainside.'"

"Oh that," Maud says. "Some Englishmen put lyrics on the ancient melody."

Dismissive. "Weren't the countess and duchess I met at your house descendants of the Wild Geese? I think one was an O'Cahan," I say.

"Many nobles left Ireland," Yeats says. "All are referred to as Wild Geese."

Nearly one o'clock when we finish our tour. Yeats wants what he calls a "proper lunch." But Maud is determined to drive on to Bayeux. A great tribute to their spiritual marriage that Willie agrees to eat baguettes, stuffed with ham and camembert cheese in the car as we drive. Great for treats, Maud, and I see why children would have loved her. For all her height and beauty, she's a child herself, delighted with our picnic on wheels.

When we do arrive at Bayeux it's after six and the cathedral's locked. But Maud says her friend, Mother Mathilde, is the superior of the nearby convent. Perhaps she will take us in to see the tapestry.

"Iseult, Seán, and I stayed in the convent during Easter," Maud says to me. "The nuns hesitated to take in Seán because males aren't allowed but I said with his long curls he could easily pass as a girl, and so they agreed. Thank God. I was sitting in the parlor with Mother Mathilde when a priest from the cathedral came to tell me about the Rising. A true Easter miracle, I'd thought. And then . . . the nuns were very good to me during those terrible weeks."

She turns to Yeats. "I was never so grateful for my conversion," Maud says, and then to me, "Willie's not fond of the Catholic hierarchy but I could not remain in the Church of Ireland."

"French Catholicism is so much more civilized. Pity the Irish couldn't be more like them," Yeats says.

"Lieutenant Cholet would disagree," I say. Of course he has no idea what I'm talking about and doesn't ask.

Yeats and I wait silently in the car while Maud goes to the door of the convent. The nuns will be at prayers or eating dinner, I think. The Mother Superior won't just come walking out. But after a few moments, here she is with Maud. She's a tall woman, wears a pleated headdress and gauzy habit. An Ursuline, I think.

We enter the darkened cathedral and follow Mother Superior's lantern across the transept to a side chapel where the tapestry stretches along all four walls. No unicorns here. The narrow piece of linen cloth, as long as a football field, is covered with figures embroidered in colors vivid even in the lantern's flickering light.

Mother Mathilde speaks English. Thank God. I could never follow the story in French, hard enough in English. Bishop Odo, she tells us, William's half brother, commissioned this work from nuns in a convent in England.

"William?"

"The duke of Normandy who became king of England," Yeats says.

"You mean William the Conqueror?" I ask. "1066?"

"Of course," Maud says.

My mind wanders to the present war as the Mother Superior talks about the fight for the English throne portrayed by the tapestry. Should America come into the fight to save France and end the slaughter? As I stand in the massive cathedral, God's House, and look at the tapestry, I think, Stay home, boys. We've gone beyond all this. Elections decide our leaders, not wars. Why get embroiled in all this history? Of course, we had our conflicts. Hadn't my own father fought to save the Union? A tapestry telling the story of our Civil War would need a very long wall. So many dead. Maybe we'd learned the cost. Maybe. Maybe.

Nearly ten o'clock when we reach Colleville, but Maud says the day out has done her good. She seems almost cheerful as we drive up to her lovely house right on edge of the beach.

"I named it Les Mouettes," she says. "The Seagulls."

Iseult and Seán run out to meet us. Boys change so quickly. Seán had been a little fellow when I met him four years ago. Now his shoulders have broadened. He's going to be tall like his mother. Iseult seems no older. Lovely but distracted, smoking a cigarette as she greets us. Barry Delaney is here, as well as their big dog, three cats, and two roosters. Maud's garden ends at the English Channel. Too dark to see much but I can smell the salt and hear the surf rolling in.

"Come, come," Barry says. "Josephine has the meal waiting."

I follow Maud into the two-storied stone house.

"I must go to my room right after dinner," Yeats says. "I'm close to finding a phrase to hang my poem on."

Poem, I think. Yeats is writing a poem right now. Sister Veronica would be thrilled.

"I finished my poem, too," Iseult says.

"Wonderful, darling," Maud says. "You must read it to us. And Willie, I'll expect a recital of your piece tomorrow."

We have a late supper at a round table: Maud, Willie, the children, and Barry Delaney. Even Seán drinks the cider, which makes me a bit lightheaded. I'm desperate for a good sleep but as soon as we finish eating, Barry takes me to a kind of porch on the side of the house filled with bookcases. She pulls out a scrapbook and opens it up.

"I've made a book of Seán's life."

Already? I think. He's only twelve years old.

"See, here are two theater tickets for the performance that Madame was to attend the night he was born," she tells me. "And here's the copy of the telegram I sent to the Pope."

I read the message: "The King of Ireland is born."

"Very nice," I say.

Maud finds us.

"Barry's our chronicler and my lieutenant. I couldn't do my work if I didn't know she was here keeping the household together," Maud says.

At that moment, the King of Ireland comes running through the room, chasing the dog, who is intent on catching the rooster. Seán shouts at the dog in French and English.

"Seán!" Maud says, but he's away.

"I'm going up to bed," I say.

"As soon as Iseult reads to us," Maud says.

I'm given a place by the fire between Maud and Barry. Iseult's poem describes the beach, "the sun-delighted strand," where she's "a sadly useless thing." Not very cheerful. A prose piece, too, with cliffs, the fringe of foam on the wet sand, all connecting to hidden gods. Confusing.

"You're being influenced by Willie and that Golden Dawn crowd," Maud says to Iseult. "I find them all too English and conventional."

"You don't understand the deeper truths. Now that I'm studying Hindu and Sanskrit," Iseult says, "I see beyond reality."

"I've been seeing beyond reality my whole life," Maud says.

"I believe in reincarnation," Iseult says to me.

"That's nice," I say.

Then Barry reads her latest, a salute to St. Thérèse of Lisieux. "I write Catholic poetry," she explains.

"And publishes in the best Church magazines," Maud adds.

Hindu, reincarnation, and the Little Flower. Quite a mixture.

"It's getting late, Barry," Maud says. Thank God. "Nora is staying for a while. Plenty of time. Besides, I have something to show her." Maud brings out copies of a French magazine, *La Illustrae*. "Pictures of Dublin after it had been shelled by English gunboats," she says as she turns the pages of photographs.

"This is O'Connell Street, Dublin's main thoroughfare. Look, rubble. How could they attack civilians? At least now the world can see the true face of the British government. For centuries they've claimed Ireland was a back door for the French invasion of England. That's how they justified their brutality. We were a security risk, a pawn for kings, the game being played for hundreds of years. You saw the Bayeux tapestry. Those same ships invaded us. I hate them, the English, and yet I'm one of them. Oh, I wish I were a peasant in Mayo and male, Celtic to the core, in Ireland for thousands of years."

"Like me?" I say. "My people were rooted in Galway for generations."

"And yet you're an American."

"Oh, Maud," I say. "Let's go to bed."

What a nice beach, I think the next morning, as I follow Maud and Yeats out onto the long stretch of sand bordering the sea. The English Channel, really. Formidable enough with loud waves hitting the shore and water as wide as any ocean though I know the coast of England's not that far away. Never could imagine Lake Michigan had a farther shore—endless to me. If only Chicago had an unbroken expanse of sand like this. And the color.

"Gold," I say to Maud.

"The sand is very fine here and that color is unusual. Not like the gray gritty stuff on so many French beaches," she says.

"No garbage either," I say, thinking about how Chicago turned its finest shoreline into a refuse dump. Wonder if Ed's still working to clear it up.

My old life seems a long way from here. A lovely fall day. Maud says Normandy is almost as bad as Ireland for the rain so good weather is especially treasured. I have the Seneca and stop to photograph the waves breaking on the shore as Maud tells me the history of this expanse of beach.

"We're lucky here," Maud says. "Colleville-sur-Mer, Saint-Laurent-sur-Mer, all these coastal towns have no real harbors. Impossible for an army to invade along the beaches of Normandy. All the historic battles took place farther away. Even the Plantagenets couldn't find men who could scale Pointe du Hoc," she says, pointing at the high cliffs a few miles away.

Yeats is far ahead of us now, not speaking to Maud this morning or me either.

"I refused his proposal again last night," Maud tells me. "Why does he keep asking? I told him years ago that ours is a spiritual marriage, much more powerful than conventional unions. We already have our children—his poems," Maud says.

"So you've never, well, umm, had carnal knowledge?"

"Once," she says. "A disaster. As I told you and Margaret, I find no plea-sure in the act and I don't see why I should endure it to satisfy a man's need."

"But you do have actual children: Seán and Iseult too."

"Yes," she says. "You might think I'm wrong to pretend Iseult is my cousin, but my work would suffer if I acknowledge I have an illegitimate daughter. And Millevoye insisted on the charade. Better to say nothing. I do believe the creation of children makes an unpleasant task bearable. But unfortunately, Willie has more carnal passion than is obvious."

Yeats is almost out of sight.

"Willie! Willie!" she shouts. "Wait for us!"

He stops, turns.

"He's been writing some poem all month," Maud says. "Once he gets stuck into something, you can't budge him. Willie does need a wife. Some-one younger who can keep house, tend to his needs, have children."

"Wouldn't you find his marriage to someone else hard to accept?" I ask her.

"Do you think I'd be jealous? Dear Nora, my connection to Willie tran-scends time and space. Someone else tidying up his drawing room would bother me not at all. Especially not now when Ireland needs me more than ever. I can't consider warming Willie's slippers by the fire when all I want to do is join the other widows of 1916 in the struggle," she says, lifting the skirt of her black dress above the sand and striding toward Yeats.

She can't help it, I think. She's an actress after all, and she's truly mourn-ing the martyred leaders, her friends. She wept this morning speaking of Patrick Pearse's mother. Both sons executed.

"They were heroes, Nora, our soldier poets. Maybe their military strat-egy was wanting but their nobility is unquestioned. They won a moral vic-tory," she says.

Moral victories don't figure in the rough-and-tumble of Chicago poli-tics and Bridgeport, I think. Ed and Mike fight to win.

Still, for all Maud's posturing and posing, she is a brave and determined woman. The nursing she and Iseult did . . .

We've caught up to Yeats now. He holds a rolled-up scroll of paper.

"Oh, Willie. You've finished."

"A decent draft," he says.

"Read it to us," Maud says.

"I wouldn't want to impose on you," I say. "I'll go back."

"Nonsense," she says. "We rarely have a witness to the birth of our children. You will be the godmother of the poem, Nora." She smiles at Yeats.

"Now, I hope it's not another one about me," she says to him.

"It's about Ireland. Though you do make an appearance."

"When Willie evokes Ireland as a woman, Erin or Scotia, he sometimes uses me as a kind of metaphor," she tells me.

Yeats is standing with the channel behind him. Great light.

"Could I take a photograph of you and Maud?" I ask him.

"Not now," he says. "Later perhaps."

He tells us to sit down on one of the large boulders.

"The title is 'Easter, 1916,'" he says.

"Very good, Willie. I was hoping you would write a poem about the heroes," Maud says.

Yeats lifts the scroll and begins:

> *"I have met them at close of day*
> *Coming with vivid faces*
> *From counter or desk among grey*
> *Eighteenth-century houses."*

"'Vivid faces,'" Maud repeats. "Yes, that's how they did look after the meetings or the demonstrations. I remember . . ."

"Please Maud," he says.

"Go on, Mr. Yeats," I say.

He nods at me, and continues:

> *"I have passed with a nod of the head*
> *Or polite meaningless words,*
> *Or have lingered awhile and said*
> *Polite meaningless words . . ."*

Easy to imagine those kinds of exchanges, I think. Yeats protecting himself with good manners, detached. He goes on:

> *"And thought before I had done*
> *Of a mocking tale or a gibe*

> To please a companion
> Around the fire at the club,
> Being certain that they and I
> But lived where motley is worn . . ."

Well, I think, he's drawing back the curtain now. The club. I can imagine his Anglo-Irish pals sitting around that fire mocking these earnest dreamers, these middle-class Catholic boys who intend to take down the mighty British Empire. "Motley" in that last line upsets Maud.

"Wearing motley?" she says. "So they're fools? Is that how you see these men? These patriots?"

Yeats only gazes at her. Not taking in her words. I hush her. Now Yeats's voice booms out accompanied somehow by the waves.

> "All changed, changed utterly:
> A terrible beauty is born."

Each word of that line seems to stand alone. A long pause. His tone becomes conversational. He looks up at us as he reads.

> "That woman's days were spent
> In ignorant good-will,
> Her nights in argument
> Until her voice grew shrill.
> What voice more sweet than hers
> When, young and beautiful,
> She rode to harriers?"

"That's Constance," Maud says. "Oh, Willie, you can't say her work is only ignorant goodwill. My God, she served food with us when the workers were locked out. The Fianna, her Boy Scouts, learned to be proud of themselves, of their country. They fought when . . ."

Oh Maud, I think. Surely you realize Yeats prefers the young Ascendancy beauty jumping the hedges in County Sligo to the armed countess in her uniform.

"'This man,'" Yeats continues, "'had kept a school.'"

"Pearse," Maud says to me.

"And rode our wingèd horse;
This other his helper and friend
Was coming into his force;
He might have won fame in the end,
So sensitive his nature seemed,
So daring and sweet his thought."

"MacDonagh," Maud says. "True. He would have been a great poet and our 'wingèd horse.' Yes, that's good."

What other insurrectionists in history had been described as having sensitive natures, daring and sweet thoughts, I wonder. Maud smiles at me, nodding.

Then Yeats's voice becomes disdainful, angry.

"This other man I had dreamed
A drunken, vainglorious lout.
He had done most bitter wrong
To some who are near my heart . . ."

"MacBride," Maud says to me. "He means John. Willie, you can't attack him now. Not when he's . . ."

Yeats reaches out and takes her hand, saying the next words looking at her.

"Yet I number him in the song;
He, too, has resigned his part
In the casual comedy;
He, too, has been changed in his turn,
Transformed utterly:
A terrible beauty is born."

Almost whispers those last two lines.

Now Yeats seems to be trying to explain something to Maud, to himself.

"Hearts with one purpose alone
Through summer and winter seem

Enchanted to a stone
To trouble the living stream."

"Hearts with one purpose alone." Maud, Constance, Peter too and Uncle Patrick, I suppose. Does their obsession divert the flow of life? Except without that kind of conviction, would tyrants ever be overthrown?

The sun, low over the ocean, is going down. The clouds catch fire. Yeats reads the next words slowly.

"The horse that comes from the road,
The rider, the birds that range
From cloud to tumbling cloud,
Minute by minute they change;
A shadow of cloud on the stream
Changes minute by minute;
A horse-hoof slides on the brim,
And a horse plashes within it;
The long-legged moor-hens dive,
And hens to moor-cocks call;
Minute by minute they live:
The stone's in the midst of all."

Hard to follow these images. Is Yeats invoking some place? Remembering Sligo? Seeing the countryside, everything transformed except for the stone, which remains hard, unmoving.

Yeats raises his voice:

"Too long a sacrifice
Can make a stone of the heart."

"Too long a sacrifice"? Clear enough. The Irish people. Eight hundred years of occupation. So many uprisings put down. The Flight of the Earls. My own family running for their lives. How many dead from the Great Starvation? More than a million. Granny Honora used to say that Ireland's a small place to hold so much suffering.

But had their hearts turned to stone? Not the Irish in Chicago, I want to say, but of course I don't.

Yeats takes Maud's other hand, looking down at her.

"O when may it suffice?"

Maud starts to speak as if answering his question. But Yeats stops her.

"That is Heaven's part, our part
To murmur name upon name,
As a mother names her child
When sleep at last has come
On limbs that had run wild.
What is it but nightfall?
No, no, not night but death . . ."

Maud lowers her head, crying now. I pat her shoulder and think Yeats has stopped. But he continues.

"Was it needless death after all?"

Maud looks up. "Needless?" she says. "Don't say needless," she begins. But Yeats interrupts her.

"For England may keep faith
For all that is done and said."

"Never," Maud says. "They will make promises only to divert and delay us."
Yeats nods, not agreeing exactly, just going on.

"We know their dream; enough
To know they dreamed and are dead;
And what if excess of love
Bewildered them till they died?"

"Excess of love." I can hear voices shouting out the songs at the Clan na Gael picnics. "A nation once again, a nation once again, and Ireland long a province be a nation once again."

Yeats drops Maud's hands, spreads his arms.

> *"I write it out in a verse—*
> *MacDonagh and MacBride*
> *And Connolly and Pearse . . ."*

Beating the names in a rhythm that sends them marching across the beach. Maud's friends, her comrades in arms.

The sun eases into the sea as Yeats finishes.

> *"Now and in time to be,*
> *Wherever green is worn,*
> *Are changed, changed utterly:*
> *A terrible beauty is born."*

"Wherever green is worn." All of us of Irish blood mourning these men but inspired by them, determined.

"Changed, changed utterly," the poem says. "A terrible beauty is born."

I sit still. Held in the spell of the words.

But Maud stands up, shakes her head, throws up her hands.

"Terrible beauty! It's awful, Willie," she says. "Awful, awful!" She pushes Yeats. "How dare you use their deaths to make this thing! How dare you! How dare you! Sacrifice doesn't turn a heart to stone. Through it alone can mankind rise to God! Oh, Willie."

She runs from the beach.

Yeats looks at me.

"Thank you." All I can think to say. "Thank you. It's beautiful. She . . ."

He walks away.

The next two days Yeats avoids Maud, taking long walks on the strand with Iseult while Maud rages at me. "Why couldn't he let John MacBride be a hero? If only for Seán's sake. His father's sacrifice atoned for the wrongs he'd done us. A true martyr," she says to me as we sit alone in the garden. "To call him 'drunken, vainglorious.' I sometimes wonder if British agents didn't buy John drink. Did he feel I had denied him his son? Not true really but fathers and sons . . . I don't know."

"Maud," I say. "MacBride was transformed. Isn't that the point of the poem?"

I've been repeating those words over and over in my mind. "A terrible beauty is born." An odd kind of comfort in the phrase. Yeats might be a stick-in-the-mud but he's certainly a very great poet.

That next afternoon Barry insists we go to St. Clair's fountain in the village. As we walk, Maud says, "I had a letter from the Franciscan priest who gave John the last rites. He told me John faced death bravely and with great faith."

Barry speaks up. "As courageous as an early Christian martyr. He told them, 'I have looked into the barrel of guns too often to be afraid of them now. Fire away.'"

The words Quinn had quoted. "I intend to use the phrase in a poem dedicated to him," Barry says.

A hive of writing here in Normandy. Every thought turned into poetry. What would people in Bridgeport think about adults spending their days this way? Is the Rising for them only one more moment in Irish history to remake into verse? But not fair to condemn them, I think. After all, weren't Pearse and the others poets too?

And Yeats is right. The executions have transformed everything. Quinn said in his letter the British care about Irish-American opinion. I can just imagine the speeches being given, not only at Clan na Gael meetings, but among the wealthy Irish at the Irish Fellowship Club who might have opposed the Rising. No division of opinion now.

We arrive in a small village. One big farm, really, and a woods with a stone fountain cut into the side of a hill. St. Clair's face has worn away, his features disappeared.

"He was Irish and a very handsome man," Barry says. "Hard on him because a noble English woman fell in love with him. She was furious when he became a celibate. He had to escape from her to Normandy. And did quite a good job of converting the pagans around here. But the woman sent her agents after him. They found him in his hermitage and split his skull." Barry says this with a certain amount of relish. "He's the patron saint of people with headaches." She stops and looks at me.

What could I say? "That's nice"? "Poor fellow"? But I have to ask her, "Does being killed by a jealous woman really count as martyrdom?"

"He died because he'd vowed purity," she says.

A trickle of water drips into the stone basin. "It comes from a stream in the hills," Barry says. She dips her finger then blesses herself. "Good for the diseases of the eye, too."

Well, St. Clair, I think, we're standing here twelve hundred years later not because you fought or conquered but because you were martyred. Like John MacBride and the others. Isn't anyone celebrated for living for a cause?

Maud stares at the broken statue. Is she picturing images of her martyred husband and friends? But dead is dead—Yeats's finest words can't bring them back.

When we come back, I find Yeats alone on the porch.

"Oh Mr. Yeats," I begin. "Your poem is a masterpiece."

He nods his head.

"I'm sorry Maud doesn't . . ." I stop.

"Maud doesn't understand what the years have done to her. Many men have admired her beauty but only I love her pilgrim soul. I want to give her rest. Make a home with her where artists can gather. Why doesn't she want that?"

What can I say? He only knows the Maud of his imagination.

"Iseult is so like the young Maud—before politics hardened her," he says.

Iseult—beautiful, young. She might stand still and let Yeats make her into a metaphor. And have his children. That night Maud tells me Yeats proposed to Iseult.

"He's too old for her," I say.

Iseult won't give Yeats an answer.

He leaves that evening.

We go to Lisieux the next day. I kneel at St. Thérèse's coffin. "Little Flower in this hour show your power," I pray. News of Peter please. Let me know he's safe.

One powerful woman, St. Thérèse, because the very next day a Connemara man shows up at Maud's door who says he was sent by Professor Keeley.

❧

"I was with the professor in the Galway unit Liam Mellows commanded," he says.

His name is Michael O'Malley. He was landed from a fishing boat down the coast and made his way to Colleville because Peter told him

Maud would help. He sits at Maud's table eating slabs of cheese on crusty bread. Someone who has actually been through the Rising. A firsthand report. He said he wasn't a member of the Volunteers or any other rebel group.

"My brothers and I were building a wall for a fellow in Galway City when we heard about the uprising in Dublin and that Mellows and the boys were going to take on the Peelers. 'We're with you,' we said. Two or three young priests came along. Gave everybody general absolution so if we were killed, we'd go straight to heaven." He pauses, then turns to Maud. "Very good tea, missus," he says.

Maud nods at Barry, who refills his cup.

"Not much of a battle really," Michael goes on. "We set up camp at a farm near Athenry. Thought we'd get the military to attack and then we could fight them from a good position but by the time the enemy came half the fellows had drifted away. The one constable we killed, Whelan, wasn't a bad fellow and a Catholic, but the inspector pushed him forward and well . . ." He shrugs. "Somebody let loose with a shotgun and Whelan got it. Too bad really. It was the bailiffs who evicted my neighbors and the battering-ram bastards knocked their homes apart I wanted to fight."

"But what about Peter Keeley?" I ask.

"I saw him during our scrimmage with the army but then everyone scattered. The Peelers started mass arrests. Jailing men and women who did no more than get together to speak Irish. The people who used to go to Pearse's cottage—have a bit of ceili with the students from Dublin—all of them were picked up. And, of course, the British knew that Professor Keeley had been telling fellows not to join the British army. They would have arrested him even if they didn't know that he had been with us at Athenry. I heard the professor was hiding out in the mountains near Carna. But that was a while ago. Cousins of mine found out there were French boats fishing out of Killybegs Harbour. Took me a month to get up there, but got on one of them and here I am. So Professor Keeley might've done the same."

"Found some way out you mean," I say.

"Could have. Mellows made it to New York. Then was arrested as a German spy. In jail now," Michael O'Malley says.

He eats the last bit of cheese.

"Jesus, if the British had just ignored us the whole Rising would have been over and forgotten by now. It's the executions that made the difference. Changed everything," he says.

"Changed utterly," I say.

Maud arranges for the café owner in town to drive Michael to Le Havre. She gives him money for his passage to New York and a letter to John Quinn.

Peter is alive, I think. He could be on his way to Paris right now.

He'll come striding across the place des Vosges to me. "Little Flower, in this hour show your power."

Except when I give Father Kevin my news, he only says, "Let's hope." Not optimistic. The two of us in the Irish College parlor.

"Tom Kettle was killed in the Battle of the Somme," he says. "Haven't found his body. Resting somewhere in the France he loved, I suppose. Serving the Cause in his way, Honora. Will no one from this generation be left to build the new Ireland?" he says.

21

DECEMBER 1916

"Here, look," Maud says, handing me her passport. "Signed at the English consulate, countersigned at the French prefecture." Permission to go to Ireland at last.

Father Kevin and I are at rue de l'Annonciation to say good-bye to Maud, Iseult, and Seán. She gave up her apartment, so we are in the attic storage space where they are staying for the next two days until their departure.

I spent the last month helping Maud pack away a lifetime in Paris. She's going home to Ireland to join the other widows of the 1916 martyrs who are continuing the fight. So many of the leaders dead or in prison. The women of the movement have taken over. I am glad to have something to do because I am still not welcome at the American hospital.

"Somebody's put the kibosh on you, Nora," Margaret told me. "I tried to speak to Mrs. Vanderbilt. But she just murmured something about the reputation of the hospital."

"Wilson, it's Henry Wilson," I said.

"We're leaving very early," Maud says. "So don't come to see us off. I hate train station farewells. Besides you will be coming to Ireland soon, Nora. We need your help."

"Doesn't look like I'll be able to, Maud," I say. Haven't dared to confront the clerk at the British consulate. Hard enough to get my residence permit approved at the police station. Not sure how far the kibosh extends. But the gendarme said to me, "Perhaps it's time for Mademoiselle to return to her own country."

"I am very impressed with my efficiency," Maud says. "I have my tickets bought and places on the boat reserved. Barry went ahead to Dublin and has found us a house. Two days camping out here, and then we're off."

Maud's convinced that John Quinn used his influence with the British to have the order banning her from Ireland lifted. Some of her old energy now.

Cold and dark in the little space. Harder and harder to get coal in Paris, and electricity is rationed. Impossible to get sugar, vegetables, or fruit.

Maud calls to Seán, "Drag over the barrel."

He's made a place for himself under the eaves and is reading by candlelight under a pile of blankets. Iseult sits in the other corner staring out the dormer window and smoking. The wooden barrel Seán pushes to the center of the floor reminds me of the ones in Piper's store in Bridgeport. Maud takes the lid off the barrel. A smell I know.

"Apples," she says. "John Quinn sends them every year for Christmas. We'll take some with us and leave the rest for you."

"Thank you, Maud," Father Kevin says. "Very kind of you."

"Yes," I say.

"Let's have some now," she says.

Sean gives each of us an apple. Bigger than the *pommes* of France, I think, as I bite into the apple. More of a crunch and so juicy. The taste of America, of home.

"John Quinn says the apples come from his native state, Ohio," Maud says.

"Apple orchards all over the Midwest," I say, "because Johnny Appleseed scattered seeds after the revolution."

"A great country, America," Father Kevin says. "After the French Revolution, the guillotine. After your revolution, apples."

"It is," I say. The imaginary cottage where I live with Peter Keeley recently moved to the shore of a lake in Wisconsin. Still no news of him.

"We'll be going, Maud," Father Kevin says, as we finish our apples. "Getting dark."

Few streetlights now and the streets of Paris very empty during these December nights.

Maud's theatricality doesn't extend to hugs and kisses but now she takes me by the shoulders.

"Thank you, Nora," she says. A quick embrace for me and one for Father Kevin. I'll miss her, I think. Might never see her again.

We are just at the door when we hear someone on the steps. "Must be the concierge," Maud says. "No one else would be coming up here." She opens the door.

"I am Major Lampton," the British officer standing in the doorway says.

"Come to make sure we're leaving?" Maud says. "I assure you we are."

"I can see that. However, I have just received a telegram from the War Office in London," he says. "You may travel to England but you are not allowed to go on to Ireland."

"You are mistaken, Major. Here, look at my documents." Maud thrusts her passport at him but he doesn't even look down.

"Countermanded," he says.

"But they can't . . ." Maud begins.

The major interrupts her. "We are fighting a war. Ireland is under martial law and you are a threat to national security."

"Me? But I've done nothing. You've released the prisoners arrested after the Rising. Constance Markievicz is free and she led a unit in the battle," Maud says.

"The War Office cannot direct political policy. Unfortunately," he says.

I remember Henry Wilson's contempt for the politicians he called "frocks."

"But Madame MacBride only wishes to visit her husband's grave. Couldn't she be allowed a short period in Ireland?" Father Kevin asks.

"You'd do well to stick to your religious duties, Father," the major says.

"Madame MacBride has been nursing soldiers and helping in the war effort . . ." Father Kevin goes on.

"You people do not seem to understand plain English. Mrs. MacBride is not allowed to go to Ireland. Perhaps her American friend, here, can suggest a place for Madame MacBride to settle in the United States. Your home is in Chicago I believe, Miss Kelly."

Oh, dear God. He knows me. The kibosh all-encompassing. Though he doesn't seem aware of my death. Probably just checked up on me in the American embassy. But he recognizes me. Scary.

"The French are losing patience with foreign nationals who spy for the enemy," he says. "And being a woman will not save you."

"That's an outrageous statement, Major," Maud says. "I demand an apology."

It's only then I notice Iseult and Seán standing right next to me. She's weeping but he's cocked his fist and is pulling his arm back. I grab his wrist and stand in front of him.

"No, Seán," I say.

The major looks over at us. He starts to laugh. "Typical Paddy. Hiding behind a woman." And then he's gone.

Ructions. Thank God the major wasn't standing behind the door or he would have heard enough sedition to hang all of us.

Maud doesn't go to England because she's told she will not be allowed to return to France. Nor will the British permit her to travel to America.

"If I could get word to Michael Collins, he would get me a false passport. He arranged one for Hanna Sheehy-Skeffington. Got her and her son to America," she says to me as we celebrate Women's Christmas in her tiny attic space. Just the two of us sipping tea and nibbling apples by the feeble fire. "You are fortunate, Nora. You can just leave. Go back."

"Oh, Maud," I say. "I'm stuck too. Besides Peter Keeley could be headed this way."

"Too dangerous for him to come to Paris," Maud says. "Now that the British have the French doing their dirty work. Support the liberation of Ireland and you're a German spy. The British have turned our oldest ally against us."

The next month the French arrest a Dutch dancer who calls herself Mata Hari as a spy. The newspapers love the story. Particularly the semi-nude photographs of Mata Hari in the native costume she designed herself. I'm selling photographs to the newspapers too. But mine are of British soldiers at the Eiffel Tower. A little money coming in until Father Kevin warns me to stop. He'd heard from his friend, Capel, that the British are watching me. "They say you are trying to get information about the movement of British units."

Oh, dear God.

At least Madame Simone's not intimidated. But there's very little for me to do at her studio.

I spend most days with Father Kevin at the Irish College helping him finish his lifework, a book entitled *Saint Columcille from Donegal to Iona and the World*.

"No Christian Europe without him," Father Kevin tells me over and over. "A prince of the O'Neills, a poet," he says. "A monk and a druid too if truth be told, who saw no contradiction between the old and the new. He scratched crosses on the ancient ogham stones and got on with it."

Father Kevin corresponds with a Church of Ireland theologian and a Presbyterian minister from Scotland. "Columcille is the only saint that Protestants, Catholics, and Dissenters revere. A good patron for a new Ireland," Father Kevin says. He is determined to complete his book. Those divided by religion will read it and make peace, he thinks.

Thousands of handwritten pages scattered everywhere. I borrow the new rector's typewriter and hunt and peck my way through the chapters, which Father Kevin takes and annotates so I type them again. A monk in a scriptorium probably made faster progress than I do. But Father Kevin is pleased and Maud stops by occasionally. I am grateful for the big lunch I eat in the parlor of the Irish College every day. It's my main meal. All my savings going for rent. I wonder does Mrs. Vanderbilt realize what the token pay given to volunteers meant to me?

APRIL 1917

"Oh Margaret, I feel so bad that I'm not helping out at the hospital," I say as we sit in my room. "But thank you, thank you so much." She's lent me enough money to pay April's rent and brought me a letter from Carolyn Wilson. Back in the States now but says she'll be returning to Paris. According to her sources, it's only a matter of time before President Wilson declares war on Germany. Just looking for an excuse according to Carolyn.

"U.S. banks have already lent billions to the allies. They'd better win or the banks won't get repaid." Helen Keller said that we'd be going to war for the capitalists, I think.

"Some other news. Paul O'Toole is dead," Margaret says.

"Poor fellow," I say.

"Wasn't killed in battle. Shot for cowardice," Margaret says. "He refused to leave the trenches."

"So they killed him for wanting to stay alive. Insane. And now our American boys will be forced into the slaughter."

"They think they're coming over to save the world. My brother John enlisted in the Marine Corps. Said if he's going to be in the fight, might as well be with the best. He says most of the men he's met in training are Irish. Ever heard of someone called Dan Daly?"

"I haven't," I say.

"Won two Medals of Honor, John says. He spoke to my brother's unit. Told them lots of the Marine Corps traditions come from the Irish like the Celtic war cry Marines yell when they go into battle," she says.

"Wouldn't that be one in the eye for the British army if Irish U.S. Marines come over here and win the war for them," I say, and laugh. Haven't laughed much lately, but the thought of General Henry Wilson thanking our Irish fellows is very funny. Margaret's not laughing.

"According to John, that's exactly what's going to happen," Margaret says.

JULY 4, 1917

So. Half of Paris crowds the Champs-Élysées waving the Stars and Stripes and yelling *"Vive l'Amérique"* with Margaret and me in the middle of it all cheering like fools as the American troops march up the avenue.

"See. Here come the Marines," Margaret says. "That's their flag."

I raise my Seneca and focus on the banner. Against a red background a gold eagle guards a globe supported by an anchor. Across the top are the words *"Semper Fidelis."* "Always faithful."

"The eagle, globe, and anchor," Margaret's telling me, "their symbol because the Marines are part of the navy. 'The Soldiers of the Sea,' John says."

The troop is close enough now so we can hear them singing:

"Admiration of the nation
We're the finest ever seen
And we glory in the title
United States Marines."

Great-looking fellows, young and smiling, marching with such energy. Keep them safe, please God . . . Keep them safe, I pray.

Margaret sees her brother.

"Johnny, Johnny!" she shouts. He's at the end of a row right near us. Tall and thin like his sister. Eyes straight ahead. Just as he passes us, he turns and smiles.

Margaret has to go back to the hospital, but I follow the parade. I know from the newspapers they are headed for the grave of Lafayette in Picpus Cemetery. We go east and now are far away from the center of Paris, but big crowds still stand along the avenues. Whole classes of schoolchildren wave American flags.

I keep my eyes on John Noll as the line of soldiers and Marines wheels left and marches along a side street into a courtyard enclosed by buildings. Where's the cemetery, I wonder. Then I see them go through a gate next to a church. I expect rows of tombstones, but instead we're in a narrow garden with trees and grass. Finally we turn and I see at the end of the space a scatter of tombstones, and against the far wall, there it is—the grave of Lafayette.

The Marines form an honor guard as their flag bearer holds the Stars and Stripes over Lafayette's grave. I recognize General Pershing from pictures in the newspaper. But it's another officer who stands front and center. I notice a group of fellows with notebooks and one or two photographers standing right behind the officer as he begins to speak. Reporters. I push my way toward them holding my Seneca in front of me like a badge and manage to reach the pressmen in time to hear the American officers say, "*Lafayette, nous ici.* Lafayette, we are here." I line the officer up in my lens and push the shutter.

"Did you get a decent shot of Stanton?" the fellow next to me asks. A short wiry man scribbling away in his notebook. "Pershing hates to speak in public. Leaves it to Colonel Stanton."

"I got the photograph," I say.

"Know some place to develop it?" he asks.

"I have my own darkroom."

"Okay, sweetheart, you're hired. Get me some close-ups of the brass and the Marines, and the flags over the grave."

"Pardon me?"

"I'm Floyd Gibbons from the Chicago *Tribune*. My photographer jumped ship and went to work for the New York *Times*. I'm desperate. I'll pay you good money for those pictures."

"All right," I say.

"And be sure to get shots of those burial plots covered in gravel," he says. "Those are the mass graves. The guillotine was just around the corner. After they cut off the victims' heads, they dumped their bodies here. Fifteen hundred or so, among them Lafayette's wife's mother, sister, and grandmother, who had the bad luck to be aristocrats at the wrong time. A bunch of nuns buried here, too. After things calmed down a bit, the families bought this ground and turned it into a cemetery."

Spooky and sad. A barbaric time I guess. But then I think of the fifteen men the British executed right after the Rising. Their bodies had been dumped into a mass grave, too, and covered with lime. I wonder if someday their families will be able to put up a monument for them.

I expect only a day's work from Floyd, but he likes my photographs— especially what he calls my casual Marines.

"Hard to get these fellows to relax. Usually they look into the camera with stone faces," he says.

"Well," I say, pointing at the photograph, "that's my friend's brother, and that's his sergeant, Dan Daly . . ."

"Who's famous," Floyd says. "Good girl. Go for the well-known ones. Who's the young kid?"

"John J. Kelly from Chicago," I say. I'd been a little nervous when I met him, but he'd been only sixteen when the *Volterra* went down. And after all, nothing unusual about running into another Kelly from Chicago.

"Listen," Floyd says to me. "I'm going down to Saint-Nazaire where the Marines are training. Want to do some human-interest stuff. How about you come with me? I'll pay you thirty francs a week and cover the hotel in St. Nazaire. What do you say?"

"Do I need any kind of credentials?" I ask him.

"I'll get them for you."

"You might have a problem. I got on the wrong side of the British army," I say, and give him a quick summary of my problems at the American hospital.

"You got in trouble because you were helping the Irish against the English?" he says.

"More or less," I say.

"The Marines will love you. Lots of them are Micks like us. You just tell Dan Daly the Brits gave you the dirty end of the stick. He'll take care of it, believe me."

Floyd's right. At Saint-Nazaire, Gunnery Sergeant Daly marches me right into Marine headquarters, and I walk out with a letter appointing me "Official photographer of the U.S. Marine Corps."

Being with this bunch of Americans lifts my spirits. Father Kevin has the address of the small hotel in the village where I'm staying. Any sign of Peter, any news, he'll telegraph me immediately. It's not that I've forgotten Peter but I must say it's fun to be with the Marines, to let go of fear. No question that these fellows will win the war once they are given the chance. Eager, they are. The Marine slogan is "First to Fight" and they are not happy to be kept out of the battle. The French and British insist that the American troops need more training. So I spent all that summer and fall photographing Marines marching along country roads carrying forty-pound packs. Or running at sacks of straw with bayonets. Some excitement when they get behind the machine guns and lay waste some empty fields. Floyd's determined to get a profile of every single Marine and sell it to their hometown papers. So I'm photographing the fellows from morning till night.

"Our boss, Robert McCormick who owns the Trib, is over here now," Floyd tells me just before Christmas. "He's on the staff of Army Intelligence."

Geeze Louise, I think. Ed's friend. He'll certainly recognize me and know the story of my drowning.

He doesn't.

I'm wondering if anybody remembers anything they read in the newspaper, which I don't say to Floyd because he seems to think getting on the front page is the greatest achievement anyone can aspire to.

The Marines want to give a Christmas party for the children of Saint-Nazaire. Floyd and I write a story for the Chicago *Tribune* about their plans. Gifts for the kids begin to arrive in the mail from America.

The biggest Marine plays Santa Claus, which confuses the children. Their St. Nicholas doesn't have the heft of ours. But each child receives a toy and shares the Christmas meal.

Dark, cold Paris seems a world away. Maud and her children are in Ireland. She'd outsmarted the British by going to England and then crossing to Ireland in disguise. Though how a six-foot-tall woman could manage that, I don't know.

It's good for me to feel useful again. I'm taking photographs of the fellows for them to send home and helping out at the medical station that's been set up to deal with training accidents and just plain sickness.

Full days but not as *"abrutissant"* as the nursing I'd done before. Being a soldier could be quite enjoyable if combat could be avoided, I think.

JUNE 1918

But of course it can't.

Floyd Gibbons comes rushing into the hotel dining room on June 2nd. Madame Guerin's serving me the coffee the Marines gave her from their stores. Wonder if anyone in Paris is drinking real coffee now.

"Come on, come on," Floyd says. "They're moving out. Petain has convinced Pershing to bring the Marines into the line. The Germans have gotten back to the Marne and this time they are pushing straight through to Paris. The Huns' last chance. I hope you've got plenty of film."

I watch Dan Daly, John Noll, and John Kelly ride by me on trucks. Smiling. Waving. The "First to Fight" Brigade finally getting into the war.

And I'm so bewitched by the Marine Corps spirit that I imagine they'll simply float across the battlefield like John Feeney's angels only with guns blazing. The marines will so frighten the Germans, the Boche will throw up their hands. Surrender. And that will be the Battle of Belleau Wood.

Except it isn't.

Floyd promotes a ride on a Red Cross truck going to Paris. Then he manages to rent a touring car and we head for Château-Thierry near the Marne River. We drive the thirty miles from Paris in the middle of the night, which turns out to be a good decision because during the day the two sides shoot at each other across the highway. We arrive late on the 5th of June. There has already been four days of fighting. I go with Floyd to find an officer to interview. No one has much time for us but a corporal takes us to Captain Lloyd Williams. He's at headquarters looking at a map of Belleau Wood, where the Germans are dug in.

"What can you tell us about the fighting yesterday, Captain Williams?"

Floyd asks. "I understand the French were retreating when you entered the wood and you told them . . ."

"Look," Captain Williams says, interupting Floyd. "I'm not even sure what I said."

"I am," the corporal says. "The French were leaving and yelled at us to join their retreat. Said the Germans had us outnumbered. Captain Williams hollered back, 'Retreat hell. We just got here.'"

Floyd writes in his notebook. Turns to me, smiles, and says, "Take the captain's photograph."

I can only get a quick candid. The captain won't pose.

"Were there many casualties?" I ask as the corporal leads us back to our car.

Floyd says, "No one knows. We won't get the names until this thing's over. But plenty dead and wounded. I think somebody screwed up. Weren't supposed to be all those German machine-gun nests in that wood."

Floyd goes off, very excited when he comes back.

"Army Intelligence intercepted a German message. The Huns are asking for reinforcements. Said the Americans fighting them here are 'Teufel Hunden,' Devil Dogs. How's that for a Marine nickname? But a bit of bad news. The Marines don't want a woman too close to combat," Floyd says.

I'm to go to a village called Bézu-le-Guéry, about five miles away, where a first-aid station's been set up in a church.

But he says there might be a silver lining.

"The doc in charge is Richard Derby. His wife is the nurse. Guess who she is? Edith Roosevelt, Teddy's daughter. Get some shots of her tending the wounded. My editors will love it. And get this. Her brother, Quentin Roosevelt, is flying missions right above us. With any luck, he'll get in a dogfight up there, crash-land, and be taken to her. She'll save his life. What a story."

"Oh for God's sake, Floyd. Listen to yourself," I say.

Already a number of casualties from the previous days of fighting when I arrive at the church. Pallets on the floor of the small stone building. Cool inside. Plain, low ceiling. I see a nurse standing over a young marine. She hears me, looks up.

"I'm Nora Kelly," I say.

"Good," she says. "I'm Edith Derby. That doctor over there is my husband Richard."

I suppose Floyd would like me to pose the two of them bandaging a wound. He's such a jerk sometimes.

"Are you trained?" Edith asks me.

"I worked at the American hospital for two years," I say.

"Fine," she says. "We're trying to stabilize the patients here until the ambulances can take them to Paris. But there is fighting all along the highway and the Germans don't always respect the Red Cross on our trucks. So we're doing our best for them here—lucky to get this place."

"Lovely church," I say.

"Thirteenth century," she tells me. "Named for St. Rufin and St. Valere, whoever they are."

"Bet they're from Ireland," I say. According to Barry most early French saints were really Irish missionaries.

"I don't know about that, but the church was a stop for pilgrims on El Camino de Santiago to Compostela, Spain."

And still a refuge I think, as we spend the night applying tourniquets and giving tetanus shots. Infection sets in so quickly. Gangrene means amputation. A shipment of serum comes from Paris by taxi. I think of Louis DuBois, and the Miracle of the Marne. It seems a long time ago.

It's dawn before I fall asleep, and I wake up three hours later. The 6th of June now. At three o'clock in the afternoon, Dr. Derby calls Edith and me over to him. "I just heard that the marines will step off at five, heading into the wood. I am afraid there's going to be a lot of casualties. I'd like to station an ambulance near the village of Belleau. Can you drive, Nora?" Dr. Derby asks me.

"I can," I say.

Hadn't Tim McShane taught me during that first year when I'd thought I loved him?

"I want you to park near the observation post at the edge of the wood. Take Moriarty with you. I set his arm, he can help. They'll wait until darkness falls to bring in the wounded. Don't take any chances," Dr. Derby says.

Would it be wrong to bring the Seneca, I wonder, get some pictures? What had I said to Carolyn Wilson? Important to tell the truth. Besides, Floyd will kill me if I don't.

Moriarty and I start at about 4:30. His arm's in a sling. But otherwise he seems in pretty good shape.

"The artillery should have hit the Germans in the wood pretty hard," he says. "Our fellows will be going in on a mopping-up operation."

We park on a rise in the road, on the other side of the wood. I see the Marines lined up, a thousand of them it seems, bunched together at the edge of a wheat field that's very different from the amber waves of grain on our prairies. Only a few acres of wheat grow right up to the edge of Belleau Wood, dense with the green leaves of June. Red and blue wildflowers are scattered across the field. I hear the Celtic war cry, "hoo-rah," and the Marines step off. They're halfway across the field, wading through wheat up to their waists, when the first booms come from the wood.

"Fuck. Fuck. Fuck," Moriarty says. "German artillery and a lot of it. They don't have a chance."

"Run away," I shout at the Marines. "Run away."

"They won't," Moriarty says to me. "They're Marines."

I close my eyes, put my head in my hands. Moriarty says to me, "You should look. They're so fucking brave." But I can't and I forget about the Seneca completely.

We get our first casualties about ten o'clock. Medics carry three young Marines to the car.

"Water, water," one says. "I'm so thirsty."

"There's a fountain in the village. After all, '*Belleau*' means 'beautiful water,'" Moriarty says to me. "It's near German headquarters in the château."

"But what about the Germans?" I ask.

"They're busy," he says.

We pull up to the yard of the château. The Germans are gone. The building is in ruins. Shelled. Moriarty gets out, runs over, and fills up the canteens. He comes back laughing. "I got the water from the mouth of a Devil Dog." He points at the stone head carved on the fountain. He hands the canteen to the young Marine. "Drink this, pal, it'll cure you."

I help him fill the canteens and all that night, as I clean blood away from one face after another, I whisper, "Water from the Devil Dog fountain." We treat nearly one hundred men but no John Noll or John Kelly or Dan Daly, thank God.

"Nora, Nora." The fellow's being carried into the church.

Floyd. Shot through the eye. "Now I know what it's like to be wounded. This is a front-page story for sure," he says.

So. The Battle of Belleau Wood becomes famous partially thanks to

Floyd Gibbons and to Dan Daly. Floyd gets very literary comparing Dan to a grizzled old sergeant in a Victor Hugo novel. The Chicago *Tribune* gives him five columns on the front page.

> A small platoon line of Marines lay on their faces and bellies under the trees at the edge of a wheat field. Two hundred yards across that flat field the enemy was located in trees. I peered into the trees but could see nothing, yet I knew that every leaf in the foliage screened scores of German machine guns that swept the field with lead. The bullets nipped the tops of the young wheat and ripped the bark from the trunks of the trees three feet from the ground on which the Marines lay. The minute for the Marine advance was approaching. An old gunnery sergeant commanded the platoon in the absence of the lieutenant who had been shot and was out of the fight. This old sergeant was a Marine veteran. His cheeks were bronzed by the wind and the sun of the seven seas. As the minute for the advance arrived, he rose from the trees first and jumped out onto the exposed edge of that field that ran with lead, across which he and his men were to charge. Then he turned to give the charge order to the men of his platoon—his mates—the men he loved. He said:

> "COME ON YOU SONS-O'BITCHES! DO YOU WANT TO LIVE FOREVER?"

Gunny Daly's words. He survives. So does John Kelly. But they find Johnny Noll's body in the wheat field the next morning.

A month later, Quentin Roosevelt will be shot down not far from his sister's small hospital, but she doesn't tend him. Only finds out he's dead when the Germans publish pictures of the ceremonial burial they gave him as the former president's son.

I ride with Floyd in the back of the ambulance to Paris. He leans on me as we walk into the American hospital. A big welcome for the hero journalist. Mrs. Vanderbilt herself is there to shake his hand.

"Hello, Nora," she says to me as if nothing at all had happened. I go to find Margaret Kirk.

Come on, you sons o'bitches. Do you want to live forever?

Stirring, I guess glorious too, I suppose. But, dear God, as I prepare to tell Margaret that her little brother is dead I wish with all my heart they'd heeded my cry, *"Run away, run away."*

NOVEMBER 11, 1918

Margaret and I are standing together in front of the Cathedral of Notre-Dame when all the church bells in Paris begin ringing at eleven minutes after eleven. Over. The war is over.

"Too late for Johnny," Margaret says.

"And millions more," I say.

But over, thank God. Over.

22

NOVEMBER 27, 1918

"Nora, Nora!" A clatter of voices yelling below my window. Still dark and me sure I'm dreaming. I open up the casement windows and look down onto the cobblestones of the place des Vosges.

"Quiet!" I shout down at the cluster of soldiers waving up at me from under the streetlamp. Fellows released from the hospital and on a tear, I suppose.

But then who do I see right in the middle of them only Margaret Kirk, laughing and calling out, "Nora! Nora, can we come up? We're desperate! Please!" she shouts.

The soldiers take up the chant. "Please, please!"

"I've nowhere to take them!" she says.

The tallest of the soldiers shouts, "Up, up, up!"

The others join in until the oldest of them, a short fellow in glasses, quiets them. "Cut it out, fellows," I hear him say.

"All right, all right," I say, "come up, but be quiet!"

"Only place I could think to take them," Margaret says as the five men find places for themselves in my room.

"They're all boys from home, friends of Johnny's," she says. "They came to me at the hospital an hour ago. The cafés are all closed and well, Nora, they've all been at the Front. Just arrived."

Months since Margaret laughed. Steeped in grief for Johnny Noll. "Such a good kid," she's told me over and over. Good to see her smiling.

"These boys are heroes, Nora," she says.

"Don't know about that but we did fire one of the last volleys of the war," the small man with glasses says. "Battery D of the Second Battalion, 129th Field Artillery, 'The Dizzy Ds.'"

"The best battery in the U.S. Army," a tall boy says.

"Or any other army," another soldier says.

"They grew up with my brother Johnny and me," Margaret says. "All from Kansas City. Meet Jimmy Pendergast, and their captain . . ." She pauses.

"Harry Truman, miss," the man with glasses says. "Sorry to disturb you but we've had a tough few weeks and just got in. Johnny had told the boys Peggy was in Paris, well, they wanted to have a drink or two in his honor. I didn't have the heart to stop them from storming the hospital, as late as it was."

"Fought our way through the mountains, miss, and that's no small feat for a bunch of prairie boys," the one called Jim Pendergast says.

I pull out three bottles of wine and hand them to Captain Truman. "Here, start on these while I get dressed," I say.

Margaret follows me into the bedroom. "Thanks, Nora. I couldn't send them away. For one thing they wouldn't leave. And they want to toast my brother. At least no more fellows will die. It's over, Nora. Really over. For the first time I believe it."

Later Captain Truman sends one of the fellows out at dawn to buy baguettes and when that fresh-baked smell fills my room, I think, Yes, yes, the war is over. Life is starting again. Oh Peter, where are you?

I watch Margaret joshing with the soldiers, trying to explain to me who is related to whom.

"We're all up from the Bottoms," one of the soldiers tells me.

"Aren't we all," I said. "My family comes from a place that was called Hardscrabble."

"Yes, but our neighborhood really is 'the Bottoms' because it's stuck into the bank of the Missouri River, buried in mud half the time. But a swell place to grow up."

"I knew Jim in St. Joe even before Kansas City," Margaret says. "Jim's family and mine have been friends since my mother worked as a laundress at the World Hotel."

"Where Jesse James lived," Jim says.

He laughs.

"Peggy's mother, Lizzie Burke, was the prettiest girl in St. Joe, according to my father. A sad day when a German fellow picked her off."

"Poor Papa," Margaret says. "Didn't live to see thirty."

"Should have married a strong Irishman," Jim says.

"A great singing voice, your mother," Jim says. "Give us a song, Peggy."

"I didn't get her talent. You've a voice, Jim. Let's have one," Margaret says.

"No, no, too many cigarettes. Captain Harry's the real musician except he needs a piano," Jim says.

I turn to the captain. "We'll find you a piano."

"Not sure if Chopin and Hayden's the kind of stuff to keep the party going," he says.

"You learned classical piano in the Bottoms?" I ask him.

"I'm from Independence, a little town outside of Kansas City. The Santa Fe Trail starts there. I only fell in with this Irish bunch recently. Just lucky, I guess."

One of the soldiers hears this. "Not what you thought at first, Captain. My name's Bill O'Hara. We were the battalion bad boys," he says to me. "Went through three captains. But this fellow is tougher than he looks."

"Yeah," a tall fellow says. "We laughed at him. This pipsqueak four-eyes giving us orders."

Captain Truman looks at me. "Those early days were interesting," he says.

"Gave us hell, Harry did, but in a quiet way. He took no guff," Jim Pendergast says. "No speeches. Just said he was determined to get us all home to Kansas City alive and in one piece. But if we acted like damn fools we'd be signing our own death warrants. He made all that army bull about cleaning the big gun over and over seem important for our own survival. Didn't care about kissing ass. Everything he did was for Battery D."

"And did you do it, Captain?" I ask. "Get them all home safely?"

"*They* did it, ma'am. No casualties. Fine men, every one of them," he says.

"And this from a Mason," Jim Pendergast says. "Who probably never met a Catholic before in his life."

"Or a Jew," another soldier puts in. "I'm Bernie Jacobson, miss. And how I got involved with this group of wild Irishmen, I'll never know, but we stuck together and did some damage to the enemy."

Jim Pendergast nods. "And we couldn't go home, though, without saying hello to Peggy, all of us together at St. Patrick's Church in St. Joe." He turns to Margaret. Hard to think of my elegant friend as "Peggy."

"My uncle Jim always had a great regard for your mother. 'Plucky,' he called her."

Margaret nods. "This was the family I told you who helped us. Three Pendergast brothers—Jim, Tom, and Mike," she says to me. "During our first winter in Kansas City, a fellow who worked for Big Jim in the bar dropped off a load of coal and a bushel of potatoes every week. We would've starved without him."

"Plenty of others," the tall fellow says, "have a lot to thank Big Jim Pendergast for."

"And Tom too," another soldier says. "Got me a job on the cops."

"And thank him you do," the captain says, "with your votes."

"Well, hell, Harry, we would have voted for the Democrats anyway!"

"I suppose," he said, "but . . ." He stops.

"You disapprove, Captain Truman?" I ask.

"Not really, but folks where I'm from, Independence, don't like bosses and block voting and jobs given out because of political connections."

Jim Pendergast laughs. "Unless they're the ones calling the shots and getting the jobs."

"You're not," I pause, "a Republican, are you, Captain Truman?"

"A Democrat born and bred, Miss Kelly, and my own father held a government job. In charge of fixing the roads in Jackson County but he was qualified and an honest man."

"Then let's drink to him," Jim says. He takes a long swallow from the wine bottle and passes it on to O'Hara.

"Can't let these boys start talking politics," Margaret says. "There are rabbits among the goats. Could start throwing punches at each other."

Jim wipes his mouth. "Don't worry, Peggy," he says. "We've been through the wars together. Aren't going to fall out over old arguments."

"Rabbits?" I say to him. "Goats?"

"You see," Jim says, "we're all Democrats, but the fellows loyal to the Pendergasts are called goats, and those following Jim Shannon are rabbits."

"Why?"

"Don't know. Something about us raising goats in the Bottoms and them having rabbits. Some people say those are Irish words that got twisted. But none of that matters. We're in Paris and we're taking you ladies to lunch at the best restaurant in town, whatever that is."

"Maxim's," I say. "A meal to write home about."

"Actually," Captain Truman says, "I was thinking that if you had some paper and a pen I'd stay right here and get a letter off. Not much time to write in the last few weeks."

"For God's sake, Captain, give it a rest," O'Hara says. He turns to me. "Never saw so much letter writing."

"The captain's in love," Jim says.

"Nothing wrong with that," I say to Truman.

"I've been in love with Bess since I met her at Sunday school when I was six years old and she was five. Cutest little thing I ever saw, with all golden ringlets. Been courting her ever since."

"A long time," I say.

"I vowed I wouldn't marry Bess until I could support her in the way she deserves," he says.

"Her family owns Queen of Pantry Flour," Jim says.

"Never heard of it," I say.

"They're important in Independence and Kansas City, though her father . . ." He stops. "Sorry, Captain." Jim stands up. "Come on, Captain. Write to her tonight. You'll have something to say. Attention! March!" And the fellows begin moving.

"Aren't you meant to be out in front?" I say to Captain Truman.

"Not with this bunch. Lucky to bring up the rear," he says. "Youth!"

"And how old are you?"

"Thirty-four."

"And your sweetheart?"

"Thirty-three."

"Don't wait too long, Captain. She'll be so glad to have you home. She won't be worrying about curtains and carpets. Marry her. Have babies.

Time goes faster than you think for a woman." I stop. What was I babbling on about, and to a complete stranger? The oldest of the bunch and younger than me.

"I know Jim said her father's a difficulty but . . ." I say.

"You don't understand," Truman says to me, "Bess's father is dead, took his own life. A family tragedy. Tough on her."

"All the more reason," I tell him. "That she'll be happy that you are alive."

We follow the men down the stairs and out into the street. Cold enough. The bells of Sainte-Clothilde ring the Angelus. Noon. Maxim's will be open.

We catch up with Margaret and Jim. "Imagine strolling the streets of Paris with a girl from Summit Avenue," he says. "My mother always said you had the prettiest wedding. Only a young girl, really, marching down that long aisle in the cathedral with that fellow with the funny name."

"You think Kirk's a funny name, Jim?" I say.

"Oh, this was the one before Kirk . . ." He caught himself. "Damn it to hell. Wasn't going to say a word about that. Ancient history."

"Obviously not in Kansas City," Margaret says.

"Which way?" the soldiers yell back to us as they came to the corner.

"Left," I say "La Gauche."

Marcel, the headwaiter, is only too delighted to lead us to the best table as the Parisians applaud *les Américains* and call out, "*Merci!*"

A lovely lunch, lots of wine and Captain Truman taking over the piano. He plays Chopin, yes, but when the boys gather around they sing "Over There," slamming out some new words,

> "And we're *going home,*
> *'Cause it's over, over there!*"

Followed by "Give My Regards to Broadway." George M. Cohan—I remember those shows at McVicker's Theatre with Mam and the family.

Being with these fellows makes me so homesick for Chicago. I'll never see it again.

"Let's go to the café on Saint-Michel that looks across at Notre-Dame," Margaret says to me.

"All right." I say.

A week after our day with the Kansas City soldiers, Paris is getting ready to celebrate its first peacetime Christmas. I wonder, will the woman from Alsace have a booth at the market on the Champs-Élysées?

The waiter brings over a bottle of champagne in a silver bucket. Vintage. He sets flutes before us, pours each of us a glass of the sparkling wine.

"But we didn't order that," I say.

"I did," Margaret says. "I'm the hostess for the Women's Christmas this year, Nora. A little early and it's only you and me."

"But Maud is with us in spirit. At least she's out of that awful Holloway Prison," I say.

The British had finally found a reason to arrest Maud.

"Will she come back to Paris?" Margaret asks me.

"Not to live," I say, "she won't desert Ireland." Maud had said as much in a short note to Father Kevin.

Yeats, Quinn, all her friends had petitioned the British government for her release because of her health.

"Not good for them to have me die in prison," she'd written to him. "I had to make promises but . . ."

"She's in London now. She had to agree not to return to Ireland. But I'm sure Maud will sneak back as soon as she's at all recovered," I say.

"Nothing stops her," Margaret says.

"A rock," I say, "though a frail one. I wonder if 'too long a sacrifice' does make a stone of the heart."

"Very poetic," Margaret says.

"Yeats," I say.

"I wish I could find some lofty words for what I'm about to say," Margaret tells me.

"Oh, oh," I say.

"I'm going home, Nora," she says. "Being with those fellows made me realize I'm an Irish girl from Kansas City. I want to be where I belong. I should be with my mother mourning Johnny. What the neighbors think doesn't seem to matter anymore."

"Well," I start, "I'm not sure anyone belongs in any one place." I stop. She's made up her mind. "I'll miss you," I say.

She says, "Never had such a good friend. That first Christmas at Maud's, when you pointed me toward Father Kevin and forgiveness, you gave me a great gift."

Late afternoon, and a small musical group has assembled for the usual polite French dance music, and indeed a few couples get up and begin to waltz sedately.

"Thank you for saying that," I tell Margaret, "and for all we shared at the hospital." She lifts her flute of champagne, I raise mine, and we touch glasses.

The door opens. A blast of cold air comes in and with it four American soldiers—all Negroes—laughing and talking to each other. The maître d' rushes up to them.

"Welcome, messieurs," he says.

"I wish some of the leftover Confederates in Kansas City could understand how grateful the French are to Negro soldiers," Margaret says.

The group sits next to us.

"Hello," I say. "Where are you from?"

"Chicago," the tall dark-skinned fellow in sergeant's stripes says to me.

"Me too," I say. "Where?"

"South Side," he says.

"So am I. Bridgeport," I say.

He smiles. "We're neighbors. I'm from Twenty-second and Wabash, St. James Parish." He turns to the other fellows. "That's how folks in Chicago talk about their neighborhood."

"You're Catholic?" Margaret blurts out.

"I'm Lorenzo Dufau. Came to Chicago from Baton Rouge. Catholic back generations. Lieutenant Dawson, there, he's from Chicago too, but a Baptist."

The lieutenant nods at us.

"I'm Nora Kelly," I say.

"Bill Dawson," the lieutenant says. "And this is Private Ben Garrison and Sergeant Jim Graham—both from South Carolina."

The waiter takes their orders. The lieutenant asks for *boeuf bourguignonne* in very good French. Lorenzo Dufau holds up three fingers—"Steak and *frites*," he says distinctly, "well done." He turns to me. "Learned our lesson."

The maître d' comes over and starts speaking to Lieutenant Dawson in rapid French.

"*Lentement,*" Dawson says. "*Je ne comprend français vite.*" And then to me, "Say a few words and they think you're an expert. You speak it?"

"Been here six years. I'd better. *Monsieur,*" I say to the maître d', "*voulez vous mon assistance?*"

"I understand that," Dawson says.

The maître d' lets loose with a stream of words, shrugs, and gestures until I say, "*D'accord.*" I turn to the soldiers. "He wants to know if any of you are musicians and can play 'le jazz hot.'"

"I wish I could," Dufau says. "If I played the trumpet I'd never have to buy a drink in Paris for the rest of my life. A musician friend of mine from New Orleans named Baneris, who lives here, thinks he's gone to heaven without even having to die. Tell the manager we're no musicians but we've got a decent singer." He turns to the fellow who's said nothing at all. "Come on, Ben, get up."

Well, it takes a lot of coaxing but finally Private Ben Garrison, the youngest of the four, goes to the bandstand. He says something to the bandleader.

"Okay, folks, this is a hit in America." He begins to sing without accompaniment: "'How you gonna keep 'em down on the farm after they've seen Paree?'"

The crowd understood only "Paris," but the band picks up the rhythm and Ben begins to throw random syllables in.

"Scatting," Lorenzo Dufau says to me as the crowd applauds.

I lean over to Lieutenant Dawson. "That song asks a good question," I say.

He nods. "Won't just be farm boys," he said. "Hard to keep anybody down after this." He gestures toward Private Garrison, who's shaking hands with the patrons as he comes back to our table. "Treat a man like a man and he's not likely to forget it."

"You got that right, Lieutenant," Jim Graham says.

"Lieutenant," Margaret repeats.

"And a good one too," Graham says. "Better than . . . Well, we could do with a few more of our own in charge."

"I was just with a pack of Irish soldiers with the same complaint. Took them three tries to get an officer who didn't see them as rowdy Micks," I say.

"Our men did all right fighting under the French, but serving under white Americans . . . My God, those were some prejudiced folks," Sergeant Dufau says.

"My dad was with the Irish Legion in the Civil War," I say. "They had Irish officers but other Irish units commanded by Yankees caught hell."

"My father fought in the Civil War too," Dufau said. "Supposed to get a medal. Never did."

"The French gave us Buffalo Soldiers the Croix de Guerre," Ben Garrison says.

"Wonderful. Congratulations," I say.

"Army gave me all I want," Lieutenant Dawson says. "A discharge and a ticket home."

The other men nod.

"Not tempted to stay in Paris?" I ask.

"This is a beautiful city," Dufau says. "The people are real human beings, kind. And the food is great. But Chicago's home and I miss it. My folks are counting the days."

"Mine too," Graham says. "Though I may not stay in South Carolina. Never liked big cities, but after this Paris I might try New York."

"Harlem, USA," Garrison says. "Lots of fellows in our outfit from there. Might give it a look-see."

"Not me," Lieutenant Dawson says. "New York's too big. Can't beat the South Side of Chicago." He points at the French musicians. "We've got the real 'le jazz hot' all right, and the blues."

"You like the blues?" Dufau asks. "A college man like you?"

"I wasn't born in college. My grandfather played blues guitar."

"But could he sing? Growl and howl and make the juke joint jump?" Dufau says.

"I'd say he could but then he married my grandmother, a preacher's daughter, and came to Chicago and we became respectable church people," Lieutenant Dawson says.

"Lace curtain," I put in.

"Oh, yes," Lieutenant Dawson says, "the curtains and a piano in the parlor, and me at Fisk, then law school."

"You're ahead of the Kellys," I said. "We haven't managed college yet. Though my cousin Ed became an engineer by going to the Atheneum at night."

Oh, God, why did I say that? And give my real name. Harder and harder to pretend I'm dead. Wrong somehow. But he won't know Ed. Then

Dawson says. "Ed? Ed Kelly? From Brighton Park. Worked on the canal, tall redheaded fellow?"

"That's him," I say.

"A boxer?"

"Right."

"Mine enemy," he says.

"Pardon me?"

He laughs. "Politically. I'm a Republican, Miss Kelly, and your cousin's as good a weapon as the Democratic Party has. I've seen him march his Brighton Park boys to the polls and every Republican knows the story of how he wrapped his arms around the ballot box and wouldn't let go until the police came to escort him to the count."

"Had to keep you Republicans from stuffing the box!" I say. "How can you let the party of Lincoln be taken over by crooks like Big Bill Thompson?"

"But it *is* the party of Lincoln," Graham speaks up, "and in the South it's the Democrats trying to keep us from voting. They're the ones behind the Jim Crow laws."

Margaret says, "I'm from Kansas City. It's the Democrats who care about the working people."

"Now, are we going to ruin this lovely afternoon by arguing about politics?" Lieutenant Dawson says. "Look how the French are staring at us. Think we're really fighting."

And indeed, the four tables closest to us have stopped talking entirely and are watching us and listening to the tone of our conversation despite not understanding the words. Imagining who knows what. Trouble with not really knowing a language.

I smile at the people at the nearest table. *"Pas problème,"* I say. *"Nous sommes amis."* They look at me blankly. *"Comprendez vous?"* I ask.

One young woman in a cloche hat says, *"Oui, je comprends, mais vous parlez un français bizarre."*

The Negro soldiers understand and we spent the next half hour laughing as Lieutenant Dawson and the others repeat "bizarre" in their best French accents, with Graham adding a Southern cadence. Then Lieutenant Dawson says the phrase using a very lawyerly diction in which he underlines each syllable of *"bizarre."*

"Américains," the man sitting next to the young woman says, shrugging away all nuance.

I've been living for seven years with people who don't really understand me or my country, I think. Even Peter looked at me sometimes as if I were an alien. These last years of war and shared fears made all Parisians one. But now I realize I am an American, a Chicagoan—and on the run. I love Paris, but it's not home. Am I losing myself? *"Je parle un français bizarre."* Not one thing or another. Oh Peter, could we go home together? You'd be so happy as an Irish American. But then I remember I'm dead.

Lieutenant Dawson orders another bottle of champagne and I let the wine ease me back into the here and now.

"I was real sorry to hear about Ed's wife," Lieutenant Dawson says.

"What?"

"Mary. Died during the flu epidemic."

"Oh, no," I say. "When?"

"Last spring," he says, "so sad to lose the child too."

"Ed's son died?"

"No it's just—well I heard that his wife was eight months pregnant."

Poor Ed, I think, poor Ed, and not a word of comfort from me, the other redhead. Poor Mary. So kind to me the morning I left Chicago. She's really gone while I only pretend to be dead.

A cruel hoax. I want to write to Ed, console him. Tell him about Peter. My life here. The war. But I can't of course. A terrible time to get a letter from me when he's mourning Mary. But how Margaret and I would rejoice if John Noll walked in right now or John Feeney, Paul O'Toole even. "A mistake," they'd say. We're alive." A great celebration would follow. Isn't that how my family would feel if I came back from the dead? I don't know.

Maybe I shouldn't write to Ed but I can send a letter to Mame and Mike explaining everything. Let them tell Ed.

And I do, writing pages and pages. I tell them that I'm married to a man I love who loves me. He's fighting for Irish freedom. But if—no, when—things are better in Ireland, we will come to Chicago for a visit. I still re-member the address of the house in Argo. Hope they still live there.

I wait for a reply. One month. The mail's still slow. Two, three, four months. No answer. They don't care. I am dead to them. What can I do?

On my fortieth birthday, April 18, 1919, a here-comes-spring day in Paris, I bob my hair. Or rather Monsieur Leon does it for me. A barber because ladies' coiffeurs do not mutilate a woman's crowning glory, as I was told by one. Leon's Russian and reminds me of Stefan, although Leon ran from the revolution instead of toward it. As he goes on about the murder of the czar and his family, I feel the scissors nicking the back of my neck. I look into the mirror when he finishes.

"Too shocking?" I ask Leon. I look so bare and the color of my hair is a deeper auburn. My eyes seem bigger framed by the bangs across my forehead.

"Not at all. Soon this style will be *la mode*," Leon says as he sweeps up my red hair and tosses the pile into the bin. "Not worth saving," he says. "The wig market kaput. No more disguises. The face, the figure—exposed. The new woman."

Is that a good thing for me at forty, I wonder. The image in the mirror smiles at me. You're a lot younger in Paris than you would be in Chicago, she seems to say.

True enough. There I'd be a spinster. Sliding into old age. Here, well, I'm years younger than Natalie Barney and Gertrude Stein. And both of them still big wheels in Paris. And Edith Wharton, at fifty-eight, has written what I think is her best novel. She had Sylvia Beach and me read the manuscript of the *The Age of Innocence*.

"Does Ellen, the countess, ring true to you?" Edith asked me.

"Absolutely," I said, and thought that New York in the 1870s was probably not all that different than Bridgeport is today. Tough on a woman with a past. Is that why Mike and Mame didn't answer my letter?

Easier to hold my head up with all that hair gone, I think. Peter will like this style, I tell myself. Still no word from him.

Poor Ireland.

The English are determined to crush the rebels.

The British army had marched from Flanders Field to Tipperary. Not a long enough way to go after all, I'd thought, when reports started coming in of the atrocities committed by members of the British force the Irish called Black and Tans because of their makeshift uniforms—khaki army pants and a policeman's dark blue jacket.

"Criminals, many recruited from English prisons," Maud says in one of her letters to Father Kevin. "Glad when they fire a house. Murderers attacking women and children. Most of our men have been arrested or are on the run. Ireland's a battlefield."

And my poor Peter in the middle of it all. Is he even alive?

Madame Simone only nods at my haircut.

"C'est la vie," she says.

We no longer copy from the old masters or other designers. Now we're stealing from the movies. I go to see *The Flapper*, starring Olive Thomas, about fifteen times.

Madame Simone's new collection is called Costumes du Cinéma.

The Seneca and I keep busy too. The Peace Conference has brought loads of Americans to Paris. Floyd Gibbons and I take pictures like crazy. Floyd gets an interview with Woodrow Wilson. To please me he asks the president about Ireland. The Irish people have voted for independence from Britain. Will the U.S. support them? After all, wasn't the war fought to protect the rights of small nations?

"We will not interfere in the internal affairs of our closest ally Great Britain," Wilson says.

So.

JULY 1919

I sit in the parlor of the Irish College listening to the members of the American Commission on Irish Independence report on their efforts to have Ireland's independence recognized in the Treaty of Versailles. About five priests, six or seven students, Father Kevin, and I are gathered. The leader of the commission, former governor Edward Dunne of Illinois, is speaking. I hide behind the priest in front of me. Dunne had been at Mike and Mame's wedding. He would know Nora Kelly.

"Woodrow Wilson presents himself as an idealist," Dunne is saying. "But I fear he's a victim of his own deep prejudices. He's an Ulsterman and a Southerner whose father served as a chaplain in the Confederate Army. He sees anyone who isn't a white Anglo-Saxon Protestant as inferior. He has implemented full segregation in federal jobs and praised the Ku Klux Klan. He disdains Irish-American Democrats. Sees them as corrupt creatures of big-city bosses. He promised during the election to support independence for Ireland. He has broken that promise. As for the treaty, itself, I understand why France wants to weaken Germany but I fear the reparations being imposed will cause such resentment among the German people that good relations with other European powers will be difficult if not impossible. And, as for Britain, she's acquired more colonies and will continue with her policy of divide and conquer. Doing to these countries what she's done to Ireland for centuries. Until they, too, will have to rebel."

Oh, dear God, I think. What a gloomy picture. But then Dunne becomes very emotional.

"Ireland should not despair," he tells the audience. "We Americans of Irish blood pledge our lives and our fortunes to the country that claims our hearts."

Afterward Father Kevin introduces me to Edward Dunne. No recognition at all. I guess the woman with the helmet of auburn hair and short skirt is not the Nora Kelly he knew.

Father Kevin asks Dunne about the address he gave to Ireland's Rebel Parliament, the Dáil. In the recent British parliamentary election the Irish people voted in representatives who favored independence. These representatives did not go to Westminster but set up their own parliament in Dublin. Democratically elected, though the British did not recognize its authority. But Dunne says the Irish Declaration of War on Britain is legitimate because the Dáil was elected by the people. "The Catholic Church will recognize Ireland's fight as a just war," he says.

The only just war is one that's over, I think. Not fair somehow that the whole world's celebrating peace and Ireland's still a battlefield.

Father Kevin asks Dunne if he's been to Galway. Looking for some news of Peter I'm sure. But Dunne did not go to Galway. So still no information about Peter.

I find myself confiding in, of all people, Leon the barber. I am seeing a lot of him. A bob needs frequent trims.

"Not even a letter from my—" Say it, Nora. "—husband in years."

But Leon gets mad at me. Don't I understand what it is to be under siege? Ireland. Russia. Armies and fighting. My husband, his mother, all struggling to survive. We must be faithful. Wait and hope.

Leon and I communicate in a mix of bad French and worse English—me speaking a kind of pidgin language that makes the customer waiting his turn with Leon ask me where I come from.

"America," I say. "Chicago."

"Then speak properly," he says.

A very dapper fellow who comes to Leon for a shave. I find myself lingering to watch Leon cover the man's face with white lather, sharpen a straight-edge razor on a strap, and begin to maneuver it. *Le coupe-chou*, the cabbage cutter, I think to myself, and laugh. The two are chatting away in Russian as Leon wraps a hot towel from chin to forehead around the fellow he calls Serge. He takes down a bottle of scent from the shelf, unwraps Serge, and splashes his face with a perfume that smells of lavender. Such a precise mustache, under plump cheeks, and dark eyes. The fellow sees me watching.

"I suppose you are waiting because you think I will give you a ticket. I am very sorry, mademoiselle. I cannot afford such gestures."

A ticket. What's he talking about?

"Nora is a photographer, Serge. Her pictures are published in the newspapers in the United States," Leon says.

"Are you a good photographer?" Serge asks me.

"I am," I say. I've learned something from Floyd Gibbons. Though he would have said, "Good? I'm the greatest."

"Chicago," Serge says. "We will play Chicago. All right, mademoiselle. You may photograph the company."

The company?

"And, of course," Leon says, "you will invite Nora to a premier. A new ballet is news."

A ballet, of course. Serge must be Sergei Diaghilev of the Ballets Russes. Famous. But I've never been able to afford a ticket for a performance.

Diaghilev takes a small leather notebook and a gold pen from his pocket. He writes a note and hands it to me.

"Here, mademoiselle. Bring this to the stage door. You may attend a rehearsal. Set up your equipment and . . ."

"But sir," I interrupt him. "My camera is small. It would be much better if I attended a performance. Stood in the wings, took photographs of the dancers from different angles." I think of Eddie Steichen praising the relaxed poses of my women clients, and Floyd, who liked my casual Marines. Perhaps I can get similar shots of the ballet dancers.

So. Christmas Eve I am in the wings as the curtain rises on *La Boutique Fantasque*. On the stage this story of a magic toy shop full of dancing dolls unfolds like a dream. The set is by Gertrude's friend Picasso. The costumes glitter. The music's enthralling. I watch the two can-can dolls, the man in evening dress and the woman in the frilly skirt of the Moulin Rouge, dance their love for each other. The dancers are Léonide Massine, the program says, and Lydia Lopokova. They move so freely through the glides, jumps, lifts. Effortless. I shoot continuously, hoping to catch some of the action. The two float into the wings only ten feet from me. But then Lydia bends over, taking great gulps of air. I see patches of perspiration on her costume. Massine is out and out sweating. A male and female attendant run up to them, patting their faces with towels and offering glasses of water. They don't notice me as I take the photographs. On stage the ballet continues. The male attendant kneels down, takes off one of Lydia's shoes, and massages her foot. I hear her groan. He replaces the shoe. The dancers move back onto the stage.

"Hard work," I say to the attendant. He turns and I think the ballet must have addled me. "Stefan," I say. How could he be here? But he is.

"Quiet," he says, but gestures to me to follow him down the staircase. We are somewhere below the stage.

"I am not Stefan anymore," he says. "You must call me Nicolai. Nic."

"What happened? Why are you here?"

"Later," he says.

I go back in to the wings for the grand finale. The dolls and the toymaker dance together. Spectacular.

"Politics," Stefan tells me. We are in my room. Christmas morning now. Instead of going to midnight Mass, I stayed at the theater as the stage was transformed into a feast. Tables of food, vodka, and the company eating and drinking and laughing.

"A Russian party is like no other," Leon said to me. He saw me as a guest of Diaghilev and was not a bit surprised that I know "Nic."

"Paris," he said.

I saw Diaghilev point his cane at Massine and touch him on each shoulder.

"Léonide has created this ballet," Nic said to me. "I think the toymaker is Diaghilev and so does he."

"Serge probably wishes his dancers were machines," Leon said.

The party finished at dawn.

And now in my room Stefan and I can finally talk.

"I chose the wrong revolutionary faction," Stefan says. "The comrades started executing each other. I had to get out."

"I somehow can't picture you working with dancers," I say.

"I presented myself as a masseur. Not bad at it now," he says.

"But ballet is so, well, aristocratic," I say.

"Diaghilev uses folktales. He's discovered how to make money from the stories of our people," Stefan says.

"Sounds familiar," I say. "Have you been to the Hôtel Jeanne d'Arc?" I ask him.

"Better not," he says. "They know Stefan, not Nicolai."

"But you'll certainly go to see Madame Simone," I say.

"I won't," he says. "It's better that I stay with my new life. I have enemies. And we shouldn't meet again either."

"But," I start, but stop. What is with these revolutionaries? Thank God Irish rebels are united.

Diaghilev hates the photographs I bring him three days after Christmas.

"You have made my dancers look like plow horses finishing a furrow. Disgusting." He tears up the prints.

Doesn't want anyone to see the reality behind the illusion, I guess. But then Paris itself has become a stage set full of players. Some, like Stefan, turning into someone else because of politics, but others like the returning American veterans are remaking themselves here because they couldn't stay down on the farm or in a factory or at a desk after they'd seen Paree. And I'm not sure if I'm an actor or merely an audience member. Missing Margaret and Maud. Longing for Peter.

MAY 16, 1920

So, Joan, you're officially a saint at last. Canonized in Rome today. Congratulations, I say, as I move through the crowd on the place des Pyramids to put my lillies on the pile of flowers in front of the statue of the Maid that so inspired me that first day in Paris. Please bless Maud and Constance and me, I pray, and all women who stand up for themselves. And send some special sign to Sister Mary Agnes. She must be over the moon. Finally got the Pope to see sense. About time. Amen.

SEPTEMBER 1920

Floyd Gibbons is back and his wife with him. He's written a best-selling book on the Battle of Belleau Wood and has a new job as a radio reporter. Very modern is Floyd. I try to get him to go to Ireland and do a program about the war for independence.

"Boring," he says, "and dangerous. A bad combination."

Instead Floyd, his wife, and I go to the Ritz. Olive Thomas, the Flapper herself, is in town with her husband Jimmy Pickford.

"An interview with a movie star always makes the front page," Floyd says. "We'll take them out. You'll take their picture. Have some fun."

"No thanks," I say.

"Paris is a party," his wife tells me. "Don't be the only one not having a good time."

"You're a Kelly from Chicago," Olive Thomas says to me when we meet. "I'm a Duffy from Pittsburgh." Beautiful. White Irish skin. Blue eyes.

"Come out with us," she says after the interview. "Let's show the French how to have fun."

And I try. I really do. Drinking champagne, dancing the Charleston with Floyd. And all I really want is to be sitting by the fire in a small cottage in the West of Ireland with Peter.

We say good night to Olive at three in the morning. Two days later she's dead. Floyd's story makes the front page in every city. An accidental overdose, he says. Little Olive Duffy from Pittsburgh gone at twenty-six.

Poor girl. Not such a party after all, I think.

23

FEBRUARY 1921

I'm working with Father Kevin in the library, typing up a storm as we try to finish his life's work.

He's not exactly on his death bed because Father Kevin won't lie down, but we both know his heart is failing; his body too frail for his spirit. Over eighty now but in the library every day. He's writing the conclusion of his book, *Saint Colmcille from Donegal to Iona and the World.*

"Colmcille's Christianity draws from the well of Celtic spirituality. The pun is intended, Nora," he says. "His insights go beyond mere doctrinal definitions and supersede any denominational divisions."

He writes, passes me the pages, and I type them. A machine-like rhythm. The new rector's a Donegal man himself. Not a stick-in-the mud like the previous fellow. We finish the very day Maud's letter comes. She wants my help.

I'd given up trying to get permission from the British consulate to go to Ireland. But Maud has a scheme.

"America's our only hope," Maud writes me. "John Quinn's part of a new organization, the American Committee for Relief in Ireland. Thousands and thousands of the most prominent men in America have joined and not only the Irish. Your President Harding's endorsed the effort and

Vice-President Coolidge, too. A delegation is coming over to investigate our 'distress.' A soft word for what's happening here. All Quakers and not an Irish American in the group. John said it's important not to give the British a chance to claim the committee's report is biased so no rebels among them. But he'd agreed that they needed photographs. I suggested you. The British can't keep you out if you're part of an official delegation. Please come Nora. We need you."

Need me?

Father Kevin doesn't want me to go. "Dear God, Nora, these fellows would shoot you as soon as look at you and then apologize later."

"But Peter," I say, and he shakes his head.

"It's been seven years and no word. He would have gotten a message to me. I'm afraid he's dead, Nora."

"But what if he's alive. I have to try to find him."

I wire Maud that I will come.

Father Kevin dies the next day. Peacefully. Asleep in his chair at the library, his head resting on the pages of his manuscript.

"We'll get this published somehow," the rector tells me, but I wonder.

Father Kevin's body will be sent to Ireland and I will travel with him.

The letter of permission arrives. I can stay in Ireland two weeks, no longer.

So. I stand on the deck with my hand on Father Kevin's coffin as dawn breaks and I first see the Irish coastline from the boat, a jagged line of rocks and inlets. But as we get closer the wide arms of the harbor open out to me. Ireland. My homeland.

Two silent priests meet the boat. I start to explain that I'm a friend of Father Kevin's and would like to be at his funeral but the taller of the two shakes his head.

"He's going back to Donegal to be buried in his home parish with his own people. Only an old aunt left and she'd not be fit for entertaining an American visitor." And he walks away, taking Father Kevin back, I guess, from his life in Paris. In control. "You never broke his spirit," I want to shout at the disappearing black back. That's when Cyril comes hopping toward me. If ever a man looks like a bird. A robin, I'd say, with a small face and a smear of a red beard, it's Cyril.

"Nora Kelly?" he says. "You must be the American. Follow me."

He doesn't even glance at the two British soldiers who lean against the wall of a shed on the pier watching the passengers disembark.

"The others are waiting at the hotel. Where's your camera gear? I hope it's not too heavy. I have a dicey back."

I show him the small case. Grateful for Eddie Steichen and my Seneca.

"All in there?" he says. "Thank God for American ingenuity,"

I suppose it couldn't but rain in Dublin the day I arrive. Cyril puts me into a taxi. "Here she is," he says to the driver, and then to me, "One of ours. We can speak freely," which Cyril does.

He's taking me to the Gresham Hotel, he says, which is still standing somehow. "Here's O'Connell Street, still full of rubble." The rain soaks into piles of gray stones and mounds of bricks. I see holes gouged out of the rows of buildings.

"Those naval guns," Cyril says. "Brought the ships right up the Liffey. Fired on us. On civilians. Women, children. And these are the same fellows who kept missing the Germans at Jutland kiss-my-foot-how-are-you. Managed to destroy buildings that didn't move. Bullies. Can you believe a so-called civilized country could do this—blow apart a whole city with the Rising over and no threat to them at all? The second city of the empire they're always calling Dublin. Well, look at it now. No concern about the innocent. Jesus, the Brits used to be content with killing us by inches, taking the land, raising the rents, starving us after the potato failed. But this? Jesus, Mary, and Holy Saint Joseph! I didn't think even they had it in them."

Cyril's a member of James Connolly's Citizen Army, he tells me, but was refused a place in the post office fight during the Rising. He has the taxi stop in front of a large pillared building.

"This is it," he says, "the General Post Office. See the nicks from the bullets? I wasn't inside. Said I had no training. But how much practice do you need to have to fire a rifle out a window? About all the military planning there was. I think it was my name. Too English. Pearse didn't want to call out 'Cyril Peterson, front and center.' My mam chose Cyril. A popular enough name on Sherriff Street. My mom loved anything English-sounding. Crazy about Queen Victoria. Called my sister Patricia, not after St. Patrick, but for Victoria's granddaughter still. Connolly never asked Pearse to call him Séamus. Oh, Jesus, I can't believe they're all dead. Why execute them? Haven't the Irish always had rebels? I know for a fact some in the British government wanted to let the whole Easter business die a natural death. You know women from the Liberties spat on Pearse and the others as they were led out to jail. The British soldiers had to protect them. No stomach for it, most of the Tommies hadn't. Plenty of lads from Sherriff Street in the British army. A good few killed at the Front. So I ask you! Hands off and the whole thing's over."

The taxi crosses O'Connell Street and stops in front of the hotel. Cyril keeps talking.

"Total British overreaction, for which I say, thank God. Wouldn't have the eyes of the world on us and you lads over here to help us, the exiles return. Sure, Nora, aren't you only gone a little while. Sent away to Amerikay prosper. I'd say some Divine plan. Only way to make sense of it all. The Great Starvation scattered our people so they could find strength in other places and come back and fight with us."

He sings:

"Some have come from the land beyond the wave;
Sworn to be brave, no more the ancient sire land,
will shelter the despot or the slave."

"But we're in it now," Cyril says. "A real war for independence. Those unionists will be wishing they took Home Rule before this is all over. The Republic of Ireland has a great ring to it. Wouldn't you say?"

He takes a breath. We get out of the taxi. A uniformed doorman reaches for my bag. Cyril waves him away.

"And now that you're here, missus, you'll be seeing some horrible scenes," Cyril says as we walk in the hotel's lobby. "Though not in here."

Impressive, the Gresham. Gold with white plaster molding and chandeliers.

Tables scattered across the wide space. Plenty of people. I get an impression of tweed and silver teapots and racks of toast. Now, toast is something I've missed in Paris.

"Breakfast and a sleep," Cyril says.

"Please," I say.

"But first meet the committee."

Five serious men sipping their tea, not unlike the silent priests who took Father Kevin away. I meet Mr. Jenson, the chairman, and nod to the others. Not much chat in any of them. Though Cyril fills in the gaps. I'm in Ireland, I think, really here. But Dublin doesn't seem that different from any city, only sadder. Is this the place Granny Honora and my mother pined for their whole lives?

I sleep the rest of the day.

That night Cyril invites us to his mother's house. The others are too tired from their crossing to go with us. But I'm delighted. The Petersons live in two rooms in a row house. The brick flats might have once been red, but layers of grime have turned them dark brown, Cyril's mother brings me close to the small coal fire. Smiling.

"A cup of tea and these lovely Jacob's biscuits. Cyril got a whole load for me. Enough for years, take plenty."

"Thank you very much."

"Have another."

"No, really."

"You will, of course."

I didn't want to take the poor woman's cookies because that's what they are, flat sugar cookies with no sugar. I look at Cyril. "Go ahead," he says. "The fellows holding Jacob's biscuit factory passed out a load of biscuits before they surrendered. Lasted all these years." He turns to his mother. "Now, Mam," he says. "Nora came all the way from America to help us out."

"Very good of you, dear. And doesn't Ireland need it! Though we're better off than most. Cyril's father made a good living as a docker. But the consumption took him young and then we were for it. But I got myself work helping at a stall on Moore Street selling odd bits of stuff. Got to be a fair hand at talking to the customers."

"A great one for the repartee you were, Mam, and still are."

"Ah, now I've lost my snap," she says

"Indeed, you have not, Mam." And he leans over and pats her shoulder. They have the same profile: small bent noses, sharp little chins. Mother bird and her baby.

Above their heads a small candle burns in front of a print of the Sacred Heart. It's very like the shrine in Granny Honora's bedroom.

"Mam's a singer too, Nora," Cyril is saying. "Give us a few belts, Mam."

"I couldn't Cyril. Throat's all closed up and scratchy."

"Here now, I have something for that." He brings out a flask.

"Jesus Christ, Cyril, where did you get something like that? It's pure silver," she says.

"A donation, Mam, to the Cause from a fellow who won't be needing it. Have some. It's good *poitín*. I got it off a priest in the country so you know it's pure." He takes a sip and passes it to me. "Go on, Nora." I tilt the flask back, feel a rush of heat, and start coughing.

"See, Mam? Clears the passages."

Water comes out of my eyes. Now, I've drunk some whiskey in my time. McKenna's served a Sunday afternoon ladies' special, but this is beyond potent.

"Don't," I say as he hands the flask to his mother. Could this old lady survive even a sip?

"Thank you, son," she says, and takes the flask with both hands, tips it back. After a long swallow she hands the flask back to Cyril. Not a bother on her.

"Very nice Cyril. Thank you."

"Now your party piece, Mam."

"One more wee sip," she says, taking back the flask. "All right. I have it now." And she begins to sing.

"'Believe me if all these endearing young charms that I gaze on so fondly today . . .'"

A clear voice, without a croak or crack. She finishes the song and smiles at us.

In that small warm room I forget all about the sad Dublin ruins around me. "Your father's favorite," Cyril's mother says. "And his charms never did fade. Young forever. Not a bad thing, I suppose. Not a bad thing at all."

"You can't judge Dublin on a dreary February day, Nora, with the British army patrolling the streets and the wind turning umbrellas inside out!" Maud says to me the next afternoon.

I'm following her to the town house she has just bought off St. Stephen's Green, a park that might be lovely if I could see it through the veil of rain.

"Stephen's Green?" I say. "Weren't characters in Joyce's book always walking back and forth across this space?"

"I don't know," she says. "Joyce makes Dublin so ugly, so squalid. Those were exciting times, Nora. The men suffering in prison today were young university students full of ideas and nobility. James Joyce's Dublin isn't mine."

A striking figure, Maud, dressed all in black with the black veil hanging from her hat that says, "I am a 1916 widow and let no one forget it." The others on the committee refer to her as Madame MacBride and she has become that. She came to lunch at the Gresham and impressed the committee. Still could focus a man's attention could Maud.

"You will see the destruction for yourselves," she said.

"You realize we are impartial observers," Mr. Jenson answered. "There must be not a repeat of the unfortunate demonstrations that happened when Edward Dunne and his group came to Ireland."

"Not so unfortunate," Maud said. "The Irish people welcomed their support." She'd turned to me and said, "Nora can you spare me the afternoon, then dinner?"

Jenson was not pleased but Maud promised she'd host a dinner for all of them on their return.

"But Nora and I need time for a good visit," she said, and led me out of the hotel.

Now she points at a cluster of buildings.

"That's University College Dublin where Joyce and Frank Skeffington studied. Frank was shot dead by that criminal Bowen-Colthurst. Seán is supposed to be there now," Maud says. "But the university's mostly empty. Our young men in prison or on the run."

"Come," she says, and leads me down some steps into an oddly shaped church and then up to a bank of vigil lights. She puts a penny into the slot of the metal box attached to an ornate stand holding lines of small candles. Maud reaches under, brings out two candles, and shoves them onto the empty spikes. Practiced in this, I think. She lights one candle and hands me the taper. I light the other.

I'm back in St. Bridget's with Granny Honora. We would light candles together—one for each of her children and their families. Me, only small, would say, "Let's light one for every single one in the family." Thinking of the blaze forty-plus candles would make. But she'd say, "No, God sees the lights and knows the prayers in our hearts."

As the flame catches, I stare at the golden tabernacle. The prayer that comes to me is "Please." Please let Peter Keeley be safe. Please protect all these Irish people. Let us do a good job. And I light three more candles.

Maud smiles at me. "So many to pray for," Maud says. "Living and dead. I always think of Kevin Barry as I stand, where he heard Mass. A student at the university, Nora. Only eighteen. He was captured in a battle against an army patrol. Tortured. Then hanged. No real trial. A military court that didn't even pretend to follow legal procedure. Thousands in front of Mountjoy Prison praying for him as he died. 'Just a lad of eighteen summers,' a song about him now. A hero. So inspiring."

Better if he were still kneeling here, I think, alive and studying. But Maud clasps my hand. "It's martyrs like him that will save us. More than fifty students joined the armed struggle after Kevin Barry's death." She makes a very dramatic sign of the cross.

Why are converts always so much more religious than Catholics themselves?

"Cardinal Newman himself was the founding rector of this college, you know, and Hopkins was here. Gerard Manley Hopkins, the poet. He hated Dublin, couldn't bear the weather," Maud says as we leave the church.

I feel a certain kinship with Hopkins as we make our way across the rainy square but then we enter her town house. Something of rue de l'Annonciation here.

We drink sherry from Waterford glasses in Maud's drawing room. A wood fire burns in her marble hearth. The velvet drapes I remember from Paris keep out drafts and muffle the noise of rain hitting the windows. We eat thick pieces of brown bread with plenty of butter.

Maud tells me she's been touring the country with Charlotte Despard, an English woman and suffragist, who's living with her. When Mrs. Despard joins us, she does seem very English in her tweed skirt and jacket, though right away she tells me that her father was born in Roscommon. "Frenchpark," she says. "My spiritual home. Spent happy days there as a child." Another one. She asks where am I from.

"Chicago," I say, "though Galway originally," adding that now that I'm on my home ground.

Mrs. Despard's incensed about the prisons she and Maud visited.

"Horrible conditions. Twenty-five men in one hut in the camp in the Curragh. No heat. They ship men off to English prisons to disguise the torture."

"Or shove them into a lunatic asylum," Maud says. "I've been trying to help Patrick Hart's mother. He broke down completely in the Broadmoor asylum. So did that poor Barnett. They told him he'd betrayed a friend. A lie. But he went completely mad."

She sighs. "Who wouldn't be driven crazy sitting in a cell watching your friends led out to be hanged on the word of some drunken shell-shocked soldier."

"Terrible," Mrs. Despard says. "Now, Nora, you must realize the British are a decent people but they're blinded by, well I have to say it, hatred of the Irish and a romantic notion about the British forces. Even my brother, John—"

"Sir John French," Maud interrupts, "head of the army during the first two years of the war. Made a mess of it. And then came to Ireland."

"None of the generals were much good," Charlotte says. "Blood on all their hands. And no lessons learned. Johnny thinks all Sinn Féiners are murderers—put Ireland under martial law. Even wanted to drop bombs on the countryside. Convinced ordinary Irish people don't want independence. It's that awful Wilson. Always whispering into Johnny's ear. More troops. Grind the rebels into the dust. Bomb them. Strafe them. Violence begetting violence. The British forces gone berserk. Johnny told them no man would be punished for shooting a rebel. License to kill."

Maud gets up, pokes at the fire, refills my sherry glass. I feel as if we're back in Paris during the war, which, it seems, will never end.

"Well, at least our committee can publicize the situation," I say. "The American people are ready to help. There are groups in every state raising money. Millions of dollars already collected and President Harding's honorary chairman."

"Your president should speak to the prime minister. You Americans don't realize how afraid the British are of losing your favor. The Sassenach hide their need so well, your lot doesn't even know your own power," Maud says. Declaiming.

"Do you have to shout, Maman? I heard you all the way upstairs." Iseult. That same flower face, long wavy hair but changed, changed utterly. Pregnant. A solid swelling visible under her dressing gown.

"*Bonsoir*, Nora," she says to me. I walk over and hug her. She smells of cigarettes.

"Good to see you," I say. "And, well, congratulations."

She nods and puts her hand on her stomach. "Thank you—I'm Mrs.

Harry Francis Stuart now. But Francis, my husband, is off with Seán and the rest. Poor baby. A hard world to be born into," she says.

"Not for long, Isuelt. We will defeat them and your child will grow up in a free Ireland!" Maud says.

Well, with one thing and another it's quite late before I think of starting back to the hotel. We'd eaten a meal *à la Normandie*, prepared by Josephine Pillon, who followed the family to Dublin. Barry joined us too, of course, along with a representative number of animals: the dog Dagda, a few birds, and a monkey. The house on St. Stephen's Green's very much Maud's space I think as we talked about Father Kevin.

Maud told stories of her first trip to Donegal, how Father Kevin had been her guide and with her when she handed over a diamond necklace given by one of her admirers to a tenant to pay his rent.

"After we left, some gombeen man offered to buy the necklace from the farmer for the exact amount of overdue rent. Poor man turned it over. The true value would have paid his rent for life."

"Oh, Maud," I finally say. "It's nearly ten. I'd better go."

"You'll have to stay here, Nora," Maud says.

"Thank you, but I need to get back," I say. "The committee will be looking for me. We're making an early start for Galway."

Galway. Even saying the word brings back Granny Honora. I can hear my uncle Mike singing to her. " 'Tried and true I'll fly to you, my own dear Galway Bay.' "

Barry speaks up. "But Nora, you can't. The curfew."

"No one's allowed on the street after nine p.m. The army patrols arrest anyone out," Maud says.

"But surely not me. An American? Part of an official delegation and . . ."

Charlotte Despard, Barry, and Maud all talk at the same time and then stop.

"Listen, Nora," Maud says, "you must not give the British any excuse to arrest you. You're a target. I am, too. I was jailed. My son hunted. Your being an American and an official will not protect you. And they know, Nora. Don't think they don't," Maud says.

"Know what?"

"Oh, Nora," Barry says. "About your connection with Peter Keeley."

"Peter. You have news? Why didn't you tell me? Where is he?" I say to Maud.

"I don't know," she says.

"Is he alive?" The question I don't want to put into words.

"He was six months ago. The Tans raided his home place near Carna. Burned it to the ground but they didn't find him. His brother's family were turned out," Maud says.

"Famine times are coming again," Barry says. "More than a hundred thousand people burned out of their homes."

"So where's Peter?" I say.

"He could be hiding in the mountains or have gotten himself on a ship and away. Connemara people don't talk," Maud says. "A hard core inside of them, like their mountains."

Barry looks at me.

"Those mountains were taller than the Alps once. Worn down until only the core is left. So ancient. Like the people." Barry half closes her eyes.

Oh God, she's going to recite one of her poems. I'll never get any information.

"Cyril will know the right people to ask in Connemara," Maud says, "But be careful."

"*Ná habair tada,*" Barry says.

"*Ná habair tada,*" I repeat. "'Whatever you say, say nothing.'"

The women nod.

A nation of conspirators and now I'm one. Can't find out the most basic facts. Not even whether Peter's alive or dead.

Barry finds a bed for me in an attic room and gives me one of her flannel nightgowns. Thank God. Freezing in this little room. I turn back the quilt and feel the sheet. Cold. Maud comes in carrying a hot water bottle.

"Here, this will help," she says.

She puts it between the sheets.

Maud wears a heavy silk kimono, Oriental-looking with flowers and dragons on it. Her hair's loose. A black shawl around her. She hands a blanket to me.

"Get into bed. Put this around you."

I do as she says and there is a promise of heat under the covers.

"How do you think Iseult looks?" Maud says.

"Aside from the obvious?" I say. "She must be due soon."

"In a month," Maud says. "She's much too thin. Her face is all pinched."

I nod. "A hard pregnancy?"

"A brutal husband. He actually tortures her, deprives her of food. He burned her dresses as a punishment. And he's a just a young fellow, not even twenty, but spoiled by an indulgent mother. They're Northern Presbyterians. He became a Catholic to marry Iseult and calls himself a republican. But in his heart he's a cruel English boarding-school boy. He struck her while they were here. He's a lunatic. You know in those schools the older boys torture the younger ones, who turn around and torture the next younger. A horrible survival-of-the-fittest culture. I knew enough of them, let me tell you. Yet Iseult says she loves him. He refuses to support her. She won't insist on a settlement. It's the curse of the Gonnes."

"Yes, I remember," I say. "Your family took land belonging to the Catholic Church and the priest said no Gonne woman would ever be happy in her marriage," I say.

"It's true," Maud says. "Miserable, all of us. Even my sister Kathleen. But Iseult. Breaks my heart."

A curse, I think, or a girl raised to pretend her own mother was her cousin. Maud left Iseult in boarding schools and with maids and governesses and was ready to marry her to a man thirty years older than she was. Poor Iseult.

"I suppose Stuart apologizes after every incident, sends flowers, blames the drink. Promises never ever to hurt her again?" I say.

"Exactly! How did you know?"

"I know, Maud and so do you," I say. "Shall I talk to Iseult tomorrow?"

"Please. She doesn't listen to me. He's turning her against me. And we were always so close. She's only here now because of the baby."

I ease further down into the bed, actually warm now, and take the hot water bottle between my feet.

"You must be tired, Nora," Maud says.

"I am and I've got to be up early and get back to the hotel," I say.

"But you'll talk to Iseult. You won't forget."

"I won't," I say.

Maud hands me a bundle. "I like your bob and your short skirt, but I think a tweed suit might be better for travel."

What can I say?

"These are Charlotte's," Maud tells me. So I'll be touring Ireland dressed as a ride-to-the-hounds Protestant.

Morning already? I wonder when I hear the pounding and shouts but the small round window in the attic room frames only darkness.

"Get up, Nora! Get up!" Maud's shouting from the hallway. Fire? I throw the covers back, wrap the blanket around me, gather Barry's nightgown, and run for the stairs. I get down the first flight. Iseult's ahead of me. We both reach the landing above the first floor at the same time.

"The Tans," Iseult says. "A raid."

A squad of a dozen or so men are standing around Maud in the hall below us.

"Army," Iseult says. "Not the Black and Tans. Thank God."

She reaches into the pocket of her dressing gown and pulls out a pack of Gauloises Bleues cigarettes and matches. A steady hand as she lights her cigarette.

"Can I have one?" I ask. I rarely smoke but I'm shaking. She takes a Gauloises and puts the tip to hers and hands it to me. Maud's talking to an officer below us but looks up when she smells the smoke. "Go back to bed, Iseult," she says.

"Sorry, ma'am," the officer says. "All occupants must go to the parlor while we search."

"Search for what?" Maud says.

And his tone changes. "Don't play the fool with me. Get into the parlor now." He looks up at us. "Come along, you two."

A captain I'd say. Twenty-five at the most. Did he fight at the Front? Doubt it. Takes himself too seriously for someone who's been in combat.

Iseult puffs on the cigarette, inhales, blows the smoke out, and descends the stairs holding on to the railing. She slumps a bit at the last step and I grab for her arm, but she waves her hand at me and recovers. Stands for a moment breathing heavily. Maud comes across to her.

"If she goes into labor, it's on your head!" she says to the officer.

Josephine lights the fire and Barry, Maud, Charlotte Despard, and I draw our chairs close to it. But Iseult sits apart, smoking cigarette after cigarette, making the parlor smell like a Paris café. I throw my half-finished cigarette into the fire.

"Thank God Seán dined with friends tonight and stayed with them.

These soldiers will arrest any young man of military age and they hate university students," Maud says.

I hear a crash. Josephine stands up and starts for the door. "It's all right, Josephine," Maud says, and then to me, "I put the good china and the silver in the bank after the last raid." She turns to Iseult. "Stop smoking. Please. I can't take it." But Iseult only smiles and lights another cigarette.

The officer and four soldiers came in. The officer's waving a pamphlet. "Seditious literature!"

Charlotte Despard walks over and takes it from his hands. "'An Appeal to the Women Workers of Ireland and England,'" she reads aloud. "And you consider this treasonous?" she says to the officer.

I see him react to her very upper-class English accent.

"I am doing my duty," he says.

"This literature is mine, sir," she says.

"And you are?"

"Charlotte Despard. You may have heard of my brother General Sir John French."

"Oh yes, ma'am, we know your connection. And Sir John would thank us for detaching you from—" He stops. "—your friends."

He takes out a small notebook.

"Nora Kelly?" he says, pointing at me.

"I am." I stand up. Such a puffy face and bits of dark hair showing under his hat.

"The British soldiers I nursed in France had better manners," I say. "They would have taken off their hats!"

One of the soldiers lets out a snort. The officer turns to him.

"Go. Continue your search."

Then he looks at me. "That was the Great War, when we knew who the enemy was. Here." And he gestures at Maud, Barry, and Josephine. "Terrorists take many forms. Some are even disguised as middle-aged American do-gooders," he says.

"Then arrest me please. Wonderful publicity. Headlines in all the American newspapers," I say.

A soldier comes to the door.

"Nobody else in the house."

"Watch yourself, Miss Kelly," the officer says. "A traitor is a traitor no matter where they come from. Tell that to the rest of your committee!"

After they leave Barry gets Iseult back to bed. I sit up with Charlotte, don't think of her as Mrs. Despard now, and Maud drinking sherry and smoking Iseult's cigarettes.

"The nerve of them!" I say. "How dare they?"

"Oh, they dare all right. Actually, that was a very civilized raid. If they were Black and Tans . . . But they'd not send the Black and Tans with you here," Maud says. "The British government wants to show the Americans how restrained they are. Only doing their duty. A sovereign government protecting itself against traitors and terrorists."

"He knew me, Maud. Knew my name."

"Of course. That's the worst of it—the sense of being watched; the heavy hand descending at any moment, the powerlessness," Maud says.

"As I said before, they hate you," Charlotte says. "Just as they hated us suffragists. I didn't understand when we began. All we were doing was asking that women be able to vote. Women—their own wives and mothers and sisters, not some alien tribe. Women. And they rode us down on horses, beat us, jailed us."

Hated her? I think. Even in her nightgown Charlotte looks exactly like the well-mannered conventional upper-class woman she was born to be. None of Maud's drama, and yet she herself had been hated and abused.

"Because we don't obey," I say. "Women and the Irish. Maud, I understand Iseult's relationship with Stuart because I was with a man who almost killed me when I revolted. Men want us under their control completely. If we do as they say, we can have lovely lives. But if not . . ."

"And England's the bullying husband of Cathleen ni Houlihan?" Maud says. "Something in that. The relationship between the two countries is so intimate."

Charlotte speaks up. "Do you know how many wives are murdered by their husbands?" she says. "Or beaten regularly? The numbers will astound you." She looks at me. "Or maybe not."

"No, I wouldn't be surprised," I say.

Charlotte sips her sherry. "I would never had known," she says. "I married Max Despard when I was twenty-six. A decent fellow from the same kind of background and family as I was."

"Charlotte's a French of Frenchpark, one of the old families of Ireland," Maud says.

"Oh? I'd say the Kellys were here when the Frenches arrived," I tell her.

Charlotte sighs. "Yes, there's that. Interlopers all of us but at least some of us have seen the light. Max did. A fierce crusader for Home Rule. Gave loads of money to Parnell."

But then, I think, Parnell was another member of their club, an Anglo-Irish Protestant. Though when he visited Chicago, Parnell talked about his American mother at every stop. "Max got richer and richer," Charlotte was saying. "Have you ever heard of the Hong Kong and Shanghai Bank?" she asks me. "He started that."

I must have smiled.

"I know, I know," she says. "Strange for a Communist like me to be proud of my capitalist husband. My dear friend Eleanor Marx often remarks on it but when Max was lost at sea, his money let me find my mission, helping the poor and oppressed."

"And do your children approve how you spent their money?" I ask.

"I have no children, Nora."

"Oh, sorry. I . . ."

"Don't apologize. I couldn't have done the work I do if I had children." She looks over at Maud. "I do admire you, Maud, for managing to have a family."

Maud takes the cigarette from her mouth, looks at it, and then grinds it out in the ashtray. "Managed? I'm not so sure. Iseult is tied up with a lunatic and Seán's been at war since he was sixteen. . . ."

"But . . ." I start.

"I know. It's a war I urged on him but sometimes I wonder . . ."

Charlotte stands up.

"No time for wondering when you get to my age." She turns to me. "I am seventy-six years old, Nora. I've come to realize regretting the past is useless. I'm going to bed."

"Amazing woman," I say to Maud after she leaves.

"She is. Kind and generous and committed. She lived a whole life with Max, traveled in the Far East. A happy marriage. A life of privilege and she put it all behind her."

"Why?"

"Why what?"

"Why does she do it? Why do you?"

"Oh, for God's sake, Nora. For Ireland of course!"

Ireland. This drawing room with its marble fireplace and ancestral portraits is very far from the Ireland Granny Honora and Mam remembered.

Maud seems to know what I'm thinking.

"Tomorrow, Nora, you will see the land of your ancestors. You'll find out what formed them and you. Don't deny us the right to love our country even if we do come from the Big Houses," she says.

She suddenly looks so old standing there in her bright kimono. The actress without her makeup. The kindly diffused amber spots gone. The harsh dawn sending cold sunlight through the windows.

My Ireland. Out there.

24

We board the train at Heuston Station in Dublin. Exciting to see that sign GALWAY over the platform.

A half hour into our journey. Cyril calls me into the corridor outside of the compartment where Jenson and the others sit, half dozing as the train pulls us further and further into the West.

"I heard about the raid," he says. "Watch yourself. My job is to make this lot look neutral, above the fray, and I'll thank you to behave."

A man's walking toward us, swinging with the movement of the train. He looks like every Irish fellow I've seen, tweed jacket and a soft cap. But Cyril stops talking and gestures for me to be quiet. The small nondescript man passes. Cyril waits until the he's through the door into the next car.

"Did you see his shoes?" he said. "Much too good for any decent man in this country."

"You think he's a British agent?"

"I think you should be careful. Don't be planning any side trips in the mountains."

"What?"

"Forget about the professor. Nothing you can do but bring him harm if he's hiding out somewhere which I'm not saying. Just keep your mind on your work. Documenting," he says, stretching out his syllables, "the atrocities, taking some photographs."

We check into a very Anglo-Irish-looking hotel called the Great Southern next to the train station, facing the square. We could be in any city, I think. Especially with fog hanging low over Galway. Hard to tell if there even is a bay, let alone what it looks like.

We eat roast beef and Yorkshire pudding for dinner.

"West Brit food," Cyril whispers to me.

Still foggy the next morning when Cyril takes us on his own tour of Galway City.

Galway wasn't shelled as Dublin was but plenty of shops along the main street were burnt out. Half standing, the roofs collapsed, windows broken.

We follow Cyril and a local priest, Father O'Flaherty, past the shops down into an open area packed with women dressed in long skirts with shawls around them, barefoot most of them. I hear them shouting. "Cockles and mussels. Alive, alive O."

"The fish market," Cyril says.

"Is this the Spanish Arch?" I ask.

"It is," he says.

"I think my own grandmother sold fish here," I say. A memory from somewhere stirring.

He looks at me. "Tough women these. I'd say you might have had an ancestor like them." We get into a very big black touring car and head west to a little town called Bearna, which the Tans had raided. I aim my Seneca at the burned thatched roofs, the white walls of the cottages striped black by the flames.

Cyril sets up a kind of parley with Bearna's parish priest, a few shopkeepers, and two fishermen in a pub. Mr. Jenson and the rest of the committee look puzzled as one of the fishermen speaks in what I recognize as Irish. The priest translates. Even the way he speaks English reminds me of Granny Honora.

Still murky outside. The pub's lit by kerosene lamps and we need a fire.

"Lorryloads of Black and Tans invade our peaceful town," Father says. "Looting, burning, driving out our young men. When our people take in their homeless neighbors, the Black and Tans come back and burn their houses down for sheltering their friends. They destroy the creameries so milk can't be processed. No income for the farmers. Their families starve. The British intend to annihilate the Irish as a people. Stop us being who we are. Trying to make us beg to be part of their empire, shameful."

I think of that General Wilson pushing Britain into a world war rather than make the least concessions to Ireland. Why can't the British allow the Irish to govern themselves? All that talk about the rights of small nations so much poppycock.

Sandwiches of brown bread and thick butter and white-meat chicken with pots of tea are brought out for us. I notice the fishermen and shopkeepers don't eat. "Please," I say, and pass half of my sandwich across to the fisherman nearest me.

"Thank you, but I won't," he says.

He looks over at the parish priest. Dear God, they're giving what little food they have to us. What to do? So I say, "Mr. Jenson, I have this money I was given to spend for dinner in Dublin and since I dined with friends perhaps . . ." Cyril catches on. "Give it over, Nora. I'll use it to stand our hosts a few rounds of sandwiches and even perhaps a drop of the *créatúr* as they say, out here."

He's off into the kitchen. I like Cyril more every day. He comes back smiling. "Nora," he says to me, "you won't believe what I saw out the kitchen window."

"What?"

"The sun. Why don't you take a dander outside while we finish listing all the crimes."

I walk out and there it is, Galway Bay. The sunlight hits the waves. Very like Lake Michigan really, except here I can see across to the other side. Wait, hills. Yes. Those are the green hills of Clare that Granny told us about.

I stand on a swath of empty ground in front of the bay. Only green grass, no houses. Strange, that, because there are cottages behind me and to the right and the left. Just none here.

Fishing boats are coming up to the pier. Small, compact little crafts with red sails.

"Púcáns," a voice says. One of the fishermen come to stand beside me.

"Púcáns," I repeat. A word I somehow know.

"My granny was born on the shores on Galway Bay," I say.

"Where would that be?"

"I don't know," I say.

"How can you not?" he asks.

Cyril, Mr. Jenson, and the other men come walking out of the pub.

Cyril says, "Decent weather for our trip to Connemara. A bleak enough place in the best of times, but desperate in the rain."

The five men climb into the back of the big touring car. Cyril driving. Me next to him and a new guide sitting in the front seat with us.

"Meet John O'Connor," Cyril says.

Very handsome, tall, early thirties I'd say. Dark hair, blue eyes. He could be one of my own uncles. The fellows in Galway are bigger than the Irishmen I've seen in Dublin. He doesn't listen to Cyril, who talks away, but looks out the window. Then turns around, watching the road behind us.

"I don't think the Black and Tans will be out yet," Cyril says to him. "Sleeping off their hangovers. Drunk half the time. What do you expect? Only convicts after all. In jail for snatching some little old lady's purse and all of a sudden they are soldiers. Given guns and the chance to do real damage."

"Well enough to keep an eye," John O'Connor says.

"The old Bog Road," he tells us as we turn straight into a circle of mountains. "The Twelve Bens," he says.

Peter's mountains, I think.

Glorious now against the blue sky, points of green amid the brown land splashed with white sheep and the yellow bushes.

"What is that bush?" I ask.

"Furze," Cyril says.

"Whin," John O'Connor says.

"Beautiful," I say.

"Too bad we can't eat scenery," John O'Connor says.

Cyril snorts but John smiles. Not immune to this startling landscape, I think.

"Turn up this lane," John says. "Something I want you to see."

Cyril's not pleased. "We don't have time. I don't want to drive these roads in the dark."

"It's important, Cyril," John says.

"A detour, gentlemen," Cyril says to the committee.

Cyril pulls up to another cottage that's black and charred, the roof falling in and the walls nothing but a few stacked stones. Abandoned, no one near. A great view though, the sea below and not far away a lake.

"Lovely and destroyed. All right, let's go," Cyril says.

"We should get out. This is Pádraic Pearse's cottage," John O'Connor says.

"Oh," Cyril says.

Peter was here when the young Dublin schoolmaster built this retreat, I think. "I watched Pearse fall in love with Ireland," Peter told me.

The committee members are out of the car. Walking up to the cottage.

"Made a party of destroying it, the Tans did," John O'Connor says. "Drinking porter and singing and cursing us all. The local farmers saw it, could do nothing to stop them."

"Poor Pearse," Cyril says.

A few of the committee nod.

"Now gentlemen," Mr. Jenson says. "You know that we can't be in any way political. This is a humanitarian mission."

"Ah but Mr. Jenson," Cyril says. "A country needs its heroes."

I walk around to the front of the cottage that faces the lake. I notice bouquets of red and yellow flowers set in the doorway.

John O'Connor follows me.

"Primroses," he says. "Used to grow wild all around the cottage. This is the time they bloom, but the Tans dug up the flower beds. Can't let anything Irish grow free."

"Somebody's tried to replace them," I say. "I had a friend who used to spend time here with Pearse. Peter Keeley from Carna, would you know him?"

John O'Connor shakes his head. "I don't," he says. I hear Cyril calling for us.

The committee members are in the car.

"We're staying with John and his wife Maura tonight," Cyril says as we turn back on the road.

"Good," I say to John. "I want to stay in a cottage, not in another fancy hotel."

Dark by the time Cyril stops in front of a very big house. I wonder where the O'Connors' cottage is. But John gets out of the car and opens the back door for the committee fellows, who are half asleep.

"You live here?" I say to John O'Connor.

"I do," he says, and laughs. "My wife and I look after the lodge for the Berridges. When they're here I do gilley, take him out fishing. Maura cooks."

"And they've invited us? How nice," I say.

"In a manner of speaking," John says.

Maura O'Connor, blond and almost as tall as John, leads us into a room with a blazing turf fire, big soft chairs, and a wall of books. No ancestral portraits on the wall. Rather an array of watercolors, all of wildflowers. I walk over to look closer as the men settle down by the fire with hot whiskeys. Maura joins me.

"Mrs. Berridge paints. Loves the countryside. She's a Lesley."

Here it comes—the Family Tree. "And he was born a MacCarthy. So."

"So what?" I ask.

"Sympathetic," she says. "They'd be delighted that you were staying here. But better not to bother them. They're over at Ballinahinch."

Now that's a name I think I know.

"Is that a famous place?"

"It is. Grace O'Malley's Castle sits on an island in the lake. And the Martins were there forever. Had to sell to some company. Berridges bought it from them."

"I think my granny had some story about Ballinahinch."

Oh why hadn't I listened, I think, for the hundredth time since I've come to Ireland.

"The Berridges rarely come here," Maura goes on. "I told them the lodge would make a wonderful hotel. A place for Irish Americans like you to come when the Troubles are over and Ireland's free."

"And you think that will happen?" I ask Maura.

"I am sure of it," she says.

The parish priest from Carna, Father Michael McHugh, joins us for dinner. I'm sure he knows Peter, so I say "I studied at the Irish College" to draw him out. Cyril kicks me under the table. I'm quiet as Father McHugh tells the same story we've heard. Shops destroyed, cottages burned, and the creameries, always the creameries targeted.

"Diabolical," he says.

Mr. Jenson writes down his words. The others ask questions. Quakers, all of them, quiet men, plainspoken, but appalled at what they are hearing.

"I expect you're an early riser," Maura says to me as she shows me to my bedroom. Solid with its mahogany furniture, canopy bed. "Your window faces Lough Inagh. The sunrise will be beautiful. Great for photographs. I think you'll want to go out into it, see the lake and have a look at the mountains."

"I thought I might sleep in," I say.

Maura shakes her head. "I'll knock on your door with early tea," she says.

Oh, well.

"Any chance it could be early coffee?" I say.

Still dark outside my window when the dawn comes. I open the door to find a scone and a pot of coffee. I drink it as I dress. Yes, I should go out for the sunrise. I take the Seneca.

The sky's lightening as I walk down a small dock and look into the lake. So clear. A mirror, reflecting the brown mountain surrounded by streaks of clouds. A red sun rising behind me. Quiet. All alone for the first time in days. I frame the mountain. Start shooting. In the lens I see a man coming slowly down the mountain across the lake. Checking his sheep, I think. How do the lambs manage to climb so high? Must be chasing one, he's moving fast. I watch as he reaches the base of the mountain then gets into a boat. A curragh? Part of Granny's stories, too. He seems to be rowing right to this dock. A message? The boat's closer now. The man waves at me. I think I hear my name. A trick of the wind in the mountains.

Then again, "Nora, Nora."

Oh, dear God.

"Peter," I call back, "Peter," because it is Peter Keeley, coming to me right out of the Connemara mountains.

I grab the bow, and pull the boat in to the dock. He jumps out.

Thinner then when I saw him last and with a thick beard. He rubs his hand along his face. "I'd have shaved if I knew. John only just came up to us. I couldn't believe you were here."

"Oh, Peter" is all I can think to say.

We stand apart staring at each other.

"So you're not alone," I say.

"A good few of us up there," he says, "the remnants of the Galway Brigade. Hiding out mostly but we've picked off a few of the Tans. We have two of the rifles the Childerses sailed into Howth."

So matter-of-fact, my gentle Peter. But after what I've seen, I understand his fierceness.

"And are you well?" he asks me.

"Me? I'm fine." This small talk is ridiculous. "I've missed you, Peter," I say. He nods.

Now I, of course, want to throw myself into his arms but have even seven years of world war, revolutions, millions dead, and a world turned upside down loosened the inner bonds that hold Peter Keeley?

Finally I say, "For God's sake, Peter, I'm your wife more or less. Are we going to stand out here chatting until a load of Black and Tans arrive?"

I take his hand, rough now and hard. Not the scholar's hand that touched me so gently in my room over the place des Vosges. I turn him toward the house.

"Late sleepers, my American colleagues," I say. "A very good chance no one is stirring and my room's near the door."

Peter shakes his head.

"Too dangerous. Informers everywhere, Nora. There's a hunger for money in this country now and the British pay big rewards for information. Someone passing by might see me go in. Even one of your own crowd."

"We'll find some place right now, Peter Keeley, or I'll turn you in myself. I haven't waited for seven years only to shake your hand and wish you well," I say.

"There's a hut a bit up that mountain behind us," he says, pointing down the road. "A shepherd's shelter," he says.

I pull his hand up the narrow sheep trail into the hut.

We have only an hour together but I find I remember every curve of that long body. He's a bit awkward at first but relaxes until the two of us move together easily with no effort at all. How I've missed him. Longed for this connection, the ease, the flood of feelings. The seven years go away, so does the hut, the mountain even. We are in the place I've imagined so often, far away from war and Black and Tans and burned-out villages.

"Ah Nora," he says. "I've been so unfair to you. Even this . . ."

"What do you mean?"

"I'm stuck here, Nora, until I get arrested or worse. No future at all for us."

"What sure future for anybody, Peter? None at all for the boys slaughtered at the Somme or Belleau Wood. You're alive. We're together. More than I ever expected."

"You must go back to America. Tell them what you've seen. Help the Cause from there. Be safe."

"I can't go home now. I owe something to Ireland. I'd be betraying Granny and Mam—all the Kellys and Keeleys—if I left. I'll finish my job with the committee then I'll come back to you," I say. "I'll photograph every wrecked cottage and creamery in the country and publish them in so many American newspapers the British government will be too ashamed to stay in Ireland."

Peter smiles.

"Hard to shame the Sassenach. They won't go easily and if they do, they'll leave bitter dissension, I'm afraid."

"Oh, Peter, why do you always expect the worst?"

"You are such an American, Nora," he says.

He lets me take his photograph and then I stand in the shed and watch Peter Keeley down to the shore into his curragh and away. I'll return in a month, I think. Set up an office of the relief committee here. Work with the Irish White Cross. Use the lodge as my base. I'm an American. What can the English do to me? I'll be representing an organization with clout. Didn't the president himself endorse us? What had Maud said? We Americans didn't know our own power.

But Maura O'Connor shakes her head.

"Come back and stay here? But, Nora, the Berridges may return. You can't stay here."

"Then there's surely a hotel somewhere nearby," I say.

"There surely isn't," she says.

The rest are ready to leave. John's loading the suitcases.

"Come on, Nora," Cyril says. "We've dozens of places waiting for us."

"I'm not leaving," I say. "Unless I'm sure I can come back. This is where my people are from. This . . ."

"You won't be returning as a representative of the Committee for Relief in Ireland, you must be appointed. The board would never approve," Mr. Jenson says.

I should have kept my plans to myself, I think. Will I never learn to keep my mouth shut? *Ná habair tada.*

"All right," I say. "Forget it. Let's go."

"About time," Cyril says. "Already getting a late start. The Tans could be out now."

"No 'could' about it," John O'Connor says. "There's a lorry full of them turning in the drive now."

"Oh, shite," Cyril says. "John, we best leave by the back door. You talk to them, Mr. Jenson. And you, Nora Kelly, keep your trap shut."

This is a very different group from the army officers who raided Maud's Dublin home. These are thugs. Pure and simple. Splintering the old oak door with their rifle butts before Maura can open it. And the uniforms, if you can call them that, dirty khaki pants, old police jackets such a dark blue as to be black. The Black and Tans in the flesh. They all need a shave and a bath from the smell of them. Not young.

We're Americans, I say to myself.

The last man through the door's better dressed than the others. Pressed pants at least. But he's got a pasty face and greasy hair.

"Officer," Mr. Jenson begins.

"Don't insult me. I'm a sergeant." The Black and Tans laugh at this. "But I am in charge."

Mr. Jenson tries again. "Now, you probably don't know who we are."

"Oh, I know who you are. Yank busybodies."

"But you may not be aware that we are all members of the Society of Friends," he says. "We do not believe in violence."

"Well bully for you," the sergeant says.

One of the Tans who is standing under the ornate mirror in the hallway takes his rifle barrel and whips it across the glass. Pieces fly all over, covering the floor.

"That belongs to the Berridges. He's a naval officer," Maura says.

"Ever so sorry, love," the fellow says.

Another Tan takes Maura by the shoulder, throws her down on the floor. "Better start cleaning that up."

"Stop that. What's wrong with you?" I say to the sergeant. "Letting these men act like barbarians?"

"Barbarians?" he says. "And this from an American."

He laughs, doubles over.

"A good one, that." He slaps me on the back, hard.

"Now, just one moment, sir," Mr. Jenson starts.

"Not 'sir' I told you. A sergeant, doing my job."

Two soldiers pick up a carved wooden table in the hall and start carrying it outside.

"Hurry up, boys. We don't have all day," the sergeant says. The men grab chairs and lamps and throw them onto the lawn. Through the open door we see the Tans throw gasoline on the pile.

Maura stands up.

"Dear God, those are valuable antiques," she says to Mr. Jenson.

The sergeant laughs at her. "Should a have thought of that before you entertained traitors, you Fenian bitch."

One of the Tans sets the furniture on fire. "Stop!" Maura says. The sergeant raises his hand to strike her.

I pull Maura to me. "Leave her alone."

"All right," he says, then makes a fist. A quick jab to my mouth. Blood.

"You can't do that," Mr. Jenson says.

"I can," the sergeant says, and he pushes the elderly man away. The rest of the committee has watched in silence, but now Mr. Smith, the youngest of them, steps forward.

"You must make your men behave," he says.

One of the Tans hits him in the stomach. He doubles over.

"This is crazy," I say.

The sergeant punches me in the face again. Blood runs from my nose and lips. My head rings.

Mr. Jenson takes a breath. "We are Quakers, peaceful people, pacifists. However, I warn you, what you do here today will be reported. You will be punished."

"We won't," the sergeant says. "Private Avery, what are our orders?"

The private starts to recite. "'No man will be reprimanded for shooting a traitor.'"

Those words. Charlotte had quoted them to me. Her own brother's. The general himself. No wonder these blackguards think they can get away with anything.

"None of you are innocent," the sergeant says. "Why are you interfering in the internal affairs of a sovereign country?"

He's quoting, I think.

"How'd you like it if another country tried to stop you handling your red Indians. Savages must be put down. A Paddy's a savage. Full stop. What did that Paddy general of yours say? No good Indian but a dead Indian? Sheridan, wasn't it? Didn't you erect statues to him? So don't tell me how to fight my war," the sergeant says.

"No killing is justified," Mr. Jenson says. "Our country has sinned but we have learned and are still learning."

I take my hand away from my bloody mouth and touch my nose. "You were glad enough for us Yanks to come and keep the Germans from beating you. No complaints about interference then."

The sergeant ignores me.

"We want a list of everyone you've met with," he says. "Tell me and you can be all on your way."

"That information is confidential," Mr. Jenson says.

"Fine, we'll just interrogate the bitch," he says. "Since you're such a gentleman, you won't let a lady suffer."

"Tell them nothing," I say. They wouldn't dare really hurt me.

"Let's see," the sergeant says. "You, Bristol," he says to a beefy fellow, "you deserve a bit of fun but I hate to show favoritism. Let me think." The sergeant looks at me. I stare right back at him. I'm too angry to be afraid. All a bluff, I think. So far all I have is a bloody nose and a split lip. Bullies. Have to stand up to them.

"I don't think these gentlemen will save you," the sergeant says to me. "Pacifist." He looks at Mr. Jenson. "Another name for coward."

"What about me, Sergeant. I got no part of that last hussy," a young fellow says.

"You didn't, did you?"

"Don't waste her on him, Sergeant. He's still a virgin," a third man says. "I carried all that heavy furniture and lit the fire. I deserve a little fun."

"I must object," Mr. Jenson says again.

"Shut your hole," the sergeant says, and hits him with the back of his hand. Mr. Jenson staggers.

The sergeant turns to the other Quakers.

"You've heard this Yankee bitch refuse to answer our questions. My men will administer the proper punishment. Don't waste time. Double quick march."

The beefy one grabs my arm. I scream and pull away.

"You can't," I say.

"Oh, but we can," the sergeant says.

"Don't. Please don't. I was a nurse in the war. I tended your wounded."

The youngest Tan reaches over and grabs my breast. "I've a wound you can heal," he says. He takes my wrist, twists it, and shoves it behind my back.

Maura tries to get my other hand, pull me away. The Tan closest kicks her from behind. She staggers. Now Mr. Jenson, Mr. Smith and the three other committee members all move toward the sergeant, shouting at him, "Stop! This is insane. You mustn't."

"Oh, they won't kill the bitch," he says. "She might well enjoy herself."

Now I'm fighting back, punching the young soldier who twisted my wrist.

"Good," says the beefy one. "I like them to fight back. That last cow only laid there and cried."

He grabs my hair and drags me toward the hallway that leads to the kitchen.

Please, God. Please, Blessed Mother, help me. Please. Peter, where are you?

The explosion's loud and so close the hall floor shakes. "What the hell?" says the sergeant. The beefy one lets go of my arm. I manage to scratch his face. A Tan comes running in.

"The lorry. They've blown up the lorry."

All the Black and Tans rush to the front door.

"Our fellows. An ambush," Maura says. "We'll get out through the kitchen."

"What about the others?" I say.

"Let them look after themselves," she says.

We go.

We're in the backyard when I see Cyril just ahead of us, waving his hand.

"Come on, come on."

We run up the steep hillside behind the lodge and down into a little valley where a stream runs over rocks. Maura steps into the water and I follow. Icy cold. The pebbles in the bottom are slippery, hard to walk on, but I'm moving faster than I ever have before, my tweed skirt dragging around me.

"Go, go," Cyril says.

We run along the stream until we come to a small stone bridge above us.

"Can you climb up there?" Cyril asks. I claw my way up the bank then reach back for Maura, who takes my hand and climbs up beside me. Cyril comes behind her. We cross the bridge and start up the mountain away from the lake.

"Peter Keeley," I say. "Peter's back there."

"No questions," Cyril says. "Keep going."

The next thing we're running through the gardens of a castle—I mean the real fairy-tale version.

"Maura, won't the people who live here turn us in?" I say to her.

"They won't," she says.

And isn't it a nun who answers the door?

"Welcome to Kylemore Abbey," she says.

Geeze Louise. We're taken to the dining room for hot soup and brown bread.

"We're Benedictines," the nun says. "Hospitality is our rule."

I find out that the community was bombed out of their convent in Ypres, Belgium, where they'd gone when religious orders were driven out of Ireland by Cromwell. Back now. They bought the castle last year when the English Duke who'd owned it gambled away all his American wife's money. A girls' school now.

So it's as two nuns accompanied by a small priest that we leave the abbey, carrying our clothes in a bundle. We change in the church at Carna. A boatman meets us at a nearby pier at dawn the next morning.

25

Cyril, Maura, and I sail back in a púcán manned by Martin O'Malley, a Recess fisherman, brother to the Michael O'Malley who landed in Normandy with us.

"A lucky wind," Martin O'Malley says as the red sail fills and the little boat skims along the surface of the bay. Granny Honora's own dear Galway Bay and me on top of it. I won't let the likes of the Black and Tans stain this beautiful land, I think, as we pass fields green with the start of spring. Somewhere on this shore, my granny Honora lived, met and married my grandfather Michael Kelly. Here my own father, Patrick, was born. Endured the Great Starvation as a boy and escaped. Somewhere here is that very piece of earth. Somewhere.

I put my hand down into the spray, rainbows in the water.

I spend an hour that afternoon soaking in a hot bath. Benefits of a fancy hotel. Finally my muscles relax. Bruises on my skin from the Black and Tans but they will fade. Dear God, what if they had raped me? Their intention surely. How could I cleanse myself of that? And yet, how many women have suffered such treatment? As I lie in the warm water, I remember my aunt Máire's ordeal. Forced to have sex with the landlord's son. Kept like a slave in the Big House bearing his children. No recourse.

"Anyone who raised a hand against the master would be evicted or worse. One more weapon they used to keep us in our place," she'd said to me. No wonder the Black and Tans assault Irish women so freely.

Well, we're avenging you, Aunt Máire.

I lather my hair, duck under the water to rinse the suds. Towel-dry my bob. A bath helped wash Tim McShane away, too, I think.

Mr. Smith drove the committee members back to Galway in the touring and brought my luggage. So I decide to forget the tweeds and wear the Madame Simone cinema-inspired dress that Maud thought was too advanced for Ireland. My version of Aunt Máire's red silk shawl.

I look into the mirror. My hair shines. A bit of rouge on my cheeks. The green crepe hits me just below the knees, a wide satin ribbon circles the drop waist. That's me. Nora Kelly, a modern woman, American citizen, resident of Paris, professional photographer. Back in the land of my ancestors. Proud of my Irish blood. Unafraid.

An army officer is sitting in the library waiting with the committee when I come down. "This is Captain Pyke," Mr. Jenson says. "He has come to talk to us about the incident."

Pyke. That name. Is this man some relation to the landlord who raped Aunt Máire? Dressed in a regular army uniform, so not a Black and Tan. Elegant, legs crossed, polished boots, a riding crop in one hand. The cliché British officer. He does have the look of my cousin Thomas, the same receding chin, concave chest. Aunt Máire's other children, my cousins Daniel and Grace, look like their mother. "Thomas was always the odd one," I'd heard Granny Honora tell my mother. Was this man his half brother? No. Too young. Thomas's father was probably this man's grandfather, which makes him Thomas's nephew, I guess.

"Pyke? It seems I've heard that name," I say. He stands, throws his narrow chest out, and says, "You well may have. We're quite a prominent family. Ours is the big gray house on the coast, about ten miles west of here."

"The Scoundrel Pykes," Maura says as she comes in the library room in that quiet way she has. Captain Pyke laughs.

"Ah, well, I did have some high-spirited ancestors. But my generation takes our responsibilities very seriously. We're at the edge of the empire here—Britain's western shore. A firm hand's always been required to keep the natives under control and maintain some semblance of civilization out here in the wilds. Quite like the American frontier. If only we could herd the Irish onto reservations. Some talk of setting up camps. Worked in South Africa.

"I understand America's turned to segregation. Important to keep the lower orders in their place. Best for everyone. Race mixing destroys society. Though I heard that the Irish in America actually intermarry with blacks."

I stare at him. Where do I start?

"I'm speechless in the face of such ignorance," I say. "Negro troops won medals fighting in France. And as for marriage, why not?"

"Oh," he says. "You're one of those—a frustrated middle-aged woman with, well, proclivities. Mutton dressed as lamb," pointing his riding crop at me. And I feel very foolish. A would-be flapper.

He turns to Mr. Jenson. "And this is the woman you say my men abused?"

"Yes," Mr. Jenson says. "Quite shocking, really. Brutal. If it wasn't for the, well, interruption, I don't know what would have happened."

Captain Pyke walks over to him, sticks his finger in Mr. Jenson's face.

"What you say was an interruption took the life of a man serving His Majesty the king. A criminal act by murderers. Barbaric. How dare you question the measures we have to take against such scum? And as for this," he pauses, "female. Are you sure she's not exaggerating, probably hoped for . . ."

"You pig," I start, and step forward, but I feel Maura's hand on my shoulder.

"Don't restrain her," Captain Pyke says. "Let her insult me."

"You could be arrested," Maura says to me. "Acting or speaking in a menacing manner toward a soldier or policeman is against the law."

Pyke hears her. "Oh, don't spoil our fun, Mrs. O'Connor. I understand Miss Kelly here was eager to be interrogated. Weren't you? Or so Sergeant Simmons said."

"I really must protest, Captain Pyke," Mr. Jenson says. "Miss Kelly is a valuable member of our delegation and on her behalf I insist that you reprimand your sergeant and those thugs."

Now he's speaking up, I think.

"A Kelly," Captain Pyke says. "When we were told only pure Americans would be part of this delegation. No Fenian sympathizers." How much does he know, I wonder. So far he's said nothing about Peter Keeley. I smooth down the skirt of my dress. A dignified retreat, I decide, and now.

"I'm an employee of the American Committee for Relief in Ireland. I have decided rather than have our important work delayed I won't pursue any complaint against your sergeant."

Captain Pyke nods.

"Very wise," he says. "Your train is leaving at nine p.m. I suggest you all stay here in the hotel until then."

"All right, Captain," Mr. Jenson says. "Since Miss Kelly has declined to press charges."

Captain Pyke touches the brim of his cap, smiles, and leaves.

Dangerous if he discovers my connection to Peter Keeley. Better to drop it. Move on.

"You did the right thing, Nora," Maura says. "They're bastards but they have all the power. Better to keep your head down and get them from behind."

We are walking along the shore of Galway Bay. Maura's found me a heavy shawl to wrap around my flapper dress, and a pair of rubber boots. I refused to sit in that library for four hours waiting for the train. I want to move fast, stomp my feet. We reach a stretch of beach. "The Silver Strand," Maura says. She leads me along a path from the beach and under an archway of tangled vines into a small clearing carpeted by tiny white flowers.

"Snowdrops," she says. "St. Bridget's flowers. Her feast is February first. In the old Irish calendar it's Imbolc, the first day of spring."

"Spring? February's often the coldest month in Chicago. The streets turn white and there's ice floes in Lake Michigan," I say. "Here I can smell the new growth."

"And primroses," Maura says, pointing to colored flowers. They should be growing at Pearse's cottage, I think.

A stone ruin in the center of the clearing, a miniature tower about two feet tall, open at the top.

"St. Enda's well," Maura says. I walk over, look down into the water. A bit of sun comes through the trees that rim the clearing and bounces on the water. I lean over and see parts of my own face reflected on the surface.

"Very ancient, this place," Maura says. "Dedicated to St. Enda, a monk and teacher. But the well's older than Christianity. A holy place of the old

Celtic religion. The druids believed you could enter the otherworld through a well, a lake, or a sudden insight," she says.

She sits on the side of the well, pats the space next to her. I sit down.

"You see, Nora, in Celtic spirituality the material world's only one part of reality. We're surrounded by the world of the spirit. Powerful. Eternal. In some stories the other world is called Tír na nÓg, the Land of the Young, an island off our coast. But I believe this other world is really inside us. And so can be accessed through our own imagination. Am I making any sense to you at all?"

I pull the shawl around me and nod.

"The Scoundrel Pykes are empty inside, Nora, for all they seem invincible. Pyke's grandmother died screaming for drugs. His father was shot by a tenant. And this one, Captain Pyke, has neither chick nor child. Barricades himself in that stone prison of a house knowing his days are numbered. The Sassenach took our land but could never capture the deep-down life that sustains us. And that drives them mad. You saw the Black and Tans. That kind of hate comes from frustration. Why won't the croppies lie down? Why do we Irish insist on fighting back century after century, no matter what they do to us? Why won't we become the obedient serfs they want?" she says.

"We wouldn't die and that annoyed them," I say. "My granny Honora told me that."

"She had it right," Maura says, "summed up in one sentence."

"I wonder if my granny ever came to this well?" I say.

"I'm sure she performed the ritual. Walk around the well three times, dropping a stone in the water each time," Maura says.

"But Father Kevin described a ceremony like that to me. Done in Donegal he said," I tell her.

"Practiced all over Ireland," Maura says. "Are you game?"

I find three smooth pebbles, one with a streak of green through the center.

Maura says, "The first stone represents the past—worries, bad memories, remorse. Understand?"

"I do," I say.

"The second stone stands for the present. The third pebble is a wish for the future. Now follow me."

I do, thinking of Father Kevin as I walk. I squeeze into the first pebble the anger I feel at the Black and Tans and at the British and all who make war on women and children. I also jam in my own regrets and guilt, then drop the stone into the water. I hear it hit the bottom.

I rub the second stone between my fingers and pray for Peter Keeley's protection and the committee's success. Then let go of the pebble. I see the splash.

I hold the last green-tinged pebble a long time. I wish Ireland free, Peter and me together. Peace. I drop the third pebble. Circles form on the water's surface. "Circles and spirals," Granny used to say. "Life is circles and spirals."

Nearly dusk when we leave the well and start back along the shore. A woman is coming from Galway. I can see the red petticoat under her long blue skirt and the black shawl very like mine wrapped around her. A young woman, I think. She moves so easily over the stones on the shore. When she reaches us, I see her gray hair and lined face.

The woman says something in Irish to Maura.

"She's greeting us. Wishing God's blessing on you."

"Thanks," I say to the woman.

More Irish. Maura replies in the same language. The woman nods.

Maura turns to me.

"She asked me if you are a stranger, a Sassenach, English. I told her you are one of us, only from America."

More questions from the woman.

"She wants to know where you're from," Maura says. "What county?"

"Well, Cook County," I say, "Chicago."

Maura laughs and speaks to the woman, who smiles.

"She's asking which county in Ireland your people come from," Maura says.

"Here," I say, "Galway. Galway Bay."

Maura translates. More questions from the woman.

"What are the family names?"

"Keeley and Kelly," I say.

When Maura relays that, the woman lets go with a rush of the language.

"Which Kellys and Keeleys? There's many."

"My grandfather was Michael Kelly," I say.

"So was mine," Maura says. "Half the men in Galway are called Michael Kelly. That doesn't help. What was his father's name?"

"I don't know."

The older woman leans forward as if to take in my words.

"My grandmother was born Honora Keeley," I say.

"And her father?" Maura asks.

"I don't know."

The old woman lets out a kind of snort then speaks to Maura.

"She can't understand why you don't know," Maura says. More talk. "Were the Lynches their landlords?" Maura asks me.

"I'm not sure but I do remember talk of a Miss Lynch. She was Henrietta Lynch, my great-aunt Máire's godmother. My sister's named for her."

When Maura translates that, the woman pulls back a little and says something under her breath. Maura laughs. "She asked me if you were a Protestant."

"No, no. Wait, I remember now. My great-grandmother had worked for the Lynches and Miss Lynch liked her. She also taught little girls in the big house." Maura translates this and the woman nods her head. A wave of Irish words.

Maura keeps nodding and then says to me, "She thinks she has you. Your great-grandmother was Mary Walsh who married John Keeley from Carna in Connemara. Nora, we were very close to Carna at Lough Inagh."

Now the woman's speech takes on a singsong rhythm. Maura repeats the words, imitating the cadence. "He was a fisherman and lived just beyond here in the townland of Freeport in Bearna." The woman points, then takes me by the hand. She pulls me along the shore. I keep stumbling on the round pebbles that make up the beach but she holds me up, gripping the stones with her toes so we don't slip. Maura comes along behind us.

"Where are we going?" I say. "Tell her we have to get back to Galway to catch a train."

Maura translates but the woman cuts her off.

"She says there are more trains," Maura says.

After about fifteen minutes of me staggering after her, we stop. She points to a swath of grass between the shore and the road. "Here," she says in English. "Freeport." And rattles off more Irish.

"This was the fishing hamlet where your Irish grandmother was born," Maura tells me.

"But there's nothing here," I say.

"Look," the woman says.

I can see that in intervals across the empty field stones are set one on top of another.

"Old walls?" I ask.

The woman understands. Nods. Explains to Maura.

"Those stones are what's left of the cottages that were here," Maura tells me.

Maura listens to a long stretch of Irish. Then she says, "There were rows and rows of cottages on this land, clustered together. Thirty families. The fishermen fished with the men of the Claddagh. It's her grandmother who told her how the púcáns would go into the bay, red sails stretched with wind, to join the fleet from Galway and go out into the sea. They would bring home the catch to the women," Maura says. "Still do. Her son has a boat. She sells fish under the Spanish Arch. Coming home now."

"I was there," I say. "And half remember my granny talking of it. But what happened to their village?"

The woman takes my two hands in hers and speaks very slowly in Irish as Maura translates.

"Everyone was evicted and their cottages burned to the ground. All on one night during the Great Starvation." The woman touches my cheek. "She says she's sorry for your troubles," Maura tells me.

"And the Lynches did this?" I said.

But the woman shakes her head and talks to Maura.

"Not the Lynches but the Scoundrel Pykes," Maura continues. "She says the Lynches sold to the Pykes, who wanted to build a seaside resort here. Imagine, Nora, to think of building a seaside resort at a time when bodies lay in the roads, dead from the Great Starvation."

"Terrible," the woman says in English, and then goes on in Irish.

Maura listens and then says, "The Scoundrel Pykes weren't able to build the resort. No one would work for them," and now Maura's almost whispering. "And from that day to this, no one has been able to build on this land." The woman gestures around her. "She says the spirits of the people who lived here are keeping it as . . ." Maura stops. "I don't know the word in English."

"A memorial?" I say.

"Yes, but more than that. A kind of evocation of the people's presence, a way to honor those driven out. Keep these empty spaces and the ruins of these cottages sacred so their souls will return here."

The woman drops my hand, bends over, and begins scrabbling in the grass. She lifts up two stones.

"From one of the hearths," Maura says. "She wants you to take it to build your own cottage in your family's home place."

I see myself living here with Peter Keeley. The two of us standing together, looking out at Galway Bay. I take the stones. "Say you'll be returning with your husband and family," Maura tells me. I do.

The moon is rising. Some story of Granny's about the moon shining on the waters of Galway Bay, helping the family escape. Granny rarely spoke of the past, but there were those nights when she and Mam and Aunt Máire would sit together in front of our fire. Granny would fill her white clay pipe with tobacco, light it up. She'd draw in the smoke and then blow smoke rings for us children to chase. But when I got older I found all the talk about the Ireland I'd never see boring. I was as Irish as I wanted to be right in Chicago. Nora Kelly embedded in the here-and-now, St. Xavier's, Montgomery Ward's, Tim McShane. No interest in the ghosts who'd gone before me.

But they were waiting for me here, I think, my ancestors. Patient. Sure I'd find my way back somehow. I heft the two rocks in my hand. Charred by thousands and thousands of fires in the hearth and then finally by the blaze that destroyed their cottages. My people's homes.

"And they were all evicted?" I say to Maura.

"They were," she says. "A death sentence. No place to go, no work, no way to earn money. I wonder how anyone survived in those days or got to Amerikay."

"Someone went ahead," I say. "For us, it was my uncle Patrick."

Those stories I'd listen to—American tales of work and survival and success. But I hadn't been able to imagine this place. Or the cruelty of the Scoundrel Pykes. And today I both meet one of them and stand on the piece of Irish earth that belongs to me.

Overwhelming, all of it. I half close my eyes, look out over the bay, and try to picture this ruin as a busy village. The fishing boats pulling up in front of the cottages, the children laughing, all of them speaking the language that I've heard from this woman. My true mother tongue.

Somehow the Irish had held on to themselves. I'm certain now England will not win. The Black and Tans will be vanquished. Ireland will be a nation once again.

A rosy glow penetrates my slitted eyes. I open them to see the red sun slip into Galway Bay surrounded by pink and purple clouds. Glorious. The old woman points to where the sun is going down. "The Blessed Isle," she says. "Tír na nÓg."

"Amerikay," I say. "Where so many went."

"But their spirits come back," the woman says in English. "To make their heaven here."

I want to stand in the water turned red by the sun. The old woman smiles as Maura and I remove our boots, pull off our stockings. My bare foot hits a sharp little stone.

"Ow!" I lift up my foot. The old woman laughs, holds up her own foot, tough on the bottom, protected by layers of calluses. She leads us through the waves.

Cold water laps against my ankles. Scarlet bubbles surround my feet as the waves ebb, leaving the beach speckled with foam and lit by the setting sun.

The old woman says something to Maura.

"I'm not sure what she's saying." Maura asks the woman a question. They go back and forth in Irish and then Maura says, "She's using a local word I don't understand. A fishermen's term. 'Mearbhall.' There's a similar word that translates as 'astounding' but that's only part of what she means. She says that sometimes at night when the men are out fishing, a light comes up from below the sea, illuminates the fish."

The old woman is nodding as Maura speaks.

"I wonder, does she mean phosphorescence?" I say.

"Perhaps," Maura says, "but the fishermen see the light as a kind of miracle and tonight the bay glows with that *mearbhall*."

A *mearbhall*. Maura said you can enter the otherworld through a well, a lake, or a sudden insight. Now as I stand here on the strand, the waves swirling around my feet, tugging me into the bay and then receding, leaving bubbles bursting into scarlet light, some deep part of myself opens up connecting me to this place, these people, this history. I thought my family had left the pain behind. We'd survived. The undertow of the past can't pull us down. We'd escaped from the Pykes and the Sergeant Simmonses of this place. But had we really? Irish Americans, Chicago Irish—we'd gained much but we'd lost a part of ourselves. What does it profit a man if he gains the whole world and suffers the loss of his soul?

My soul, I'd managed to ignore my soul during my time with Tim Mc-Shane. Not flooded with guilt until that day in Notre-Dame. But Father Kevin had absolved me, practically given me Peter in lieu of saying three Hail Marys. A decent woman again though dead to my family and to Chicago. No time to worry about my soul during the war—move, act, serve, survive. But standing here I know my soul's not under the jurisdiction of the Church or the nuns, or even my own to control. Does it belong here? Does my innermost self speak this old woman's language? In losing the words, did I lose a part of me?

Mearbhall, an idea I can't put English on. The light inside me that I can't explain even to myself.

The sun slides down below the western horizon. The red and amber sky goes dark. The moon rises. My feet and ankles are numb with cold. I step back, stamp my feet on the sand, bend down, rub my right foot, and then the old woman's there, kneading and rubbing my left one.

"It hurts," I say to Maura.

"Life coming back," she says. "Blood circulating."

My Irish blood.

26

When we return to the hotel, Mr. Jenson and the other committee members still sit in the library, leaning back in the armchairs that face the fire. Wood, not turf, and I've been in Galway long enough to know that those big logs in a country of so few trees cost big money. Maura pointed out the Barna Woods as we walked back on the high road to Galway.

"Belongs to the Lynch estate," she told me. "The tenants can't even pick up fallen branches. Landlords own the trees. 'Ireland thrice clad and thrice bare,'" she quoted. "Words from Geoffrey Keating's *History of Ireland*. We were once called 'the Isle of Woods Covered with Forests.' Each wave of invaders cut down the trees, the Vikings for their raiding ships, the Normans for their castles, and then the English for their navy vessels. 'Heart of oaks' but they were our oaks. Very few trees left in Ireland except on the estates of the rich."

So tenants can't have wood fires but the Great Southern Hotel affords them no problem.

Cyril hurries up to us. "And where have you been? The train's leaving in half an hour!"

"But you said the Donegal train doesn't go until nine o'clock and it's only eight," I say.

Mr. Jenson speaks up.

"You're not going to Donegal, Miss Kelly. You're returning to Dublin and taking the boat to France. I can't afford another incident like today's."

"So you're firing me?" I say.

"We purposely did not include Irish Americans in the survey group so our report would not be clouded by racial bias," he says.

"What? Racial bias? You saw the destruction. You were there this morning when . . ."

"After you left, Miss Kelly, Captain Pyke returned. He'd learned that you did consort with a known criminal. You used this committee for personal reasons. You put us all at risk. We must be seen to be objective for our own protection and so our recommendations will be taken seriously."

Now, I'm not about to apologize for meeting Peter Keeley. And as far as objectivity, what is there to be objective about? England's had its foot on Ireland's neck for eight hundred years. We're throwing it off. The Sassenach are fighting to retain control. A ruthless, dirty war waged on ordinary people.

"You think if we're polite to the British, they will treat the Irish people better?" I ask Mr. Jenson. "Come on, Cyril," I say. "Maud particularly wanted me to record the atrocities in Donegal. That's where she first understood the injustice of the oppression, the . . ."

"Listen to yourself, Miss Kelly," Mr. Jenson says. "That kind of emotion works against our purposes."

"All right," I say. "Then if I'm fired, I'm just going to stay here."

"Not a good idea, Nora," Cyril says. "Pyke will arrest you."

"Good, headlines in the papers and . . ."

"Hold on there, Nora," he says. "You'd be playing right into the Sassenach's hands. Discredit the whole shebang and draw attention to a friend who," he raises his voice, "wants none."

And then I think, my picture in the paper? What if someone in Chicago saw it? Nora Kelly is not dead. She's a jailbird.

"We don't have time for this argument," Mr. Jenson says. "Go back to Paris. We'll send you your fee."

I remember how happy Peter was that I'd be the one documenting the evidence. "We need photographs," he said. "The English are so good at convincing the world that they're the honest broker, not criminals."

"Don't fire me please," I say. "The photographs are important. Where will you get another photographer? And I promised Maud and John Quinn."

"You know John Quinn?" Mr. Smith says.

"I do. He recommended me."

Smith's listening to me.

"I actually know many of the members of the National Council and lots of fellows on the state committees," I say. "Why, Patrick Nash of Chicago is a close family friend."

"Nash," Mr. Smith says. "I've met Pat Nash. He contributed quite generously to underwrite the expenses of this trip."

"I know Cardinal Mundelein and even went to school with Paul Drymalski's daughter and . . ." I say.

"All right, all right," Cyril says.

He turns to Mr. Jenson. "Would you be willing to let Nora have another go at being an impartial observer who keeps her trap shut and takes photographs as she's being paid to do?"

Mr. Jenson doesn't reply.

Maura speaks up. "Nora has a feel for the place, the landscape and the people. Surely you want the photographs to touch hearts don't you? Isn't the point to raise money? Perhaps a bit of passion is needed," she says.

"Very quiet passion," I say. "I promise, I'll be absolutely understated. Please. God's given me this opportunity to use my skills for a good purpose. Don't deny me the chance."

These are Quakers after all, I think. Mr. Smith says something about Grace in earthen vessels. They huddle and I'm rehired.

So.

We make ninety-five stops in the next three weeks, travel from Gortahork in northwest Donegal to Timoleague on the extreme southern coast, and cover the Midlands. We prove what the British government has denied. That ninety percent of the damage being inflicted by British forces is on civilian property to the tune of twenty million dollars lost, a fortune. One hundred and fifty towns have been destroyed, which Mr. Jenson says would translate into five thousand in the United States.

One hundred thousand people are starving, which would equal three million Americans.

We see hundreds of burned-out creameries. The centerpiece of the Irish rural economy destroyed. A pretty emotional Mr. Jenson by the end of our tour. It's me who arranges for them to meet Maud and members of the Irish White Cross when we come back to Dublin.

Delighted with me is Maud. Thank God I don't have to tell her I was almost fired.

"I'm hopeful that the committee's findings will pressure the British government into agreeing to withdraw their troops," she tells me when we assemble at her house on our last evening in Dublin.

"Charlotte Despard's heard the king himself is disgusted with the Black and Tans," she says.

I tell Maud I bring her greetings from every crossroads in Donegal. And say that I visited Father Kevin's grave in a lovely cemetery at the foot of a cliff in Glencolmcille and discovered that Kevin's favorite saint defined Donegal.

"At every stop, we were taken to one of the holy wells dedicated to him," I tell Maud. And I give her white clay from St. Colmcille's birthplace, Gartan. Only a woman of the O'Friel clan could give out the clay, and Cyril took a half a day finding Ann O'Friel. Now Maud rolls the white balls between her fingers.

"Gives protection from fire," she says. "We need it. Another raid last week."

Maud serves us one of Josephine's dinners in her own dining room and she invites Alice Stopford Green and Mary Spring Rice, two of my money-smuggling clients. Both on the board of the White Cross.

"I'm still wearing Madame Simone's lovely creation," Alice says to me, and winks.

Maud charms the men. In the candlelight, she looks very like the young woman who became Yeats's muse. Although I'm not sure these gentlemen could quote any lines about Maud's yellow hair. Let alone her pilgrim soul.

Barry is cutting slices of Josephine's tarte tatin when Maud leans forward and says, to Mr. Jenson, "You must influence your government. Convince your president to speak to Lloyd George."

Jenson shakes his head. "Madame, I think you misunderstand our mission. We are here for humanitarian purposes. No politics."

"But you can't separate them," I say. "As long as Ireland is ruled by a government that sees its people as savages, scum—Captain Pyke's words."

"Very well said, miss." The words come from a tall, broad-shouldered man who walks into the dining room. Dark hair and very blue eyes, handsome, smiling. Dressed in a khaki uniform with a Sam Browne belt and wearing a slouch hat.

Maud rushes over to him.

"Mick. Thank you for coming. But really, should you have taken the chance?"

She goes to the window and looks out. Mick, Michael. Could it be?

"I wasn't followed, Maud," he says. "I came through your back garden. Some of our fellows are watching."

"You're Michael Collins," I say.

He takes off his hat and half bows to me.

"I am," he says.

"General Michael Collins, commandant of the Irish Republican Army," Maud says.

Mr. Jenson stands up. But Michael Collins speaks to me. "And who are you?" he says, taking my hand.

"I'm Nora Kelly, from Chicago."

"Ah, Chicago. My brother lives there, Patrick Collins. Do you know him?" He laughs. "I forgot Chicago's a big place. Not like Ireland, where everyone knows everyone."

"Chicago's not that much different," I say. "Is your brother a police captain by any chance?"

"He is."

"I've met him. A friend of my cousin's."

"Well now, isn't that a lovely coincidence? Pat had a job lined up for me in a Chicago a few years back. I was working in London. Lonesome. Almost went but the . . ." He shrugs. "And you're a member of this august committee?"

"Not really, I'm the photographer," I say.

"Ah," he says. "An artist, too."

He turns to Maud. "How splendid our Irish women are. I am grateful to all of you," he says, smiling at Alice and Mary.

Our Irish women, including me! I'm one of them, approved by the commandant himself.

"And, of course," Collins goes on, "I thank you, gentlemen, our American friends, and I mean that in both senses. I understand you are Quakers, a group that has served Ireland in so many ways over the generations. Your aid during the Great Starvation is still remembered."

"Thank you, sir," Mr. Jenson says, "but as members of the Society of Friends, we are opposed to any kind of violence. It's good of you to come here. But really, our mission cannot be seen to have any connection to your, well, army."

"Our, well, army?"

Michael Collins laughs.

"I'd say we're the least militaristic bunch you could imagine. Believe me, we'd be happy enough to lay down our arms if the British would withdraw their troops and put the Black and Tans back in the prisons they left. But we can't leave our people defenseless. We have thirty-five hundred fighters. There are fifty-seven thousand British forces here, gentlemen. They outnumber us, are better armed, but we've shown them they can't murder the innocent without retaliation."

"Violence begets violence," Mr. Smith says, "and the violent are carried away."

Collins nods. "Probably true. But then Jesus himself drove the money changers out of the temple, and I'd say King David gave as good as he got. The Brits have never faced an armed and unified Ireland. I think most of them do want out."

"I don't know, Mick," Maud says. "There's Churchill and Henry Wilson and too many in the army pledged to keeping Ireland at all cost."

"True enough," Collins says.

"Thrust into hell Satan and all those who roam the world seeking the ruin of souls," I say.

Mr. Jenson and the other Quakers look at each other completely befuddled and even the converted super-Catholic Maud Gonne MacBride has no idea of what I'm saying.

But Michael Collins laughs. "I wouldn't say my fighters are exactly the Heavenly Host but I do believe we are on the side of the angels and that we will prevail."

Cyril steps into the room. "Better go, Mick," he says. Collins turns to the committee, touches Maud's shoulder.

"*Slán a bhaile*," Collins says. "Safe Journey back to America."

"Wait," I say. "Peter Keeley. Do you know Peter Keeley?"

"I do," he says.

"Tell him . . . tell him I'll be back."

"I believe you will be," Collins says.

Maud follows him out. Mr. Jenson sits down.

"Well," he says. "Well, well."

I can't go, I think. I can't leave Ireland. I am ready to enlist in the struggle. Any army led by Michael Collins with Peter Keeley in the ranks has me. I imagine myself photographing battle scenes, carrying messages. "A Nation Once Again" and me in the center. How proud my uncle Patrick would be.

I go after Maud and Michael Collins. They're standing together in her study.

"I have to stay," I say. "Please give me something to do."

"You have a job," Maud says. "Using your photographs to tell our story."

Michael Collins looks me right in the eye.

"More important than ever for America to pressure the Brits. Old Orange Henry Wilson is telling Lloyd George to give him a hundred thousand soldiers and he'll end all this nonsense. Jesus, Maud, look what Dyer did in India last year. Massacred three hundred and seventy Indians. Opened fire on a peaceful demonstration, killed people who had no weapons. The army practically gave him a medal. Britain is very close to being governed by its soldiers, Nora. Wilson and Macready openly advocate the 'Indian solution' in Ireland. They've already imposed martial law. Wilson wants to replace what he calls 'indiscriminate reprisals' with official arrests and executions. He said he'll have the 'full approval and backing of the English people.' They want to set up prison camps over the whole of Ireland like they did in South Africa. Some British politicians see the danger. Want a truce. Negotiations. They'll want to keep the North."

"That's impossible, Mick," Maud says.

"I don't know," Mick says. He's standing by a bookcase, runs his fingers along the spines of the books, reads the authors' names aloud. "Lady Gregory, Douglas Hyde, the Irish story as told by the gentry," he says, "all very high-minded and full of ideals."

And then he turns to me. "You saw those people in Connemara and Donegal. They were living from day to day in the best of times and now they're afraid the Tans will descend at any moment."

"The people will fight on," Maud says.

"The people. You speak of the people. I don't see 'the people' much when I'm out and about. Only individual families, widows and sonless mothers, fatherless children. Why not buy ourselves some peace? The North won't stay separated. The men of Ulster, the O'Neills O'Donnells and O'Cahans, were the last free chieftains in Ireland. Their descendants can't be anything but Irish, no matter what lines are drawn on a map."

"But Mick," Maud says. "Dev and the rest, they wouldn't stand for it."

"I know that. If I put my name on a treaty, it's my own death warrant I'll be signing," he says.

"But surely, the British wouldn't dare assassinate you," I say.

"Oh, it's somebody who loves me will kill me, Nora Kelly," he says.

"No," I say. "No, the Irish revolution's not going to have a reign of terror like the French. It can't," I say.

"We'd be bucking history if we came out with a clean pair of heels," Michael Collins says.

"But we did," I say. "America."

"Seems to me you had a bit of a civil war. Worse maybe for being delayed," he says.

"But that was different," I say.

"Always different, he says. "Ah well. I might wish I'd taken that job Pat had for me in Chicago."

❧

The rest of the committee sails from Queenstown directly to New York, but I'm to take a late-night ferry to London, then the boat to Paris. Cyril takes me to the docks. Two British soldiers are checking each embarking passenger.

"Those army lads will be gone out of Ireland soon enough," Cyril says.

And glad to be gone, I think. Practically holding their noses. The older one overweight with a bristly mustache. The younger soldier hollow-cheeked, slight.

Cyril carries my suitcase and camera case. As I hold my passport out to the official at the bottom of the gangplank, the older British soldier steps in front of me.

"Come with us," he says.

"Am I under arrest?" No answer. I look around for Cyril. Not there.

A military car's waiting and the husky soldier pushes me into it.

"Leave me alone," I say. "I'm part of an official delegation. I'm an American . . ."

"Fenian scum," he says. Bad teeth and breath to match.

"Where are you taking me? I'll miss the ferry," I say.

"The least of your worries," the young soldier says.

"I was a Red Cross nurse," I say to him. "Cared for fellows like you on the Front. At least tell me where we're going."

"Kilmainham—where the leaders of the Easter Rising were held and executed," the slight one says. "Official retaliations now. Arrest. Quick military trials. Execution. Ireland's under martial law. The army can do what it wants."

But they wouldn't kill me, I think. I'm not important enough, I'm just ordinary. And then I remember those burned-out shops, the destroyed cottages. The Tans in Donegal set a cottage on fire then shot the inhabitants as they came running out. Hit a mother carrying a two-year-old child. Both dead. Killed on their own doorstep.

But these men are regular army soldiers, I think. Not Tans or the auxiliaries.

Little comfort in that, I think, as one on each side they march me down a long corridor.

Calm yourself, Nora, I think. I repeat words in my head—official delegation, an observer, impartial, an American for God's sake. The fat soldier pushes me into an office.

An officer at the desk. An older man, gray-haired. Surely he fought in France. Who do I know in the British army? All those soldiers passing through the hospital wards. Somebody we must know in common and I realize I'm acting the way I would if this were a Chicago police station and I'd been arrested for drunkenness or something, trying to come up with a relative of the desk sergeant, a friend of the lieutenant. Tell him I'm connected, special.

The gray-haired officer looks up. Hard to get so much disdain in one expression. I'm in for it, I think.

"Who are you?" he asks.

"Nora Kelly," I say, and take my passport out of my bag and put it on his desk.

He flicks his finger and it knocks the passport back toward me.

"Who are you?" he asks again.

"Nora Kelly, 2703 South Hillock, Chicago, though I've lived in Paris for almost ten years. I work for the couturier Madame Simone and take pictures."

I'm babbling I know but I can't stop myself.

"Who are you?"

"Nora Kelly," I start again.

"Nora Kelly of Chicago is dead," he says. "Drowned on the *Volterra* in 1914. Where did you get this passport? How long have you been impersonating her and why?"

"I'm not impersonating Nora Kelly. I am Nora Kelly," I say.

The door opens and who comes in only Captain Pyke. Bad to worse. Pyke salutes.

"Good evening, General Macready."

Macready? The general in charge of all the troops in Ireland?

"Is this the woman?" Macready asks him.

Pyke nods, then says to me, "I thought you were just a fool, but I seem to have underestimated you."

"You didn't. I am just a fool. I mean, I really am Nora Kelly from Chicago."

Oh dear God. Groveling and I've been in custody less than an hour. Help me, God. Joan of Arc, where are you? I take my passport, open it to the photo. "Look," I say to Macready, "that's me."

"The passport is obviously forged," he says. "So you took the identity of this Nora Kelly. Why? I insist you tell me who you are."

"I am Nora Kelly," I said. "I was born in Chicago, but my father was born here in Galway. Patrick Kelly, his parents were Honora Keeley and Michael Kelly. You must have records somewhere. Look them up. For God's sake, the Pykes were their landlords."

And now I lean forward, desperate to get Macready to believe me.

"My great-aunt has children by this man's grandfather. My cousins are his uncles and aunt!" There, I think.

Macready looks at Pyke.

"What is she talking about?" he asks.

Pyke laughs. "You're surely not asking me to explain my grandfather's bastards are you? We'll be here the rest of the night."

"Ireland," Macready says. "Sometimes I think you Irish landlords deserve what you're getting. I loathe this country and people, with a depth deeper than the sea and more violent than what I felt against the Boche."

Then to me, "You're a spy, madame. We hang spies."

"A spy? I was traveling with an official party, Quakers for God's sake. Openly taking photographs. You saw my camera. I'll show you."

My camera. All those pictures on the rolls of film. The people we met. Peter. But Cyril had been carrying my Seneca and he's long gone. Thank God.

"I suppose we can have the trial as soon as he comes," Macready says. And then to me, "We need three for a proper military court."

"Proper court? What? A trial? Don't I get a lawyer? Where's the jury?"

Pyke laughs again. "Maybe she's an American after all."

"I am."

"You are what?" A third army officer is coming in from the door behind me, walks over to the desk. Pyke straightens up, salutes.

"As you were, Captain. Hello, Macready."

Wilson. Henry Wilson's the third judge. The man who wants to shut the natives into concentration camps. The fellow who warned me off before the war. Damn.

"*Bonjour, mademoiselle,*" he says. "Or is it *madame*? Have you married some rebel? Is that why you're betraying the laws of civilized society?"

"Civilized?" I start, then stop. No smart mouth, Nora. Surely they wouldn't hang me. The British spared Constance and she'd commanded a unit in the Rising. Shot English soldiers. Probably wish now they had executed her. And what did Wilson say about marrying a rebel? Just a random insult or does he know about Peter Keeley? I have to be very calm and logical.

"Now, General Wilson," I say. "You remember the night I met you with Maud Gonne, Millevoye, and Arthur Capel?" I ask.

"I remember you disregarded some well-meant advice," he says.

"But didn't Maud introduce me as Nora Kelly? And that was before I died, or I mean the *Volterra* went down."

"I'd hardly use Madame McBride in your defense," Wilson says.

"But listen, I left Chicago because of a man and . . ."

Now Wilson laughs. That awful bray I remember from the Procope restaurant.

"Always put the blame on some fellow." This from Pyke, how he dares.

"His name was Tim McShane," I go on. "A gangster, I was afraid of him. I got away to Paris, but I heard he was coming after me so when the

Volterra went down I had someone get word to my family to pretend I'd been on it and . . ."

Couldn't tell them my own sister had engineered my death. Not to protect me but to get rid of me. Some pride left after all.

"A fairy story," Wilson says. "The natives are so imaginative. Maybe that's why they're all such bloody liars."

To the others he says, "Even if this woman, whatever her name, is American, there's a good chance she was born in Ireland and so is the subject of the Crown. Treason is a capital offense. Let's declare her guilty and get it over with."

"It's just we've never executed a woman in Ireland," Macready says.

"No time like the present," Wilson says. "Deadlier than the male. Hey, Pyke. Heard a few tales about your family. The Scoundrel Pykes, aren't they? From some place near Galway City? And that's where this woman was operating. Interesting, I wonder who she met out there. Maybe you can save yourself, madame. We're always grateful for information. There was an attack on a police barracks in Clifden last night. Give us a few possible names."

So this is how it happens, I think. How someone becomes an informer. Up to now, I've felt as if I were in a bad play, that this couldn't be real. Hadn't Father Kevin said Wilson was all bluff and bluster? But anything can happen in the middle of the night at Kilmainham jail. I have to be careful. I can't lead them to Michael Collins or Peter Keeley.

"You're losing," I say. "That's what this is all about. You outnumber Michael Collins and his men twenty or thirty to one and yet they're beating you. You're having a tantrum and taking it out on me. Well, go ahead hang me and see what happens. I *am* Nora Kelly from Bridgeport in Chicago. When my family finds out you've hanged me, they won't care if I was already dead. My brothers, my cousins, the whole Democratic Party of Cook County will come after you and . . ."

Wilson's braying again. "Don't waste time hanging her. Shoot her now as she tries to escape. A terrible accident, a frightful misunderstanding for which we'll all be very sorry indeed."

And now I *am* scared. These bastards are going to kill me. I hear a clicking sound. My teeth are chattering. I won't even get the last rites. An Act of Perfect Contrition. How does it go? "Oh my God, I'm heartily sorry . . ." But I'm not sorry for fighting these bastards. I wish . . .

There's a kind of crash. The door opens. Maud, Charlotte Despard, and Mary Spring Rice march, no other word for it, up to the desk.

"Stop this ridiculous charade, immediately," Maud says.

"No charade," Wilson says. "We've arrested a spy. We've tried her, we . . ."

"Be quiet, Wilson," Charlotte says.

"What are you women doing here? How did you get in?" Macready asks.

"I'm afraid they came with me." I hadn't noticed the man behind the women. Macready stands up.

"What are you doing here?" he asks.

"Hello, Johnny," Wilson says. "Don't think this is anything you need to be concerned with."

General Sir John French, Charlotte's brother. But he's an enemy too, as bad as the others. Worse. Old now. White-haired, pot belly. Wheezing. Tired. The Lord Lieutenant of Ireland.

"Let this woman go," French says.

"There are serious charges against her. She's impersonating a dead woman."

"She is the dead woman," Maud says. And repeats my story of Tim McShane and the *Volterra*.

"See?" I say. "Who'd make up something like that? And how would Maud know?"

"A story agreed upon between you," Pyke says.

"Who are you?" French asks him.

"Captain George Pyke," he says.

"From Galway?"

"Yes, sir."

"The Scoundrel Pykes I suppose. A captain? Who do you command?"

"A squad of auxiliaries, sir."

"Black and Tans," I say. "He's never been on a real battlefield. Didn't set foot in France. I was a nurse at the Front, General French, British troops and with the U.S. Marines and . . ." But French isn't listening. He yawns.

"You heard my brother," Charlotte says. "Release Nora this minute."

Now Mary Spring Rice speaks up. "May I remind you that my cousin is the British ambassador to the United States. I will wire him right now unless Nora leaves with us this minute."

"Now I am in charge here and . . ." Wilson says.

"Don't listen to him, Johnny," Charlotte says. "He's always manipulated you—putting you out front while he schemes behind your back. Pushing you and those other officers at the Curragh to resign. And did he? No. Let others risk themselves while he stays safe in the shadows."

"Some truth in that, Henry," French says.

"But . . ." Wilson starts.

"Best release this woman, Macready," French says. "She is an American. There'll be a fuss if she's dead. Look at the publicity de Valera got in the States. The money he raised. All those Irish over there—power, influence."

"De Valera," Macready says. "Your Cuban Jew compatriot, Wilson. But then you've Irish roots too, don't you, Johnny? A pity."

Macready sits down, opens my passport again, looks at the picture and then at me.

"Perhaps a mistake has been made. You may go," he says. Then he writes something in my passport. "But you are forbidden to return to Ireland ever." He looks at French. "I trust you don't object, General?"

"Fine, fine," French says.

"But you can't ban me from Ireland," I say.

"Come along, Nora," Maud says.

In a kind of daze as Maud, Charlotte, Mary, and I get into a waiting taxi. It's nearly dawn.

"We'll put you on the early boat," Maud says. "Best to be on your way."

"But they detained me, threatened me. I can't just leave and let them get away with it."

"Get away with it? Those three—French, Macready, Wilson—by their blind stupidity and arrogance murdered hundreds of thousands of their own British soldiers. Not held accountable. Promoted. Sent over here to murder more," Maud says.

"You have a lot of work to do, Nora. Develop those photographs and get them out," Charlotte says.

"But my camera and my film are gone," I say.

Maud only smiles.

Cyril's at the dock holding my suitcase and my camera case.

"Come on. We got you a cabin."

The official checking embarking passengers flips through my passport, then stops. Looks up. He's about to say something, but Cyril stops him.

"Don't mind that auld writing in her passport. It won't mean anything in a few months," Cyril says.

The official nods.

"Welcome aboard," he says. A Dublin accent, an Irish man.

"You'll be back one day, Nora," Cyril says. "As a special guest of the Republic of Ireland. Now, I believe you have photographs to develop."

27

PARIS
SPRING 1921

I spend the weeks after I return from Ireland in the darkroom. The sheer discipline of keeping the film in the chemical bath just so many seconds and no more distracts me from thoughts of Peter and Pyke, the Black and Tans and Wilson.

Do your job, Nora, I tell myself.

I make the first prints dramatic. Women and children stand numb, staring, next to the ruins of their homes. Shadowed. But the results seem theatrical and somehow diminish the reality. So instead I print the photographs flatly. Documents. No bias. Let the destruction speak for itself, illustrate the committee's report, stay with the facts.

Though I'd like to write a paragraph or two for some newspaper explaining how I felt when the Tans broke into Lough Inagh Lodge. Those filthy hands grabbing me, Nora Kelly, from Bridgeport, Chicago. An American citizen, for crying out loud. Nothing to them. An Irish woman so fair game. Rape me. Murder me. No consequences for them. Nothing to fear.

"Police, police!" I would've yelled if some blackguard had pulled me into an alley in Chicago. But what to do if your rapist and murderer is the police?

I wish I could describe my arrest, quote Wilson and Macready. Macready had said "I loathe this country" to Wilson. And then called de Valera "Your Cuban Jew compatriot."

Yet Maud told me Macready has Irish roots and his wife is from Cork.

A web of connections. The gentry saving Ireland from the Irish.

I get a check from John Quinn for one hundred francs. The committee's very pleased, he writes. My photographs were powerful. Ten million dollars has been raised for Ireland.

No word from Peter and the only real news about Ireland comes from what I hear after Mass on Sundays at the Irish College.

A slow grinding war, hidden from the rest of the world. Tourists keep Madame Simone and me busy. Paris has never been so full of visitors.

I keep an eye out for the rugby man or anyone like him but the British seem to have lost interest in me.

Five o'clock on an April morning I hear the soft knock at the door of my studio.

Peter, I think.

"Peter," I say as I open the door.

"Sorry, missus. Only me."

"Cyril! For God's sake, what are you doing here?"

"Not sure it's for God's sake, more my own."

I smile at him but I'm disappointed.

This is the scene I've imagined so many times. Peter's arrival, our reunion, our . . .

"Very hungry, missus," Cyril is saying. "I'd welcome a fry."

"I do have eggs. I can make you an omelette," I say.

"I prefer to see my eggs. You get out the skillet and plenty of butter and I'll do the honors," he says.

Cyril even fries slices of a baguette and talks all through his breakfast.

"Tans raided the ma's place. Been doing that. Terrorizing the slums. Come driving up a street in lorries. Tanks even. Ridiculous. We've heard there are plans to strafe Dublin. Imagine planes flying over the flats. Shooting civilians as if they were enemy troops. The Brits shine bright lights on the buildings. Frightening, the sirens, the rumpus. Soldiers go from flat to flat breaking down the doors, getting people out of bed, sending them out into the cold. Children with little enough warm to wear in the best of times shivering in the night. Claim they're looking for Fenians, for guns. But really they want to scare the people. Keep mothers from letting their sons join the fight. Of course it does the opposite. After every raid we get more recruits. Mick says we should write the Tans a thank-you letter. They're so brutal even King George wants them gone. Dev's back in Ireland. There'll be elections in May for the little hop-o'-my-thumb Parliament the Brits have given us. Too little, too late. Always the mistake they make. But when Sinn Féin carries the day and are democratically elected . . ." Cyril sends the words up and down the scale, making music of them. "Then the world will take notice. Who knows? Dev wants Mick to stop the guerrilla carry-on and go toe-to-toe with the British army, Marquis of Queensbury style. Mick only laughed and told him to talk to some of the lads who'd fought at the Somme or Wipers. Anyway . . ."

Amazing how Cyril times his chewing so as not to lose a word. I jump in. "But you're here," I say.

"I am because as I said, they raided me ma's. Thank God I wasn't there. But they took her. Put her in Mountjoy jail, would you believe. Maud found out and dragged Yeats himself down there. Gave them a song and dance about how Ma had worked for his family. That did the trick. Well, me ma almost scuttled the whole effort saying she was an Irish patriot and proud of it and go ahead and hang her. Raving to beat the band and telling the officer she had the power to curse him and his family. All Maud and Yeats could do to get her out of there. But it seemed time for me to get out of the country for a while, do a bit of business over here," Cyril says.

"Peter?" I ask him. "What about Peter?"

"Still out in the mountain somewhere causing the Tans and the police bother," Cyril says.

"Have you seen him?"

"I haven't but I would probably know if he were dead."

"Probably?"

"Nothing sure of these days, Nora. Now, you have a bit of an assignment, too."

"What?"

"We want plenty of publicity about the elections. Lots of stories in the newspapers in America. A profile of each candidate. The British are trying to portray our fellows as madmen and women. Good few women standing. We want to tell the real story. Show them as people."

"But I'm not a writer, I take pictures."

"I presume your camera can copy photographs too."

"Well, I suppose."

He takes an envelope from the inside pocket of his jacket and dumps out a whole load of snapshots. Some are wedding photographs. Some college graduation shots, others family groups.

"Let them see us as people," Cyril says. "Make it harder for the other side to murder us."

He pushes the pictures over to me.

"Do you know what Macready was heard to say?" Cyril says.

"What?" I say.

"'Let them take their seats. We'll round them up and shoot the whole bloody lot by mistake.' Harder to do if the world knows who we are," Cyril says.

So, we enlist May Quinlivan as the writer. She's back to finish her degree. A position awaits her at the convent school for girls in Donaghmore, County Tyrone.

"The new Ireland will need educated women," she says.

May and I want Cyril to let us do a special feature on the five women candidates. The three of us work in my room. May lines up the photographs of Constance Markievicz, Kathleen Clarke, Margaret Pearse, Kathleen O'Callaghan, Mary MacSwiney, and Ada English.

"No other country has so many women standing for office," May says. "Important to put them front and center."

Cyril resists. "You don't have to tell me about women fighting for the Cause," he says. "I saw a young girl ride her bicycle right through a Tan roadblock carrying a message. But this election is serious business. It's the men we have to concentrate on."

"But women in America just got the vote last year. They'll be fascinated with these stories. I bet the *Woman's Home Companion* will run the whole feature," I say.

"What's that?" Cyril asks, "A ladies' magazine?"

"Cyril," I say, "get the women on our side and they'll get the men." He sighs but agrees.

We couldn't ask for a better cast of characters. There's Constance Markievicz. What drama. A privileged young beauty falls for a foreign nobleman, marries him, the two of them become the center of a group of artists in Dublin, and then her awakening. She joins the Irish Citizen Army, founds her rebel Boy Scouts, the Fianna, and commands a fighting unit during the Rising. Then after her almost execution, she's elected to the British parliament—the first woman—and made a minister of state in the rebel govern-ment. The first woman minister in any European government.

Who could invent such a tale?

We print a photograph of the young Constance in a ball gown next to one of her in uniform.

And then Margaret Pearse. Cyril has a portrait of her, with white hair and a half smile, that seems to embody Mother Machree, this woman whose two sons were executed, who as her son said in his poem, did not grudge her two strong sons to the Cause.

Next we tell Kathleen O'Callaghan's story. Her husband was a a former mayor of Limerick, shot in the hallway of their house, right in front of her eyes.

"But let's put in that she was a businesswoman," I say to May. "Had her own shop. Still does."

Kathleen Clarke and her husband Tom were living in Brooklyn doing well for themselves. Three children born in America. She goes back to Ireland only to have both her husband and brother executed for their part in the Uprising. May tells me that when Kathleen Clarke went to the prison to try to see her husband, she was pregnant and then miscarried. "Do we dare put that in?" I wonder. But decide even the *Woman's Home Companion* won't report such an intimate detail.

We write about Mary MacSwiney, sister of Terence MacSwiney, who died on hunger strike. She's a graduate of Cambridge University, a scholar, a teacher, and now a candidate. Ada English is one of the first women psychiatrists.

What an impressive group.

May and I finish the article in a week.

Cyril reads it and nods.

"I hope they win," I say.

"Bound to. Running unopposed."

"But . . ."

Will I ever understand?

John Quinn sends the article and photographs to the *Woman's Home Companion* and after they publish it he has twenty thousand copies of our article printed and distributed in the U.S. and Britain. May and I are over the moon. Every one of the women is very pleased. All refuse to take their seats in the Westminister Parliament but meet as the Irish Parliament, the Dáil, a few weeks after the election. But the war in Ireland grinds on.

I'm surprised when the note inviting me to Gertrude Stein's Saturday salon comes to Madame Simone's.

"Probably wants someone there who remembers her from before the war," Madame Simone says.

May would enjoy looking at the paintings, I think, and we both need a break from Ireland. So I put on my green crepe dress and we go.

Hard to even see the walls, the atelier's so crowded.

Americans voices. Loud.

One fellow is standing alone in the doorway of the atelier as we arrive. Good-looking, dark hair, blue eyes, better dressed then the others.

"Hello," I say, "I'm Nora Kelly and this is May Quinlivan."

"Scott Fitzgerald," he says. He points with his glass of whiskey at the crowd. "Most of these fellows are former soldiers. Went through the war. I missed the fighting. Too damn young to have a real war. Not good for a writer to miss the big event of his times," he says.

"I thought a writer could make a good story out of anything," I say.

"Yeah? Well, I suppose that's what I've been trying to do. I can sell anything as long as it's set in New York and full of flappers and wild parties," he says. "This is the Jazz Age, lady."

"There's a war going on in Ireland right now. You could cover that," I say.

"No market for it," he says.

"But you're Irish," I say.

"Born and bred. Catholic schools all my life. Zelda and I were married in St. Patrick's Cathedral. Another world, another time."

He finishes his drink and leaves. May and I wander into the kitchen. Alice is entertaining the wives. I guess Gertrude likes the women segregated. Probably thinks they'll interfere in the serious discussions taking place among the men.

"Here comes the Irish woman Gertrude told you about," Alice says to the woman sitting at the kitchen table. She's about my age with the round face and deep-set eyes I knew from my Bridgeport neighbors, the map of Ireland on her face.

She smiles at me. "What county?"

Oh, well, here we go.

"I'm Irish American," I say. "From Chicago."

"Oh," she says. "I thought you were really Irish."

"Well, my friend May here's from Tyrone. And I've just discovered my people are from Bearna in County Galway."

"Bearna," she says, all delighted. "I know Bearna. I've an aunt married to a fellow from there."

"Was he a Keeley or a Kelly?"

"He wasn't," she says.

"Ah, well," I say. I've become so used to every Irish person I meet being somehow connected to every other that I see myself in that web, and am disappointed. She senses that.

"I suppose if we went back far enough, I'd have Kellys or Keeleys somewhere. Barnacle's my name. Nora Barnacle."

"I'm Nora, too," I say. "Well, Honora, originally."

"Me too," she said, "but it seems such an old-fashioned name. So culchie."

"Culchie?"

"Country—what the Dublin jackeens call us. But the real Ireland's in the West, as I keep reminding Jim."

"Your husband?"

"James Joyce. For God's sake, you must have heard of him. The greatest writer in the world or will be."

Alice intervenes. "Now, Nora. I wouldn't make claims like that. Lots of competitors for that title."

"Best of luck to them," Nora says. "None of them beat Jim for sheer hard work, writing away until his eyes gave out." She turns to May. "But you're really Irish?"

"I am," May says. "County Tyrone."

"May's got a job waiting for her teaching at a convent," I say.

"I was at Presentation Convent in Galway for years," Nora says.

"You were a nun?"

And Nora laughs. A wonderful burst of sound through her nose, her mouth. Her shoulders shake. I didn't believe someone could really laugh until they cry but Nora does.

She is doubled over when a fellow I guess is her husband comes into the kitchen. Tall, very thin, thick glasses, dark hair, wears a tweed suit. "Nora, let's get out of here. I can't take the shite any longer."

Then he really looks at her. "What is this?" And then to us, "Is she having some kind of a fit?"

Nora straightens up. "I'm laughing, Jim."

He doesn't like it. "She's not telling you one of her stories, is she? With me as the punch line?"

"Not about you at all," she says. "Nora here has the same name as me. She wondered if I'd been a nun. As you well know, it's far from being a nun I was reared and you should thank your lucky stars or you'd never have met the chambermaid from Finn's Hotel who took you walking across Stephen's Green and you never would have been able to—what did you say? Oh, I remember, free yourself from the nets of false piety and guilt." She starts to laugh again. "How's that for a fancy name for courting, ladies," Nora says.

"So you are laughing at me," he says, offended.

"Ah, Jim. Get over yourself. It's myself I'm laughing at and having a bit of fun with these two. And don't start looking around for empty glasses. I've barely a drop taken though I'd see you've done the honors for both of us."

Joyce seems completely sober but I suppose a wife knows when her husband's had a few too many. How innocent that sounds. And yet next door is a room full of men well on their way to being drunk, relying on their women to get them home.

"Mr. Joyce," I say, "I really enjoyed your book, *The Portrait of an Artist—*"

"*A Portrait of the Artist as a Young Man,*" he corrects me.

"Oh, sorry. But I did read it."

He staggers just the slightest bit and leans on Nora's shoulder.

"Would you ever give me a hand, girls?" Nora says. "To get this boyo out the door and into a taxi."

Well, one thing I learned nursing is how to get a fellow unsteady on his feet moving in the right direction. Joyce bids good-bye to the rest of the party as we walk him through the crowd and to the front door.

Gertrude comes to see us out.

"You Irish," she says as if everyone else in the room weren't drunk. A squarish fellow with a loud voice stands in a corner lecturing a group of men and a very young woman, all the while pointing his finger.

"That fellow doesn't look Irish and he's about to put a finger through your Picasso," I say.

She looks. "That's Hemingway. But he's a genius."

"And what's my husband?" Nora says.

"Now I hardly would compare . . ." Gertrude starts, but I interrupt.

"All those geniuses," I said, "and every one of them pissed to the eyebrows."

Joyce straightens up. "Is that an Americanism?" he says, and starts fumbling in his pockets. "I'll write it down."

"We'll do it at home, Jim," Nora says. "Good night, Miss Stein. Jim's, well . . ."

But Gertrude cuts her off, laughing. "All in good fun. At least your wife stays sober, Mr. Joyce. Look at Zelda."

She points at a very pretty dark-haired girl dancing to some unheard music, while an audience of six men stand around her clapping in time.

"That's the Charleston," May says.

Gertrude Stein sniffs. "Not much art to it."

Now Joyce begins to do a stiff-legged imitation.

"That's it," Nora says. "Let's go."

"The Fitzgeralds are only visiting," Gertrude says. "He's had success in New York, returning there I'd say." She sounds disappointed. "But he'll come back. That whole lost generation are coming to Paris," she said. "They need the inspiration and camaraderie, the . . ."

". . . cheap living," I put in.

James Joyce is tottering but we manage to move him out onto the street. We help him into a taxi. He leans his head back and closes his eyes.

"Will you be able to get him into the house?" I ask Nora.

"Oh, a sleep in the taxi and he'll be fine. My sister's here visiting, at home with Lucia and Giorgio, she'll help."

"You have children?" I say.

"I do. Doesn't everybody?" She laughs again and then says, "Oh, you don't?" I shake my head. So does May. "Well, Jim says some of the women here in Paris live together as if they were married to each other. Fair play to them, I say, but you two don't seem the type."

"We're not a couple," I say.

Joyce opens his eyes. Oh God, I think, more questions from him, too?

Are May and I the only single women in Paris without partners of one sex or the other?

"St. Fiacre," he says, "an Irish monk, gave his name to these conveyances; patron of the drivers."

Hadn't one of the Alices told me that?

"Very nice, Jim," Nora says. "Now, go back to sleep." And the taxi leaves.

May and I start laughing. "I don't know, Nora. I think the Jazz Age will have to do without me," May says.

"Me too," I agree.

Hot for the start of July, and Madame Collard has decorated the window of L'Impasse with red, white, and blue bunting for Bastille Day, July 14th, when I come in for lunch with Nora Barnacle.

"Jim told me women didn't go to lunch without a male escort," she says as we settle in. Nora wears a navy blue dress with a white collar.

"Maybe in most restaurants but not at L'Impasse," I say.

She's interested in my work with Madame Simone. My photography.

We walk to the Irish College after lunch. Nora has never been there and tells me Jim wants her to investigate the library. "He's feuding with the church and doesn't want to be seen in the college," she says.

The place is in an uproar when we arrive. Priests and students milling around in the courtyard, everybody talking at once. I see May Quinlivan. She waves at us to come over.

"Isn't it wonderful!"

"What?"

"The truce! It's over. The British have surrendered."

Not quite, but a cease-fire's been agreed and negotiations for a treaty will begin soon. So no more killings. May tells us that Michael Collins said to the British after they signed the truce, "Are you mad? We were out of ammunition. Couldn't have lasted another week."

"I must tell Jim," Nora says. "Come with me. We live quite close."

I follow her up the rue Mouffetard into rue du Cardinal-Lemoine. A workaday *quartier.* Narrow buildings. Little shops. Busy. She points across the street.

"Valery told us Hemingway lived there," Nora says. "Looks like a pokey place. Ours is nicer."

She turns up a small lane onto a kind of green, set in front of three buildings.

Some young fellows are playing soccer. One kicks a ball toward us. Nora raises her foot, stops the ball. Kicks it back.

"That's my Giorgio," she says. "Sixteen this month. My daughter's fourteen."

She leads me into the center building. Newish.

"This *is* nice," I say as we climb up the stairs to the third floor.

"Belongs to Valery Larbaud, a writer, lent it to us because Jim's good at borrowing and says he's giving them a chance to support his genius like that McCormick one from Chicago used to send money every month." Nora stops. "You're from Chicago," she says.

"But I'm not rich. Barely making ends meet."

She laughs. "I know how that is."

The flat's spread out. Reminds me of Maud's place on rue de l'Annunciation. Big windows.

"Jim," Nora calls out. "Jim. Good news. There's a truce."

"In the study," we hear.

The genius is hunched over a desk. Piles of paper cover the surface. He's not alone. I'm surprised to see Sylvia Beach and Adrienne Monnier with him.

"Sylvia," I say, "Adrienne."

"You know Miss Beach?" Joyce says, "Ah, Americans, of course."

Always take my clients to Sylvia's bookstore. Gives them a chance to feel Bohemian and speak English.

"That fool of an Englishman from the embassy refused to let his wife finish typing my 'Cyclops' chapter," Joyce says to Nora. "Said the language was obscene. How does he think men in pubs talk?"

"We're publishing Mr. Joyce's book," Sylvia tells me. "But having a hard time getting the manuscript ready for the printer."

I can see lines of tiny letters covering the sheets on Joyce's desk. Reminds me a bit of the Kelly fragment and Father Kevin's pages. Another Irishman in his scriptorium.

"I can hunt and peck now, Sylvia," I say. "Can I help?"

"Would that be all right, Mr. Joyce?" she asks.

Joyce cocks his head. Looks at me sideways. "You're the pissed-to-the-eyebrows woman," he says.

"I am."

We laugh.

"This would be a good chapter for you to type," he says.

"Because it's set in a bar?" I say.

On my high horse a bit.

"Because there are great Dublin phrases in it," he says.

"But do you have a typewriter?" Sylvia asks me.

"I can get the use of one," I say, thinking of the rector's machine. "Belongs to the Irish College. I could work in their library."

"When can you finish? The printer must have the manuscript soon if we're to have copies by February 2, 1922."

"My fortieth birthday," Joyce says.

Younger than me, I think.

Doesn't look it.

"I celebrated mine by bobbing my hair," I say.

He doesn't answer. He's turned to Nora, who's said nothing. "What were you shouting about, Nora?" he asks her.

"A truce, Jim, in Ireland. The fighting's over," she says.

"A day for the history books," I say.

"History," Joyce says. "History is a nightmare from which I'm trying to awake," he says.

"But . . ." I start.

Nora interrupts me. "Come on, ladies, I'll make us some tea. Let Jim get back to work."

She shoos us out. Shuts the study door.

"Don't get him going on politics," Nora says to me. "He's still angry about Parnell."

Nora goes into the kitchen. Sylvia and Adrienne walk into the drawing room, knowing the way.

"Hello, Lucia," Sylvia says to the young girl sitting in a chair by the empty fireplace staring at a sketchbook on her lap. She holds a drawing pencil and doesn't respond. Looks very like Nora and I think of Iseult. Here's another young woman who's a blurred copy of her powerful mother. Not easy.

Nora comes in carrying a tray. "Don't sit there mooning, Lucia," she says. "Help me."

"How?" Lucia says.

"Never mind."

Nora sets down the tray, hands out cups, pours the tea, all the while glancing at Lucia.

"A dreamer like her father," Nora says to me. "Living in her head."

"Have you spent much time in Ireland, Lucia?" I ask her.

"Some," she says. "Have you?"

"A little," I say. "But I plan to go now that the fighting's over."

"I wouldn't be in any rush," Nora says. "Lots of ways to make a bollocks of the truce."

"You can't go now, Nora," Sylvia says. "You promised to type for us."

Which I do. No problem with getting the loan of the rector's typewriter and the library from four to six in the afternoon. Only difficulty is to keep myself from laughing out loud at the Dublin characters jumping out at me from Joyce's manuscript. I can picture Cyril up at the bar muttering away. Sometimes I have to ask Joyce to decipher bits. Always very formal with me except when he reads the dialogue. Then he takes on different accents, and cadences. Hilarious. Peter made ancient Ireland live for me and now this fellow's taking me into Barney McKiernan's Pub twenty years ago. Reminds me of McKenna's in Bridgeport on a Saturday night.

I'm working away in the first week in September when the French-Irish duchess finds me.

❧❦❧

"What exactly is the Irish Race Convention?" I ask the duchess. She and the countess are at Mass at the Irish College on this September Sunday. Haven't seen them since the St. Patrick's Day celebration at Our Lady of Victory.

Now here they are. It seems Sheila and Antoinette have returned to Ireland and the women need two new aides-de-camp, they say. May and I are it.

"The convention will be a gathering of those of Irish blood from all over the world," the countess says, "under the patronage of the Duke of Tetuan— the O'Donnell, descendant of one of the Wild Geese who went to Spain." It's to take place the last week of January.

"I'm not sure I'll be in Paris," I say. "I'm planning to go to Ireland."

"Better wait," May says. "The talks might break down and the war will start again."

So in addition to being Joyce's typist, I join May as a staff member for the convention.

And then early in December, May comes shouting into the little office at the Irish College that's been given to the race convention.

"It's done, it's done. The treaty's signed! We're free!"

I jump up and hug her. "Free," we say together. "Free, free." A nation once again.

That afternoon I suggest to the duchess that Professor Keeley be placed on our program. She agrees. I write to Maud and include money for Peter's fare. Ask her to get word to him through Cyril or Maura O'Connor. And won't she please come *early* and celebrate Nollaig na mBan and so much else.

I get a strange reply. "I have spent my life fighting for the Republic of Ireland. I will not accept half measures nor will any real patriot such as Peter Keeley," Maud writes. What?

May tells me that the treaty sticks in a lot of people's craw. The King of England will still be head of state and Ireland a dominion and member of the Commonwealth with elected members of the Irish Parliament required to swear an oath of allegiance to the king but as May says, "It's only words." We're in our little office the first week of January.

"Right," I agree. "They can cross their fingers."

"Collins said we don't have freedom but we have the conditions for freedom. Have to go step by step," May says. "It's better than having the Black and Tans burning the place down around us. And as for the North. Well, Mick's already shipping guns there."

May's own Tyrone has been lopped off and made part of Northern Ireland, a new state with a Protestant majority that would stay united to Britain. Unionists.

"But we're a small island," May says. "We can't be split like that."

"A house divided against itself cannot stand," I say.

"Did Dev say that, may I ask?"

"Abraham Lincoln, actually talking about our Civil War," I said.

"Dear God, don't even say those words," she says. "We can't have a civil war though if Dev keeps pushing . . ." She looks at me. "You know who Dev is, don't you?"

"Of course," I said. "Eamon de Valera. For heaven's sakes, May. I may be American but I'm not a complete idiot. Besides, he's an American citizen, too."

"When de Valera was in jail and Collins helped him escape, de Valera was the president of our new state, and now he's opposing the treaty," May says.

A few days later May arrives, red-eyed.

"Have you been crying?" I ask.

"De Valera's left the government in protest. Said Collins betrayed the Republic. It's bad, Nora. The country's splitting apart."

So. Not a great time to have a Congress of Unity, I think.

28

JANUARY 1922

"I wonder, will Peter come," I ask Cyril, as May and I follow him through the lobby of the Grand Hotel. The Irish Race Convention opening reception's tonight.

"Only the muckety-mucks from both sides," he says.

"Michael Collins and the government picked four delegates and asked Dev as head of the opposition party to choose four. Countess Markievicz is one and so's Mary Mac Swiney," May says.

All the women in the Dáil voted against the treaty and walked out with de Valera, which seems a mistake to me. I mean what if aldermen in Chicago quit the City Council when a vote went against them?

Still Cyril thinks the opposing sides will use the race convention to make a deal.

"A lot of snorting and stomping then Mick and Dev will work out some agreement. Have to," Cyril says.

We join the crush of delegates, mostly men but a good few women, moving into the ballroom. Each group gathers under one of a dozen or so banners. I see Australia, Argentina, Brazil, Canada, Chile, one for Tasmania, of all places, South Africa, India, France, of course, Switzerland, Germany, Italy, Portugal, and Spain. Big crowds near the England and

Scotland banners and almost as many United States delegates. Though in their section handwritten signs specify New York, Boston, Philadelphia, and San Francisco. And there's Chicago sticking up with at least a dozen men standing around it. Don't recognize anyone, thank God. I move to the side of the ballroom, find the duchess and the countess.

We rigged a kind of throne for the Duke of Tetuan, the O'Donnell, by covering a chair with cloth-of-gold embroidered with an Irish harp, shamrocks, the O'Donnell crest, and the duke's own Spanish coat of arms. The duchess's footman stands next to the throne. I talked her out of having him wear a powdered wig but the footman's still very grand, in brocade britches and a lace jabot. He'll present each delegation to the duke.

The duke enters. He's a hefty fellow and I hear a creak as he settles down on what is only a rather frail chair.

The countess and the duchess approach him first. They curtsy in a smooth movement many of the other women try to match. The men half bow. The duke says a few words to each in Spanish. A priest from the Irish College translates.

Eamon de Valera doesn't wait for the footman's announcement but walks right up to the duke.

"I am Eamon de Valera, president of the Republic of Ireland," he says.

The duke stands up. "And I am the Duke of Tetuan, and the O'Donnell," he says in accented English.

Now, of the two, De Valera's hands down the more regal, a foot taller than the duke and very Spanish-looking—dark, one of those Roman noses.

"That man is rude," the duchess says to me. "He has no sense of protocol."

He knows exactly what he's doing, I think. The Republic of Ireland. No titles allowed except for his own, I guess.

"No bowing and scraping for Dev," someone says.

I turn. *"Bichon,"* I say.

"Haven't heard that for a while," Seán MacBride says to me.

"You're a delegate?" I ask.

I mean he can't be more than eighteen.

"I'm President de Valera's secretary," he says. Didn't grow to his mother's height, but those are her eyes.

"Is your mother here? Constance?" I ask him.

"They're too republican to attend this show," he says.

The duke is addressing the group now. Speaking in Spanish again, the priest translating. And doesn't de Valera step right up next to the duke and start talking to him in Irish, which the priest puts into Spanish.

The duke nods. Gestures. Presenting de Valera, who turns to the crowd, raises his voice. He delivers a full-blown speech—all in the Irish language, and when the priest tries to translate the words into English de Valera stops him with a chop of his hand as if to say, You who call yourselves Irish will learn the language.

"Dev's always been great at the old one-upmanship," Cyril says to me. "Balls of brass. Look at Mick's fellows. Fuming."

Supposed to be no politics at the convention. A united front to the world. So much for that.

After the speech Seán takes my arm and walks me into the corridor outside the ballroom.

"Listen, Nora, President de Valera wants to host a private luncheon away from the conference," he says.

"That's nice," I say.

"Well, we want you to give us your place and make a meal for say, four people. Tomorrow. Lunchtime."

"Seán, my place is tiny and as for cooking . . ." I say.

"Food's not important to Dev. But get some decent wine. He's a pioneer at home but likes wine on the Continent. Here." He gives me a load of francs. "Tomorrow at one o'clock."

"Is your mother coming?"

"No women," he says. "Serious business. Private."

"No women? For God's sake, Seán. Where would all of you be without women?"

"Nora, please. Other people are looking at us." And they are. The delegates pass us as they leave the reception.

"I'm sorry I asked you," Seán says. "We'll find some other place."

"No, no. It's all right but don't expect some kind of feast." Seán laughs and then looks around and whispers, "Dev's in touch with Liam Mellows. After the meeting, I'll get him to talk to you."

"Liam Mellows. He's the fellow Peter was with."

"Quiet, Nora. See you tomorrow," he says.

I ask May to help me. Omelettes are the only thing I'd ever cooked in my little kitchen. All well and good for Seán to say the food doesn't matter but what would Mam or Granny Honora think if I didn't feed the president of Ireland a proper meal? I ask Madame Simone for a recipe, a suggestion.

"L'Impasse," she says.

Of course. So May and I carry a cauldron of beef bourguignonne, a pan of roasted potatoes with rosemary, and a bowl of ratatouille from the restaurant to my apartment. I buy a large apple tarte from the corner patisserie.

"At least I can make the coffee," I say to May as we shove the meal into my tiny oven.

"They'll want tea," she says, and produces a tin of Barry's. May and I put two of my small tables together. Madame Collard lent us linens and silver. I borrowed some candles from the sacristy of the Irish College. We're ready.

Seán and de Valera arrive first. Something very clerical about de Valera. Ascetic but not celibate. I mean the man has six children.

A decent wine, Seán said, and he nods at me as he sips the Pommard I pour him. I hand de Valera a glass and fill it.

"Nora's from Chicago," Seán says to de Valera as he leads him over to the fireplace. De Valera's glad enough to warm himself. He nods and says nothing to me.

Seán goes on. "Of course, the president's more familiar with New York."

"My mother and her family lived near New York when they first arrived in America," I say, which doesn't seem to interest de Valera, but I keep talking, anything to fill the silence. "In Jersey City," I say, "across the harbor . . ."

"I know where Jersey City is," de Valera says. "My parents were married in St. Patrick's Church in Jersey City."

"Well, small world," I say. "My aunt was in that parish. Maybe she knew your parents."

"Is she alive?" he asks.

"My aunt? Yes," I say.

"Get me the name," he says to Seán.

May speaks up. "My people know yours, Mr. de Valera. In fact, we're related to the Colls of Bruree."

"What's your name?" de Valera asks.

"May Quinlivan."

"From?"

"Well, Tyrone now. My father's the schoolmaster there but his people are from Bruree. They tell stories about you, sir. Your growing up there and all," May says.

"After the president's father died his mother sent him to her parents," Seán says to me.

"How could a lone woman support a two-year-old child?" de Valera says. "My uncle Ned took me back to Ireland."

My granny Honora and Aunt Máire raised nine children between them, I think. I wonder would they have sent any back to Ireland? Can't picture it.

"Is she still alive?" I ask.

"She is," he says. "She married again. My brother Thomas was ordained two months after the Rising."

"My da says they always thought around home you'd go for a priest," May tells de Valera.

Seán cuts her off. "Well now, I'm sure you ladies have things to do in the kitchen. We'll have lunch as soon as the president's guests arrive."

He takes May's arm and mine and steers us out of the room.

"What was that about?" I ask May as we ladle out the bourguignonne.

"I think I put my foot in it," she says. "There were some problems with de Valera getting into the seminary." And now she whispers, "Priests have to be, well, legitimate you know. . . ."

"And de Valera?"

"Well, there's some at home think the whole story of the Spanish husband is dodgy. His mother had worked in the Big House and went to America very sudden."

Dear God, I think. Was de Valera's mother another landlord's victim?

Seán comes to the kitchen door. "Almost ready?" he says. Which means "Hurry up."

"Not polite to quiz the president," Seán says to May.

"I didn't mean . . ." she starts.

"Oh, for God's sake, Seán," I say. "Who cares who de Valera's father was?"

"He does," Seán says. A knock at the door.

"I'll go," Seán says.

Both May and I expect a representative from the government. I imagine the pro- and anti-treaty forces reconciling over lunch in my apartment. I'd take the historic photograph.

But when we look out who is standing there? Only the Duke of Tetuan. Alone. Wrapped in a cloak, a fedora hat pulled down to his eyebrows.

"You weren't followed?" Seán asks as he takes the duke's cloak and hat, which gives me a chance to go into the room.

"I'll take those," I say to Seán.

The duke walks straight over to de Valera, who sets down his wineglass.

"Well?" he says, standing up.

"Yes," says the duke. "I believe the evidence is clear. Your father, Juan Vivion de Valera, is related to the Marqués de Auñón. Members of the family did go to Cuba."

"My mother always said the de Valeras had a sugar plantation," de Valera says.

The duke nods. "Exactly. You are a descendant, sir, of Spanish nobility."

The duke takes de Valera by the shoulder and kisses him on both cheeks.

"Wow," I say.

Seán turns me toward the kitchen.

"Lunch," he says.

As May and I fill their plates in the kitchen I hear a fourth man arrive. An American from his voice.

May and I set out the lunch on the tables by the fire. "Don't you have to go somewhere," Seán asks me.

"No," I say. I'll stay in the kitchen but I won't leave my own house.

Of course my place is so small May and I can hear every word through the closed kitchen door. The American seems to be giving de Valera a report. "Your mother was born December 23, 1858, in Bruree, County Limerick," he starts.

"I know that. You're wasting my time," de Valera says.

"Please, sir, I prefer to proceed chronologically," the man says.

"This is nonsense," de Valera says.

"Easy," I hear Seán say.

The man continues. "After your grandfather Patrick Coll died, she, at the age of sixteen, went into service in the home of Thomas Atkinson."

In the kitchen, May squeezes my hand. "That's it, the landlord," she whispers.

"She left his employ, sailed for New York on the S.S. *Nevada* arriving October 2, 1879, and you of course were born in October 1882, three years later." He pauses.

"So not the landlord's son," May says. I wonder if de Valera's thinking the same thing. The man speaking must be a detective.

"I found a record of her residing at 98 Blossom Street, Brooklyn," the man says.

"Brooklyn," says de Valera. "She never mentioned Brooklyn."

"She was living with quite a prominent American family," the detective says. "In service, of course."

"Prominent?" de Valera says. "What were they? Judges? Attorneys? Businessmen?"

"No," the man says. "Their names were Martha and Frank Giraud, but Frank was known professionally as Frank Girard."

"Professionally?" de Valera says.

"Yes," the detective says. "He was a well-known vaudevillian."

"Vaudevillian?" de Valera asks.

"A performer. He acted in musical shows," the man says. "And then did an act as a strong man. I have a photograph."

"But I've seen him," I whisper to May. "Frank Girard. He played the McVicker's Theatre with Tony Pastor. Come on."

We walk over to the table and pick up the plates. "Hope you enjoyed it," I say. "Some nice apple tart for you."

DeValera's holding the photograph.

"Oh," I say. "Frank Girard and Charles Wurley. I saw their act."

The duke recovers first. "Mademoiselle, you are interrupting us."

"Oh, I'm sorry," I say. "But I do know vaudeville."

I lean over and point at the figures.

"See, Mr. de Valera, the tall man there dressed like Roman centurion? That's Frank. He played the strong man, and the other fellow kind of balancing on his shoulder, his feet up in the air, his face blackened and his clothes raggedy? Well, that's Charles Wurley."

De Valera looks at Seán. "What is this woman going on about?"

"Sir," I say, "think of it. If your mother lived with the Girards, she must have met all kinds of exciting people. Nora Bay and Daisy Ring and . . ."

"Your father," the detective says, "was a friend of Girard's perhaps."

"My mother always said he was a musician," de Valera says.

"But maybe your father was in vaudeville too," I say.

"I doubt if a descendant of the Marqués de Auñón would be a performer," the Duke of Tetuan says.

"We'll bring dessert," May says, and walks me into the kitchen.

"Why did you pull me away?" I say.

"For heaven's sakes, Nora. Don't be going on about that big man Girard. Sounds as if you're suggesting *he* was de Valera's father."

"I didn't mean that," I say.

"Dev was Eddie Coll growing up. Let him be related to a duke. Might make him less prickly," May says.

We serve the apple tarte just as the detective is saying, "So I have been unable to find a record of a de Valera–Coll marriage at St. Patrick's in Jersey City." He stops talking.

May and I close the kitchen door. We still hear every word.

"Now, your mother told you your father went to Colorado for his health soon after you were born and died out there." The man coughs. "Unfortunately, I could find no death certificate for a Juan Vivion de Valera in the state of Colorado from 1880 to 1890."

"New Mexico," de Valera said. "Maybe New Mexico."

"I checked," the detective says. "Nothing."

"But he must have died by 1888," de Valera says, "because . . ." He stops.

"Because your mother married Charles Wheelwright May 7, 1888, in St. Francis Xavier Church, New York, New York," the detective says.

De Valera's father better have been dead or his mother is a bigamist. Unless she did make up the Spanish husband.

"I advise you to accept your mother's story," the detective says.

"Story? It's no story. It's fact. Now, thanks to Your Grace, I know about the origins of my father's family."

"You do, Señor de Valera," I hear the duke say. "And as for documents, I assure you, the memories of your mother are far superior to any clerk's records."

"He's right, Dev," Seán says. "Look at me. Best thing my father ever did for me was to die in the 1916 uprising before he and my mother destroyed each other entirely."

Easier to make heroes of dead fathers, I think.

"All right," I say to May. "Let's bring in the tea."

As I set down a cup in front of de Valera I ask him straight out.

"Peter Keeley, Mr. de Valera. He was a professor here at the Irish College and he fought with Liam Mellows in Galway. I was wondering if you know where he is now."

"What I do know and don't know must remain my business," de Valera says.

"Oh, come on, Dev," Seán says. "Nora here's a special friend of the pro-fessor. No harm to reassure her."

"MacBride, you astonish me. Where's your discipline? Your father for all his shortcomings understood the need for military discipline."

"Can we at least tell Nora Peter Keeley's a valuable man who's devoted to the Republic?" he asks.

De Valera nods. I guess Peter is with them against the treaty. I remem-ber Michael Collins at Maud's. Now, there was a fellow who'd inspire you. How could Peter support this frozen-faced stick of a fellow with his cat's cradle of questions and insecurity?

The detective leaves first.

It's the duke, not de Valera, who thanks May and me for our hospitality. Very charming, his English has a Spanish accent and an Irish lilt.

"You know," he says to me, "my ancestors went to Spain partly because of the old Irish belief that Ireland's salvation would somehow come from Spain. One reason why I support Mr. de Valera even though he is a repub-lican."

And he sings in a low voice,

> O My Dark Rosaleen, do not sigh, do not weep!
> The priests are on the ocean green, they march along the deep.
> There's wine from the royal Pope,
> Upon the ocean green.

He pauses, then lets his voice swell. "'And Spanish ale shall give you hope, My Dark Rosaleen!'"

Seán's light tenor joins in and I even think I hear a rumble from de Valera.

> My Dark Rosaleen, My own Rosaleen.
> Shall glad your heart, shall give you hope,
> Shall give you health, and help, and hope,
> My Dark Rosaleen.

"So," the duke says, and claps de Valera on the shoulder, "Catherine Coll meets Juan Vivion de Valera in the home of a vaudeville performer, and the prophecy is fulfilled."

De Valera's mouth moves. Smiling, I think.

De Valera's at Mass the next morning, Sunday. As soon as the priest finishes doesn't Dev go right up to the Communion rail and address the congregation.

Speaking in English this time.

"I hope all of you students return to Ireland as good republicans," he says.

Balls of brass indeed.

He and Seán go off to the priests' refectory.

Still no sign of Maud or Constance. But the next day I spot Seán in the lobby of the Grand Hotel, which hasn't changed much from when Molly Childers stayed there.

Very close to Michael Collins, the Childerses were. I remember Molly talking about the pistol Collins gave Erskine. Had they stuck with him or were they supporting de Valera?

I'm determined to get more information from Seán about Peter.

I manage to grab Seán's arm.

"Please," I say. "Have you seen Peter? Where is he? What's he doing?"

Seán looks around the lobby at the knots of delegates.

"Let's sit down," he says. We find a table in the corner.

"I haven't seen him myself but I hear he's still in the mountains," Seán says.

"But why?" I say. "The war's over."

Seán shakes his head. "I hope Mick sees sense and tells the Brits Ireland's a republic no matter what the treaty says. We'd all unite behind him," he says.

"But won't the British send in troops?" I say.

"We beat them once. We can do it again," he says. "But it won't come to that. Look at all the support we have." He points to the crowd.

"But half of these people agree with Collins and the government. They accept the treaty," I say.

"We'll have to change their minds one way or another," he says. "Why our army can't disband quite yet."

He leans forward.

"Look, Nora, Peter Keeley runs a kind of training camp for new recruits in the Connemara mountains. They do the military stuff of course but the professor teaches them Irish, tells them the old stories of the Fianna. That's us, the Fianna Fáil, Soldiers of Destiny."

All I hear is "military stuff." My gentle Peter. Training Irish boys to fight each other?

Enough I think. Enough.

Get out, Peter.

"Seán," I start, but there's a fellow bending over us—a head of thick white hair. He's slim, smiling. Gray suit with a waistcoat.

"Mr. MacBride," he says. "Let me introduce myself. I'm Frank McCord. I heard your parents speak in Chicago twenty years ago."

"You did?" Seán says. "Sit down, Mr. McCord. Let me buy you a drink. We'll all have a glass." He stands up, waves for a waiter.

"We'll talk more later, Nora," he says to me.

I bet.

I don't know McCord, thank God, but I'm not taking any chances.

"Nothing for me," I say, and get up.

"Well if you must go," Seán says. Relieved, he stands. So does McCord.

"You're American?" McCord says.

"She's from Chicago too," Seán says.

I see he's about to introduce me, so I pretend to wave to someone across the lobby and start to walk away.

But McCord's saying, "I don't live in Chicago. I moved to a suburb called Argo. Not a place you'd have heard of. Don't think they sell Argo starch in Ireland."

Argo. Mike and Mame's town, and I can't help myself. The words pop out.

"Do you know Mike Kelly?" I ask.

"Owns a plumbing company? Just became president of the bank?" McCord says.

I nod.

"Good friend of mine. In the Knights of Columbus together. How do you know Mike?"

"I went to school with his wife," I say.

McCord's ready for a good gossip and I long for news but I take a step away.

"My wife's very friendly with Mike's sister who lives with them," Mc-Cord says.

That stops me.

"A widow with a son. She tells my wife that young Mrs. Kelly couldn't manage without her," McCord says.

Mike let my sister Henrietta move in with them? Is he crazy? Poor Mame.

Wonder was Henrietta there when my letter came? Is that why Mike didn't answer? Did Henrietta intercept it? McCord's going on, telling Seán that young Mrs. Kelly was the first woman to drive in Argo. Always had a carload of kids though she hasn't been seen around much lately. Not well, the sister told his wife.

"What's wrong? Is Mame sick?" I ask.

Too interested. Saying her name. Giving myself away. McCord's going to start quizzing me. Change the subject.

"Have you seen anything of Paris, Mr. McCord?" I ask him.

"Went to a show last night, all colored musicians. Not my kind of music. I like the old songs. You remember Dolly McKee, Miss, er . . ."

Expecting me to fill in my name but all I hear is "Dolly McKee."

"I remember her," I say.

"Such a tragic ending," McCord says. He looks at Seán. "Murdered."

Now I should say "So sad" and leave, but I have to ask.

"She was married to her manager, wasn't she? Can't remember his name," I say.

"Tim McShane," McCord says.

To hear that name.

"He left Chicago, didn't he?" Hoping.

"Oh, no. Owns a casino and a bunch of racehorses," McCord says. "But now what's *your* name so I can tell Mike I ran into you. Small world."

"Oh, look at the time," I say, pointing to the clock on the lobby wall. "The session's starting."

I shake McCord's hand. Grab Seán's arm. Look at him. He nods. Raised in conspiracy. He won't tell McCord my name.

I leave the Grand Hotel and go home to the place des Vosges and finish the bottle of wine I bought for de Valera.

I've been keeping Peter and my family in separate parts of my mind. Characters in a story I tell myself.

Now Peter's training young men to kill and Henrietta's making Mame's life a misery.

And Tim McShane.

I had him living far away somewhere or dead. Very late before I fall asleep.

❧

"The best lack all conviction, while the worst are full of passionate intensity." Yeats lets the words spread out through the room. Ripples from a pebble dropped into the Lake Isle of Innisfree. A good crowd for his talk. The last of the convention.

We are in the library of the Irish College, where I first learned from Peter "what the heart feels," to quote James Joyce, who is not attending the convention.

When I came into the room Yeats lifted one finger in greeting, then mouthed "Maud?" I shrugged and shook my head. I still haven't seen her and she may not come to hear Yeats speak, since the poet has sided with Michael Collins and the government against de Valera and the republicans. Now the audience, similarly divided, looks straight ahead, avoiding the eyes of the opposition, each thinking, We are the best; they are the worst. The unity of the Irish Race Convention has splintered after days of too much talk.

"I wrote this poem," Yeats explained in his introduction, "as the Great War was ending and revolution was sweeping through Russia like a bloody tide. History teaches a sad lesson—great hopes are too often followed by a reign of terror—a lesson we in Ireland seem doomed to learn. I'm appealing to you to consider the consequences."

He cleared his throat, smoothed back his hair, all-over gray now but somehow he was better-looking, more substantial, a father himself now. It changes a man, I guess.

Self-assured, not the fellow who shouted his verses into the wind on that beach in Normandy. "Changed, changed utterly"—the words still stick in my head.

"I've titled this poem 'The Second Coming.'" A strange beginning: "Turning and turning in the widening gyre the falcon cannot hear the falconer."

Now, where did he get that image? I wondered. Are there falcons in

Ireland? Probably imagining himself a desert sheik in one of those past lives he told Maud he had. But the next lines were not hard to understand.

"Things fall apart; the center cannot hold."

True.

Then I heard the door open. De Valera and Seán came in and stood in the back. De Valera and Michael Collins had once been the center of the Irish struggle but that center didn't hold. Battling each other.

Yeats went on, telling us that "mere anarchy and a blood-dimmed tide" have been loosed upon the world. He looked over at de Valera. But surely it's not too late for Ireland. Ireland can't dissolve into the kind of conflict that is tearing apart Russia and wiped out a generation of young men in Europe.

"The ceremony of innocence is drowned," Yeats said, but what did that mean? For some reason I think of Iseult, her flower face, her little daughter. Seán told me the baby had died. "Almost destroyed Iseult," he said. I can imagine Iseult letting go of life altogether, drowning.

And then Yeats says the line that stirs this audience: "The best lack all conviction, while the worst are full of passionate intensity."

"The best." Jesus, I think, he could be talking about Mr. Jenson and the Quakers who'd been afraid to stand up to Captain Pyke, his power trampling over their goodness. "The worst." Does he mean de Valera? Full of passionate intensity, no question. But then, Collins's followers are just as convinced they are right.

Yeats lowers his voice. "Surely some revelation is at hand," he says. Good, maybe he's offering some solution, some way to reach common ground before a blood-dimmed tide does break against those rocky shores I saw in Connemara and Donegal.

Yeats looks up from his text, stops. I know who has come in before I turn around. Maud. And Constance with her. The two of them try to move quietly into the back row. Fat chance. Two men immediately stand up, offer them their seats. I watch Maud and Constance smile as they sit down. A fellow two seats away leans over to shake hands with each one of them.

Ireland's Joans of Arc—leave it to us to have two. An older man waves to them. "Douglas Hyde," May whispers to me. The man who started it all, I think. Maud sees Seán, starts to get up. He gives her a thumbs-up and gestures her back into her seat.

Yeats clears his throat, tries to resume the reading, but no one's paying one bit of attention. Now a woman is embracing Maud. "Mary Mac-Swiney," May says.

"Excuse me," Yeats says, "excuse me, ladies and gentlemen. There is another stanza to this poem."

"Oh, Willie," Maud says. "We are so sorry. Con and I were delayed . . ."

"Better late than never," a voice shouts out, "like the Irish Republic!" This gets a laugh.

The distraction is a relief. Enough about the best and the worst, blood-dimmed tides. But the crowd does quiet and looks up at him. Yeats doesn't say anything.

"Go on, Willie," Maud says. "We're waiting."

"Surely some revelation is at hand," Yeats repeats. "Surely the Second Coming is at hand. The Second Coming!"

He loses me with the next lines. Something about a lion's body and the desert. The heavyset fellow next to me is asleep, little half snores coming out of him.

"'And what rough beast, its hour come round at last, slouches towards Bethlehem to be born?'" Yeats stops. That seems to be the end of the poem.

"Bethlehem?" That wakes the fellow next to me. "Did he say 'Bethlehem'?" he asks me, then shouts out to Yeats. "Are you mocking our beliefs, Mr. Yeats? I know you are not a Catholic but I expect you to respect our religion."

Conversations and comments all around me. Yeats doesn't move. I wonder if he's remembering the riots at the Abbey Theatre after *The Playboy of the Western World*.

The duchess stands up. "Ladies and gentlemen, please," but no one hears her.

I get up and go over to Maud.

"For God's sake, Maud, do something," I say. "Go up there. If you and Con stand with him now . . ."

"We can't, Nora," she says, and points over at de Valera, who is watching us.

"Jesus, Mary, and Joseph," I say, and start for the front. Not my place to interfere. But the duchess is completely flustered and . . .

And then who comes bobbing up to Yeats? Only Cyril. Hadn't even seen him come in.

"Thank you kindly, Mr. Yeats," Cyril says. "Very profound altogether I'm sure, but some of us would like to get a blast of your old stuff. Wouldn't we?" he asks the audience.

"My own favorite's the one that got a tune put on it," he says.

Cyril starts to sing:

> Down by the salley gardens, my love and I did meet;
> She passed the salley gardens with little snow-white feet.

Not exactly the blood-dimmed tide, and I wonder if Yeats likes being reminded of a time when he spoke so simply. The audience is listening to Cyril. The man next to me smiles.

"'She bid me take love easy,'" Cyril sings, "'as the leaves grow on the tree.'"

And for a moment, all of us—whether from Australia or Africa, South America or North, Portugal, Spain, Tasmania—are in the Ireland of the mind and heart that exerts such a pull on anyone of Irish blood. It's a song we all know, and so we sing too. Finishing the verses, luxuriating in the lovely, sad ending.

"'But I was young and foolish, and now am full of tears.'"

Applause. For ourselves together.

The moment of unity doesn't last. The audience forms into knots of dissension. De Valera, Seán, Maud, and Constance leave without speaking to Yeats. May follows them, and I think, Get out of there, Peter, please. Just get out of Ireland.

FEBRUARY 1922

May and I find seats in Sylvia's Shakspeare and Company on February 2, James Joyce's birthday. Copies of *Ulysses* are stacked up on a table in the front of the shop, the title bold on the blue paper spine. A very different audience here than the group at the Irish Race Convention. French and Americans mostly. Sylvia leads Nora and Joyce out from the back of the store to sit on chairs behind the small table.

I'm hoping Joyce will read from the chapter in Barney McKiernan's Pub but he tells us his sight's so bad he can't see his own text. Instead he thanks

Sylvia and Adrienne and all who helped him get *Ulysses* into print and urges the audience to "buy the damn book and read it yourselves."

We laugh.

Nora speaks up. "And me, Jim, thank me," she says.

"I do, of course," Joyce says.

"The whole book takes place on June 16, 1904," Nora says, "the day Jim and I went walking."

"It does," Joyce says.

"And pay attention to that last chapter," she says, "he's taking off the way I talk says I don't bother with punctuation just let whatever's in my head roll out."

"Yes," Joyce says. "Yes, you do."

He smiles.

"And now will those who wish to buy copies," Sylvia begins.

But then some fellow shouts out from the back. "Given Ireland's history of conflict, Mr. Joyce, do you expect an all-out civil war?"

And I know how Joyce will respond. "History is a nightmare from which I'm trying to awake," he says.

I look at May. She shakes her head.

"Mick and Dev will work out a compromise, they will," she says as we leave.

I spend four weeks of tips on my signed copy of *Ulysses*. Eager to get to Nora's last chapter. But slow going. I only read a few pages a night, saying the words aloud to myself.

But then I doubt James Joyce wants readers galloping through his masterpiece. I develop the photo I took of Nora and Joyce. A portrait of the artist and the woman who said "Yes."

JUNE 1922

May twists the dial on the rector's radio, trying to bring in the signal. I hold the antenna out a window. Only at midnight do the radio waves from Ireland seem able to cross the Irish Sea and the English Channel, bounce off the Eiffel Tower, and be picked up by the rector's radio. Early to bed, the rector, thank God, doesn't seem aware that in the oldest parts of the college, one key fits every door. I've kept the key from the office we used during the convention. After the delegates went home to Ireland, the divisions deepened. De Valera gave speeches calling on Irishmen to kill other Irishmen, to wade through blood for the republic.

And then when he and Mick Collins do work out a compromise and agree on a Constitution, the British government insists that all elected officials must take an oath to the king, which the republicans refuse to do. Cyril says the Brits want to force a civil war, have Ireland collapse, bring in British troops and take the whole place over.

"Henry Wilson's pulling the strings, mark my words," Cyril said, and then left Paris. "Good-bye, girls," he said. "Going back on active duty."

He's supporting Collins.

Lots of to-ing and fro-ing during the spring and early summer, but no shooting.

But now the crisis has come. For weeks the anti-treaty fellows have occupied the Four Courts, the building that housed the British administration and now belongs to the Irish government. Michael Collins refused to attack. Let them sit there until they tire themselves out, he said. A kind of reverse siege. After all, these were his friends, his comrades.

But then we heard Winston Churchill had issued an ultimatum. The Irish government must retake the Four Courts or he'd order the British army to do it for them. A few rounds of artillery will sort out the rebels, he said. He accused Michael Collins of ordering General Henry Wilson's assassination. He was shot last week in London. Not true, May said.

"Two IRA fellows took advantage of an opportunity," May told me. "Spontaneous. They saw him in front of his house and shot him. Not planned really."

Both men had been in the British army during the World War. One lost his leg. Ironic if Wilson's death sent British troops back into Ireland, I think. Is he visiting disaster on the "natives" from his grave?

Though May says if the British do attack, the two sides will unite against them.

A week now since Wilson was killed and the Brits haven't invaded. The stalemate continues.

Nothing but static on the rector's radio tonight. May hits the receiver.

"Damn this thing," she says. Finally the static resolves into the announcer's voice:

"Two hours ago artillery pieces were moved into position facing the Four Courts. An order from the Irish Government signed by Michael Collins has been delivered to the rebels. They must surrender immediately or the Free State army will open fire."

Static. Then, "I can hear gunfire." The announcer loses his detached tone.

"Dear God," May says. "They're shooting at each other."

"They can't," I say. "They can't. Jesus Christ, Peter could be in the Four Courts."

I thought of the Michael Collins I'd met. An easygoing fellow, very different from the stubborn, stiff-necked de Valera. Collins didn't seem a man bent on impressing a father he'd never known. Why couldn't he find a way to compromise?

"This is terrible!" May says. "One of my brothers is inside the Four Courts, and the other on the outside, shooting at him."

She's crying now.

"They made Mick do it," May says. "The Brits made him. Why did he listen to them? They want us to destroy each other."

I remember the song Granny Honora would sing. *"Siúil, siúil, siúil, á rún."* A woman asking the man she loves to walk home safely to her. Aren't Irish women on both sides praying for the same thing? *Walk, walk, walk, my love, walk home safely to me.*

Now we hear the boom of artillery. The sound that shattered Belleau Wood. Coming across to us from Dublin. I remember the piles of rubble, the damage the British naval guns caused. And now this.

"What is wrong with men?" I ask May. "Can't they ever leave well enough alone? Collins said, 'If we don't have freedom, we have the conditions for freedom.' Why can't they work together on that?"

"And bow to King George, like the Brits want us to? No, Nora. Too many have died to settle for half measures," May says. "I see that now. Collins is wrong. We'll have to fight."

Too many have died, so more should?

29

DECEMBER 1922

Paris is a city of war widows. No reason I should be spared. Yet I've convinced myself Peter will survive. A man who so loves Ireland cannot be murdered by another Irishman I think. And then in August Michael Collins is assassinated by the IRA. Ambushed in Cork. Traveling with little security to a secret meeting with a republican leader, trying to negotiate a truce. "They won't kill me in my own county," he said. They did.

Only thirty-one—a full dozen years younger than I am. I can almost hear his brother Pat saying, "If only Mick had come out to me in Chicago. Took that job in the bank. He'd be married now with family, living here on the South Side." If only . . .

The Free State government retaliates. Executes Liam Mellows and three other republicans in November. Then Erskine Childers is arrested for violating the government's ban on weapons by carrying a pistol that Michael Collins himself had given him. He's tried, convicted, and shot. How can Molly Childers bear such a senseless loss?

"Nora, Nora. It's me Cyril, open up," he says.

Almost midnight. Cold. Snow on Cyril's jacket. Christmas soon. I think of Peter. That long-ago walk on Christmas Eve.

"I thought you were in Ireland," I say to Cyril.

"I was."

"Did you see Peter?" I say.

"I did."

"Well, how is he?"

Cyril says nothing.

"You're very serious-looking, Cyril," I say, and then I know.

"No, no, not Peter. Please, not Peter. Please, please," I say.

Cyril puts his arm around my shoulders, walks me over to the couch in front of the fireplace. Still a sheen of red on ashy coals that give off no heat. He makes me sit down.

"He's dead?"

"He is," Cyril says. "I am sorry for your troubles, Nora."

"How?"

"Shot by a young fellow at the training camp. A former student of the professor's. You might have known him. McCarthy's his name. A red-headed fellow from Cork."

"James McCarthy?"

Cyril nods.

The student who noticed me that first day. The one who asked all the questions.

"But he was a republican," I say.

"Everyone was once," Cyril says. "But McCarthy's a Corkman. His family and the Collinses were neighbors. All those boys went a bit crazy when Mick was killed. And then Griffith drops dead. No restraining voice. The executions. And the IRA up to high do. Burning the houses of Free State senators. This fellow McCarthy hears about the camp. Goes to Carna. Starts asking around. Telling people he was a student of the professor's in Paris and wants to continue his studies. Way of saying he wants to join up. John O'Connor questions him. But this McCarthy's full of stories about the Irish College and even mentions you, Nora, which convinces John."

"Used me?" I say.

"He did," Cyril says. "He's taken to the camp. A bunch of caves. Hard to find. After a few weeks McCarthy is sent down to get supplies. He goes to the Free State army barracks in Galway. They raid the camp. They only meant to arrest the professor but somebody started shooting. Not even sure which side. And the professor . . ."

Cyril stops.

"Are you sure he's dead?" I say. "In a fight like that there must have been a lot of confusion. Maybe he got away. Maybe he was arrested. Maybe . . ."

"Ah Nora. I saw him die."

"No. No," I say.

"I went in with the army, Nora."

And now I stand up.

"You what?"

"The killing's got to stop, Nora. Dev will never give up. Peter Keeley shouldn't have died. None of them should. But the government of Ireland can't be destroyed."

"Go," I say. "Leave now. Get out. I can't listen to you." I push him out the door.

I take Peter's photograph from my bedside table.

"Peter, I hardly knew you," I say. So little time together. Days scattered across years. Memories I'd woven into a great love. Gentle Peter. A man who was the opposite of Tim McShane in every way. We could have been so happy together. I want to weep. To sob. But I can only sit in silence staring at the picture.

"He died for Ireland," May says when she finds me the next morning still sitting up. The fire out. The room freezing. She piles up coals and bits of paper, strikes a match. Talking about honor and bravery and Ireland as the fire catches.

"Damn Ireland," I say. "Not a country. A fantasy. I hate Ireland."

"Oh no, Nora," May says. "Don't say that."

"This all has to stop, May," I say.

"Stop, how?" she says. "We can't surrender to an unjust government."

"That the Irish people elected," I say.

"The people didn't understand. The professor would tell you that," she says.

"But he can't, May. He can't tell me anything."

Yeats warned us. The blood-dimmed tide. The monster who was, what was his word? Slouching. Yes, slouching toward Bethlehem. Yeats is right. Some evil thing has been loosed.

"Don't you see, May? A divided Ireland is what the British want. Now they can say the Irish got their pathetic country only to tear it apart. Wilson's somewhere laughing at Irishmen killing one another."

"For now," May says. "But not forever. You must believe that, Nora. Peter died to make the dream come true and it will. It will," she says.

We don't notice Cyril, who's let himself in. Holds up a bottle of whiskey.

"How dare you . . ." I start.

"We'll have a truce, girls. And a wake for Peter Keeley."

"'Down by the salley gardens,'" he sings as he finds glasses, pours us each a whiskey, and stands in front of the fire.

"'But I was young and foolish, and now am full of tears,'" he finishes. And I find that I'm crying at last.

"Slainté," Cyril says and drinks down the whiskey. May and I do the same.

We sit talking about Peter till nightfall. And then I sleep.

FEBRUARY 1923

"A plague on both their houses," I say to Madame Simone.

"Is there some equivalent French phrase?" I ask her as we eat dinner at L'Impasse.

"Many," she says.

Two months now since Peter's death and still the fighting goes on in Ireland. Not a war really, but a kind of tit-for-tat violence, hard to support either side. What was Peter thinking when he realized his student, this young man he'd inspired to love Ireland, had betrayed him? When he saw Cyril with the army? To die because of politics. Horrible. I'm so angry I can't even mourn Peter properly. I say all this to Madame Simone, who makes the kind of "ptt" sound only a French woman can. A stream of French follows.

"Lentement s'il vous plaît," I beg her.

And then slowly and deliberately Madame Simone gives me a history lesson. Don't I realize that every time I walk through la place de la Concorde I pass the site of the guillotine?

"A popular entertainment, the executions, not just of the king and queen and aristocrats," she says, "but of the revolutionaries themselves. Comrades who had become enemies. Robespierre decapitated his former friends until eventually his head fell. *O Liberté, que de crimes on commet en ton nom!*"

"Liberty," I translate aloud. "What crimes are committed in your name. Why, that's profound, Madam Simone."

She exhales expressively. Did I think those words were hers? *Non,* no. Hadn't I ever heard of Madame Roland? Jeanne-Marie Phlipon?

Madame Roland had a salon, Madame Simone tells me, where the French revolutionaries met to conspire. Americans came too.

"Benjamin Franklin?" I ask. "Thomas Jefferson?"

"I suppose," she says.

All of them grateful for the good food and drink. Hard going for revolutionaries who didn't come from wealthy families, she tells me.

And then after all Madame Roland did for the revolution, doesn't she get marched up to the guillotine and beheaded.

"Oh, no," I say. "That's terrible. I can't believe . . ."

"Pttt," says Madame Simone. "Only an American would be so surprised." She shakes her head. "A kind of strength in such naïveté, perhaps."

"Laughing like an ignorant fighter laughs who's never lost a battle," I say.

"Well put, Nora," Madame Simone says.

"It's a poem," I tell her, "Called 'Chicago.' About my city. Young and tough and optimistic." Eddie Stiechen had sent it to me, written by his brother-in-law. Power in the fellow Carl Sandburg's words.

Now I quote the last of Sandburg's lines: "Proud to be Hog Butcher, Tool Maker, Stacker of Wheat, Player with Railroads and Freight Handler to the Nation.'"

Madame Simone hasn't understood half of what I've said.

"My cousin Ed would hate that poem," I say to her. "He wants Chicago to be beautiful, more like Paris."

"Perhaps your city can be both beautiful and strong," Madame Simone says. "This war ended not in peace but in smothered enmity. I'm leaving Paris. I will live with my nephew and his family in Bordeaux. Make dresses for my grandnieces. I am not Gabrielle Chanel. I wish to be with my family. Go home, Nora. Back to your Chicago."

"But my family doesn't want me," I say to her.

"You don't know that," she says.

"I wrote to my brother," I say. "Though I wonder if he got the letter."

"Write again," she says. "So many have been lost. Wonderful to have someone return alive."

"But it was my sister Henrietta who killed me," I say.

"She may be sorry," Madame Simone says.

"I doubt it."

"Find out. Ask her."

"Me speak to her? Never. I loathe her. I . . ."

Jesus, I sound like Macready or Wilson. Maybe it would be a relief to stop hating Henrietta. And after all I have one or two things to apologize for myself.

"But how can I leave Paris?" I say. "I'm not the same Nora who arrived here. I don't know if I can live in Chicago."

"Find out. You have been in a play, Nora. A spectacle. You've spoken lines in a language you don't really know. Imagined yourself in love with a man you never saw, and joined a revolution you didn't understand."

"That's not fair. I did love Peter and I am of Irish blood just like they are and . . ."

"But you're also an American, Nora. Americans always go home in the end."

"But Tim McShane," I start.

"You survived a war, Nora. You fear a bully?" she says.

Late that night in my room at the place des Vosges I pick up the framed photograph I took of Peter at Lough Inagh. A wild man with that beard and those runaway curls. Still the shy scholar though. The slight smile, and I'd gotten his eyes—that seeing-beyond expression in them.

I've placed Peter at the Center of my Altar of Remembrance. A collection of pictures of the living and the dead. The photographs I'd taken of my soldier patients, one of Louis DuBois, Lieutenant Cholet, a nice shot of Maud and Constance, Molly Childers and the Alices, Margaret Kirk, Madame Simone, James Joyce and Nora.

I'd propped up the memorial card from the duchess's funeral against the wall. On the front Notre-Dame de Paris, Our Lady as a medieval princess, her baby on her hip.

I pick up the card, turn it over.

St. Patrick's Prayer on the back. I read:

> *I arise today through the light of the sun*
> *The radiance of the moon*
> *The swiftness of the wind*
> *The depth of the sea . . .*
> *Christ before me*
> *Christ behind me*
> *Christ in me*

Madame Simone is right and wrong. Maybe my imagination did create my relationship with Peter but then so much of what I believe I can't see.

Like Holy Communion. The body and blood of Jesus in the host, on my tongue. Faith.

And all those Irish songs and stories that propelled the Rising.

Invisible.

I remember Maura O'Connor at St. Enda's well. We can enter the otherworld through a lake, a well, a sudden insight.

Yet on the shores of Galway Bay the real and imagined Ireland met and mingled for me.

Funny, one reason I do want to go home is to tell the family I found Granny Honora's birthplace, stood on the actual piece of Irish earth that's uniquely ours. I would show them the hearth stones from the burned cottages.

I set Peter's picture down. He'd told me to go back to America. Work for Ireland from Chicago.

I wonder if the Irish Fellowship Club would do something to end Ireland's civil war. Tell both sides no more money from America until they stop killing each other.

I have two small bottles of holy water on my altar—one from Lourdes and the other from the Devil Dog fountain. I sprinkle myself with both, then write a letter to Rose, put a few drops on the envelope, and address it to the grocery at Larney's Corner.

I tell Rose I'll come home in the spring. Need that long to save my fare.

Two weeks later a telegram is delivered to the room on the place des Vosges. It's from Rose:

Mame dying. We need you. We love you. Come home.

Mame dying? Can't wait six months. I have to go now. Money, I need money. I look up at the framed Matisse sketch. Here's a work of imagination with a price tag.

That day I wire John Quinn. He advances me enough for passage on the next ship. I will give him the sketch in New York. Meet the fellow at last.

I pack my clothes, my photos, my Seneca, and the stones from the hearth at Bearna.

The first morning out at sea I come up on the deck. Land to the west of us. Ireland.

So long, Ireland, I think. I'm leaving you as my ancestors did. Making the same journey.

"*Slán abhaile.*" I hear Peter's voice.

"Safe home."